W9-AVD-803

A Fabulous Formless Darkness
contains stories to delight any reader. Those unfamiliar with
the genre will discover a wide range of styles and subjects;
the fan will encounter old favorites and new treasures.

Robert Aickman
Ambrose Bierce
Algernon Blackwood
Robert W. Chambers
Walter de la Mare
Philip K. Dick
Charles Dickens
Thomas M. Disch
Shirley Jackson
Stephen King
Fritz Leiber
Joyce Carol Oates
Fitz-James O'Brien
Oliver Onions
Ivan Turgenev
Edith Wharton
Gene Wolfe

"[An] outstanding anthology. Included is excellent work by most of the major writers of supernatural fiction. This book can offer many hours of enjoyment from both the familiar and the unfamiliar."

—E.F. Bleiler
author of *The Guide to Supernatural Fiction*

"Hartwell's insights into horror, and his brief introductions to each story, are thoughtful as well as informative."

—*Newsday*

"A gigantic, superlatively edited historical overview of horror fiction."

—*Chicago Sun-Times*

"A must-read for all readers [of] horror. It provides an overview of past and contemporary horror that's unmatched in any other collection."

—*Weird Tales*

"Undoubtedly the most important anthology of the year, if not the decade. An incredible book, which attempts to detail the history of horror literature in its short story form . . . [and] succeeds brilliantly.

"Hartwell is a man who knows where the richest blood lies and has skillfully tapped that vein for our own gruesome pleasures."

—*Fangoria*

THE DARK DESCENT
edited by David G. Hartwell

The Color of Evil
The Medusa in the Shield
A Fabulous Formless Darkness

A FABULOUS FORMLESS DARKNESS

The Dark Descent Vol. 3

edited by David G. Hartwell

TOR
HORROR

A TOM DOHERTY ASSOCIATES BOOK
NEW YORK

This is a work of fiction. All the characters and events portrayed in this book are fictitious, and any resemblance to real people or events is purely coincidental.

A FABULOUS FORMLESS DARKNESS

Copyright © 1987 by David G. Hartwell
Introduction to this volume copyright © 1992 by David G. Hartwell

This book first appeared as part of the Tor hardcover THE DARK DESCENT.

A Tor Book

Published by Tom Doherty Associates, Inc.
49 West 24th Street
New York, N.Y. 10010

ISBN: 0-812-50967-6

First printing: January 1992

Printed in the United States of America

0 9 8 7 6 5 4 3 2 1

DEDICATION

To Tom Doherty and Harriet P. McDougal and the Tor Books Horror imprint, and especially Melissa Ann Singer, editor, for support and patience.

To Kathryn Cramer and Peter D. Pautz for their hard work and enthusiasm, as well as provocative discussion.

To Patricia W. Hartwell for letting the books pile up and the piles of paper fall over throughout the house and still loving me.

ACKNOWLEDGMENTS

This anthology grew out of three years of weekly discussions with Peter D. Pautz and Kathryn Cramer on the nature and virtues of horror literature, and its evolution. Peter's knowledge of the contemporary field and Kathryn's theoretical bent were seminal in the genesis of my own thoughts on what horror literature is and has become. Jack Sullivan, Kirby McCauley and Peter Straub were particularly helpful in discussing aspects of horror, and Samuel R. Delany contributed valuable insights, as well as the title for Part III. And I owe an incalculable debt to the great anthologists—from M. R. James and Dashiell Hammett, Elizabeth Bowen, Dorothy Sayers through Wise and Fraser, Boris Karloff and August Derleth to Kirby McCauley, Ramsey Campbell and Jack Sullivan—whose research and scholarship and taste guided my reading over the decades. Robert Hadji and Jessica Salmonson gave valuable support in late-night convention discussions, and the World Fantasy Convention provided an annual environment for advancing ideas in the context of the fine working writers and experts who make horror literature a vigorous and growing form in our time. Finally, my sincere thanks to Stephen King for *Danse Macabre*.

Copyright Acknowledgments

CONTENTS

Introduction to
A Fabulous Formless Darkness

This is the third volume of the three volume work, *The Dark Descent*, an anthology that examines the nature of horror literature and offers examples from Poe to the present. Together, the three volumes, *The Color of Evil*, *The Medusa in the Shield*, and *A Fabulous Formless Darkness*, cover the history and evolution of horror in literature to our times. As is made clear in the general introduction, there are three currents or streams of horror that persist and intermingle throughout history. These streams are discernible in individual stories, in terms of what is more or less central to the aesthetic of an individual work.

I have chosen the pieces included in *A Fabulous Formless Darkness* to represent literary investigations of horror based upon doubt and dread of the nature of reality. These stories create an atmosphere of anxiety and discomfort as you become more and more aware that something terrible, something you cannot quite pin down, is happening before your very eyes. What happens may be monstrous or evil, or both, but you cannot confront it directly and disperse or thwart it. So it is truly horrifying. Some of these stories are supernatural, some are not, but all embody a transaction between the reader and the text that creates horrific sensations. These powerful feelings aroused are the point of horror in fiction, and these stories deliver.

As will be evident, my enterprise in *The Dark Descent* has been to redefine and clarify horror for our era, when it has become such a vital force in contemporary literature. Throughout history until today, the short story has been the form in which the evolution of horror has taken place. The classics of horror fiction are, for the most part, short stories and novellas, and this work represents the largest and most comprehensive collection of them in existence. It allows the contemporary reader access to the whole tradition of horror in the English language.

Each story in *A Fabulous Formless Darkness* is an intense, meticulous portrayal of an atmosphere that surrounds and enfolds you in doubt and dread, an experience in reading you will not soon forget. The power of horror, as one critic has suggested, is to bring to consciousness, if only for a moment, material we could otherwise not bear to look at. In the case of the stories in this volume, a kind of metaphysical doubt must be confronted. Thereby, the story reawakens our emotions and strengthens us through awe and fear and wonder.

Here, then, is *A Fabulous Formless Darkness* . . .

David G. Hartwell

A Fabulous Formless Darkness

Introduction to
The Dark Descent

To taste the full flavor of these stories you must bring
an orderly mind to them, you must have a reasonable
amount of confidence, if not in what used to be called
the laws of nature, at least in the currently suspected
habits of nature. . . . To the truly superstitious the
"weird" has only its Scotch meaning: "Something
which actually takes place."

—Dashiell Hammett, *Creeps by Night*

The appeal of the spectrally macabre is generally narrow because it demands from the reader a certain degree of imagination and a capacity for detachment from
everyday life. Relatively few are free enough from the
spell of daily routine to respond. . . .

—H. P. Lovecraft, *Supernatural Horror in
    Literature*

1

On a July Sunday morning, I was moderating a panel
discussion at Necon, a small New England convention
devoted to dark fantasy. The panelists included Alan Ryan,
Whitley Strieber, Peter Straub, Charles L. Grant and, I believe, Les Daniels, all of them horror novelists. The theme
of the discussion was literary influences, with each partici-
pant naming the horror writers he felt significant in the genesis of his career. As the minutes rolled by and the litany of
names, Poe and Bradbury and Leiber and Lovecraft and
Kafka and others, was uttered, I realized that except for a
ritual bow to Stephen King, every single influential writer

named had been a short story writer. So I interrupted the panel and asked them all to spend the last few minutes commenting on my observation. What they said amounted to this: the good stuff is pretty much all short fiction.

After a few months of thought, I spent a late Halloween night with Peter Straub at the World Fantasy Convention, getting his response to my developing ideas on the recent evolution of horror from a short story to a novel genre. My belief that the long-form horror story is avant-garde and experimental, an unsolved aesthetic problem being attacked with energy and determination by Straub and King and others in our time, solidified as a result of that conversation.

But it seemed to me too early to generalize as to the nature of the new horror novel form. What, then, I asked myself, has happened to the short story? The horror story has certainly not up and vanished after 160 years of development and popularity; far from it. As an administrator of the annual World Fantasy Awards since 1975, I was aware of significant growth in short fiction in the past decade. And so the idea of this book was conceived, to conclude the era of the dominance of short-form horror with a definitive anthology that attempts to represent the entire evolution of the form to date and to describe and point out the boundaries of horror as it has been redefined in our contemporary field. For it seemed apparent to me that the conventional approach to horror codified by the great anthologies of the 1940s is obsolete, was indeed becoming obsolete as those books were published, and has persisted to the detriment of a clearer understanding of the literature to the present. It has persisted to the point where fans of horror fiction most often restrict their reading to books and stories given the imprimateur of a horror category label, thus missing some of the finest pleasures of this century in that fictional mode. I have gathered as many as could be confined within one huge volume here in *The Dark Descent*, with the intent of clearing the air and broadening future considerations of horror.

Fear has its own aesthetic—as Le Fanu, Henry James, Montagu James and Walter de la Mare have repeatedly shown—and also its own propriety. A story dealing in fear ought, ideally, to be kept at a certain pitch. And that austere other world, the world of the ghost, should inspire, when it impacts on our own, not so much revulsion or shock as a sort of awe.

—Elizabeth Bowen, *The Second Ghost Book*

The one test of the really weird is simply this—whether or not there be excited in the reader a profound sense of dread, and of contact with unknown spheres and powers.

—H. P. Lovecraft, *Supernatural Horror in Literature*

II   The Evolution of Horror Fiction

For more than 150 years horror fiction has been a vital component of English and American literature, invented with the short story form itself and contributing intimately to the evolution of the short story. Until the last decade, the dominant literary form of horror fiction was the short story and novella. This is simply no longer the case. Shortly after the beginning of the 1970s, within a very few years, the novel form assumed the position of leadership. First came a scattering of exceptionally popular novels—*Rosemary's Baby*, *The Other*, *The Exorcist*, *The Mephisto Waltz*, with attendant film successes—then, in 1973, the deluge, with Stephen King on the crest of the wave, altering the nature of horror fiction for the foreseeable future and sweeping along with it all the living generations of short fiction writers. Very few writers of horror fiction, young or old, resisted the commercial or aesthetic temptation to expand into the novel form, leading to the creation of some of the best horror novels of all time as well as a large amount of popular trash rushed into print. The models for these works were the previous bestsellers, popular films and the short fiction masterpieces of previous decades.

When the tide ebbed in the 1980s, much of the trash was left dead in the backlists of paperback publishers, but the horror novel had become firmly established. This is significant from a number of perspectives. Rapid evolution and experimentation was encouraged. All kinds of horror literature benefited from the incorporation of every conceivable element of horrific effect and technique from other literature and film and video and comics.

The most useful and provocative view we can take on the horror novel in recent years is that it constitutes an avant-garde and experimental literary form which attempts to translate the horrific effects previously thought to be the nearly exclusive domain of the short forms into newly conceived long forms that maintain the proper atmosphere and effects. Certainly isolated examples of more or less successful novel-length horror fiction exist, from *Frankenstein* and *Dracula* to *The Haunting of Hill House*, but they are comparatively infrequent next to the constant, rich proliferation and development of horror in shorter forms in every decade from Poe to the present. The horror novels of the past do not in aggregate form a body of traditional literature and technique from which the present novels spring and upon which they depend.

It is evident both from the recent novels themselves and from the public statements of many of the writers that Stephen King, Peter Straub and Ramsey Campbell, and a number of other leading novelists, have been discussing among themselves—and trying to solve in their works—the perceived problems of developing the horror novel into a sophisticated and effective form. In so doing, they have highlighted the desirability of a volume such as *The Dark Descent*, which represents the context from which the literature springs and attempts to elucidate the whole surround of horror today.

Horror novels grow to a very large extent out of the varied and highly evolved novellas and short stories exemplified in this book. Our perceptions of the nature of horror literature had been changing and evolving rapidly in recent decades, to the point where a compilation of the horror story, organized according to new principles, is needed to manifest the broadened nature of the literature.

Before proceeding in the next section to begin an anatomy of horror, it is interesting to note that there has been a renewed fashion for horror in every decade since the First World War, but this is the first such "revival" that has produced numerous novels.

There was a general increase in horror, particularly the ghost story, in the 1920s under the influence of M. R. James, both a prominent writer and anthologist, and such masters as Algernon Blackwood, Walter de la Mare, Edith Wharton and others. At that time the great horror magazine, *Weird Tales*, was founded in the U.S. In the 1930s, the dark fantasy story or weird tale became prominent, influenced by the magazine mentioned above, the growth of the H. P. Lovecraft circle of writers, and a proliferation of anthologies, either in series or as huge compendiums celebrating the first century of horror fiction. After the films and books of the 1930s, the early 1940s produced the finest "great works" collections, epitomized by *And the Darkness Falls*, edited by Boris Karloff, and *Great Tales of Terror and the Supernatural*, edited by Herbert Wise and Phyllis Fraser; and Arkham House, the great specialty publisher devoted to this day to bringing into print collections by great horror authors, was founded by writer Donald Wandrei to print the collected works of H. P. Lovecraft. After the war came the science fiction horrors of the 1950s, in all those monster films and in the works of Richard Matheson, Jack Finney, Theodore Sturgeon and Ray Bradbury. In the early sixties we had the craze for "junk food" paperback horror anthologies and collections, under the advent of the midnight horror movie boom on TV. But as we remarked above, short fiction always remained at the forefront. Even the novelists were famous for their short stories.

A lot has changed.

Atmosphere is the all-important thing, for the final criterion of authenticity is not the dovetailing of a plot but the creation of a given sensation.

—H. P. Lovecraft, *Supernatural Horror in Literature*

Much as we ask for it, the *frisson* of horror, among the many oddities of our emotional life, is one of the oddest. For one thing, it is usually a response to something that is not there. Under normal circumstances, that is, it attends only such things as nightmares, phobias and literature. In that respect it is unlike terror, which is extreme and sudden fear in the face of a material threat. . . . The terror can be dissipated by a round of buckshot. Horror, on the other hand, is fascinated dread in the presence of an immaterial cause. The frights of nightmares cannot be dissipated by a round of buckshot; to flee them is to run into them at every turn.

—Sigmund Freud, *The Uncanny*

III   What It Is

Sigmund Freud remarked that we immediately recognize scenes that are supposed to provoke horror, "even if they actually provoke titters." It seems to me, however, that horror fiction has usually been linked to or categorized by manifest signs in texts, and this has caused more than a little confusion among commentators over the years. Names such as weird tales, gothic tales, terror tales, ghost stories, supernatural tales, macabre stories—all clustered around the principle of a real or implied or fake intrusion of the supernatural into the natural world, an intrusion which arouses fear—have been used as appellations for the whole body of literature, sometimes interchangeably by the same writer. So often, and in so many of the best works, has the intrusion been a ghost, that nearly half the time you will find "horror story" and "ghost story" used interchangeably. And this is so in spite of the acknowledged fact that supernatural horror in literature embodies many manifestations (from demons to vampires to werewolves to pagan gods and more) and, further, that ghosts are recognizably not supposed to horrify in a fair number of ghost stories.

J. A. Cuddon, a thorough scholar, has traced the early

connections between ghost and horror stories from the 1820s to the 1870s, viewing them as originally separable: "The growth of the ghost story and the horror story in this mid-century period tended to coalesce; indeed, it is difficult to establish objective criteria by which to distinguish between the two. A taxonomical approach invariably begins to break down at an early stage. . . . On balance, it is probable that a ghost story will contain an element of horror." Jack Sullivan, another distinguished scholar and anthologist, sums up the problems of definition and terminology thusly: "We find ourselves in a tangled morass of definitions and permutations that grows as relentlessly as the fungus in the House of Usher." Sullivan chooses "ghost story" as generic, presumably to have one leg to stand on facing in each direction.

We choose "horror" as our term, both in accordance with the usage of the marketplace (Tor Books has a Tor Horror line; horror is a label for the marketing category under which novels and collections appear), and because it points toward a transaction between the reader and the text that is the essence of the experience of reading horror fiction, and not any thing contained within that text (such as a ghost, literal or implied). And moreover, H. P. Lovecraft, the theoretician and critic who most carefully described the literature in his *Supernatural Horror in Literature*, who was certainly the most important American writer of horror fiction in the first half of this century, has to the best of my memory not a single conventional ghost story in the corpus of his works.

It is Lovecraft's essay that provides the keystone upon which any architecture of horror must be built: atmosphere. And it seems to me that Freud is in accord. What this means is that you can experience true horror in, potentially, any work of fiction, be it a western, a contemporary gothic, science fiction, mystery, whatever category of content the writer may choose. A work may be a horror story (and indeed included in this anthology) no matter what, as long as the atmosphere allows. This means that horror is set free from the supernatural, that it is unnecessary for the story to contain any overt or implied device or manifestation whatsoever. The emotional transaction is paramount and definitive, and we recognize its presence even when it doesn't work as it is supposed to.

> To them [people who don't read horror] it is a kind of pornography, inducing horripilation instead of erection. And the reader who appears to relish such sensations— why he's an emotional masochist, the slave of an unholy drug, a decadent psychotic beast.
>
> —David Aylward, *Revenge of the Past*

> First, the longing for mystic experience which seems always to manifest itself in periods of social confusion, when political progress is blocked: as soon as we feel that our own world has failed us, we try to find evidence for another world; second, the instinct to inoculate ourselves against panic at the real horrors loose on the earth . . . by injections of imagery horror, which soothe us with the momentary illusion that the forces of madness and murder may be tamed and compelled to provide us with a mere dramatic entertainment.
>
> —Edmund Wilson, *A Literary Chronicle*

> I used to read horror when I was depressed to jump-start my emotions—but it only gave me temporary relief.
>
> —Kathryn Cramer (personal correspondence)

> It proves that the tale of horror and/or the supernatural *is* serious, *is* important, *is* necessary . . . not only to those human beings who read to think, but to those who read to feel; the volume may even go a certain distance toward proving the idea that, as this mad century races toward its conclusion—a conclusion which seems ever more ominous and ever more absurd—it may be the

most important and useful form of fiction which the moral writer may command.

—Stephen King, Introduction to *The Arbor House Treasury of Horror and the Supernatural*

IV   The Death of Horror

The death of the novel and the death of the short story are literary topics we joke about, so it should come as no particular surprise that a recent, and otherwise excellent, collection of essays on supernatural fiction in America from 1820–1920 states that supernatural fiction died around 1920 ("dematerialized"), to be replaced by psychoanalysis, which took over its function. Now it seems to me surprising to maintain that fiction that embodies psychological truth in metaphor is replaceable by science—it sounds rather too much like replacing painting with photography. Yet this is only a recent example of the obituary approach, an effective gambit when dealing with material you wish to exterminate, and often used by self-appointed arbiters of taste.

Let's resurrect the great Modernist critic, Edmund Wilson, for a few minutes. Wilson wrote an essay on horror in the early 1940s that challenged the whole canon of significant works established by the anthologists of the 1930s and '40s, from Dorothy Sayers and M. R. James and Hugh Walpole and Marjorie Bowen to Wise and Fraser, and Karloff. Wilson proposed his own list of masterpieces, from Poe and Gogol ("the greatest master") and Melville and Turgenev through Hardy, Stevenson, Kipling, Conrad's *The Heart of Darkness* and Henry James' *The Turn of the Screw* to Walter de la Mare and, ultimately, Kafka ("he went straight for the morbidities of the psyche"). He, Wilson, seems to be reaching toward a redefinition of horror literature, but unfortunately his essay vibrates with the discomfort of the humanist and rationalist confronting the supernatural. He rejects nearly every classic story in the horror canon and every single writer principally known for work in the field, reserving particular antipathy for H. P. Lovecraft, the anti-Modernist (to whom he devoted a whole separate essay of demolition).

Wilson's comments on Kafka are instructive. Kafka's "visions of moral horror" are "narratives that compel our attention, and fantasies that generate more shudders than the whole of Algernon Blackwood or M. R. James combined." Kafka's characters "have turned into the enchanted denizens of a world in which, prosaic though it is, we can find no firm foothold in reality and in which we can never even be certain whether souls are being saved or damned . . . he went straight for the morbidities of the psyche with none of the puppetry of specters and devils that earlier writers still carried with them." Wilson's view of the evolution of horror is implicit in these comments. He sees the literature as evolving in a linear fashion into fantasies of the psyche removed entirely from supernatural trappings. Any audience interested in these trappings is regressive. He sees no value to a modern reader in obsolete fiction.

Since Wilson's presupposition is that the evolution of horror ended with Kafka, his theory of horror reading among his contemporaries—that they are indulging in a "revived" taste for an obsolete form—allows him to start from the premise that the ghost story is dead, that it died with the advent of the electric light, and to conclude immediately that contemporary versions are doomed attempts to revive the corpse of the form. Sound familiar? It's the familiar "death of literature" obituary approach. Well, back to the grave, Edmund. You're dead, and horror literature is alive and well, happily evolving and diversifying.

But Wilson's approach to the horror canon was and remains generally stimulating. For it appears that as horror has evolved in this century it has grown significantly in the areas of "the morbidities of the psyche" and fantasies of "a world in which, prosaic though it is, we can find no firm foothold in reality."

In order to achieve the fantastic, it is neither necessary nor sufficient to portray extraordinary things. The strangest event will enter into the order of the universe if it is alone in a world governed by laws. . . . You cannot impose limits on the fantastic; either it does not exist at all, or else it extends throughout the universe. It is an entire world in which things manifest a captive, tormented thought, a thought both whimsical and enchained, that gnaws away from below at the mechanism's links without ever managing to express itself. In this world, matter is never entirely matter, since it offers only a constantly frustrated attempt at determinism, and mind is never completely mind, because it has fallen into slavery and has been impregnated and dulled by matter. All is woe. Things suffer and tend towards inertia, without ever attaining it; the debased, enslaved mind unsuccessfully strives toward consciousness and freedom.

—Jean-Paul Sartre, *AMINADAB or The Fantastic Considered as a Language*

V   The Three Streams

We return to the life and state of horror fiction in the present. Contemporary horror fiction occurs in three streams, in three principal modes or clusters of emphasis: 1. moral allegorical 2. psychological metaphor 3. fantastic. The stories in this anthology are separated according to these categories. These modes are not mutually exclusive, but usually a matter of emphasis along a spectrum from the overtly moral at one extreme to the nearly totally ambiguous at the other, with human psychology always a significant factor but only sometimes the principal focus. Perhaps we might usefully imagine them as three currents in the same ocean.

Stories that cluster at the first pole are characteristically supernatural fiction, most usually about the intrusion of supernatural evil into consensus reality, most often about the horrid and colorful special effects of evil. These are the stories of children possessed by demons, of hauntings by evil ghosts from the past (most ghost stories), stories of bad places (where evil persists from past times), of witchcraft and satanism. In our day they are often written and read by lapsed Christians, who have lost their firm belief in good but still have a discomforting belief in evil. Stories in this stream imply or state the Manichean universe that is so difficult to perceive in everyday life, wherein evil is so evident, horror so common that we are left with our sensitivities partly or fully deadened to it in our post-Holocaust, post-Vietnam, six-o'clock news era. A strong extra-literary appeal of such fiction, it seems to me, is to jump-start the readers' deadened emotional sensitivities.

And the moral allegory has its significant extra-literary appeal in itself to that large audience that desires the attribution of a moral calculus (usually teleological) deriving from ultimate and metaphysical forms of good and evil behind events in an everyday reality. Ginjer Buchanan says that "all the best horror is written by lapsed Catholics."

In speaking of stories and novels in this first stream, we are speaking of the most popular form of horror fiction today, the commercial bestseller lineage of *Rosemary's Baby* and *The Exorcist*, and a majority of the works of Stephen King. These stories are taken to the heart of the commercial-category audience that is characteristically style-deaf (regardless of the excellence of some of the works), the audience that requires repeated doses of such fiction for its emotional effect to persist. This stream is the center of category horror publishing.

The second group of horror stories, stories of aberrant human psychology embodied metaphorically, may be either purely supernatural, such as *Dracula*, or purely psychological, such as Robert Bloch's *Psycho*. What characterizes them as a group is the monster at the center, from the monster of Frankenstein, to Carmilla, to the chain-saw murderer—an overtly abnormal human or creature, from whose acts and on account of whose being the horror arises. D. H. Lawrence's little boy, Faulkner's Emily, and, more subtly, the New Yorker of Henry James' "The Jolly Corner" show the extent to which this stream interpenetrates and blends with the mainstream of psychological fiction in this century. Both Lovecraft and Edmund Wilson, from differing perspectives, see

Joseph Conrad's *The Heart of Darkness* as essentially horror fiction. There has been strong resistance on the part of critics, from Wilson to the present, to admitting nonsupernatural psychological horror into consideration of the field, allowing many to declare the field a dead issue for contemporary literature, of antiquarian interest only since the 1930s. This trend was probably aided by the superficial examination of the antiquarianism of both M. R. James and H. P. Lovecraft.

But by 1939 an extremely significant transition is apparent, particularly in the U.S. *Weird Tales* and the Lovecraft circle of writers, as well as the popular films, had made horror a vigorous part of popular culture, had built a large audience among the generally nonliterary readership for pulp fiction, a "lower-class" audience. And in 1939 John W. Campbell, the famous science fiction editor, founded the revolutionary pulp fantasy magazine, *Unknown*. From 1923 to 1939, the leading source of horror and supernatural fiction in the English language was *Weird Tales*, publishing all traditional styles but tending toward the florid and antiquarian. *Unknown* was an aesthetic break with traditional horror fiction. Campbell demanded stories with contemporary, particularly urban, settings, told in clear, unornamented prose style. *Unknown* featured stories by all the young science fiction writers whose work was changing that genre in Campbell's *Astounding*. Alfred Bester, Eric Frank Russell, Robert A. Heinlein, A. E. Van Vogt, L. Ron Hubbard and others, particularly such fantasists as Theodore Sturgeon, Jane Rice, Anthony Boucher, Fredric Brown and Fritz Leiber.

The stories tended to focus equally on the supernatural and the psychological. Psychology was often quite overtly the underpinning for horror, as in, for example, Hubbard's "He Didn't Like Cats," in which there is an extended discussion between the two supporting characters as to whether the central character's problem is supernatural or psychological . . . and we never know, for either way he's doomed. *Unknown* broke the dominance of *Weird Tales* and influenced such significant young talents as Ray Bradbury and Shirley Jackson. The magazine encouraged the genrification of certain types of psychological fiction and, at the same time, crossbred a good bit of horror into the growing science fiction field. This reinforced a cultural trend apparent in the monster and mad scientist films of the 1930s, giving us the enormous spawn of SF/horror films of the 1950s and beyond.

It is interesting to note that as our perceptions of horror fiction and what the term includes change over the decades, differing works seem to fall naturally into or out of the category. The possibilities of psychological horror seem in the end to blur distinctions, and there is no question that horror is becoming ever more inclusive.

Stories of the third stream have at their center ambiguity as to the nature of reality, and it is this very ambiguity that generates the horrific effects. Often there is an overtly supernatural (or certainly abnormal) occurrence, but we know of it only by allusion. Often, essential elements are left undescribed so that, for instance, we do not know whether there was really a ghost or not. But the difference is not merely supernatural versus psychological explanation: third stream stories lack any explanation that makes sense in everyday reality—we don't know, and that doubt disturbs us, horrifies us. This is the fiction to which Sartre's analysis alludes, the fantastic. At its extreme, from Kafka to the present, it blends indistinguishably with magic realism, the surreal, the absurd, all the fictions that confront reality through paradoxical distance. It is the fiction of radical doubt. Thomas M. Disch once remarked that Poe can profitably be considered as a contemporary of Kierkegaard, and it is evident that this stream develops from the beginnings of horror fiction in the short story. In the contemporary field it is a major current.

Third stream stories tend to cross all category lines but usually they do not use the conventional supernatural as a distancing device. While most horror fiction declares itself at some point as violating the laws of nature, the fantastic worlds of third stream fiction use as a principal device what Sartre has called the language of the fantastic.

At the end of a horror story, the reader is left with a new perception of the nature of reality. In the moral allegory strain, the point seems to be that this is what reality was and has been all along (i.e., literally a world in which supernatural forces are at work) only you couldn't or wouldn't recognize it. Psychological metaphor stories basically use the intrusion of abnormality to release repressed or unarticulated psychological states. In her book, *Powers of Horror*, critic Julia Kristeva says that horror deals with material just on the edge of repression but not entirely repressed and inaccessible. Stories from our second stream use the heightening effect on the monstrously abnormal to achieve this release. Third stream stories maintain the pretense of everyday reality only to annihilate it, leaving us with another world entirely, one in which we are disturbingly imprisoned. It is in perceiving the changed reality and its nature that the pleasure and illumination of third stream stories lies, that raises this part of horror fiction above the literary level of most of its generic relations. So the transaction between the reader and the text that identifies all horror fiction is to an extent modified in third stream stories (there is rarely, if ever, any terror), making them more difficult to classify and identify than even the borderline cases in the psychological category. Gene Wolfe's "Seven American Nights" is, in my opinion, a story on the borderline of third stream, deeply disturbing but not conventionally horrifying. The mass horror audience is not much taken with third stream stories, regardless of craft or literary merit, because they modify the emotional jolt.

Although the manifest images of horror fiction are legion, their latent meanings are few. Readers and writers of horror fiction, like those of all the popular genres, seem under a compulsion to repeat. Certainly the needs satisfied by horror fiction are recurrent and ineradicable.

—George Stade, *The New York Times*,
Oct. 27, 1985

I recognize terror as the finest emotion and so I will try to terrorize the reader. But if I find that I cannot terrify, I will try to horrify, and if I find that I cannot horrify, I'll go for the gross-out.

—Stephen King, *Danse Macabre*

VI   The Dark Descent

The descent of horror fiction from its origins in the nine-teenth century to the many and sophisticated forms of the contemporary field has taken place in shorter stories. Now that the novel has taken over, the major writers are unlikely to devote their principal efforts to short fiction. So we have reached a point in the evolution of this literary mode at which we can take stock of its achievements in short fiction and assess its qualities and contributions to all of literature. The stories assembled in this book are divided according to the three streams we have identified, both to provide extended examples and to provoke further discussion. The short story is vigorously alive in horror today, in magazines, antholo-gies, and collections. Let it, for a moment, occupy the center of your attention. The best short fiction in modern horror is the equal of the best of all times and places.

Fritz Leiber

SMOKE GHOST

Fritz Leiber's most famous short story of the 1940s is the urban horror piece, "Smoke Ghost." The impact of this story on horror writing in the U.S. can scarcely be overestimated. It is a revolutionary ghost story that re-thinks the entire tradition and re-imagines the supernat-ural in our time. Leiber uses the traditional device of the ghost in an aggressively new way—as a projection of the group unconscious of civilized and rational humanity that alters the nature of reality—that must be wor-shipped. Combining the moral and psychological tradi-tions, Leiber transforms them into an ambiguous and unsettling other reality. Perhaps a descendent of the sto-ries of other dimensions such as Blackwood's "The Wil-lows" or Bierce's "The Damned Thing" or Frank Belknap Long's "The Hounds of Tindalos," "Smoke Ghost" influ-ences the field from Bradbury to Ramsey Campbell and is representative of the transition from old to new styles in horror fiction influenced by *Unknown* magazine. Lei-ber was the recipient of the Grand Master Award for life achievement at the World Fantasy Convention in 1976.

Miss Millick wondered just what had happened to Mr. Wran. He kept making the strangest remarks when she took dictation. Just this morning he had quickly turned around and asked, "Have you ever seen a ghost, Miss Millick?" And she had tittered nervously and replied, "When I was a girl there was a thing in white that used to come out of the closet in the attic bedroom when I slept there, and moan. Of course it was just my imagination. I was frightened of lots of things.'' And he had said, ''I don't mean that kind of ghost. I mean a ghost from the world today, with the soot of the factories on its face and the pounding of machinery in its soul. The kind that would haunt coal yards and slip around at night through deserted office buildings like this one. A real ghost. Not something out of books.'' And she hadn't known what to say.

He'd never been like this before. Of course he might be joking, but it didn't sound that way. Vaguely Miss Millick wondered whether he mightn't be seeking some sort of sympathy from her. Of course, Mr. Wran was married and had a little child, but that didn't prevent her from having daydreams. The daydreams were not very exciting, still they helped fill up her mind. But now he was asking her another of those unprecedented questions.

''Have you ever thought what a ghost of our times would look like, Miss Millick? Just picture it. A smoky composite face with the hungry anxiety of the unemployed, the neurotic restlessness of the person without purpose, the jerky tension of the high-pressure metropolitan worker, the uneasy resentment of the striker, the callous opportunism of the scab, the aggressive whine of the panhandler, the inhibited terror of the bombed civilian, and a thousand other twisted emotional patterns. Each one overlying and yet blending with the other, like a pile of semi-transparent masks?''

Miss Millick gave a little self-conscious shiver and said, ''That would be terrible. What an awful thing to think of.''

She peered furtively across the desk. She remembered having heard that there had been something impressively abnormal about Mr. Wran's childhood, but she couldn't recall what it was. If only she could do something—laugh at his mood or ask him what was really wrong. She shifted the extra pencils in her left hand and mechanically traced over some of the shorthand curlicues in her notebook.

''Yet, that's just what such a ghost or vitalized projection would look like, Miss Millick,'' he continued, smiling in a tight way. ''It would grow out of the real world. It would reflect the tangled, sordid, vicious things. All the loose ends. And it would be very grimy. I don't think it would seem white or wispy, or favor graveyards. It wouldn't moan. But it would mutter unintelligibly, and twitch at your sleeve. Like a sick, surly ape. What would such a thing want from a person, Miss Millick? Sacrifice? Worship? Or just fear? What could you do to stop it from troubling you?"

Miss Millick giggled nervously. There was an expression beyond her powers of definition in Mr. Wran's ordinary, flat-cheeked, thirtyish face, silhouetted against the dusty window. He turned away and stared out into the gray downtown atmosphere that rolled in from the railroad yards and the mills. When he spoke again his voice sounded far away.

"Of course, being immaterial, it couldn't hurt you physically—at first. You'd have to be peculiarly sensitive to see it, or be aware of it at all. But it would begin to influence your actions. Make you do this. Stop you from doing that. Although only a projection, it would gradually get its hooks into the world of things as they are. Might even get control of suitably vacuous minds. Then it could hurt whomever it wanted."

Miss Millick squirmed and read back her shorthand, like the books said you should do when there was a pause. She became aware of the failing light and wished Mr. Wran would ask her to turn on the overhead. She felt scratchy, as if soot were sifting down on to her skin.

"It's a rotten world, Miss Millick," said Mr. Wran, talking at the window. "Fit for another morbid growth of superstition. It's time the ghosts, or whatever you call them, took over and began a rule of fear. They'd be no worse than men."

"But"—Miss Millick's diaphragm jerked, making her titter inanely—"of course, there aren't any such things as ghosts."

Mr. Wran turned around.

"Of course there aren't, Miss Millick," he said in a loud, patronizing voice, as if she had been doing the talking rather than he. "Science and common sense and psychiatry all go to prove it."

She hung her head and might even have blushed if she

hadn't felt so all at sea. Her leg muscles twitched, making her stand up, although she hadn't intended to. She aimlessly rubbed her hand along the edge of the desk.

"Why, Mr. Wran, look what I got off your desk," she said, showing him a heavy smudge. There was a note of clumsily playful reproof in her voice. "No wonder the copy I bring you always gets so black. Somebody ought to talk to those scrubwomen. They're skimping on your room."

She wished he would make some normal joking reply. But instead he drew back and his face hardened.

"Well, to get back," he rapped out harshly, and began to dictate.

When she was gone, he jumped up, dabbed his finger experimentally at the smudged part of the desk, frowned worriedly at the almost inky smears. He jerked open a drawer, snatched out a rag, hastily swabbed off the desk, crumpled the rag into a ball and tossed it back. There were three or four other rags in the drawer, each impregnated with soot.

Then he went over to the window and peered out anxiously through the dusk, his eyes searching the panorama of roofs, fixing on each chimney and water tank.

"It's a neurosis. Must be. Compulsions. Hallucinations," he muttered to himself in a tired, distraught voice that would have made Miss Millick gasp. "It's that damned mental abnormality cropping up in a new form. Can't be any other explanation. But it's so damned real. Even the soot. Good thing I'm seeing the psychiatrist. I don't think I could force myself to get on the elevated tonight." His voice trailed off, he rubbed his eyes, and his memory automatically started to grind.

It had all begun on the elevated. There was a particular little sea of roofs he had grown into the habit of glancing at just as the packed car carrying him homeward lurched around a turn. A dingy, melancholy little world of tar-paper, tarred gravel, and smoky brick. Rusty tin chimneys with odd conical hats suggested abandoned listening posts. There was a washed-out advertisement of some ancient patent medicine on the nearest wall. Superficially it was like ten thousand other drab city roofs. But he always saw it around dusk, either in the smoky half-light, or tinged with red by the flat rays of a dirty sunset, or covered by ghostly windblown white sheets of rain-splash, or patched with blackish snow; and it seemed unusually bleak and suggestive; almost beautifully ugly though in no sense picturesque; dreary, but meaningful. Unconsciously it came to symbolize for Catesby Wran certain disagreeable aspects of the frustrated, frightened century in which he lived, the jangled century of hate and heavy industry and total wars. The quick daily glance into the half darkness became an integral part of his life. Oddly, he never saw it in the morning, for it was then his habit to sit on the other side of the car, his head buried in the paper.

One evening toward winter he noticed what seemed to be a shapeless black sack lying on the third roof from the tracks. He did not think about it. It merely registered as an addition to the well-known scene and his memory stored away the impression for further reference. Next evening, however, he decided he had been mistaken in one detail. The object was a roof nearer than he had thought. Its color and texture, and the grimy stains around it, suggested that it was filled with coal dust, which was hardly reasonable. Then, too, the following evening it seemed to have been blown against a rusty ventilator by the wind—which could hardly have happened if it were at all heavy. Perhaps it was filled with leaves. Catesby was surprised to find himself anticipating his next daily glance with a minor note of apprehension. There was something unwholesome in the posture of the thing that stuck in his mind—a bulge in the sacking that suggested a misshaped head peering around the ventilator. And his apprehension was justified, for that evening the thing was on the nearest roof, though on the farther side, looking as if it had just flopped down over the low brick parapet.

Next evening the sack was gone. Catesby was annoyed at the momentary feeling of relief that went through him, because the whole matter seemed too unimportant to warrant feelings of any sort. What difference did it make if his imagination had played tricks on him, and he'd fancied that the object was slowly crawling and hitching itself closer across the roofs? That was the way any normal imagination worked.

He deliberately chose to disregard the fact that there were reasons for thinking his imagination was by no means a normal one. As he walked home from the elevated, however, he found himself wondering whether the sack was really gone. He seemed to recall a vague, smudgy trail leading across the gravel to the nearer side of the roof, which was masked by a parapet. For an instant an unpleasant picture formed in his mind—that of an inky, humped creature crouched behind the parapet, waiting.

The next time he felt the familiar grating lurch of the car, he caught himself trying not to look out. That angered him. He turned his head quickly. When he turned it back, his compact face was definitely pale. There had been only time for a fleeting rearward glance at the escaping roof. Had he actually seen in silhouette the upper part of a head of some sort peering over the parapet? Nonsense, he told himself. And even if he had seen something, there were a thousand explanations which did not involve the supernatural or even true hallucination. Tomorrow he would take a good look and clear up the whole matter. If necessary, he would visit the roof personally, though he hardly knew where to find it and disliked in any case the idea of pampering a silly fear.

He did not relish the walk home from the elevated that evening, and visions of the thing disturbed his dreams, and were in and out of his mind all next day at the office. It was then that he first began to relieve his nerves by making jokingly serious remarks about the supernatural to Miss Millick, who seemed properly mystified. It was on the same day, too, that he became aware of a growing antipathy to grime and soot. Everything he touched seemed gritty, and he found himself mopping and wiping at his desk like an old lady with a morbid fear of germs. He reasoned that there was no real change in his office, and that he'd just now become sensitive to the dirt that had always been there, but there was no denying an increasing nervousness. Long before the car reached the curve, he was straining his eyes through the murky twilight, determined to take in every detail.

Afterward he realized he must have given a muffled cry of some sort, for the man beside him looked at him curiously, and the woman ahead gave him an unfavorable stare. Conscious of his own pallor and uncontrollable trembling, he stared back at them hungrily, trying to regain the feeling of security he had completely lost. They were the usual reassuringly wooden-faced people everyone rides home with on the elevated. But suppose he had pointed out to one of them what he had seen—that sodden, distorted face of sacking and coal dust, that boneless paw which waved back and forth, unmistakably in his direction, as if reminding him of a future appointment—he involuntarily shut his eyes tight. His thoughts were racing ahead to tomorrow evening. He pictured this same windowed oblong of light and packed humanity surging around the curve—then an opaque monstrous form leaping out from the roof in a parabolic swoop—an unmentionable face pressed close against the window, smearing it with wet coal dust—huge paws fumbling sloppily at the glass—

Somehow he managed to turn off his wife's anxious inquiries. Next morning he reached a decision and made an appointment for that evening with a psychiatrist a friend had told him about. It cost him a considerable effort, for Catesby had a well-grounded distaste for anything dealing with psychological abnormality. Visiting a psychiatrist meant raking up an episode in his past which he had never fully described even to his wife. Once he had made the decision, however, he felt considerably relieved. The psychiatrist, he told himself, would clear everything up. He could almost fancy him saying, "Merely a bad case of nerves. However, you must consult the oculist whose name I'm writing down for you, and you must take two of these pills in water every four hours," and so on. It was almost comforting, and made the coming revelation he would have to make seem less painful.

But as the smoky dusk rolled in, his nervousness had returned and he had let his joking mystification of Miss Millick run away with him until he had realized he wasn't frightening anyone but himself.

He would have to keep his imagination under better control, he told himself, as he continued to peer out restlessly at the massive, murky shapes of the downtown office buildings.

Why, he had spent the whole afternoon building up a kind of neo-medieval cosmology of superstition. It wouldn't do. He realized then that he had been standing at the window much longer than he'd thought, for the glass panel in the door was dark and there was no noise coming from the outer office. Miss Millick and the rest must have gone home.

It was then he made the discovery that there would have been no special reason for dreading the swing around the curve that night. It was, as it happened, a horrible discovery. For, on the shadowed roof across the street and four stories below, he saw the thing huddle and roll across the gravel and, after one upward look of recognition, merge into the blackness beneath the water tank.

As he hurriedly collected his things and made for the elevator, fighting the panicky impulse to run, he began to think of hallucination and mild psychosis as very desirable conditions. For better or for worse, he pinned all his hopes on the psychiatrist.

"So you find yourself growing nervous and . . . er . . . jumpy, as you put it," said Dr. Trevethick, smiling with dignified geniality. "Do you notice any more definite physical symptoms? Pain? Headache? Indigestion?"

Catesby shook his head and wet his lips. "I'm especially nervous while riding in the elevated," he murmured swiftly.

"I see. We'll discuss that more fully. But I'd like you first to tell me about something you mentioned earlier. You said there was something about your childhood that might predispose you to nervous ailments. As you know, the early years are critical ones in the development of an individual's behavior pattern."

Catesby studied the yellow reflections of frosted globes in the dark surface of the desk. The palm of his left hand aimlessly rubbed the thick nap of the armchair. After a while he raised his head and looked straight into the doctor's small brown eyes.

"From perhaps my third to my ninth year," he began, choosing the words with care, "I was what you might call a sensory prodigy."

The doctor's expression did not change. "Yes?" he inquired politely.

"What I mean is that I was supposed to be able to see through walls, read letters through envelopes and books through their covers, fence and play ping-pong blindfolded, find things that were buried, read thoughts." The words tumbled out.

"And could you?" The doctor's voice was toneless.

"I don't know. I don't suppose so," answered Catesby, long-lost emotions flooding back into his voice. "It's all confused now. I thought I could, but then they were always encouraging me. My mother . . . was . . . well . . . interested in psychic phenomena. I was . . . exhibited. I seem to remember seeing things other people couldn't. As if most opaque objects were transparent. But I was very young. I didn't have any scientific criteria for judgment."

He was reliving it now. The darkened rooms. The earnest assemblages of gawking, prying adults. Himself alone on a little platform, lost in a straight-backed wooden chair. The black silk handkerchief over his eyes. His mother's coaxing, insistent questions. The whispers. The gasps. His own hate of the whole business, mixed with hunger for the adulation of adults. Then the scientists from the university, the experiments, the big test. The reality of those memories engulfed him and momentarily made him forget the reason why he was disclosing them to a stranger.

"Do I understand that your mother tried to make use of you as a medium for communicating with the . . . er . . . other world?"

Catesby nodded eagerly.

"She tried to, but she couldn't. When it came to getting in touch with the dead, I was a complete failure. All I could do—or thought I could do—was see real, existing, three-dimensional objects beyond the vision of normal people. Objects anyone could have seen except for distance, obstruction, or darkness. It was always a disappointment to mother."

He could hear her sweetish, patient voice saying, "Try again, dear, just this once. Katie was your aunt. She loved you. Try to hear what she's saying." And he had answered,

"I can see a woman in a blue dress standing on the other side of Dick's house." And she had replied, "Yes, I know, dear. But that's not Katie. Katie's a spirit. Try again. Just this once, dear." The doctor's voice gently jarred him back into the softly gleaming office.

"You mentioned scientific criteria for judgment, Mr. Wran. As far as you know, did anyone ever try to apply them to you?"

Catesby's nod was emphatic.

"They did. When I was eight, two young psychologists from the university got interested in me. I guess they did it for a joke at first, and I remember being very determined to show them I amounted to something. Even now I seem to recall how the note of polite superiority and amused sarcasm drained out of their voices. I suppose they decided at first that it was very clever trickery, but somehow they persuaded mother to let them try me out under controlled conditions. There were lots of tests that seemed very businesslike after mother's slipshod little exhibitions. They found I was clair-voyant—or so they thought. I got worked up and on edge. They were going to demonstrate my supernormal sensory powers to the university psychology faculty. For the first time I began to worry about whether I'd come through. Perhaps they kept me going at too hard a pace, I don't know. At any rate, when the test came, I couldn't do a thing. Everything became opaque. I got desperate and made things up out of my imagination. I lied. In the end I failed utterly, and I be-lieve the two young psychologists got into a lot of hot water as a result."

He could hear the brusque, bearded man saying, "You've been taken in by a child, Flaxman, a mere child. I'm greatly disturbed. You've put yourself on the same plane as common charlatans. Gentlemen, I ask you to banish from your minds this whole sorry episode. It must never be referred to." He winced at the recollection of his feeling of guilt. But at the same time he was beginning to feel exhilarated and almost light-hearted. Unburdening his long-repressed memories had altered his whole viewpoint. The episodes on the elevated began to take on what seemed their proper proportions as merely the bizarre workings of overwrought nerves and an overly suggestible mind. The doctor, he anticipated confidently, would disentangle the obscure subconscious causes, whatever they might be. And the whole business would be finished off quickly, just as his childhood experience—which was beginning to seem a little ridiculous now—had been finished off.

"From that day on," he continued, "I never exhibited a trace of my supposed powers. My mother was frantic and tried to sue the university. I had something like a nervous breakdown. Then the divorce was granted, and my father got custody of me. He did his best to make me forget it. We went on long outdoor vacations and did a lot of athletics, associated with normal matter-of-fact people. I went to business college eventually. I'm in advertising now. But," Catesby paused, "now that I'm having nervous symptoms, I've wondered if there mightn't be a connection. It's not a question of whether I was really clairvoyant or not. Very likely my mother taught me a lot of unconscious deceptions, good enough to fool even young psychology instructors. But don't you think it may have some important bearing on my present condition?"

For several moments the doctor regarded him with a professional frown. Then he said quietly, "And is there some . . . er . . . more specific connection between your experiences then and now? Do you by any chance find that you are once again beginning to . . . er . . . see things?"

Catesby swallowed. He had felt an increasing eagerness to unburden himself of his fears, but it was not easy to make a beginning, and the doctor's shrewd question rattled him. He forced himself to concentrate. The thing he thought he had seen on the roof loomed up before his inner eye with unexpected vividness. Yet it did not frighten him. He groped for words.

Then he saw that the doctor was not looking at him but over his shoulder. Color was draining out of the doctor's face and his eyes did not seem so small. Then the doctor sprang to his feet, walked past Catesby, threw up the window and peered into the darkness.

As Catesby rose, the doctor slammed down the window and said in a voice whose smoothness was marred by a slight, persistent gasping, "I hope I haven't alarmed you. I saw the face of . . . er . . . a Negro prowler on the fire escape. I must have frightened him, for he seems to have gotten out of sight in a hurry. Don't give it another thought. Doctors are frequently bothered by *voyeurs* . . . er . . . Peeping Toms."

"A Negro?" asked Catesby, moistening his lips.

The doctor laughed nervously. "I imagine so, though my first odd impression was that it was a white man in blackface. You see, the color didn't seem to have any brown in it. It was dead-black."

Catesby moved toward the window. There were smudges on the glass. "It's quite all right, Mr. Wran." The doctor's voice had acquired a sharp note of impatience, as if he were trying hard to reassume his professional authority. "Let's continue our conversation. I was asking you if you were"— he made a face—"seeing things."

Catesby's whirling thoughts slowed down and locked into place. "No, I'm not seeing anything that other people don't see, too. And I think I'd better go now. I've been keeping you too long." He disregarded the doctor's half-hearted gesture of denial. "I'll phone you about the physical examination. In a way you've already taken a big load off my mind." He smiled woodenly. "Goodnight, Dr. Trevethick."

Catesby Wran's mental state was a peculiar one. His eyes searched every angular shadow, he glanced sideways down each chasm-like alley and barren basement passageway, and kept stealing looks at the irregular line of the roofs, yet he was hardly conscious of where he was going. He pushed away the thoughts that came into his mind, and kept moving. He became aware of a slight sense of security as he turned into a lighted street where there were people and high buildings and blinking signs. After a while he found himself in the dim lobby of the structure that housed his office. Then he realized why he couldn't go home, why he daren't go home—after what had happened at the office of Dr. Trevethick.

"Hello, Mr. Wran," said the night elevator man, a burly

figure in overalls, sliding open the grille-work door to the old-fashioned cage. "I didn't know you were working nights now, too."

Catesby stepped in automatically. "Sudden rush of orders," he murmured inanely. "Some stuff that has to be gotten out."

The cage creaked to a stop at the top floor. "Be working very late, Mr. Wran?"

He nodded vaguely, watched the car slide out of sight, found his keys, swiftly crossed the outer office, and entered his own. His hand went out to the light switch, but then the thought occurred to him that the two lighted windows, standing out against the dark bulk of the building, would indicate his whereabouts and serve as a goal toward which something could crawl and climb. He moved his chair so that the back was against the wall and sat down in the semidarkness. He did not remove his overcoat.

For a long time he sat there motionless, listening to his own breathing and the faraway sounds from the streets below: the thin metallic surge of the crosstown streetcar, the farther one of the elevated, faint lonely cries and honkings, indistinct rumblings. Words he had spoken to Miss Millick in nervous jest came back to him with the bitter taste of truth. He found himself unable to reason critically or connectedly, but by their own volition thoughts rose up into his mind and gyrated slowly and rearranged themselves with the inevitable movement of planets.

Gradually his mental picture of the world was transformed. No longer a world of material atoms and empty space, but a world in which the bodiless existed and moved according to its own obscure laws or unpredictable impulses. The new picture illuminated with dreadful clarity certain general facts which had always bewildered and troubled him and from which he had tried to hide: the inevitability of hate and war, the diabolically timed mischances which wreck the best of human intentions, the walls of willful misunderstanding that divide one man from another, the eternal vitality of cruelty and ignorance and greed. They seemed appropriate now, necessary parts of the picture. And superstition only a kind of wisdom.

Then his thoughts returned to himself and the question he had asked Miss Millick, "What would such a thing want from a person? Sacrifices? Worship, Or just fear? What could you do to stop it from troubling you?" It had become a practical question.

With an explosive jangle, the phone began to ring. "Cate, I've been trying everywhere to get you," said his wife. "I never thought you'd be at the office. What are you doing? I've been worried."

He said something about work.

"You'll be home right away?" came the faint anxious question. "I'm a little frightened. Ronny just had a scare. It woke him up. He kept pointing to the window saying, 'Black man, black man.' Of course it's something he dreamed. But I'm frightened. You will be home? What's that, dear? Can't you hear me?"

"I will. Right away," he said. Then he was out of the office, buzzing the night bell and peering down the shaft.

He saw it peering up the shaft at him from the deep shadows three floors below, the sacking face pressed against the iron grille-work. It started up the stair at a shockingly swift, shambling gait, vanishing temporarily from sight as it swung into the second corridor below.

Catesby clawed at the door to the office, realized he had not locked it, pushed it in, slammed and locked it behind him, retreated to the other side of the room, cowered between the filing cases and the wall. His teeth were clicking. He heard the groan of the rising cage. A silhouette darkened the frosted glass of the door, blotting out part of the grotesque reverse of the company name. After a little the door opened.

The big-globed overhead light flared on and, standing inside the door, her hand on the switch, was Miss Millick.

"Why, Mr. Wran," she stammered vacuously, "I didn't know you were here. I'd just come in to do some extra typing after the movie. I didn't . . . but the lights weren't on. What were you—"

He stared at her. He wanted to shout in relief, grab hold of her, talk rapidly. He realized he was grinning hysterically.

"Why, Mr. Wran, what's happened to you?" she asked embarrassedly, ending with a stupid titter. "Are you feeling sick? Isn't there something I can do for you?"

He shook his head jerkily and managed to say, "No, I'm just leaving. I was doing some extra work myself."

"But you *look* sick," she insisted, and walked over toward him. He inconsequentially realized she must have stepped in mud, for her high-heeled shoes left neat black prints.

"Yes, I'm sure you must be sick. You're so terribly pale." She sounded like an enthusiastic, incompetent nurse. Her face brightened with a sudden inspiration. "I've got something in my bag, that'll fix you up right away," she said. "It's for indigestion."

She fumbled at her stuffed oblong purse. He noticed that she was absent-mindedly holding it shut with one hand while she tried to open it with the other. Then, under his very eyes, he saw her bend back the thick prongs of metal locking the purse as if they were tinfoil, or as if her fingers had become a pair of steel pliers.

Instantly his memory recited the words he had spoken to Miss Millick that afternoon. "It couldn't hurt you physically—at first . . . gradually get its hooks into the world . . . might even get control of suitably vacuous minds. Then it could hurt whomever it wanted." A sickish, cold feeling grew inside him. He began to edge toward the door.

But Miss Millick hurried ahead of him.

"You don't have to wait, Fred," she called. "Mr. Wran's decided to stay a while longer."

The door to the cage shut with a mechanical rattle. The cage creaked. Then she turned around in the door.

"Why, Mr. Wran," she gurgled reproachfully, "I just couldn't think of letting you go home now. I'm sure you're terribly unwell. Why, you might collapse in the street. You've just got to stay here until you feel different."

The creaking died away. He stood in the center of the office, motionless. His eyes traced the coal-black course of Miss Millick's footprints to where she stood blocking the door.

Then a sound that was almost a scream was wrenched out of him, for it seemed to him that the blackness was creeping up her legs under the thin stockings.

"Why, Mr. Wran," she said, "you're acting as if you were crazy. You must lie down for a while. Here, I'll help you off with your coat."

The nauseously idiotic and rasping note was the same; only it had been intensified. As she came toward him he turned and ran through the storeroom, clattered a key desperately at the lock of the second door to the corridor. "Why, Mr. Wran," he heard her call, "are you having some kind of a fit? You must let me help you."

The door came open and he plunged out into the corridor and up the stairs immediately ahead. It was only when he reached the top that he realized the heavy steel door in front of him led to the roof. He jerked up the catch.

"Why, Mr. Wran, you mustn't run away. I'm coming after you."

Then he was out on the gritty gravel of the roof. The night sky was clouded and murky, with a faint pinkish glow from the neon signs. From the distant mills rose a ghostly spurt of flame. He ran to the edge. The street lights glared dizzily upward. Two men were tiny round blobs of hat and shoulders. He swung around.

The thing was in the doorway. The voice was no longer solicitous but moronically playful, each sentence ending in a titter.

"Why, Mr. Wran, why have you come up here? We're all alone. Just think, I might push you off."

The thing came slowly toward him. He moved backward until his heels touched the low parapet. Without knowing why, or what he was going to do, he dropped to his knees. He dared not look at the face as it came nearer, a focus for the worst in the world, a gathering point for poisons from everywhere. Then the lucidity of terror took possession of his mind, and words formed on his lips.

"I will obey you. You are my god," he said. "You have supreme power over man and his animals and his machines. You rule this city and all others. I recognize that."

Again the titter, closer. "Why, Mr. Wran, you never talked like this before. Do you mean it?"

"The world is yours to do with as you will, save or tear to pieces," he answered fawningly, the words automatically fitting themselves together in vaguely liturgical patterns. "I recognize that. I will praise, I will sacrifice. In smoke and soot I will worship you for ever."

The voice did not answer. He looked up. There was only Miss Millick, deathly pale and swaying drunkenly. Her eyes were closed. He caught her as she wobbled toward him. His knees gave way under the added weight and they sank down together on the edge of the roof.

After a while she began to twitch. Small noises came from her throat and her eyelids edged open.

"Come on, we'll go downstairs," he murmured jerkily, trying to draw her up. "You're feeling bad."

"I'm terribly dizzy," she whispered. "I must have fainted, I didn't eat enough. And then I'm so nervous lately, about the war and everything, I guess. Why, we're on the roof! Did you bring me up here to get some air? Or did I come up without knowing it? I'm awfully foolish. I used to walk in my sleep, my mother said."

As he helped her down the stairs, she turned and looked at him. "Why, Mr. Wran," she said, faintly, "you've got a big black smudge on your forehead. Here, let me get it off for you." Weakly she rubbed at it with her handkerchief. She started to sway again, and he steadied her.

"No, I'll be all right," she said. "Only I feel cold. What happened, Mr. Wran? Did I have some sort of fainting spell?"

He told her it was something like that.

Later, riding home in the empty elevated car, he wondered how long he would be safe from the thing. It was a purely practical problem. He had no way of knowing, but instinct told him he had satisfied the brute for some time. Would it want more when it came again? Time enough to answer that question when it arose. It might be hard, he realized, to keep out of an insane asylum. With Helen and Ronny to protect, as well as himself, he would have to be careful and tight-lipped. He began to speculate as to how many other men and women had seen the thing or things like it.

The elevated slowed and lurched in a familiar fashion. He looked at the roofs near the curve. They seemed very ordinary, as if what made them impressive had gone away for a while.

Gene Wolfe

SEVEN AMERICAN NIGHTS

Gene Wolfe is the finest writer in the contemporary science fiction field and is reviewed as a major American writer. His works range throughout the varieties of the fantastic to stories and novels of contemporary life. "Seven American Nights" is a masterpiece of SF by a former fan of *Weird Tales*, a complex and horrifying vision of the future: strange, elusive, ambiguous. It is a direct descendent of Poe's "Mellonta Tauta" and J. Leslie Mitchell's *The Last American*, classic satires set in the future; the humor is subtle and ironic. Overtly a simple story, in the end it is a Poesian cryptogram. The theme of drug-induced hallucination is an old one in the literature of the fantastic, never more gracefully or effectively handled than in "Seven American Nights."

ESTEEMED AND LEARNED MADAME:

As I last wrote you, it appears to me likely that your son Nadan (may Allah preserve him!) has left the old capital and traveled—of his own will or another's—north into the region about the Bay of Delaware. My conjecture is now confirmed by the discovery in those regions of the notebook I enclose. It is not of American manufacture, as you see; and though it holds only the records of a single week, several suggestive items therein provide us new reason to hope.

I have photocopied the contents to guide me in my investigations; but I am alert to the probability that you,

Madame, with your superior knowledge of the young man we seek, may discover implications I have overlooked. Should that be the case, I urge you to write me at once.

Though I hesitate to mention it in connection with so encouraging a finding, your most recently due remission has not yet arrived. I assume that this tardiness results from the procrastination of the mails, which is here truly abominable. I must warn you, however, that I shall be forced to discontinue the search unless funds sufficient for my expenses are forthcoming before the advent of winter.

With inexpressible respect,
HASSAN KERBELAI

Here I am at last! After twelve mortal days aboard the *Princess Fatimah*—twelve days of cold and ennui—twelve days of bad food and throbbing engines—the joy of being on land again is like the delight a condemned man must feel when a letter from the shah snatches him from beneath the very blade of death. America! America! Dull days are no more! They say that everyone who comes here either loves or hates you, America—by Allah I love you now!

Having begun this record at last, I find I do not know where to begin. I had been reading travel diaries before I left home; and so when I saw you, O Book, lying so square and thick in your stall in the bazaar—why should I not have adventures too, and write a book like Osman Aga's? Few come to this sad country at the world's edge after all, and most who do land farther up the coast.

And that gives me the clue I was looking for—how to begin. America began for me as colored water. When I went out on deck yesterday morning, the ocean had changed from green to yellow. I had never heard of such a thing before, neither in my reading, nor in my talks with Uncle Mirza, who was here thirty years ago. I am afraid I behaved like the greatest fool imaginable, running about the ship babbling, and looking over the side every few minutes to make certain

the rich mustard color was still there and would not vanish
the way things do in dreams when we try to point them out
to someone else. The steward told me he knew. Golam Gassem the grain merchant (whom I had tried to avoid meeting
for the entire trip until that moment) said, "Yes, yes," and
turned away in a fashion that showed he had been avoiding
me too, and that it was going to take more of a miracle than
yellow water to change his feelings.

One of the few native Americans in first class came out
just then: Mister—as the style is here—Tallman, husband of
the lovely Madam Tallman, who really deserves such a tall
man as myself. (Whether her husband chose that name in
self-derision, or in the hope that it would erase others' memory of his infirmity; or whether it was his father's, and is
merely one of the countless ironies of fate, I do not know.
There was something wrong with his back.) As if I had
not made enough spectacle of myself already, I took this
Mr. Tallman by the sleeve and told him to look over the side,
explaining that the sea had turned yellow. I am afraid Mr.
Tallman turned white himself instead, and turned something
else too—his back—looking as though he would have struck
me if he dared. It was comic enough, I suppose—I heard
some of the other passengers chuckling about it afterward—
but I don't believe I have seen such hatred in a human face
before. Just then the captain came strolling up, and I—considerably deflated but not flattened yet, and thinking that he
had not overheard Mr. Tallman and me—mentioned for the
final time that day that the water had turned yellow. "I
know," the captain said. "It's his country"—there he jerked
his head in the direction of the pitiful Mr. Tallman—"bleeding to death."

Here it is evening again, and I see that I stopped writing
last night before I had so much as described my first sight of
the coast. Well, so be it. At home it is midnight, or nearly,
and the life of the cafés is at its height. How I wish that I
were there now, with you, Yasmin, not webbed among these
red- and purple-clad strangers, who mob their own streets
like an invading army, and duck into their houses like rats

into their holes. But you, Yasmin, or Mother, or whoever may read this, will want to know of my day—only you are sometimes to think of me as I am now, bent over an old, scarred table in a decayed room with two beds, listening to the hastening feet in the streets outside.

I slept late this morning; I suppose I was more tired from the voyage than I realized. By the time I woke, the whole of the city was alive around me, with vendors crying fish and fruits under my shuttered window, and the great wooden wains the Americans call *trucks* rumbling over the broken concrete on their wide iron wheels, bringing up goods from the ships in the Potomac anchorage. One sees very odd teams here, Yasmin. When I went to get my breakfast (one must go outside to reach the lobby and dining room in these American hotels, which I would think would be very inconvenient in bad weather) I saw one of these *trucks* with two oxen, a horse, and a mule in the traces, which would have made you laugh. The drivers crack their whips all the time.

The first impression one gets of America is that it is not as poor as one has been told. It is only later that it becomes apparent how much has been handed down from the previous century. The streets here are paved, but they are old and broken. There are fine, though decayed, buildings everywhere (this hotel is one—the Inn of Holidays, it is called), more modern in appearance than the ones we see at home, where for so long traditional architecture was enforced by law. We are on Maine Street, and when I had finished my breakfast (it was very good, and very cheap by our standards), though I am told it is impossible to get anything out of season here), I asked the manager where I should go to see the sights of the city. He is a short and phenomenally ugly man, something of a hunchback, as so many of them are. "There are no tours," he said. "Not any more."

I told him that I simply wanted to wander about by myself, and perhaps sketch a bit.

"You can do that. North for the buildings, south for the theater, west for the park. Do you plan to go to the park, Mr. Jaffarzadeh?"

"I haven't decided yet."

"You should hire at least two securities if you go to the park—I can recommend an agency."

"I have my pistol."

"You'll need more than that, sir."

Naturally, I decided then and there that I would go to the park, and alone. But I have determined not to spend this, the sole, small coin of adventure this land has provided me so far, before I discover what else it may offer to enrich my existence.

Accordingly, I set off for the north when I left the hotel. I have not, thus far, seen this city, or any American city, by night. What they might be like if these people thronged the streets then, as we do, I cannot imagine. Even by clearest day, there is the impression of carnival, of some mad circus whose performance began a hundred or more years ago and has not ended yet.

At first it seemed that only every fourth or fifth person suffered some trace of the genetic damage that destroyed the old America, but as I grew more accustomed to the streets, and thus less quick to dismiss as Americans and no more the unhappy old woman who wanted me to buy flowers and the boy who dashed shrieking between the wheels of a *truck*, and began instead to look at them as human beings—in other words, just as I would look at some chance-met person on one of our own streets—I saw that there was hardly a soul not marked in some way. These deformities, though they are individually hideous, in combination with the bright, ragged clothing so common here, give the meanest assemblage the character of a pageant. I sauntered along, hardly out of earshot of one group of street musicians before encountering another, and in a few strides passed a man so tall that he was taller seated on a low step than I standing; a bearded dwarf with a withered arm; and a woman whose face had been divided by some devil into halves, one large-eyed and idiotically despairing, the other squinting and sneering.

There can be no question about it—Yasmin must not read this. I have been sitting here for an hour at least, staring at the flame of the candle. Sitting and listening to something that from time to time beats against the steel shutters that close the window of this room. The truth is that I am paralyzed by a fear that entered me—I do not know from where—yesterday, and has been growing ever since.

Everyone knows that these Americans were once the most skilled creators of consciousness-altering substances the world has ever seen. The same knowledge that permitted them to forge the chemicals that destroyed them, so that they might have bread that never staled, innumerable poisons for vermin, and a host of unnatural materials for every purpose, also contrived synthetic alkaloids that produced endless feverish imaginings.

Surely some, at least, of these skills remain. Or if they do not, then some of the substances themselves, preserved for eighty or a hundred years in hidden cabinets, and no doubt growing more dangerous as the world forgets them. I think that someone on the ship may have administered some such drug to me.

That is out at last! I felt so much better at having written it—it took a great deal of effort—that I took several turns about this room. Now that I have written it down, I do not believe it at all.

Still, last night I dreamed of that bread, of which I first read in the little schoolroom of Uncle Mirza's country house. It was no complex, towering "literary" dream such as I have sometimes had, and embroidered, and boasted of afterward over coffee. Just the vision of a loaf of soft white bread lying on a plate in the center of a small table: bread that retained the fragrance of the oven (surely one of the most delicious in the world) though it was smeared with gray mold. Why would the Americans wish such a thing? Yet all the historians agree that they did, just as they wished their own corpses to appear living forever.

It is only this country, with its colorful, fetid streets, deformed people, and harsh, alien language, that makes me feel as drugged and dreaming as I do. Praise Allah that I can speak Farsi to you, O Book. Will you believe that I have taken out every article of clothing I have, just to read the makers' labels? Will *I* believe it, for that matter, when I read this at home?

The public buildings to the north—once the great center, as I understand it, of political activity—offer a severe contrast to the streets of the still-occupied areas. In the latter, the old buildings are in the last stages of decay, or have been repaired by makeshift and inappropriate means; but they seethe with the life of those who depend upon such commercial activity as the port yet provides, and with those who depend on them, and so on. The monumental buildings, because they were constructed of the most imperishable materials, appear almost whole, though there are a few fallen columns and sagging porticos, and in several places small trees (mostly the sad *carpinus caroliniana*, I believe) have rooted in the crevices of walls. Still, if it is true, as has been written, that Time's beard is gray not with the passage of years but with the dust of ruined cities, it is here that he trails it. These imposing shells are no more than that. They were built, it would seem, to be cooled and ventilated by machinery. Many are windowless, their interiors now no more than sunless caves, reeking of decay; into these I did not venture. Others had had fixed windows that once were mere walls of glass; and a few of these remained, so that I was able to sketch their construction. Most, however, are destroyed. Time's beard has swept away their very shards.

Though these old buildings (with one or two exceptions) are deserted, I encountered several beggars. They seemed to be Americans whose deformities preclude their doing useful work, and one cannot help but feel sorry for them, though their appearance is often as distasteful as their importunities. They offered to show me the former residence of their Padshah, and as an excuse to give them a few coins I accompanied them, making them first pledge to leave me when I had seen it.

The structure they pointed out to me was situated at the end of a long avenue lined with impressive buildings; so I suppose they must have been correct in thinking it once important. Hardly more than the foundation, some rubble, and one ruined wing remain now, and it cannot have been originally of an enduring construction. No doubt it was actually a summer palace or something of that kind. The beggars have now forgotten its very name, and call it merely "the white house."

When they had guided me to this relic, I pretended that I wanted to make drawings, and they left as they had promised. In five or ten minutes, however, one particularly enterprising fellow returned. He had no lower jaw, so that I had quite a lot of difficulty in understanding him at first; but after we had shouted back and forth a good deal—I telling him to depart and threatening to kill him on the spot, and he protesting—I realized that he was forced to make the sound of d for b, n for m, and t for p; and after that we got along better.

I will not attempt to render his speech phonetically, but he said that since I had been so generous, he wished to show me a great secret—something foreigners like myself did not even realize existed.

"Clean water," I suggested.

"No, no. A great, great secret, Captain. You think all this is dead." He waved a misshapen hand at the desolated structures that surrounded us.

"Indeed I do."

"One still lives. You would like to see it? I will guide. Don't worry about the others—they're afraid of me. I will drive them away."

"If you are leading me into some kind of ambush, I warn you, you will be the first to suffer."

He looked at me very seriously for a moment, and a man seemed to stare from the eyes in that ruined face, so that I felt a twinge of real sympathy. "See there? The big building to the south, on Pennsylvania? Captain, my father's father's father was chief of a department" ("detartnent") "there. I would not betray you."

From what I have read of this country's policies in the days of his father's father's father, that was little enough reassurance, but I followed him.

We went diagonally across several blocks, passing through two ruined buildings. There were human bones in both, and remembering his boast, I asked him if they had belonged to the workers there.

"No, no." He tapped his chest again—a habitual gesture, I suppose—and scooping up a skull from the floor, held it beside his own head so that I could see that it exhibited cranial deformities much like his own. "We sleep here, to be shut behind strong walls from the things that come at night. We die here, mostly in wintertime. No one buries us."

"You should bury each other," I said.

He tossed down the skull, which shattered on the terrazzo floor, waking a thousand dismal echoes. "No shovel, and few are strong. But come with me."

At first sight the building to which he led me looked more decayed than many of the ruins. One of its spires had fallen, and the bricks lay in the street. Yet when I looked again, I saw that there must be something in what he said. The broken windows had been closed with ironwork at least as well made as the shutters that protect my room here; and the door, though old and weathered, was tightly shut, and looked strong.

"This is the museum," my guide told me. "The only part left, almost, of the Silent City that still lives in the old way. Would you like to see inside?"

I told him that I doubted that we would be able to enter.

"Wonderful machines." He pulled at my sleeve. "You *see* in, Captain. Come."

We followed the building's walls around several corners, and at last entered a sort of alcove at the rear. Here there was a grill set in the weed-grown ground, and the beggar gestured toward it proudly. I made him stand some distance off, then knelt as he had indicated to look through the grill.

There was a window of unshattered glass beyond the grill. It was very soiled now, but I could see through into the basement of the building, and there, just as the beggar had said, stood an orderly array of complex mechanisms.

I stared for some time, trying to gain some notion of their purpose; and at length an old American appeared among them, peering at one and then another, and whisking the shining bars and gears with a rag.

The beggar had crept closer as I watched. He pointed at the old man, and said, "Still come from north and south to study here. Someday we are great again." Then I thought of my own lovely country, whose eclipse—though without genetic damage—lasted twenty-three hundred years. And I gave him money, and told him that, yes, I was certain America would be great again someday, and left him, and returned here.

I have opened the shutters so that I can look across the city to the obelisk and catch the light of the dying sun. Its fields and valleys of fire do not seem more alien to me, or more threatening, than this strange, despondent land. Yet I know that we are all one—the beggar, the old man moving among the machines of a dead age, those machines themselves, the sun, and I. A century ago, when this was a thriving city, the philosophers used to speculate on the reason that each neutron and proton and electron exhibited the same mass as all the others of its kind. Now we know that there is only one particle of each variety, moving backward and forward in time, an electron when it travels as we do, a positron when its temporal displacement is retrograde, the same few particles appearing billions of billions of times to make up a single object, and the same few particles forming all the objects, so that we are all the sketches, as it were, of the same set of pastels.

I have gone out to eat. There is a good restaurant not far from the hotel, better even than the dining room here. When I came back the manager told me that there is to be a play tonight at the theater, and assured me that because it is so close to his hotel (in truth, he is very proud of this theater, and no doubt its proximity to his hotel is the only circumstance that permits the hotel to remain open) I will be in no danger if I go without an escort. To tell the truth, I am a little ashamed that I did not hire a boat today to take me across the channel to the park; so now I will attend the play, and dare the night streets.

Here I am again, returned to this too-large, too-bare, uncarpeted room, which is already beginning to seem a second home, with no adventures to retail from the dangerous benighted streets. The truth is that the theater is hardly more than a hundred paces to the south. I kept my hand on the butt of my pistol and walked along with a great many other people (mostly Americans) who were also going to the theater, and felt something of a fool.

The building is as old as those in the Silent City, I should think; but it has been kept in some repair. There was more of a feeling of gaiety (though to me it was largely an alien gaiety) among the audience than we have at home, and less of the atmosphere of what I may call the sacredness of Art. By that I knew that the drama really is sacred here, as the colorful clothes of the populace make clear in any case. An exaggerated and solemn respect always indicates a loss of faith.

Having recently come from my dinner, I ignored the stands in the lobby at which the Americans—who seem to eat constantly when they can afford it—were selecting various cold meats and pastries, and took my place in the theater proper. I was hardly in my seat before a pipe-puffing old gentleman, an American, desired me to move in order that he might reach his own. I stood up gladly, of course, and greeted him as "Grandfather," as our own politeness (if not theirs) demands. But while he was settling himself and I was still standing beside him, I caught a glimpse of his face from the exact angle at which I had seen it this afternoon, and recognized him as the old man I had watched through the grill.

Here was a difficult situation. I wanted very much to draw him into conversation, but I could not well confess that I had been spying on him. I puzzled over the question until the lights were extinguished and the play began.

It was Vidal's *Visit to a Small Planet*, one of the classics of the old American theater, a play I have often read about but never (until now) seen performed. I would have liked it much better if it had been done with the costumes and settings of its proper period; unhappily, the director had chosen to "modernize" the entire affair, just as we sometimes present *Rustam Beg* as if Rustam had been a hero of the war just past. General Powers was a contemporary American soldier with the mannerisms of a cowardly bandit, Spelding a publisher of libelous broadsheets, and so on. The only characters that gave me much pleasure were the limping spaceman, Kreton, and the ingenue, Ellen Spelding, played as and by a radiantly beautiful American blonde.

All through the first act my mind had been returning (particularly during Spelding's speeches) to the problem of the old man beside me. By the time the curtain fell, I had decided that the best way to start a conversation might be to offer to fetch him a kebab—or whatever he might want—from the lobby, since his thread-bare appearance suggested that he might be ready enough to be treated, and the weakness of his legs would provide an admirable excuse. I tried the gambit as soon as the flambeaux were relit, and it worked as well as I could have wished. When I returned with a paper tray of sandwiches and bitter drinks, he remarked to me quite spontaneously that he had noticed me flexing my right hand during the performance.

"Yes," I said, "I had been writing a good deal before I came here."

That set him off, and he began to discourse, frequently with a great deal more detail than I could comprehend, on the topic of writing machines. At last I halted the flow with some question that must have revealed that I knew less of the subject than he had supposed. "Have you ever," he asked me, "carved a letter in a potato, and moistened it with a stamp pad, and used it to imprint paper?"

"As a child, yes. We use a turnip, but no doubt the principle is the same."

"Exactly; and the principle is that of extended abstraction. I ask you—on the lowest level, what is communication?"

"Talking, I suppose."

His shrill laugh rose above the hubbub of the audience. "Not at all! Smell"—here he gripped my arm—"smell is the essence of communication. Look at that word *essence* itself. When you smell another human being, you take chemicals from his body into your own, analyze them, and from the analysis you accurately deduce his emotional state. You do it so constantly and so automatically that you are largely unconscious of it, and say simply, 'He seemed frightened,' or 'He was angry.' You see?''

I nodded, interested in spite of myself.

''When you speak, you are telling another how you would smell if you smelled as you should and if he could smell you properly from where he stands. It is almost certain that speech was not developed until the glaciations that terminated the Pliocene stimulated mankind to develop fire, and the frequent inhalation of wood smoke had dulled the olfactory organs.''

''I see.''

''No, you hear—unless you are by chance reading my lips, which in this din would be a useful accomplishment.'' He took an enormous bite of his sandwich, spilling pink meat that had surely come from no natural animal. ''When you write, you are telling the other how you would speak if he could hear you, and when you print with your turnip, you are telling him how you would write. You will notice that we have already reached the third level of abstraction.''

I nodded again.

''It used to be believed that only a limited number K of levels of abstraction were possible before the original matter disappeared altogether—some very interesting mathematical work was done about seventy years ago in an attempt to derive a generalized expression for K for various systems. Now we know that the number can be infinite if the array represents an open curve, and that closed curves are also possible.''

''I don't understand.''

''You are young and handsome—very fine looking, with your wide shoulders and black mustache; let us suppose a young woman loves you. If you and I and she were crouched now on the limb of a tree, you would scent her desire. Today, perhaps she tells you of that desire. But it is also possible, is it not, that she may write you of her desire?''

Remembering Yasmin's letters, I assented.

''But suppose those letters are perfumed—a musky, sweet perfume. You understand? A closed curve—the perfume is not the odor of her body, but an artificial simulation of it. It may not be what she feels, but it is what she tells you she feels. Your real love is for a whale, a male deer, and a bed of roses.'' He was about to say more, but the curtain went up for the second act.

I found that act both more enjoyable, and more painful, than the first. The opening scene, in which Kreton (soon joined by Ellen) reads the mind of the family cat, was exceptionally effective. The concealed orchestra furnished music to indicate cat thoughts; I wish I knew the identity of the composer, but my playbill does not provide the information. The bedroom wall became a shadow screen, where we saw silhouettes of cats catching birds, and then, when Ellen tickled the real cat's belly, making love. As I have said, Kreton and Ellen were the play's best characters. The juxtaposition of Ellen's willowy beauty and high-spirited naîveté and Kreton's clear desire for her illuminated perfectly the Paphian difficulties that would confront a powerful telepath, were such persons to exist.

On the other hand, Kreton's summoning of the presidents, which closes the act, was as objectionable as it could possibly have been made. The foreign ruler conjured up by error was played as a Turk, and as broadly as possible. I confess to feeling some prejudice against that bloodthirsty race myself, but what was done was indefensible. When the president of the World Council appeared, he was portrayed as an American.

By the end of that scene I was in no very good mood. I think that I have not yet shaken off the fatigues of the crossing; and they, combined with a fairly strenuous day spent prowling around the ruins of the Silent City, had left me now in that state in which the smallest irritation takes on the dimensions of a moral insult. The old curator beside me discerned my irascibility, but mistook the reason for it, and began to apologize for the state of the American stage, saying that all the performers of talent emigrated as soon as they gained recognition, and returned only when they had failed on the eastern shore of the Atlantic.

''No, no,'' I said. ''Kreton and the girl are very fine, and the rest of the cast is at least adequate.''

He seemed not to have heard me. ''They pick them up

wherever they can—they choose them for their faces. When they have appeared in three plays, they call themselves actors. At the Smithsonian—I am employed there, perhaps I've already mentioned it—we have tapes of real theater: Laurence Olivier, Orson Welles, Katharine Cornell. Spelding is a barber, or at least he was. He used to put his chair under the old Kennedy statue and shave the passers-by. Ellen is a trollop, and Powers a drayman. That lame fellow Kreton used to snare sailors for a singing house on Portland Street.''

His disparagement of his own national culture embarrassed me, though it put me in a better mood. (I have noticed that the two often go together—perhaps I am secretly humiliated to find that people of no great importance can affect my interior state with a few words or some mean service.) I took my leave of him and went to the confectioner's stand in the lobby. The Americans have a very pretty custom of duplicating the speckled eggs of wild birds in marzipan, and I bought a box of these—not only because I wanted to try them myself, but because I felt certain they would prove a treat for the old man, who must seldom have enough money to afford luxuries of that kind. I was quite correct—he ate them eagerly. But when I sampled one, I found its odor (as though I were eating artificial violets) so unpleasant that I did not take another.

''We were speaking of writing,'' the old man said. ''The closed curve and the open curve. I did not have time to make the point that both could be achieved mechanically; but the monograph I am now developing turns upon that very question, and it happens that I have examples with me. First the closed curve. In the days when our president was among the world's ten most powerful men—the reality of the Paul Laurent you see on the stage there—each president received hundreds of requests every day for his signature. To have granted them would have taken hours of his time. To have refused them would have raised a brigade of enemies.''

''What did they do?''

''They called upon the resources of science. That science devised the machine that wrote this.''

From within his clean, worn coat he drew a folded sheet of paper. I opened it and saw that it was covered with the text of what appeared to be a public address, written in a childish scrawl. Mentally attempting to review the list of the American presidents I had seen in some digest of world history long ago, I asked whose hand it was.

"The machine's. Whose hand is being imitated here is one of the things I am attempting to discover."

In the dim light of the theater it was almost impossible to make out the faded script, but I caught the word *Sardinia*. "Surely, by correlating the contents to historical events it should be possible to date it quite accurately."

The old man shook his head. "The text itself was composed by another machine to achieve some national psychological effect. It is not probable that it bears any real relationship to the issues of its day. But now look here." He drew out a second sheet, and unfolded it for me. So far as I could see, it was completely blank. I was still staring at it when the curtain went up.

As Kreton moved his toy aircraft across the stage, the old man took a final egg and turned away to watch the play. There was still half a carton left, and I, thinking that he might want more later, and afraid that they might be spilled from my lap and lost underfoot, closed the box and slipped it into the side pocket of my jacket.

The special effects for the landing of the second spaceship were well done; but there was something else in the third act that gave me as much pleasure as the cat scene in the second. The final curtain hinges on the device our poets call *the Peri's asphodel*, a trick so shopworn now that it is acceptable only if it can be presented in some new light. The one used here was to have John—Ellen's lover—find Kreton's handkerchief and, remarking that it seemed perfumed, bury his nose in it. For an instant, the shadow wall used at the beginning of the second act was illuminated again to graphically (or I should say, pornographically) present Ellen's desire, conveying to the audience that John had, for that moment, shared the telepathic abilities of Kreton, whom all of them had now entirely forgotten.

The device was extremely effective, and left me feeling that I had by no means wasted my evening. I joined the general applause as the cast appeared to take their bows; then, as I was turning to leave, I noticed that the old man appeared very ill. I asked if he were all right, and he confessed ruefully that he had eaten too much, and thanked me again for my kindness—which must at that time have taken a great deal of resolution.

I helped him out of the theater, and when I saw that he had no transportation but his feet, told him I would take him home. He thanked me again, and informed me that he had a room at the museum.

Thus the half-block walk from the theater to my hotel was transformed into a journey of three or four kilometers, taken by moonlight, much of it through rubble-strewn avenues of the deserted parts of the city.

During the day I had hardly glanced at the stark skeleton of the old highway. Tonight, when we walked beneath its ruined overpasses, they seemed inexpressibly ancient and sinister. It occurred to me then that there may be a time-flaw, such as astronomers report from space, somewhere in the Atlantic. How is it that this western shore is more antiquated in the remains of a civilization not yet a century dead than we are in the shadow of Darius? May it not be that every ship that plows that sea moves through ten thousand years?

For the past hour—I find I cannot sleep—I have been debating whether to make this entry. But what good is a travel journal, if one does not enter everything? I will revise it on the trip home, and present a cleansed copy for my mother and Yasmin to read.

It appears that the scholars at the museum have no income but that derived from the sale of treasures gleaned from the past; and I bought a vial of what is supposed to be the greatest creation of the old hallucinatory chemists from the woman who helped me get the old man into bed. It is—it was—about half the height of my smallest finger. Very probably it was alcohol and nothing more, though I paid a substantial price.

I was sorry I had bought it before I left, and still more sorry when I arrived here; but at the time it seemed that this would be my only opportunity, and I could think of nothing but to seize the adventure. After I have swallowed the drug I will be able to speak with authority about these things for the remainder of my life.

Here is what I have done. I have soaked the porous sugar of one of the eggs with the fluid. The moisture will soon dry up. The drug—if there is a drug—will remain. Then I will rattle the eggs together in an empty drawer, and each day, beginning tomorrow night, I will eat one egg.

I am writing today before I go down to breakfast, partly because I suspect that the hotel does not serve so early. Today I intend to visit the park on the other side of the channel. If it is as dangerous as they say, it is very likely I will not return to make an entry tonight. If I do return—well, I will plan for that when I am here again.

After I had blown out my candle last night I could not sleep, though I was tired to the bone. Perhaps it was only the excitement of the long walk back from the museum; but I could not free my mind from the image of Ellen. My wandering thoughts associated her with the eggs, and I imagined myself Kreton, sitting up in bed with the cat on my lap. In my daydream (I was not asleep) Ellen brought me my breakfast on a tray, and the breakfast consisted of the six candy eggs.

When my mind had exhausted itself with this kind of imagery, I decided to have the manager procure a girl for me so that I could rid myself of the accumulated tensions of the voyage. After about an hour, during which I sat up reading, he arrived with three; and when he had given me a glimpse of them through the half-open door, he slipped inside and shut it behind him, leaving them standing in the corridor. I told him I had only asked for one.

"I know, Mr. Jaffarzadeh, I know. But I thought you might like to have a choice."

None of them—from the glimpse I had had—resembled Ellen; but I thanked him for his thoughtfulness and suggested that he bring them in.

"I wanted to tell you first, sir, that you must allow me to set the price with them—I can get them for much less than you, sir, because they know they cannot deceive me, and they must depend on me to bring them to my guests in the future.'' He named a sum that was in fact quite trivial.

"That will be fine,'' I said. "Bring them in.''

He bowed and smiled, making his pinched and miserly face as pleasant as possible and reminding me very much of a picture I had once seen of an imp summoned before the court of Suleiman. "But first, sir, I wished to inform you that if you would like all three—together—you may have them for the price of two. And should you desire only two of the three, you may have them for one and one-half the price of one. All are very lovely, and I thought you might want to consider it.''

"Very well, I have considered it. Show them in.''

"I will light another candle,'' he said, bustling about the room. "There is no charge, sir, for candles at the rate you're paying. I can put the girls on your bill as well. They'll be down as room service—you understand, I'm sure.''

When the second candle was burning and he had positioned it to his liking on the nightstand between the two beds, he opened the door and waved in the girls, saying, "I'll go now. Take what you like and send out the others.'' (I feel certain this was a stratagem—he felt I would have difficulty in getting any to leave, and so would have to pay for all three.)

Yasmin must never see this—that is decided. It is not just that this entire incident would disturb her greatly, but because of what happened next. I was sitting on the bed nearest the door, hoping to decide quickly which of the three most resembled the girl who had played Ellen. The first was too short, with a wan, pinched face. The second was tall and blonde, but plump. The third, who seemed to stumble as she entered, exactly resembled Yasmin.

For a few seconds I actually believed it was she. Science has so accustomed us to devising and accepting theories to account for the facts we observe, however fantastic, that our minds must begin their manufacture before we are aware of it. Yasmin had grown lonely for me. She had booked passage a few days after my own departure, or perhaps had flown, daring the notorious American landing facilities. Arriving here, she had made inquiries at the consulate, and was approaching my door as the manager lit his candle, and not knowing what was taking place had entered with prostitutes he had engaged.

It was all moonshine, of course. I jumped to my feet and held up the candle, and saw that the third girl, though she had Yasmin's large, dark eyes and rounded little chin, was not she. For all her night-black hair and delicate features, she was indisputably an American; and as she came toward me (encouraged, no doubt, because she had attracted my attention) I saw that like Kreton in the play she had a club foot.

As you see, I returned alive from the park after all. Tonight before I retire I will eat an egg; but first I will briefly set down my experiences.

The park lies on the opposite side of the Washington Channel, between the city and the river. It can be reached by land only at the north end. Not choosing to walk so far and return, I hired a little boat with a tattered red sail to carry me to the southern tip, which is called Hains Point. Here there was a fountain, I am told, in the old times; but nothing remains of it now.

We had clear, sunny spring weather, and made our way over exhilarating swells of wave with nothing of the deadly wallowing that oppressed me so much aboard the *Princess Fatimah*. I sat in the bow and watched the rolling greenery of the park on one side of the channel and the ruins of the old fort on the other, while an elderly man handled the tiller, and his thin, sun-browned granddaughter, aged about eleven, worked the sail.

When we rounded the point, the old man told me that for very little more he would take me across to Arlington to see the remains of what is supposed to be the largest building of the country's antiquity. I refused, determined to save that experience for another time, and we landed where a part of the ancient concrete coping remained intact.

The tracks of old roads run up either shore; but I decided to avoid them, and made my way up the center, keeping to the highest ground in so far as I could. Once, no doubt, the whole area was devoted to pleasure. Very little remains, however, of the pavilions and statuary that must have dotted the ground. There are little, worn-away hills that may once have been rockeries but are now covered with soil, and many stagnant pools. In a score of places I saw the burrows of the famous giant American rats, though I never saw the animals themselves. To judge from the holes, their size has not been exaggerated—there were several I could have entered with ease.

The wild dogs, against which I had been warned by both the hotel manager and the old boatman, began to follow me after I had walked about a kilometer north. They are short-haired, and typically blotched with black and brown flecked with white. I would say their average weight was about twenty-five kilos. With their erect ears and alert, intelligent faces they did not seem particularly dangerous; but I soon noticed that whichever way I turned, the ones in back of me edged nearer. I sat on a stone with my back to a pool and made several quick sketches of them, then decided to try my pistol. They did not seem to know what it was, so I was able to center the red aiming laser very nicely on one big fellow's chest before I pressed the stud for a high energy pulse.

For a long time afterward, I heard the melancholy howling of these dogs behind me. Perhaps they were mourning their fallen leader. Twice I came across rusting machines that may have been used to take invalids through the gardens in such fair weather as I myself experienced today. Uncle Mirza says I am a good colorist, but I despair of ever matching the green-haunted blacks with which the declining sun painted the park.

I met no one until I had almost reached the piers of the abandoned railway bridge. Then four or five Americans who pretended to beg surrounded me. The dogs, who as I understand it live mostly upon the refuse cast up by the river, were more honest in their intentions and cleaner in their persons. If these people had been like the pitiful creatures I had met in the Silent City, I would have thrown them a few coins; but they were more or less able-bodied men and women who could have worked, and chose instead to rob. I told them that

I had been forced to kill a fellow countryman of theirs (not mentioning that he was a dog) who had assaulted me; and asked where I could report the matter to the police. At that they backed off, and permitted me to walk around the northern end of the channel in peace, though not without a thousand savage looks. I returned here without further incident, tired and very well satisfied with my day.

I have eaten one of the eggs! I confess I found it difficult to take the first taste; but marshaling my resolution was like pushing at a wall of glass—all at once the resistance snapped, and I picked the thing up and swallowed it in a few bites. It was piercingly sweet, but there was no other flavor. Now we will see. This is more frightening than the park by far.

Nothing seemed to be happening, so I went out to dinner. It was twilight, and the carnival spirit of the streets was more marked than ever—colored lights above all the shops, and music from the rooftops where the wealthier natives have private gardens. I have been eating mostly at the hotel, but was told of a "good" American-style restaurant not too far south on Maine Street.

It was just as described—people sitting on padded benches in alcoves. The tabletops are of a substance like fine-grained, greasy, artificial stone. They looked very old. I had the Number One Dinner—buff-colored fish soup with the pasty American bread on the side, followed by a sandwich of ground meat and raw vegetables doused with a tomato sauce and served on a soft, oily roll. To tell the truth, I did not much enjoy the meal; but it seems a sort of duty to sample more of the American food than I have thus far.

I am very tempted to end the account of my day here, and in fact I laid down this pen when I had written *thus far*, and made myself ready for bed. Still, what good is a dishonest record? I will let no one see this—just keep it to read over after I get home.

Returning to the hotel from the restaurant, I passed the theater. The thought of seeing Ellen again was irresistible; I bought a ticket and went inside. It was not until I was in my seat that I realized that the bill had changed.

The new play was *Mary Rose*. I saw it done by an English company several years ago, with great authenticity; and it struck me that (like Mary herself) It had far outlived its time. The American production was an inauthentic as the other had been correct. For that reason, it retained—or I should have said it had acquired—a good deal of interest.

Americans are superstitious about the interior of their country, not its coasts, so Mary Rose's island had been shifted to one of the huge central lakes. The highlander, Cameron, had accordingly become a Canadian, played by General Powers' former aide. The Speldings had become the Morelands, and the Morelands had become Americans. Kreton was Harry, the knife-throwing wounded soldier; and my Ellen had become Mary Rose.

The role suited her so well that I imagined the play had been selected as a vehicle for her. Her height emphasized the character's unnatural immaturity, and her slenderness, and the vulnerability of her pale complexion, would have told us, I think, if the play had not, that she had been victimized unaware. More important than any of these things was a wild and innocent affinity for the supernatural, which she projected to perfection. It was that quality alone (as I now understood) that had made us believe on the preceding night that Kreton's spaceship might land in the Speldings' rose garden—he would have been drawn to Ellen, though he had never seen her. Now it made Mary Rose's disappearances and reappearances plausible and even likely; it was as likely that unseen spirits lusted for Mary Rose as that Lieutenant Blake (previously John Randolf) loved her.

Indeed, it was more likely. And I had no sooner realized that than the whole mystery of *Mary Rose*—which had seemed at once inexplicable and banal when I had seen it well played in Teheran—lay clear before me. We of the audience were the envious and greedy spirits. If the Morelands could not see that one wall of their comfortable drawing room was but a sea of dark faces, if Cameron had never noticed that we were the backdrop of his island, the fault was theirs. By rights then, Mary Rose should have been drawn to us when she vanished. At the end of the second act I began to look for her, and in the beginning of the third I found her, standing silent and unobserved behind the last row of seats. I was only four rows from the stage, but I slipped out of my place as unobtrusively as I could, and crept up the aisle toward her.

I was too late. Before I had gone halfway, it was nearly time for her entrance at the end of the scene. I watched the rest of the play from the back of the theater, but she never returned.

Same night. I am having a good deal of trouble sleeping, though while I was on the ship I slept nine hours at night, and was off as soon as my head touched the pillow.

The truth is that while I lay in bed tonight I recalled the old curator's remark that the actresses were all prostitutes. If it is true and not simply an expression of hatred for younger people whose bodies are still attractive, then I have been a fool to moan over the thought of Mary Rose and Ellen when I might have had the girl herself.

Her name is Ardis Dahl—I just looked it up in the playbill. I am going to the manager's office to consult the city directory there.

Writing before breakfast. Found the manager's office locked last night. It was after two. I put my shoulder against the door and got it open easily enough. (There was no metal socket for the bolt such as we have at home—just a hole mortised in the frame.) The directory listed several Dahls in the city, but since it was nearly eight years out of date it did not inspire a great deal of confidence. I reflected, however, that in a backwater like this people were not likely to move about so much as we do at home, and that if it were not still of some utility, the manager would not be likely to retain it; so I selected the one that appeared from its address to be nearest the theater, and set out.

The streets were completely deserted. I remember thinking that I was now doing what I had previously been so afraid to do, having been frightened of the city by reading. How ridiculous to suppose that robbers would be afoot now, when no one else was. What would they do, stand for hours at the empty corners?

The moon was full and high in the southern sky, showering the street with the lambent white fluid of its light. If it had not been for the sharp, unclean odor so characteristic of American residential areas, I might have thought myself walking through an illustration from some old book of wonder tales, or an actor in a children's pantomime, so bewitched by the scenery that he has forgotten the audience.

(In writing that—which to tell the truth I did not think of at the time, but only now, as I sat here at my table—I realized that that is in fact what must happen to the American girl I have been in the habit of calling Ellen but must now learn to call Ardis. She could never perform as she does if it were not that in some part of her mind her stage became her reality.)

The shadows about my feet were a century old, tracing faithfully the courses they had determined long before New Tabriz came to jewel the lunar face with its sapphire. Webbed with thoughts of her—my Ellen, my Mary Rose, my Ardis!— and with the magic of that pale light that commands all the tides, I was elevated to a degree I cannot well describe.

Then I was seized by the thought that everything I felt might be no more than the effect of the drug.

At once, like someone who falls from a tower and clutches at the very wisps of air, I tried to return myself to reality. I bit the interiors of my cheeks until the blood filled my mouth, and struck the unfeeling wall of the nearest building with my fist. In a moment the pain sobered me. For a quarter hour or more I stood at the curbside, spitting into the gutter and trying to clean and bandage my knuckles with strips torn from my handkerchief. A thousand times I thought what a sight I would be if I did in fact succeed in seeing Ellen, and I comforted myself with the thought that if she were indeed a prostitute it would not matter to her—I could afford her a few additional rials and all would be well.

Yet that thought was not really much comfort. Even when a woman sells her body, a man flatters himself that she would not do so quite so readily were he not who he is. At the very moment I drooled blood into the street, I was congratulating myself on the strong, square face so many have admired; and wondering how I should apologize if in kissing her I smeared her mouth with red.

Perhaps it was some faint sound that brought me to myself; perhaps it was only the consciousness of being watched. I drew my pistol and turned this way and that, but saw nothing.

Yet the feeling endured. I began to walk again; and if there was any sense of unreality remaining, it was no longer the unearthly exultation I had felt earlier. After a few steps I stopped and listened. A dry sound of rattling and scraping had followed me. It too stopped now.

I was nearing the address I had taken from the directory. I confess my mind was filled with fancies in which I was rescued by Ellen herself, who in the end should be more frightened than I, but who would risk her lovely person to save mine. Yet I knew these *were* but fancies, and the thing pursuing me was not, though it crossed my mind more than once that it might be, some *druj* made to seem visible and palpable to me.

Another block, and I had reached the address. It was a house no different from those on either side—built of the rubble of buildings that were older still, three-storied, heavy-doored, and almost without windows. There was a bookshop on the ground floor (to judge by an old sign) with living quarters above it. I crossed the street to see it better, and stood, wrapped again in my dreams, staring at the single thread of yellow light that showed between the shutters of a gable window.

As I watched that light, the feeling of being watched myself grew upon me. Time passed, slipping through the waist of the universe's great hourglass like the eroded soil of this continent slipping down her rivers to the seas. At last my fear and desire—desire for Ellen, fear of whatever it was that glared at me with invisible eyes—drove me to the door of the house. I hammered the wood with the butt of my pistol, though I knew how unlikely it was that any American would answer a knock at such a time of night, and when I had knocked several times, I heard slow steps from within.

The door creaked open until it was caught by a chain. I saw a gray-haired man, fully dressed, holding an old-fashioned long-barreled gun. Behind him a woman lifted a stub of smoking candle to let him see; and though she was clearly much older than Ellen, and was marked, moreover, by the deformities so prevalent here, there was a certain nobility in her features and a certain beauty as well, so that I was reminded of the fallen statue that is said to have stood on an island farther north, and which I have seen pictured.

I told the man that I was a traveler—true enough!—and that I had just arrived by boat from Arlington and had no place to stay, and so had walked into the city until I had noticed the light of his window. I would pay, I said, a silver rial if they would only give me a bed for the night and breakfast in the morning, and I showed them the coin. My plan was to become a guest in the house so that I might discover whether Ellen was indeed one of the inhabitants; if she were, it would have been an easy matter to prolong my stay.

The woman tried to whisper in her husband's ear, but save for a look of nervous irritation he ignored her. "I don't dare let a stranger in." From his voice I might have been a lion, and his gun a trainer's chair. "Not with no one here but my wife and myself."

"I see," I told him. "I quite understand your position."

"You might try the house on the corner," he said, shutting the door, "but don't tell them Dahl sent you." I heard the heavy bar dropped into place at the final word.

I turned away—and then by the mercy of Allah who is indeed compassionate happened to glance back one last time at the thread of yellow between the shutters of that high window. A flicker of scarlet higher still caught my attention, perhaps only because the light of the setting moon now bathed the rooftop from a new angle. I think the creature I glimpsed there had been waiting to leap upon me from behind, but when our eyes met it launched itself toward me. I had barely time to lift my pistol before it struck me and slammed me to the broken pavement of the street.

For a brief period I think I lost consciousness. If my shot had not killed the thing as it fell, I would not be sitting here writing this journal this morning. After half a minute or so I came to myself enough to thrust its weight away, stand up, and rub my bruises. No one had come to my aid; but neither had anyone rushed from the surrounding houses to kill and rob me. I was as alone with the creature that lay dead at my feet as I had been when I only stood watching the window in the house from which it had sprung.

After I found my pistol and assured myself that it was still in working order, I dragged the thing to a spot of moonlight. When I glimpsed it on the roof, it had seemed a feral dog, like the one I had shot in the park. When it lay dead before me, I had thought it a human being. In the moonlight I saw it was neither, or perhaps both. There was a blunt muzzle; and the height of the skull above the eyes, which anthropologists say is the surest badge of humanity and speech, had been stunted until it was not greater than I have seen in a macaque. Yet the arms and shoulders and pelvis—even a few filthy rags of clothing—all bespoke mankind. It was a female, with small, flattened breasts still apparent on either side of the burn channel.

At least ten years ago I read about such things in Osman Aga's *Mystery Beyond the Sun's Setting*; but it was very different to stand shivering on a deserted street corner of the old capital and examine the thing in the flesh. By Osman Aga's account (which no one, I think, but a few old women has ever believed) these creatures were in truth human beings—or at least the descendants of human beings. In the last century, when the famine gripped their country and the irreversible damage done to the chromosomal structures of the people had already become apparent, some few turned to the eating of human flesh. No doubt the corpses of the famine supplied their food at first; and no doubt those who ate of them congratulated themselves that by so doing they had escaped the effects of the enzymes that were then still used to bring slaughter animals to maturity in a matter of months. What they failed to realize was that the bodies of the human beings they ate had accumulated far more of these unnatural substances than were ever found in the flesh of the short-lived cattle. From them, according to *Mystery Beyond the Sun's Setting*, rose such creatures as the thing I had killed.

But Osman Aga has never been believed. So far as I know, he is a mere popular writer, with a reputation for glorifying Caspian resorts in recompense for free lodging, and for indulging in absurd expeditions to breed more books and publicize the ones he has already written—crossing the desert on a camel and the Alps on an elephant—and no one else has ever, to my knowledge, reported such things from this continent. The ruined cities filled with rats and rabid bats, and the terrible whirling dust storms of the interior, have been enough for other travel writers. Now I am sorry I did not contrive a way to cut off the thing's head; I feel sure its skull would have been of interest to science.

As soon as I had written the preceding paragraph, I realized that there might still be a chance to do what I had failed to do last night. I went to the kitchen, and for a small bribe was able to secure a large, sharp knife, which I concealed beneath my jacket.

It was still early as I ran down the street, and for a few minutes I had high hopes that the thing's body might still be lying where I had left it; but my efforts were all for nothing. It was gone, and there was no sign of its presence—no blood, no scar from my beam on the house. I poked into alleys and waste cans. Nothing. At last I came back to the hotel for breakfast, and I have now (it is mid-morning) returned to my room to make my plans for the day.

Very well, I failed to meet Ellen last night—I shall not fail today. I am going to buy another ticket for the play, and tonight I will not take my seat, but wait behind the last row where I saw her standing. If she comes to watch at the end of the second act as she did last night, I will be there to compliment her on her performance and present her with some gift. If she does not come, I will make my way backstage—from what I have seen of these Americans, a quarter rial should get me anywhere, but I am willing to loosen a few teeth if I must.

* * *

What absurd creatures we are! I have just reread what I wrote this morning, and I might as well have been writing of the philosophic speculations of the Congress of Birds or the affairs of the demons in Domdaniel, or any other subject on which neither I nor anyone else knows or can know a thing. O Book, you have heard what I supposed would occur, now let me tell you what actually took place.

I set out as I had planned to procure a gift for Ellen. On the advice of the hotel manager, I followed Maine Street north until I reached the wide avenue that passes close by the obelisk. Around the base of this still imposing monument is held a perpetual fair in which the merchants use the stone blocks fallen from the upper part of the structure as tables. What remains of the shaft is still, I should say, upwards of one hundred meters high; but it is said to have formerly stood three or four times that height. Much of the fallen material has been carted away to build private homes.

There seems to be no logic to the prices in this country, save for the general rule that foodstuffs are cheap and imported machinery—cameras and the like—costly. Textiles are expensive, which no doubt explains why so many of the people wear ragged clothes that they mend and dye in an effort to make them look new. Certain kinds of jewelry are quite reasonable; others sell for much higher prices than they would in Teheran. Rings of silver or white gold set, usually, with a single modest diamond, may be had in great numbers for such low prices that I was tempted into buying a few to take home as an investment. Yet I saw bracelets that would have sold at home for no more than half a rial, for which the seller asked ten times that much. There were many interesting antiques, all of which are alleged to have been dug from the ruined cities of the interior at the cost of someone's life. When I had talked to five or six vendors of such items, I was able to believe that I knew how the country was depopulated.

After a good deal of this pleasant, wordy shopping, during which I spent very little, I selected a bracelet made of old coins—many of them silver—as my gift to Ellen. I reasoned that women always like jewelry, and that such a showy piece might be of service to an actress in playing some part or other, and that the coins must have a good deal of intrinsic value. Whether she will like it or not—if she ever receives it—I do not know; it is still in the pocket of my jacket.

When the shadow of the obelisk had grown long, I returned here to the hotel and had a good dinner of lamb and rice, and retired to groom myself for the evening. The five remaining candy eggs stood staring at me from the top of my dresser. I remembered my resolve, and took one. Quite suddenly I was struck by the conviction that the demon I believed I had killed the night before had been no more than a phantom engendered by the action of the drug.

What if I had been firing my pistol at mere empty air? That seemed a terrible thought—indeed, it seems so to me still. A worse one is that the drug really may have rendered visible—as some say those ancient preparations were intended to—a real but spiritual being. If such things in fact walk what we take to be unoccupied rooms and rooftops, and the empty streets of night, it would explain many sudden deaths and diseases, and perhaps the sudden changes for the worse we sometimes see in others and others in us, and even the birth of evil men. This morning I called the thing a *druj*; it may be true.

Yet if the drug had been in the egg I ate last night, then the egg I held was harmless. Concentrating on that thought, I forced myself to eat it all, then stretched myself upon the bed to wait.

Very briefly I slept and dreamed. Ellen was bending over me, caressing me with a soft, long-fingered hand. It was only for an instant, but sufficient to make me hope that dreams are prophecies.

If the drug was in the egg I consumed, that dream was its only result. I got up and washed, and changed my clothes, sprinkling my fresh shirt liberally with our Pamir rosewater, which I have observed the Americans hold in high regard. Making certain my ticket and pistol were both in place, I left for the theater.

The play was still *Mary Rose*. I intentionally entered late (after Harry and Mrs. Otery had been talking for several minutes), then lingered at the back of the last row as though I were too polite to disturb the audience by taking my seat. Mrs. Otery made her exit; Harry pulled his knife from the wood of the packing case and threw it again, and when the mists of the past had marched across the stage, Harry was gone, and the Moreland and the parson were chatting to the tune of Mrs. Moreland's knitting needles. Mary Rose would be on stage soon. My hope that she would come out to watch the opening scene had come to nothing; I would have to wait until she vanished at the end of Act II before I could expect to see her.

I was looking for a vacant seat when I became conscious of someone standing near me. In the dim light I could tell little except that he was rather slender, and a few centimeters shorter than I.

Finding no seat, I moved back a step or two. The newcomer touched my arm and asked in a whisper if I could light his cigarette. I had already seen that it was customary to smoke in the theaters here, and I had fallen into the habit of carrying matches to light the candles in my room. The flare of the flame showed the narrow eyes and high cheekbones of Harry—or as I preferred to think of him, Kreton. Taken somewhat aback, I murmured some inane remark about the excellence of his performance.

"Did you like it? It is the least of all parts—I pull the curtain to open the show, then pull it again to tell everyone it's time to go home."

Several people in the audience were looking angrily at us, so we retreated to a point at the head of the aisle that was at least legally in the lobby, where I told him I had seen him in *Visit to a Small Planet* as well.

"Now *there* is a play. The character—as I am sure you saw—is good and bad at once. He is benign, he is mischievous, he is hellish."

"You carried it off wonderfully well, I thought."

"Thank you. This turkey here—do you know how many roles it has?"

"Well, there's yourself, Mrs. Otery, Mr. Amy—"

"No, no." He touched my arm to stop me. "I mean *roles*, parts that require real acting. There's one—the girl. She gets to skip about the stage as an eighteen-year-old whose brain atrophied at ten; and at least half what she does is wasted on the audience because they don't realize what's wrong with her until Act I is almost over.''

''She's wonderful,'' I said. ''I mean Mlle. Dahl.''

Kreton nodded and drew on his cigarette. ''She is a very competent ingenue, though it would be better if she weren't quite so tall.''

''Do you think there's any chance that she might come out here—as you did?''

''Ah,'' he said, and looked me up and down.

For a moment I could have sworn that the telepathic ability he was credited with in *Visit to a Small Planet* was no fiction; nevertheless, I repeated my question: ''Is it probable or not?''

''There's no reason to get angry—no, it's not likely. Is that enough payment for your match?''

''She vanishes at the end of the second act, and doesn't come on stage again until near the close of the third.''

Kreton smiled. ''You've read the play?''

''I was here last night. She must be off for nearly forty minutes, including the intermission.''

''That's right. But she won't be here. It's true she goes out front sometimes—as I did myself tonight—but I happen to know she has company backstage.''

''Might I ask who?''

''You might. It's even possible I might answer. You're Moslem, I suppose—do you drink?''

''I'm not a *strict* Moslem; but no, I don't. I'll buy you a drink gladly though, if you want one, and have coffee with you while you drink it.''

We left by a side door and elbowed our way through the crowd in the street. A flight of narrow and dirty steps descending from the sidewalk led us to a cellar tavern that had all the atmosphere of a private club. There was a bar with a picture (now much dimmed by dirt and smoke) of the cast of a play I did not recognize behind it, three tables, and a few alcoves. Kreton and I slipped into one of these and ordered from a barman with a misshapen head. I suppose I must have stared at him, because Kreton said, ''I sprained my ankle stepping out of a saucer, and now I am a convalescent soldier. Should we make up something for him, too? Can't we just say the potter is angry sometimes?"

"The potter?" I asked.

" 'None answered this; but after Silence spake/A Vessel of a more ungainly Make:/They sneer at me for leaning all awry;/What! Did the Hand then of the Potter shake?' "

I shook my head. "I've never heard that; but you're right, he looks as though his head had been shaped in clay, then knocked in on one side while it was still wet."

"This is a republic of hideousness, as you have no doubt already seen. Our national symbol is supposed to be an extinct eagle; it is in fact the nightmare."

"I find it a very beautiful country," I said. "Though I confess that many of your people are unsightly. Still, there are the ruins, and you have such skies as we never see at home."

"Our chimneys have been filled with wind for a long time."

"That may be for the best. Blue skies are better than most of the things made in factories."

"And not all our people are unsightly," Kreton murmured.

"Oh, no. Mlle. Dahl—"

"I had myself in mind."

I saw that he was baiting me, but I said, "No, you aren't hideous—in fact, I would call you handsome in an exotic way. Unfortunately, my tastes run more toward Mlle. Dahl."

"Call her Ardis—she won't mind."

The barman brought Kreton a glass of green liqueur, and me a cup of the weak, bitter American coffee.

"You were going to tell me who she is entertaining."

"Behind the scenes." Kreton smiled. "I just thought of that—I've used the phrase a thousand times, as I suppose everyone has. This time it happens to be literally correct, and its birth is suddenly made plain, like Oedipus's. No, I don't think I promised I would tell you that—though I suppose I said I might. Aren't there other things you would really rather know? The secret hidden beneath Mount Rushmore, or how you might meet her yourself?''

"I will give you twenty rials to introduce me to her, with some assurance that something will come of the introduction. No one need ever find out."

Kreton laughed. "Believe me, I would be more likely to boast of my profit than keep it secret—though I would probably have to divide my fee with the lady to fulfill the guarantee."

"You'll do it then?"

He shook his head, still laughing. "I only pretend to be corrupt; it goes with this face. Come backstage after the show tonight, and I'll see that you meet Ardis. You're very wealthy, I presume, and if you're not, we'll say you are anyway. What are you doing here?"

"Studying your art and architecture."

"Great reputation in your own country, no doubt?"

"I am a pupil of Akhon Mirza Ahmak; he has a great reputation, surely. He even came here, thirty years ago, to examine the miniatures in your National Gallery of Art."

"Pupil of Akhon Mirza Ahmak, pupil of Akhon Mirza Ahmak," Kreton muttered to himself. "That is very good— I must remember it. But now"—he glanced at the old clock behind the bar—"it's time we got back. I'll have to freshen my makeup before I go on in the last act. Would you prefer to wait in the theater, or just come around to the stage door when the play's over? I'll give you a card that will get you in."

"I'll wait in the theater," I said, feeling that would offer less chance for mishap; also because I wanted to see Ellen play the ghost again.

"Come along then—I have a key for that side door."

I rose to go with him, and he threw an arm about my shoulder that I felt it would be impolite to thrust away. I could feel his hand, as cold as a dead man's, through my clothing, and was reminded unpleasantly of the twisted hands of the beggar in the Silent City.

We were going up the narrow stairs when I felt a gentle touch inside my jacket. My first thought was that he had seen the outline of my pistol, and meant to take it and shoot me. I gripped his wrist and shouted something—I do not remember what. Bound together and struggling, we staggered up the steps and into the street.

In a few seconds we were the center of a mob—some taking his side, some mine, most only urging us to fight, or asking each other what the disturbance was. My pocket sketchpad, which he must have thought held money, fell to the ground between us. Just then the American police arrived—not by air as the police would have come at home, but astride shaggy, hulking horses, and swinging whips. The crowd scattered at the first crackling arc from the lashes, and in a few seconds they had beaten Kreton to the ground. Even at the time I could not help thinking what a terrible thing it must be to be one of these people, whose police are so quick to prefer any prosperous-looking foreigner to one of their own citizens.

They asked me what had happened (my questioner even dismounted to show his respect for me), and I explained that Kreton had tried to rob me, but that I did not want him punished. The truth was that seeing him sprawled unconscious with a burn across his face had put an end to any resentment I might have felt toward him; out of pity, I would gladly have given him the few rials I carried. They told me that if he had attempted to rob me he must be charged, and that if I would not accuse him they would do so themselves.

I then said that Kreton was a friend; and that on reflection I felt certain that what he had attempted had been intended as a prank. (In maintaining this I was considerably handicapped by not knowing his real name, which I had read on the playbill but forgotten, so that I was forced to refer to him as "this poor man.")

At last the policeman said, "We can't leave him in the street, so we'll have to bring him in. How will it look if there's no complaint?"

Then I understood that they were afraid of what their superiors might say if it became known that they had beaten him unconscious when no charge was made against him; and when I became aware that if I would not press charges, the charges they would bring themselves would be far more serious—assault or attempted murder—I agreed to do what they wished, and signed a form alleging the theft of my sketchbook.

When they had gone at last, carrying the unfortunate Kreton across a saddlebow, I tried to reenter the theater. The side door through which we had left was locked, and though I would gladly have paid the price of another ticket, the box office was closed. Seeing that there was nothing further to be done, I returned here, telling myself that my introduction to Ellen, if it ever came, would have to wait for another day.

Very truly it is written that we walk by paths that are always turning. In recording these several pages I have managed to restrain my enthusiasm, though when I described my waiting at the back of the theater for Ardis, and again when I recounted how Kreton had promised to introduce me to her, I was forced for minutes at a time to lay down my pen and walk about the room singing and whistling, and—to reveal everything—jumping over the beds! But now I can conceal no longer. I have seen her! I have touched her hand; I am to see her again tomorrow; and there is every hope that she will become my mistress!

I had undressed and laid myself on the bed (thinking to bring this journal up to date in the morning) and had even fallen into the first doze of sleep when there was a knock at the door. I slipped into my robe and pressed the release.

It was the only time in my life that for even an instant I thought I might be dreaming—actually asleep—when in truth I was up and awake.

How feeble it is to write that she is more beautiful in person than she appears on the stage. It is true, and yet it is a supreme irrelevance. I have seen more beautiful women—indeed, Yasmin is, I suppose, by the formal standards of art, more lovely. It is not Ardis' beauty that draws me to her—the hair like gold, the translucent skin that then still showed traces of the bluish makeup she had worn as a ghost, the flashing eyes like the clear, clean skies of America. It is something deeper than that; something that would remain if all that were somehow taken away. No doubt she has habits that would disgust me in someone else, and the vanity that is said to be so common in her profession, and yet I would do anything to possess her.

Enough of this. What is it but empty boasting, now that I am on the point of winning her?

She stood in my doorway. I have been trying to think how I can express what I felt then. It was as though some tall flower, a lily perhaps, had left the garden and come to tap at my door, a thing that had never happened before in all the history of the world, and would never happen again.

"You are Nadan Jaffarzadeh?"

I admitted that I was, and shamefacedly, twenty seconds too late, moved out of her way.

She entered, but instead of taking the chair I indicated, turned to face me; her blue eyes seemed as large as the colored eggs on the dresser, and they were filled with a melting hope. "You are the man, then, that Bobby O'Keene tried to rob tonight."

I nodded.

"I know you—I mean, I know your face. This is insane. You came to *Visit* on the last night and brought your father, and then to *Mary Rose* on the first night, and sat in the third or fourth row. I thought you were an American, and when the police told me your name, I imagined some greasy fat man with gestures. Why on earth would Bobby want to steal from *you*?"

"Perhaps he needed the money."

She threw back her head and laughed. I had heard her laugh in *Mary Rose* when Simon was asking her father for her hand; but that had held a note of childishness that (however well suited to the part) detracted from its beauty. This laugh was the merriment of houris sliding down a rainbow. "I'm sure he did. He always needs money. You're sure, though, that he meant to rob you? You couldn't have . . ."

She saw my expression and let the question trail away. The truth is that I was disappointed that I could not oblige her, and at last I said, "If you want me to be mistaken, Ardis, then I was mistaken. He only bumped against me on the steps, perhaps, and tried to catch my sketchbook when it fell.''

She smiled, and her face was the sun smiling upon roses. "You would say that for me? And you know my name?"

"From the program. I came to the theater to see you—and that was not my father, who it grieves me to say is long dead, but only an old man, an American, whom I had met that day.''

"You brought him sandwiches at the first intermission—I was watching you through the peephole in the curtain. You must be a very thoughtful person.''

"Do you watch everyone in the audience so carefully?"

She blushed at that, and for a moment could not meet my eyes.

"But you will forgive Bobby, and tell the police that you want them to let him go? You must love the theater, Mr. Jef—Jaff—''

"You've forgotten my name already. It is Jaffarzadeh, a very commonplace name in my country.''

"I hadn't forgotten it—only how to pronounce it. You see, when I came here I had learned it without knowing who you were, and so I had no trouble with it. Now you're a real person to me and I can't say it as an actress should.'' She seemed to notice the chair behind her for the first time, and sat down.

I sat opposite her. "I'm afraid I know very little about the theater.''

"We are trying to keep it alive here, Mr. Jaffar, and—"

"Jaffarzadeh. Call me Nadan—then you won't have so many syllables to trip over.''

She took my hand in hers, and I knew quite well that the gesture was as studied as a salaam and that she felt she was playing me like a fish; but I was beside myself with delight. To be played by *her*! To have *her* eager to cultivate my affection! And the fish will pull her in yet—wait and see!

"I will,'' she said, "Nadan. And though you may know little of the theater, you feel as I do—as we do—or you would not come. It has been such a long struggle; all the history of the stage is a struggle, the gasping of a beautiful child born at the point of death. The moralists, censorship and oppression, technology, and now poverty have all tried to destroy her. Only we, the actors and audiences, have kept her alive. We have been doing well here in Washington, Nadan.''

"Very well indeed," I said. "Both the productions I have seen have been excellent."

"But only for the past two seasons. When I joined the company it had nearly fallen apart. We revived it—Bobby and Paul and I. We could do it because we cared, and because we were able to find a few naturally talented people who can take direction. Bobby is the best of us—he can walk away with any part that calls for a touch of the sinister . . ."

She seemed to run out of breath. I said, "I don't think there will be any trouble about getting him free."

"Thank God. We're getting the theater on its feet again now. We're attracting new people, and we've built up a following—people who come to see every production. There's even some money ahead at last. But *Mary Rose* is supposed to run another two weeks, and after that we're doing *Faust*, with Bobby as Mephistopheles. We've simply no one who can take his place, no one who can come close to him."

"I'm sure the police will release him if I ask them to."

"They *must*. We have to have him tomorrow night. Bill—someone you don't know—tried to go on for him in the third act tonight. It was just ghastly. In Iran you're very polite; that's what I've heard."

"We enjoy thinking so."

"We're not. We never were; and as . . ."

Her voice trailed away, but a wave of one slender arm evoked everything—the cracked plaster walls became as air, and the decayed city, the ruined continent, entered the room with us. "I understand," I said.

"They—we—were betrayed. In our souls we have never been sure by whom. When we feel cheated we are ready to kill; and maybe we feel cheated all the time."

She slumped in her chair, and I realized, as I should have long before, how exhausted she was. She had given a performance that had ended in disaster, then had been forced to plead with the police for my name and address, and at last had come here from the station house, very probably on foot. I asked when I could obtain O'Keene's release.

"We can go tomorrow morning, if you'll do it."

"You wish to come too?"

She nodded, smoothed her skirt, and stood. "I'll have to know. I'll come for you about nine, if that's all right."

"If you'll wait outside for me to dress, I'll take you home."

"That's not necessary."

"It will only take a moment," I said.

The blue eyes held something pleading again. "You're going to come in with me—that's what you're thinking, I know. You have two beds here—bigger, cleaner beds than the one I have in my little apartment; if I were to ask you to push them together, would you still take me home afterward?"

It was as though I were dreaming indeed: a dream in which everything I wanted—the cosmos purified—delivered itself to me. I said, "You won't have to leave at all—you can spend the night with me. Then we can breakfast together before we go to release your friend."

She laughed again, lifting that exquisite head. "There are a hundred things at home I need. Do you think I'd have breakfast with you without my cosmetics, and in these dirty clothes?"

"Then I will take you home—yes, though you lived in Kazvin. Or on Mount Kaf."

She smiled. "Get dressed, then. I'll wait outside, and I'll show you my apartment; perhaps you won't want to come back here afterward."

She went out, her wooden-soled American shoes clicking on the bare floor, and I threw on trousers, shirt, and jacket, and jammed my feet into my boots. When I opened the door, she was gone. I rushed to the barred window at the end of the corridor, and was in time to see her disappear down a side street. A last swirl of her skirt in a gust of night wind, and she had vanished into the velvet dark.

For a long time I stood there looking out over the ruinous buildings. I was not angry—I do not think I could be angry with her. I was, though here it is hard to tell the truth, in some way glad. Not because I feared the embrace of love—I have no doubt of my ability to suffice any woman who can be sated by man—but because an easy exchange of my co-operation for her person would have failed to satisfy my need for romance, for adventure of a certain type, in which danger and love are twined like coupling serpents. Ardis, my Ellen, will provide that, surely, as neither Yasmin nor the pitiful wanton who was her double could. I sense that the world is opening for me only now; that I am being born; that that corridor was the birth canal, and that Ardis in leaving me was drawing me out toward her.

When I returned to my own door, I noticed a bit of paper on the floor before it. I transcribe it exactly here, though I cannot transmit its scent of lilacs.

You are a most attractive man and I want very much to stretch the truth and tell you you can have me freely when Bobby is free but I won't sell myself etc. Really I *will* sell myself for Bobby but I have other fish to fry tonight. I'll see you in the morning and if you can get Bobby out or even try hard you'll have (real) love from the vanishing

Mary Rose

Morning. Woke early and ate here at the hotel as usual, finishing about eight. Writing this journal will give me something to do while I wait for Ardis. Had an American breakfast today, the first time I have risked one. Flakes of pastry dough toasted crisp and drenched with cream, and with it strudel and the usual American coffee. Most natives have spiced pork in one form or another, which I cannot bring myself to try; but several of the people around me were having egg dishes and oven-warmed bread, which I will sample tomorrow.

I had a very unpleasant dream last night; I have been trying to put it out of my mind ever since I woke. It was dark, and I was under an open sky with Ardis, walking over ground much rougher than anything I saw in the park on the farther side of the channel. One of the hideous creatures I shot night before last was pursuing us—or rather, lurking about us, for it appeared first to the left of us, then to the right, silhouetted against the night sky. Each time we saw it, Ardis grasped my arm and urged me to shoot, but the little indicator light on my pistol was glowing red to show that there was not enough charge left for a shot. All very silly, of course, but I am going to buy a fresh powerpack as soon as I have the opportunity.

It is late afternoon—after six—but we have not had dinner yet. I am just out of the tub, and sit here naked, with today's candy egg laid (pinker even than I) beside this book on my table. Ardis and I had a sorry, weary time of it, and I have come back here to make myself presentable. At seven we will meet for dinner; the curtain goes up at eight, so it can't be a long one, but I am going backstage to watch the play from the wings, where I will be able to talk to her when she isn't performing.

I just took a bite of the egg—no unusual taste, nothing but an unpleasant sweetness. The more I reflect on it, the more inclined I am to believe that the drug was in the first I ate. No doubt the monster I saw had been lurking in my brain since I read *Mysteries*, and the drug freed it. True, there were bloodstains on my clothes (the Peri's asphodel!) but they could as easily have come from my cheek, which is still sore. I have had my experience, and all I have left is my candy. I am almost tempted to throw out the rest. Another bite.

Still twenty minutes before I must dress and go for Ardis— she showed me where she lives, only a few doors from the theater. To work then.

Ardis was a trifle late this morning, but came as she had promised. I asked where we were to go to free Kreton, and when she told me—a still-living building at the eastern end of the Silent City—I hired one of the rickety American caleches to drive us there. Like most of them, it was drawn by a starved horse; but we made good time.

The American police are organized on a peculiar system. The national secret police (officially, the Federated Enquiry Divisions) are in a tutorial position to all the others, having power to review their decisions, promote, demote, and discipline, and as the ultimate reward, enroll personnel from the other organizations. In addition they maintain a uniformed force of their own. Thus when an American has been arrested by uniformed police, his friends can seldom learn whether he has been taken by the local police, by the F.E.D. uniformed national force, or by members of the F.E.D. secret police posing as either of the foregoing.

Since I had known nothing of these distinctions previously, I had no way of guessing which of the three had O'Keene; but the local police to whom Ardis had spoken the night before had given her to understand that he had been taken by them. She explained all this to me as we rattled along, then added that we were now going to the F.E.D. Building to secure his release. I must have looked as confused as I felt at this, because she added, "Part of it is a station for the Washington Police Department—they rent the space from the F.E.D."

My own impression (when we arrived) was that they did no such thing—that the entire apparatus was no more real than one of the scenes in Ardis's theater, and that all the men and women to whom we spoke were in fact agents of the secret police, wielding ten times the authority they pretended to possess, and going through a solemn ritual of deception. As Ardis and I moved from office to office, explaining our simple errand, I came to think that she felt as I did, and that she had refrained from expressing these feelings to me in the cab not only because of the danger, the fear that I might betray her or the driver be a spy, but because she was ashamed of her nation, and eager to make it appear to me, a foreigner, that her government was less devious and meretricious than is actually the case.

If this is so—and in that windowless warren of stone I was certain it was—then the very explanation she proffered in the cab (which I have given in its proper place) differentiating clearly between local police, uniformed F.E.D. police, and secret police, was no more than a children's fable, concealing an actuality less forthright and more convoluted.

Our questioners were courteous to me, much less so to Ardis, and (so it seemed to me) obsessed by the idea that something more lay behind the simple incident we described over and over again—so much so in fact that I came to believe it myself. I have neither time nor patience enough to describe all these interviews, but I will attempt to give a sample of one.

We went into a small, windowless office crowded between two others that appeared empty. A middle-aged American woman was seated behind a metal desk. She appeared normal and reasonably attractive until she spoke; then her scarred gums showed that she had once had two or three times the proper number of teeth—forty or fifty, I suppose, in each jaw—and that the dental surgeon who had extracted the supernumerary ones had not always, perhaps, selected those he suffered to remain as wisely as he might. She asked, "How is it outside? The weather? You see, I don't know, sitting in here all day."

Ardis said, "Very nice."

"Do you like it, *Hajji*? Have you had a pleasant stay in our great country?"

"I don't think it has rained since I've been here."

She seemed to take the remark as a covert accusation. "You came too late for the rains, I'm afraid. This is a very fertile area, however. Some of our oldest coins show heads of wheat. Have you seen them?" She pushed a small copper coin across the desk, and I pretended to examine it. There are one or two like it in the bracelet I bought for Ardis, and which I still have not presented to her. "I must apologize on behalf of the District for what happened to you," the woman continued. "We are making every effort to control crime. You have not been victimized before this?"

I shook my head, half suffocated in that airless office, and said I had not been.

"And now you are here." She shuffled the papers she held, then pretended to read from one of them. "You are here to secure the release of the thief who assaulted you. A very commendable act of magnanimity. May I ask why you brought this young woman with you? She does not seem to be mentioned in any of these reports."

I explained that Ardis was a coworker of O'Keene's, and that she had interceded for him.

"Then it is you, Ms. Dahl, who are really interested in securing this prisoner's release. Are you related to him?"

And so on.

At the conclusion of each interview we were told either that the matter was completely out of the hands of the person to whom we had just spent half an hour or an hour talking, that it was necessary to obtain a clearance from someone else, or that an additional deposition had to be made. About two o'clock we were sent to the other side of the river—into what my guidebooks insist is an entirely different jurisdiction—to visit a penal facility. There we were forced to look for Kreton among five hundred or so miserable prisoners, all of whom stank and had lice. Not finding him, we returned to the F.E.D. Building past the half-overturned and yet still brooding figure called the Seated Man, and the ruins and beggars of the Silent City, for another round of interrogations. By five, when we were told to leave, we were both exhausted, though Ardis seemed surprisingly hopeful. When I left her at the door of her building a few minutes ago, I asked her what they would do tonight without Kreton.

"Without Harry, you mean." She smiled. "The best we can, I suppose, if we must. At least Paul will have someone ready to stand in for him tonight."

We shall see how well it goes.

I have picked up this pen and replaced it on the table ten times at least. It seems very likely that I should destroy this journal instead of continuing with it, were I wise; but I have discovered a hiding place for it which I think will be secure.

When I came back from Ardis's apartment tonight there were only two candy eggs remaining. I am certain—absolutely certain—that three were left when I went to meet Ardis. I am almost equally sure that after I had finished making the entry in this book, I put it, as I always do, at the left side of the drawer. It was on the right side.

It is possible that all this is merely the doing of the maid who cleans the room. She might easily have supposed that a single candy egg would not be missed, and have shifted this book while cleaning the drawer, or peeped inside out of curiosity.

I will assume the worst, however. An agent sent to investigate my room might be equipped to photograph these pages—but he might not, and it is not likely that he himself would have a reading knowledge of Farsi. Now I have gone through the book and eliminated all the passages relating to my reason for visiting this leprous country. Before I leave this room tomorrow I will arrange indicators—hairs and other objects whose positions I shall carefully record—that will tell me if the room has been searched again.

Now I may as well set down the events of the evening, which were truly extraordinary enough.

I met Ardis as we had planned, and she directed me to a small restaurant not far from her apartment. We had no sooner seated ourselves than two heavy-looking men entered. At no time could I see plainly the face of either, but it appeared to me that one was the American I had met aboard the *Princess Fatimah* and that the other was the grain dealer I had so assiduously avoided there, Golam Gassem. It is impossible, I think, for my divine Ardis ever to look less than beautiful; but she came as near to it then as the laws of nature permit—the blood drained from her face, her mouth opened slightly, and for a moment she appeared to be a lovely corpse. I began to ask what the trouble was, but before I could utter a word she touched my lips to silence me, and then, having somewhat regained her composure, said, "They have not seen us. I am leaving now. Follow me as though we were finished eating." She stood, feigned to pat her lips with a napkin (so that the lower half of her face was hidden) and walked out into the street.

I followed her, and found her laughing not three doors away from the entrance to the restaurant. The change in her could not have been more startling if she had been released from an enchantment. "It is so funny," she said. "Though it wasn't then. Come on, we'd better go; you can feed me after the show."

I asked her what those men were to her.

"Friends," she said, still laughing.

"If they are friends, why were you so anxious that they not see you? Were you afraid they would make us late?" I knew that such a trivial explanation could not be true, but I wanted to leave her a means of evading the question if she did not want to confide in me.

She shook her head. "No, no. I didn't want either to think I did not trust him. I'll tell you more later, if you want to involve yourself in our little charade."

"With all my heart."

She smiled at that—that sun-drenched smile for which I would gladly have entered a lion pit. In a few more steps we were at the rear entrance to the theater, and there was no time to say more. She opened the door, and I heard Kreton arguing with a woman I later learned was the wardrobe mistress. "You are free," I said, and he turned to look at me.

"Yes. Thanks to you, I think. And I do thank you."

Ardis gazed on him as though he were a child saved from drowning. "Poor Bobby. Was it very bad?"

"It was frightening, that's all. I was afraid I'd never get out. Do you know Terry is gone?"

She shook her head, and said, "What do you mean?" but I was certain—and here I am not exaggerating or coloring the facts, though I confess I have occasionally done so elsewhere in this chronicle—that she had known it before he spoke.

"He simply isn't here. Paul is running around like a lunatic. I hear you missed me last night."

"God, yes," Ardis said, and darted off too swiftly for me to follow.

Kreton took my arm. I expected him to apologize for having tried to rob me, but he said, "You've met her, I see."

"She persuaded me to drop the charges against you."

"Whatever it was you offered me—twenty rials? I'm morally entitled to it, but I won't claim it. Come and see me when you're ready for something more wholesome—and meanwhile, how do you like her?"

"That is something for me to tell her," I said, "not you."

Ardis returned as I spoke, bringing with her a balding black man with a mustache. "Paul, this is Nadan. His English is very good—not so British as most of them. He'll do, don't you think?''

''He'll have to—you're sure he'll do it?''

''He'll love it,'' Ardis said positively, and disappeared again.

It seemed that ''Terry'' was the actor who played Mary Rose's husband and lover, Simon; and I—who had never acted in so much as a school play—was to be pressed into the part. It was about half an hour before curtain time, so I had all of fifty minutes to learn my lines before my entrance at the end of the first act.

Paul, the director, warned me that if my name were used, the audience would be hostile; and since the character (in the version of the play they were presenting) was supposed to be an American, they would see errors where none existed. A moment later, while I was still in frantic rehearsal, I heard him saying, ''The part of Simon Blake will be taken by Ned Jefferson.''

The act of stepping onto the stage for the first time was really the worst part of the entire affair. Fortunately I had the advantage of playing a nervous young man come to ask for the hand of his sweetheart, so that my shaky laughter and stammer became ''acting.''

My second scene—with Mary Rose and Cameron on the magic island—ought by rights to have been much more difficult than the first. I had had only the intermission in which to study my lines, and the scene called for pessimistic apprehension rather than mere anxiety. But all the speeches were short, and Paul had been able by that time to get them lettered on large sheets of paper, which he and the stage manager held up in the wings. Several times I was forced to extemporize, but though I forgot the playwright's words, I never lost my sense of the *trend* of the play, and was always able to contrive something to which Ardis and Cameron could adapt their replies.

In comparison to the first and second acts, my brief appearance in the third was a holiday; yet I have seldom been so exhausted as I was tonight when the stage darkened for Ardis's final confrontation with Kreton, and Cameron and I, and the middle-aged people who had played the Morelands were able to creep away.

We had to remain in costume until we had taken our bows, and it was nearly midnight before Ardis and I got something to eat at the same small, dirty bar outside which Kreton had tried to rob me. Over the steaming plates she asked me if I had enjoyed acting, and I had to nod.

"I thought you would. Under all that solidity you're a very dramatic person, I think."

I admitted it was true, and tried to explain why I feel that what I call *the romance of life* is the only thing worth seeking. She did not understand me, and so I passed it off as the result of having been brought up on the *Shah Namah*, of which I found she had never heard.

We went to her apartment. I was determined to take her by force if necessary—not because I would have enjoyed brutalizing her, but because I felt she would inevitably think my love far less than it was if I permitted her to put me off a second time. She showed me about her quarters (two small rooms in great disorder), then, after we had lifted into place the heavy bar that is the sigil of every American dwelling, put her arms about me. Her breath was fragrant with the arrack I had bought for her a few minutes before. I feel sure now that for the rest of my life that scent will recall this evening to me.

When we parted, I began to unloose the laces that closed her blouse, and she at once pinched out the candle. I pleaded that she was thus depriving me of half the joy I might have had of her love; but she would not permit me to relight it, and our caresses and the embraces of our couplings were exchanged in perfect darkness. I was in ecstasy. To have seen her, I would have blinded myself; yet nothing could have increased my delight.

When we separated for the last time, both spent utterly, and she left to wash, I sought for matches. First in the drawer of the unsteady little table beside the bed, then among the disorder of my own clothes, which I had dropped to the floor and we had kicked about. I found some eventually, but could not find the candle—Ardis, I think, had hidden it. I struck a match; but she had covered herself with a robe. I said, "Am I never to see you?"

"You will see me tomorrow. You're going to take me boating, and we'll picnic by the water, under the cherry trees. Tomorrow night the theater will be closed for Easter, and you can take me to a party. But now you are going home, and I am going to go to sleep." When I was dressed and standing in her doorway, I asked her if she loved me; but she stopped my mouth with a kiss.

I have already written about the rest—returning to find two eggs instead of three, and this book moved. I will not write of that again. But I have just—between this paragraph and the last—read over what I wrote earlier tonight, and it seems to me that one sentence should have had more weight than I gave it: when I said that in my role as Simon I never lost the *trend* of the play.

What the fabled secret buried by the old Americans beneath their carved mountain may be I do not know; but I believe that if it is some key to the world of human life, it must be some form of that. Every great man, I am sure, consciously or not, in those terms or others, has grasped that secret—save that in the play that is our life we can grapple that trend and draw it to left or right if we have the will.

So I am doing now. If the taking of the egg was not significant, yet I will make it so—indeed I already have when I infused one egg with the drug. If the scheme in which Ardis is entangled—with Golam Gassem and Mr. Tallman if it be they—is not some affair of statecraft and dark treasure, yet I will make it so before the end. If our love is not a great love, destined to live forever in the hearts of the young and the mouths of the poets, it will be so before the end.

Once again I am here; and in all truth I am beginning to wonder if I do not write this journal only to read it. No man was ever happier than I am now—so happy, indeed, that I was sorely tempted not to taste either of the two eggs that remain. What if the drug, in place of hallucination, self-knowledge, and euphoria, brings permanent and despairing madness? Yet I have eaten it nonetheless, swallowing the whole sweet lump in a few bites. I would rather risk whatever may come than think myself a coward. With equanimity I await the effects.

The fact is that I am too happy for all the Faustian determination I penned last night. (How odd that *Faust* will be the company's next production. Kreton will be Mephistopheles, of course—Ardis said as much, and it would be certain in any case. Ardis herself will be Margaret. But who will play the Doctor?) Yet now, when all the teeth-gritting, table-pounding determination is gone, I know that I will carry out the essentials of the *plan* more surely than ever—with the ease, in fact, of an accomplished violinist sawing out some simple tune while his mind roves elsewhere. I have been looking at the ruins of the Jeff (as they call it), and it has turned my mind again to the fate of the old Americans. How often they, who chose their leaders for superficial appearances of strength, wisdom, and resolution, must have elected them only because they were as fatigued as I was last night.

I had meant to buy a hamper of delicacies, and call for Ardis about one, but she came for me at eleven with a little basket already packed. We walked north along the bank of the channel until we reached the ruins of the old tomb to which I have already referred, and the nearly circular artificial lake the Americans call the Basin. It is rimmed with flowering trees—old and gnarled, but very beautiful in their robes of white blossom. For some little American coin we were given command of a bright blue boat with a sail twice or three times the size of my handkerchief, in which to dare the halcyon waters of the lake.

When we were well away from the people on shore, Ardis asked me, rather suddenly, if I intended to spend all my time in America here in Washington.

I told her that my original plan had been to stay here no more than a week, then make my way up the coast to Philadelphia and the other ancient cities before I returned home; but that now that I had met her I would stay here forever if she wished it.

"Haven't you ever wanted to see the interior? This strip of beach we live on is kept half alive by the ocean and the trade that crosses it; but a hundred miles inland lies the wreck of our entire civilization, waiting to be plundered.''

''Then why doesn't someone plunder it?'' I asked.

''They do. A year never passes without someone bringing some great prize out—but it is so large . . .'' I could see her looking beyond the lake and the fragrant trees. ''So large that whole cities are lost in it. There was an arch of gold at the entrance to St. Louis—no one knows what became of it. Denver, the Mile-High City, was nested in silver mines; no one can find them now.''

''Many of the old maps must still be in existence.''

Ardis nodded slowly, and I sensed that she wanted to say more than she had. For a few seconds there was no sound but the water lapping against the side of the boat.

''I remember having seen some in the museum in Teheran—not only our maps, but some of your own from a hundred years ago.''

''The courses of the rivers have changed,'' she said. ''And when they have not, no one can be sure of it.''

''Many buildings must still be standing, as they are here, in the Silent City.''

''That was built of stone—more solidly than anything else in the country. But yes, some, many, are still there.''

''Then it would be possible to fly in, land somewhere, and pillage them.''

''There are many dangers, and so much rubble to look through that anyone might search for a lifetime and only scratch the surface.''

I saw that talking of all this only made her unhappy, and tried to change the subject. ''Didn't you say that I could escort you to a party tonight? What will that be like?''

''Nadan, I have to trust someone. You've never met my father, but he lives close to the hotel where you are staying, and has a shop where he sells old books and maps.'' (So I had visited the right house—almost—after all!) ''When he was younger, he wanted to go into the interior. He made three or four trips, but never got farther than the Appalachian foothills. Eventually he married my mother and didn't feel any longer that he could take the risks . . .''

"I understand."

"The things he had sought to guide him to the wealth of the past became his stock in trade. Even today, people who live farther inland bring him old papers; he buys them and resells them. Some of those people are only a step better than the ones who dig up the cemeteries for the wedding rings of the dead women."

I recalled the rings I had bought in the shadow of the broken obelisk, and shuddered, though I do not believe Ardis observed it.

"I said that some of them were hardly better than the grave robbers. The truth is that some are worse—there are people in the interior who are no longer people. Our bodies are poisoned—you know that, don't you? All of us Americans. They have adapted—that's what Father says—but they are no longer human. He made his peace with them long ago, and he trades with them still."

"You don't have to tell me this."

"Yes, I do—I must. Would you go into the interior, if I went with you? The government will try to stop us if they learn of it, and to confiscate anything we find."

I assured her with every oath I could remember that with her beside me I would cross the continent on foot if need be.

"I told you about my father. I said that he sells the maps and records they bring him. What I did not tell you is that he reads them first. He has never given up, you see, in his heart."

"He has made a discovery?" I asked.

"He's made many—hundreds. Bobby and I have used them. You remember those men in the restaurant? Bobby went to each of them with a map and some of the old letters. He's persuaded them to help finance an expedition into the interior, and made each of them believe that we'll help him cheat the other—that keeps them from combining to cheat us, you see."

"And you want me to go with you?" I was beside myself with joy.

"We weren't going to go at all—Bobby was going to take the money, and go to Baghdad or Marrakesh, and take me with him. But, Nadan"—here she leaned forward, I remember, and took my hand in hers—"there really is a secret. There are many, but one better—more likely to be true, more likely to yield truly immense wealth than all the others. I know you would share fairly with me. We'll divide everything, and I'll go back to Teheran with you."

I know that I have never been more happy in my life than I was then, in that silly boat. We sat together in the stern, nearly sinking it, under the combined shade of the tiny sail and Ardis's big straw hat, and kissed and stroked one another until we would have been pilloried a dozen times in Iran.

At last, when I could bear no more unconsummated love, we ate the sandwiches Ardis had brought, and drank some warmish, fruit-flavored beverage, and returned to shore.

When I took her home a few minutes ago, I very strongly urged her to let me come upstairs with her; I was on fire for her, sick to impale her upon my own flesh and pour myself into her as some mad god before the coming of the Prophet might have poured his golden blood into the sea. She would not permit it—I think because she feared that her apartment could not be darkened enough to suit her modesty. I am determined that I will yet see her.

I have bathed and shaved to be ready for the party, and as there is still time I will insert here a description of the procession we passed on the way back from the lake. As you see, I have not yet completely abandoned the thought of a book of travels.

A very old man—I suppose a priest—carried a cross on a long pole, using it as a staff, and almost as a crutch. A much younger one, fat and sweating, walked backward before him swinging a smoking censer. Two robed boys carrying large candles preceded them, and they were followed by more robed children, singing, who fought with nudges and pinches when they felt the fat man was not watching them.

Like everyone else, I have seen this kind of thing done much better in Rome; but I was more affected by what I saw here. When the old priest was born, the greatness of America must have been a thing of such recent memory that few can have realized it had passed forever; and the entire procession—from the flickering candles in clear sunshine, to the dead leader lifted up, to his inattentive, bickering followers behind—seemed to me to incarnate the philosophy and the dilemma of these people. So I felt, at least, until I saw that they watched it as uncomprehendingly as they might if they themselves were only travelers abroad, and I realized that its ritualized plea for life renewed was more foreign to them than to me.

It is very late—three, my watch says.

I resolved again not to write in this book. To burn it or tear it to pieces, or to give it to some beggar; but now I am writing once again because I cannot sleep. The room reeks of my vomit, though I have thrown open the shutters and let in the night.

How could I have loved that? (And yet a few moments ago, when I tried to sleep, visions of Ellen pursued me back to wakefulness.)

The party was a masque, and Ardis had obtained a costume for me—a fantastic gilded armor from the wardrobe of the theater. She wore the robes of an Egyptian princess, and a domino. At midnight we lifted our masks and kissed, and in my heart I swore that tonight the mask of darkness would be lifted too.

When we left, I carried with me the bottle we had brought, still nearly half full; and before she pinched out the candle I persuaded her to pour out a final drink for us to share when the first frenzy of our desire was past. She—it—did as I asked, and set it on the little table near the bed. A long time afterward, when we lay gasping side by side, I found my pistol with one groping hand and fired the beam into the wide-bellied glass. Instantly it filled with a blue fire from the burning alcohol. Ardis screamed, and sprang up.

I ask myself now how I could have loved; but then, how could I in one week have come so near to loving this corpse-country? Its eagle is dead—Ardis is the proper symbol of its rule.

One hope, one very small hope remains. It is possible that

what I saw tonight was only an illusion, induced by the egg. I know now that the thing I killed before Ardis's father's house was real, and between this paragraph and the last I have eaten the last egg. If hallucinations now begin, I will know that what I saw by the light of the blazing arrack was in truth a thing with which I have lain, and in one way or another will see to it that I never return to corrupt the clean wombs of the women of our enduring race. I might seek to claim the miniatures of our heritage after all, and allow the guards to kill me—but what if I were to succeed? I am not fit to touch them. Perhaps the best end for me would be to travel alone into this maggot-riddled continent; in that way I will die at fit hands.

Later. Kreton is walking in the hall outside my door, and the tread of his twisted black shoe jars the building like an earthquake. I heard the word *police* as though it were thunder. My dead Ardis, very small and bright, has stepped out of the candle-flame, and there is a hairy face coming through the window.

The old woman closed the notebook. The younger woman, who had been reading over her shoulder, moved to the other side of the small table and seated herself on a cushion, her feet politely positioned so that the soles could not be seen. "He is alive then," she said.

The older woman remained silent, her gray head bowed over the notebook, which she held in both hands.

"He is certainly imprisoned, or ill, otherwise he would have been in touch with us." The younger woman paused, smoothing the fabric of her *chador* with her right hand, while the left toyed with the gem simulator she wore on a thin chain. "It is possible that he has already tried, but his letters have miscarried."

"You think this is his writing?" the older woman asked, opening the notebook at random. When the younger did not answer, she added, "Perhaps. Perhaps."

Charles Dickens

THE SIGNAL-MAN

Charles Dickens is the most important force in the popularity of the ghost story in the nineteenth century. Dickens gave the ghost story a traditional home in the Christmas issues of the influential magazines he edited, and wrote the most enduring classic in the Christmas ghost sub-genre himself, "A Christmas Carol." He solidified the scattered tradition of telling ghost stories of all types during the Christmas season into a cultural ritual as not only the most popular writer in English of his era but also as one of the most powerful editors. His active career extends from the 1830s to the 1870s and by the end of that career, Dickens had brought into print some of the finest horror stories of the century and made them fashionable. Dickens' own short fiction was nearly always sentimental and in the moral allegory mode . . . certainly all of his once famous Christmas stories are. But "The Signal-Man" is something else entirely, a penetrating psychological story and a disturbingly ambiguous questioning of the nature of reality, a story of "nameless horror." It is perhaps Dickens' best horror story.

"Halloa! Below there!"

When he heard a voice thus calling to him, he was standing at the door of his box, with a flag in his hand, furled round its short pole. One would have thought, considering the nature of the ground, that he could not have doubted from what quarter the voice came; but instead of looking up to where I stood on the top of the steep cutting nearly over his head, he turned himself about, and looked down the Line. There was something remarkable in his manner of doing so, though I could not have said for my life what. But I know it was remarkable enough to attract my notice, even though his figure was foreshortened and shadowed, down in the deep trench, and mine was high above him, so steeped in the glow of an angry sunset, that I had shaded my eyes with my hand before I saw him at all.

"Halloa! Below!"

From looking down the Line, he turned himself about again, and, raising his eyes, saw my figure high above him.

"Is there any path by which I can come down and speak to you?"

He looked up at me without replying, and I looked down at him without pressing him too soon with a repetition of my idle question. Just then there came a vague vibration in the earth and air, quickly changing into a violent pulsation, and an oncoming rush that caused me to start back, as though it had force to draw me down. When such vapour as rose to my height from this rapid train had passed me, and was skimming away over the landscape, I looked down again, and saw him refurling the flag he had shown while the train went by.

I repeated my inquiry. After a pause, during which he seemed to regard me with fixed attention, he motioned with his rolled-up flag towards a point on my level, some two or three hundred yards distant. I called down to him, "All right!" and made for that point. There, by dint of looking closely about me, I found a rough zigzag descending path notched out, which I followed.

The cutting was extremely deep and unusually precipitous. It was made through a clammy stone, that became oozier and wetter as I went down. For these reasons, I found the way long enough to give me time to recall a singular air of reluctance or compulsion with which he had pointed out the path.

When I came down low enough upon the zigzag descent to see him again, I saw that he was standing between the rails on the way by which the train had lately passed, in an attitude as if he were waiting for me to appear. He had his left hand at his chin, and that left elbow rested on his right hand, crossed over his breast. His attitude was one of such expectation and watchfulness that I stopped a moment, wondering at it.

I resumed my downward way, and stepping out upon the level of the railroad, and drawing nearer to him, saw that he was a dark, sallow man, with a dark beard and rather heavy eyebrows. His post was in as solitary and dismal a place as ever I saw. On either side a dripping-wet wall of jagged stone, excluding all view but a strip of sky; the perspective one way only a crooked prolongation of this great dungeon; the shorter perspective in the other direction terminating in a gloomy red light, and the gloomier entrance to a black tunnel, in whose massive architecture there was a barbarous, depressing, and forbidding air. So little sunlight ever found its way to this spot that it had an earthy, deadly smell; and so much cold wind rushed through it that it struck chill to me, as if I had left the natural world.

Before he stirred, I was near enough to him to have touched him. Not even then removing his eyes from mine, he stepped back one step, and lifted his hand.

This was a lonesome post to occupy (I said), and it had riveted my attention when I looked down from up yonder. A visitor was a rarity, I should suppose; not an unwelcome rarity, I hoped? In me he merely saw a man who had been shut up within narrow limits all his life, and who, being at last set free, had a newly-awakened interest in these great works. To such purpose I spoke to him; but I am far from sure of the terms I used, for, besides that I am not happy in opening any conversation, there was something in the man that daunted me.

He directed a most curious look towards the red light near the tunnel's mouth, and looked all about it, as if something were missing from it, and then looked at me.

That light was part of his charge, was it not?

He answered in a low voice, ''Don't you know it is?''

The monstrous thought came into my mind, as I perused the fixed eyes and the saturnine face, that this was a spirit, not a man. I have speculated since whether there may have been infection in his mind.

In my turn I stepped back. But in making the action, I detected in his eyes some latent fear of me. This put the monstrous thought to flight.

"You look at me," I said, forcing a smile, "as if you had a dread of me."

"I was doubtful," he returned, "whether I had seen you before."

"Where?"

He pointed to the red light he had looked at.

"There?" I said.

Intently watchful of me, he replied (but without sound), "Yes."

"My good fellow, what should I do there? However, be that as it may, I never was there, you may swear."

"I think I may," he rejoined. "Yes; I am sure I may."

His manner cleared, like my own. He replied to my remarks with readiness, and in well-chosen words. Had he much to do there? Yes—that was to say, he had enough responsibility to bear; but exactness and watchfulness were what was required of him, and of actual work—manual labour—he had next to none. To change that signal, to trim those lights, and to turn this iron handle now and then, was all he had to do under that head. Regarding those many long and lonely hours of which I seemed to make so much, he could only say that the routine of his life had shaped itself into that form, and he had grown used to it. He had taught himself a language down here—if only to know it by sight, and to have formed his own crude ideas of its pronunciation, could be called learning it. He had also worked at fractions and decimals, and tried a little algebra; but he was, and had been as a boy, a poor hand at figures. Was it necessary for him when on duty always to remain in that channel of damp air, and could he never rise into the sunshine from between those high stone walls? Why that depended upon times and circumstances. Under some conditions there would be less upon the Line than under others; and the same held good as to certain hours of the day and night. In bright weather, he did choose occasions for getting a little above those lower shadows; but, being at all times liable to be called by his electric bell, and at such times listening for it with redoubled anxiety, the relief was less than I would suppose.

He took me into his box, where there was a fire, a desk for an official book in which he had to make certain entries, a telegraphic instrument with its dial, face, and needles, and the little bell of which he had spoken. On my trusting that he would excuse the remark that he had been well educated, and (I hoped I might say without offence) perhaps educated above that station, he observed that instances of slight incongruity in such wise would rarely be found wanting among large bodies of men; that he had heard it was so in workhouses, in the police force, even in that last desperate resource the army; and that he knew it was so, more or less, in any great railway staff. He had been, when young (if I could believe it, sitting in that hut—he scarcely could), a student of natural philosophy, and had attended lectures; but he had run wild, misused his opportunities, gone down, and never risen again. He had no complaint to offer about that. He had made his bed, and he lay upon it. It was far too late to make another.

All that I have here condensed he said in a quiet manner, with his grave dark regards divided between me and the fire. He threw in the word ''Sir'' from time to time, and especially when he referred to his youth—as though to request me to understand that he claimed to be nothing but what I found him. He was several times interrupted by the little bell, and had to read off messages, and send replies. Once he had to stand without the door, and display a flag as a train passed, and make some verbal communication to the driver. In the discharge of his duties, I observed him to be remarkably exact and vigilant, breaking off his discourse at a syllable, and remaining silent until what he had to do was done.

In a word, I should have set this man down as one of the safest of men to be employed in that capacity, but for the circumstance that while he was speaking to me he twice broke off with a fallen colour, turned his face towards the little bell when it did NOT ring, opened the door of the hut (which was kept shut to exclude the unhealthy damp), and looked out towards the red light near the mouth of the tunnel. On both of those occasions, he came back to the fire with the inexplicable air upon him which I had remarked, without being able to define, when we were so far asunder.

Said I, when I rose to leave him, "You almost make me think that I have met with a contented man."

(I am afraid I must acknowledge that I said it to lead him on.)

"I believe I used to be so," he rejoined, in the low voice in which he had first spoken; "but I am troubled, sir, I am troubled."

He would have recalled the words if he could. He had said them, however, and I took them up quickly.

"With what? What is your trouble?"

"It is very difficult to impart, sir. It is very, very difficult to speak of. If ever you make me another visit, I will try to tell you."

"But I expressly intend to make you another visit. Say, when shall it be?"

"I go off early in the morning, and I shall be on again at ten tomorrow night, sir."

"I will come at eleven."

He thanked me, and went out at the door with me. "I'll show my white light, sir," he said, in his peculiar low voice, "till you have found the way up. When you have found it, don't call out! And when you are at the top, don't call out!"

His manner seemed to make the place strike colder to me, but I said no more than, "Very well."

"And when you come down to-morrow night, don't call out! Let me ask you a parting question. What made you cry, 'Halloa! Below there!' to-night?"

"Heaven knows," said I. "I cried something to that effect—"

"Not to that effect, sir. Those were the very words. I know them well."

"Admit those were the very words. I said them, no doubt, because I saw you below."

"For no other reason?"

"What other reason could I possibly have?"

"You had no feeling that they were conveyed to you in any supernatural way?"

"No."

He wished me good-night, and held up his light. I walked by the side of the down Line of rails (with a very disagreeable sensation of a train coming behind me) until I found the path. It was easier to mount than to descend, and I got back to my inn without any adventure.

Punctual to my appointment, I placed my foot on the first notch of the zigzag next night, as the distant clocks were striking eleven. He was waiting for me at the bottom, with his white light on. "I have not called out," I said, when we came close together; "may I speak now?" "By all means, sir." "Good-night, then, and here's my hand." "Good-night, sir, and here's mine." With that we walked side by side to his box, entered it, closed the door, and sat down by the fire.

"I have made up my mind, sir," he began, bending forward as soon as we were seated, and speaking in a tone but a little above a whisper, "that you shall not have to ask me twice what troubles me. I took you for some one else yesterday evening. That troubles me."

"That mistake?"

"No. That Some one else."

"Who is it?"

"I don't know."

"Like me?"

"I don't know. I never saw the face. The left arm is across the face, and the right arm is waved—violently waved. This way."

I followed his action with my eyes, and it was the action of an arm gesticulating, with the utmost passion and vehemence, "For God's sake, clear the way!"

"One moonlight night," said the man, "I was sitting here, when I heard a voice cry, 'Halloa! Below there!' I started up, looked from that door, and saw this Some one else standing by the red light near the tunnel, waving as I just now showed you. The voice seemed hoarse with shouting, and it cried, 'Look out! Look out!' And then again, 'Halloa! Below there!

Look out!' I caught up my lamp, turned it on red, and ran towards the figure, calling, 'What's wrong? What has happened? Where?' It stood just outside the blackness of the tunnel. I advanced so close upon it that I wondered at its keeping the sleeve across its eyes. I ran right up at it, and had my hand stretched out to pull the sleeve away, when it was gone.''

''Into the tunnel?'' said I.

''No. I ran on into the tunnel, five hundred yards. I stopped, and held my lamp above my head, and saw the figures of the measured distance, and saw the wet stains stealing down the walls and trickling through the arch. I ran out again faster than I had run in (for I had a mortal abhorrence of the place upon me), and I looked all round the red light with my own red light, and I went up the iron ladder to the gallery atop of it, and I came down again, and ran back here. I telegraphed both ways, 'An alarm has been given. Is anything wrong?' The answer came back, both ways, 'All well.' ''

Resisting the slow touch of a frozen finger tracing out my spine, I showed him how that this figure must be a deception of his sense of sight; and how that figures, originating in disease of the delicate nerves that minister to the functions of the eye, were known to have often troubled patients, some of whom had become conscious of the nature of their affliction, and had even proved it by experiments upon themselves. ''As to an imaginary cry,'' said I, ''do but listen for a moment to the wind in this unnatural valley while we speak so low, and to the wild harp it makes of the telegraph wires.''

That was all very well, he returned, after we had sat listening for a while, and he ought to know something of the wind and the wires—he who so often passed long winter nights there, alone and watching. But he would beg to remark that he had not finished.

I asked his pardon, and he slowly added these words, touching my arm,—

''Within six hours after the Appearance, the memorable accident on this Line happened, and within ten hours the dead and wounded were brought along through the tunnel over the spot where the figure had stood.''

A disagreeable shudder crept over me, but I did my best against it. It was not to be denied, I rejoined, that this was a remarkable coincidence, calculated deeply to impress his mind. But it was unquestionable that remarkable coincidences did continually occur, and they must be taken into account in dealing with such a subject. Though to be sure I must admit, I added (for I thought I saw that he was going to bring the objection to bear upon me), men of common sense did not allow much for coincidences in making the ordinary calculations of life.

He again begged to remark that he had not finished.

I again begged his pardon for being betrayed into interruptions.

"This," he said, again laying his hand upon my arm, and glancing over his shoulder with hollow eyes, "was just a year ago. Six or seven months passed, and I had recovered from the surprise and shock, when one morning, as the day was breaking, I, standing at the door, looked towards the red light, and saw the spectre again." He stopped, with a fixed look at me.

"Did it cry out?"

"No. It was silent."

"Did it wave its arm?"

"No. It leaned against the shaft of the light, with both hands before the face. Like this."

Once more I followed his action with my eyes. It was an action of mourning. I have seen such an attitude in stone figures on tombs.

"Did you go up to it?"

"I came in and sat down, partly to collect my thoughts, partly because it had turned me faint. When I went to the door again, daylight was above me, and the ghost was gone."

"But nothing followed? Nothing came of this?"

He touched me on the arm with his forefinger twice or thrice, giving a ghastly nod each time:—

"That very day, as a train came out of the tunnel, I noticed, at a carriage window on my side, what looked like a confusion of hands and heads, and something waved. I saw it just in time to signal the driver, Stop! He shut off, and put his brake on; but the train drifted past here a hundred and fifty yards or more. I ran after it, and, as I went along, heard terrible screams and cries. A beautiful young lady had died instantaneously in one of the compartments, and was brought in here, and laid down on this floor between us.''

Involuntarily I pushed my chair back, as I looked from the boards at which he pointed to himself.

"True, sir. True. Precisely as it happened, so I tell it you."

I could think of nothing to say, to any purpose, and my mouth was very dry. The wind and the wires took up the story with a long lamenting wail.

He resumed. "Now, sir, mark this, and judge how my mind is troubled. The spectre came back a week ago. Ever since, it has been there, now and again, by fits and starts."

"At the light?"

"At the Danger-light."

"What does it seem to do?"

He repeated, if possible with increased passion and vehemence, that former gesticulation of, "For God's sake, clear the way!"

Then he went on: "I have no peace or rest for it. It calls to me, for many minutes together, in an agonized manner, 'Below there! Look out! Look out!' It stands waving to me. It rings my little bell——"

I caught at that. "Did it ring your bell yesterday evening when I was here, and you went to the door?"

"Twice."

"Why, see," said I, "how your imagination misleads you. My eyes were on the bell, and my ears were open to the bell, and if I am a living man, it did NOT ring at those times. No, nor at any other time, except when it was rung in the natural course of physical things by the station communicating with you."

He shook his head. "I have never made a mistake as to that yet, sir. I have never confused the spectre's ring with the man's. The ghost's ring is a strange vibration in the bell that it derives from nothing else, and I have not asserted that the bell stirs to the eye. I don't wonder that you failed to hear it. But *I* heard it.''

"And did the spectre seem to be there when you looked out?''

"It WAS there.''

"Both times?''

He repeated firmly, "Both times.''

"Will you come to the door with me and look for it now?''

He bit his under lip, as though he were somewhat unwilling, but arose. I opened the door, and stood on the step, while he stood in the doorway. There was the Danger-light. There was the dismal mouth of the tunnel. There were the high, wet stone walls of the cutting. There were the stars above them.

"Do you see it?'' I asked him, taking particular note of his face. His eyes were prominent and strained, but not very much more so, perhaps, than my own had been when I had directed them earnestly towards the same spot.

"No,'' he answered. "It is not there.''

"Agreed,'' said I.

We went in again, shut the door, and resumed our seats. I was thinking how best to improve this advantage, if it might be called one, when he took up the conversation in such a matter-of-course way, so assuming that there could be no serious question of fact between us, that I felt myself placed in the weakest of positions.

"By this time you will fully understand, sir,'' he said, "that what troubles me so dreadfully is the question, What does the spectre mean?''

I was not sure, I told him, that I did fully understand.

"What is its warning against?'' he said, ruminating, with his eyes on the fire, and only by times turning them on me. "What is the danger? Where is the danger? There is danger overhanging somewhere on the Line. Some dreadful calamity will happen. It is not to be doubted this third time, after what has gone before. But surely this is a cruel haunting of *me*. What can *I* do?''

He pulled out his handkerchief, and wiped the drops from his heated forehead.

"If I telegraph Danger, on either side of me, or on both, I can give no reason for it," he went on, wiping the palms of his hands. "I should get into trouble, and do no good. They would think I was mad. This is the way it would work:— Message: 'Danger! Take care!' Answer: 'What Danger? Where?' Message: 'Don't know. But, for God's sake, take care!' They would displace me. What else could they do?"

His pain of mind was most pitiable to see. It was the mental torture of a conscientious man, oppressed beyond endurance by an unintelligible responsibility involving life.

"When it first stood under the Danger-light," he went on, putting his dark hair back from his head, and drawing his hands outward across his temples in an extremity of feverish distress, "why not tell me where that accident was to happen—if it must happen? Why not tell me how it could be averted—if it could have been averted? When on its second coming it hid its face, why not tell me, instead, 'She is going to die. Let them keep her at home'? If it came, on those two occasions, only to show me that its warnings were true, and so to prepare me for the third, why not warn me plainly now? And I, Lord help me! A mere poor signal-man on this solitary station! Why not go to somebody with credit to be believed, and power to act?"

When I saw him in this state, I saw that for the poor man's sake, as well as for the public safety, what I had to do for the time was to compose his mind. Therefore, setting aside all question of reality or unreality between us, I represented to him that whoever thoroughly discharged his duty must do well, and that at least it was his comfort that he understood his duty, though he did not understand these confounding Appearances. In this effort I succeeded far better than in the attempt to reason him out of his conviction. He became calm; the occupations incidental to his post as the night advanced began to make larger demands on his attention; and I left him at two in the morning. I had offered to stay through the night, but he would not hear of it.

That I more than once looked back at the red light as I ascended the pathway, that I did not like the red light, and that I should have slept but poorly if my bed had been

under it, I see no reason to conceal. Nor did I like the two
sequences of the accident and the dead girl. I see no reason
to conceal that either.

But what ran most in my thoughts was the consideration
how ought I to act, having become the recipient of this disclosure? I had proved the man to be intelligent, vigilant,
painstaking, and exact; but how long might he remain so, in
his state of mind? Though in a subordinate position, still he
held a most important trust; and would I (for instance) like
to stake my own life on the chances of his continuing to
execute it with precision?

Unable to overcome a feeling that there would be something treacherous in my communicating what he had told me
to his superiors in the Company, without first being plain
with himself and proposing a middle course to him, I ultimately resolved to offer to accompany him (otherwise keeping his secret for the present) to the wisest medical
practitioner we could hear of in those parts, and to take his
opinion. A change in his time of duty would come round next
night, he had apprised me, and he would be off an hour or
two after sunrise, and on again soon after sunset. I had appointed to return accordingly.

Next evening was a lovely evening, and I walked out early
to enjoy it. The sun was not yet quite down when I traversed
the field-path near the top of the deep cutting. I would extend
my walk for an hour, I said to myself, half an hour on and
half an hour back, and it would then be time to go to my
signal-man's box.

Before pursuing my stroll, I stepped to the brink, and mechanically looked down from the point from which I had first
seen him. I cannot describe the thrill that seized upon me
when, close at the mouth of the tunnel, I saw the appearance
of a man, with his left sleeve across his eyes, passionately
waving his right arm.

The nameless horror that oppressed me passed in a moment, for in a moment I saw that this appearance of a man
was a man indeed, and that there was a little group of other
men, standing at a short distance, to whom he seemed to be
rehearsing the gesture he made. The Danger-light was not yet

lighted. Against its shaft, a little low hut, entirely new to me, had been made of some wooden supports and tarpaulin. It looked no bigger than a bed.

With an irresistible sense that something was wrong—with a flashing self-reproachful fear that fatal mischief had come of my leaving the man there, and causing no one to be sent to overlook or correct what he did—I descended the notched path with all the speed I could make.

"What is the matter?" I asked the men.

"Signal-man killed this morning, sir."

"Not the man belonging to that box?"

"Yes, sir."

"Not the man I know?"

"You will recognize him, sir, if you knew him," said the man who spoke for the others, solemnly uncovering his own head, and raising an end of the tarpaulin, "for his face is quite composed."

"Oh, how did this happen—how did this happen?" I asked, turning from one to another as the hut closed in again.

"He was cut down by an engine, sir. No man in England knew his work better. But somehow he was not clear of the outer rail. It was just at broad day. He had struck the light, and had the lamp in his hand. As the engine came out of the tunnel, his back was towards her, and she cut him down. That man drove her, and was showing how it happened. Show the gentleman, Tom."

The man who wore a rough dark dress, stepped back to his former place at the mouth of the tunnel.

"Coming round the curve in the tunnel, sir," he said, "I saw him at the end, like as if I saw him down a perspective-glass. There was no time to check speed, and I knew him to be very careful. As he didn't seem to take heed of the whistle, I shut it off when we were running down upon him, and called to him as loud as I could call."

"What did you say?"

"I said, "Below there! Look out! Look out! For God's sake, clear the way!' "

I started.

"Ah! it was a dreadful time, sir. I never left off calling to him. I put this arm before my eyes not to see, and I waved this arm to the last; but it was no use.''

Without prolonging the narrative to dwell on any one of its curious circumstances more than on any other, I may, in closing it, point out the coincidence that the warning of the Engine-Driver included, not only the words which the unfortunate Signal-man had repeated to me as haunting him, but also the words which I myself—not he—had attached, and that only in my own mind, to the gesticulation he had imitated.

Stephen King

CROUCH END

It is a tribute to King's range of talent that he, like Dickens, can work outside his ordinary métier upon occasion. He is in fact the Dickens of the contemporary horror field: his unparallelled popularity and moral stance, his irrevocable commitment to popular culture and commerce, his flair for storytelling and entertainment, his seemingly tireless energy, his rejection by the majority of the guardians of high art. While Stephen King's "The Mist" is the premier example to date in his works of a story concerned with shifting realities, "Crouch End," King's Lovecraftian Cthulhu mythos story, occupies a more borderline position. This story is the closest King approaches, except in the odd, surreal "Big Wheels," and perhaps in "Mrs. Todd's Shortcut" to a concern with alterations in base or consensus reality. And he does so here only by adopting the borrowed posture of "The Call of Cthulhu," that the elder gods are real, distinguishing his own approach by maintaining that they are real in an other or alternate universe connected to ours only at spots such as Crouch End in London. In Lovecraft there is only one reality, cosmic and evilly inhuman. At this writing King is just past forty and already a phenomenal worldwide success, and the evolution of the horror novel has been advanced more by his works than those of any writer in the history of the genre. And he is so exceedingly generous in his support of the work of other writers that his name stands behind (or on the paperback cover) of many books every year by others. He is a one-man boom in the publishing of horror in our time.

By the time the woman had finally gone, it was nearly two-thirty in the morning. Outside the Crouch End police station, Tottenham Lane was a small dead river. London was asleep—but of course, London never sleeps deeply, and its dreams are uneasy.

PC Vetter closed his notebook, which he'd almost filled as the American woman's strange frenzied story had poured out. He looked at the typewriter and the stack of blank forms on the shelf beside it.

"This one'll look odd come the morning light," PC Vetter said.

PC Farnham was drinking a Coke. He didn't speak for a long time. "She was an American woman," he said finally, as if that might explain the story she had told.

"It'll go in the back file," Vetter agreed, and looked around for a cigarette. "But I wonder . . ."

Farnham laughed. "You don't mean you believe any part of it?"

"Didn't say that, did I? No. But you're new here."

PC Farnham sat a little straighter. He was twenty-seven, and it was hardly his fault that he had been posted here from Muswell Hill to the north, or that Vetter, who was nearly twice his age, had spent his entire uneventful career in the quiet London backwater of Crouch End.

"Perhaps so, sir," he said, "but, respectfully, I still think I know a piece of whole cloth when I see one . . . or hear one."

"Give us a fag, Farnham," Vetter said, looking a little amused. "There's a good boy." He lit it with a wooden match from a bright red railway box, shook it out, and tossed the match stub into Farnham's ashtray. He peered at Farnham through a haze of drifting smoke. His face was deeply lined and his nose was a map of broken veins—he liked his six cans of Harp a night, did PC Vetter.

"You think Crouch End's a very quiet place, don't you?"

Farnham shrugged. He thought Crouch End was suburban and, tell the truth, dull as dishwater. "Quiet, yes."

"And you're right. It is. Goes to sleep by eleven, most nights. But I've seen a lot of strange things in Crouch End.

If you're here half as long as I've been, you'll see your share, too. There are more strange things happen right here in this quiet six or eight blocks than anywhere else in London, I'll take my oath. And that's saying a lot. It scares me. So I have my lager, and then I'm not so scared. You look at Sergeant Gordon sometime, Farnham, and ask yourself why his hair is dead white at forty. Or I'd say take a look at Petty, but you can't very well, can you? Petty committed suicide in the summer of 1976. Our hot summer. It was . . .'' Vetter seemed to consider his words. "It was quite bad that summer. Quite bad. There were a lot of us who were afraid . . . they might break through.''

"Who might break through what?'' Farnham asked. He felt a contemptuous smile turning up the corners of his mouth, knew it was far from politic, but was unable to stop it. In his way, Vetter was raving as badly as the American woman had. He had always been a bit queer. The booze, probably. Then he saw Vetter smiling right back at him.

"You think I'm dotty,'' he said.

"Not at all,'' Farnham protested, groaning inwardly.

"You're a good boy,'' Vetter said. "Won't be riding a desk here in the station when you're my age. Not if you stick on the force. D'you plan to stick it, Farnham?''

"Yes,'' Farnham said firmly. It was true. He meant to stick it even though Sheila wanted him off the police force and somewhere she could count on him. The Ford assembly line, perhaps. The thought of it curdled his stomach.

"I thought you did,'' Vetter said, crushing his smoke. "Gets in your blood, doesn't it? And you could go far. And it'll not be Crouch End you finish up in, either. Still, you don't know everything. Crouch End is . . . strange. You ought to look in the back file sometime, Farnham. Oh, a lot of it's the usual . . . girls and boys run away from home to be hippies . . . punks, they call themselves now . . . men who went out for a pack of fags and just never came back . . . and when you clap an eye to their wives you understand why . . . unsolved arsons . . . purse-snatching . . . all of that. But in between, there's enough stories to curdle your blood. And some to sick your stomach.''

"Is that true?" Farnham demanded suddenly.

Vetter didn't seem offended by the question. He just nodded. "Stories very much like the one that poor American girl told us. She'll not see her husband no more, that girl won't." He looked at Farnham and shrugged. "Believe me, believe me not. It's all one, isn't it? The file's there. We call it the open file because it's more polite than the back file or the unsolved file. Study it up, Farnham. Study it up."

Farnham said nothing, but he intended to study it up. The idea that there might be a whole series of stories such as the one the American woman had told was . . . was disturbing.

"Sometimes," Vetter said, stealing another of Farnham's Silk Cut cigarettes, "I wonder about Dimensions. Science fiction writers are always going on about Dimensions, aren't they? Ever read science fiction, Farnham?"

"No," Farnham said. He had decided this was some sort of elaborate leg-pull.

"Ever read Lovecraft?"

"Never heard of him."

"Well, this fellow Lovecraft was always writing about Dimensions," Vetter said, producing his box of railway matches. "Dimensions close to ours. Full of these immortal monsters that would drive a man mad at one look. Frightful rubbish, what? Except, whenever one of these people straggles in, I think it all might just be true. I say to myself then—when it's quiet and late at night, like it is now—that our whole world, everything we think of as nice and normal and sane, is like a big leather ball filled with air. Only in some places, the leather's scuffed almost down to nothing. Places where . . . where the barriers are thinner. Do you get me?"

"Yes," Farnham said. He did not get PC Vetter at all.

"And then I think, Crouch End's one of those thin places. Highgate's mostly all right, it's just as thick as you'd want between us and the Dimensions in Muswell Hill and Highgate, but now you take Archway and Finsbury Park. They border on Crouch End, too. I've got friends in both places, and they know of my . . . my interest in certain things that don't seem to be any way rational. Certain things related, we'll say, by people with nothing to gain by making up a crazy story. Did you ask yourself, Farnham, why the woman would have told us the things she did if they weren't true?'' He struck a match and looked at Farnham over it. ''Pretty young woman, twenty-six, two kiddies back at her hotel, husband's a young lawyer doing well in Milwaukee or someplace? What's to gain by coming in here and raving about monsters?''

''I don't know,'' Farnham said stiffly. ''But there may be an ex—''

''So I say to myself,'' Vetter overrode him, ''that if there were such things as 'thin spots,' this one would begin at Archway and Finsbury Park . . . but the real thin place is here at Crouch End. And I say to myself, wouldn't it be a day if whatever was left just . . . rubbed away? Wouldn't it be a day if even half of what that woman told us was true?''

Farnham was silent. He had decided that PC Vetter probably also believed in palmistry and phrenology and the Rosicrucians.

''Read the back file,'' Vetter said, getting up. There was a crackling sound as he put his hands in the small of his back and stretched. ''I'm going out to get some fresh air.''

He strolled out. Farnham looked after him with a mixture of amusement and resentment. Vetter was dotty, all right. He was also a bloody fag-mooch. Fags didn't come cheap in this brave new world of socialism and the welfare state. He picked up Vetter's notebook and began leafing through the girl's story again.

And, yes, he would go through the back file.

He would do it for laughs.

The girl—the young woman—had burst into the station at quarter past ten the previous evening, her hair in damp strings around her face, her eyes bulging. She was dragging her purse by the strap.

''Lonnie,'' she said. ''Oh, my God, you've got to find Lonnie.''

''Well, we'll do our best, won't we?'' Vetter said. ''But you've got to tell us who Lonnie is.''

''He's dead,'' the young woman said. ''I know he is.'' She

began to cry. Then she began to laugh—to cackle, really. She dropped her purse in front of her. She was hysterical.

The station was fairly deserted at that hour on a weeknight. Sergeant Raymond was listening to a Pakistani woman tell, with almost unearthly calm, how her purse had been nicked on Hillfield Avenue. He half rose, and PC Farnham came in front of the anteroom, where he had been taking down old posters (HAVE YOU ROOM IN YOUR HEART FOR AN UNWANTED CHILD?) and putting up new ones (SIX RULES FOR SAFE NIGHT-CYCLING).

Vetter nodded for Farnham and waved Sergeant Raymond back. Raymond, who liked to break pickpockets' fingers for them, was not the man for a hysterical woman.

"Lonnie!" she shrieked. "Oh, my God, Lonnie, they've got him—!"

The Pakistani woman turned the steady brown moon of her face toward the young American woman, studied her for a moment, and then turned back to Sergeant Raymond, her calm unbroken. Farnham came forward.

"Miss—" PC Farnham began.

"What's going *on* out there?" she whispered. Her breath was coming in quick pants. Farnham noticed there was a slight scratch on her left cheek. She was a pretty thing with auburn hair. Her clothes were moderately expensive. The heel had come off one of her shoes.

"What's going *on* out there?" she repeated, and then she said it for the first time: "Monsters—"

The Pakistani woman looked over again . . . and smiled. Her teeth were rotten. The smile was gone like a conjurer's trick, and she was looking at the lost/stolen property form Raymond had handed her.

"Get the lady a cup of coffee and bring it down to room three," Vetter said. "Could you do with a cup of coffee, mum?"

"Lonnie," she whispered. "I know he's dead."

"Now, you just come with old Ted Vetter and we'll see what this is about," he said, and helped her to her feet. She was still talking in a low moaning voice when he led her away, one arm around her. She was rocking unsteadily because of the broken shoe.

Farnham got the coffee and brought it into room three, a plain white cubicle furnished with a scarred table, four chairs, and a water cooler in the corner. He put the coffee in front of her.

"Here, mum," he said, "this'll do you good. I've got sugars if—"

"I can't drink it," she said. "I couldn't—" And then she clutched the porcelain cup—someone's long-forgotten souvenir of Blackpool—in her hands as if for warmth. Her hands were shaking quite badly, and Farnham wanted to tell her to put it down before she slopped the coffee and burned herself.

"I couldn't," she said again, and then drank, still holding the cup two-handed, the way a child will hold his cup of broth. And when she looked at them, it was a child's look—simple, exhausted, appealing . . . and at bay. It was as if whatever had happened had somehow made her roughly young; as if some invisible hand had swooped down from the sky and roughly slapped the last twenty years from her, leaving a child in grown-up American clothes in this small white interrogation room in Crouch End. Yes, it had been like that.

"Lonnie," she said. "The monsters," she said. "Will you help me? Will you please help me? Maybe he isn't dead. Maybe . . . I'm an American citizen!" she cried out suddenly, and then, as if she had said something deeply shameful, she began to sob.

Vetter patted her shoulder. "There, mum. I think we can help find your Lonnie. Your husband, is he?"

Still sobbing, she nodded. "Danny and Norma are back at the hotel . . . with the sitter . . . they'll be sleeping . . . expecting him to kiss them when he comes in . . ."

"Now if you could relax and tell us what happened—"

"And where it happened," Farnham added. Vetter looked up at him swiftly, frowning.

"But that's just it!" she cried. "I don't know *where* it happened! I'm not even sure what happened, except that it was h-h-hor—"

Vetter had taken out his notebook. "What's your name, mum?"

"My name is Doris Freeman. My husband is Leonard Freeman. We're staying at the Hotel Inter-Continental. We're American citizens." This recital seemed to steady her a little. She sipped her coffee and put the mug down. Farnham saw that the palms of her hands were quite red.

Vetter was writing all of this down in his notebook. Now he looked momentarily at PC Farnham, just an unobtrusive flick of the eyes.

"Are you on holiday?" he asked.

"Yes . . . two weeks here and one week in Spain. We were supposed to have a week in Spain . . . but this isn't helping find Lonnie! Why are you asking me these stupid questions?"

"Just trying to get the background, Mrs. Freeman," Farnham said. Without really thinking about it, both of them had adopted low soothing voices. "Now you go ahead and tell us what happened. Tell it in your own words."

"Why is it so hard to get a taxi in London?" she asked abruptly.

Farnham hardly knew what to say, but Vetter responded as if the question was utterly germane to the discussion.

"Hard to say, mum. The tourists, maybe. And it can be specially hard around five o'clock. That's when they start changing drivers, you know. Day shift goes off, night shift comes on. Why? Did you have a problem getting someone who'd take you from in town out here to Crouch End?"

"Yes," she said, and looked at him gratefully. "We left the hotel at three and came down to Foyle's Bookshop. Is that Cambridge Circus?"

"Near there," Vetter agreed. "Lovely big bookshop, mum, isn't it?"

"We had no trouble getting a cab from the Inter-Continental . . . they were lined up outside. But when we came out of Foyle's, it was like you said. They went by, but their lights on top were always off and when the first one did stop, when Lonnie said Crouch End, the driver just laughed and shook his head. Said it wasn't his cab."

"Aye, that's right," Farnham said.

"He even refused a pound tip," Doris Freeman said, and a very American perplexity had crept into her tone. "We waited for almost half an hour before we got a driver who said he'd take us out. It was five-thirty by then, or maybe quarter of six. And that was when Lonnie discovered he'd lost the address . . ."

She clutched the mug again.

"Who were you going to see?" Vetter asked.

"A colleague of my husband's. A lawyer named John Squales. My husband had never met him, but their two firms were—" She gestured vaguely.

"Affiliated?"

"Yes, that's right. And over the last four years Lonnie and Mr. Squales have had a lot of correspondence back and forth. And when Mr. Squales found out we were going to be in London on vacation, he invited us to his home for dinner. Lonnie had always written him at his office, of course, but he had Mr. Squales's home address on a slip of paper. After we got in the cab, he discovered he'd lost it. And all he could remember was that it was in Crouch End."

She looked at them.

"Crouch End. That's an ugly name."

Vetter said, "So what did you do then?"

She began to talk. By the time she finished, her first cup of coffee and another one were gone, and PC Vetter had filled up several pages in his notebook with his blocky, sprawling script . . .

Lonnie Freeman was a big man, and hunched forward in the roomy back seat of the black London cab so he could talk to the driver, he looked to her amazingly as he had looked when she had first seen him at a college basketball game in their senior year—sitting on the bench, his knees somewhere up around his ears, his hands on their big wrists dangling between his legs. Only then he had been wearing basketball shorts and a towel around his neck, and now he was in a business suit and tie. He had never gotten in many games, she remembered fondly, because he just wasn't that good. And he lost addresses.

The cabby listened indulgently to the tale of the lost address after all of Lonnie's pockets had been duly investigated. He was an elderly man impeccably turned out in a grey summer-weight suit, the antithesis of the slouching New York cab driver. Only the checked wool cap on the driver's head clashed, but it was an agreeable clash; it lent him a touch of rakish charm. Outside, the traffic flowed endlessly past on Cambridge Circus; the theater nearby announced that *Jesus Christ Superstar* was entering its eighth year of continuous performances.

"Well, I tell you what, guy," the cabby said. "I'll take you out to Crouch End, but I'm not going to just put yer down there. Because Crouch End's a big place, en't it?"

And Lonnie, who had never been in Crouch End—or out of the United States, for that matter—in his life, nodded sagely.

"Yes, it is," the cabby agreed with himself. "So I take yer there, and we'll stop at a call box, and you check your friend's address, and off we go, right to the door."

"That's wonderful," Doris said, really meaning it. They had been in London six days now, and she could not recall ever having been in a place where the people were more polite, kinder, or . . . or more civilized.

"Thank you," Lonnie said, and sat back. He put his arm around Doris and smiled. "See? No problem."

"No thanks to you," she mock-growled, and threw a light punch at his midsection. There was plenty of room for even a tall man like Lonnie to stretch out; the black London cabs were roomier than the New York Checkers, too.

"Right," the cabby said. "Off we go, then. Heigh-ho for Crouch End."

It was late August, and a steady hot wind rattled the trash across the roads and whipped at the coats and skirts of the men and women going home from work. The sun had settled below the tops of the buildings, but when it shone between them, Doris saw that it was beginning to take on the reddish cast of evening. The cabby hummed. She relaxed with Lonnie's arm around her—she had seen more of him in the last six days than she had all year, it seemed, and she was very pleased to discover that she liked it. She had never been out of America before, either, and she had to keep reminding herself that she was in England, she was in *London*, thousands should be so lucky.

Very quickly she had lost any sense of direction. Cab rides in London did that to you, she had discovered. The city was a great sprawling warren of Roads and Mews and Hills and Closes (and even Inns), and she couldn't understand how anyone could get around. When she had mentioned it to Lonnie the day before, he had replied that they got around very carefully . . . hadn't she noticed that they all kept the *London Streetfinder* tucked cozily away beneath the dash?

This was the longest cab ride they had taken. The fashionable section of town dropped behind them (in spite of that perverse going-around-in-circles feeling). They passed through an area of monolithic housing developments that might have been utterly deserted for all the signs of life they showed (no, she corrected herself to Vetter and Farnham in the small white room; she had seen one small boy sitting on the curb, striking matches), then an area of small, rather tatty-looking shops and fruit stalls, and then—no wonder driving in London seemed to produce such a disorienting round-and-round feeling—they seemed to have driven smack into the fashionable section again.

"There was even a McDonald's hamburger place," she told Vetter and Farnham, in a tone of voice usually reserved for the Sphinx and the Hanging Gardens.

"Was there?" Vetter replied, being properly amazed and respectful—she had achieved a kind of total recall, and he wanted nothing to break that mood, at least until she had told them everything she could.

The fashionable section with the McDonald's as its centerpiece dropped behind. Now the sun was a solid orange ball sitting above the horizon, washing the streets with a strange clear light that nevertheless made all the pedestrians look as if their faces were aflame.

"It was then that things began to . . . to change," she

said. Her voice had dropped a little. Her hands were trembling again.

Vetter leaned forward, intent. "Changed? How? How did things change, Mrs. Freeman?"

They had passed a newsagent's window, she remembered, and the signboard outside had read SIXTY LOST IN UNDERGROUND HORROR.

"Lonnie, look at that!"

"What?" He craned around, but the newsagent's was already behind them.

"It said, 'Sixty Lost in Underground Horror.' Isn't that what they call the subways?"

"Yes," Lonnie said, "the underground or the tubes. Was it a crash?"

"I don't know." She leaned forward. "Driver, do you know what that was about? Was there a subway crash?"

"A collision, mum? Not that I know of."

"Do you have a radio?"

"Not in me cab, mum."

"Lonnie?"

"Hmm?"

But she could see that Lonnie had lost interest. He was going through his pockets again (and because he was wearing his three-piece suit, there were a lot of them to go through), having another hunt for the scrap of paper with John Squales's address written on it.

The message chalked on the board played over and over in her mind. SIXTY KILLED IN TUBE CRASH, it should have read. SIXTY KILLED AS UNDERGROUND TRAINS COLLIDE, it should have read. But . . . SIXTY LOST IN UNDERGROUND HORROR. It made her uneasy. It didn't say "killed," it said "lost" . . . the way sailors were referred to when they drowned at sea.

UNDERGROUND HORROR.

She didn't like it. It made her think of graveyards, sewers, and flabby-pale, noisome things swarming suddenly out of the tubes themselves, wrapping their arms (tentacles, maybe) around the hapless commuters on the platforms, dragging them away to darkness . . .

They turned right. Standing on the corner beside their

parked motorcycles were three boys in leathers. They looked up at the cab and for a moment—the setting sun was almost full in her face from this angle—it seemed that the bikers did not have human heads at all. For that one moment she was nastily sure that the sleek, flat, and sloping heads of rats sat atop those black leather jackets, rats with beady black eyes staring at the cab. Then the light shifted just a tiny bit and she saw of course she had been mistaken; there were only three boys in their late teens there, smoking cigarettes and standing in front of the British version of the American candy store.

"Here we go," Lonnie said, giving up the search and pointing out the window. They were passing a sign which read "Crouch Hill Road." Elderly brick houses like sleepy dowagers had closed in, seeming to look down at the cab from their blank windows. A few kids passed back and forth, riding bikes or trikes. Two others were trying to ride a skateboard with no notable success. Fathers home from work sat together, smoking and talking and watching the children. It all looked reassuringly normal.

The cab drew up in front of a dismal-looking restaurant with a small spotted sign in the corner of the window reading FULLY LICENSED and a much larger one in the center which informed that within one could purchase curries to take away. On the inner ledge there slept a gigantic grey cat. Beside the restaurant was a call box.

"Here you are, guy," the cab driver said. "You find your friend's address and I'll track him down."

"Fair enough," Lonnie said, and got out.

Doris sat in the cab for a moment and then also emerged, feeling like stretching her legs. The hot wind was still blowing. It whipped her skirt around her knees and then plastered an old ice-cream wrapper to her shin. She removed it with a grimace of disgust. When she looked up, she was staring directly through the plate-glass window at the big grey tom. It stared back at her, one-eyed. The rest of its face had been clawed away in some long-ago but gigantic battle, and all that remained was a twisted pinkish mass of scar tissue, one milky cataract, and a few tufts of fur.

It miaowed at her, silently through the glass.

Feeling a surge of disgust, she went to the call box and peered in through one of the dirty panes. Lonnie made a circle at her with his thumb and forefinger and winked. Then he pushed tenpence into the slot and talked with someone. He laughed—soundlessly through the glass. Like the cat. She looked over, but now the window was empty. In the dimness beyond she could see chairs up on tables and an old man pushing a broom. When she looked back, she saw that Lonnie was jotting something down. He put his pen away, held the paper in his hand—she could see an address was jotted on it—said one or two other things, then hung up and came out.

He waggled the address at her in mild triumph. "Okay, that's th—" His eyes went past her shoulder and he frowned. "Where's the cab gone?"

She turned around. The taxi had vanished. Where it had stood there was only curbing and a few papers blowing lazily up the gutter. Across the street, two kids were clutching at each other and giggling. Doris noticed that one of them had a hand that was deformed into something like a claw—she had thought the National Health was supposed to take care of things like that. The children looked across the street, saw her observing them, and fell into each other's arms giggling again.

"Well . . . I don't know," Doris said. She felt disoriented and a little stupid. The heat, the wind that seemed to blow constantly with no gusts or drops, like the draft from a furnace, the almost painted quality of the light . . .

("What time was it then?" Farnham asked suddenly.

("I don't know," Doris Freeman said, startled out of her recital. "Six, I suppose. No later than twenty past."

("I see, go on," Farnham said, knowing perfectly well that in August the setting of the sun would not have begun—even by the loosest standards—until seven o'clock or after.)

"Don't know?" Lonnie repeated. "What did he do, just pick up and leave?"

"Maybe when you put your hand up," Doris said, raising her own hand and making the thumb-and-forefinger circle

Lonnie had made in the call box, ''maybe when you did that he thought you were waving him on.''

''I'd have to wave a long time to send him on with two pounds-five on the meter,'' Lonnie grunted, and walked over to the curb. On the other side of Crouch Hill Road, the two small children were still giggling. ''Hey!'' Lonnie called. ''You kids!''

''You an American, sir?'' one of them called back. It was the boy with the claw hand.

''Yes,'' Lonnie said, smiling. ''Did you see a cab over here? Did the driver pull away up the road?''

The two children seemed to consider the question. The boy's companion was a girl of about five with an untidy tangle of brown hair. She stepped forward to the opposite curb, formed her hands into a megaphone, and still smiling—she screamed it through her megaphoned hands and her smile— she cried at them: *''Fuck you, Joe!''*

Lonnie's mouth dropped open.

''Sir! Sir! Sir!'' the boy screeched, and made an obscene gesture with his deformed hand. Then the two of them took to their heels and fled around the corner and out of sight, leaving only their laughter to echo back.

Lonnie looked at Doris, dumbstruck.

''I . . . I guess they don't like Americans,'' he said lamely.

She looked around nervously. The street appeared totally deserted.

He slipped an arm around her. ''Well, kid, looks like we hike it.''

''I'm not sure I want to, Lonnie,'' she said. ''Those two might have gone to get their big brothers.'' She laughed to show it was a joke, but there was a shrill quality to it she didn't like. Come to think of it, the evening had taken on a decidedly surreal quality she didn't much like. She wished they had stayed at the hotel.

''Not much else we can do,'' he said. ''The street's not exactly overflowing with taxis, is it?''

''Lonnie, why would he do that? Just—what do they say?— just scarper like that.''

''I don't have the slightest idea. But John gave me good

directions for the taxi driver. He lives in a street called Brass End, which is a very minor dead-end street, and he said it wasn't in the *Streetfinder*." As he talked he was moving her away from the call box, from the restaurant that sold curries to take away, from the now-empty curb. They were walking up Crouch Hill Road again. "We take a right onto Hillfield Avenue, a left halfway down, then our first right . . . or was it left? Anyway, onto Petrie Street. Second left is Brass End."

"Can you remember all that?"

"Try me," he said bravely, and she just had to laugh. Lonnie had a way of making things seem better.

There was a map of the Crouch End area on the wall. Farnham approached it and studied it with his hands stuffed into his pockets. The station seemed very quiet, now. Vetter was still outside—clearing some of the witchmoss from his brains, one hoped—and Raymond had finished with the woman who'd had her purse nicked.

Farnham put his finger on the spot where the cabby had most likely let them off (if anything about the woman's story was to be believed, that was). Yes, their route to the lawyer's house looked pretty straightforward. Crouch Hill Road to Hillfield Avenue, a left onto Vickers Lane, left onto Petrie Street, from Petrie Street into Brass End, which was no more than six or eight houses long. No more than a mile all told. Ought to have been able to do that walking on their hands.

"Raymond!" he called. "You still here?"

Raymond came in. He had changed into street clothes and was zipping up a light poplin windcheater. "Only just, my beardless darling."

"Cut it," Farnham said, smiling all the same. Raymond frightened him a little. He was one of those people you could take one look at and know they were standing close to the law-and-order fence . . . on one side or the other. There was a twisted white line of scar running down from the left corner of Raymond's mouth almost all the way to his Adam's apple. He claimed a pickpocket had once nearly cut his throat with a jagged bit of bottle. Claimed that's why he broke their fingers for them. Farnham thought that was shit. He thought Raymond broke their fingers because he liked to break them.

"Got a cig?" Raymond asked.

Farnham sighed and gave him one. His pack was becoming rapidly depleted. As he lit Raymond's smoke he said, "Is there a curry shop on Crouch Hill Road?"

"Not to my knowledge, love," Raymond said.

"That's what I thought."

"Has my poppet got a problem?"

"No," Farnham said, a little too sharply, remembering Doris Freeman's clotted hair and staring eyes.

Near the top of Crouch Hill Road, Doris and Lonnie turned onto Hillfield Avenue, which was lined with imposing and gracious-looking homes—nothing but shells, she thought, probably cut up into apartments and bed-sitters inside with surgical precision.

"So far, so good," Lonnie said.

"Yes, it's—" she began, and that was when the low moaning arose.

They both stopped. The moaning was coming almost directly from their right, where a high hedge ran around a small yard. Lonnie started toward the sound, and she grasped his arm. "Lonnie, no—"

"What do you mean, no?" he said. "Someone's hurt."

She stepped after him nervously. The hedge was high but thin. He was able to brush it aside and reveal a small square of lawn outlined with flowers. The lawn was very green. In the center of it was a black, smoking patch—or at least that was her first impression. When she peered around Lonnie's shoulder again—his shoulder was too high for her to peer over—she saw it was a hole, vaguely man-shaped. The tendrils of smoke were emanating from it.

SIXTY LOST IN UNDERGROUND HORROR, she thought abruptly.

The moaning was coming from the hole, and Lonnie began to force himself through the hedge toward it.

"Lonnie," she said. "No, don't."

"Someone's hurt," he said, and pushed himself the rest

of the way through with a bristly tearing sound. She saw him going toward the hole, and then the hedge snapped back, leaving her nothing but a vague impression of his shape as he went toward it. She tried to push through after him and was scratched by the short, stiff branches of the hedge for her trouble. She was wearing a sleeveless blouse.

"Lonnie?" she called, suddenly very afraid. "Lonnie, come back!"

"Just a minute, hon—"

The house looked at her impassively over the top of the hedge.

The moaning sounds continued, but now they sounded lower—guttural and somehow gleeful. Couldn't Lonnie *hear* that?

"Hey, is somebody down there?" she heard Lonnie ask. "Is there—oh! Hey! Jesus!" And suddenly Lonnie screamed. She had never heard him scream before, and it was a terrible sound. Her legs seemed to turn to waterbags. She looked wildly for the entrance path through the hedge and couldn't see it. Anywhere. Images swirled before her eyes—the bikies who had looked like large sleek-headed rats for a moment, the cat with the pink chewed face, the small boy with the claw hand.

Lonnie! She tried to scream, but no words came out.

Now there were sounds of struggle. The moaning had stopped. But there were sounds—wet, sloshing sounds—from the other side of the hedge. Then, suddenly, Lonnie came flying back through the hedge as if he had been given a tremendous push. The left arm of his suit-coat was torn, and the entire suit was splattered with runnels of black stuff that seemed to be smoking, as the pit in the lawn had been smoking.

"Doris, run!"

"Lonnie, what—"

"Run!" His face was totally devoid of color.

Doris looked around wildly, for a cop or anyone else. But Hillfield Avenue might have been a part of some great deserted city for all the life or movement she saw. Then she glanced back at the hedge and saw something else was moving behind there, something that was more than black; it seemed ebony, the antithesis of all light.

And it was sloshing.

A moment later, the short, stiff branches of the hedge began to rustle. She stared, hypnotized with dreadful fascination. She might have stood there forever (so she told Vetter and Farnham) if Lonnie hadn't grabbed her arm roughly and shrieked at her—yes, Lonnie, who never even raised his voice at the kids, had *shrieked*—she might have been standing there yet. Standing there, or . . .

But they ran.

Where? Farnham had asked her.

She didn't know. Lonnie was totally undone. He was in a hysteria of panic and revulsion. He didn't talk. His fingers clamped over her wrist like a handcuff. They ran away from the house looming over the hedge, they ran away from the smoking hole in the lawn. She knew those things for sure; all the rest was vague impressions.

At first it had been hard to run, and then it got easier because they were going downhill. They turned, then turned again. Houses stared at them, grey houses with high stoops and drawn green shades. She remembered Lonnie pulling off his jacket which had been splattered with that black goo, and throwing it away. Then they had come to a wider street.

'Stop,'' she panted. "Lonnie . . . stop . . . I can't . . .'' Her free hand was pressed to her side. There seemed to be a red-hot spike planted in there.

And he did stop. They had come out of the residential area and were standing at the corner of Crouch Lane and Norris Road. A sign on the far side of Norris Road proclaimed that they were but one mile from Slaughter Towen. Town? Vetter suggested. No, Doris Freeman said, Slaughter *Towen*, with an "e."

Raymond crushed out the cigarette he had "borrowed" from Farnham. "I'm off," he announced, and then looked more closely at Farnham. "My poppet should take better care of himself. He's got big dark circles under his eyes. Any hair on your palms, poppet?" He laughed uproariously.

"Ever hear of a Crouch Lane?" Farnham asked.

"Crouch Hill Road, you mean."

"No, I mean Crouch Lane."

"Never heard of it."

"What about Norris Road?"

"There's a Norris Road cuts off from the high street in Basingstoke—"

"No, here."

"Not by me, poppet."

For some reason he couldn't understand—the woman was obviously crackers—Farnham persisted. "What about Slaughter Towen?"

"Towen, you said? Not Town?"

"Yes, that's right."

"Never heard of it, poppet, but if I do, I believe I'll steer clear."

"Why's that?"

"Because in the old Druidic lingo, a touen or towen was a place for ritual sacrifice. That's where they took out your liver and lights. Sleep tight, love." And, zipping his wind-cheater up to the chin, Raymond glided out.

Farnham looked after him uneasily. He made that last up, he told himself. What a hard copper like Sid Raymond knows about the druids you could carve on the head of a pin and still have room for the Lord's Prayer. Right. And even if he had picked up a piece of information like that, it didn't change the fact that the woman was . . .

"Must be going crazy," Lonnie said, and laughed shakily.

Doris had looked at her watch earlier and saw that some-how it had gotten to be quarter of eight. The light had changed; from a clear orange it had gone to a thick and murky red that glared off the windows of the shops in Norris Road and seemed to face a church steeple across the way in fresh-clotted blood. The sun itself sat on the horizon now, an oblate sphere.

"What happened back there?" Doris asked. "What was it, Lonnie?"

"Lost my jacket, too. Hell of a note."

"You didn't lose it, you took it off. It was covered with . . ."

"Don't be foolish!" he snapped at her. But his eyes were not snappish; they were soft, shocked, wandering. "I lost it, that's all."

"Lonnie, what happened when you went through the hedge?"

"Nothing," he said briskly. "Let's not talk about it. Where are we?"

"Lonnie—"

"I can't remember," he said softly, looking at her. "It's all a blank. We were there . . . we heard a sound . . . then I was running. That's all I can remember." And then he added in a frighteningly childish voice: "Did I throw my jacket away? I liked that one. It matched the pants." He laughed suddenly, idiotically.

This was something new to be frightened of. Whatever he had seen beyond the hedge seemed to have partially unhinged him. She was not sure the same wouldn't have happened to her . . . if she had seen. It didn't matter. They had to get out of here. Get back to the hotel with the kids.

"Let's get a cab. I want to go home."

"But John—"

"Never mind John!" she said, and now she was shrill herself. "It's wrong, everything's wrong, we're getting a cab and going home!"

"Yes, all right. Okay." Lonnie passed a shaking hand across his forehead. "But there aren't any."

There was, in fact, no traffic at all on Norris Road, which was wide and cobbled. Directly down the center of it ran a set of old tram-tracks. On the other side, in front of a flower shop, an old and rusty three-wheeled D-car was parked. Farther down on their own side, a Yamaha bike stood aslant on its kickstand. That was all. They could *hear* cars, but the sound was faraway, diffuse.

"Maybe the street's closed for repairs," he muttered, and then Lonnie had done a strange thing . . . strange, at least, for him; he was always so easy and self-assured. He looked back over his shoulder as if afraid they had been followed.

"We'll walk," she said.

"Where?"

"Anywhere. Away from Crouch End. We can get a taxi if we get away from here." She was suddenly positive of that, if nothing else.

"All right." Now he seemed perfectly willing to entrust the leadership of the whole matter over to her.

They began walking toward the setting sun along Norris Road. The faraway hum of the traffic remained constant, not seeming to diminish, but not seeming to grow any, either. The desertion was beginning to get on her nerves. She felt they were being watched, tried to dismiss the feeling, and found that she couldn't. The sound of their footfalls

(SIXTY LOST IN UNDERGROUND HORROR)

echoed back to them. The business at the hedge played on her mind more and more, and finally she had to ask again.

"Lonnie, what *was* it?"

He answered simply: "I don't remember, Doris. And I don't want to."

They passed a market that was closed—a pile of coconuts like shrunken heads seen back-to were piled in the window. They passed a laundromat where white machines had been pulled from the washed-out pink plasterboard walls like square teeth from dying gums—the image made her feel queasy. They passed a soap-streaked show window with an old SHOP TO LEASE sign in the front. Something moved behind the soap streaks, and Doris saw, peering out at her, the pink and tufted battle-scarred face of the cat.

She consulted the workings and tickings of her body and discovered that she was in a state of slowly building terror. It felt as if her intestines had begun to crawl slightly inside her. Her mouth had a sharp unpleasant taste, almost as if she had dosed with a strong mouthwash. The cobbles of Norris Road bled fresh blood in the sunset.

They were approaching an underpass. And it was dark under there. *I can't,* her mind informed her in a matter-of-fact sort of way. *I can't go under there, anything might be under there. Don't ask me because I just can't.*

Another part of her mind asked if she could bear to retrace

their steps . . . past the empty shop with the cat in it (how had he gotten there from the restaurant by the call box? best not to think about that), the somehow oral shambles of the laundromat, the market of severed shrunken heads. She didn't think she could.

They had drawn closer to the underpass now. A six-car train lunged over it with startling suddenness, a crazy bride rushing to meet her groom with unseemly rapaciousness, trailing a train of sparks. They both leaped back involuntarily, but it was Lonnie who cried out aloud. She looked at him and she saw that he had aged and turned into someone she didn't think she knew in the last hour . . . had it been an hour? She didn't know. But she did know that his hair looked somehow greyer, and while she told herself firmly—as firmly as she could—that it was just a trick of the light, it decided her. Lonnie was in no shape to go back. Therefore, the underpass.

"Doris—" he said, pulling back a little.

"Come on," she said, and took his hand. She took it brusquely so he would not feel it trembling. She walked forward and he followed docilely.

They were almost out—it was a very short underpass, she thought with ridiculous relief—when the hand grasped her upper arm.

She didn't scream. Her lungs seemed to have collapsed like small crumpled paper sacks. Her mind wanted to leave her body behind and just . . . just fly. Lonnie's hand parted from her own. He seemed unaware. He walked out on the other side—she saw him for just one moment silhouetted, tall and lanky, against the bloody, furious colors of the sunset, and then he was gone. She had not seen him again since.

The hand grasping her upper arm was hairy, like an ape's hand. It turned her remorselessly toward a heavy slumped shape leaning against the sooty concrete wall. It leaned there in the double shadow of two concrete supporting pillars, and the shape was all she could make out . . . the shape, and two luminous green eyes.

"Got a cigarette, love?" a husky cockney voice asked her, and she smelled raw meat and deep-fat-fried chips and something sweet and awful, like the residue at the bottom of garbage cans.

Those green eyes were cat's eyes. And suddenly she became sure, horribly sure, that if the big slumped shape stepped out of the shadows, she would see the milky cataract of eye, the pink ridges of scar tissue, the tufts of ginger hair.

She tore free, backed up, and felt something part the air near her . . . a hand? Claws? A spitting, hissing sound—

Another train charged overhead. The roar was huge, brain-rattling. Soot sifted down like black snow. She fled in blind panic, for the second time that evening not knowing where . . . or for how long.

What brought her back to herself was the realization that Lonnie was gone. She had half collapsed against a dirty brick wall, breathing in great tearing gasps. She was still in Norris Road (at least she believed herself to be, she told the two constables; the wide way was still cobbled, and the tram tracks still ran directly down the center of the road), but the deserted, decaying shops had given way to deserted, decaying warehouses. DAWGLISH & SONS read the soot-begrimed signboard on one. A second had the name ALHAZRED emblazoned across ancient and peeling green paint. Below the name was a series of Arabian pothooks and dashes.

"Lonnie!" she called. There was no echo, no carrying in spite of the silence (no, not complete silence, she told them; there was still the sound of traffic, and it might have been closer . . . but not much). The word that stood for her husband seemed to drop from her mouth and fall dead at her feet. The blood of sunset had been replaced by the cool grey ashes of twilight. For the first time it occurred to her that night might fall upon her here in Crouch End—if she was still indeed in Crouch End—and that thought brought fresh terror.

She told Vetter and Farnham that there had been absolutely no reflection on her part during that unknowable length of time between being dropped off at the call box and the final horror. She had reacted like a frightened animal. Stimulus was applied; they fled. And now she was alone. She wanted Lonnie, her husband. She was aware of that. But it did not occur to her to wonder much—if at all—about why this area, which must surely lie within five miles of Cambridge Circus, should be utterly deserted. It did not occur to her to wonder how the disfigured cat could have gotten from the restaurant to the shop-to-let. She did not even wonder much about the inexplicable pit in the lawn of that house, except as it bore on Lonnie. Those questions came later, when it was too late, and they would (she said) haunt her for the rest of her life.

Doris Freeman set off walking, calling for Lonnie. Her voice did not echo, but her footfalls seemed to. The shadows began to fill Norris Road. Overhead, the sky was now purple. It might have been some distorting effect of the twilight, or her own exhaustion, but the warehouses seemed to lean over the road now. The windows, caked with the dirt of decades—of centuries, perhaps—seemed to be staring at her. And the names on the signboards (she said) became progressively stranger, lunatic, and certainly unpronounceable. The vowels were in the wrong places, and consonants had been strung together in a way that would make it impossible for any human tongue to get around them. CTHULU KRYON read one, with more of those Arabian pothooks beneath it YOGSOGGOTH read another. R'YELEH said yet another. There was one that she remembered particularly: NRTESN NYARLAHOTEP.

("How could you remember such gibberish?" Farnham asked her.)

(And Doris Freeman had shook her head, slowly and tiredly. "I don't know. I really don't know.")

Norris Road seemed to stretch on into infinity, cobbled, split by tram tracks. And although she continued to walk—she wouldn't have believed she could run, although later, she said, she did—she no longer called for Lonnie. She was now in the grip of the greatest fear she had ever known, a fear she would not have believed a human being could endure without going mad or dropping stone dead. Yet it was impossible for her to articulate her fear except in one way, and even this, although concrete, was not satisfactory.

She said it was as if she was no longer on earth. As if she was on a different planet, a place so alien that the human mind could not even begin to comprehend it. The *angles*

seemed different, she said. The *colors* seemed different. The
. . . but it was hopeless.

She could only walk under a sky that seemed twisted and
strange between the dark bulking buildings, and hope that it
would end.

And it did.

She became aware of two figures standing on the sidewalk
ahead of her. It was the two children—the boy with the deformed claw hand and the little girl. Her hair was in braids.

"It's the American woman," the boy said.

"She's lost," said the girl.

"Lost her husband."

"Lost her way."

"Found the darker way."

"Found the way into the funnel."

"Lost her hope."

"Found the Whistler from the Stars—"

"—Eater of Dimensions—"

"—the Blind Piper who is not named for a thousand
years—"

Faster and faster their words came, a breathless liturgy, a
flashing loom. Her head spun with them. The buildings
leaned. The stars were out, but they were not *her* stars, the
ones she had wished on as a girl or courted under as a young
woman, these were crazed stars in lunatic constellations, and
her hands went to her ears and her hands did not shut out the
sounds and finally she screamed at them:

*"Where's my husband? Where's Lonnie? What have you
done to him?"*

There was silence. And then the girl said: "He's gone beneath."

The boy: "Gone to Him Who Waits."

The girl smiled—a malicious smile full of evil innocence.
"He couldn't well not go, could he? The mark was on him.
And you'll go. You'll go now."

"Lonnie! *What have you done with—*"

The boy raised his hand and chanted in a high fluting language that she could not understand—but the sound of the
words drove Doris Freeman nearly mad with fear.

"The street began to move then," she told Vetter and Farnham. "The cobbles began to . . . to undulate like a carpet. They rose and fell, rose and fell. The tram tracks came loose and flew into the air—I remember that, I remember the starlight shining on them—and then the cobbles themselves began to come loose, one by one at first, and then in bunches. They just flew off into the darkness. There was a tearing sound when they came loose. A grinding, tearing sound . . . the way an earthquake must sound. And—something started to come through—"

"What?" Vetter asked. He was hunched forward, his eyes boring into Doris Freeman. "What did you see? What was it?"

"Tentacles," she said, slowly and haltingly. "I think . . . I think it was tentacles. But they were as thick as old banyan trees, as if each of them was made up of a thousand squirming smaller tentacles . . . and there were pink things like suckers . . . but sometimes they looked like faces . . . like Lonnie's face, some of them, some like other faces, all of them in agony . . . screaming in agony . . . but below them, in the darkness under the street . . . in the darkness *beneath* . . . there was something else. Something like great . . . great *eyes* . . ."

At that point she had broken down, unable to go on for some time.

And as it turned out, there was really no more to tell. She had no coherent memory of what happened after that. The next thing she remembered was cowering in the doorway of a closed newsagent's shop. She might be there yet, she had told them, except that she had seen cars passing back and forth, and the reassuring glow of arc-sodium streetlights. Two people had passed in front of her, and Doris had cringed farther back into the shadows, afraid of the two evil children. But these were not children, she saw; they were a teenage boy and girl walking hand in hand. The boy was saying something about the new Francis Coppola film.

She had come out onto the sidewalk warily, ready to dart back into the convenient bolthole the newsagent's doorway made—but there was no need. Fifty yards up on her left was a moderately busy intersection, with cars and lorries standing at a stop-and-go light. Across the way was a jeweler's shop with a large lighted clock in the show window. A steel accordion grille had been drawn across the window, but she could still make out the time. It was five minutes of ten.

She had walked up to the intersection then, and despite the streetlights and the comforting rumble of traffic, she had kept shooting terrified glances over her shoulder. She ached all over. She was limping on one broken heel. Somehow she had kept her purse. She had pulled muscles in her belly and both legs—her right leg was particularly bad, as if she had strained something in it.

At the intersection she saw that somehow she had come around to Hillfield Avenue and Tottenham Road. A woman of about sixty with her greying hair escaping from the rag it was done up in was talking to a man of about the same age under a streetlamp. They both looked at Doris as she approached them as if she were some sort of dreadful apparition.

"Police," Doris Freeman had croaked. "Where's the police station? I . . . I'm an American citizen and . . . I've lost my husband . . . and I need the police."

"What's happened, then, love?" the woman asked, not unkindly. "You look like you've been through the wringer, you do."

"Car accident?" her companion asked.

"No," she managed. "Please . . . is there a police station somewhere near?"

"Right up Tottenham Road," the man said. He took a package of Players from his pocket. "Like a cigarette? You look like you could use one, mum."

"Thank you," she said, and took the cigarette although she had quit nearly four years ago. The elderly man had to follow the jittering tip of it with his lighted match to get it going for her.

He glanced at the woman with her hair bound up in the rag. "I'll just take a little stroll up with her, Evvie. Make sure she gets there all right."

"I'll come along as well, then, won't I?" Evvie said, and

put an arm around Doris's shoulders. "Now what is it, love? Did someone try to mug you?"

"No," Doris said. "It . . . I . . . I . . . the street . . . there was a cat with only one eye . . . the street . . . the street opened up . . . I saw it . . . He Who Waits, they called it . . . Lonnie . . . I've got to find Lonnie . . ."

She was aware that she was speaking incoherencies, but she seemed helpless to be any clearer. And at any rate, she told Vetter and Farnham, she hadn't been all *that* incoherent, because the man and woman had drawn away from her, as if, when Evvie asked what the matter was, Doris had told her it was bubonic plague.

The man said something then, and Doris thought it was: "Happened again."

The woman pointed. "Station house is right up there. Globes hanging in front. You'll see it." And very quickly the two of them began to walk away . . . but now they were the ones glancing back over their shoulders.

Doris took two steps toward them. "Don't you come near!" Evvie called shrilly . . . and forked the sign of the evil eye at Doris, simultaneously cringing against the man, who put an arm about her. "Don't you come near, if you've been to Crouch End Towen!"

And with that, the two of them had disappeared into the night.

Now PC Farnham stood leaning in the doorway between the common room and the main filing room—the back files Vetter had spoken of were certainly not kept here. Farnham had made himself a fresh cup of tea and was smoking the last cigarette in his pack—the woman had also bummed several—smoking op's, he believed they called it in the States.

The woman had gone back to her hotel, in the company of the nurse Vetter had called—the nurse would be staying with her tonight, and would make a judgment in the morning as to whether the woman would need to go in hospital. The children made that difficult, Farnham supposed, and where the woman was an American national (as she kept proclaiming), it became that much more complicated. And what was

she going to tell the kiddies when they woke up? That the
big bad monster of Crouch End Town

(Towen)

had eaten up daddy?

Farnham grimaced and put down his teacup. It wasn't his
problem, none of it. For good or for ill, Mrs. Doris Freeman
had become sandwiched between the National State and the
American Embassy in the great waltz of governments. It was
none of his affair; he was only a PC who wanted to forget
the whole thing. And he intended to let Vetter write the report. It was Vetter's baby. Vetter could afford to put his name
to such a bouquet of lunacy; he was an old man, used up.
He would still be a PC on the night shift when he got his
gold watch, his pension, and his council flat. Farnham, on
the other hand, had ambitions of making sergeant soon, and
that meant he had to watch every little thing.

And speaking of Vetter, where was he? He'd been taking
the night air for quite a while now.

Farnham crossed the common room and went out. He stood
between the two lighted globes and stared across Tottenham
Road. Vetter was nowhere in sight. It was past three A.M.,
and silence lay thick and even, like a shroud. What was that
line from Wordsworth? "All that great heart lying still,"
something like that.

He went down the steps and stood on the sidewalk. He felt
a trickle of unease now. It was silly, of course it was. He was
angry with himself, angry that the woman's mad story should
have had even this slight effect on him. Perhaps he deserved
to be afraid of a hard copper like Sid Raymond.

Farnham walked slowly up to the corner, thinking he would
meet Vetter coming back from his night stroll. But he would
go no farther than the corner, if the station was left empty
even for a few moments, there would be hell to pay—if it
was discovered.

He went up to the corner and looked around. It was funny,
but all the arc-sodiums seemed to have gone out up here. The
entire street looked different without them. Would it have to
be reported, he wondered? And where was Vetter?

He would take a little walk up, he decided, and see just

what was what. But not far. It wouldn't do to leave the station unattended, that would be a sure and simple way of assuring an end like Vetter's, an old man on the night shift in a quiet part of town, mostly concerned with kids congregating on the corners after midnight . . . and crazy American women.

He would walk up just a little way.

Not far.

Vetter came in less than five minutes after Farnham had left. Farnham had gone in the opposite direction, and if Vetter had come along a minute earlier, he would have seen the young constable stand at the corner for a moment and then disappear from sight.

"Farnham?" he called.

There was no answer but the buzz of the clock on the wall.

"Farnham?" he called again, and wiped his mouth with the palm of his hand.

Lonnie Freeman was never found. Eventually his wife—who had begun to grey around the temples—flew back to America with her children. They went on the Concorde. A month later she attempted suicide. She spent a year in a rest home. She came out much improved.

PC Robert Farnham was never seen or heard from again. He left a wife and a two-year-old set of twin girls. His wife wrote a series of angry letters to her MP, insisting that something was going on, something was being covered up, that her Bob had been enticed into taking some dangerous sort of undercover assignment or other, like that fellow Hackett on the BBC. He would have done anything to make sergeant, she told the MP repeatedly. Eventually, the MP stopped answering her letters, and at about the same time that Doris Freeman was coming out of the rest home, her hair almost entirely white now, Sheila Farnham moved back to Sussex, where her parents lived. Eventually she married a man in a steadier line of work than that of policing London—Frank Hobbs worked on the Ford assembly line. It had been necessary to get a divorce from her Bob first on grounds of desertion, but that was no problem.

Vetter took early retirement about four months after Doris

Freeman had stumbled her way into the station in Tottenham Road in Crouch End. He did indeed move into council housing, a two-above-the-shops in the town of Frimley. Six months later he was found dead of a heart attack, a can of Harp Lager in his hand.

The hot end-of-summer night when Doris Freeman told her tale was August 19, 1974. Better than three and a half years have passed since then. And Doris's Lonnie and Sheila's Bob are together.

Vetter would have known where.

By the entirely democratic and accidental process of alphabetical order, they are together in the back file, the place where unsolved cases and tales too wild to bear any credence are kept.

FARNHAM, ROBERT is written on the tab of one thin folder. FREEMAN, LEONARD is written on the tab of the folder directly behind. Both folders contain a single page—a badly typed report by the investigating officer. In both cases, the signature is Vetter's.

And in Crouch End, which is really a quiet suburb of London, strange things still happen. From time to time.

Joyce Carol Oates

NIGHT-SIDE

Joyce Carol Oates is one of the major talents in contemporary American literature, a poet, novelist, essayist and short story writer of the first rank. Her contributions to horror literature include many stories in the Gothic mold of William Faulkner and Flannery O'Connor, but she sometimes writes more nearly in the tradition of Shirley Jackson, as in "Night-Side," which is perhaps her finest horror story. It is the title piece of one of her many short story collections, the one that contains a large part of her significant work in the horror mode. In this story, she deals with the occult directly, in an uncharacteristic (for her) fashion most comparable to, say, Robert Aickman, or Edith Wharton. She is in the main tradition of horror in American literature in this century, though she works outside category boundaries. If there is such a thing as supernatural mainstream, Henry James, Edith Wharton, Shirley Jackson, Joyce Carol Oates and Peter Straub define it.

6 February 1887. Quincy, Massachusetts.
Montague House.

Disturbing experience at Mrs. A——'s home yesterday evening. Few theatrics—comfortable though rather pathetically shabby surroundings—an only mildly sinister atmosphere (especially in contrast to the Walpurgis Night presented by that shameless charlatan in Portsmouth: the Dwarf Eustace who presumed to introduce me to Swedenborg himself, under the erroneous impression that I am a member of the Church of the New Jerusalem—*I!*). Nevertheless I came away disturbed, and my conversation with Dr. Moore afterward, at dinner, though dispassionate and even, at times, a bit flippant, did not settle my mind. Perry Moore is of course a hearty materialist, an Aristotelian-Spencerian with a love of good food and drink, and an appreciation of the more nonsensical vagaries of life; when in his company I tend to support that general view, as I do at the University as well—for there is a terrific pull in my nature toward the gregarious that I cannot resist. (That I do not wish to resist.) Once I am alone with my thoughts, however, I am accursed with doubts about my own position and nothing seems more precarious than my intellectual ''convictions.''

The more hardened members of our Society, like Perry Moore, are apt to put the issue bluntly: Is Mrs. A——of Quincy a conscious or unconscious fraud? The conscious frauds are relatively easy to deal with; once discovered, they prefer to erase themselves from further consideration. The unconscious frauds are not, in a sense, ''frauds'' at all. It would certainly be difficult to prove criminal intention. Mrs. A——, for instance, does not accept money or gifts so far as we have been able to determine, and both Perry Moore and I noted her courteous but firm refusal of the Judge's offer to send her and her husband (presumably ailing?) on holiday to England in the spring. She is a mild, self-effacing, rather stocky woman in her mid-fifties who wears her hair parted in the center, like several of my maiden aunts, and whose sole item of adornment was an old-fashioned cameo brooch; her black dress had the appearance of having been homemade, though it was attractive enough, and freshly ironed. According to the Society's records she has been a practicing medium now for six years. Yet she lives, still, in an undistinguished section of Quincy, in a neighborhood of modest frame dwellings. The A——s' house is in fairly good condition, especially considering the damage routinely done by our winters, and the only room we saw, the parlor, is quite ordinary, with overstuffed chairs and the usual cushions and a monstrous horsehair sofa and, of course, the oaken table; the atmosphere would have been so conventional as to have seemed disappointing had not Mrs. A——made an attempt to brighten it, or perhaps to give it a glamourously occult air, by hanging certain watercolors about the room. (She claims that the watercolors were "done" by one of her contact spirits, a young Iroquois girl who died in the seventeen seventies of smallpox. They are touchingly garish—mandalas and triangles and stylized eyeballs and even a transparent Cosmic Man with Indian-black hair.)

At last night's sitting there were only three persons in addition to Mrs. A——. Judge T——of the New York State Supreme Court (now retired); Dr. Moore; and I, Jarvis Williams. Dr. Moore and I came out from Cambridge under the aegis of the Society for Psychical Research in order to make a preliminary study of the kind of mediumship Mrs. A——affects. We did not bring a stenographer along this time though Mrs. A——indicated her willingness to have the sitting transcribed; she struck me as being rather warmly cooperative, and even interested in our formal procedures, though Perry Moore remarked afterward at dinner that she had struck him as "noticeably reluctant." She was, however, flustered at the start of the séance and for a while it seemed as if we and the Judge might have made the trip for nothing. (She kept waving her plump hands about like an embarrassed hostess, apologizing for the fact that the spirits were evidently in a "perverse uncommunicative mood tonight.")

She did go into trance eventually, however. The four of us were seated about the heavy round table from approximately 6:50 P.M. to 9 P.M. For nearly forty-five minutes Mrs. A—— made abortive attempts to contact her Chief Communicator and then slipped abruptly into trance (dramatically, in fact: her eyes rolled back in her head in a manner that alarmed me at first), and a personality named Webley appeared. "Webley's" voice appeared to be coming from several directions during the course of the sitting. At all times it was a least three yards from Mrs. A——; despite the semi-dark of the parlor I believe I could see the woman's mouth and throat clearly enough, and I could not detect any obvious signs of ventriloquism. (Perry Moore, who is more experienced than I in psychical research, and rather more casual about the whole phenomenon, claims he has witnessed feats of ventriloquism that would make poor Mrs. A——look quite shabby in comparison.) "Webley's" voice was raw, singsong, peculiarly disturbing. At times it was shrill and at other times so faint as to be nearly inaudible. Something brattish about it. Exasperating. "Webley" took care to pronounce his final *g*'s in a self-conscious matter, quite unlike Mrs. A——. (Which could be, of course, a deliberate ploy.)

This Webley is one of Mrs. A——'s most frequent manifesting spirits, though he is not the most reliable. Her Chief Communicator is a Scots patriarch who lived "in the time of Merlin" and who is evidently very wise; unfortunately he did not choose to appear yesterday evening. Instead, Webley presided. He is supposed to have died some seventy-five years ago at the age of nineteen in a house just up the street from the A——s'. He was either a butcher's helper or an apprentice tailor. He died in a fire—or by a "slow dreadful crippling disease"—or beneath a horse's hooves, in a freakish accident; during the course of a sitting he alluded self-pityingly to his death but seemed to have forgotten the exact details. At the very end of the evening he addressed me directly as Dr. Williams of Harvard University, saying that since I had influential friends in Boston I could help him with his career—it turned out he had written hundreds of songs and poems and parables but none had been published; would I please find a publisher for his work? Life had treated him so unfairly. His talent—his genius—had been lost to humanity. I had it within my power to help him, he claimed, was I not *obliged* to help him . . . ? He then sang one of his songs, which sounded to me like an old ballad; many of the words were so shrill as to be unintelligible, but he sang it just the same, repeating the verses in a haphazard order:

> This ae nighte, this ae nighte,
> —Every nighte and alle,
> Fire and fleet and candle-lighte,
> And Christe receive thy saule.

When thou from hence away art past,
  —Every nighte and alle,
To Whinny-muir though com'st at last:
  And Christe receive thy saule.

From Brig o' Dread when thou may'st pass,
  —Every nighte and alle,
The whinnes sall prick thee to the bare bane:
  And Christe receive thy saule.

The elderly Judge T——had come up from New York City in order, as he earnestly put it, to "speak directly to his deceased wife as he was never able to do while she was living"; but Webley treated the old gentleman in a high-handed, cavalier manner, as if the occasion were not at all serious. He kept saying, "Who is there tonight? *Who* is there? Let them introduce themselves again—I don't *like* strangers! I tell you I don't *like* strangers!" Though Mrs. A——had informed us beforehand that we would witness no physical phenomena, there were, from time to time, glimmerings of light in the darkened room, hardly more than the tiny pulsations of light made by fireflies; and both Perry Moore and I felt the table vibrating beneath our fingers. At about the time when Webley gave way to the spirit of Judge T——'s wife, the temperature in the room seemed to drop suddenly and I remember being gripped by a sensation of panic—but it lasted only an instant and I was soon myself again. (Dr. Moore claimed not to have noticed any drop in temperature and Judge T——was so rattled after the sitting that it would have been pointless to question him.)

The séance proper was similar to others I have attended. A spirit—or a voice—laid claim to being the late Mrs. T——; this spirit addressed the survivor in a peculiarly intense, urgent manner, so that it was rather embarrassing to be present. Judge T——was soon weeping. His deeply creased face glistened with tears like a child's.

"Why Darrie! *Darrie*! Don't cry! Oh don't cry!" the spirit said. "No one is dead, Darrie. There is no death. No death! . . . Can you hear me, Darrie? Why are you so fright-

ened? So upset? No need, Darrie, no need! Grandfather and
Lucy and I are together here—happy together. Darrie, look
up! Be brave, my dear! My poor frightened dear! We never
knew each other, did we? My poor dear! My love! . . . I saw
you in a great transparent house, a great burning house; poor
Darrie, they told me you were ill, you were weak with fever;
all the rooms of the house were aflame and the staircase was
burnt to cinders, but there were figures walking up and
down, Darrie, great numbers of them, and you were among
them, dear, stumbling in your fright—so clumsy! Look up, dear,
and shade your eyes, and you will see me. Grandfather helped
me—did you know? Did I call out his name at the end? My
dear, my darling, it all happened so quickly—we never knew
each other, did we? Don't be hard on Annie! Don't be cruel!
Darrie? Why are you crying?'' And gradually the spirit voice
grew fainter; or perhaps something went wrong and the channels of communication were no longer clear. There were repetitions, garbled phrases, meaningless queries of ''Dear? Dear?''
that the Judge's replies did not seem to placate. The spirit spoke
of her gravesite, and of a trip to Italy taken many years before,
and of a dead or unborn baby, and again of Annie—evidently
Judge T——'s daughter; but the jumble of words did not always
make sense and it was a great relief when Mrs. A——suddenly
woke from her trance.

Judge T——rose from the table, greatly agitated. He wanted
to call the spirit back; he had not asked her certain crucial
questions; he had been overcome by emotion and had found
it difficult to speak, to interrupt the spirit's monologue. But
Mrs. A——(who looked shockingly tired) told him the spirit
would not return again that night and they must not make
any attempt to call it back.

''The other world obeys its own laws,'' Mrs. A——said in
her small, rather reedy voice.

We left Mrs. A——'s home shortly after 9:00 P.M. I too
was exhausted; I had not realized how absorbed I had been
in the proceedings.

Judge T——is also staying at Montague House, but he was
too upset after the sitting to join us for dinner. He assured

us, though, that the spirit was authentic—the voice had been his wife's, he was certain of it, he would stake his life on it. She had never called him "Darrie" during her lifetime, wasn't it odd that she called him "Darrie" now?—and was so concerned for him, so loving?—and concerned for their daughter as well? He was very moved. He had a great deal to think about. (Yes, he'd had a fever some weeks ago—a severe attack of bronchitis and a fever; in fact, he had not completely recovered.) What was extraordinary about the entire experience was the wisdom revealed: There is no death.

There is no death.

Dr. Moore and I dined heartily on roast crown of lamb, spring potatoes with peas, and buttered cabbage. We were served two kinds of bread—German rye and sour-cream rolls; the hotel's butter was superb; the wine excellent; the dessert—crepes with cream and toasted almonds—looked marvelous, though I had not any appetite for it. Dr. Moore was ravenously hungry. He talked as he ate, often punctuating his remarks with rich bursts of laughter. It was his opinion, of course, that the medium was a fraud—and not a very skillful fraud, either. In his fifteen years of amateur, intermittent investigations he had encountered far more skillful mediums. Even the notorious Eustace with his levitating tables and hobgoblin chimes and shrieks was cleverer than Mrs. A——; one knew of course that Eustace was a cheat, but one was hard pressed to explain his method. Whereas Mrs. A——was quite transparent.

Dr. Moore spoke for some time in his amiable, dogmatic way. He ordered brandy for both of us, though it was nearly midnight when we finished our dinner and I was anxious to get to bed. (I hoped to rise early and work on a lecture dealing with Kant's approach to the problem of Free Will, which I would be delivering in a few days.) But Dr. Moore enjoyed talking and seemed to have been invigorated by our experience at Mrs. A——'s.

At the age of forty-three Perry Moore is only four years my senior, but he has the air, in my presence at least, of being considerably older. He is a second cousin of my mother, a very successful physician with a bachelor's flat and office in Louisburg Square; his failure to marry, or his refusal, is one of Boston's perennial mysteries. Everyone agrees that he is learned, witty, charming, and extraordinarily intelligent. Striking rather than conventionally handsome, with a dark, lustrous beard and darkly bright eyes, he is an excellent amateur violinist, an enthusiastic sailor, and a lover of literature—his favorite writers are Fielding, Shakespeare, Horace, and Dante. He is, of course, the perfect investigator in spiritualist matters since he is detached from the phenomena he observes and yet he is indefatigably curious; he has a positive love, a mania, for facts. Like the true scientist he seeks facts that, assembled, may possibly give rise to hypotheses: he does not set out with a hypothesis in mind, like a sort of basket into which certain facts may be tossed, helter-skelter, while others are conveniently ignored. In all things he is an empiricist who accepts nothing on faith.

"If the woman is a fraud, then," I say hesitantly, "you believe she is a self-deluded fraud? And her spirits' information is gained by means of telepathy?"

"Telepathy indeed. There can be no other explanation," Dr. Moore says emphatically. "By some means not yet known to science . . . by some uncanny means she suppresses her conscious personality . . . and thereby releases other, secondary personalities that have the power of seizing upon others' thoughts and memories. It's done in a way not understood by science at the present time. But it will be understood eventually. Our investigations into the unconscious powers of the human mind are just beginning; we're on the threshold, really, of a new era."

"So she simply picks out of her clients' minds whatever they want to hear," I say slowly. "And from time to time she can even tease them a little—insult them, even: she can unloose a creature like that obnoxious Webley upon a person like Judge T—without fear of being discovered. Telepathy. . . . Yes, that would explain a great deal. Very nearly everything we witnessed tonight."

"*Everything*, I should say," Dr. Moore says.

* * *

In the coach returning to Cambridge I set aside Kant and my lecture notes and read Sir Thomas Browne: *Light that makes all things seen, makes some things invisible. The greatest mystery of Religion is expressed by adumbration.*

19 March 1887. Cambridge. 11 P.M.

Walked ten miles this evening; must clear cobwebs from mind.

Unhealthy atmosphere. Claustrophobic. Last night's sitting in Quincy—a most unpleasant experience.

(Did not tell my wife what happened. Why is she so curious about the Spirit World?—about Perry Moore?)

My body craves more violent physical activity. In the summer, thank God, I will be able to swim in the ocean: the most strenuous and challenging of exercises.

Jotting down notes re the Quincy experience:

I. Fraud

Mrs. A——, possibly with accomplices, conspires to deceive; she does research into her clients' lives beforehand, possibly bribes servants. She is either a very skillful ventriloquist or works with someone who is. (Husband? Son? The husband is a retired cabinetmaker said to be in poor health; possibly consumptive. The son, married, lives in Waterbury.)

Her stated wish to avoid publicity and her declining of payment may simply be ploys; she may intend to make a great deal of money at some future time.

(Possibility of blackmail?—might be likely in cases similar to Perry Moore's.)

II. Non-fraud

Naturalistic

1. Telepathy. She reads minds of clients.
2. "Multiple personality" of medium. Aspects of her own buried psyche are released as her con-

scious personality is suppressed. These second-ary beings are in mysterious rapport with the "secondary" personalities of the clients.

Spiritualistic

1. The controls are genuine communicators, inter-mediaries between our world and the world of the dead. These spirits give way to other spirits, who then speak through the medium; or

2. These spirits *influence* the medium, who relays their messages using her own vocabulary. Their personalities are then filtered through and limited by hers.

3. The spirits are not those of the deceased; they are perverse, willful spirits. (Perhaps demons? But there are no demons.)

III. Alternative hypothesis

Madness: the medium is mad, the clients are mad, even the detached, rationalist investigators are mad.

Yesterday evening at Mrs. A——'s home, the second sitting Perry Moore and I observed together, along with Miss Brad-ley, a stenographer from the Society, and two legitimate cli-ents—a Brookline widow, Mrs. P——, and her daughter Clara, a handsome young woman in her early twenties. Mrs. A——exactly as she appeared to us in February; possibly a little stouter. Wore black dress and cameo brooch. Served Lapsang tea, tiny sandwiches, and biscuits when we arrived shortly after 6 P.M. Seemed quite friendly to Perry, Miss Bradley, and me; fussed over us, like any hostess; chattered a bit about the cold spell. Mrs. P——and her daughter arrived at six-thirty and the sitting began shortly thereafter.

Jarring from the very first. A babble of spirit voices. Mrs. A——in trance, head flung back, mouth gaping, eyes rolled upward. Queer. Unnerving. I glanced at Dr. Moore but he seemed unperturbed, as always. The widow and her daughter, however, looked as frightened as I felt.

Why are we here, sitting around this table?

What do we believe we will discover?

What are the risks we face . . . ?

"Webley" appeared and disappeared in a matter of minutes. His shrill, raw, aggrieved voice was supplanted by that of a creature of indeterminate sex who babbled in Gaelic. This creature in turn was supplanted by a hoarse German, a man who identified himself as Felix; he spoke a curiously ungrammatical German. For some minutes he and two or three other spirits quarreled. (Each declared himself Mrs. A——'s Chief Communicator for the evening.) Small lights flickered in the semi-dark of the parlor and the table quivered beneath my fingers and I felt, or believed I felt, something brushing against me, touching the back of my head. I shuddered violently but regained my composure at once. An unidentified voice proclaimed in English that the Spirit of our Age was Mars: there would be a catastrophic war shortly and most of the world's population would be destroyed. All atheists would be destroyed. Mrs. A——shook her head from side to side as if trying to wake. Webley appeared, crying "Hello? Hello? I can't see anyone! Who is there? Who has called me?" but was again supplanted by another spirit who shouted long strings of words in a foreign language. [Note: I discovered a few days later that this language was Walachian, a Romanian dialect. Of course Mrs. A——, whose ancestors are English, could not possibly have known Walachian, and I rather doubt that the woman has even heard of the Walachian people.]

The sitting continued in this chaotic way for some minutes. Mrs. P——must have been quite disappointed, since she had wanted to be put in contact with her deceased husband. (She needed advice on whether or not to sell certain pieces of property.) Spirits babbled freely in English, German, Gaelic, French, even in Latin, and at one point Dr. Moore queried a spirit in Greek, but the spirit retreated at once as if not equal to Dr. Moore's wit. The atmosphere was alarming but at the same time rather maniac; almost jocular. I found myself suppressing laughter. Something touched the back of my head and I shivered violently and broke into perspiration, but the experience was not altogether unpleasant; it would be very difficult for me to characterize it.

And then—

And then, suddenly, everything changed. There was complete calm. A spirit voice spoke gently out of a corner of the room, addressing Perry Moore by his first name in a slow, tentative, groping way. "Perry? Perry . . . ?" Dr. Moore jerked about in his seat. He was astonished; I could see by his expression that the voice belonged to someone he knew.

"Perry . . . ? This is Brandon. I've waited so long for you, Perry, how could you be so selfish? I forgave you. Long ago. You couldn't help your cruelty and I couldn't help my innocence. Perry? My glasses have been broken—I can't see. I've been afraid for so long, Perry, please have mercy on me! I can't bear it any longer. I didn't *know* what it would be like. There are crowds of people here, but we can't see one another, we don't know one another, we're strangers, there is a universe of strangers—I can't see anyone clearly—I've been lost for twenty years, Perry, I've been waiting for you for twenty years! You don't dare turn away again, Perry! Not again! Not after so long!"

Dr. Moore stumbled to his feet, knocking his chair aside.

"No—Is it—I don't believe—"

"Perry? Perry? Don't abandon me again, Perry! Not again!"

"What is this?" Dr. Moore cried.

He was on his feet now; Mrs. A——woke from her trance with a groan. The women from Brookline were very upset and I must admit that I was in a mild state of terror, my shirt and my underclothes drenched with perspiration.

The sitting was over. It was only seven-thirty.

"Brandon?" Dr. Moore cried. "Wait. Where are—? Brandon? Can you hear me? Where are you? Why did you do it, Brandon? Wait! Don't leave! Can't anyone call him back—Can't anyone help me—"

Mrs. A——rose unsteadily. She tried to take Dr. Moore's hands in hers but he was too agitated.

"I heard only the very last words," she said. "They're always that way—so confused, so broken—the poor things— Oh, what a pity! It wasn't murder, was it? Not murder! Suicide—? I believe suicide is even worse for them! The poor broken things, they wake in the other world and are utterly, utterly lost—they have no guides, you see—no help in crossing over— They are completely alone for eternity—"

"Can't you call him back?" Dr. Moore asked wildly. He was peering into a corner of the parlor, slightly stooped, his face distorted as if he were staring into the sun. "Can't someone help me? . . . Brandon? Are you here? Are you here somewhere? For God's sake can't someone help!"

"Dr. Moore, please, the spirits are gone—the sitting is over for tonight—"

"You foolish old woman, leave me alone! Can't you see I—I—I must not lose him—Call him back, will you? I insist! I insist!"

"Dr. Moore, please—You mustn't shout—"

"I said call him back! At once! *Call him back!*"

Then he burst into tears. He stumbled against the table and hid his face in his hands and wept like a child; he wept as if his heart had been broken.

And so today I have been reliving the séance. Taking notes, trying to determine what happened. A brisk windy walk of ten miles. Head buzzing with ideas. Fraud? Deceit? Telepathy? Madness?

What a spectacle! Dr. Perry Moore calling after a spirit, begging it to return—and then crying, afterward, in front of four astonished witnesses.

Dr. Perry Moore of all people.

My dilemma: whether I should report last night's incident to Dr. Rowe, the president of the Society, or whether I should say nothing about it and request that Miss Bradley say nothing. It would be tragic if Perry's professional reputation were to be damaged by a single evening's misadventure; and before long all of Boston would be talking.

In his present state, however, he is likely to tell everyone about it himself.

At Montague House the poor man was unable to sleep. He would have kept me up all night had I had the stamina to endure his excitement.

There *are* spirits! There have always been spirits!

His entire life up to the present time has been misspent!

And of course, most important of all—there is no death!

He paced about my hotel room, pulling at his beard nervously. At times there were tears in his eyes. He seemed to want a response of some kind from me but whenever I started to speak he interrupted; he was not really listening.

"Now at last I know. I can't undo my knowledge," he said in a queer hoarse voice. "Amazing, isn't it, after so many years . . . so many wasted years . . . Ignorance has been my lot, darkness . . . and a hideous complacency. My God, when I consider my deluded smugness! I am so ashamed, so ashamed. All along people like Mrs. A——have been in contact with a world of such power . . . and people like me have been toiling in ignorance, accumulating material achievements, expending our energies in idiotic transient things . . . But all that is changed now. Now I know. I *know*. There is no death, as the Spiritualists have always told us."

"But, Perry, don't you think—Isn't it possible that—"

"I *know*," he said quietly. "It's as clear to me as if I had crossed over into that other world myself. Poor Brandon! He's no older now than he was *then*. The poor boy, the poor tragic soul! To think that he's still living after so many years . . . Extraordinary. . . . It makes my head spin," he said slowly. For a moment he stood without speaking. He pulled at his beard, then absently touched his lips with his fingers, then wiped at his eyes. He seemed to have forgotten me. When he spoke again his voice was hollow, rather ghastly. He sounded drugged. "I . . . I had been thinking of him as . . . as dead, you know. As dead. Twenty years. Dead. And now, tonight, to be forced to realize that . . . that he isn't dead after all . . . It was laudanum he took. I found him. His rooms on the third floor of Weld Hall. I found him, I had no real idea, none at all, not until I read the note . . . and of course I destroyed the note . . . I had to, you see: for his sake. For his sake more than mine. It was because he realized

there could be no . . . no hope. . . . Yet he called me cruel!
You heard him, Jarvis, didn't you? Cruel! I suppose I was.
Was I? I don't know what to think. I must talk with him
again. I . . . I don't know what to . . . what to think. I . . ."

"You look awfully tired, Perry. It might be a good idea to
go to bed," I said weakly.

". . . recognized his voice at once. Oh at once: no doubt.
None. What a revelation! And my life so misspent. . . .
Treating people's *bodies*. Absurd. I know now that nothing
matters except that other world . . . nothing matters except
our dead, our beloved dead . . . who are *not dead*. What a
colossal revelation . . . ! Why, it will change the entire course
of history. It will alter men's minds throughout the world.
You were there, Jarvis, so you understand. You were a witness. . . ."

"But—"

"You'll bear witness to the truth of what I am saying?"

He stared at me, smiling. His eyes were bright and threaded
with blood.

I tried to explain to him as courteously and sympathetically
as possible that his experience at Mrs. A——'s was not substantially different from the experiences many people have
had at séances. "And always in the past psychical researchers
have taken the position—"

"You were *there*," he said angrily. "You heard Brandon's
voice as clearly as I did. Don't deny it!"

"—have taken the position that—that the phenomenon
can be partly explained by the telepathic powers of the medium—"

"That was Brandon's *voice*," Perry said. "I felt this presence, I tell you! *His*. Mrs. A——had nothing to do with it—
nothing at all. I feel as if . . . as if I could call Brandon back
by myself. . . . I feel his presence even now. Close about
me. He isn't dead, you see; no one is dead, there's a universe
of . . . of people who are not dead. . . . Parents, grandpar-
ents, sisters, brothers, everyone . . . everyone. . . . How can
you deny, Jarvis, the evidence of our own senses? You were
there with me tonight and you know as well as I do. . . ."

"Perry, I don't *know*. I did hear a voice, yes, but we've

heard voices before at other sittings, haven't we? There are always voices. There are always 'spirits.' The Society has taken the position that the spirits could be real, of course, but that there are other hypotheses that are perhaps more likely—''

"Other hypotheses indeed!" Perry said irritably. "You're like a man with his eyes shut tight who refuses to open them out of sheer cowardice. Like the cardinals refusing to look through Galileo's telescope! And you have pretensions of being a man of learning, of science. . . . Why, we've got to destroy all the records we've made so far; they're a slander on the world of the spirits. Thank God we didn't file a report yet on Mrs. A——! It would be so embarrassing to be forced to call it back . . .''

"Perry, please. Don't be angry. I want only to remind you of the fact that we've been present at other sittings, haven't we?—and we've witnessed others responding emotionally to certain phenomena. Judge T——, for instance. He was convinced he'd spoken with his wife. But you must remember, don't you, that you and I were not at all convinced . . . ? It seemed to us more likely that Mrs. A——is able, through extrasensory powers we don't quite understand, to read the minds of her clients, and then to project certain voices out into the room so that it sounds as if they are coming from other people. . . . You even said, Perry, that she wasn't a very skillful ventriloquist. You said—''

"What does it matter what, in my ignorance, I said?" he cried. "Isn't it enough that I've been humiliated? That my entire life has been turned about? Must you insult me as well—sitting there so smugly and insulting *me*? I think I can make claim to being someone whom you might respect.''

And so I assured him that I did respect him. And he walked about the room, wiping at his eyes, greatly agitated. He spoke again of his friend, Brandon Gould, and of his own ignorance, and of the important mission we must undertake to inform men and women of the true state of affairs. I tried to talk with him, to reason with him, but it was hopeless. He scarcely listened to me.

". . . must inform the world . . . crucial truth. . . . There is no death, you see. Never was. Changes civilization, changes the course of history. Jarvis?'' he said groggily. ''You see? *There is no death.*''

25 March 1887. Cambridge.

Disquieting rumors re Perry Moore. Heard today at the University that one of Dr. Moore's patients (a brother-in-law of Dean Barker) was extremely offended by his behavior during a consultation last week. Talk of his having been drunk—which I find incredible. If the poor man appeared to be excitable and not his customary self, it was not because he was *drunk*, surely.

Another far-fetched tale told me by my wife, who heard it from her sister Maude: Perry Moore went to church (St. Ai-dan's Episcopal Church on Mount Street) for the first time in a decade, sat alone, began muttering and laughing during the sermon, and finally got to his feet and walked out, creating quite a stir. *What delusions!* What delusions!—he was said to have muttered.

I fear for the poor man's sanity.

31 March 1887. Cambridge. 4 A.M.

Sleepless night. Dreamed of swimming . . . swimming in the ocean . . . enjoying myself as usual when suddenly the water turns thick . . . turns to mud. Hideous! Indescribably awful. I was swimming nude in the ocean, by moonlight, I believe, ecstatically happy, entirely alone, when the water turned to mud. . . . Vile, disgusting mud; faintly warm; sucking at my body. Legs, thighs, torso, arms. Horrible. Woke in terror. Drenched with perspiration: pajamas wet. One of the most frightening nightmares of my adulthood.

A message from Perry Moore came yesterday just before dinner. Would I like to join him in visiting Mrs. A——sometime soon, in early April perhaps, on a noninvestigative basis . . . ?

He is uncertain now of the morality of our "investigating" Mrs. A——or any other medium.

4 April 1887. Cambridge.

Spent the afternoon from two to five at William James's home on Irving Street, talking with Professor James of the inexplicable phenomenon of consciousness. He is robust as always, rather irreverent, supremely confident in a way I find enviable; rather like Perry Moore before his conversion. (Extraordinary eyes—so piercing, quick, playful; a graying beard liberally threaded with white; close-cropped graying hair; a large, curving, impressive forehead; a manner intelligent and graceful and at the same time rough-edged, as if he anticipates or perhaps even hopes for recalcitration in his listeners.) We both find conclusive the ideas set forth in Binét's *Alterations of Personality* . . . . unsettling as these ideas may be to the rationalist position. James speaks of a *peculiarity* in the constitution of human nature: that is, the fact that we inhabit not only our ego-consciousness but a wide field of psychological experience (most clearly represented by the phenomenon of memory, which no one can adequately explain) over which we have no control whatsoever. In fact, we are not generally aware of this field of consciousness.

We inhabit a lighted sphere, then; and about us is a vast penumbra of memories, reflections, feelings, and stray uncoordinated thoughts that "belong" to us theoretically, but that do not seem to be part of our conscious identity. (I was too timid to ask Professor James whether it might be the case that we do not inevitably own these aspects of the personality—that such phenomena belong as much to the objective world as to our subjective selves.) It is quite possible that there is an element of some indeterminate kind: oceanic, timeless, and living, against which the individual being constructs temporary barriers as part of an ongoing process of unique, particularized survival; like the ocean itself, which appears to separate islands that are in fact not "islands" at all, but aspects of the earth firmly joined together below the surface of the water. Our lives, then, resemble these islands. . . . All this is no more than a possibility, Professor James and I agreed.

James is acquainted, of course, with Perry Moore. But he declined to speak on the subject of the poor man's increasingly eccentric behavior when I alluded to it. (It may be that he knows even more about the situation than I do—he enjoys a multitude of acquaintances in Cambridge and Boston.) I brought our conversation round several times to the possibility of the *naturalness* of the conversion experience in terms of the individual's evolution of self, no matter how his family, his colleagues, and society in general viewed it, and Professor James appeared to agree; at least he did not emphatically disagree. He maintains a healthy skepticism, of course, regarding Spiritualist claims, and all evangelical and enthusiastic religious movements, though he is, at the same time, a highly articulate foe of the "rationalist" position and he believes that psychical research of the kind some of us are attempting will eventually unearth riches—revealing aspects of the human psyche otherwise closed to our scrutiny.

"The fearful thing," James said, "is that we are at all times vulnerable to incursions from the 'other side' of the personality. . . . We cannot determine the nature of the total personality simply because much of it, perhaps most, is hidden from us. . . . When we are invaded, then, we are overwhelmed and surrender immediately. Emotionally charged intuitions, hunches, guesses, even ideas may be the least aggressive of these incursions; but there are visual and auditory hallucinations, and forms of automatic behavior not controlled by the conscious mind. . . . Ah, you're thinking I am simply describing insanity?"

I stared at him, quite surprised.

"No. Not at all. Not at all," I said at once.

Reading through my grandfather's journals, begun in East Anglia many years before my birth. Another world then. Another language, now lost to us. *Man is sinful by nature. God's justice takes precedence over His mercy.* The dogma of Original Sin: something brutish about the innocence of that belief. And yet consoling. . . .

Fearful of sleep since my dreams are so troubled now. The voices of impudent spirits (Immanuel Kant himself come to chide me for having made too much of his categories—!), stray shouts and whispers I cannot decipher, the faces of my own beloved dead hovering near, like carnival masks, insubstantial and possibly fraudulent. Impatient with my wife, who questions me too closely on these personal matters; annoyed from time to time, in the evenings especially, by the silliness of the children. (The eldest is twelve now and should know better.) Dreading to receive another lengthy letter—sermon, really—from Perry Moore re his "new position," and yet perversely hoping one will come soon.

I must know.

(Must know what . . . ?)

I must know.

10 April 1887. Boston. St. Aidan's Episcopal Church.

Funeral service this morning for Perry Moore; dead at forty-three.

17 April 1887. Seven Hills, New Hampshire.

A weekend retreat. No talk. No need to think.

Visiting with a former associate, author of numerous books. Cartesian specialist. Elderly. Partly deaf. Extraordinarily kind to me. (Did not ask about the Department or about my work.) Intensely interested in animal behavior now, in observation primarily; fascinated with the phenomenon of hibernation.

He leaves me alone for hours. He sees something in my face I cannot see myself.

* * *

The old consolations of a cruel but just God: ludicrous today.

In the nineteenth century we live free of God. We live in the illusion of freedom-of-God.

Dozing off in the guest room of this old farmhouse and then waking abruptly. *Is someone here? Is someone here?* My voice queer, hushed, childlike. *Please: is someone here?*

Silence.

Query: Is the penumbra outside consciousness all that was ever meant by "God"?

Query: Is inevitability all that was ever meant by "God"?

God—the body of fate we inhabit, then; no more and no less.

God pulled Perry down into the body of fate: into Himself. (Or Itself.) As Professor James might say, Dr. Moore was "vulnerable" to an assault from the other side.

At any rate he is dead. They buried him last Saturday.

25 April 1887. Cambridge.

Shelves of books. The sanctity of books. Kant, Plato, Schopenhauer, Descartes, Hume, Hegel, Spinoza. The others. All. Nietzsche, Spencer, Leibnitz (on whom I did a torturous Master's thesis). Plotinus. Swedenborg. *The Transactions of the American Society for Psychical Research.* Voltaire. Locke. Rousseau. And Berkeley: the good Bishop adrift in a dream.

An etching by Halbrech above my desk, The Thames 1801. Water too black. Inky-black. Thick with mud . . . ? Filthy water in any case.

Perry's essay, forty-five scribbled pages. "The Challenge of the Future." Given to me several weeks ago by Dr. Rowe, who feared rejecting it for the *Transactions* but could not, of course, accept it. I can read only a few pages at a time, then push it aside, too moved to continue. Frightened also.

The man had gone insane.

Died insane.

Personality broken: broken bits of intellect.

His argument passionate and disjointed, with no pretense of objectivity. Where some weeks ago he had taken the stand that it was immoral to investigate the Spirit World, now he took the stand that it was imperative we do so. We are on the brink of a new age . . . new knowledge of the universe . . . comparable to the stormy transitional period between the Ptolemaic and the Copernican theories of the universe. . . . More experiments required. Money. Donations. Subsidies by private institutions. All psychological research must be channeled into a systematic study of the Spirit World and the ways by which we can communicate with that world. Mediums like Mrs. A——must be brought to centers of learning like Harvard and treated with the respect their genius deserves. Their value to civilization is, after all, beyond estimation. They must be rescued from arduous and routine lives where their genius is drained off into vulgar pursuits . . . they must be rescued from a clientele that is mainly concerned with being put into contact with deceased relatives for utterly trivial, self-serving reasons. Men of learning must realize the gravity of the situation. Otherwise we will fail, we will stagger beneath the burden, we will be defeated, ignobly, and it will remain for the twentieth century to discover the existence of the Spirit Universe that surrounds the Material Universe, and to determine the exact ways by which one world is related to another.

Perry Moore died of a stroke on the eighth of April; died instantaneously on the steps of the Bedford Club shortly after 2 P.M. Passers-by saw a very excited, red-faced gentleman with an open collar push his way through a small gathering at the top of the steps—and then suddenly fall, as if shot down.

In death he looked like quite another person: his features sharp, the nose especially pointed. Hardly the handsome Perry Moore everyone had known.

He had come to a meeting of the Society, though it was suggested by Dr. Rowe and by others (including myself) that he stay away. Of course he came to argue. To present his "new position." To insult the other members. (He was contemptuous of a rather poorly organized paper on the medium Miss E——of Salem, a young woman who works with objects like rings, articles of clothing, locks of hair, et cetera; and quite angry with the evidence presented by a young geologist that would seem to discredit, once and for all, the claims of Eustace of Portsmouth. He interrupted a third paper, calling the reader a "bigot" and an "ignorant fool.")

Fortunately the incident did not find its way into any of the papers. The press, misunderstanding (deliberately and maliciously) the Society's attitude toward Spiritualism, delights in ridiculing our efforts.

There were respectful obituaries. A fine eulogy prepared by Reverend Tyler of St. Aidan's. Other tributes. *A tragic loss. . . . Mourned by all who knew him. . . .* (I stammered and could not speak. I cannot speak of him, of it, even now. Am I mourning, am I aggrieved? Or merely shocked? Terrified?) Relatives and friends and associates glossed over his behavior these past few months and settled upon an earlier Perry Moore, eminently sane, a distinguished physician and man of letters. I did not disagree, I merely acquiesced; I could not make any claim to have really known the man.

And so he has died, and so he is dead. . . .

Shortly after the funeral I went away to New Hampshire for a few days. But I can barely remember that period of time now. I sleep poorly, I yearn for summer, for a drastic change of climate, of scene. It was unwise for me to take up the responsibility of psychical research, fascinated though I am by it; my classes and lectures at the University demand most of my energy.

How quickly he died, and so young: so relatively young.

No history of high blood pressure, it is said.

At the end he was arguing with everyone, however. His personality had completely changed. He was rude, impetuous, even rather profane; even poorly groomed. (Rising to challenge the first of the papers, he revealed a shirtfront that appeared to be stained.) Some claimed he had been drinking all along, for years. Was it possible . . . ? (He had clearly enjoyed the wine and brandy in Quincy that evening, but I would not have said he was intemperate.) Rumors, fanciful tales, outright lies, slander. . . . It is painful, the vulnerability death brings.

Bigots, he called us. Ignorant fools. Unbelievers—atheists —traitors to the Spirit World—heretics. Heretics! I believe he looked directly at me as he pushed his way out of the meeting room: his eyes glaring, his face dangerously flushed, no recognition in his stare.

After his death, it is said, books continue to arrive at his home from England and Europe. He spent a small fortune on obscure, out-of-print volumes—commentaries on the Kabbala, on Plotinus, medieval alchemical texts, books on astrology, witchcraft, the metaphysics of death. Occult cosmologies. Egyptian, Indian, and Chinese "wisdom." Blake, Swedenborg, Cozad. *The Tibetan Book of the Dead.* Datsky's *Lunar Mysteries*. His estate is in chaos because he left not one but several wills, the most recent made out only a day before his death, merely a few lines scribbled on scrap paper, without witnesses. The family will contest, of course. Since in this will he left his money and property to an obscure woman living in Quincy, Massachusetts, and since he was obviously not in his right mind at the time, they would be foolish indeed not to contest.

Days have passed since his sudden death. Days continue to pass. At times I am seized by a sort of quick, cold panic; at other times I am inclined to think the entire situation has been exaggerated. In one mood I vow to myself that I will never again pursue psychical research because it is simply too dangerous. In another mood I vow I will never again pursue it because it is a waste of time and my own work, my own career, must come first.

Heretics, he called us. Looking straight at me.

Still, he was mad. And is not to be blamed for the vagaries of madness.

19 June 1887. Boston.

Luncheon with Dr. Rowe, Miss Madeleine van der Post, young Lucas Matthewson; turned over my personal records and notes re the mediums Dr. Moore and I visited. (Destroyed jottings of a private nature.) Miss van der Post and Matthewson will be taking over my responsibilities. Both are young, quick-witted, alert, with a certain ironic play about their features; rather like Dr. Moore in his prime. Matthewson is a former seminary student now teaching physics at the Boston University. They questioned me about Perry Moore, but I avoided answering frankly. Asked if we were close, I said *No*. Asked if I had heard a bizarre tale making the rounds of Boston salons—that a spirit claiming to be Perry Moore has intruded upon a number of séances in the area—I said honestly that I had not; and I did not care to hear about it.

Spinoza: *I will analyze the actions and appetites of men as if it were a question of lines, of planes, and of solids.*

It is in this direction, I believe, that we must move. Away from the phantasmal, the vaporous, the unclear; toward lines, planes, and solids.

Sanity.

8 July 1887. Mount Desert Island, Maine.

Very early this morning, before dawn, dreamed of Perry Moore: a babbling gesticulating spirit, bearded, bright-eyed, obviously mad. Jarvis? Jarvis? Don't deny me! he cried. I am so . . . so bereft. . . .

Paralyzed, I faced him: neither awake nor asleep. His words were not really *words* so much as unvoiced thoughts. I heard them in my own voice; a terrible raw itching at the back of my throat yearned to articulate the man's grief.

Perry?

You don't dare deny me! Not now!

He drew near and I could not escape. The dream shifted,

lost its clarity. Someone was shouting at me. Very angry, he
was, and baffled—as if drunk—or ill—or injured.

Perry? I can't hear you—

—our dinner at Montague House, do you remember?
Lamb, it was. And crepes with almonds for dessert. You
remember! You remember! You can't deny me! We were both
nonbelievers then, both abysmally ignorant—you can't deny
me!

(I was mute with fear or with cunning.)

—that idiot Rowe, how humiliated he will be! All of them!
All of you! The entire rationalist bias, the—the conspiracy
of—of fools—bigots— In a few years—In a few short years—
Jarvis, where are you? Why can't I see you? Where have you
gone?—My eyes can't focus; will someone help me? I seem
to have lost my way. Who is here? Who am I talking with?
You remember me, don't you?

(He brushed near me, blinking helplessly. His mouth was
a hole torn into his pale ravaged flesh.)

Where are you? Where is everyone? I thought it would be
crowded here but—but there's no one—I am forgetting so
much! My name—what was my name? Can't see. Can't remember. Something very important—something very important I must accomplish—can't remember—Why is there no
God? No one here? No one in control? We drift this way and
that way, we come to no rest, there are no landmarks—no
way of judging—everything is confused—disjointed—Is
someone listening? Would you read to me, please? Would
you read to me?—anything!—that speech of Hamlet's—*To be
or not*—a sonnet of Shakespeare's—any sonnet, anything—
That time of year thou may in me behold—is that it?—is that
how it begins? *Bare ruin'd choirs where the sweet birds once
sang.* How does it go? Won't you tell me? I'm lost—there's
nothing here to see, to touch—isn't anyone listening? I
thought there was someone nearby, a friend: isn't anyone
here?

(I stood paralyzed, mute with caution: he passed by.)

—*When in the chronicle of wasted time*—*the wide world
dreaming of things to come*—is anyone listening?—can anyone help?—I am forgetting so much—my name, my life—my

life's work—to penetrate the mysteries—the veil—to do justice to the universe of—of what—what had I intended?—am I in the place of repose now, have I come home? Why is it so empty here? Why is no one in control? My eyes—my head—mind broken and blown about—slivers—shards—annihilating all that's made to a—a green thought—a green shade—Shakespeare? Plato? Pascal? Will someone read me Pascal again? I seem to have lost my way—I am being blown about—Jarvis, was it? My dear young friend Jarvis? But I've forgotten your last name—I've forgotten so much—

(I wanted to reach out to touch him—but could not move, could not wake. The back of my throat ached with sorrow. Silent! Silent! I could not utter a word.)

—my papers, my journal—twenty years—a key somewhere hidden—where?—ah, yes: the bottom drawer of my desk—do you hear?—my desk—house—Louisburg Square—the key is hidden there—wrapped in a linen handkerchief—the strongbox is—the locked box is—hidden—my brother Edward's house—attic—trunk—steamer trunk—initials R. W. M.—Father's trunk, you see—strongbox hidden inside—my secret journals—life's work—physical and spiritual wisdom—must not be lost—are you listening?—is anyone listening? I am forgetting so much, my mind is in shreds—but if you could locate the journal and read it to me—if you could salvage it—me—I would be so very grateful—I would forgive you anything, all of you—Is anyone there? Jarvis? Brandon? No one?—My journal, my soul: will you salvage it? Will—

(He stumbled away and I was alone again.)

Perry—?

But it was too late: I awoke drenched with perspiration.

Nightmare.
Must forget.

Best to rise early, before the others. Mount Desert Island lovely in July. Our lodge on a hill above the beach. No spirits here: wind from the northeast, perpetual fresh air, perpetual waves. Best to rise early and run along the beach and plunge into the chilly water.

Clear the cobwebs from one's mind.

How beautiful the sky, the ocean, the sunrise!

No spirits here on Mount Desert Island. Swimming: skillful exertion of arms and legs. Head turned this way, that way. Eyes half shut. The surprise of the cold rough waves. One yearns almost to slip out of one's human skin at such times . . . ! Crude blatant beauty of Maine. Ocean. Muscular exertion of body. How alive I am, how living, how invulnerable; what a triumph in my every breath. . . .

Everything slips from my mind except the present moment. I am living, I am alive. I am immortal. Must not weaken: must not sink. Drowning? No. Impossible. Life is the only reality. It is not extinction that awaits but a hideous dreamlike state, a perpetual groping, blundering—far worse than extinction—incomprehensible: so it is life we must cling to, arm over arm, swimming, conquering the element that sustains us.

Jarvis? someone cried. *Please hear me—*

How exquisite life is, the turbulent joy of life contained in flesh! I heard nothing except the triumphant waves splashing about me. I swam for nearly an hour. Was reluctant to come ashore for breakfast, though our breakfasts are always pleasant rowdy sessions: my wife and my brother's wife and our seven children thrown together for the month of July. Three boys, four girls: noise, bustle, health, no shadows, no spirits. No time to think. Again and again I shall emerge from the surf, face and hair and body streaming water, exhausted but jubilant, triumphant. Again and again the children will call out to me, excited, from the dayside of the world that they inhabit.

I will not investigate Dr. Moore's strongbox and his secret journal; I will not even think about doing so. The wind blows words away. The surf is hypnotic. I will not remember this morning's dream once I sit down to breakfast with the family. I will not clutch my wife's wrist and say *We must not die! We dare not die!*—for that would only frighten and offend her.

Jarvis? she is calling at this very moment.

And I say *Yes—? Yes, I'll be there at once.*

Walter de la Mare

SEATON'S AUNT

Walter de la Mare, after Henry James, until Robert Aickman, is the master of dreadful uncertainty in the horror story. His finest tales most often suggest the supernatural without confirming it, which method Aickman later raised to a primary aesthetic principle of the ghost story. He has an excellent and refined style and a thorough, Jamesian attitude toward the buildup of detail and the psychological rounding of character. He is a major figure in the literature of the fantastic, one who has fallen out of fashion as the popularity of the overtly monstrous and the overtly moral horror story has risen since the 1930s. "Seaton's Aunt" is one of his most famous pieces and, with "Out of the Deep," often considered his best by connoisseurs and commentators. The slow accretion of effect does not give the audience looking for immediate thrills satisfaction; de la Mare is for that category of readers whom Stephen King alluded to as "human beings who read to think." "Seaton's Aunt" is an example of the twentieth-century development of the fantastic as the third major mode of horror. "De la Mare was happy to live with uncertainties, conscious of the infinite possibilities created by the imagination but exclusively committed to none of them," says the scholar Julia Briggs. His purpose was to awaken his readers to the life of the imagination. Horror was often his primary tool.

I had heard rumors of Seaton's aunt long before I actually encountered her. Seaton, in the hush of confidence, or at any little show of toleration on our part, would remark, "My aunt," or "My old aunt, you know," as if his relative might be a kind of cement to an *entente cordiale*.

He had an unusual quantity of pocket-money; or, at any rate, it was bestowed on him in unusually large amounts; and he spent it freely, though none of us would have described him as an "awfully generous chap." "Hullo, Seaton," we would say, "the old Begum?" At the beginning of term, too, he used to bring back surprising and exotic dainties in a box with a trick padlock that accompanied him from his first appearance at Gummidge's in a billycock hat to the rather abrupt conclusion of his schooldays.

From a boy's point of view he looked distastefully foreign with his yellowish skin, slow chocolate-coloured eyes, and lean weak figure. Merely for his looks he was treated by most of us true-blue Englishmen with condescension, hostility, or contempt. We used to call him "Pongo," but without any much better excuse for the nickname than his skin. He was, that is, in one sense of the term what he assuredly was not in the other sense, a sport.

Seaton and I, as I may say, were never in any sense intimate at school; our orbits only intersected in class. I kept deliberately aloof from him. I felt vaguely he was a sneak, and remained quite unmollified by advances on his side, which, in a boy's barbarous fashion, unless it suited me to be magnanimous, I haughtily ignored.

We were both of us quick-footed, and at Prisoner's Base used occasionally to hide together. And so I best remember Seaton—his narrow watchful face in the dusk of a summer evening; his peculiar crouch, and his inarticulate whisperings and mumblings. Otherwise he played all games slackly and limply; used to stand and feed at his locker with a crony or two until his "tuck" gave out; or waste his money on some outlandish fancy or other. He bought, for instance, a silver bangle, which he wore above his left elbow, until some of the fellows showed their masterly contempt of the practice by dropping it nearly red-hot down his neck.

It needed, therefore, a rather peculiar taste, and a rather rare kind of schoolboy courage and indifferent to criticism, to be much associated with him. And I had neither the taste nor, probably, the courage. None the less, he did make advances, and on one memorable occasion went to the length of bestowing on me a whole pot of some outlandish mulberry-coloured jelly that had been duplicated in his term's supplies. In the exuberance of my gratitude I promised to spend the next half-term holiday with him at his aunt's house.

I had clean forgotten my promise when, two or three days before the holiday, he came up and triumphantly reminded me of it.

"Well, to tell you the honest truth, Seaton, old chap—" I began graciously: but he cut me short.

"My aunt expects you," he said; "she is very glad you are coming. She's sure to be quite decent to *you*, Withers."

I looked at him in sheer astonishment; the emphasis was so uncalled for. It seemed to suggest an aunt not hitherto hinted at, and a friendly feeling on Seaton's side that was far more disconcerting than welcome.

We reached his aunt's house partly by train, partly by a lift in an empty farm-cart, and partly by walking. It was a whole-day holiday, and we were to sleep the night; he lent me extraordinary night-gear, I remember. The village street was unusually wide, and was fed from a green by two converging roads, with an inn, and a high green sign at the corner. About a hundred yards down the street was a chemist's shop—a Mr. Tanner's. We descended the two steps into his dusky and odorous interior to buy, I remember, some rat poison. A little beyond the chemist's was the forge. You then walked along a very narrow path, under a fairly high wall, nodding here and there with weeds and tufts of grass, and so came to the iron garden-gates, and saw the high flat house behind its huge sycamore. A coach-house stood on the left of the house, and on the right a gate led into a kind of rambling orchard. The lawn lay away over to the left again, and at the bottom (for the whole garden sloped gently to a sluggish and rushy pond-like stream) was a meadow.

We arrived at noon, and entered the gates out of the hot dust beneath the glitter of the dark-curtained windows. Seaton led me at once through the little garden-gate to show me his tadpole pond, swarming with what (being myself not in the least interested in low life) seemed to me the most horrible creatures—of all shapes, consistencies, and sizes, but with which Seaton was obviously on the most intimate of terms. I can see his absorbed face now as, squatting on his heels he fished the slimy things out in his sallow palms. Wearying at last of these pets, we loitered about awhile in an aimless fashion. Seaton seemed to be listening, or at any rate waiting for something to happen or for someone to come. But nothing did happen and no one came.

That was just like Seaton. Anyhow, the first view I got of his aunt was when, at the summons of a distant gong, we turned from the garden, very hungry and thirsty, to go into luncheon. We were approaching the house when Seaton suddenly came to a standstill. Indeed, I have always had the impression that he plucked at my sleeve. Something, at least, seemed to catch me back, as it were, as he cried, "Look out, there she is!"

She was standing at an upper window which opened wide on a hinge, and at first sight she looked an excessively tall and overwhelming figure. This, however, was mainly because the window reached all but to the floor of her bedroom. She was in reality rather an undersized woman, in spite of her long face and big head. She must have stood, I think, unusually still, with eyes fixed on us, though this impression may be due to Seaton's sudden warning and to my consciousness of the cautious and subdued air that had fallen on him at sight of her. I know that without the least reason in the world I felt a kind of guiltiness, as if I had been "caught." There was a silvery star pattern sprinkled on her black silk dress, and even from the ground I could see the immense coils of her hair and the rings on her left hand which was held fingering the small jet buttons of her bodice. She watched our united advance without stirring, until, imperceptibly, her eyes raised and lost themselves in the distance, so that it was out of an assumed reverie that she appeared suddenly to awaken to our presence beneath her when we drew close to the house.

"So this is your friend, Mr. Smithers, I suppose?" she said, bobbing to me.

"Withers, Aunt," said Seaton.

"It's much the same," she said, with eyes fixed on me. "Come in, Mr. Withers, and bring him along with you."

She continued to gaze at me—at least, I think she did so. I know that the fixity of her scrutiny and her ironical "Mr." made me feel peculiarly uncomfortable. None the less she was extremely kind and attentive to me, though, no doubt, her kindness and attention showed up more vividly against her complete neglect of Seaton. Only one remark that I have any recollection of she made to him: "When I look on my nephew, Mr. Smithers, I realize that dust we are, and dust shall become. You are hot, dirty, and incorrigible, Arthur."

She sat at the head of the table, Seaton at the foot, and I, before a wide waste of damask tablecloth, between them. It was an old and rather close dining-room, with windows thrown wide to the green garden and a wonderful cascade of fading roses. Miss Seaton's great chair faced this window, so that its rose-reflected light shone full on her yellowish face, and on just such chocolate eyes as my schoolfellow's, except that hers were more than half-covered by unusually long and heavy lids.

There she sat, steadily eating, with those sluggish eyes fixed for the most part on my face; above them stood the deep-lined fork between her eyebrows; and above that the wide expanse of a remarkable brow beneath its strange steep bank of hair. The lunch was copious, and consisted, I remember, of all such dishes as are generally considered too rich and too good for the schoolboy digestion—lobster mayonnaise, cold game sausages, an immense veal and ham pie farced with eggs, truffles, and numberless delicious flavours; besides kickshaws, creams, and sweetmeats. We even had a wine, a half-glass of old darkish sherry each.

Miss Seaton enjoyed and indulged an enormous appetite. Her example and a natural schoolboy voracity soon overcame my nervousness of her, even to the extent of allowing me to enjoy to the best of my bent so rare a spread. Seaton was singularly modest; the greater part of his meal consisted of almonds and raisins, which he nibbled surreptitiously and as if he found difficulty in swallowing them.

I don't mean that Miss Seaton "conversed" with me. She merely scattered trenchant remarks and now and then twinkled a baited question over my head. But her face was like a dense and involved accompaniment to her talk. She presently dropped the "Mr.," to my intense relief, and called me now Withers, or Wither, now Smithers, and even once towards the close of the meal distinctly Johnson, though how on earth my name suggested it, or whose face mine had reanimated in memory, I cannot conceive.

"And is Arthur a good boy at school, Mr. Wither?" was one of her many questions. "Does he please his masters? Is he first in his class? What does the reverend Dr. Gummidge think of him, eh?"

I knew she was jeering at him, but her face was adamant against the least flicker of sarcasm or facetiousness. I gazed fixedly at a blushing crescent of lobster.

"I think you're eighth, aren't you, Seaton?"

Seaton moved his small pupils towards his aunt. But she continued to gaze with a kind of concentrated detachment at me.

"Arthur will never make a brilliant scholar, I fear," she said, lifting a dexterously burdened fork to her wide mouth . . .

After luncheon she preceded me up to my bedroom. It was a jolly little bedroom, with a brass fender and rugs and a polished floor, on which it was possible, I afterwards found, to play "snow-shoes." Over the washstand was a little black-framed water-colour drawing, depicting a large eye with an extremely fishlike intensity in the spark of light on the dark pupil; and in "illuminated" lettering beneath was printed very minutely, "Thou God Seest ME," followed by a long looped monogram, "S.S.," in the corner. The other pictures were all of the sea: brigs on blue water; a schooner overtopping chalk cliffs; a rocky island of prodigious steepness, with two tiny sailors dragging a monstrous boat up a shelf of beach.

"This is the room, Withers, my poor dear brother William died in when a boy. Admire the view!"

I looked out of the window across the tree-tops. It was a day hot with sunshine over the green fields, and the cattle were standing swishing their tails in the shallow water. But the view at the moment was no doubt made more vividly impressive by the apprehension that she would presently inquire after my luggage, and I had brought not even a toothbrush. I need have had no fear. Hers was not that highly civilized type of mind that is stuffed with sharp, material details. Nor could her ample presence be described as in the least motherly.

"I would never consent to question a schoolfellow behind my nephew's back," she said, standing in the middle of the room, "but tell me, Smithers, why is Arthur so unpopular? You, I understand, are his only close friend." She stood in a dazzle of sun, and out of it her eyes regarded me with such leaden penetration beneath their thick lids that I doubt if my face concealed the least thought from her. "But there, there," she added very suavely, stooping her head a little, "don't trouble to answer me. I never extort an answer. Boys are queer fish. Brains might perhaps have suggested his washing his hands before luncheon; but—not my choice, Smithers. God forbid! And now, perhaps, you would like to go into the garden again. I cannot actually see from here, but I should not be surprised if Arthur is now skulking behind that hedge."

He was. I saw his head come out and take a rapid glance at the windows.

"Join him, Mr. Smithers; we shall meet again, I hope, at the teatable. The afternoon I spend in retirement."

Whether or not, Seaton and I had not been long engaged with the aid of two green switches in riding round and round a lumbering old grey horse we found in the meadow, before a rather bunched-up figure appeared, walking along the field-path on the other side of the water, with a magenta parasol studiously lowered in our direction throughout her slow progress, as if that were the magnetic needle and we the fixed Pole. Seaton at once lost all nerve and interest. At the next lurch of the old mare's heels he toppled over into the grass, and I slid off the sleek broad back to join him where he stood, rubbing his shoulder and sourly watching the rather pompous figure till it was out of sight.

"Was that your aunt, Seaton?" I enquired; but not till then.

He nodded.

"Why didn't she take any notice of us, then?"

"She never does."

"Why not?"

"Oh,. she knows all right, without; that's the damn awful part of it." Seaton was one of the very few fellows at Gummidge's who had the ostentation to use bad language. He had suffered for it too. But it wasn't, I think, bravado. I believe he really felt certain things more intensely than most of the other fellows, and they were generally things that fortunate and average people do not feel at all—the peculiar quality, for instance, of the British schoolboy's imagination.

"I tell you, Withers," he went on moodily, slinking across the meadow with his hands covered up in his pockets, "she sees everything. And what she doesn't see, she knows without."

"But how?" I said, not because I was much interested, but because the afternoon was so hot and tiresome and purposeless, and it seemed more of a bore to remain silent. Seaton turned gloomily and spoke in a very low voice.

"Don't appear to be talking of her, if you wouldn't mind. It's—because she's in league with the Devil." He nodded his head and stooped to pick up a round flat pebble. "I tell you," he said, still stooping, "you fellows don't realize what it is. I know I'm a bit close and all that. But so would you be if you had that old hag listening to every thought you think."

I looked at him, then turned and surveyed one by one the windows of the house.

"Where's your *pater*?" I said awkwardly.

"Dead, ages and ages ago, and my mother too. She's not my aunt even by rights."

"What is she, then?"

"I mean she's not my mother's sister, because my grandmother married twice; and she's one of the first lot. I don't know what you call her, but anyhow she's not my real aunt.''

"She gives you plenty of pocket-money."

Seaton looked steadfastly at me out of his flat eyes. "She can't give me what's mine. When I come of age half of the whole lot will be mine; and what's more"—he turned his back on the house—"I'll make her hand over every blessed shilling of it."

I put my hands in my pockets and stared at Seaton. "Is it much?"

He nodded.

"Who told you?" He got suddenly very angry; a darkish red came into his cheeks, his eyes glistened, but he made no answer, and we loitered listlessly about the garden until it was time for tea . . .

Seaton's aunt was wearing an extraordinary kind of lace jacket when we sidled sheepishly into the drawing-room together. She greeted me with a heavy and protracted smile, and bade me bring a chair close to the little table.

"I hope Arthur has made you feel at home," she said as she handed me my cup in her crooked hand. "He don't talk much to me; but then I'm an old woman. You must come again, Wither, and draw him out of his shell. You old snail!" She wagged her head at Seaton, who sat munching cake and watching her intently.

"And we must correspond, perhaps." She nearly shut her eyes at me. "You must write and tell me everything behind the creature's back." I confess I found her rather disquieting company. The evening drew on. Lamps were brought in by a man with a nondescript face and very quiet footsteps. Seaton was told to bring out the chessmen. And we played a game, she and I, with her big chin thrust over the board at every move as she gloated over the pieces and occasionally croaked "Check!"—after which she would sit back inscrutably staring at me. But the game was never finished. She simply hemmed me in with a gathering cloud of pieces that held me impotent, and yet one and all refused to administer to my poor flustered old king a merciful *coup de grâce*.

"There," she said, as the clock struck ten—"a drawn game, Withers. We are very evenly matched. A very creditable defense, Withers. You know your room. There's supper on a tray in the dining-room. Don't let the creature over-eat himself. The gong will sound three-quarters of an hour *before* a punctual breakfast." She held out her cheek to Seaton, and he kissed it with obvious perfunctoriness. With me she shook hands.

"An excellent game," she said cordially, "but my memory is poor, and"—she swept the pieces helter-skelter into the box—"the result will never be known." She raised her great head far back. "Eh?"

It was a kind of challenge, and I could only murmur: "Oh, I was absolutely in a hole, you know!" when she burst out laughing and waved us both out of the room.

Seaton and I stood and ate our supper, with one candlestick to light us, in a corner of the dining room. "Well, and how would you like it?" he said very softly, after cautiously poking his head round the doorway.

"Like what?"

"Being spied on—every blessed thing you do and think?"

"I shouldn't like it at all," I said, "if she does."

"And yet you let her smash you up at chess!"

"I didn't let her!" I said indignantly.

"Well, you funked it, then."

"And I didn't funk it either," I said, "she's so jolly clever with her knights."

Seaton stared at the candle. "Knights," he said slowly. "You wait, that's all." And we went upstairs to bed.

I had not been long in bed, I think, when I was cautiously awakened by a touch on my shoulder. And there was Seaton's face in the candlelight—and his eyes looking into mine.

"What's up?" I said, lurching on to my elbow.

"*Ssh*! Don't scurry," he whispered. "She'll hear. I'm sorry for waking you, but I didn't think you'd be asleep so soon."

"Why, what's the time, then?" Seaton wore, what was then rather unusual, a night-suit, and he hauled his big silver watch out of the pocket in his jacket.

"It's a quarter to twelve. I never get to sleep before twelve—not here."

"What do you do, then?"

"Oh, I read: and listen."

"Listen?"

Seaton stared into his candle-flame as if he were listening even then. "You can't guess what it is. All you read in ghost stories, that's all rot. You can't see much, Withers, but you know all the same."

"Know what?"

"Why, that they're there."

"Who's there?" I asked fretfully, glancing at the door.

"Why, in the house. It swarms with 'em. Just you stand still and listen outside my bedroom door in the middle of the night. I have, dozens of times; they're all over the place."

"Look here, Seaton," I said, "you asked me to come here, and I didn't mind chucking up a leave just to oblige you and because I'd promised; but don't get talking a lot of rot, that's all, or you'll know the difference when we get back."

"Don't fret," he said coldly, turning away. "I shan't be at school long. And what's more, you're here now, and there isn't anybody else to talk to. I'll chance the other."

"Look here, Seaton," I said, "you may think you're going to scare me with a lot of stuff about voices and all that. But I'll just thank you to clear out; and you may please yourself about pottering about all night."

He made no answer; he was standing by the dressing-table looking across his candle into the looking-glass; he turned and stared slowly round the walls.

"Even this room's nothing more than a coffin. I suppose she told you—'It's all exactly the same as when my brother William died'—trust her for that! And good luck to him, say I. Look at that." He raised his candle close to the little water-colour I have mentioned. "There's hundreds of eyes like that in his house; and even if God does see you, He takes precious good care you don't see Him. And it's just the same with them. I tell you what, Withers, I'm getting sick of all this. I shan't stand it much longer."

The house was silent within and without, and even in the yellowish radiance of the candle a faint silver showed through the open window on my blind. I slipped off the bedclothes, wide awake, and sat irresolute on the bedside.

"I know you're only guying me," I said angrily, "but why is the house full of—what you say? Why do you hear—what you *do* hear? Tell me that, you silly fool!"

Seaton sat down on a chair and rested his candlestick on his knee. He blinked at me calmly. "She brings them," he said, with lifted eyebrows.

"Who? Your aunt?"

He nodded.

"How?"

"I told you," he answered pettishly. "She's in league. You don't know. She as good as killed my mother, I know that. But it's not only her by a long chalk. She just sucks you dry. I know. And that's what she'll do for me; because I'm like her—like my mother, I mean. She simply hates to see me alive. I wouldn't be like that old she-wolf for a million pounds. And so"—he broke off, with a comprehensive wave of his candlestick—"they're always here. Ah, my boy, wait till she's dead! She'll hear something then, I can tell you. It's all very well now, but wait till then! I wouldn't be in her shoes when she has to clear out—for something. Don't you go and believe I care for ghosts, or whatever you like to call them. We're all in the same box. We're all under her thumb."

He was looking almost nonchalantly at the ceiling at the moment, when I saw his face chance, saw his eyes suddenly drop like shot birds and fix themselves on the cranny of the door he had left just ajar. Even from where I sat I could see his cheek change colour; it went greenish. He crouched without stirring, like an animal. And I, scarcely daring to breathe, sat with creeping skin, sourly watching him. His hands relaxed, and he gave a kind of sigh.

"Was *that* one?" I whispered, with a timid show of jauntiness. He looked round, opened his mouth, and nodded. "What?" I said. He jerked his thumb with meaningful eyes, and I knew that he meant that his aunt had been there listening at our door cranny.

"Look here, Seaton," I said once more, wriggling to my feet. "You may think I'm a jolly noodle; just as you please. But your aunt has been civil to me and all that, and I don't believe a word you say about her, that's all, and never did. Every fellow's a bit off his pluck at night, and you may think it a fine sport to try your rubbish on me. I heard your aunt come upstairs before I fell asleep. And I'll bet you a level tanner she's in bed now. What's more, you can keep your blessed ghosts to yourself. It's a guilty conscience, I should think."

Seaton looked at me intently, without answering for a moment. "I'm not a liar, Withers; but I'm not going to quarrel either. You're the only chap I care a button for; or, at any rate, you're the only chap that's ever come here; and it's something to tell a fellow what you feel. I don't care a fig for fifty thousand ghosts; although I swear on my solemn oath that I know they're here. But she"—he turned deliberately—"you laid a tanner she's in bed, Withers; well, I know different. She's never in bed much of the night, and I'll prove it, too, just to show you I'm not such a nolly as you think I am. Come on!"

"Come on where?"

"Why, to see."

I hesitated. He opened a large cupboard and took out a small dark dressing-gown and a kind of shawl-jacket. He threw the jacket on the bed and put on the gown. His dusky face was colourless, and I could see by the way he fumbled at the sleeves he was shivering. But it was no good showing the white feather now. So I threw the tasselled shawl over my shoulders and, leaving our candle brightly burning on the chair, we went out together and stood in the corridor.

"Now then, listen!" Seaton whispered.

We stood leaning over the staircase. It was like leaning over a well, so still and chill the air was all around us. But presently, as I suppose happens in most old houses, began to echo and answer in my ears a medley of infinite small stirrings and whisperings. Now out of the distance an old timber would relax its fibres, or a scurry die away behind the perishing wainscot. But amid and behind such sounds as these I seemed to begin to be conscious, as it were, of the lightest of footfalls, sounds as faint as the vanishing remembrance of voices in a dream. Seaton was all in obscurity except his face; out of that his eyes gleamed darkly, watching me.

"You'd hear, too, in time, my fine soldier," he muttered. "Come on!"

He descended the stairs, slipping his lean fingers lightly along the balusters. He turned to the right at the loop, and I followed him barefooted along a thickly carpeted corridor. At the end stood a door ajar. And from here we very stealthily and in complete blackness ascended five narrow stairs. Seaton, with immense caution, slowly pushed open a door, and we stood together, looking into a great pool of duskiness, out of which, lit by the feeble clearness of a night-light, rose a vast bed. A heap of clothes lay on the floor; beside them two slippers dozed, with noses each to each, a foot or two apart. Somewhere a little clock ticked huskily. There was a close smell; lavender and eau de Cologne, mingled with the fragrance of ancient sachets, soap, and drugs. Yet it was a scent even more peculiarly compounded than that.

And the bed! I stared warily in; it was mounded gigantically, and it was empty.

Seaton turned a vague pale face, all shadows: "What did I say?" he muttered. "Who's—who's the fool now, I say? How are we going to get back without meeting her, I say? Answer me that! Oh, I wish to God you hadn't come here, Withers."

He stood audibly shivering in his skimpy gown, and could hardly speak for his teeth chattering. And very distinctly, in the hush that followed his whisper, I heard approaching a faint unhurried voluminous rustle. Seaton clutched my arm, dragged me to the right across the room to a large cupboard, and drew the door close to on us. And, presently, as with bursting lungs I peeped out into the long, low, curtained bedroom, waddled in that wonderful great head and body. I can see her now, all patched and lined with shadow, her tied-up hair (she must have had enormous quantities of it for so old a woman), her heavy lids above those flat, slow, vigilant eyes.

She just passed across my ken in the vague dusk; but the bed was out of sight.

We waited on and on, listening to the clock's muffled ticking. Not the ghost of a sound rose up from the great bed. Either she lay archly listening or slept a sleep serener than an infant's. And when, it seemed, we had been hours in hiding and were cramped, chilled, and half suffocated, we crept out on all fours, with terror knocking at our ribs, and so down the five narrow stairs and back to the little candle-lit blue-and-gold bedroom.

Once there, Seaton gave in. He sat livid on a chair with closed eyes.

"Here," I said, shaking his arm, "I'm going to bed; I've had enough of this foolery; I'm going to bed." His lips quivered, but he made no answer. I poured out some water into my basin and, with that cold pictured azure eye fixed on us, bespattered Seaton's sallow face and forehead and dabbled his hair. He presently sighed and opened fish-like eyes.

"Come one!" I said. "Don't get shamming, there's a good chap. Get on my back, if you like, and I'll carry you into your bedroom."

He waved me away and stood up. So, with my candle in one hand, I took him under the arm and walked him along according to his direction down the corridor. His was a much dingier room than mine, and littered with boxes, paper, cages, and clothes. I huddled him into bed and turned to go. And suddenly, I can hardly explain it now, a kind of cold and deadly terror swept over me. I almost ran out of the room, with eyes fixed rigidly in front of me, blew out my candle, and buried my head under the bedclothes.

When I awoke, roused not by a gong, but by a long-continued tapping at my door, sunlight was raying in on cornice and bedpost, and birds were singing in the garden. I got up, ashamed of the night's folly, dressed quickly, and went downstairs. The breakfast room was sweet with flowers and fruit and honey. Seaton's aunt was standing in the garden beside the open French window, feeding a great flutter of birds. I watched her for a moment, unseen. Her face was set in a deep reverie beneath the shadow of a big loose sun-hat.

It was deeply lined, crooked, and, in a way I can't describe, fixedly vacant and strange. I coughed politely, and she turned with a prodigious smiling grimace to ask how I had slept. And in that mysterious fashion by which we learn each other's secret thoughts without a syllable said, I knew that she had followed every word and movement of the night before, and was triumphing over my affected innocence and ridiculing my friendly and too easy advances.

We returned to school, Seaton and I, lavishly laden, and by rail all the way. I made no reference to the obscure talk we had had, and resolutely refused to meet his eyes or to take up the hints he let fall. I was relieved—and yet I was sorry—to be going back, and strode on as fast as I could from the station, with Seaton almost trotting at my heels. But he insisted on buying more fruit and sweets—my share of which I accepted with a very bad grace. It was uncomfortably like a bribe, and, after all, I had no quarrel with his rum old aunt, and hadn't really believed half the stuff he had told me.

I saw as little of him as I could after that. He never referred to our visit or resumed his confidences, though in class I would sometimes catch his eye fixed on mine, full of a mute understanding, which I easily affected not to understand. He left Gummidge's, as I have said, rather abruptly, though I never heard of anything to his discredit. And I did not see him or have any news of him again till by chance we met one summer afternoon in the Strand.

He was dressed rather oddly in a coat too large for him and a bright silky tie. But we instantly recognized one another under the awning of a cheap jeweller's shop. He immediately attached himself to me and dragged me off, not too cheerfully, to lunch with him at an Italian restaurant near by. He chattered about our old school, which he remembered only with dislike and disgust; told me cold-bloodedly of the disastrous fate of one or two of the older fellows who had been among his chief tormentors; insisted on an expensive wine and the whole gamut of the foreign menu; and finally informed me, with a good deal of niggling, that he had come up to town to buy an engagement-ring.

And of course: "How is your aunt?" I enquired at last.

He seemed to have been awaiting the question. It fell like a stone into a deep pool, so many expressions flitted across his long, sad, sallow, un-English face.

"She's aged a good deal," he said softly, and broke off.

"She's been very decent," he continued presently after, and paused again. "In a way." He eyed me fleetingly. "I dare say you heard that—she—that is, that we—had lost a good deal of money."

"No," I said.

"Oh, yes!" said Seaton, and paused again.

And somehow, poor fellow, I knew in the clink and clatter of glass and voices that he had lied to me; that he did not possess, and never had possessed, a penny beyond what his aunt had squandered on his too ample allowance of pocket-money.

"And the ghosts?" I enquired quizzically.

He grew instantly solemn, and, though it may have been my fancy, slightly yellowed. But "You are making game of me, Withers," was all he said.

He asked for my address, and I rather reluctantly gave him my card.

"Look here, Withers," he said, as we stood together in the sunlight on the kerb, saying goodbye, "here I am, and—and it's all very well. I'm not perhaps as fanciful as I was. But you are practically the only friend I have on earth—except Alice . . . And there—to make a clean breast of it, I'm not sure that my aunt cares much about my getting married. She doesn't say so, of course. You know her well enough for that." He looked sidelong at the rattling gaudy traffic.

"What I was going to say is this: Would you mind coming down? You needn't stay the night unless you please, though, of course, you know you would be awfully welcome. But I should like you to meet my—to meet Alice; and then, perhaps, you might tell me your honest opinion of—of the other too."

I vaguely demurred. He pressed me. And we parted with a half promise that I would come. He waved his ball-topped cane at me and ran off in his long jacket after a bus.

A letter arrived soon after, in his small weak handwriting, giving me full particulars regarding route and trains. And without the least curiosity, even perhaps with some little annoyance that chance should have thrown us together again, I accepted his invitation and arrived one hazy midday at his out-of-the-way station to find him sitting on a low seat under a clump of "double" hollyhocks, awaiting me.

He looked preoccupied and singularly listless; but seemed, none the less, to be pleased to see me.

We walked up the village street, past the little dingy apothecary's and the empty forge, and, as on my first visit, skirted the house together, and, instead of entering by the front door, made our way down the green path into the garden at the back. A pale haze of cloud muffled the sun; the garden lay in a grey shimmer—its old trees, its snap-dragoned faintly glittering walls. But now there was an air of slovenliness where before all had been neat and methodical. In a patch of shallowly dug soil stood a worn-down spade leaning against a tree. There was an old decayed wheelbarrow. The roses had run to leaf and briar; the fruit-trees were unpruned. The goddess of neglect had made it her secret resort.

"You ain't much of a gardener, Seaton," I said at last, with a sigh of relief.

"I think, do you know, I like it best like this," said Seaton. "We haven't any man now, of course. Can't afford it." He stood staring at his little dark oblong of freshly turned earth. "And it always seems to me," he went on ruminatingly, "that, after all, we are all nothing better than interlopers on the earth, disfiguring and staining wherever we go. It may sound shocking blasphemy to say so; but then it's different here, you see. We are further away."

"To tell you the truth, Seaton, I *don't* quite see," I said; "but it isn't a new philosophy, is it? Anyhow, it's a precious beastly one."

"It's only what I think," he replied, with all his odd old stubborn meekness. "And one thinks as one *is*."

We wandered on together, talking little, and still with that expression of uneasy vigilance on Seaton's face. He pulled out his watch as we stood gazing idly over the green meadows and the dark motionless bulrushes.

"I think, perhaps, it's nearly time for lunch," he said. "Would you like to come in?"

We turned and walked slowly towards the house, across whose windows I confess my own eyes, too, went restlessly meandering in search of its rather disconcerting inmate. There was a pathetic look of bedraggledness, of want of means and care, rust and overgrowth and faded paint. Seaton's aunt, a little to my relief, did not share our meal. So he carved the cold meat, and dispatched a heaped-up plate by an elderly servant for his aunt's private consumption. We talked little and in half-suppressed tones, and sipped some Madeira which Seaton after listening for a moment or two fetched out of the great mahogany sideboard.

I played him a dull and effortless game of chess, yawning between the moves he himself made almost at haphazard, and with attention elsewhere engaged. Towards five o'clock came the sound of a distant ring, and Seaton jumped up, overturning the board, and so ended a game that else might have fatuously continued to this day. He effusively excused himself, and after some little while returned with a slim, dark, pale-faced girl of about nineteen, in a white gown and hat, to whom I was presented with some little nervousness as his "dear old friend and schoolfellow."

We talked on in the golden afternoon light, still, as it seemed to me, and even in spite of our efforts to be lively and gay, in a half-suppressed, lack-lustre fashion. We all seemed, if it were not my fancy, to be expectant, to be almost anxiously awaiting an arrival, the appearance of someone whose image filled our collective consciousness. Seaton talked least of all, and in a restless interjectory way, as he continually fidgeted from chair to chair. At last he proposed a stroll in the garden before the sun should have quite gone down.

Alice walked between us. Her hair and eyes were conspicuously dark against the whiteness of her gown. She carried herself not ungracefully, and yet with peculiarly little movement of her arms and body, and answered us both without turning her head. There was a curious provocative reserve in that impassive melancholy face. It seemed to be haunted by some tragic influence of which she herself was unaware.

And yet somehow I knew—I believe we all knew—that this walk, this discussion of their future plans, was a futility. I had nothing to base such skepticism on, except only a vague sense of oppression, a foreboding consciousness of some inert invincible power in the background, to whom optimistic plans and love-making and youth are as chaff and thistle-down. We came back, silent, in the last light. Seaton's aunt was there—under an old brass lamp. Her hair was as barbarously massed and curled as ever. Her eyelids, I think, hung even a little heavier in age over their slow-moving inscrutable pupils. We filed in softly out of the evening, and I made my bow.

"In this short interval, Mr. Withers," she remarked amiably, "you have put off youth, put on the man. Dear me, how sad it is to see the young days vanishing! Sit down. My nephew tells me you met by chance—or act of Providence, shall we call it?—and in my beloved Strand! You, I understand, are to be best man—yes, best man! Or am I divulging secrets?" She surveyed Arthur and Alice with overwhelming graciousness. They sat apart on two low chairs and smiled in return.

"And Arthur—how do you think Arthur is looking?"

"I think he looks very much in need of a change," I said.

"A change! Indeed?" She all but shut her eyes at me and with an exaggerated sentimentality shook her head. "My dear Mr. Withers! Are we not *all* in need of a change in this fleeting, fleeting world?" She mused over the remark like a connoisseur. "And you," she continued, turning abruptly to Alice, "I hope you pointed out to Mr. Withers all my pretty bits?"

"We only walked round the garden," the girl replied; then, glancing at Seaton, added almost inaudibly, "it's a very beautiful evening."

"*Is* it?" said the old lady, starting up violently. "Then on this very beautiful evening we will go in to supper. Mr. Withers, your arm; Arthur, bring your bride."

We were a queer quartet, I thought to myself, as I solemnly

led the way into the faded, chilly dining-room, with this indefinable old creature leaning wooingly on my arm—the large flat bracelet on the yellow-laced wrist. She fumed a little, breathing heavily, but as if with an effort of the mind rather than of the body; for she had grown much stouter and yet little more proportionate. And to talk into that great white face, so close to mine, was a queer experience in the dim light of the corridor, and even in the twinkling crystal of the candles. She was naïve; she was crafty and challenging; she was even arch; and all these in the brief, rather puffy passage from one room to the other, with these two tongue-tied children bringing up the rear. The meal was tremendous. I have never seen such a monstrous salad. But the dishes were greasy and over-spiced, and were indifferently cooked. One thing only was quite unchanged—my hostess's appetite was as gargantuan as ever. The heavy silver candelabra that lighted us stood before her high-backed chair. Seaton sat a little removed, his plate almost in darkness.

And throughout this prodigious meal his aunt talked, mainly to me, mainly *at* him, but with an occasional satirical sally at Alice and muttered explosions of reprimand to the servant. She had aged, and yet, if it be not nonsense to say so, seemed no older. I suppose to the Pyramids a decade is but as the rustling down of a handful of dust. And she reminded me of some such unshakeable prehistoricism. She certainly was an amazing talker—rapid, egregious, with a delivery that was perfectly overwhelming. As for Seaton—her flashes of silence were for him. On her enormous volubility would suddenly fall a hush; acid sarcasm would be left implied; and she would sit softly moving her great head, with eyes fixed full in a dreamy smile; but with her whole attention, one could see, slowly, joyously, absorbing his mute discomfiture.

She confided in us her views on a theme vaguely occupying at the moment, I suppose, all our minds. "We have barbarous institutions, and so must put up, I suppose, with a never-ending procession of fools—of fools *ad infinitum*. Marriage, Mr. Withers, was instituted in the privacy of a garden; *sub rosa*, as it were. Civilization flaunts it in the glare of day.

The dull marry the poor; the rich the effete; and so our New Jerusalem is peopled with naturals, plain and coloured, at either end. I detest folly; I detest still more (if I must be frank, dear Arthur) mere cleverness. Mankind has simply become a tailless host of uninstinctive animals. We should never have taken to Evolution, Mr. Withers. 'Natural Selection!'—little gods and fishes!—the deaf for the dumb. We should have used our brains—intellectual pride, the ecclesiastics call it. And by brains I mean—what do I mean, Alice?—I mean, my dear child,'' and she laid two gross fingers on Alice's narrow sleeve, "I mean courage. Consider it, Arthur. I read that the scientific world is once more beginning to be afraid of spiritual agencies. Spiritual agencies that tap, and actually float, bless their hearts! I think just one more of those mulberries—thank you.

"They talk about 'blind Love,' " she ran on derisively as she helped herself, her eyes roving over the dish, "but why blind? I think, Mr. Withers, from weeping over its rickets. After all, it is we plain women that triumph, is it not so—beyond the mockery of time. Alice, now! Fleeting, fleeting is youth, my child. What's that you were confiding to your plate, Arthur? Satirical boy. He laughs at his old aunt: nay, but thou didst laugh. He detests all sentiment. He whispers the most acid asides. Come, my love, we will leave these cynics; we will go and commiserate with each other on our sex. The choice of two evils, Mr. Smithers!'' I opened the door, and she swept out as if borne on a torrent of unintelligible indignation; and Arthur and I were left in the clear four-flamed light alone.

For a while we sat in silence. He shook his head at my cigarette-case, and I lit a cigarette. Presently he fidgeted in his chair and poked his head forward into the light. He paused to rise and shut again the shut door.

"How long will you be?'' he asked me.

I laughed.

"Oh, it's not that!'' he said, in some confusion. "Of course, I like to be with her. But it's not that. The truth is, Withers, I don't care about leaving her too long with my aunt.''

I hesitated. He looked at me questioningly.

"Look here, Seaton," I said, "you know well enough that I don't want to interfere in your affairs, or to offer advice where it is not wanted. But don't you think perhaps you may not treat your aunt quite in the right way? As one gets old, you know, a little give and take. I have an old godmother, or something of the kind. She's a bit queer, too . . . A little allowance; it does no harm. But hang it all, I'm no preacher."

He sat down with his hands in his pockets and still with his eyes fixed almost increduously on mine. "How?" he said.

"Well, my dear fellow, if I'm any judge—mind, I don't say that I am—but I can't help thinking she thinks you don't care for her; and perhaps takes your silence for—for bad temper. She has been very decent to you, hasn't she?"

" 'Decent'? My God!" said Seaton.

I smoked on in silence; but he continued to look at me with that peculiar concentration I remembered of old.

"I don't think, perhaps, Withers," he began presently, "I don't think you quite understand. Perhaps you are not quite our kind. You always did, just like the other fellows, guy me at school. You laughed at me that night you came to stay here—about the voices and all that. But I don't mind being laughed at—because I know."

"Know what?" It was the same old system of dull question and evasive answer.

"I mean I know that what we see and hear is only the smallest fraction of what is. I know she lives quite out of this. She *talks* to you; but it's all make-believe. It's all a 'parlour game.' She's not really with you; only pitting her outside wits against yours and enjoying the fooling. She's living on inside on what you're rotten without. That's what it is—a cannibal feast. She's a spider. It doesn't much matter what you call it. It means the same kind of thing. I tell you, Withers she hates me; and you can scarcely dream what that hatred means. I used to think I had an inkling of the reason. It's oceans deeper than that. It just lies behind: herself against myself. Why, after all, how much do we really understand of anything? We don't even know our own histories, and not a tenth, not a tenth of the reasons. What has life been to me?—

nothing but a trap. And when one sets oneself free for a while, it only begins again. I thought you might understand; but you are on a different level: that's all.''

"What on earth are you talking about?" I said contemptuously, in spite of myself.

"I mean what I say," he said gutturally. "All this outside's only make-believe—but there! what's the good of talking? So far as this is concerned I'm as good as done. You wait.''

Seaton blew out three of the candles and, leaving the vacant room in semi-darkness, we groped our way along the corridor to the drawing-room. There a full moon stood shining in at the long garden windows. Alice sat stooping at the door, with her hands clasped in her lap, looking out, alone.

"Where is she?" Seaton asked in a low tone.

She looked up; and their eyes met in a glance of instantaneous understanding, and the door immediately afterwards opened behind us.

"*Such* a moon!" said a voice, that once heard, remained unforgettably on the ear. "A night for lovers, Mr. Withers, if ever there was one. Get a shawl, my dear Arthur, and take Alice for a little promenade. I dare say we old cronies will manage to keep awake. Hasten, hasten, Romeo! My poor, poor Alice, how laggard a lover!''

Seaton returned with a shawl. They drifted out into the moonlight. My companion gazed after them till they were out of hearing, turned to me gravely, and suddenly twisted her white face into such a convulsion of contemptuous amusement that I could only stare blankly in reply.

"Dear innocent children!" she said, with inimitable unctuousness. "Well, well, Mr. Withers, we poor seasoned old creatures must move with the times. Do you sing?''

I scouted the idea.

"Then you must listen to my playing. Chess"—she clasped her forehead with both cramped hands—"chess is now completely beyond my poor wits.''

She sat down at the piano and ran her fingers in a flourish over the keys. "What shall it be? How shall we capture them, those passionate hearts? That first fine careless rapture? Poetry itself." She gazed softly into the garden a moment, and

presently, with a shake of her body, began to play the opening bars of Beethoven's "Moonlight" Sonata. The piano was
old and woolly. She played without music. The lamplight was
rather dim. The moonbeams from the window lay across the
keys. Her head was in shadow. And whether it was simply
due to her personality or to some really occult skill in her
playing, I cannot say; I only know that she gravely and deliberately set herself to satirize the beautiful music. It brooded
on the air, disillusioned, charged with mockery and bitter-
ness. I stood at the window; far down the path I could see
the white figure glimmering in that pool of colourless light.
A few faint stars shone, and still that amazing woman behind
me dragged out of the unwilling keys her wonderful grotesquerie of youth and love and beauty. It came to an end. I
knew the player was watching me. "Please, please, go on!"
I murmured, without turning. "*Please* go on playing, Miss
Seaton."

No answer was returned to this honeyed sarcasm, but I
realized in some vague fashion that I was being acutely scru-
tinized, when suddenly there followed a procession of quiet,
plaintive chords which broke at last softly into the hymn, "A
Few More Years Shall Roll."

I confess it held me spellbound. There is a wistful, strained
plangent pathos in the tune; but beneath those masterly old
hands it cried softly and bitterly the solitude and desperate
estrangement of the world. Arthur and his lady-love vanished
from my thoughts. No one could put into so hackneyed an
old hymn tune such an appeal who had never known the
meaning of the words. Their meaning, anyhow, isn't commonplace.

I turned a fraction of an inch to glance at the musician.
She was leaning forward a little over the keys, so that at the
approach of my silent scrutiny she had but to turn her face
into the thin flood of moonlight for every feature to become
distinctly visible. And so, with the tune abruptly terminated,
we steadfastly regarded one another; and she broke into a
prolonged chuckle of laughter.

"Not quite so seasoned as I supposed, Mr. Withers. I see

you are a real lover of music. To me it is too painful. It evokes too much thought . . .''

I could scarcely see her little glittering eyes under their penthouse lids.

''And now,'' she broke off crisply, ''tell me, as a man of the world, what do you think of my new niece?''

I was not a man of the world, nor was I much flattered in my stiff and dullish way of looking at things by being called one; and I could answer her without the least hesitation.

''I don't think, Miss Seaton, I'm much of a judge of character. She's very charming.''

''A brunette?''

''I think I prefer dark women.''

''And why? Consider, Mr. Withers; dark hair, dark eyes, dark cloud, dark night, dark vision, dark death, dark grave, dark DARK!''

Perhaps the climax would have rather thrilled Seaton, but I was too thick-skinned. ''I don't know much about all that,'' I answered rather pompously. ''Broad daylight's difficult enough for most of us.''

''Ah,'' she said, with a sly inward burst of satirical laughter.

''And I suppose,'' I went on, perhaps a little nettled, ''it isn't the actual darkness one admires, it's the contrast of the skin, and the colour of the eyes, and—and their shining. Just as,'' I went blundering on, too late to turn back, ''just as you only see the stars in the dark. It would be a long day without any evening. As for death and the grave, I don't suppose we shall much notice that.'' Arthur and his sweetheart were slowly returning along the dewy path. ''I believe in making the best of things.''

''How very interesting!'' came the smooth answer. ''I see you are a philosopher, Mr. Withers. H'm! 'As for death and the grave, I don't suppose we shall much notice that.' Very interesting . . . And I'm sure,'' she added in a particularly suave voice, ''I profoundly hope so.'' She rose slowly from her stool. ''You will take pity on me again, I hope. You and I would get on famously—kindred spirits—elective affinities. And, of course, now that my nephew's going to leave me, now that his affections are centred on another, I shall be a very lonely old woman . . . Shall I not, Arthur?"

Seaton blinked stupidly. "I didn't hear what you said, Aunt."

"I was telling our old friend, Arthur, that when you are gone I shall be a very lonely old woman."

"Oh, I don't think so," he said in a strange voice.

"He means, Mr. Withers, he means, my dear child," she said, sweeping her eyes over Alice, "he means that I shall have memory for company—heavenly memory—the ghosts of other days. Sentimental boy! And did you enjoy our music, Alice? Did I really stir that youthful heart? . . . O, O, O," continued the horrible old creature, "you billers and cooers, I have been listening to such flatteries, such confessions! Beware, beware, Arthur, there's many a slip." She rolled her little eyes at me, she shrugged her shoulders at Alice, and gazed an instant stonily into her nephew's face.

I held out my hand. "Good night, good night!" she cried. "He that fights and runs away. Ah, good night, Mr. Withers; come again soon!" She thrust out her cheek at Alice, and we all three filed slowly out of the room.

Black shadow darkened the porch and half the spreading sycamore. We walked without speaking up the dusty village street. Here and there a crimson window glowed. At the fork of the high-road I said goodbye. But I had hardly more than a dozen paces when a sudden impulse seized me.

"Seaton!" I called.

He turned in the cool stealth of the moonlight.

"You have my address; if by any chance, you know, you should care to spend a week or two in town between this and the—the Day, we should be delighted to see you."

"Thank you, Withers, thank you," he said in a low voice.

"I dare say"—I waved my stick gallantly at Alice—"I dare say you will be doing some shopping; we could all meet," I added, laughing.

"Thank you, thank you, Withers—immensely," he repeated.

And so we parted.

* * *

But they were out of the jog-trot of my prosaic life. And being of a stolid and incurious nature, I left Seaton and his marriage, and even his aunt, to themselves in my memory, and scarcely gave a thought to them until one day I was walking up the Strand again, and passed the flashing gloaming of the second-rate jeweller's shop where I had accidentally encountered my old schoolfellow in the summer. It was one of those stagnant autumnal days after a night of rain. I cannot say why, but a vivid recollection returned to my mind of our meeting and of how suppressed Seaton had seemed, and of how vainly he had endeavoured to appear assured and eager. He must be married by now, and had doubtless returned from his honeymoon. And I had clean forgotten my manners, had sent not a word of congratulation, nor—as I might very well have done, and as I knew he would have been pleased at my doing—even the ghost of a wedding present. It was just as of old.

On the other hand, I pleaded with myself, I had had no invitation. I paused at the corner of Trafalgar Square, and at the bidding of one of those caprices that seize occasionally on even an unimaginative mind, I found myself pelting after a green bus, and actually bound on a visit I had not in the least intended or foreseen.

The colours of autumn were over the village when I arrived. A beautiful late afternoon sunlight bathed thatch and meadow. But it was close and hot. A child, two dogs, a very old woman with a heavy basket I encountered. One or two incurious tradesmen looked idly up as I passed by. It was all so rural and remote, my whimsical impulse had so much flagged, that for a while I hesitated to venture under the shadow of the sycamore-tree to enquire after the happy pair. Indeed I first passed by the faint-blue gates and continued my walk under the high, green and tufted wall. Hollyhocks had attained their topmost bud and seeded in the little cottage gardens beyond; the Michaelmas daisies were in flower, a sweet warm aromatic smell of fading leaves was in the air. Beyond the cottages lay a field where cattle were grazing, and beyond that I came to a little churchyard. Then the road wound on, pathless and houseless, among gorse and bracken.

I turned impatiently and walked quickly back to the house and rang the bell.

The rather colourless elderly woman who answered my enquiry informed me that Miss Seaton was at home, as if only taciturnity forbade her adding, "But she doesn't want to see *you*."

"Might I, do you think, have Mr. Arthur's address?" I said.

She looked at me with quiet astonishment, as if waiting for an explanation. Not the faintest of smiles came into her thin face.

"I will tell Miss Seaton," she said after a pause. "Please walk in."

She showed me into the dingy undusted drawing-room, filled with evening sunshine and with the green-dyed light that penetrated the leaves overhanging the long French windows. I sat down and waited on and on, occasionally aware of a creaking footfall overhead. At last the door opened a little, and the great face I had once known peered round at me. For it was enormously changed; mainly, I think, because the aged eyes had rather suddenly failed, and so a kind of stillness and darkness lay over its calm and wrinkled pallor.

"Who is it?" she asked.

I explained myself and told her the occasion of my visit.

She came in, shut the door carefully after her, and, though the fumbling was scarcely perceptible, groped her way to a chair. She had on an old dressing-gown, like a cassock, of a patterned cinnamon colour.

"What is it you want?" she said, seating herself and lifting her blank face to mine.

"Might I just have Arthur's address?" I said deferentially. "I am so sorry to have disturbed you."

"H'm. You have come to see my nephew?"

"Not necessarily to see him, only to hear how he is, and, of course, Mrs. Seaton, too. I am afraid my silence must have appeared . . ."

"He hasn't noticed your silence," croaked the old voice out of the great mask; "besides, there isn't any Mrs. Seaton."

"Ah, then, " I answered, after a momentary pause, "I have not seemed so black as I painted myself! And how is Miss Outram?"

"She's gone into Yorkshire," answered Seaton's aunt.

"And Arthur too?"

She did not reply, but simply sat blinking at me with lifted chin, as if listening, but certainly not for what I might have to say. I began to feel rather at a loss.

"You were no close friend of my nephew's, Mr. Smithers?" she said presently.

"No," I answered, welcoming the cue, "and yet, do you know, Miss Seaton, he is one of the very few of my old school-fellows I have come across in the last few years, and I suppose as one gets older one begins to value old associations . . ." My voice seemed to trail off into a vacuum. "I thought Miss Outram," I hastily began again, "a particularly charming girl. I hope they are both quite well."

Still the old face solemnly blinked at me in silence.

"You must find it very lonely, Miss Seaton, with Arthur away?"

"I was never lonely in my life," she said sourly. "I don't look to flesh and blood for my company. When you've got to be my age, Mr. Smithers (which God forbid), you'll find life a very different affair from what you seem to think it is now. You won't seek company then, I'll be bound. It's thrust on you." Her face edged round into the clear green light, and her eyes groped, as it were, over my vacant, disconcerted face. "I dare say, now," she said, composing her mouth,."I dare say my nephew told you a good many tarradiddles in his time. Oh, yes, a good man, eh? He was always a liar. What, now, did he say of me? Tell me, now." She leant forward as far as she could, trembling, with an ingratiating smile.

"I think he is rather superstitious," I said coldly, "but, honestly, I have a very poor memory, Miss Seaton."

"Why?" she said. "*I* haven't."

"The engagement hasn't been broken off, I hope."

"Well, between you and me," she said, shrinking up and with an immensely confidential grimace, "it has."

"I'm sure I'm very sorry to hear it. And where is Arthur?"

"Eh?"

"Where is Arthur?"

We faced each other mutely among the dead old bygone furniture. Past all my analysis was that large, flat, grey, cryptic countenance. And then, suddenly, our eyes for the first time really met. In some indescribable way out of that thick-lidded obscurity a far small something stooped and looked out at me for a mere instant of time that seemed of almost intolerable protraction. Involuntarily I blinked and shook my head. She muttered something with great rapidity, but quite inarticulately; rose and hobbled to the door. I thought I heard, mingled in broken mutterings, something about tea.

"Please, please, don't trouble," I began, but could say no more, for the door was already shut between us. I stood and looked out on the long-neglected garden. I could just see the bright weedy greenness of Seaton's tadpole pond. I wandered about the room. Dusk began to gather, the last birds in that dense shadowiness of trees had ceased to sing. And not a sound was to be heard in the house. I waited on and on, vainly speculating. I even attempted to ring the bell; but the wire was broken, and only jangled loosely at my efforts.

I hesitated, unwilling to call or to venture out, and yet more unwilling to linger on, waiting for a tea that promised to be an exceedingly comfortless supper. And as darkness drew down, a feeling of the utmost unease and disquietude came over me. All my talks with Seaton returned on me with a suddenly enriched meaning. I recalled again his face as we had stood hanging over the staircase, listening in the small hours to the inexplicable stirrings of the night. There were no candles in the room; every minute the autumnal darkness deepened. I cautiously opened the door and listened, and with some little dismay withdrew, for I was uncertain of my way out. I even tried the garden, but was confronted with a veritable thicket of foliage by a padlocked gate. It would be a little too ignominious to be caught scaling a friend's garden fence!

Cautiously returning into the still and musty drawing-room, I took out my watch, and gave the incredible old woman ten minutes in which to reappear. And when that tedious ten minutes had ticked by, I could scarcely distinguish its hands. I determined to wait no longer, drew open the door and, trusting to my sense of direction, groped my way through the corridor that I vaguely remembered led to the front of the house.

I mounted three or four stairs and, lifting a heavy curtain, found myself facing the starry fanlight of the porch. From here I glanced into the gloom of the dining-room. My fingers were on the latch of the outer door when I heard a faint stirring in the darkness above the hall. I looked up and became conscious of, rather than saw, the huddled old figure looking down on me.

There was an immense hushed pause. Then, "Arthur, Arthur," whispered an inexpressibly peevish rasping voice, "is that you? Is that you, Arthur?"

I can scarcely say why, but the question horribly startled me. No conceivable answer occurred to me. With head craned back, hand clenched on my umbrella, I continued to stare up into the gloom, in this fatuous confrontation.

"Oh, oh," the voice croaked. "It is *you*, is it? *That* disgusting man! . . . Go away out. Go away out."

At this dismissal, I wrenched open the door and, rudely slamming it behind me, ran out into the garden, under the gigantic old sycamore, and so out at the open gate.

I found myself half up the village street before I stopped running. The local butcher was sitting in his shop reading a piece of newspaper by the light of a small oil-lamp. I crossed the road and enquired the way to the station. And after he had with minute and needless care directed me, I asked casually if Mr. Arthur Seaton still lived with his aunt at the big house just beyond the village. He poked his head in at the little parlour door.

"Here's a gentleman enquiring after young Mr. Seaton, Millie," he said. "He's dead, ain't he?"

"Why, yes, bless you," replied a cheerful voice from within. "Dead and buried these three months or more—young Mr. Seaton. And just before he was to be married, don't you remember, Bob?"

I saw a fair young woman's face peer over the muslin of the little door at me.

"Thank you," I replied, "then I go straight on?"

"That's it, sir; past the pond, bear up the hill a bit to the left, and then there's the station lights before your eyes."

We looked intelligently into each other's faces in the beam of the smoky lamp. But not one of the many questions in my mind could I put into words.

And again I paused irresolutely a few paces further on. It was not, I fancy, merely a foolish apprehension of what the raw-boned butcher might "think" that prevented my going back to see if I could find Seaton's grave in the benighted churchyard. There was precious little use in pottering about in the muddy dark merely to discover where he was buried. And yet I felt a little uneasy. My rather horrible thought was that, so far as I was concerned—one of his extremely few friends—he had never been much better than "buried" in my mind.

Ivan Turgenev

CLARA MILITCH

Ivan Turgenev was one of the few masters of supernatural horror fiction outside the English language in the nineteenth century. He was a Russian writer of enormous prestige and influence, and his supernatural works span his entire career, the best of them coming from his mature years. *Clara Militch* is a short novel and perhaps the best of all his works in the horror mode. Turgenev maintained that love is a supernatural phenomenon, an intriguing notion that underpins this story of requited love and horror. Turgenev's works were widely read in translation at the end of the nineteenth century. One might also note that in a contemporary scholarly edition of the text, the last word of the novella is "horror."

I

In the spring of 1878 there was living in Moscow, in a small wooden house in Shabolovka, a young man of five-and-twenty, called Yakov Aratov. With him lived his father's sister, an elderly maiden lady, over fifty, Platonida Ivanovna. She took charge of his house, and looked after his household expenditure, a task for which Aratov was utterly unfit. Other relations he had none. A few years previously, his father, a provincial gentleman of small property, had moved to Moscow together with him and Platonida Ivanovna, whom he always, however, called Platosha; her nephew, too, used the same name. On leaving the country-place where they had always lived up till then, the elder Aratov settled in the old capital, with the object of putting his son to the university, for which he had himself prepared him; he bought for a trifle a little house in one of the outlying streets, and established himself in it, with all his books and scientific odds and ends. And of books and odds and ends he had many—for he was a man of some considerable learning . . . "an out-and-out eccentric," as his neighbours said of him. He positively passed among them for a sorcerer; he had even been given the title of an "insectivist." He studied chemistry, mineralogy, entomology, botany, and medicine; he doctored patients gratis with herbs and metallic powders of his own invention, after the method of Paracelsus. These same powders were the means of his bringing to the grave his pretty, young, too delicate wife, whom he passionately loved, and by whom he had an only son. With the same powders he fairly ruined his son's health too, in the hope and intention of strengthening it, as he detected anæmia and a tendency to consumption in his constitution inherited from his mother. The name of "sorcerer" had been given him partly because he regarded himself as a descendant—not in the direct line, of course—of the great Bruce, in honour of whom he had called his son Yakov, the Russian form of James.

He was what is called a most good-natured man, but of melancholy temperament, pottering, and timid, with a bent for everything mysterious and occult. . . . A half-whispered ah! was his habitual exclamation; he even died with this exclamation on his lips, two years after his removal to Moscow.

His son, Yakov, was in appearance unlike his father, who had been plain, clumsy, and awkward; he took more after his mother. He had the same delicate pretty features, the same soft ash-coloured hair, the same little aquiline nose, the same pouting childish lips, and great greenish-grey languishing eyes, with soft eyelashes. But in character he was like his father; and the face, so unlike the father's face, wore the father's expression; and he had the triangular-shaped hands and hollow chest of the old Aratov, who ought, however, hardly to be called old, since he never reached his fiftieth year. Before his death, Yakov had already entered the university in the faculty of physics and mathematics; he did not, however, complete his course; not through laziness, but because, according to his notions, you could learn no more in the university than you could studying alone at home; and he did not go in for a diploma because he had no idea of entering the government service. He was shy with his fellow-students, made friends with scarcely any one, especially held aloof from women, and lived in great solitude buried in books. He held aloof from women, though he had a heart of the tenderest, and was fascinated by beauty. . . . He had even obtained a sumptuous English keepsake, and (oh shame!) gloated adoringly over its ''elegantly engraved'' representations of the various ravishing Gulnaras and Medoras. . . . But his innate modesty always kept him in check. In the house he used to work in what had been his father's study, it was also his bedroom, and his bed was the very one in which his father had breathed his last.

The mainstay of his whole existence, his unfailing friend and companion, was his aunt Platosha, with whom he exchanged barely a dozen words in the day, but without whom he could not stir hand or foot. She was a long-faced, long-toothed creature, with pale eyes, and a pale face, with an invariable expression, half of dejection, half of anxious dismay. For ever garbed in a grey dress and a grey shawl, she wandered about the house like a spirit, with noiseless steps, sighed, murmured prayers—especially one favourite one, consisting of three words only, ''Lord, succour us!''—and looked after the house with much good sense, taking care of every halfpenny, and buying everything herself. Her nephew she adored; she was in a perpetual fidget over his health—afraid of everything—not for herself but for him; and directly she fancied the slightest thing wrong, she would steal in softly, and set a cup of herb tea on his writing-table, or stroke him on the spine with her hands, soft as wadding. Yakov was not annoyed by these attentions—though the herb tea he left untouched—he merely nodded his head approvingly. However, his health was really nothing to boast of. He was very impressionable, nervous, fanciful, suffered from palpitations of the heart, and sometimes from asthma; like his father, he believed that there are in nature, and in the soul of man, mysteries which may sometimes be divined, but to which one can never penetrate; he believed in the existence of certain powers and influences, sometimes beneficient, but more often malignant, . . . and he believed too in science, in its dignity and importance. Of late he had taken a great fancy to photography. The smell of the chemicals used in this pursuit was a source of great uneasiness to his old aunt—not on her own account again, but on Yasha's, on account of his chest; but for all the softness of his temper, there was not a little obstinacy in his composition, and he persisted in his favourite pursuit. Platosha gave in, and only sighed more than ever, and murmured, "Lord, succour us!" whenever she saw his fingers stained with iodine.

Yakov, as we have already related, had held aloof from his fellow-students; with one of them he had, however, become fairly intimate, and saw him frequently, even after the fellow-student had left the university and entered the service, in a position involving little responsibility. He had, in his own words, got on to the building of the Church of our Saviour, though, of course, he knew nothing whatever of architecture. Strange to say, this one solitary friend of Aratov's, by name Kupfer, a German, so far Russianised that he did not know one word of German, and even fell foul of "the Germans," this friend had apparently nothing in common with him. He was a black-haired, red-cheeked young man, very jovial, talkative, and devoted to the feminine society Aratov so assiduously avoided. It is true Kupfer both lunched and dined with him pretty often, and even, being a man of small means, used to borrow trifling sums of him; but this was not what induced the free and easy German to frequent the humble little house in Shabolovka so diligently. The spiritual purity, the idealism of Yakov pleased him, possibly as a contrast to what he was seeing and meeting every day; or possibly this very attachment to the youthful idealist betrayed him of German blood after all. Yakov liked Kupfer's simple-hearted frankness; and besides that, his accounts of the theatres, concerts, and balls, where he was always in attendance—of the unknown world altogether, into which Yakov could not make up his mind to enter—secretly interested and even excited the young hermit, without, however, arousing any desire to learn all this by his own experience. And Platosha made Kupfer welcome; it is true she thought him at times excessively unceremonious, but instinctively perceiving and realising that he was sincerely attached to her precious Yasha, she not only put up with the noisy guest, but felt kindly towards him.

II

At the time with which our story is concerned, there was in Moscow a certain widow, a Georgian princess, a person of somewhat dubious, almost suspicious character. She was close upon forty; in her youth she had probably bloomed with that peculiar Oriental beauty, which fades so quickly; now she powdered, rouged, and dyed her hair yellow. Various reports, not altogether favourable, nor altogether definite, were in circulation about her; her husband no one had known, and she had never stayed long in any one town. She had no children, and no property, yet she kept open house, in debt or otherwise; she had a salon, as it is called, and received a rather mixed society, for the most part young men. Everything in her house from her own dress, furniture, and table, down to her carriage and her servants, bore the stamp of something shoddy, artificial, temporary, . . . but the princess herself, as well as her guests, apparently desired nothing better. The princess was reputed a devotee of music and literature, a patroness of artists and men of talent, and she really was interested in all these subjects, even to the point of enthusiasm, and an enthusiasm not altogether affected. There was an unmistakeable fibre of artistic feeling in her. Moreover she was very approachable, genial, free from presumption or pretentiousness, and, though many people did not suspect it, she was fundamentally good-natured, soft-hearted, and kindly disposed. . . . Qualities rare—and the more precious for their rarity—precisely in persons of her sort! "A fool of a woman!" a wit said of her: "but she'll get into heaven, not a doubt of it! Because she forgives everything, and everything will be forgiven her.'' It was said of her too that when she disappeared from a town, she always left as many creditors behind as persons she had befriended. A soft heart readily turned in any direction.

Kupfer, as might have been anticipated, found his way into her house, and was soon on an intimate—evil tongues said a too intimate—footing with her. He himself always spoke of her not only affectionately but with respect; he called her a heart of gold—say what you like! and firmly believed both in her love for art and her comprehension of art! One day after dinner at the Aratovs', in discussing the princess and her evenings, he began to persuade Yakov to break for once from his anchorite seclusion, and to allow him, Kupfer, to present him to his friend. Yakov at first would not even hear of it. ''But what do you imagine?'' Kupfer cried at last: ''what sort of presentation are we talking about? Simply, I take you, just as you are sitting now, in your everyday coat, and go with you to her for an evening. No sort of etiquette is necessary there, my dear boy! You're learned, you know, and fond of literature and music''—(there actually was in Aratov's study a piano on which he sometimes struck minor chords)—''and in her house there's enough and to spare of all those goods! . . . and you'll meet there sympathetic people, no nonsense about them! And after all, you really can't at your age, with your looks (Aratov dropped his eyes and waved his hand deprecatingly), yes, yes, with your looks, you really can't keep aloof from society, from the world, like this! Why, I'm not going to take you to see generals! Indeed, I know no generals myself! . . . Don't be obstinate, dear boy! Morality is an excellent thing, most laudable. . . . But why fall a prey to asceticism? You're not going in for becoming a monk!''

Aratov was, however, still refractory; but Kupfer found an unexpected ally in Platonida Ivanovna. Though she had no clear idea what was meant by the word asceticism, she too was of the opinion that it would be no harm for dear Yasha to take a little recreation, to see people, and to show himself.

''Especially,'' she added, ''as I've perfect confidence in Fyodor Fedoritch! He'll take you to no bad place! . . .'' ''I'll bring him back in all his maiden innocence,'' shouted Kupfer, at which Platonida Ivanovna, in spite of her confidence, cast uneasy glances upon him. Aratov blushed up to his ears, but ceased to make objections.

It ended by Kupfer taking him next day to spend an evening at the princess's. But Aratov did not remain there long. To begin with, he found there some twenty visitors, men and women, sympathetic people possibly, but still strangers, and this oppressed him, even though he had to do very little talking; and that, he feared above all things. Secondly, he did not like their hostess, though she received him very graciously and simply. Everything about her was distasteful to him: her painted face, and her frizzed curls, and her thickly-sugary voice, her shrill giggle, her way of rolling her eyes and looking up, her excessively low-necked dress, and those fat, glossy fingers with their multitude of rings! . . . Hiding himself away in a corner, he took from time to time a rapid survey of the faces of all the guests, without even distinguishing them, and then stared obstinately at his own feet. When at last a stray musician with a worn face, long hair, and an eyeglass stuck into his contorted eyebrow sat down to the grand piano and flinging his hands with a sweep on the keys and his foot on the pedal, began to attack a fantasia of Liszt on a Wagner motive, Aratov could not stand it, and stole off, bearing away in his heart a vague, painful impression; across which, however, flitted something incomprehensible to him, but grave and even disquieting.

III

Kupfer came next day to dinner; he did not begin, however, expatiating on the preceding evening, he did not even reproach Aratov for his hasty retreat, and only regretted that he had not stayed to supper, when there had been champagne! (of the Novgorod brand, we may remark in parenthesis). Kupfer probably realised that it had been a mistake on his part to disturb his friend, and that Aratov really was a man "not suited" to that circle and way of life. On his side, too, Aratov said nothing of the princess, nor of the previous evening. Platonida Ivanovna did not know whether to rejoice at the failure of this first experiment or to regret it. She decided at last that Yasha's health might suffer from such outings, and was comforted. Kupfer went away directly after dinner, and did not show himself again for a whole week. And it was not that he resented the failure of his suggestion, the good fellow was incapable of that, but he had obviously found some interest which was absorbing all his time, all his thoughts; for later on, too, he rarely appeared at the Aratovs', had an absorbed look, spoke little and quickly vanished. . . . Aratov went on living as before; but a sort of—if one may so express it—little hook was pricking at his soul. He was continually haunted by some reminiscence, he could not quite tell what it was himself, and this reminiscence was connected with the evening he had spent at the princess's. For all that, he had not the slightest inclination to return there again, and the world, a part of which he had looked upon at her house, repelled him more than ever. So passed six weeks.

And behold one morning Kupfer stood before him once more, this time with a somewhat embarrassed countenance. "I know," he began with a constrained smile, "that your visit that time was not much to your taste; but I hope for all that you'll agree to my proposal . . . that you won't refuse me my request!"

"What is it?" inquired Aratov.

"Well, do you see," pursued Kupfer, getting more and more heated: "there is a society here of amateurs, artistic people, who from time to time get up readings, concerts, even theatrical performances for some charitable object."

"And the princess has a hand in it?" interposed Aratov.

"The princess has a hand in all good deeds, but that's not the point. We have arranged a literary and musical matinée . . . and at this matinée you may hear a girl . . . an extraordinary girl! We cannot make out quite yet whether she is to be a Rachel or a Viardot . . . for she sings exquisitely, and recites and plays. . . . A talent of the very first rank, my dear boy! I'm not exaggerating. Well then, won't you take a ticket? Five roubles for a seat in the front row."

"And where has this marvellous girl sprung from?" asked Aratov.

Kupfer grinned. "That I really can't say. . . . Of late she's found a home with the princess. The princess you know is a protector of every one of that sort. . . . But you saw her, most likely, that evening."

Aratov gave a faint inward start . . . but he said nothing.

"She has even played somewhere in the provinces," Kupfer continued, "and altogether she's created for the theater. There! you'll see for yourself!"

"What's her name?" asked Aratov.

"Clara . . ."

"Clara?" Aratov interrupted a second time. "Impossible!"

"Why impossible? Clara . . . Clara Militch; it's not her real name . . . but that's what she's called. She's going to sing a song of Glinka's . . . and of Tchaykovsky's; and then she'll recite the letter from *Yevgeny Oniegin*. Well; will you take a ticket?"

"And when will it be?"

"To-morrow . . . to-morrow, at half-past one, in a private drawing-room, in Ostozhonka. . . . I will come for you. A five-rouble ticket? . . . Here it is . . . no, that's a three-rouble one. Here . . . and here's the programme. . . . I'm one of the stewards."

Aratov sank into thought. Platonida Ivanovna came in at that instant, and glancing at his face, was in a flutter of agitation at once. "Yasha," she cried, "what's the matter with you? Why are you so upset? Fyodor Fedoritch, what is it you've been telling him?"

Aratov did not let his friend answer his aunt's question, but hurriedly snatching the ticket held out to him, told Platonida Ivanovna to give Kupfer five roubles at once.

She blinked in amazement. . . . However, she handed Kupfer the money in silence. Her darling Yasha had ejaculated his commands in a very imperative manner.

"I tell you, a wonder of wonders!" cried Kupfer, hurrying to the door. "Wait till tomorrow."

"Has she black eyes?" Aratov called after him.

"Black as coal!" Kupfer shouted cheerily, as he vanished.

Aratov went away to his room, while Platonida Ivanovna stood rooted to the spot, repeating in a whisper, "Lord, succour us! Succour us, Lord!"

IV

The big drawing-room in the private house in Ostozhonka was already half full of visitors when Aratov and Kupfer arrived. Dramatic performances had sometimes been given in this drawing-room, but on this occasion there was no scenery nor curtain visible. The organisers of the matinée had confined themselves to fixing up a platform at one end, putting upon it a piano, a couple of reading-desks, a few chairs, a table with a bottle of water and a glass on it, and hanging red cloth over the door that led to the room allotted to the performers. In the first row was already sitting the princess in a bright green dress. Aratov placed himself at some distance from her, after exchanging the barest of greetings with her. The public was, as they say, of mixed materials; for the most part young men from educational institutions. Kupfer, as one of the stewards, with a white ribbon on the cuff of his coat, fussed and bustled about busily; the princess was obviously excited, looked about her, shot smiles in all directions, talked with those next to her . . . none but men were sitting near her. The first to appear on the platform was a flute-player of consumptive appearance, who most conscientiously dribbled away—what am I saying?—piped, I mean— a piece also of consumptive tendency; two persons shouted bravo! Then a stout gentleman in spectacles, of an exceedingly solid, even surly aspect, read in a bass voice a sketch of Shtchedrin; the sketch was applauded, not the reader; then the pianist, whom Aratov had seen before, came forward and strummed the same fantasia of Liszt; the pianist gained an encore. He bowed with one hand on the back of the chair, and after each bow he shook back his hair, precisely like Liszt! At last after a rather long interval the red cloth over the door on to the platform stirred and opened wide, and

Clara Militch appeared. The room resounded with applause. With hesitating steps, she moved forward on the platform, stopped and stood motionless, clasping her large handsome ungloved hands in front of her, without a curtsy, a bend of the head, or a smile.

She was a girl of nineteen, tall, rather broad-shouldered, but well-built. A dark face, of a half-Jewish half-gipsy type, small black eyes under thick brows almost meeting in the middle, a straight, slightly turned-up nose, delicate lips with a beautiful but decided curve, an immense mass of black hair, heavy even in appearance, a low brow still as marble, tiny ears . . . the whole face dreamy, almost sullen. A nature passionate, willful—hardly good-tempered, hardly very clever, but gifted—was expressed in every feature.

For some time she did not raise her eyes; but suddenly she started, and passed over the rows of spectators a glance intent, but not attentive, absorbed, it seemed, in herself. . . . "What tragic eyes she has!" observed a man sitting behind Aratov, a grey-headed dandy with the face of a Revel harlot, well known in Moscow as a prying gossip and writer for the papers. The dandy was an idiot, and meant to say something idiotic . . . but he spoke the truth. Aratov, who from the very moment of Clara's entrance had never taken his eyes off her, only at that instant recollected that he really had seen her at the princess's; and not only that he had seen her, but that he had even noticed that she had several times, with a peculiar insistency, gazed at him with her dark intent eyes. And now too—or was it his fancy?—on seeing him in the front row she seemed delighted, seemed to flush, and again gazed intently at him. Then, without turning round, she stepped away a couple of paces in the direction of the piano, at which her accompanist, a long-haired foreigner, was sitting. She had to render Glinka's ballad: "As soon as I knew you . . ." She began at once to sing, without changing the attitude of her hands or glancing at the music. Her voice was soft and resonant, a contralto; she uttered the words distinctly and with emphasis, and sang monotonously, with little light and shade, but with intense expression. "The girl sings with conviction," said the same dandy sitting behind Aratov, and again he spoke the truth. Shouts of "Bis!" "Bravo!" resounded over the room; but she flung a rapid glance on Aratov, who neither shouted nor clapped—he did not particularly care for her singing—gave a slight bow, and walked out without taking the hooked arm proffered her by the long-haired pianist. She was called back . . . not very soon, she reappeared, with the same hesitating steps approached the piano, and whispering a couple of words to the accompanist, who picked out and put before him another piece of music, began Tchaykovsky's song: "No, only he who knows the thirst to see." . . . This song she sang differently from the first—in a low voice, as though she were tired . . . and only the line next the last, "He knows what I have suffered," broke from her in a ringing, passionate cry. The last line, "And how I suffer" . . . she almost whispered, with a mournful prolongation of the last word. This song produced less impression on the audience than the Glinka ballad; there was much applause, however. . . . Kupfer was particularly conspicuous; folding his hands in a peculiar way, in the shape of a barrel, at each clap he produced an extraordinarily resounding report. The princess handed him a large, straggling nosegay for him to take to the singer; but she, seeming not to observe Kupfer's bowing figure, and outstretched hand with the nosegay, turned and went away, again without waiting for the pianist, who skipped forward to escort her more hurriedly than before, and when he found himself so unjustifiably deserted, tossed his hair as certainly Liszt had never tossed his!

During the whole time of the singing, Aratov had been watching Clara's face. It seemed to him that her eyes, through the drooping eyelashes, were again turned upon him; but he was especially struck by the immobility of the face, the forehead, the eyebrows; and only at her outburst of passion he caught through the hardly-parted lips the warm gleam of a close row of white teeth. Kupfer came up to him.

"Well, my dear boy, what do you think of her?" he asked, beaming all over with satisfaction.

"It's a fine voice," replied Aratov; "but she doesn't know how to sing yet; she's no real musical knowledge." (Why he said this, and what conception he had himself of "musical knowledge," the Lord only knows!)

Kupfer was surprised. "No musical knowledge," he repeated slowly. . . . "Well, as to that . . . she can acquire that. But what soul! Wait a bit, though; you shall hear her in Tatiana's letter."

He hurried away from Aratov, while the latter said to himself, "Soul! with that immovable face!" He thought that she moved and held herself like one hypnotised, like a somnambulist. And at the same time she was unmistakably . . . yes! unmistakably looking at him.

Meanwhile the matinée went on. The fat man in spectacles appeared again; in spite of his serious exterior, he fancied himself a comic actor, and recited a scene from Gogol, this time without eliciting a single token of approbation. There was another glimpse of the flute-player; another thunder-clap from the pianist; a boy of twelve, frizzed and pomaded, but with tearstains on his cheeks, thrummed some variations on a fiddle. What seemed strange was that in the intervals of the reading and music, from the performers' room, sounds were heard from time to time of a French horn; and yet this instrument never was brought into requisition. In the sequel it appeared that the amateur, who had been invited to perform on it, had lost courage at the moment of facing the public. At last Clara Militch made her appearance again.

She held a volume of Pushkin in her hand; she did not, however, glance at it once during her recitation. . . . She was obviously nervous, the little book shook slightly in her fingers. Aratov observed also the expression of weariness which now overspread all her stern features. The first line, "I write to you . . . what more?" she uttered exceedingly simply, almost naïvely, and with a naïve, genuine, helpless gesture held both hands out before her. Then she began to hurry a little; but from the beginning of the lines: "Another! no! To no one in the whole world I have given my heart!" she mastered her powers, gained fire; and when she came to the words, "My whole life has but been a pledge of a meeting true with thee," her hitherto thick voice rang out boldly and enthusiastically, while her eyes just as boldly and directly fastened upon Aratov. She went on with the same fervour, and only towards the end her voice dropped again; and in it, and in her face, the same weariness was reflected again. The last four lines she completely "murdered," as it is called; the volume of Pushkin suddenly slid out of her hand, and she hastily withdrew.

The audience fell to applauding desperately, encoring. . . . One Little-Russian divinity student bellowed in so deep a bass, "Mill-itch! Mill-itch!" that his neighbour civilly and sympathetically advised him "to take care of his voice, it would be the making of a protodeacon." But Aratov at once rose and made for the door. Kupfer overtook him. . . . "I say, where are you off to?" he called; "would you like me to present you to Clara?" "No, thanks," Aratov returned hurriedly, and he went homewards almost at a run.

V

He was agitated by strange sensations, incomprehensible to himself. In reality, Clara's recitation, too, had not been quite to his taste . . . though he could not quite tell why. It disturbed him, this recitation; it struck him as crude and inharmonious. . . . It was as though it broke something within him, forced itself with a certain violence upon him. And those fixed, insistent, almost importunate looks—what were they for? what did they mean?

Aratov's modesty did not for one instant admit of the idea that he might have made an impression on this strange girl, that he might have inspired in her a sentiment akin to love, to passion! . . . And indeed, he himself had formed a totally different conception of the still unknown woman, the girl to whom he was to give himself wholly, who would love him, be his bride, his wife. . . . He seldom dwelt on this dream—in spirit as in body he was virginal; but the pure image that arose at such times in his fancy was inspired by a very different figure, the figure of his dead mother, whom he scarcely remembered, but whose portrait he treasured as a sacred relic. The portrait was a water-colour, painted rather unskilfully by a lady who had been a neighbour of hers; but the likeness, as every one declared, was a striking one. Just such a tender profile, just such kind, clear eyes and silken hair, just such a smile and pure expression, was the woman, the girl, to have, for whom as yet he scarcely dared to hope. . . .

But this swarthy, dark-skinned creature, with coarse hair, dark eyebrows, and a tiny moustache on her upper lip, she was certainly a wicked, giddy . . . "gipsy" (Aratov could not imagine a harsher appellation)—what was she to him?

And yet Aratov could not succeed in getting out of his head this dark-skinned gipsy, whose singing and reading and very appearance were displeasing to him. He was puzzled, he was angry with himself. Not long before he had read Sir Walter Scott's novel, *St. Ronan's Well* (there was a complete edition of Sir Walter Scott's works in the library of his father, who had regarded the English novelist with esteem as a serious, almost a scientific, writer). The heroine of that novel is called Clara Mowbray. A poet who flourished somewhere about 1840, Krasov, wrote a poem on her, ending with the words:

"Unhappy Clara! poor frantic Clara!
Unhappy Clara Mowbray!"

Aratov knew this poem also. . . . And now these words were incessantly haunting his memory. . . . "Unhappy Clara! Poor, frantic Clara!" . . . (This was why he had been so surprised when Kupfer told him the name of Clara Militch.)

Platosha herself noticed, not a change exactly in Yasha's temper—no change in reality took place in it—but something unsatisfactory in his looks and in his words. She cautiously questioned him about the literary matinée at which he had been present; muttered, sighed, looked at him from in front, from the side, from behind; and suddenly clapping her hands on her thighs, she exclaimed: "To be sure, Yasha; I see what it is!"

"Why? what?" Aratov queried.

"You've met for certain at that matinée one of those long-tailed creatures"—this was how Platonida Ivanovna always spoke of all fashionably-dressed ladies of the period—"with a pretty dolly face; and she goes prinking *this* way . . . and pluming *that* way''—Platonida presented these fancied manœuvers in mimicry—''and making saucers like this with her eyes''—and she drew big, round circles in the air with her forefinger—''You're not used to that sort of thing. So you fancied . . but that means nothing, Yasha . . . no-o-thing at all! Drink a cup of posset at night . . . it'll pass off! . . . Lord, succour us!''

Platosha ceased speaking, and left the room. . . . She had hardly ever uttered such a long and animated speech in her life. . . . While Aratov thought, ''Auntie's right, I dare say. . . . I'm not used to it; that's all . . .''—it actually was the first time his attention had ever happened to be drawn to a person of the female sex . . . at least he had never noticed it before—''I mustn't give way to it.''

And he set to work on his books, and at night drank some lime-flower tea; and positively slept well that night, and had no dreams. The next morning he took up his photography again as though nothing had happened. . . .

But towards evening his spiritual repose was again disturbed.

VI

And this is what happened. A messenger brought him a note, written in a large irregular woman's hand, and containing the following lines:

''If you guess who it is writes to you, and if it is not a bore to you, come to-morrow after dinner to the Tversky boulevard—about five o'clock—and wait. You shall not be kept long. But it is very important. Do come.''

There was no signature. Aratov at once guessed who was his correspondent, and this was just what disturbed him. ''What folly,'' he said, almost aloud; ''this is too much. Of course I shan't go.'' He sent, however, for the messenger, and from him learned nothing but that the note had been handed him by a maidservant in the street. Dismissing him, Aratov read the letter through and flung it on the ground. . . .

But, after a little while, he picked it up and read it again: a second time he cried, "Folly!"—he did not, however, throw the note on the floor again, but put it in a drawer. Aratov took up his ordinary occupations, first one and then another; but nothing he did was successful or satisfactory. He suddenly realised that he was eagerly expecting Kupfer! Did he want to question him, or perhaps even to confide in him? . . . But Kupfer did not make his appearance. Then Aratov took down Pushkin, read Tatiana's letter, and convinced himself again that the "gipsy girl" had not in the least understood the real force of the letter. And that donkey Kupfer shouts: Rachel! Viardot! Then he went to his piano, as it seemed, unconsciously opened it, and tried to pick out by ear the melody of Tchaykovsky's song; but he slammed it to again directly in vexation, and went up to his aunt to her special room, which was for ever baking hot, smelled of mint, sage, and other medicinal herbs, and was littered up with such a multitude of rugs, side-tables, stools, cushions, and padded furniture of all sorts, that any one unused to it would have found it difficult to turn round and oppressive to breathe in it. Platonida Ivanovna was sitting at the window, her knitting in her hands (she was knitting her darling Yasha a comforter, the thirty-eighth she had made him in the course of his life!), and was much astonished to see him. Aratov rarely went up to her, and if he wanted anything, used always to call, in his delicate voice, from his study: "Aunt Platosha!" However, she made him sit down, and sat all alert, in expectation of his first words, watching him through her spectacles with one eye, over them with the other. She did not inquire after his health nor offer him tea, as she saw he had not come for that. Aratov was a little disconcerted . . . then he began to talk . . . talked of his mother, of how she had lived with his father and how his father had got to know her. All this he knew very well . . . but it was just what he wanted to talk about. Unluckily for him, Platosha did not know how to keep up a conversation at all; she gave him very brief replies, as though she suspected that was not what Yasha had come for.

"Eh!" she repeated, hurriedly, almost irritably plying her knitting-needles. "We all know: your mother was a darling

. . . a darling that she was. . . . And your father loved her as a husband should, truly and faithfully even in her grave; and he never loved any other woman": she added, raising her voice and taking off her spectacles.

"And was she of a retiring disposition?" Aratov inquired, after a short silence.

"Retiring! to be sure she was. As a woman should be. Bold ones have sprung up nowadays."

"And were there no bold ones in your time?"

"There were in our time too . . . to be sure there were! But who were they? A pack of strumpets, shameless hussies. Draggle-tails—for ever gadding about after no good. . . . What do they care? It's little they take to heart. If some poor fool comes in their way, they pounce on him. But sensible folk looked down on them. Did you ever see, pray, the like of such in our house?"

Aratov made no reply, and went back to his study. Platonida Ivanovna looked after him, shook her head, put on her spectacles again, and again took up her comforter . . . but more than once sank into thought, and let her knitting-needles fall on her knees.

Aratov up till very late kept telling himself, no! no! but with the same irritation, the same exasperation, he fell again into musing on the note, on the "gipsy girl," on the appointed meeting, to which he would certainly not go! And at night she gave him no rest. He was continually haunted by her eyes—at one time half-closed, at another wide open—and their persistent gaze fixed straight upon him, and those motionless features with their dominating expression. . . .

The next morning he again, for some reason, kept expecting Kupfer; he was on the point of writing a note to him . . . but did nothing, however, . . . and spent most of the time walking up and down his room. He never for one instant admitted to himself even the idea of going to this idiotic rendezvous . . . and at half-past three, after a hastily swallowed dinner, suddenly throwing on his cloak and thrusting his cap on his head, he dashed out into the street, unseen by his aunt, and turned towards the Tversky boulevard.

VII

Aratov found few people walking in it. The weather was damp and rather cold. He tried not to reflect on what he was doing, to force himself to turn his attention to every object that presented itself, and, as it were, persuaded himself that he had simply come out for a walk like the other people passing to and fro. . . . The letter of the day before was in his breast-pocket, and he was conscious all the while of its presence there. He walked twice up and down the boulevard, scrutinised sharply every feminine figure that came near him—and his heart throbbed. . . . He felt tired and sat down on a bench. And suddenly the thought struck him: "What if that letter was not written by her, but to some one else by some other woman?" In reality this should have been a matter of indifference to him . . . and yet he had to admit to himself that he did not want this to be so. "That would be too silly," he thought, "even sillier than *this*!" A nervous unrest began to gain possession of him; he began to shiver—not outwardly, but inwardly. He several times took his watch out of his waistcoat pocket, looked at the face, put it back, and each time forgot how many minutes it was to five. He fancied that every passer-by looked at him in a peculiar way, with a sort of sarcastic astonishment and curiosity. A wretched little dog ran up, sniffed at his legs, and began wagging his tail. He threatened it angrily. He was particularly annoyed by a factory lad in a greasy smock, who seated himself on a seat on the other side of the boulevard, and by turns whistling, scratching himself, and swinging his feet in enormous tattered boots, persistently stared at him. "And his master," thought Aratov, "is waiting for him, no doubt, while he, lazy scamp, is kicking up his heels here. . . ."

But at that very instant he felt that someone had come up and was standing close behind him . . . there was a breath of something warm from behind. . . .

He looked round. . . . She!

He knew her at once, though a thick, dark blue veil hid her features. He instantaneously leapt up from the seat, but

stopped short, and could not utter a word. She too was silent.
He felt great embarrassment; but her embarrassment was no
less. Aratov, even through the veil, could not help noticing
how deadly pale she had turned. Yet she was the first to
speak.

"Thanks," she began in an unsteady voice, "thanks for
coming. I did not expect . . ." She turned a little away and
walked along the boulevard. Aratov walked after her.

"You have, perhaps, thought ill of me," she went on,
without turning her head; "indeed, my conduct is very
strange. . . . But I had heard so much about you . . . but no!
I . . . that was not the reason. . . . If only you knew . . .
There was so much I wanted to tell you, my God! . . . But
how to do it . . . how to do it!"

Aratov was walking by her side, a little behind her; he
could not see her face; he saw only her hat and part of her
veil . . . and her long black shabby cape. All his irritation,
both with her and with himself, suddenly came back to him;
all the absurdity, the awkwardness of this interview, these
explanations between perfect strangers in a public promenade, suddenly struck him.

"I have come on your invitation," he began in his turn.
"I have come, my dear madam" (her shoulders gave a faint
twitch, she turned off into a side passage, he followed her),
"simply to clear up, to discover to what strange misunderstanding it is due that you are pleased to address me, a
stranger to you . . . who . . . only *guessed*, to use your expression in your letter, that it was your writing to him . . .
guessed it because during that literary matinée, you saw fit
to pay him such . . . such obvious attention."

All this little speech was delivered by Aratov in that ringing but unsteady voice in which very young people answer at
examinations on a subject in which they are well prepared. . . . He was angry; he was furious. . . . It was just
this fury which loosened his ordinarily not very ready tongue.

She still went on along the walk with rather slower
steps. . . . Aratov, as before, walked after her, and as before
saw only the old cape and the hat, also not a very new one.

His vanity suffered at the idea that she must now be thinking: "I had only to make a sign—and he rushed at once!"

Aratov was silent . . . he expected her to answer him; but she did not utter a word.

"I am ready to listen to you," he began again, "and shall be very glad if I can be of use to you in any way . . . though I am, I confess, surprised . . . considering the retired life I lead. . . ."

At these last words of his, Clara suddenly turned to him, and he beheld such a terrified, such a deeply-wounded face, with such large bright tears in the eyes, such a pained expression about the parted lips, and this face was so lovely, that he involuntarily faltered, and himself felt something akin to terror and pity and softening.

"Ah, why . . . why are you like that?" she said, with an irresistibly genuine and truthful force, and how movingly her voice rang out! "Could my turning to you be offensive to you? . . . is it possible you have understood nothing? . . . Ah, yes! you have understood nothing, you did not understand what I said to you, God knows what you have been imagining about me, you have not even dreamed what it cost me—to write to you! . . . You thought of nothing but yourself, your own dignity, your peace of mind! . . . But is it likely I" . . . (she squeezed her hands raised to her lips so hard that the fingers gave a distinct crack). . . . "As though I made any sort of demands of you, as though explanations were necessary first. . . . 'My dear madam, . . . I am, I confess, surprised, . . . if I can be of any use' . . . Ah! I am mad!—I was mistaken in you—in your face! . . . when I saw you the first time . . . ! Here . . . you stand. . . . If only one word. What, not one word?"

She ceased. . . . Her face suddenly flushed, and as suddenly took a wrathful and insolent expression. "Mercy! how idiotic this is!" she cried suddenly, with a shrill laugh. "How idiotic our meeting is! What a fool I am! . . . and you too. . . . Ugh!"

She gave a contemptuous wave of her hand, as though motioning him out of her road, and passing him, ran quickly out of the boulevard, and vanished.

The gesture of her hand, the insulting laugh, and the last exclamation, at once carried Aratov back to his first frame of mind, and stifled the feeling that had sprung up in his heart when she turned to him with tears in her eyes. He was angry again, and almost shouted after the retreating girl: "You may make a good actress, but why did you think fit to play off this farce on me?"

He returned home with long strides, and though he still felt anger and indignation all the way, yet across these evil, malignant feelings, unconsciously, the memory forced itself of the exquisite face he had seen for a single moment only. . . . He even put himself the question, "Why did I not answer her when she asked of me only a word? I had not time," he thought. "She did not let me utter the word . . . and what word could I have uttered?"

But he shook his head at once, and murmured reproachfully, "Actress!"

And again, at the same time, the vanity of the inexperienced nervous youth, at first wounded, was now, as it were, flattered at having any way inspired such a passion. . . .

"Though by now," he pursued his reflections, "it's all over, of course. . . . I must have seemed absurd to her." . . .

This idea was disagreeable to him, and again he was angry . . . both with her . . . and with himself. On reaching home, he shut himself up in his study. He did not want to see Platosha. The good old lady came twice to his locked door, put her ear to the keyhole, and only sighed and murmured her prayer.

"It has begun!" she thought. . . . "And he only five-and-twenty! Ah, it's early, it's early!"

VIII

All the following day Aratov was in very low spirits. "What is it, Yasha?" Platonida Ivanovna said to him: "you seem somehow all loose ends to-day!" . . . In her own peculiar idiom the old lady's expression described fairly accurately Aratov's mental condition. He could not work and he did not know himself what he wanted. At one time he was eagerly on the watch for Kupfer, again he suspected that it was from Kupfer that Clara had got his address . . . and from where else could she "have heard so much about him"? Then he wondered: was it possible his acquaintance with her was to end like this? Then he fancied she would write to him again; then he asked himself whether he ought not to write her a letter, explaining everything, since he did not at all like leaving an unfavorable impression of himself. . . . But exactly what to explain? Then he stirred up in himself almost a feeling of repulsion for her, for her insistence, her impertinence; and then again he saw that unutterably touching face and heard an irresistible voice; then he recalled her singing, her recitation—and could not be sure whether he had been right in his wholesale condemnation of it. In fact, he was all loose ends! At last he was heartily sick of it, and resolved to keep a firm hand over himself, as it is called, and to obliterate the whole incident, as it was unmistakably hindering his studies and destroying his peace of mind. It turned out not so easy to carry out this resolution . . . more than a week passed by before he got back into his old accustomed groove. Luckily Kupfer did not turn up at all; he was in fact out of Moscow. Not long before the incident, Aratov had begun to work at painting in connection with his photographic plans; he set to work upon it now with redoubled zest.

So, imperceptibly, with a few (to use the doctors' expression) "symptoms of relapse," manifested, for instance, in his once almost deciding to call upon the princess, two months passed . . . then three months . . . and Aratov was the old Aratov again. Only somewhere down below, under the surface of his life, something like a dark and burdensome secret dogged him wherever he went. So a great fish just caught on the hook, but not yet drawn up, will swim at the bottom of a deep stream under the very boat where the angler sits with a stout rod in his hand.

And one day, skimming through a not quite new number of the *Moscow Gazette*, Aratov lighted upon the following paragraph:

"With the greatest regret," wrote some local contributor from Kazan, "we must add to our dramatic record the news of the sudden death of our gifted actress Clara Militch, who had succeeded during the brief period of her engagement in becoming a favorite of our discriminating public. Our regret is the more poignant from the fact that Miss Militch by her own act cut short her young life, so full of promise, by means of poison. And this dreadful deed was the more awful through the talented actress taking the fatal drug in the theater itself. She had scarcely been taken home when to the universal grief, she expired. There is a rumor in the town that an unfortunate love affair drove her to this terrible act."

Aratov slowly laid the paper on the table. In outward appearance he remained perfectly calm . . . but at once something seemed to strike him a blow in the chest and the head—and slowly the shock passed on through all his limbs. He got up, stood still on the spot, and sat down again, again read through the paragraph. Then he got up again, lay down on the bed, and clasping his hands behind, stared a long while at the wall, as though dazed. By degrees the wall seemed to fade away . . . vanished . . . and he saw facing him the boulevard under the grey sky, and *her* in her black cape . . . then her on the platform . . . saw himself even close by her. That something which had given him such a violent blow in the chest at the first instant, began mounting now . . . mounting into his throat. . . . He tried to clear his throat; tried to call some one—but his voice failed him—and, to his own astonishment, tears rushed in torrents from his eyes . . . what called forth these tears? Pity? Remorse? Or was it simply his nerves could not stand the sudden shock?

Why, she was nothing to him? was she?

"But, perhaps, it's not true after all," the thought came as a sudden relief to him. "I must find out! But from whom? From the princess? No, from Kupfer . . . from Kupfer? But they say he's not in Moscow—no matter, I must try him first!"

With these reflections in his head, Aratov dressed himself in haste, called a cab and drove to Kupfer's.

IX

Though he had not expected to find him, he found him. Kupfer had, as a fact, been away from Moscow for some time, but he had now been back a week, and was indeed on the point of setting off to see Aratov. He met him with his usual heartiness, and was beginning to make some sort of explanation . . . but Aratov at once cut him short with the impatient question, "Have you heard it? Is it true?"

"Is what true?" replied Kupfer, puzzled.

"About Clara Militch?"

Kupfer's face expressed commiseration. "Yes, yes, my dear boy, it's true; she poisoned herself! Such a sad thing!"

Aratov was silent for a while. "But did you read it in the paper too?" he asked—"or perhaps you have been in Kazan yourself?"

"I have been in Kazan, yes; the princess and I accompanied her there. She came out on the stage there, and had a great success. But I didn't stay up to the time of the catastrophe . . . I was in Yaroslav at the time."

"In Yaroslav?"

"Yes—I escorted the princess there. . . . She is living now at Yaroslav."

"But you have trustworthy information?"

"Trustworthy . . . I have it at first-hand!—I made the acquaintance of her family in Kazan. But, my dear boy . . . this news seems to be upsetting you? Why, I recollect you didn't care for Clara at one time? You were wrong, though! She was a marvelous girl—only what a temper! I was terribly brokenhearted about her!"

Aratov did not utter a word, he dropped into a chair, and after a brief pause, asked Kupfer to tell him . . . he stammered.

"What?" inquired Kupfer.

"Oh . . . everything," Aratov answered brokenly, "all about her family . . . and the rest of it. Everything you know!"

"Why, does it interest you? By all means!" And Kupfer,

whose face showed no traces of his having been so terribly broken-hearted about Clara, began his story.

From his account Aratov learnt that Clara Militch's real name was Katerina Milovidov; that her father, now dead, had held the post of drawing-master in a school in Kazan, had painted bad portraits and holy pictures of the regulation type; that he had besides had the character of being a drunkard and a domestic tyrant; that he had left behind him, first a widow, of a shopkeeper's family, a quite stupid body, a character straight out of an Ostrovsky comedy; and secondly, a daughter much older than Clara and not like her—a very clever girl, and enthusiastic, only sickly, a remarkable girl—and very advanced in her ideas, my dear boy! That they were living, the widow and daughter, fairly comfortably, in a decent little house, obtained by the sale of the bad portraits and holy pictures; that Clara . . . or Katia, if you like, from her child-hood up impressed every one with her talent, but was of an insubordinate, capricious temper, and used to be for ever quarrelling with her father; that having an inborn passion for the theater, at sixteen she had run away from her parents' house with an actress . . .

"With an actor?" put in Aratov.

"No, not with an actor, with an actress, to whom she became attached. . . . It's true this actress had a protector, a wealthy gentleman, no longer young, who did not marry her simply because he happened to be married—and indeed I fancy the actress was a married woman." Furthermore Kupfer informed Aratov that Clara had even before her coming to Moscow acted and sung in provincial theatres, that, having lost her friend the actress—the gentleman, too, it seemed, had died, or else he had made it up with his wife—Kupfer could not quite remember this—she had made the acquaintance of the princess, "that heart of gold, whom you, my dear Yakov Andreitch," the speaker added with feeling, "were incapable of appreciating properly"; that at last Clara had been offered an engagement in Kazan, and that she had accepted it, though before then she used to declare that she would never leave Moscow! But then how the people of Kazan liked her—it was really astonishing! Whatever the performance was, nothing but nosegays and presents! nosegays and presents! A wholesale miller, the greatest swell in the province, had even presented her with a gold inkstand! Kupfer related all this with great animation, without giving expression, however, to any special sentimentality, and interspersing his narrative with the questions, "What is it to you?" and "Why do you ask?" when Aratov, who listened to him with devouring attention, kept asking for more and more details. All was told at last, and Kupfer was silent, rewarding himself for his exertions with a cigar.

"And why did she take poison?" asked Aratov. "In the paper it was stated . . ."

Kupfer waved his hand. "Well . . . that I can't say . . . I don't know. But the paper tells a lie. Clara's conduct was exemplary . . . no love affairs of any kind. . . . And indeed how should there be with her pride! She was proud—as Satan himself—and unapproachable! A headstrong creature! Hard as rock! You'll hardly believe it—though I knew her so well— I never saw a tear in her eyes!"

"But I have," Aratov thought to himself.

"But there's one thing," continued Kupfer, "of late I noticed a great change in her: she grew so dull, so silent, for hours together there was no getting a word out of her. I asked her even, 'Has any one offended you, Katerina Semyonovna?' For I knew her temper; she could never swallow an affront! But she was silent, and there was no doing anything with her! Even her triumphs on the stage didn't cheer her up; bouquets fairly showered on her . . . but she didn't even smile! She gave one look at the gold inkstand—and put it aside! She used to complain that no one had written the real part for her, as she conceived it. And her singing she'd given up altogether. It was my fault, my dear boy! . . . I told her that you thought she'd no musical knowledge. But for all that . . . why she poisoned herself—is incomprehensible! And the way she did it! . . ."

"In what part had she the greatest success?" . . . Aratov wanted to know in what part she had appeared for the last time, but for some reason he asked a different question.

"In Ostrovosky's *Gruna*, as far as I remember. But I tell

you again she'd no love affairs! You may be sure of that from one thing. She lived in her mother's house. . . . You know the sort of shopkeepers' houses: in every corner a holy picture and a little lamp before it, a deadly stuffiness, a sour smell, nothing but chairs along the walls in the drawing-room, a geranium in the window, and if a visitor drops in, the mistress sighs and groans, as if they were invaded by an enemy. What chance is there for gallantry or lovemaking? Sometimes they wouldn't even admit me. Their servant, a muscular female, in a red sarafan, with an enormous bust, would stand right across the passage, and growl, 'Where are you coming?' No, I positively can't understand why she poisoned herself. Sick of life, I suppose," Kupfer concluded his cogitations philosophically.

Aratov sat with downcast head. "Can you give me the address of that house in Kazan?" he said at last.

"Yes; but what do you want it for? Do you want to write a letter there?"

"Perhaps."

"Well, you know best. But the old lady won't answer, for she can't read and write. The sister, though, perhaps . . . Oh, the sister's a clever creature! But I must say again, I wonder at you, my dear boy! Such indifference before . . . and now such interest! All this, my boy, comes from too much solitude!"

Aratov made no reply, and went away, having provided himself with the Kazan address.

When he was on his way to Kupfer's, excitement, bewilderment, expectation had been reflected on his face. . . . Now he walked with an even gait, with downcast eyes, and hat pulled over his brows; almost every one who met him sent a glance of curiosity after him . . . but he did not observe any one who passed . . . it was not as on the Tversky boulevard!

"Unhappy Clara! poor frantic Clara!" was echoing in his soul.

X

The following day Aratov spent, however, fairly quietly. He was even able to give his mind to his ordinary occupations. But there was one thing: both during his work and during his leisure he was continually thinking of Clara, of what Kupfer had told him the evening before. It is true that his meditations, too, were of a fairly tranquil character. He fancied that this strange girl interested him from the psychological point of view, as something of the nature of a riddle, the solution of which was worth racking his brains over. "Ran away with an actress living as a kept mistress," he pondered, "put herself under the protection of that princess, with whom she seems to have lived—and no *love affairs*? It's incredible! . . . Kupfer talked of pride! But in the first place we know" (Aratov ought to have said: we have read in books), . . . "we know that pride can exist side by side with levity of conduct; and secondly, how came she, if she were so proud, to make an appointment with a man who might treat her with contempt . . . and did treat her with it . . . and in a public place, moreover . . . in a boulevard!" At this point Aratov recalled all the scene in the boulevard, and he asked himself, Had he really shown contempt for Clara? "No," he decided, . . . "it was another feeling . . . a feeling of doubt . . . lack of confidence, in fact!" "Unhappy Clara!" was again ringing in his head. "Yes, unhappy," he decided again. . . . "That's the most fitting word. And, if so, I was unjust. She said truly that I did not understand her. A pity! Such a remarkable creature, perhaps, came so close . . . and I did not take advantage of it, I repulsed her. . . . Well, no matter! Life's all before me. There will be, very likely, other meetings, perhaps more interesting!

"But on what grounds did she fix on *me* of all the world?" He glanced into a looking-glass by which he was passing. "What is there special about me? I'm not a beauty, am I? My face . . . is like any face. . . . She was not a beauty either, though.

"Not a beauty . . . and such an expressive face! Immobile

. . . and yet expressive! I never met such a face. . . . And talent, too, she has . . . that is, she had, unmistakable. Untrained, undeveloped, even coarse, perhaps . . . but unmistakable talent. And in that case I was unjust to her.'' Aratov was carried back in thought to the literary musical matinée . . . and he observed to himself how exceedingly clearly he recollected every word she had sung or recited, every intonation of her voice. . . . ''That would not have been so had she been without talent. And now it is all in the grave, to which she has hastened of herself. . . . But I've nothing to do with that . . . I'm not to blame! It would be positively ridiculous to suppose that I'm to blame.''

It again occurred to Aratov that even if she had had ''anything of the sort'' in her mind, his behavior during their interview must have effectually disillusioned her. . . . ''That was why she laughed so cruelly, too, at parting. Besides, what proof is there that she took poison because of unrequited love? That's only the newspaper correspondents, who ascribe every death of that sort to unrequited love! People of a character like Clara's readily feel life repulsive . . . burdensome. Yes, burdensome. Kupfer was right; she was simply sick of life.

''In spite of her successes, her triumphs?'' Aratov mused. He got a positive pleasure from the psychological analysis to which he was devoting himself. Remote till now from all contact with women, he did not even suspect all the significance for himself of this intense realization of a woman's soul.

''It follows,'' he pursued his meditations, ''that art did not satisfy her, did not fill the void in her life. Real artists exist only for art, for the theater. . . . Everything else is pale beside what they regard as their vocation. . . . She was a dilettante.''

At this point Aratov fell to pondering again. ''No, the word dilettante did not accord with that face, the expression of that face, those eyes. . . .''

And Clara's image floated again before him, with eyes, swimming in tears, fixed upon him, with clenched hands pressed to her lips. . . .

"Ah, no, no," he muttered, "what's the use?"

So passed the whole day. At dinner Aratov talked a great deal with Platosha, questioned her about the old days, which she remembered, but described very badly, as she had so few words at her command, and except her dear Yasha, had scarcely ever noticed anything in her life. She could only rejoice that he was nice and good-humored to-day; towards evening Aratov was so far calm that he played several games of cards with his aunt.

So passed the day . . . but the night!

XI

It began well; he soon fell asleep, and when his aunt went into him on tip-toe to make the sign of the cross three times over him in his sleep—she did so every night—he lay breathing as quietly as a child. But before dawn he had a dream.

He dreamed he was on a bare steppe, strewn with big stones, under a lowering sky. Among the stones curved a little path; he walked along it.

Suddenly there rose up in front of him something of the nature of a thin cloud. He looked steadily at it; the cloud turned into a woman in a white gown with a bright sash round her waist. She was hurrying away from him. He saw neither her face nor her hair . . . they were covered by a long veil. But he had an intense desire to overtake her, and to look into her face. Only, however much he hastened, she went more quickly than he.

On the path lay a broad flat stone, like a tombstone. It blocked up the way. The woman stopped. Aratov ran up to her; but yet he could not see her eyes . . . they were shut. Her face was white, white as snow; her hands hung lifeless. She was like a statue.

Slowly, without bending a single limb, she fell backwards, and sank down upon the tombstone. . . . And then Aratov lay down beside her, stretched out straight like a figure on a monument, his hands folded like a dead man's.

But now the woman suddenly rose, and went away. Aratov

tried to get up too . . . but he could neither stir nor unclasp his hands, and could only gaze after her in despair.

Then the woman suddenly turned round, and he saw bright living eyes, in a living but unknown face. She laughed, she waved her hand to him . . . and still he could not move.

She laughed once more, and quickly retreated, merrily nodding her head, on which there was a crimson wreath of tiny roses.

Aratov tried to cry out, tried to throw off this awful nightmare. . . .

Suddenly all was darkness around . . . and the woman came back to him. But this was not the unknown statue . . . it was Clara. She stood before him, crossed her arms, and sternly and intently looked at him. Her lips were tightly pressed together, but Aratov fancied he heard the words, "If you want to know what I am, come over here!"

"Where?" he asked.

"Here!" he heard the wailing answer. "Here!"

Aratov woke up.

He sat up in bed, lighted the candle that stood on the little table by his bedside—but did not get up—and sat a long while, chill all over, slowly looking about him. It seemed to him as if something had happened to him since he went to bed; that something had taken possession of him . . . something was in control of him. "But is it possible?" he murmured unconsciously. "Does such a power really exist?"

He could not stay in his bed. He quickly dressed, and till morning he was pacing up and down his room. And, strange to say, of Clara he never thought for a moment, and did not think of her, because he had decided to go next day to Kazan!

He thought only of the journey, of how to manage it, and what to take with him, and how he would investigate and find out everything there, and would set his mind at rest. "If I don't go," he reasoned with himself, "why, I shall go out of my mind!" He was afraid of that, afraid of his nerves. He was convinced that when once he had seen everything there with his own eyes, every obsession would vanish like that nightmare. "And it will be a week lost over the journey," he thought; "what is a week? else I shall never shake it off."

The rising sun shone into his room; but the light of day did not drive away the shadows of the night that lay upon him, and did not change his resolution.

Platosha almost had a fit when he informed her of his intention. She positively sat down on the ground . . . her legs gave way beneath her. "To Kazan? why to Kazan?" she murmured, her dim eyes round with astonishment. She would not have been more surprised if she had been told that her Yasha was going to marry the baker woman next door, or was starting for America. "Will you be long in Kazan?" "I shall be back in a week," answered Aratov, standing with his back half-turned to his aunt, who was still sitting on the floor.

Platonida Ivanova tried to protest more, but Aratov answered her in an utterly unexpected and unheard-of way: 'I'm not a child," he shouted, and he turned pale all over, his lips trembled, and his eyes glittered wrathfully. "I'm twenty-six, I know what I'm about, I'm free to do what I like! I suffer no one . . . give me the money for the journey, pack my box with my clothes and linen . . . and don't torture me! I'll be back in a week, Platosha," he added, in a somewhat softer tone.

Platosha got up, sighing and groaning, and, without further protest, crawled to her room. Yasha had alarmed her. "I've no head on my shoulders," she told the cook, who was helping her to pack Yasha's things; "no head at all, but a hive full of bees all a-buz and a-hum! He's going off to Kazan, my good soul, to Ka-a-zan!" The cook, who had observed their dvornik the previous evening talking for a long time with a police officer, would have liked to inform her mistress of this circumstance, but did not dare, and only reflected, "To Kazan! if only it's nowhere farther still!" Platonida Ivanovna was so upset that she did not even utter her usual prayer. "In such a calamity the Lord God Himself cannot aid us!"

The same day Aratov set off for Kazan.

XII

He had no sooner reached that town and taken a room in a hotel than he rushed off to find out the house of the widow Milovidov. During the whole journey he had been in a sort of benumbed condition, which had not, however, prevented him from taking all the necessary steps, changing at Nizhni-Novgorod from the railway to the steamer, getting his meals at the stations, etc., etc. He was convinced as before that *there* everything would be solved; and therefore he drove away every sort of memory and reflection, confining himself to one thing, the mental rehearsal of the *speech*, in which he would lay before the family of Clara Militch the real cause of his visit. And now at last he reached the goal of his efforts, and sent up his name. He was admitted . . . with perplexity and alarm—still he was admitted.

The house of the widow Milovidov turned out to be exactly as Kupfer had described it; and the widow herself really was like one of the tradesmen's wives in Ostrovsky, though the widow of an official; her husband had held his post under government. Not without some difficulty, Aratov, after a preliminary apology for his boldness, for the strangeness of his visit, delivered the speech he had prepared, explaining that he was anxious to collect all the information possible about the gifted artist so early lost, that he was not led to this by idle curiosity, but by profound sympathy for her talent, of which he was the devoted admirer (he said that, devoted admirer!), that, in fact, it would be a sin to leave the public in ignorance of what it had lost—and why its hopes were not realized. Madame Milovidov did not interrupt Aratov; she did not understand very well what this unknown visitor was saying to her, and merely opened her eyes rather wide and rolled them upon him, thinking, however, that he had a quiet respectable air, was well dressed . . . and not a pickpocket . . . hadn't come to beg.

"You are speaking of Katia?" she inquired, directly Aratov was silent.

"Yes . . . of your daughter."

"And you have come from Moscow for this?"

"Yes, from Moscow."

"Only on this account?"

"Yes."

Madame Milovidov gave herself a sudden shake. "Why, are you an author? Do you write for the newspapers?"

"No, I'm not an author—and hitherto I have not written for the newspapers."

The widow bowed her head. She was puzzled.

"Then, I suppose . . . it's from your own interest in the matter?" she asked suddenly. Aratov could not find an answer for the minute.

"Through sympathy, from respect for talent," he said at last.

The word "respect" pleased Madame Milovidov. "Eh!" she pronounced with a sigh . . . "I'm her mother, any way—and terribly I'm grieved for her. . . . Such a calamity all of a sudden! . . . But I must say it: a crazy girl she always was—and what a way to meet with her end! Such a disgrace. . . . Only fancy what it was for a mother? we must be thankful indeed that they gave her a Christian burial. . . ." Madame Milovidov crossed herself. "From a child up she minded no one—she left her parents' house . . . and at last—sad to say!—turned actress! Every one knows I never shut my doors upon her; I loved her, to be sure! I was her mother, any way! she'd no need to live with strangers . . . or to go begging! . . ." Here the widow shed tears . . . "But if you, my good sir," she began, again wiping her eyes with the ends of her kerchief, "really have any idea of the kind, and you are not intending anything dishonorable to us, but on the contrary, wish to show us respect, you'd better talk a bit with my other daughter. She'll tell you everything better than I can. . . . Annotchka!" called Madame Milovidov, "Annotchka, come here! Here is a worthy gentleman from Moscow wants to have a talk about Katia!"

There was a sound of something moving in the next room; but no one appeared. "Annotchka!" the widow called again, "Anna Semyonovna! come here, I tell you!"

The door softly opened, and in the doorway appeared a

girl no longer very young, looking ill—and plain—but with very soft and mournful eyes. Aratov got up from his seat to meet her, and introduced himself, mentioning his friend Kupfer. "Ah! Fyodor Fedoritch?" the girl articulated softly, and softly she sank into a chair.

"Now, then, you must talk to the gentleman," said Madam Milovidov, getting up heavily: "he's taken trouble enough, he's come all the way from Moscow on purpose—he wants to collect information about Katia. And will you, my good sir," she added, addressing Aratov—"excuse me . . . I'm going to look after my housekeeping. You can get a very good account of everything from Annotchka; she will tell you about the theatre . . . and all the rest of it. She is a clever girl, well educated: speaks French, and reads books as well as her sister did. One may say indeed she gave her her education . . . she was older—and so she looked after it."

Madame Milovidov withdrew. On being left alone with Anna Semyonovna, Aratov repeated his speech to her; but realizing at the first glance that he had to do with a really cultivated girl, not a typical tradesman's daughter, he went a little more into particulars and made use of different expressions; but towards the end he grew agitated, flushed and felt that his heart was throbbing. Anna listened to him in silence, her hands folded on her lap; a mournful smile never left her face . . . bitter grief, still fresh in its poignancy, was expressed in that smile.

"You knew my sister?" she asked Aratov.

"No, I did not actually know her," he answered. "I met her and heard her once . . . but one need only hear and see your sister once to . . ."

"Do you wish to write her biography?" Anna questioned him again.

Aratov had not expected this inquiry; however, he replied promptly, "Why not? But above all, I wanted to acquaint the public . . ."

Anna stopped him by a motion of her hand.

"What is the object of that? The public caused her plenty of suffering as it is; and indeed Katia had only just begun life. But if you yourself—(Anna looked at him and smiled again a smile as mournful but more friendly . . . as though she were saying to herself, Yes, you make me feel I can trust you) . . . if you yourself feel such interest in her, let me ask you to come and see us this afternoon . . . after dinner. I can't just now . . . so suddenly . . . I will collect my strength . . . I will make an effort . . . Ah, I loved her too much!''

Anna turned away; she was on the point of bursting into sobs.

Aratov rose hurriedly from his seat, thanked her for her offer, said he should be sure . . . oh, very sure!—to come—and went off, carrying away with him an impression of a soft voice, gentle and sorrowful eyes, and burning in the tortures of expectation.

XIII

Aratov went back the same day to the Milovidovs and spent three whole hours in conversation with Anna Semyonovna. Madame Milovidov was in the habit of lying down directly after dinner—at two o'clock—and resting till evening tea at seven. Aratov's talk with Clara's sister was not exactly a conversation; she did almost all the talking, at first with hesitation, with embarrassment, then with a warmth that refused to be stifled. It was obvious that she had adored her sister. The confidence Aratov had inspired in her grew and strengthened; she was no longer stiff; twice she even dropped a few silent tears before him. He seemed to her to be worthy to hear an unreserved account of all she knew and felt . . . in her own secluded life nothing of this sort had ever happened before! . . . As for him . . . he drank in every word she uttered.

This was what he learned . . . much of it, of course, half-said . . . much he filled in for himself.

In her early years, Clara had undoubtedly been a disagreeable child; and even as a girl, she had not been much gentler; self-willed, hot-tempered, sensitive, she had never got on with her father, whom she despised for his drunkenness and incapacity. He felt this and never forgave her for it. A gift for music showed itself early in her; her father gave it no encouragement, acknowledging no art but painting, in which he himself was so conspicuously unsuccessful though it was the means of support of himself and his family. Her mother Clara loved, . . . but in a careless way, as though she were her nurse; her sister she adored, though she fought with her and had even bitten her. . . . It is true she fell on her knees afterwards and kissed the place she had bitten. She was all fire, all passion, and all contradiction; revengeful and kind; magnanimous and vindictive; she believed in fate—and did not believe in God (these words Anna whispered with horror); she loved everything beautiful, but never troubled herself about her own looks, and dressed anyhow; she could not bear to have young men courting her, and yet in books she only read the pages which treated of love; she did not care to be liked, did not like caresses, but never forgot a caress, just as she never forgot a slight; she was afraid of death and killed herself! She used to say sometimes, "Such a one as I want I shall never meet . . . and no other will I have!" "Well, but if you meet him?" Anna would ask. "If I meet him . . . I will capture him." "And if he won't let himself be captured?" "Well, then . . . I will make an end of myself. It will prove I am no good." Clara's father—he used sometimes when drunk to ask his wife, "Who got you your blackbrowed she-devil there? Not I!"—Clara's father, anxious to get her off his hands as soon as possible, betrothed her to a rich young shopkeeper, a great blockhead, one of the so-called "refined" sort. A fortnight before the wedding-day—she was only sixteen at the time—she went up to her betrothed, her arms folded and her fingers drumming on her elbows—her favorite position—and suddenly gave him a slap on his rosy cheek with her large powerful hand! He jumped and merely gaped; it must be said he was head over ears in love with her . . . He asked: "What's that for?" She laughed scornfully and walked off. "I was there in the room," Anna related, "I saw it all, I ran after her and said to her, 'Katia, why did you do that, really?' And she answered me: 'If he'd been a real man he would have punished me, but he's no more pluck than a drowned hen! And then he asks, "What's that for?"

If he loves me, and doesn't bear malice, he had better put up with it and not ask, "What's that for?" I will never be anything to him—never, never!' And indeed she did not marry him. It was soon after that she made the acquaintance of that actress, and left her home. Mother cried, but father only said, 'A stubborn beast is best away from the flock!' And he did not bother about her, or try to find her out. My father did not understand Katia. On the day before her flight," added Anna, "she almost smothered me in her embraces, and kept repeating: 'I can't, I can't help it! . . . My heart's torn, but I can't help it! your cage is too small . . . it cramps my wings! And there's no escaping one's fate. . . .'

"After that," observed Anna, "we saw each other very seldom. . . . When my father died, she came for a couple of days, would take nothing of her inheritance, and vanished again. She was unhappy with us . . . I could see that. Afterwards she came to Kazan as an actress."

Aratov began questioning Anna about the theater, about the parts in which Clara had appeared, about her triumphs. . . . Anna answered in detail, but with the same mournful, though keen fervor. She even showed Aratov a photograph, in which Clara had been taken in the costume of one of her parts. In the photograph she was looking away, as though turning from the spectators; her thick hair tied with a ribbon fell in a coil on her bare arm. Aratov looked a long time at the photograph, thought it like, asked whether Clara had taken part in public recitations, and learnt that she had not; that she had needed the excitement of the theatre, the scenery . . . but another question was burning on his lips.

"Anna Semyonovna!" he cried at last, not loudly, but with a peculiar force, "tell me, I implore you, tell me why did she . . . what led her to this fearful step?" . . .

Anna looked down. "I don't know," she said, after a pause of some instants. "By God, I don't know!" she went on strenuously, supposing from Aratov's gesture that he did not believe her. . . . "Since she came back here certainly she was melancholy, depressed. Something must have happened to her in Moscow—what, I could never guess. But on the other hand, on that fatal day she seemed as it were . . . if not more cheerful, at least more serene than usual. Even I had no presentiment,'' added Anna with a bitter smile, as though reproaching herself for it.

"You see,'' she began again, "it seemed as though at Katia's birth it had been decreed that she was to be unhappy. From her early years she was convinced of it. She would lean her head on her hand, sink into thought, and say, 'I shall not live long!' She used to have presentiments. Imagine! she used to see beforehand, sometimes in a dream and sometimes awake, what was going to happen to her! 'If I can't live as I want to live, then I won't live,' . . . was a saying of hers too. . . . 'Our life's in our own hands, you know.' And she proved that!''

Anna hid her face in her hands and stopped speaking. "Anna Semyonovna,'' Aratov began after a short pause, "you have perhaps heard to what the newspapers ascribed . . . 'To an unhappy love affair?' '' Anna broke in, at once pulling away her hands from her face. "That's a slander, a fabrication! . . . My pure, unapproachable Katia . . . Katia! . . . an unhappy, unrequited love? And shouldn't I have known of it? . . . Every one was in love with her . . . while she . . . And whom could she have fallen in love with here? Who among all the people here, who was worthy of her? Who was up to the standard of honesty, truth, purity . . . yes, above all, of purity which she, with all her faults, always held up as an ideal before her? . . . She repulsed! . . . she! . . .''

Anna's voice broke. . . . Her fingers were trembling. All at once she flushed crimson . . . crimson with indignation, and for that instant, and that instant only, she was like her sister.

Aratov was beginning an apology.

"Listen,'' Anna broke in again. "I have an intense desire that you should not believe that slander, and should refute it, if possible! You want to write an article or something about her: that's your opportunity for defending her memory! That's why I talk so openly to you. Let me tell you; Katia left a diary . . .''

Aratov trembled. "A diary?'' he muttered.

"Yes, a diary . . . that is, only a few pages. Katia was not fond of writing . . . for months at a time she would write nothing, and her letters were so short. But she was always, always truthful, she never told a lie. . . . She, with her pride, tell a lie! I . . . I will show you this diary! You shall see for yourself whether there is the least hint in it of any unhappy love affair!''

Anna quickly took out of a table-drawer a thin exercise-book, ten pages, no more, and held it out to Aratov. He seized it eagerly, recognized the irregular sprawling hand-writing, the handwriting of that anonymous letter, opened it at random, and at once lighted upon the following lines.

"Moscow, Tuesday . . . June.—Sang and recited at a literary matinée. To-day is a vital day for me. *It must decide my fate.* (These words were twice underlined.) I saw again . . .'' Here followed a few lines carefully erased. And then, "No! no! no! . . . Must go back to the old way, if only . . .''

Aratov dropped the hand that held the diary, and his head slowly sank upon his breast.

"Read it!'' cried Anna. "Why don't you read it? Read it through from the beginning. . . . It would take only five min-utes to read it all, though the diary extends over two years. In Kazan she used to write down nothing at all. . . . ''

Aratov got up slowly from his chair and flung himself on his knees before Anna.

She was simply petrified with wonder and dismay.

"Give me . . . give me that diary,'' Aratov began with failing voice, and he stretched out both hands to Anna. "Give it me . . . and the photograph . . . you are sure to have some other one, and the diary I will return. . . . But I want it, oh, I want it! . . .''

In his imploring words, in his contorted features there was something so despairing that it looked positively like rage, like agony . . . And he was in agony, truly. He could not himself have foreseen that such pain could be felt by him, and in a frenzy he implored forgiveness, deliverance . . .

"Give it me,'' he repeated.

"But . . . you . . . you were in love with my sister?'' Anna said at last.

Aratov was still on his knees.

"I only saw her twice . . . believe me! . . . and if I had not been impelled by causes, which I can neither explain nor fully understand myself, . . . if there had not been some power over me, stronger than myself . . . I should not be entreating you . . . I should not have come here. I want . . . I must . . . you yourself said I ought to defend her memory!"

"And you were not in love with my sister?" Anna asked a second time.

Aratov did not at once reply, and he turned aside a little, as though in pain.

"Well, then! I was! I was—I'm in love now," he cried in the same tone of despair.

Steps were heard in the next room.

"Get up . . . get up . . ." said Anna hurriedly. "Mamma is coming."

Aratov rose.

"And take the diary and the photograph, in God's name! Poor, poor Katia! . . . But you will give me back the diary," she added emphatically. "And if you write anything, be sure to send it me. . . . Do you hear?"

The entrance of Madame Milovidov saved Aratov from the necessity of a reply. He had time, however, to murmur, "You are an angel! Thanks! I will send anything I write. . . ."

Madame Milovidov, half awake, did not suspect anything. So Aratov left Kazan with the photograph in the breast-pocket of his coat. The diary he gave back to Anna; but, unobserved by her, he cut out the page on which were the words underlined.

On the way back to Moscow he relapsed again into a state of petrification. Though he was secretly delighted that he had attained the object of his journey, still all thoughts of Clara he deferred till he should be back at home. He thought much more about her sister Anna. "There," he thought, "is an exquisite, charming creature. What delicate comprehension of everything, what a loving heart, what a complete absence of egoism! And how girls like that spring up among us, in the provinces, and in such surroundings too! She is not strong, and not good-looking, and not young; but what a splendid helpmate she would be for a sensible, cultivated man! That's the girl I ought to have fallen in love with!'' Such were Aratov's reflections . . . but on his arrival in Moscow things put on quite a different complexion.

XIV

Platonida Ivanovna was unspeakably rejoiced at her nephew's return. There was no terrible chance she had not imagined during his absence. ''Siberia at least!'' she muttered, sitting rigidly still in her little room; ''at least for a year!'' The cook too had terrified her by the most well-authenticated stories of the disappearance of this and that young man of the neighborhood. The perfect innocence and absence of revolutionary ideas in Yasha did not in the least reassure the old lady. ''For indeed . . . if you come to that, he studies photography . . . and that's quite enough for them to arrest him!'' And behold, here was her darling Yasha back again, safe and sound. She observed, indeed, that he seemed thinner, and looked hollow in the face; natural enough, with no one to look after him! but she did not venture to question him about his journey. She asked at dinner. ''And is Kazan a fine town?'' ''Yes,'' answered Aratov. ''I suppose they're all Tartars living there?'' ''Not only Tartars.'' ''And did you get a Kazan dressing-gown while you were there?'' ''No, I didn't.'' With that the conversation ended.

But as soon as Aratov found himself alone in his own room, he quickly felt as though something were enfolding him about, as though he were once more *in the power*, yes, in the power of another life, another being. Though he had indeed said to Anna in that sudden delirious outburst that he was in love with Clara, that saying struck even him now as senseless and frantic. No, he was not in love; and how could he be in love with a dead woman, whom he had not even liked in her lifetime, whom he had almost forgotten? No, but he was in *her* power . . . he no longer belonged to himself. He was *captured*. So completely captured, that he did not even attempt to free himself by laughing at his own absurdity, nor by trying to arouse if not a conviction, at least a hope in himself that it would all pass, that it was nothing but nerves, nor by seeking for proofs, nor by anything! "If I meet him, I will capture him," he recalled those words of Clara's Anna had repeated to him. Well, he was captured. But was not she dead? Yes, her body was dead . . . but her soul? . . . is not that immortal? . . . does it need corporeal organs to show its power? Magnetism has proved to us the influence of one living human soul over another living human soul. . . . Why should not this influence last after death, if the soul remains living? But to what end? What can come of it? But can we, as a rule, apprehend what is the object of all that takes place about us? These ideas so absorbed Aratov that he suddenly asked Platosha at tea-time whether she believed in the immortality of the soul. She did not for the first minute understand what his question was, then she crossed herself and answered. "She should think so indeed! The soul not immortal!" "And, if so, can it have any influence after death?" Aratov asked again. The old lady replied that it could . . . pray for us, that is to say; at least, when it had passed through all its ordeals, awaiting the last dread judgment. But for the first forty days the soul simply hovered about the place where its death had occurred.

"The first forty days?"

"Yes; and then the ordeals follow."

Aratov was astounded at his aunt's knowledge, and went off to his room. And again he felt the same thing, the same power over him. This power showed itself in Clara's image being constantly before him to the minutest details, such details as he seemed hardly to have observed in her lifetime; he saw . . . saw her fingers, her nails, the little hairs on her cheeks near her temples, the little mole under her left eye; he saw the slight movement of her lips, her nostrils, her eyebrows . . . and her walk, and how she held her head a little on the right side . . . he saw everything. He did not by any means take a delight in it all, only he could not help thinking of it and seeing it. The first night after his return he did not, however, dream of her . . . he was very tired, and slept like a log. But directly he waked up, she came back into his room again, and seemed to establish herself in it, as though she were the mistress, as though by her voluntary death she had purchased the right to it, without asking him or needing his permission. He took up her photograph, he began reproducing it, enlarging it. Then he took it into his head to fit it to the stereoscope. He had a great deal of trouble to do it . . . at last he succeeded. He fairly shuddered when through the glass he looked upon her figure, with the semblance of corporeal solidity given it by the stereoscope. But the figure was grey, as though covered with dust . . . and moreover the eyes—the eyes looked always to one side, as though turning away. A long, long while he stared at them, as though expecting them to turn to him . . . he even half-closed his eyelids on purpose . . . but the eyes remained immovable, and the whole figure had the look of some sort of doll. He moved away, flung himself in an armchair, took out the leaf from her diary, with the words underlined, and thought, "Well, lovers, they say, kiss the words traced by the hand of the beloved—but I feel no inclination to do that—and the handwriting I think ugly. But that line contains my sentence." Then he recalled the promise he had made Anna about the article. He sat down to the table, and set to work upon it, but everything he wrote struck him as so false, so rhetorical . . . especially so false . . . as though he did not believe in what he was writing nor in his own feelings. . . . And Clara herself seemed so utterly unknown and uncomprehended! She seemed to withhold herself from him. "No!" he thought, throwing down the pen . . . "either authorship's altogether not my line, or I must wait a little!" He fell to recalling his visit to the Milovidovs, and all Anna had told him, that sweet, delightful Anna. . . . A word she had uttered—"pure"—suddenly struck him. It was as though something scorched him, and shed light. "Yes," he said aloud, "she was pure, and I am pure. . . . That's what gave her this power."

Thoughts of the immortality of the soul, of the life beyond the grave, crowded upon him again. Was it not said in the Bible: "Death, where is thy sting?" And in Schiller: "And the dead shall live!" *(Auch die Todten sollen leben!)*

And too, he thought, in Mitskevitch: "I will love thee to

the end of time . . . and beyond it!'' And an English writer had said: ''Love is stronger than death.'' The text from Scripture produced particular effect on Aratov. . . . He tried to find the place where the words occurred. . . . He had no Bible; he went to ask Platosha for one. She wondered, she brought out, however, a very old book in a wrapped leather binding, with copper clasps, covered with candle wax, and handed it over to Aratov. He bore it off to his own room, but for a long time he could not find the text . . . he stumbled, however, on another: ''Greater love hath no man than this, that a man lay down his life for his friends'' (S. John xv. 13).

He thought: ''That's not right. It ought to be: Greater *power* hath no man.''

''But if she did not lay down her life for me at all? If she made an end of herself simply because life had become a burden to her? What if, after all, she did not come to that meeting for anything to do with love at all?''

But at that instant he pictured to himself Clara before their parting on the boulevard. . . . He remembered the look of pain on her face, and the tears and the words, ''Ah, you understood nothing!''

No! he could have no doubt why and for whom she had laid down her life. . . .

So passed that whole day till night-time.

XV

Aratov went to bed early, without feeling specially sleepy, but he hoped to find repose in bed. The strained condition of his nerves brought about an exhaustion far more unbearable than the bodily fatigue of the journey and the railway. However, exhausted as he was, he could not get to sleep. He tried to read . . . but the lines danced before his eyes. He put out the candle, and darkness reigned in his room. But still he lay sleepless, with his eyes shut. . . . And it began to seem to him some one was whispering in his ear. . . . ''The beating of the heart, the pulse of the blood,'' he thought. . . . But the whisper passed into connected speech.

Some one was talking in Russian hurriedly, plaintively, and indistinctly. Not one separate word could he catch. . . . But it was the voice of Clara.

Aratov opened his eyes, raised himself, leaned on his elbow. . . . The voice grew fainter, but kept up its plaintive, hurried talk, indistinct as before. . . .

It was unmistakably Clara's voice.

Unseen fingers ran light arpeggios up and down the keys of the piano . . . then the voice began again. More prolonged sounds were audible . . . as it were moans . . . always the same over and over again. Then apart from the rest the words began to stand out . . . "Roses . . . roses . . . roses. . . ."

"Roses," repeated Aratov in a whisper. "Ah, yes! it's the roses I saw on the woman's head in the dream." . . . "Roses," he heard again.

"Is that you?" Aratov asked in the same whisper. The voice suddenly ceased.

Aratov waited . . . and waited, and dropped his head on the pillow. "Hallucinations of hearing," he thought. "But if . . . if she really were here, close at hand? . . . If I were to see her, should I be frightened? or glad? But what should I be frightened of? or glad of? Why, of this, to be sure; it would be a proof that there is another world, that the soul is immortal. Though, indeed, even if I did see something, it too might be a hallucination of the sight. . . ."

He lighted the candle, however, and in a rapid glance, not without a certain dread, scanned the whole room . . . and saw nothing in it unusual. He got up, went to the stereoscope . . . again the same grey doll, with its eyes averted. The feeling of dread gave way to one of annoyance. He was, as it were, cheated in his expectations . . . the very expectation indeed struck him as absurd.

"Well, this is positively idiotic!" he muttered, as he got back into bed, and blew out the candle. Profound darkness reigned once more.

Aratov resolved to go to sleep this time. . . . But a fresh sensation started up in him. He fancied some one was standing in the middle of the room, not far from him, and scarcely perceptibly breathing. He turned round hastily and opened his eyes. . . . But what could be seen in impenetrable darkness? He began to feel for a match on his little bedside table . . . and suddenly it seemed to him that a sort of soft, noiseless hurricane was passing over the whole room, over him, through him, and the word "I!" sounded distinctly in his ears. . . .

"I! . . . I . . . !"

Some instants passed before he succeeded in getting the candle alight.

Again there was no one in the room; and he now heard nothing, except the uneven throbbing of his own heart. He drank a glass of water, and stayed still, his head resting on his hand. He was waiting.

He thought: "I will wait. Either it's all nonsense . . . or she is here. She is not going to play cat and mouse with me like this!" He waited, waited long . . . so long that the hand on which he was resting his head went numb . . . but not one of his previous sensations was repeated. Twice his eyes closed. . . . He opened them promptly . . . at least he believed that he opened them. Gradually they turned towards the door and rested on it. The candle burned dim, and it was once more dark in the room . . . but the door made a long streak of white in the half darkness. And now this patch began to move, to grow less, to disappear . . . and in its place, in the doorway, appeared a woman's figure. Aratov looked intently at it . . . Clara! And this time she was looking straight at him, coming towards him. . . . On her head was a wreath of red roses. . . . He was all in agitation, he sat up. . . .

Before him stood his aunt in a nightcap adorned with a broad red ribbon, and in a white dressing-jacket.

"Platosha!" he said with an effort. "Is that you?"

"Yes, it's I," answered Platonida Ivanovna . . . "I, Yasha darling, yes."

"What have you come for?"

"You waked me up. At first you kept moaning as it were . . . and then you cried out all of a sudden, 'Save me! help me!' "

"I cried out?"

"Yes, and such a hoarse cry, 'Save me!' I thought, Mercy on us! He's never ill, is he? And I came in. Are you quite well?"

"Perfectly well."

"Well, you must have had a bad dream then. Would you like me to burn a little incense?"

Aratov once more stared intently at his aunt, and laughed aloud. . . . The figure of the good old lady in her nightcap and dressing-jacket, with her long face and scared expression, was certainly very comic. All the mystery surrounding him, oppressing him—everything weird was sent flying instantaneously.

"No, Platosha dear, there's no need," he said. "Please forgive me for unwittingly troubling you. Sleep well, and I will sleep too."

Platonida Ivanovna remained a minute standing where she was, pointed to the candle, grumbled, "Why not put it out . . . an accident happens in a minute?" and as she went out, could not refrain, though only at a distance, from making the sign of the cross over him.

Aratov fell asleep quickly, and slept till morning. He even got up in a happy frame of mind . . . though he felt sorry for something. . . . He felt light and free. "What romantic fancies, if you come to think of it!" he said to himself with a smile. He never once glanced either at the stereoscope, or at the page torn out of the diary. Immediately after breakfast, however, he set off to go to Kupfer's.

What drew him there . . . he was dimly aware.

XVI

Aratov found his sanguine friend at home. He chatted a little with him, reproached him for having quite forgotten his aunt and himself, listened to fresh praises of that heart of gold, the princess, who had just sent Kupfer from Yaroslav a smoking-cap embroidered with fishscales . . . and all at once, sitting just opposite Kupfer and looking him straight in the face, he announced that he had been a journey to Kazan.

"You have been to Kazan; what for?"

"Oh, I wanted to collect some facts about that . . . Clara Militch."

"The one that poisoned herself?"

"Yes."

Kupfer shook his head. "Well, you are a chap! And so quiet about it! Toiled a thousand miles out there and back . . . for what? Eh? If there'd been some woman in the case now! Then I can understand anything! anything! any madness!" Kupfer ruffled up his hair. "But simply to collect materials, as it's called among you learned people. . . . I'd rather be excused! There are statistical writers to do that job! Well, and did you make friends with the old lady and the sister? Isn't she a delightful girl?"

"Delightful," answered Aratov, "she gave me a great deal of interesting information."

"Did she tell you exactly how Clara took poison?"

"You mean . . . how?"

"Yes, in what manner?"

"No . . . she was still in such grief . . . I did not venture to question her too much. Was there anything remarkable about it?"

"To be sure there was. Only fancy; she had to appear on the stage that very day, and she acted her part. She took a glass of poison to the theatre with her, drank it before the first act, and went through all that act afterwards. With the poison inside her! Isn't that something like strength of will? Character, eh? And, they say, she never acted her part with such feeling, such passion! The public suspected nothing, they clapped, and called for her. . . . And directly the curtain fell, she dropped down there, on the stage. Convulsions . . . and convulsions, and within an hour she was dead! But didn't I tell you all about it? And it was in the papers too!"

Aratov's hands had grown suddenly cold, and he felt an inward shiver.

"No, you didn't tell me that," he said at last. "And you don't know what play it was?"

Kupfer thought a minute. "I did hear what the play was . . . there is a betrayed girl in it. . . . Some drama, it must have been. Clara was created for dramatic parts. . . . Her very appearance . . . But where are you off to?'' Kupfer interrupted himself, seeing that Aratov was reaching after his hat.

''I don't feel quite well,'' replied Aratov. ''Good-bye . . . I'll come in another time.''

Kupfer stopped him and looked into his face. ''What a nervous fellow you are, my boy! Just look at yourself. . . . You're as white as chalk.''

''I'm not well,'' repeated Aratov, and, disengaging himself from Kupfer's detaining hands, he started homewards. Only at that instant it became clear to him that he had come to Kupfer with the sole object of talking of Clara . . .

''UNHAPPY CLARA, POOR FRANTIC CLARA. . . .''

On reaching home, however, he quickly regained his composure to a certain degree.

The circumstances accompanying Clara's death had at first given him a violent shock . . . but later on this performance ''with the poison inside her,'' as Kupfer had expressed it, struck him as a kind of monstrous pose, a piece of bravado, and he was already trying not to think about it, fearing to arouse a feeling in himself, not unlike repugnance. And at dinner, as he sat facing Platosha, he suddenly recalled her midnight appearance, recalled that abbreviated dressing-jacket, the cap with the high ribbon—and why a ribbon on a nightcap?—all the ludicrous apparition which, like the scene-shifter's whistle in a transformation scene, had dissolved all his visions into dust! He even forced Platosha to repeat her description of how she had heard his scream, had been alarmed, had jumped up, could not for a minute find either his door or her own, and so on. In the evening he played a game of cards with her, and went off to his room rather depressed, but again fairly composed.

Aratov did not think about the approaching night, and was not afraid of it: he was sure he would pass an excellent night. The thought of Clara had sprung up within him from time to time; but he remembered at once how ''affectedly'' she had killed herself, and turned away from it. This piece of "bad taste" blocked out all other memories of her. Glancing cursorily into the stereoscope, he even fancied that she was averting her eyes because she was ashamed. Opposite the stereoscope on the wall hung a portrait of his mother. Aratov took it from its nail, scrutinised it a long while, kissed it and carefully put it away in a drawer. Why did he do that? Whether it was that it was not fitting for this portrait to be so close to that woman . . . or for some other reason Aratov did not inquire of himself. But his mother's portrait stirred up memories of his father . . . of his father, whom he had seen dying in this very room, in this bed. "What do you think of all this, Father?" he mentally addressed himself to him. "You understand all this; you too believed in Schiller's world of spirits. Give me advice!"

"Father would have advised me to give up all this idiocy," Aratov said aloud, and he took up a book. He could not, however, read for long, and feeling a sort of heaviness all over, he went to bed earlier than usual, in the full conviction that he would fall asleep at once.

And so it happened . . . but his hopes of a quiet night were not realised.

XVII

It had not struck midnight when he had an extraordinary and terrifying dream.

He dreamed that he was in a rich manorhouse of which he was the owner. He had lately bought both the house and the estate attached to it. And he kept thinking, "It's nice, very nice now, but evil is coming!" Beside him moved to and fro a little tiny man, his steward; he kept laughing, bowing, and trying to show Aratov how admirably everything was arranged in his house and his estate. "This way, pray, this way, pray," he kept repeating, chuckling at every word; "kindly look how prosperous everything is with you! Look at the horses . . . what splendid horses!" And Aratov saw a row of immense horses. They were standing in their stalls with their backs to him; their manes and tails were magnificent . . . but as soon as Aratov went near, the horses' heads turned towards him, and they showed their teeth viciously. "It's very nice," Aratov thought! "but evil is coming!" "This way, pray, this way," the steward repeated again, "pray come into the garden: look what fine apples you have!" The apples certainly were fine, red, and round; but as soon as Aratov looked at them, they withered and fell . . . "Evil is coming," he thought. "And here is the lake," lisped the steward, "isn't it blue and smooth? And here's a little boat of gold . . . will you get into it? . . . it floats of itself." "I won't get into it," thought Aratov, "evil is coming!" and for all that he got into the boat. At the bottom lay huddled up a little creature like a monkey; it was holding in its paws a glass full of a dark liquid. "Pray don't be uneasy," the steward shouted from the bank . . . "It's of no consequence! It's death! Good luck to you!" The boat darted swiftly along . . . but all of a sudden a hurricane came swooping down on it, not like the hurricane of the night before, soft and noiseless—no; a black, awful, howling hurricane! Everything was confusion. And in the midst of the whirling darkness Aratov saw Clara in a stage-dress; she was lifting a glass to her lips, listening to shouts of "Bravo! bravo!" in the distance, and some coarse voice shouted in Aratov's ear: "Ah! did you think it would all end in a farce? No; it's a tragedy! a tragedy!"

Trembling all over, Aratov awoke. In the room it was not dark. . . . A faint light streamed in from somewhere, and showed every thing in the gloom and stillness. Aratov did not ask himself whence this light came. . . . He felt one thing only: Clara was there, in that room . . . he felt her presence . . . he was again and for ever in her power!

The cry broke from his lips, "Clara, are you here?"

"Yes!" sounded distinctly in the midst of the lighted, still room.

Aratov inaudibly repeated his question. . . .

"Yes!" he heard again.

"Then I want to see you!" he cried, and he jumped out of bed.

For some instants he stood in the same place, pressing his

bare feet on the chill floor. His eyes strayed about. "Where? where?" his lips were murmuring. . . .

Nothing to be seen, not a sound to be heard. . . . He looked round him, and noticed that the faint light that filled the room came from a night-light, shaded by a sheet of paper and set in a corner, probably by Platosha while he was asleep. He even discerned the smell of incense . . . also, most likely, the work of her hands.

He hurriedly dressed himself: to remain in bed, to sleep, was not to be thought of. Then he took his stand in the middle of the room, and folded his arms. The sense of Clara's presence was stronger in him than it had ever been.

And now he began to speak, not loudly, but with solemn deliberation, as though he were uttering an incantation.

"Clara," he began, "if you are truly here, if you see me, if you hear me—show yourself! . . . If the power which I feel over me is truly your power, show yourself! If you understand how bitterly I repent that I did not understand you, that I repelled you—show yourself! If what I have heard was truly your voice; if the feeling overmastering me is love; if you are now convinced that I love you, I, who till now have neither loved nor known any woman; if you know that since your death I have come to love you passionately, inconsolably; if you do not want me to go mad—show yourself, Clara!"

Aratov had hardly uttered this last word when all at once he felt that some one was swiftly approaching him from behind—as that day on the boulevard—and laying a hand on his shoulder. He turned round, and saw no one. But the sense of *her* presence had grown so distinct, so unmistakable, that once more he looked hurriedly about him. . . .

What was that? On an easy-chair, two paces from him, sat a woman, all in black. Her head was turned away, as in the stereoscope. . . . It was she! It was Clara! But what a stern, sad face!

Aratov slowly sank on his knees. Yes; he was right then. He felt neither fear nor delight, not even astonishment. . . . His heart even began to beat more quietly. He had one sense, one feeling, "Ah! at last! at last!"

"Clara," he began, in a faint but steady voice, "why do

you not look at me? I know that it is you . . . but I may fancy my imagination has created an image like *that one* . . ."—he pointed towards the stereoscope—"prove to me that it is you. . . . Turn to me, look at me, Clara!"

Clara's hand slowly rose . . . and fell again.

"Clara! Clara! turn to me!"

And Clara's head slowly turned, her closed lids opened, and her dark eyes fastened upon Aratov.

He fell back a little, and uttered a single, long-drawn-out, trembling "Ah!"

Clara gazed fixedly at him . . . but her eyes, her features, retained their former mournfully stern, almost displeased expression. With just that expression on her face she had come on to the platform on the day of the literary matinée, before she caught sight of Aratov. And, just as then, she suddenly flushed, her face brightened, her eyes kindled, and a joyful, triumphant smile parted her lips. . . .

"I have come!" cried Aratov. "You have conquered. . . . Take me! I am yours, and you are mine!"

He flew to her; he tried to kiss those smiling, triumphant lips, and he kissed them. He felt their burning touch: he even felt the moist chill of her teeth: and a cry of triumph rang through the half-dark room.

Platonida Ivanovna, running in, found him in a swoon. He was on his knees; his head was lying on the arm-chair; his outstretched arms hung powerless; his pale face was radiant with the intoxication of boundless bliss.

Platonida Ivanovna fairly dropped to the ground beside him; she put her arms round him, faltered, "Yasha! Yasha, darling! Yasha, dearest!" tried to lift him in her bony arms . . . he did not stir. Then Platonida Ivanovna fell to screaming in a voice unlike her own. The servant ran in. Together they somehow roused him, began throwing water over him— even took it from the holy lamp before the holy picture. . . .

He came to himself. But in response to his aunt's questions he only smiled, and with such an ecstatic face that she was more alarmed than ever, and kept crossing first herself and then him. . . . Aratov, at last, put aside her hand, and, still with the same ecstatic expression of face, said: "Why, Platosha, what is the matter with you?"

"What is the matter with you, Yasha darling?"

"With me? I am happy . . . happy, Platosha . . . that's what's the matter with me. And now I want to lie down, to sleep. . . ." He tried to get up, but felt such a sense of weakness in his legs, and in his whole body, that he could not, without the help of his aunt and the servant, undress and get into bed. But he fell asleep very quickly, still with the same look of blissful triumph on his face. Only his face was very pale.

XVIII

When Platonida Ivanovna came in to him next morning, he was still in the same position . . . but the weakness had not passed off and he actually preferred to remain in bed. Platonida Ivanovna did not like the pallor of his face at all. "Lord, have mercy on us! what is it?" she thought; "not a drop of blood in his face, refuses broth, lies there and smiles, and keeps declaring he's perfectly well!" He refused breakfast too. "What is the matter with you, Yasha?" she questioned him; "do you mean to lie in bed all day?" "And what if I did?" Aratov answered gently. This very gentleness again Platonida Ivanovna did not like at all. Aratov had the air of a man who has discovered a great, very delightful secret, and is jealously guarding it and keeping it to himself. He was looking forward to the night, not impatiently, but with curiosity. "What next?" he was asking himself; "what will happen?" Astonishment, incredulity, he had ceased to feel; he did not doubt that he was in communication with Clara, that they loved one another . . . that, too, he had no doubt about. Only . . . what could come of such love? He recalled that kiss . . . and a delicious shiver ran swiftly and sweetly through all his limbs. "Such a kiss," was his thought, "even Romeo and Juliet knew not! But next time I will be stronger. . . . I will master her. . . . She shall come with a wreath of tiny roses in her dark curls. . . .

"But what next? We cannot live together, can we? Then must I die so as to be with her? Is it not for that she has come; and is it not *so* she means to take me captive?

"Well; what then? If I must die, let me die. Death has no terrors for me now. It cannot, then, annihilate me? On the contrary, only *thus* and *there* can I be happy . . . as I have not been happy in life, as she has not. . . . We are both pure! Oh, that kiss!"

Platonida Ivanovna was incessantly coming into Aratov's room. She did not worry him with questions; she merely looked at him, muttered, sighed, and went out again. But he refused his dinner too: this was really too dreadful. The old lady set off to an acquaintance of hers, a district doctor, in whom she placed some confidence, simply because he did not drink and had a German wife. Aratov was surprised when she brought him in to see him; but Platonida Ivanovna so earnestly implored her darling Yashenka to allow Paramon Paramonitch (that was the doctor's name) to examine him—if only for her sake—that Aratov consented. Paramon Paramonitch felt his pulse, looked at his tongue, asked a question, and announced at last that it was absolutely necessary for him to "auscultate" him. Aratov was in such an amiable frame of mind that he agreed to this too. The doctor delicately uncovered his chest, delicately tapped, listened, hummed and hawed, prescribed some drops and a mixture, and, above all, advised him to keep quiet and avoid any excitement. "I dare say!" thought Aratov; "that idea's a little too late, my good friend!" "What is wrong with Yasha?" queried Platonida Ivanovna, as she slipped a three-rouble note into Paramon Paramonitch's hand in the doorway. The district doctor, who like all modern physicians—especially those who wear a government uniform—was fond of showing off with scientific terms, announced that her nephew's diagnosis showed all the symptoms of neurotic cardialgia, and there were febrile symptoms also. "Speak plainer, my dear sir; do," cut in Platonida Ivanovna; "don't terrify me with your Latin; you're not in your surgery!" "His heart's not right," the doctor explained; "and, well—there's a little fever too"

. . . and he repeated his advice as to perfect quiet and absence of excitement. "But there's no danger, is there?" Platonida Ivanovna inquired severely. ("You dare rush off into Latin again," she implied.) "No need to anticipate any at present!"

The doctor went away . . . and Platonida Ivanovna grieved. . . . She sent to the surgery, though, for the medicine, which Aratov would not take, in spite of her entreaties. He refused any herb-tea too. "And why are you so uneasy, dear?" he said to her; "I assure you, I'm at this moment the sanest and happiest man in the whole world!" Platonida Ivanovna could only shake her head. Towards evening he grew rather feverish; and still he insisted that she should not stay in his room, but should go to sleep in her own. Platonida Ivanovna obeyed; but she did not undress, and did not lie down. She sat in an arm-chair, and was all the while listening and murmuring her prayers.

She was just beginning to doze, when suddenly she was awakened by a terrible piercing shriek. She jumped up, rushed into Aratov's room, and as on the night before, found him lying on the floor.

But he did not come to himself as on the previous night, in spite of all they could do. He fell the same night into a high fever, complicated by failure of the heart.

A few days later he passed away.

A strange circumstance attended his second fainting-fit. When they lifted him up and laid him on his bed, in his clenched right hand they found a small tress of a woman's dark hair. Where did this lock of hair come from? Anna Semyonovna had such a lock of hair left by Clara; but what could induce her to give Aratov a relic so precious to her? Could she have put it somewhere in the diary, and not have noticed it when she lent the book?

In the delirium that preceded his death, Aratov spoke of himself as Romeo . . . after the poison, spoke of marriage, completed and perfect; of his knowing now what rapture meant. Most terrible of all for Platosha was the minute when Aratov, coming a little to himself, and seeing her beside his bed, said to her, "Aunt, what are you crying for?—because

I must die? But don't you know that love is stronger than death? . . . Death! death! where is thy sting? You should not weep, but rejoice, even as I rejoice. . . .''

And once more on the face of the dying man shone out the rapturous smile, which gave the poor old woman such cruel pain.

Robert W. Chambers

THE REPAIRER OF REPUTATIONS

Robert W. Chambers' first book, *The King in Yellow* (1895), is a monument in the development of horror literature in the U.S. In the stories therein, Chambers achieved a unique blend of Poe, Ambrose Bierce and the decadence of Wilde and Beardsley to produce a landmark collection. "The Yellow Sign" is generally accorded the primary status in the book as a masterpiece of horror, but the lead story, "The Repairer of Reputations," is in some ways an even more extraordinary achievement, a horrific tale that is also a sophisticated, avant garde work of science fiction set in New York twenty-five years in the future after the great war with Germany, a world of revolutions and suicide parlors, unconventional in many ways. Chambers became rich and famous as a novelist of romance and of historical adventure, and rarely returned to horror, never again reaching the heights of perfervid intensity of the stories in *The King in Yellow*. It is now obvious that great horror stories exist in all the sub-genres of fiction, and that SF, with its concern with alternate realities, is a particularly amenable genre for the horror writer. Many of the stories that contribute to the evolution of SF are also in fact horror; none more powerful than "The Repairer of Reputations."

I

"Ne raillon pas les fous; leur folie dure plus longtemps
que la nôtre . . . Voilà toute la différence."

Toward the end of the year 1920 the Government of the
United States had practically completed the programme,
adopted during the last months of President Winthrop's ad-
ministration. The country was apparently tranquil. Everybody knows how the Tariff and Labor questions were settled.
The war with Germany, incident on that country's seizure of
the Samoan Islands, had left no visible scars upon the republic, and the temporary occupation of Norfolk by the invading
army had been forgotten in the joy over repeated naval vic-
tories and the subsequent ridiculous plight of General Von
Gartenlaube's forces in the State of New Jersey. The Cuban
and Hawaiian investments had paid one hundred per cent,
and the territory of Samoa was well worth its cost as a coal-
ing station. The country was in a superb state of defence.
Every coast city had been well supplied with land fortifications; the army under the parental eye of the General Staff,
organized according to the Prussian system, had been
increased to 300,000 men with a territorial reserve of a million; and six magnificent squadrons of cruisers and battle-
ships patrolled the six stations of the navigable seas, leaving
a steam reserve amply fitted to control home waters. The
gentlemen from the West had at last been constrained to acknowledge that a college for the training of diplomats was as
necessary as law schools are for the training of barristers.
Consequently we were no longer represented abroad by incompetent patriots. The nation was prosperous. Chicago, for
a moment paralyzed after a second great fire, had risen from
its ruins, white and imperial, and more beautiful than the
white city which had been built for its plaything in 1893.
Everywhere good architecture was replacing bad, and even
in New York, a sudden craving for decency had swept away
a great portion of the existing horrors. Streets had been wid-

ened, properly paved and lighted, trees had been planted, squares laid out, elevated structures demolished and underground roads built to replace them. The new government buildings and barracks were fine bits of architecture, and the long system of stone quays which completely surrounded the island had been turned into parks which proved a godsend to the population. The subsidizing of the state theatre and state opera brought its own reward. The United States National Academy of Design was much like European institutions of the same kind. Nobody envied the Secretary of Fine Arts, either his cabinet position or his portfolio. The Secretary of Forrestry and Game Preservation had a much easier time, thanks to the new system of National Mounted Police. We had profited well by the latest treaties with France and England; the exclusion of foreign-born Jews as a measure of national self-preservation, the settlement of the new independent negro state of Suanee, the checking of immigration, the new laws concerning naturalization, and the gradual centralization of power in the executive all contributed to national calm and prosperity. When the Government solved the Indian problem and squadrons of Indian cavalry scouts in native costume were substituted for the pitiable organizations tacked on to the tail of skeletonized regiments by a former Secretary of War, the nation drew a long sigh of relief. When, after the colossal Congress of Religions, bigotry and intolerance were laid in their graves and kindness and charity began to draw warring sects together, many thought the millennium had arrived, at least in the new world, which after all is a world by itself.

But self-preservation is the first law, and the United States had to look on in helpless sorrow as Germany, Italy, Spain and Belgium writhed in the throes of Anarchy, while Russia, watching from the Caucasus, stooped and bound them one by one.

In the city of New York the summer of 1899 was signalized by the dismantling of the Elevated Railroads. The summer of 1900 will live in the memories of New York people for many a cycle; the Dodge Statue was removed in that year. In the following winter began that agitation for the repeal of the laws prohibiting suicide, which bore its final fruit in the month of April, 1920, when the first Government Lethal Chamber was opened on Washington Square.

I had walked down that day from Dr. Archer's house on Madison Avēnue, where I had been as a mere formality. Ever since that fall from my horse, four years before, I had been troubled at times with pains in the back of my head and neck, but now for months they had been absent, and the doctor sent me away that day saying there was nothing more to be cured in me. It was hardly worth his fee to be told that; I knew it myself. Still I did not grudge him the money. What I minded was the mistake which he made at first. When they picked me up from the pavement where I lay unconscious, and somebody had mercifully sent a bullet through my horse's head, I was carried to Doctor Archer, and he, pronouncing my brain affected, placed me in his private asylum where I was obliged to endure treatment for insanity. At last he decided that I was well, and I, knowing that my mind had always been as sound as his, if not sounder, "paid my tuition" as he jokingly called it, and left. I told him, smiling, that I would get even with him for his mistake, and he laughed heartily, and asked me to call once in a while. I did so, hoping for a chance to even up accounts, but he gave me none, and I told him I would wait.

The fall from my horse had fortunately left no evil results; on the contrary, it had changed my whole character for the better. From a lazy young man about town, I had become active, energetic, temperate, and above all—oh, above all else—ambitious. There was only one thing which troubled me. I laughed at my own uneasiness, and yet it troubled me.

During my convalescence I had bought and read for the first time *The King in Yellow*. I remember after finishing the first act that it occurred to me that I had better stop. I started up and flung the book into the fireplace; the volume struck the barred grate and fell open on the hearth in the fire-light. If I had not caught a glimpse of the opening words in the second act I should never have finished it, but as I stooped to pick it up, my eyes became riveted to the open page, and with a cry of terror, or perhaps it was of joy so poignant that I suffered in every nerve, I snatched the thing out of the coals and crept shaking to my bedroom, where I read it and reread it, and wept and laughed and trembled with a horror which at times assails me yet. This is the thing that troubles me, for I cannot forget Carcosa where black stars hang in the heavens; where the shadows of men's thoughts lengthen in the afternoon, when the twin suns sink into the Lake of Hali; and my mind will bear forever the memory of the Pallid Mask. I pray God will curse the writer, as the writer has cursed the world with this beautiful, stupendous creation, terrible in its simplicity, irresistible in its truth—a world which now trembles before the King in Yellow. When the French Government seized the translated copies which had just arrived in Paris, London, of course, became eager to read it. It is well known how the book spread like an infectious disease, from city to city, from continent to continent, barred out here, confiscated there, denounced by press and pulpit, censured even by the most advanced of literary anarchists. No definite principles had been violated in those wicked pages, no doctrine promulgated, no convictions outraged. It could not be judged by any known standard, yet, although it was acknowledged that the supreme note of art had been struck in *The King in Yellow*, all felt that human nature could not bear the strain, nor thrive on words in which the essence of purest poison lurked. The very banality and innocence of the first act only allowed the blow to fall afterward with more awful effect.

It was, I remember, the 13th day of April, 1920, that the first Government Lethal Chamber was established on the south side of Washington Square, between Wooster Street and South Fifth Avenue. The block which had formerly consisted of a lot of shabby old buildings, used as cafés and restaurants for foreigners, had been acquired by the Government in the winter of 1898. The French and Italian cafés and restaurants were torn down; the whole block was enclosed by a gilded iron railing, and converted into a lovely garden with lawns, flowers and fountains. In the centre of the garden stood a small, white building, severely classical in architecture, and surrounded by thickets of flowers. Six Ionic columns supported the roof, and the single door was of bronze. A splendid marble group of "The Fates" stood before the door, the work of a young American sculptor, Boris Yvain, who had died in Paris when only twenty-three years old.

The inauguration ceremonies were in progress as I crossed University Place and entered the square. I threaded my way through the silent throng of spectators, but was stopped at Fourth Street by a cordon of police. A regiment of United States lancers were drawn up in a hollow square around the Lethal Chamber. On a raised tribune facing Washington Park stood the Governor of New York, and behind him were grouped the Mayor of New York and Brooklyn, the Inspector-General of Police, the Commandant of the state troops, Colonel Livingston, military aide to the President of the United States, General Blount, commanding at Governor's Island, Major-General Hamilton, commanding the garrison of New York and Brooklyn, Admiral Buffby of the fleet in the North River, Surgeon General Lanceford, the staff of the National Free Hospital, Senators Wyse and Franklin of New York, and the Commissioner of Public Works. The tribune was surrounded by a squadron of hussars of the National Guard.

The Governor was finishing his reply to the short speech of the Surgeon-General. I heard him say: ''The laws prohibiting suicide and providing punishment for any attempt at self-destruction have been repealed. The Government has seen fit to acknowledge the right of man to end an existence which may have become intolerable to him, through physical suffering or mental despair. It is believed that the community will be benefited by the removal of such people from their midst. Since the passage of this law, the number of suicides in the United States has not increased. Now that the Government has determined to establish a Lethal Chamber in every city, town and village in the country, it remains to be seen whether or not that class of human creatures from whose desponding ranks new victims of self-destruction fall daily will accept the relief thus provided.'' He paused, and turned to the white Lethal Chamber. The silence in the street was absolute. ''There a painless death awaits him who can no longer bear the sorrows of this life. If death is welcome let him seek it there.'' Then quickly turning to the military aide of the President's household, he said, ''I declare the Lethal

Chamber open," and again facing the vast crowd, he cried in a clear voice: "Citizens of New York and of the United States of America, through me the Government declares the Lethal Chamber to be open."

The solemn hush was broken by a sharp cry of command, the squadron of hussars filed after the Governor's carriage, the lancers wheeled and formed along Fifth Avenue to wait for the commandant of the garrison, and the mounted police followed them. I left the crowd to gape and stare at the white marble Death Chamber, and, crossing South Fifth Avenue, walked along the western side of that thoroughfare to Bleecker Street. Then I turned to the right and stopped before a dingy shop which bore the sign,

HAWBERK, ARMORER.

I glanced into the doorway and saw Hawberk busy in his little shop at the end of the hall. He looked up at the same moment, and catching sight of me cried in his deep, hearty voice, "Come in, Mr. Castaigne!" Constance, his daughter, rose to meet me as I crossed the threshold, and held out her pretty hand, but I saw the blush of disappointment on her cheeks, and knew that it was another Castaigne she had expected, my cousin Louis. I smiled at her confusion and complimented her on the banner which she was embroidering from a colored plate. Old Hawberk sat riveting the worn greaves of some ancient suit of armor, and the ting! ting! ting! of his little hammer sounded pleasantly in the quaint shop. Presently he dropped his hammer, and fussed about for a moment with a tiny wrench. The soft clash of the mail sent a thrill of pleasure through me. I loved to hear the music of steel brushing against steel, the mellow shock of the mallet on thigh pieces, and the jingle of chain armor. That was the only reason I went to see Hawberk. He had never interested me personally, nor did Constance, except for the fact of her being in love with Louis. This did occupy my attention, and sometimes even kept me awake at night. But I knew in my heart that all would come right, and that I should arrange their future as I expected to arrange that of my kind doctor,

John Archer. However, I should never have troubled myself about visiting them just then had it not been, as I say, that the music of the tinkling hammer had for me this strong fascination. I would sit for hours, listening and listening, and when a stray sunbeam struck the inlaid steel, the sensation it gave me was almost too keen to endure. My eyes would become fixed, dilating with a pleasure that stretched every nerve almost to breaking, until some movement of the old armorer cut off the ray of sunlight, then, still thrilling secretly, I leaned back and listened again to the sound of the polishing rag, swish! swish! rubbing rust from the rivets.

Constance worked with the embroidery over her knees, now and then pausing to examine more closely the pattern in the colored plate from the Metropolitan Museum.

"Who is this for?" I asked.

Hawberk explained that in addition to the treasures of armor in the Metropolitan Museum of which he had been appointed armorer, he also had charge of several collections belonging to rich amateurs. This was the missing greave of a famous suit which a client of his had traced to a little shop in Paris on the Quai d'Orsay. He, Hawberk, had negotiated for and secured the greave, and now the suit was complete. He laid down his hammer and read me the history of the suit, traced since 1450 from owner to owner until it was acquired by Thomas Stainbridge. When his superb collection was sold, this client of Hawberk's bought the suit, and since then the search for the missing greave had been pushed until it was, almost by accident, located in Paris.

"Did you continue the search so persistently without any certainty of the greave being still in existence?" I demanded.

"Of course," he replied coolly.

Then for the first time I took a personal interest in Hawberk.

"It was worth something to you," I ventured.

"No," he replied, laughing, "my pleasure in finding it was my reward."

"Have you no ambition to be rich?" I asked, smiling.

"My one ambition is to be the best armorer in the world," he answered gravely.

Constance asked me if I had seen the ceremonies at the Lethal Chamber. She herself had noticed cavalry passing up Broadway that morning, and had wished to see the inauguration, but her father wanted the banner finished, and she had stayed at his request.

"Did you see your cousin, Mr. Castaigne, there?" she asked, with the slightest tremor of her soft eyelashes.

"No," I replied carelessly. "Louis' regiment is manoeuvring out in Westchester County." I rose and picked up my hat and cane.

"Are you going upstairs to see the lunatic again?" laughed old Hawberk. If Hawberk knew how I loathe that word "lunatic," he would never use it in my presence. It rouses certain feelings within me which I do not care to explain. However, I answered him quietly: "I think I shall drop in and see Mr. Wilde for a moment or two."

"Poor fellow," said Constance, with a shake of her head, "it must be hard to live alone year after year, poor, crippled and almost demented. It is very good of you, Mr. Castaigne, to visit him as often as you do."

"I think he is vicious," observed Hawberk, beginning again with his hammer. I listened to the golden tinkle on the greave plates; when he had finished I replied:

"No, he is not vicious, nor is he in the least demented. His mind is a wonder chamber, from which he can extract treasures that you and I would give years of our lives to acquire."

Hawberk laughed.

I continued a little impatiently: "He knows history as no one else could know it. Nothing, however trivial, escapes his search, and his memory is so absolute, so precise in details, that were it known in New York that such a man existed, the people could not honor him enough."

"Nonsense," muttered Hawberk, searching on the floor for a fallen rivet.

"Is it nonsense," I asked, managing to suppress what I felt, "is it nonsense when he says that the tassets and cuissards of the enamelled suit of armor commonly known as the 'Prince's Emblazoned' can be found among a mass of rusty theatrical properties, broken stoves and ragpickers' refuse in a garret in Pell Street?''

Hawberk's hammer fell to the ground, but he picked it up and asked, with a great deal of calm, how I knew that the tassets and left cuissard were missing from the ''Prince's Emblazoned.''

''I did not know until Mr. Wilde mentioned it to me the other day. He said they were in the garret of 998 Pell Street.''

''Nonsense,'' he cried, but I noticed his hand trembling under his leathern apron.

''Is this nonsense too?'' I asked pleasantly. ''Is it nonsense when Mr. Wilde continually speaks of you as the Marquis of Avonshire and of Miss Constance—''

I did not finish, for Constance had started to her feet with terror written on every feature. Hawberk looked at me and slowly smoothed his leathern apron. ''That is impossible,'' he observed. ''Mr. Wilde may know a great many things—''

''About armor, for instance, and the 'Prince's Emblazoned,' '' I interposed, smiling.

''Yes,'' he continued, slowly, ''about armor also—may be—but he is wrong in regard to the Marquis of Avonshire, who, as you know, killed his wife's traducer years ago, and went to Australia where he did not long survive his wife.''

''Mr. Wilde is wrong,'' murmured Constance. Her lips were blanched but her voice was sweet and calm.

''Let us agree, if you please, that in this one circumstance Mr. Wilde is wrong,'' I said.

II

I climbed the three dilapidated flights of stairs, which I had so often climbed before, and knocked at a small door at the end of the corridor. Mr. Wilde opened the door and I walked in.

When he had double-locked the door and pushed a heavy chest against it, he came and sat down beside me, peering up into my face with his little light-colored eyes. Half a dozen new scratches covered his nose and cheeks, and the silver wires which supported his artificial ears had become displaced. I thought I had never seen him so hideously fascinating. He had no ears. The artificial ones, which now stood out at an angle from the fine wire, were his one weakness. They were made of wax and painted a shell pink, but the rest of his face was yellow. He might better have revelled in the luxury of some artificial fingers for his left hand, which was absolutely fingerless, but it seemed to cause him no inconvenience, and he was satisfied with his wax ears. He was very small, scarcely higher than a child of ten, but his arms were magnificently developed, and his thighs as thick as any athlete's. Still, the most remarkable thing about Mr. Wilde was that a man of his marvellous intelligence and knowledge should have such a head. It was flat and pointed, like the heads of many of those unfortunates whom people imprison in asylums for the weak-minded. Many called him insane but I knew him to be as sane as I was.

I do not deny that he was eccentric; the mania he had for keeping that cat and teasing her until she flew at his face like a demon, was certainly eccentric. I never could understand why he kept the creature, nor what pleasure he found in shutting himself up in his room with the surly, vicious beast. I remember once glancing up from the manuscript I was studying by the light of some tallow dips and seeing Mr. Wilde squatting motionless on his high chair, his eyes fairly blazing with excitement, while the cat, which had risen from her place before the stove, came creeping across the floor right at him. Before I could move she flattened her belly to the ground, crouched, trembled, and sprang into his face. Howling and foaming, they rolled over and over on the floor, scratching and clawing, until the cat screamed and fled under the cabinet, and Mr. Wilde turned over on his back, his limbs contracting and curling up like the legs of a dying spider. He *was* eccentric.

Mr. Wilde had climbed into his high chair, and, after studying my face, picked up a dog's-eared ledger and opened it.

"Henry B. Matthews," he read, "bookkeeper with Whysot Whysot and Company, dealers in church ornaments.

Called April 3d. Reputation damaged on the race-track. Known as a welcher. Reputation to be repaired by August 1st. Retainer Five Dollars.'' He turned the page and ran his fingerless knuckles down the closely-written columns.

"P. Greene Dusenberry, Minister of the Gospel, Fair-beach, New Jersey. Reputation damaged in the Bowery. To be repaired as soon as possible. Retainer $100.''

He coughed and added, "Called, April 6th.''

"Then you are not in need of money, Mr. Wilde,'' I inquired.

"Listen,'' he coughed again.

"Mrs. C. Hamilton Chester, of Chester Park, New York City, called April 7th. Reputation damaged at Dieppe, France. To be repaired by October 1st. Retainer $500.

"Note.—C. Hamilton Chester, Captain U.S.S. 'Avalanche' ordered home from South Sea Squadron October 1st.''

"Well,'' I said, "the profession of a Repairer of Reputations is lucrative.''

His colorless eyes sought mine. "I only wanted to demonstrate that I was correct. You said it was impossible to succeed as a Repairer of Reputations; that even if I did succeed in certain cases, it would cost me more than I would gain by it. To-day I have five hundred men in my employ, who are poorly paid, but who pursue the work with an enthusiasm which possibly may be born of fear. These men enter every shade and grade of society; some even are pillars of the most exclusive social temples; others are the prop and pride of the financial world; still others hold undisputed sway among the 'Fancy and the Talent.' I choose them at my leisure from those who reply to my advertisements. It is easy enough, they are all cowards. I could treble the number in twenty days if I wished. So you see, those who have in their keeping the reputations of their fellow-citizens, *I* have in my pay.''

"They may turn on you,'' I suggested.

He rubbed his thumb over his cropped ears, and adjusted the wax substitutes. "I think not,'' he murmured thoughtfully, "I seldom have to apply the whip, and then only once. Besides, they like their wages."

"How do you apply the whip?" I demanded.

His face for a moment was awful to look upon. His eyes dwindled to a pair of green sparks.

"I invite them to come and have a little chat with me," he said in a soft voice.

A knock at the door interrupted him, and his face resumed its amiable expression.

"Who is it?" he inquired.

"Mr. Steylette," was the answer.

"Come to-morrow," replied Mr. Wilde.

"Impossible," began the other, but was silenced by a sort of bark from Mr. Wilde.

"Come to-morrow," he repeated.

We heard somebody move away from the door and turn the corner by the stairway.

"Who is that?" I asked.

"Arnold Steylette, Owner and Editor in Chief of the great New York daily."

He drummed on the ledger with his fingerless hand, adding: "I pay him very badly, but he thinks it a good bargain."

"Arnold Steylette!" I repeated, amazed.

"Yes," said Mr. Wilde with a self-satisfied cough.

The cat, which had entered the room as he spoke, hesitated, looked up at him and snarled. He climbed down from the chair and squatting on the floor, took the creature into his arms and caressed her. The cat ceased snarling and presently began a loud purring which seemed to increase in timbre as he stroked her.

"Where are the notes?" I asked. He pointed to the table, and for the hundredth time I picked up the bundle of manuscript entitled

"THE IMPERIAL DYNASTY OF AMERICA."

One by one I studied the well-worn pages, worn only by my own handling, and although I knew all by heart, from the beginning, "When from Carcosa, the Hyades, Hastur, and

Aldebaran," to "Castaigne, Louis de Calvados, born December 19th, 1877," I read it with an eager rapt attention, pausing to repeat parts of it aloud, and dwelling especially on "Hildred de Calvados, only son of Hildred Castaigne and Edythe Landes Castaigne, first in succession," etc., etc.

When I finished, Mr. Wilde nodded and coughed.

"Speaking of your legitimate ambition," he said, "how do Constance and Louis get along?"

"She loves him," I replied simply.

The cat on his knee suddenly turned and struck at his eyes, and he flung her off and climbed on to the chair opposite me.

"And Doctor Archer! But that's a matter you can settle any time you wish," he added.

"Yes," I replied, "Doctor Archer can wait, but it is time I saw my cousin Louis."

"It is time," he repeated. Then he took another ledger from the table and ran over the leaves rapidly.

"We are now in communication with ten thousand men," he muttered. "We can count on one hundred thousand within the first twenty-eight hours, and in forty-eight hours the state will rise *en masse*. The country follows the state, and the portion that will not, I mean California and the Northwest, might better never have been inhabited. I shall not send them the Yellow Sign."

The blood rushed to my head, but I only answered, "A new broom sweeps clean."

"The ambition of Cæsar and of Napoleon pales before that which could not rest until it had seized the minds of men and controlled even their unborn thoughts," said Mr. Wilde.

"You are speaking of the King in Yellow," I groaned with a shudder.

"He is a king whom Emperors have served."

"I am content to serve him," I replied.

Mr. Wilde sat rubbing his ears with his crippled hand. "Perhaps Constance does not love him," he suggested.

I started to reply, but a sudden burst of military music from the street below drowned my voice. The twentieth dragoon regiment, formerly in garrison at Mount St. Vincent, was returning from the manœuvres in Westchester County, to its new barracks on East Washington Square. It was my cousin's regiment. They were a fine lot of fellows, in their pale-blue, tight-fitting jackets, jaunty busbys and white riding breeches with the double yellow stripe, into which their limbs seemed molded. Every other squadron was armed with lances, from the metal points of which fluttered yellow and white pennons. The band passed, playing the regimental march, then came the colonel and staff, the horses crowding and trampling, while their heads bobbed in unison, and the pennons fluttered from their lance points. The troopers, who rode with the beautiful English seat, looked brown as berries from their bloodless campaign among the farms of Westchester, and the music of their sabres against the stirrups, and the jingle of spurs and carbines, was delightful to me. I saw Louis riding with his squadron. He was as handsome an officer as I have ever seen. Mr. Wilde, who had mounted a chair by the window, saw him too, but said nothing. Louis turned and looked straight at Hawberk's shop as he passed, and I could see the flush on his brown cheeks. I think Constance must have been at the window. When the last troopers had clattered by, and the last pennons vanished into South 5th Avenue, Mr. Wilde clambered out of his chair and dragged the chest away from the door.

"Yes," he said, "it is time that you saw your cousin Louis."

He unlocked the door and I picked up my hat and stick and stepped into the corridor. The stairs were dark. Groping about, I set my foot on something soft, which snarled and spit, and I aimed a murderous blow at the cat, but my cane shivered to splinters against the balustrade, and the beast scurried back into Mr. Wilde's room.

Passing Hawberk's door again I saw him still at work on the armor, but I did not stop, and stepping out into Bleecker Street, I followed it to Wooster, skirted the grounds of the Lethal Chamber, and crossing Washington Park, went straight to my rooms in the Benedick. Here I lunched comfortably, read the *Herald* and the *Meteor*, and finally went to the steel safe in my bedroom and set the time combination. The three and three-quarter minutes which it is necessary to wait, while the time lock is opening, are to me golden moments. From the instant I set the combination to the moment when I grasp the knobs and swing back the solid steel doors, I live in an ecstasy of expectation. Those moments must be like moments passed in Paradise. I know what I am to find at the end of the time limit. I know what the massive safe holds secure for me, for me alone, and the exquisite pleasure of waiting is hardly enhanced when the safe opens and I lift, from its velvet crown, a diadem of purest gold, blazing with diamonds. I do this every day, and yet the joy of waiting and at last touching again the diadem only seems to increase as the days pass. It is a diadem fit for a King among kings, an Emperor among emperors. The King in Yellow might scorn it, but it shall be worn by his royal servant.

I held it in my arms until the alarm on the safe rang harshly, and then tenderly, proudly, I replaced it and shut the steel doors. I walked slowly back into my study, which faces Washington Square, and leaned on the window sill. The afternoon sun poured into my windows, and a gentle breeze stirred the branches of the elms and maples in the park, now covered with buds and tender foliage. A flock of pigeons circled about the tower of the Memorial Church; sometimes alighting on the purple tiled roof, sometimes wheeling downward to the lotos fountain in front of the marble arch. The gardeners were busy with the flower beds around the fountain, and the freshly-turned earth smelled sweet and spicy. A lawn mower, drawn by a fat white horse, clinked across the green sward, and watering carts poured showers of spray over the asphalt drives. Around the statue of Peter Stuyvesant, which in 1897 had replaced the monstrosity supposed to represent Garibaldi, children played in the spring sunshine, and nurse girls wheeled elaborate baby-carriages with a reckless disregard for the pasty-faced occupants, which could probably be explained by the presence of half a dozen trim dragoon troopers languidly lolling on the benches. Through the trees, the Washington Memorial Arch glistened like silver in the sunshine, and beyond, on the eastern extremity of the square, the gray stone barracks of the dragoons and the white granite artillery stables were alive with color and motion.

I looked at the Lethal Chamber on the corner of the square opposite. A few curious people still lingered about the gilded iron railing, but inside the grounds the paths were deserted. I watched the fountains ripple and sparkle; the sparrows had already found this new bathing nook, and the basins were crowded with the dusty-feathered little things. Two or three white peacocks picked their way across the lawns, and a drab-colored pigeon sat so motionless on the arm of one of the Fates that it seemed to be a part of the sculptured stone.

As I was turning carelessly away, a slight commotion in the group of curious loiterers around the gates attracted my attention. A young man had entered, and was advancing with nervous strides along the gravel path which leads to the bronze doors of the Lethal Chamber. He paused a moment before the Fates, and as he raised his head to those three mysterious faces, the pigeon rose from its sculptured perch, circled about for a moment and wheeled to the east. The young man pressed his hands to his face, and then with an undefinable gesture sprang up the marble steps, the bronze doors closed behind him, and half an hour later the loiterers slouched away, and the frightened pigeon returned to its perch in the arms of Fate.

I put on my hat and went out into the park for a little walk before dinner. As I crossed the central driveway a group of officers passed, and one of them called out, "Hello, Hildred," and came back to shake hands with me. It was my cousin Louis, who stood smiling and tapping his spurred heels with his riding-whip.

"Just back from Westchester," he said; "been doing the bucolic; milk and curds, you know, dairy-maids in sunbonnets, who say 'haeow' and 'I don't think' when you tell them they are pretty. I'm nearly dead for a square meal at Delmonico's. What's the news?"

"There is none," I replied pleasantly. "I saw your regiment coming in this morning."

"Did you? I didn't see you. Where were you?"

"In Mr. Wilde's window."

"Oh, hell!" he began impatiently, "that man is stark mad! I don't understand why you————"

He saw how annoyed I felt by this outburst, and begged my pardon.

"Really, old chap," he said, "I don't mean to run down a man you like, but for the life of me, I can't see what the deuce you find in common with Mr. Wilde. He's not well-bred, to put it generously; he's hideously deformed; his head is the head of a criminally insane person. You know yourself he's been in an asylum————"

"So have I," I interrupted calmly.

Louis looked startled and confused for a moment, but recovered and slapped me heartily on the shoulder.

"You were completely cured," he began, but I stopped him again.

"I suppose you mean that I was simply acknowledged never to have been insane."

"Of course that—that's what I meant," he laughed.

I disliked his laugh because I knew it was forced, but I nodded gaily and asked him where he was going. Louis looked after his brother officers who had now almost reached Broadway.

"We had intended to sample a Brunswick cocktail, but to tell you the truth I was anxious for an excuse to go and see Hawberk instead. Come along, I'll make you my excuse."

We found old Hawberk, neatly attired in a fresh spring suit, standing at the door of his shop and sniffing the air.

"I had just decided to take Constance for a little stroll before dinner," he replied to the impetuous volley of questions from Louis. "We thought of walking on the park terrace along the North River."

At that moment Constance appeared and grew pale and rosy by turns as Louis bent over her small gloved fingers. I tried to excuse myself, alleging an engagement up-town, but Louis and Constance would not listen, and I saw I was expected to remain and engage old Hawberk's attention. After all, it would be just as well if I kept my eye on Louis, I thought, and when they hailed a Spring Street horsecar, I got in after them and took my seat beside the armorer.

The beautiful line of parks and granite terraces overlooking the wharves along the North River, which were built in 1910 and finished in the autumn of 1917, had become one of the most popular promenades in the metropolis. They extended from the battery to 190th Street, overlooking the noble river and affording a fine view of the Jersey shore and the Highlands opposite. Cafés and restaurants were scattered here and there among the trees, and twice a week military bands from the garrison played in the kiosques on the parapets.

We sat down in the sunshine on the bench at the foot of the equestrian statue of General Sheridan. Constance tipped her sunshade to shield her eyes, and she and Louis began a murmuring conversation which was impossible to catch. Old Hawberk, leaning on his ivory-headed cane, lighted an excellent cigar, the mate to which I politely refused, and smiled at vacancy. The sun hung low above the Staten Island woods, and the bay was dyed with golden hues reflected from the sunwarmed sails of the shipping in the harbor.

Brigs, schooners, yachts, clumsy ferry-boats, their decks swarming with people, railroad transports carrying lines of brown, blue and white freight cars, stately sound steamers, *declassé* tramp steamers, coasters, dredgers, scows, and everywhere pervading the entire bay impudent little tugs puffing and whistling officiously—these were the crafts which churned the sunlit waters as far as the eye could reach. In calm contrast to the hurry of sailing vessel and steamer, a silent fleet of white warships lay motionless in midstream.

Constance's merry laugh aroused me from my reverie.

"What *are* you staring at?" she inquired.

"Nothing—the fleet," I smiled.

Then Louis told us what the vessels were, pointing out each by its relative position to the old Red Fort on Governor's Island.

"That little cigar-shaped thing is a torpedo boat," he explained; "there are four more lying close together. They are the 'Tarpon,' the 'Falcon,' the 'Sea Fox' and the 'Octopus.' The gun-boats just above are the 'Princeton,' the 'Champlain,' the 'Still Water' and the 'Erie.' Next to them lie the cruisers 'Farragut' and 'Los Angeles,' and above them the battle-ships 'California' and 'Dakota,' and the 'Washington' which is the flag-ship. Those two squatty-looking chunks of metal which are anchored there off Castle William are the double-turreted monitors 'Terrible' and 'Magnificent'; behind them lies the ram, 'Osceola.' "

Constance looked at him with deep approval in her beautiful eyes. "What loads of things you know for a soldier," she said, and we all joined in the laugh which followed.

Presently Louis rose with a nod to us and offered his arm to Constance, and they strolled away along the river wall. Hawberk watched them for a moment and then turned to me.

"Mr. Wilde was right," he said. "I have found the missing tassets and left cuissard of the 'Prince's Emblazoned' in a vile old junk garret in Pell Street."

"998?" I inquired, with a smile.

"Yes."

"Mr. Wilde is a very intelligent man," I observed.

"I want to give him the credit of this most important discovery," continued Hawberk. "And I intend it shall be known that he is entitled to the fame of it."

"He won't thank you for that," I answered sharply; "please say nothing about it."

"Do you know what it is worth?" said Hawberk.

"No, fifty dollars, perhaps."

"It is valued at five hundred, but the owner of the 'Prince's Emblazoned' will give two thousand dollars to the person who completes his suit; that reward also belongs to Mr. Wilde."

"He doesn't want it! He refuses it!" I answered angrily. "What do you know about Mr. Wilde? He doesn't need the money. He is rich—or will be—richer than any living man except myself. What will we care for money then—what will we care, he and I, when—when———"

"When what?" demanded Hawberk, astonished.

"You will see," I replied, on my guard again.

He looked at me narrowly, much as Doctor Archer used to, and I knew he thought I was mentally unsound. Perhaps it was fortunate for him that he did not use the world lunatic just then.

"No," I replied to his unspoken thought, "I am not mentally weak; my mind is as healthy as Mr. Wilde's. I do not care to explain just yet what I have on hand, but it is an investment which will pay more than mere gold, silver and precious stones. It will secure the happiness and prosperity of a continent—yes, a hemisphere!''

"Oh," said Hawberk.

"And eventually," I continued more quietly, "it will secure the happiness of the whole world.''

"And incidentally your own happiness and prosperity as well as Mr. Wilde's?''

"Exactly," I smiled. But I could have throttled him for taking that tone.

He looked at me in silence for a while and then said very gently, "Why don't you give up your books and studies, Mr. Castaigne, and take a tramp among the mountains somewhere or other? You used to be fond of fishing. Take a cast or two at the trout in the Rangelys.''

"I don't care for fishing any more," I answered, without a shade of annoyance in my voice.

"You used to be fond of everything," he continued; "athletics, yachting, shooting, riding————''

"I have never cared to ride since my fall," I said quietly.

"Ah, yes, your fall," he repeated, looking away from me.

I thought this nonsense had gone far enough, so I turned the conversation back to Mr. Wilde; but he was scanning my face again in a manner highly offensive to me.

"Mr. Wilde," he repeated, "do you know what he did this afternoon? He came downstairs and nailed a sign over the hall door next to mine; it read:

Mr. Wilde,
Repairer of Reputations.
3d Bell.

Do you know what a Repairer of Reputations can be?''

"I do," I replied, suppressing the rage within.

"Oh," he said again.

Louis and Constance came strolling by and stopped to ask if we would join them. Hawberk looked at his watch. At the same moment a puff of smoke shot from the casemates of

Castle William, and the boom of the sunset gun rolled across the water and was re-echoed from the Highlands opposite. The flag came running down from the flag-pole, the bugles sounded on the white decks of the warships, and the first electric light sparkled out from the Jersey shore.

As I turned into the city with Hawberk I heard Constance murmur something to Louis which I did not understand; but Louis whispered, "My darling," in reply; and again, walking ahead with Hawberk through the square I heard a murmur of "sweetheart," and "my own Constance," and I knew the time had nearly arrived when I should speak of important matters with my cousin Louis.

III

One morning early in May I stood before the steel safe in my bedroom, trying on the golden jewelled crown. The diamonds flashed fire as I turned to the mirror, and the heavy beaten gold burned like a halo about my head. I remembered Camilla's agonized scream and the awful words echoing through the dim streets of Carcosa. They were the last lines in the first act, and I dared not think of what followed—dared not, even in the spring sunshine, there in my own room, surrounded with familiar objects, reassured by the bustle from the street and the voices of the servants in the hallway outside. For those poisoned words had dropped slowly into my heart, as death-sweat drops upon a bed-sheet and is absorbed. Trembling, I put the diadem from my head and wiped my forehead, but I thought of Hastur and of my own rightful ambition, and I remembered Mr. Wilde as I had last left him, his face all torn and bloody from the claws of that devil's creature, and what he said—ah, what he said! The alarm bell in the safe began to whirr harshly, and I knew my time was up; but I would not heed it, and replacing the flashing circlet upon my head, I turned defiantly to the mirror. I stood for a long time absorbed in the changing expression of my own eyes. The mirror reflected a face which was like my own, but whiter, and so thin that I hardly recognized it. And all the time I kept repeating between my clenched teeth, "The day has come! the day has come!" while the alarm in the safe whirred and clamored, and the diamonds sparkled and flamed above my brow. I heard a door open but did not heed it. It was only when I saw two faces in the mirror—it was only when another face rose over my shoulder, and two other eyes met mine. I wheeled like a flash and seized a long knife from my dressing-table, and my cousin sprang back very pale, crying: "Hildred! for God's sake!" Then as my hand fell, he said: "It is I, Louis, don't you know me?" I stood silent. I could not have spoken for my life. He walked up to me and took the knife from my hand.

"What is all this?" he inquired, in a gentle voice. "Are you ill?"

"No," I replied. But I doubt if he heard me.

"Come, come, old fellow," he cried, "take off that brass crown and toddle into the study. Are you going to a masquerade? What's all this theatrical tinsel anyway?"

I was glad he thought the crown was made of brass and paste, yet I didn't like him any the better for thinking so. I let him take it from my hand, knowing it was best to humor him. He tossed the splendid diadem in the air, and catching it, turned to me smiling.

"It's dear at fifty cents," he said. "What's it for?"

I did not answer, but took the circlet from his hands, and placing it in the safe, shut the massive steel door. The alarm ceased its infernal din at once. He watched me curiously, but did not seem to notice the sudden ceasing of the alarm. He did, however, speak of the safe as a biscuit box. Fearing lest he might examine the combination, I led the way into my study. Louis threw himself on the sofa and flicked at flies with his eternal riding-whip. He wore his fatigue uniform with the braided jacket and jaunty cap, and I noticed that his riding-boots were all splashed with red mud.

"Where have you been?" I inquired.

"Jumping mud creeks in Jersey," he said. "I haven't had time to change yet; I was rather in a hurry to see you. Haven't you got a glass of something? I'm dead tired; been in the saddle twenty-four hours."

I gave him some brandy from my medicinal store, which he drank with a grimace.

"Damned bad stuff," he observed. "I'll give you an address where they sell brandy that is brandy."

"It's good enough for my needs," I said indifferently. "I use it to rub my chest with." He stared and flicked at another fly.

"See here, old fellow," he began, "I've got something to suggest to you. It's four years now that you've shut yourself up here like an owl, never going anywhere, never taking any healthy exercise, never doing a damn thing but poring over those books up there on the mantelpiece."

He glanced along the row of shelves. "Napoleon, Napoleon, Napoleon!" he read. "For heaven sake, have you nothing but Napoleons there?"

"I wish they were bound in gold," I said. "But wait, yes, there is another book, The King in Yellow." I looked him steadily in the eye.

"Have you never read it?" I asked.

"I? No, thank God! I don't want to be driven crazy."

I saw he regretted his speech as soon as he had uttered it. There is only one word which I loathe more than I do lunatic and that word is crazy. But I controlled myself and asked him why he thought The King in Yellow dangerous.

"Oh, I don't know," he said, hastily. "I only remember the excitement it created and the denunciations from pulpit and press. I believe the author shot himself after bringing forth this monstrosity, didn't he?"

"I understand he is still alive," I answered.

"That's probably true," he muttered; "bullets couldn't kill a fiend like that."

"It is a book of great truths," I said.

"Yes," he replied, "of 'truths' which send men frantic and blast their lives. I don't care if the thing is, as they say, the very supreme essence of art. It's a crime to have written it and I for one shall never open its pages."

"Is that what you have come to tell me?" I asked.

"No," he said, "I came to tell you that I am going to be married."

I believe for a moment my heart ceased to beat, but I kept my eyes on his face.

"Yes," he continued, smiling happily, "married to the sweetest girl on earth."

"Constance Hawberk," I said mechanically.

"How did you know?" he cried, astonished. "I didn't know it myself until that evening last April, when we strolled down to the embankment before dinner."

"When is it to be?" I asked.

"It was to have been next September, but an hour ago a despatch came ordering our regiment to the Presidio, San Francisco. We leave at noon to-morrow. To-morrow," he repeated. "Just think, Hildred, to-morrow I shall be the happiest fellow that ever drew breath in this jolly world, for Constance will go with me."

I offered him my hand in congratulation, and he seized and shook it like the good-natured fool he was—or pretended to be.

"I am going to get my squadron as a wedding present," he rattled on. "Captain and Mrs. Louis Castaigne, eh, Hildred?"

Then he told me where it was to be and who were to be there, and made me promise to come and be best man. I set my teeth and listened to his boyish chatter without showing what I felt, but—

I was getting to the limit of my endurance, and when he jumped up, and, switching his spurs till they jingled, said he must go, I did not detain him.

"There's one thing I want to ask of you," I said quietly.

"Out with it, it's promised," he laughed.

"I want you to meet me for a quarter of an hour's talk to-night."

"Of course, if you wish," he said, somewhat puzzled. "Where?"

"Anywhere, in the park there."

"What time, Hildred?"

"Midnight."

"What in the name of—" he began, but checked himself and laughingly assented. I watched him go down the stairs and hurry away, his sabre banging at every stride. He turned into Bleecker Street, and I knew he was going to see Constance. I gave him ten minutes to disappear and then followed in his footsteps, taking with me the jewelled crown and the silken robe embroidered with the Yellow Sign. When I turned into Bleecker Street, and entered the doorway which bore the sign,

MR. WILDE,
REPAIRER OF REPUTATIONS.
3d Bell.

I saw old Hawberk moving about in his shop, and imagined I heard Constance's voice in the parlor; but I avoided them both and hurried up the trembling stairways to Mr. Wilde's apartment. I knocked, and entered without ceremony. Mr. Wilde lay groaning on the floor, his face covered with blood, his clothes torn to shreds. Drops of blood were scattered about over the carpet, which had also been ripped and frayed in the evidently recent struggle.

"It's that cursed cat," he said, ceasing his groans, and turning his colorless eyes to me; "she attacked me while I was asleep. I believe she will kill me yet."

This was too much, so I went into the kitchen and seizing a hatchet from the pantry, started to find the infernal beast and settle her then and there. My search was fruitless, and after a while I gave it up and came back to find Mr. Wilde squatting on his high chair by the table. He had washed his face and changed his clothes. The great furrows which the cat's claws had ploughed up in his face he had filled with collodion, and a rag hid the wound in his throat. I told him I should kill the cat when I came across her, but he only shook his head and turned to the open ledger before him. He read name after name of the people who had come to him in regard to their reputation, and the sums he had amassed were startling.

"I put on the screws now and then," he explained.

"One day or other some of these people will assassinate you," I insisted.

"Do you think so?" he said, rubbing his mutilated ears.

It was useless to argue with him, so I took down the manuscript entitled *Imperial Dynasty of America*, for the last time I should ever take it down in Mr. Wilde's study. I read it through, thrilling and trembling with pleasure. When I had finished, Mr. Wilde took the manuscript and, turning to the dark passage which leads from his study to his bedchamber, called out in a loud voice, "Vance." Then for the first time, I noticed a man crouching there in the shadow. How I had overlooked him during my search for the cat, I cannot imagine.

"Vance, come in," cried Mr. Wilde.

The figure rose and crept toward us, and I shall never forget the face that he raised to mine, as the light from the window illuminated it.

"Vance, this is Mr. Castaigne," said Mr. Wilde. Before he had finished speaking, the man threw himself on the ground before the table, crying and gasping, "Oh, God! Oh, my God! Help me! Forgive me—Oh, Mr. Castaigne, keep that man away. You cannot, you cannot mean it! You are different—save me! I am broken down—I was in a madhouse and now—when all was coming right—when I had forgotten the King—the King in Yellow and—but I shall go mad again— I shall go mad—"

His voice died into a choking rattle, for Mr. Wilde had leapt on him and his right hand encircled the man's throat. When Vance fell in a heap on the floor, Mr. Wilde clambered nimbly into his chair again, and rubbing his mangled ears with the stump of his hand, turned to me and asked me for the ledger. I reached it down from the shelf and he opened it. After a moment's searching among the beautifully written pages, he coughed complacently, and pointed to the name Vance.

"Vance," he read aloud, "Osgood Oswald Vance." At the sound of his voice, the man on the floor raised his head and turned a convulsed face to Mr. Wilde. His eyes were injected with blood, his lips tumefied. "Called April 28th," continued Mr. Wilde. "Occupation, cashier in the Seaforth National Bank; has served a term of forgery at Sing Sing, from whence he was transferred to the Asylum for the Criminal Insane. Pardoned by the Governor of New York, and discharged from the Asylum, January 19, 1918. Reputation damaged at Sheepshead Bay. Rumors that he lives beyond his income. Reputation to be repaired at once. Retainer $1,500.

"Note.—Has embezzled sums amounting to $30,000 since March 20th, 1919, excellent family, and secured present position through uncle's influence. Father President of Seaforth Bank."

I looked at the man on the floor.

"Get up, Vance," said Mr. Wilde in a gentle voice. Vance rose as if hypnotized. "He will do as we suggest now," observed Mr. Wilde, and opening the manuscript, he read the entire history of the Imperial Dynasty of America. Then in a kind and soothing murmur he ran over the important points with Vance, who stood like one stunned. His eyes were so blank and vacant that I imagined he had become half-witted, and remarked it to Mr. Wilde who replied that it was of no consequence anyway. Very patiently we pointed out to Vance what his share in the affair would be, and he seemed to understand after a while. Mr. Wilde explained the manuscript, using several volumes on Heraldry, to substantiate the result of his researches. He mentioned the establishment of the Dynasty in Carcosa, the lakes which connected Hastur, Aldebaron and the mystery of the Hyades. He spoke of Cassilda and Camilla, and sounded the cloudy depths of Demhe, and the Lake of Hali. "The scalloped tatters of the King in Yellow must hide Yhtill forever," he muttered, but I do not believe Vance heard him. Then by degrees he led Vance along the ramifications of the Imperial family, to Uoht and Thale, from Naotalba and Phantom of Truth, to Aldones, and then tossing aside his manuscript and notes, he began the wonderful story of the Last King. Fascinated and thrilled, I watched him. He threw up his head, his long arms were stretched out in a magnificent gesture of pride and power, and his eyes blazed deep in their sockets like two emeralds. Vance listened stupefied. As for me, when at last Mr. Wilde had finished, and pointing to me, cried, "The cousin of the King!" my head swam with excitement.

Controlling myself with a superhuman effort, I explained to Vance why I alone was worthy of the crown and why my cousin must be exiled or die. I made him understand that my cousin must never marry, even after renouncing all his claims, and how that least of all he should marry the daughter of the Marquis of Avonshire and bring England into the question. I showed him a list of thousands of names which Mr. Wilde had drawn up; every man whose name was there had received the Yellow Sign which no living human being dared disregard. The city, the state, the whole land, were ready to rise and tremble before the Pallid Mask.

The time had come, the people should know the son of Hastur, and the whole world bow to the Black Stars which hang in the sky over Carcosa.

Vance leaned on the table, his head buried in his hands. Mr. Wilde drew a rough sketch on the margin of yesterday's *Herald* with a bit of lead pencil. It was a plan of Hawberk's rooms. Then he wrote out the order and affixed the seal, and shaking like a palsied man, I signed my first writ of execution with my name Hildred-Rex.

Mr. Wilde clambered to the floor and unlocking the cabinet, took a long square box from the first shelf. This he brought to the table and opened. A new knife lay in the tissue paper inside and I picked it up and handed it to Vance, along with the order and the plan of Hawberk's apartment. Then Mr. Wilde told Vance he could go; and he went, shambling like an outcast of the slums.

I sat for a while watching the daylight fade behind the square tower of the Judson Memorial Church, and finally, gathering up the manuscript and notes, took my hat and started for the door.

Mr. Wilde watched me in silence. When I had stepped into the hall I looked back. Mr. Wilde's small eyes were still fixed on me. Behind him, the shadows gathered in the fading light. Then I closed the door behind me and went out into the darkening streets.

I had eaten nothing since breakfast, but I was not hungry. A wretched half-starved creature, who stood looking across the street at the Lethal Chamber, noticed me and came up to tell me a tale of misery. I gave him money, I don't know why, and he went away without thanking me. An hour later another outcast approached and whined his story. I had a blank bit of paper in my pocket, on which was traced the Yellow Sign and I handed it to him. He looked at it stupidly for a moment, and then with an uncertain glance at me, folded it with what seemed to me exaggerated care and placed it in his bosom.

The electric lights were sparkling among the trees, and the new moon shone in the sky above the Lethal Chamber. It was tiresome waiting in the square; I wandered from the Marble Arch to the artillery stables, and back again to the lotos fountain. The flowers and grass exhaled a fragrance which troubled me. The jet of the fountain played in the moonlight, and the musical splash of falling drops reminded me of the tinkle of chained mail in Hawberk's shop. But it was not so fascinating, and the dull sparkle of the moonlight on the water brought no such sensations of exquisite pleasure, as when the sunshine played over the polished steel of a corselet on Hawberk's knee. I watched the bats darting and turning above the water plants in the fountain basin, but their rapid, jerky flight set my nerves on edge, and I went away again to walk aimlessly to and fro among the trees.

The artillery stables were dark, but in the cavalry barracks the officers' windows were brilliantly lighted, and the sally-port was constantly filled with troopers in fatigue, carrying straw and harness and baskets filled with tin dishes.

Twice the mounted sentry at the gates was changed while I wandered up and down the asphalt walk. I looked at my watch. It was nearly time. The lights in the barracks went out one by one, the barred gate was closed, and every minute or two an officer passed in through the side wicket, leaving a rattle of accoutrements and a jingle of spurs on the night air. The square had become very silent. The last homeless loiterer had been driven away by the gray-coated park policeman, the car tracks along Wooster Street were deserted, and the only sound which broke the stillness was the stamping of the sentry's horse and the ring of his sabre against the saddle pommel. In the barracks, the officers' quarters were still lighted, and military servants passed and repassed before the bay windows. Twelve o'clock sounded from the new spire of St. Francis Xavier, and at the last stroke of the sad-toned bell a figure passed through the wicket beside the portcullis, returned the salute of the sentry, and crossing the street, entered the square and advanced toward the Benedick apartment house.

"Louis," I called.

The man pivoted on his spurred heels and came straight toward me.

"Is that you, Hildred?"

"Yes, you are on time."

I took his offered hand, and we strolled toward the Lethal Chamber.

He rattled on about his wedding and the graces of Constance, and their future prospects, calling my attention to his captain's shoulderstraps, and the triple gold arabesque on his sleeve and fatigue cap. I believe I listened as much to the music of his spurs and sabre as I did to his boyish babble, and at last we stood under the elms on the Fourth Street corner of the square opposite the Lethal Chamber. Then he laughed and asked me what I wanted with him. I motioned him to a seat on a bench under the electric light, and sat down beside him. He looked at me curiously, with that same searching glance which I hate and fear so in doctors. I felt the insult of his look, but he did not know it, and I carefully concealed my feelings.

"Well, old chap," he enquired, "what can I do for you?"

I drew from my pocket the manuscript and notes of the *Imperial Dynasty of America*, and looking him in the eye, said:

"I will tell you. On your word as a soldier, promise me to read this manuscript from beginning to end, without asking me a question. Promise me to read these notes in the same way, and promise me to listen to what I have to tell later."

"I promise, if you wish it," he said pleasantly. "Give me the paper, Hildred."

He began to read, raising his eyebrows with a puzzled whimsical air, which made me tremble with suppressed anger. As he advanced, his eyebrows contracted, and his lips seemed to form the word, "rubbish."

Then he looked slightly bored, but apparently for my sake read, with an attempt at interest, which presently ceased to be an effort. He started when in the closely-written pages he came to his own name, and when he came to mine he lowered the paper, and looked sharply at me for a moment. But he kept his word, and resumed his reading, and I let the half-formed question die on his lips unanswered. When he came to the end and read the signature of Mr. Wilde, he folded the paper carefully and returned it to me. I handed him the notes, and he settled back, pushing his fatigue cap up to his forehead, with a boyish gesture, which I remembered so well in school. I watched his face as he read, and when he finished I took the notes with the manuscript, and placed them in my pocket. Then I unfolded a scroll marked with the Yellow Sign. He saw the sign, but he did not seem to recognize it, and I called his attention to it somewhat sharply.

"Well," he said, "I see it. What is it?"

"It is the Yellow Sign," I said, angrily.

"Oh, that's it, is it?" said Louis, in that flattering voice, which Dr. Archer used to employ with me, and would probably have employed again, had I not settled his affair for him.

I kept my rage down and answered as steadily as possible, "Listen, you have engaged your word?"

"I am listening, old chap," he replied soothingly.

I began to speak very calmly.

"Dr. Archer, having by some means become possessed of the secret of the Imperial Succession, attempted to deprive me of my right, alleging that because of a fall from my horse four years ago, I had become mentally deficient. He presumed to place me under restraint in his own house in hopes of either driving me insane or poisoning me. I have not forgotten it. I visited him last night and the interview was final."

Louis turned quite pale, but did not move. I resumed triumphantly, "There are yet three people to be interviewed in the interests of Mr. Wilde and myself. They are my cousin Louis, Mr. Hawberk, and his daughter Constance.''

Louis sprang to his feet and I arose also, and flung the paper marked with the Yellow Sign to the ground.

"Oh, I don't need that to tell you what I have to say," I cried with a laugh of triumph. "You must renounce the crown to me, do you hear, to *me*."

Louis looked at me with a startled air, but recovering himself said kindly, "Of course I renounce the—what is it I must renounce?''

"The crown," I said angrily.

"Of course," he answered, "I renounce it. Come, old chap, I'll walk back to your rooms with you.''

"Don't try any of your doctor's tricks on me," I cried, trembling with fury. "Don't act as if you think I am insane.''

"What nonsense," he replied. "Come, it's getting late, Hildred.''

"No," I shouted, "you must listen. You cannot marry, I forbid it. Do you hear? I forbid it. You shall renounce the crown, and in reward I grant you exile, but if you refuse you shall die.''

He tried to calm me but I was roused at last, and drawing my long knife barred his way.

Then I told him how they would find Dr. Archer in the cellar with his throat open, and I laughed in his face when I thought of Vance and his knife, and the order signed by me.

"Ah, you are the King," I cried, "but I shall be King. Who are you to keep me from Empire over all the habitable earth? I was born the cousin of a king, but I shall be King!''

Louis stood white and rigid before me. Suddenly a man came running up Fourth Street, entered the gate of the Lethal Temple, traversed the path to the bronze doors at full speed, and plunged into the death chamber with the cry of one demented, and I laughed until I wept with tears, for I had recognized Vance, and knew that Hawberk and his daughter were no longer in my way.

"Go," I cried to Louis, "you have ceased to be a menace. You will never marry Constance now, and if you marry any one else in your exile, I will visit you as I did my doctor last night. Mr. Wilde takes charge of you to-morrow." Then I turned and darted into South Fifth Avenue, and with a cry of terror Louis dropped his belt and sabre and followed me like the wind. I heard him close behind me at the corner of Bleecker Street, and I dashed into the doorway under Hawberk's sign. He cried, "Halt, or I fire!" but when he saw that I flew up the stairs leaving Hawberk's shop below, he left me, and I heard him hammering and shouting at their door as though it were possible to arouse the dead.

Mr. Wilde's door was open, and I entered crying, "It is done, it is done! Let the nations rise and look upon their King!" but I could not find Mr. Wilde, so I went to the cabinet and took the splendid diadem from its case. Then I drew on the white silk robe, embroidered with the Yellow Sign, and placed the crown upon my head. At last I was King, King by my right in Hastur, King because I knew the mystery of the Hyades, and my mind had sounded the depths of the Lake of Hali. I was King! The first gray pencillings of dawn would raise a tempest which would shake two hemispheres. Then as I stood, my every nerve pitched to the highest tension, faint with the joy and splendor of my thought, without, in the dark passage, a man groaned.

I seized the tallow dip and sprang to the door. The cat passed me like a demon, and the tallow dip went out, but my long knife flew swifter than she, and I heard her screech, and I knew that my knife had found her. For a moment I listened to her tumbling and thumping about in the darkness, and then when her frenzy ceased, I lighted a lamp and raised it over my head. Mr. Wilde lay on the floor with his throat torn open. At first I thought he was dead, but as I looked, a green sparkle came into his sunken eyes, his mutilated hand trembled, and then a spasm stretched his mouth from ear to ear. For a moment my terror and despair gave place to hope, but as I bent over him his eyeballs rolled clean around in his head, and he died. Then while I stood transfixed with rage and despair, seeing my crown, my empire, every hope and every ambition, my very life, lying prostrate there with the dead master, *they* came, seized me from behind, and bound me until my veins stood out like cords, and my voice failed with the paroxysms of my frenzied screams. But I still raged, bleeding and infuriated among them, and more than one policeman felt my sharp teeth. Then when I could no longer move they came nearer; I saw old Hawberk, and behind him my cousin Louis' ghastly face, and farther away, in the corner, a woman, Constance, weeping softly.

"Ah! I see it now!" I shrieked. "You have seized the throne and the empire. Woe! woe to you who are crowned with the crown of the King in Yellow!"

[EDITOR'S NOTE—Mr. Castaigne died yesterday in the Asylum for Criminal Insane.]

Oliver Onions

THE BECKONING FAIR ONE

Oliver Onions is one of the most powerful and elegant
of all ghost story writers and his masterpiece is the novella, "The Beckoning Fair One." As a study of gradual
mental deterioration, it is admired by Lovecraft, Blackwood and Aickman, and has been called the greatest
single ghost story. It also represents complex levels of
interpretation, all tightly woven and consistent. It is, for
instance, an allegory of the fate of a man who rejects
reality for art. It may well be a realistic portrayal of descent into psychosis. It is certainly a story that calls the
nature of reality into doubt. Onions' first book of ghost
stories, *Widdershins* (1911), is one of the rarest and
best ghost books of the century; the stories are widely
reprinted and influential, including the one herein. It is
interesting to note the similarities between "The Beckoning Fair One" and "How Love Came to Professor
Guildea" and "Clara Militch," its apparent precursors.
It is in some ways superior even to "The Turn of the
Screw."

1

The three or four "To Let" boards had stood within the
low paling as long as the inhabitants of the little triangular "square" could remember, and if they had ever been
vertical it was a very long time ago. They now overhung the
palings each at its own angle, and resembled nothing so much

as a row of wooden choppers, ever in the act of falling upon some passer-by, yet never cutting off a tenant for the old house from the stream of his fellows. Not that there was ever any great "stream" through the square; the stream passed a furlong and more away, beyond the intricacy of tenements and alleys and byways that had sprung up since the old house had been built, hemming it in completely; and probably the house itself was only suffered to stand pending the falling-in of a lease or two, when doubtless a clearance would be made of the whole neighborhood.

It was of bloomy old red brick, and built into its walls were the crowns and clasped hands and other insignia of insurance companies long since defunct. The children of the secluded square had swung upon the low gate at the end of the entrance-alley until little more than the solid top bar of it remained, and the alley itself ran past boarded basement windows on which tramps had chalked their cryptic marks. The path was washed and worn uneven by the spilling of water from the eaves of the encroaching next house, and cats and dogs had made the approach their own. The chances of a tenant did not seem such as to warrant the keeping of the "To Let" boards in a state of legibility and repair, and as a matter of fact they were not so kept.

For six months Oleron had passed the old place twice a day or oftener, on his way from his lodgings to the room, ten minutes' walk away, he had taken to work in; and for six months no hatchet-like notice-board had fallen across his path. This might have been due to the fact that he usually took the other side of the square. But he chanced one morning to take the side that ran past the broken gate and the rain-worn entrance alley, and to pause before one of the inclined boards. The board bore, besides the agent's name, the announcement, written apparently about the time of Oleron's own early youth, that the key was to be had at Number Six.

Now Oleron was already paying for his separate bedroom and workroom, more than an author who, without private means, habitually disregards his public, can afford; and he was paying in addition a small rent for the storage of the greater part of his grandmother's furniture. Moreover, it invariably happened that the book he wished to read in bed was at his working-quarters half a mile and more away, while the note or letter he had sudden need of during the day was as likely as not to be in the pocket of another coat hanging behind his bedroom door. And there were other inconveniences in having a divided domicile. Therefore Oleron, brought suddenly up by the hatchet-like notice-board, looked first down through some scanty privet bushes at the boarded basement windows, then up at the blank and grimy windows of the first floor, and so up to the second floor and the flat stone coping of the leads. He stood for a minute thumbing his lean and shaven jaw; then, with another glance at the board, he walked slowly across the square to Number Six.

He knocked, and waited for two or three minutes, but, although the door stood open, received no answer. He was knocking again when a long-nosed man in shirt-sleeves appeared.

"I was arsking a blessing on our food," he said in severe explanation.

Oleron asked if he might have the key of the old house; and the long-nosed man withdrew again.

Oleron waited for another five minutes on the step; then the man, appearing again and masticating some of the food of which he had spoken, announced that the key was lost.

"But you won't want it," he said. "The entrance door isn't closed, and a push'll open any of the others. I'm a agent for it, if you're thinking of taking it—"

Oleron recrossed the square, descended the two steps at the broken gate, passed along the alley, and turned in at the old wide doorway. To the right, immediately within the door, steps descended to the roomy cellars, and the staircase before him had a carved rail, and was broad and handsome and filthy. Oleron ascended it, avoiding contact with the rail and wall, and stopped at the first landing. A door facing him had been boarded up, but he pushed at that on his right hand, and an insecure bolt or staple yielded. He entered the empty first floor.

He spent a quarter of an hour in the place, and then came out again. Without mounting higher, he descended and recrossed the square to the house of the man who had lost the key.

"Can you tell me how much the rent is?" he asked.

The man mentioned a figure, the comparative lowness of which seemed accounted for by the character of the neighbourhood and the abominable state of unrepair of the place.

"Would it be possible to rent a single floor?"

The long-nosed man did not know; they might. . . .

"Who are they?"

The man gave Oleron the name of a firm of lawyers in Lincoln's Inn.

"You might mention my name—Barrett," he added.

Pressure of work prevented Oleron from going down to Lincoln's Inn that afternoon, but he went on the morrow, and was instantly offered the whole house as a purchase for fifty pounds down, the remainder of the purchase money to remain on mortgage. It took him half an hour to disabuse the lawyer's mind of the idea that he wished anything more of the place than to rent a single floor of it. This made certain hums and haws of a difference, and the lawyer was by no means certain that it lay within his power to do as Oleron suggested; but it was finally extracted from him that, provided the notice-boards were allowed to remain up, and that, provided it was agreed that in the event of the whole house letting, the arrangement should terminate automatically without further notice, something might be done. That the old place should suddenly let over his head seemed to Oleron the slightest of risks to take, and he promised a decision within a week. On the morrow he visited the house again, went through it from top to bottom, and then went home to his lodgings to take a bath.

He was immensely taken with that portion of the house he had already determined should be his own. Scraped clean and repainted, and with that old furniture of Oleron's grandmother's, it ought to be entirely charming. He went to the storage warehouse to refresh his memory of his half-forgotten belongings, and to take the measurements; and thence he went to a decorator's. He was very busy with his regular work, and could have wished that the notice-board had caught his attention either a few months earlier or else later in the year; but the quickest way would be to suspend work entirely until after his removal. . . .

A fortnight later his first floor was painted throughout in a tender, elder-flower white, the paint was dry, and Oleron was in the middle of his installation. He was animated, delighted; and he rubbed his hands as he polished and made disposals of his grandmother's effects—the tall lattice-paned china cupboard with its Derby and Mason and Spode, the large folding Sheraton table, the long, low bookshelves (he had had two of them "copied"), the chairs, the Sheffield candlesticks, the riveted rose-bowls. These things he set against his newly painted elder-white walls—walls of wood paneled in the happiest proportions, and molded and coffered to the low-seated window-recesses in a mood of gaiety and rest that the builders of rooms no longer know. The ceilings were lofty, and faintly painted with an old pattern of stars; even the tapering moldings of his iron fireplace were as delicately designated as jewelry; and Oleron walked about rubbing his hands, frequently stopping for the mere pleasure of the glimpses from white room to white room. . . .

"Charming, charming!" he said to himself. "I wonder what Elsie Bengough will think of this!"

He bought a bolt and a Yale lock for his door, and shut off his quarters from the rest of the house. If he now wanted to read in bed, his book could be had for stepping into the next room. All the time, he thought how exceedingly lucky he was to get the place. He put up a hat-rack in the little square hall, and hung up his hats and caps and coats; and passers through the small triangular square late at night, looking up over the little serried row of wooden "To Let" hatchets, could see the light within Oleron's red blinds, or else the sudden darkening of one blind and the illumination of another, as Oleron, candlestick in hand, passed from room to room, making final settlings of his furniture, or preparing to resume the work that his removal had interrupted.

2

As far as the chief business of his life—his writing—was concerned, Paul Oleron treated the world a good deal better than he was treated by it; but he seldom took the trouble to strike a balance, or to compute how far, at forty-four years of age, he was behind his points on the handicap. To have done so wouldn't have altered matters, and it might have depressed Oleron. He had chosen his path, and was committed to it beyond possibility of withdrawal. Perhaps he had chosen it in the days when he had been easily swayed by something a little disinterested, a little generous, a little noble; and had he ever thought of questioning himself, he would still have held to it that a life without nobility and generosity and disinterestedness was no life for him. Only quite recently, and rarely, had he even vaguely suspected that there was more in it than this; but it was no good anticipating the day when, he supposed, he would reach that maximum point of his powers beyond which he must inevitably decline, and be left face to face with the question whether it would not have profited him better to have ruled his life by less exigent ideals.

In the meantime, his removal into the old house with the insurance marks built into its brick merely interrupted *Romilly Bishop* at the fifteenth chapter.

As this tall man with the lean, ascetic face moved about his new abode, arranging, changing, altering, hardly yet into his working stride again, he gave the impression of almost spinster-like precision and nicety. For twenty years past, in a score of lodgings, garrets, flats, and rooms furnished and unfurnished, he had been accustomed to do many things for himself, and he had discovered that it saves time and temper to be methodical. He had arranged with the wife of the long-nosed Barrett, a stout Welsh woman with a falsetto voice, the Merionethshire accent of which long residence in London had not perceptibly modified, to come across the square each morning to prepare his breakfast and also to "turn the place out" on Saturday mornings; and for the rest, he even welcomed a little housework as a relaxation from the strain of writing.

His kitchen, together with the adjoining strip of an apartment into which a modern bath had been fitted, overlooked the alley at the side of the house; and at one end of it was a large closet with a door, and a square sliding hatch in the upper part of the door. This had been a powder-closet, and through the hatch the elaborately dressed head had been thrust to receive the click and puff on the powder-pistol. Oleron puzzled a little over this closet; then, as its use occurred to him, he smiled faintly, a little moved, he knew not by what. . . . He would have to put it to a very different purpose from its original one; it would probably have to serve as a larder. . . . It was in this closet that he made a discovery. The back of it was shelved, and, rummaging on an upper shelf that ran deeply into the wall, Oleron found a couple of mushroom-shaped old wooden wig-stands. He did not know how they had come to be there. Doubtless the painters had turned them up somewhere or other, and had put them there. But his five rooms, as a whole, were short of cupboard and closet-room; and it was only by the exercise of some ingenuity that he was able to find places for the bestowal of his household linen, his boxes, and his seldom-used but not-to-be-destroyed accumulation of papers.

It was early spring that Oleron entered on his tenancy, and he was anxious to have *Romilly* ready for publication in the coming autumn. Nevertheless, he did not intend to force its production. Should it demand longer in the doing, so much the worse; he realized its importance, its crucial importance, in his artistic development, and it must have its own length and time. In the workroom he had recently left he had been making excellent progress; *Romilly* had begun, as the saying is, to speak and act of herself; and he did not doubt she would continue to do so the moment the distraction of his removal was over. This distraction was almost over; he told himself it was time he pulled himself together again; and on a March morning he went out and returned again with two great bunches of yellow daffodils, placed one bunch on his mantelpiece between the Sheffield sticks and the other on the table before him, and took out the half-completed manuscript of *Romilly Bishop*.

But before beginning work he went to a small rosewood cabinet and took from a drawer his check-book and pass-book. He totted them up, and his monk-like face grew thoughtful. His installation had cost him more than he had intended it should, and his balance was rather less than fifty pounds, with no immediate prospect of more.

"Hm! I'd forgotten rugs and chintz curtains and so forth mounted up so," said Oleron. "But it would have been a pity to spoil the place for the want of ten pounds or so. . . . Well, *Romilly* simply *must* be out for the autumn, that's all. So here goes————"

He drew his papers toward him.

But he worked badly; or, rather, he did not work at all. The square outside had its own noises, frequent and new, and Oleron could only hope that he would speedily become accustomed to these. First came hawkers, with their carts and cries; at midday the children, returning from school, trooped into the square and swung on Oleron's gate; and when the children had departed again for afternoon school, an itinerant musician with a mandoline posted himself beneath Oleron's window and began to strum. This was a not unpleasant distraction, and Oleron, pushing up his window, threw the man a penny. Then he returned to his table again. . . .

But it was no good. He came to himself, at long intervals, to find that he had been looking about his room and wondering how it had formerly been furnished—whether a settee in buttercup or petunia satin had stood under the farther window, whether from the center molding of the light lofty ceiling had depended a glimmering crystal chandelier, or where the tambour-frame or the piquet-table had stood. . . . No, it was no good; he had far better be frankly doing nothing than getting fruitlessly tired; and he decided that he would take a walk, but, chancing to sit down for a moment, dozed in his chair instead.

"This won't do," he yawned when he awoke at half-past four in the afternoon; "I must do better than this to-morrow————"

And he felt so deliciously lazy that for some minutes he even contemplated the breach of an appointment he had for the evening.

The next morning he sat down to work without even permitting himself to answer one of his three letters—two of them tradesmen's accounts, the third a note from Miss Bengough, forwarded from his old address. It was a jolly day of white and blue, with a gay noisy wind and a subtle turn in the color of growing things; and over and over again, once or twice a minute, his room became suddenly light and then subsided again, as the shining white cloud rolled northeastward over the square. The soft fitful illumination was reflected in the polished surface of the table and even in the footworn old floor; and the morning noises had begun again.

Oleron made a pattern of dots on the paper before him, and then broke off to move the jar of daffodils exactly opposite the center of a creamy panel. Then he wrote a sentence that ran continuously for a couple of lines, after which it broke off into notes and jottings. For a time he succeeded in persuading himself that in making these memoranda he was really working; then he rose and began to pace his room. As he did so, he was struck by an idea. It was that the place might possibly be a little better for more positive color. It was, perhaps, a thought *too* pale—mild and sweet as a kind old face, but a little devitalized, even wan. . . . Yes, decidedly it would bear a robuster note—more and richer flowers, and possibly some warm and gay stuff for cushions for the window-seats. . . .

"Of course, I really can't afford it," he muttered, as he went for a two-foot and began to measure the width of the window recesses. . . .

In stooping to measure a recess, his attitude suddenly changed to one of interest and attention. Presently he rose again, rubbing his hands with gentle glee.

"Oho, oho!" he said. "These look to me very much like windowboxes, nailed up. We must look into this! Yes, those are boxes, or I'm . . . oho, this is an adventure!"

On that wall of his sitting-room there were two windows (the third was in another corner), and, beyond the open bedroom door, on the same wall, was another. The seats of all had been painted, repainted, and painted again; and Oleron's investigating finger had barely detected the old nailheads beneath the paint. Under the ledge over which he stooped an old keyhole also had been puttied up. Oleron took out his penknife.

He worked carefully for five minutes, and then went into the kitchen for a hammer and chisel. Driving the chisel cautiously under the seat, he started the whole lid slightly. Again using the penknife, he cut along the hinged edge and outward along the ends; and then he fetched a wedge and a wooden mallet.

"Now for our little mystery————" he said.

The sound of the mallet on the wedge seemed, in that sweet and pale apartment, somehow a little brutal—nay, even shocking. The paneling rang and rattled and vibrated to the blows like a sounding-board. The whole house seemed to echo; from the roomy cellarage to the garrets above, a flock of echoes seemed to awake; and the sound got a little on Oleron's nerve. All at once he paused, fetched a duster, and muffled the mallet. . . . When the edge was sufficiently raised he put his fingers under it and lifted. The paint flaked and starred a little; the rusty old nails squeaked and grunted; and the lid came up, laying open the box beneath. Oleron looked into it. Save for a couple of inches of scurf and mold and old cobwebs it was empty.

"No treasure there," said Oleron, a little amused that he should have fancied there might have been. "*Romilly* will still have to be out by the autumn. Let's have a look at the others."

He turned to the second window.

The raising of the two remaining seats occupied him until well into the afternoon. That of the bedroom, like the first, was empty; but from the second seat of his sitting-room he drew out something yielding and folded and furred over an inch thick with dust. He carried the object into the kitchen, and having swept it over a bucket, took a duster to it.

It was some sort of a large bag, of an ancient frieze-like material, and when unfolded it occupied the greater part of the small kitchen floor. In shape it was an irregular, a very irregular, triangle, and it had a couple of wide flaps, with the remains of straps and buckles. The patch that had been uppermost in the folding was of a faded yellowish brown; but the rest of it was of shades of crimson that varied according to the exposure of the parts of it.

"Now whatever can that have been?" Oleron mused as he stood surveying it. . . . "I give it up. Whatever it is, it's settled my work for today, I'm afraid————"

He folded the object up carelessly and thrust it into a corner of the kitchen; then, taking pans and brushes and an old knife, he returned to the sitting-room and began to scrape and to wash and to line with paper his newly discovered receptacles. When he had finished, he put his spare boots and books and papers into them; and he closed the lids again, amused with his little adventure, but also a little anxious for the hour to come when he should settle fairly down to his work again.

3

It piqued Oleron a little that his friend, Miss Bengough, should dismiss with a glance the place he himself had found so singularly winning. Indeed she scarcely lifted her eyes to it. But then she had always been more or less like that—a little indifferent to the graces of life, careless of appearances, and perhaps a shade more herself when she ate biscuits from a paper bag than when she dined with greater observance of the convenances. She was an unattached journalist of thirty-four, large, showy, fair as butter, pink as a dog-rose, reminding one of a florist's picked specimen bloom, and given to sudden and ample movements and moist and explosive utterances. She "pulled a better living out of the pool" (as she expressed it) than Oleron did; and by cunningly disguised puffs of drapers and haberdashers she "pulled" also the greater part of her very varied wardrobe. She left small whirlwinds of air behind her when she moved, in which her veils and scarves fluttered and spun.

Oleron heard the flurry of her skirts on his staircase and her single loud knock at his door when he had been a month in his new abode. Her garments brought in the outer air, and she flung a bundle of ladies' journals down on a chair.

"Don't knock off for me," she said across a mouthful of large-headed hatpins as she removed her hat and veil. "I didn't know whether you were straight yet, so I've brought some sandwiches for lunch. You've got coffee, I suppose?— No, don't get up—I'll find the kitchen————"

"Oh, that's all right, I'll clear these things away. To tell the truth, I'm rather glad to be interrupted," said Oleron.

He gathered his work together and put it away. She was already in the kitchen; he heard the running of water into the kettle. He joined her, and ten minutes later followed her back to the sitting-room with the coffee and sandwiches on a tray. They sat down, with the tray on a small table between them.

"Well, what do you think of the new place?" Oleron asked as she poured out coffee.

"Hm! . . . Anybody'd think you were going to get married, Paul."

He laughed.

"Oh, no. But it's an improvement on some of them, isn't it?"

"Is it? I suppose it is; I don't know. I liked the last place, in spite of the black ceiling and no watertap. How's *Romilly*?"

Oleron thumbed his chin.

"Hm! I'm rather ashamed to tell you. The fact is, I've not got on very well with it. But it will be all right on the night, as you used to say."

"Stuck?"

"Rather stuck."

"Got any of it you care to read to me? . . ."

Oleron had long been in the habit of reading portions of his work to Miss Bengough occasionally. Her comments were always quick and practical, sometimes directly useful, sometimes indirectly suggestive. She, in return for his confidence, always kept all mention of her own work sedulously from him. His, she said, was "real work"; hers merely filled space, not always even grammatically.

"I'm afraid there isn't," Oleron replied, still meditatively dry-shaving his chin. Then he added, with a little burst of candor, "The fact is, Elsie, I've not written—not actually written—very much more of it—*any* more of it, in fact. But, of course, that doesn't mean I haven't progressed. I've progressed, in one sense, rather alarmingly. I'm now thinking of reconstructing the whole thing."

Miss Bengough gave a gasp. "Reconstructing!"

"Making Romilly herself a different type of woman. Somehow, I've begun to feel that I'm not getting the most out of her. As she stands, I've certainly lost interest in her to some extent."

"But—but———" Miss Bengough protested, "you had her so real, *so living*, Paul!"

Oleron smiled faintly. He had been quite prepared for Miss Bengough's disapproval. He wasn't surprised that she liked Romilly as she at present existed; she would. Whether she realized it or not, there was much of herself in his fictitious creation. Naturally Romilly would seem "real," "living," to her. . . .

"But are you really serious, Paul?" Miss Bengough asked presently, with a round-eyed stare.

"Quite serious."

"You're really going to scrap those fifteen chapters?"

"I didn't exactly say that."

"That fine, rich love-scene?"

"I should only do it reluctantly, and for the sake of something I thought better."

"And that beautiful, *beautiful* description of Romilly on the shore?"

"It wouldn't necessarily be wasted," he said a little uneasily.

But Miss Bengough made a large and windy gesture, and then let him have it.

"Really, you are *too* trying!" she broke out. "I do wish sometimes you'd remember you're human, and live in a world! You know I'd be the *last* to wish you to lower your standard one inch, but it wouldn't be lowering it to bring it within human comprehension. Oh, you're sometimes altogether too godlike! . . . Why, it would be a wicked, criminal waste of your powers to destroy those fifteen chapters! Look at it reasonably, now. You've been working for nearly twenty years; you've now got what you've been working for almost within your grasp; your affairs are at a most critical stage (oh, don't tell me; I know you're about at the end of your money); and here you are, deliberately proposing to withdraw a thing that will probably make your name, and to substitute for it something that ten to one nobody on earth will ever want to read—and small blame to them! Really, you try my patience!''

Oleron had shaken his head slowly as she had talked. It was an old story between them. The noisy, able practical journalist was an admirable friend—up to a certain point; beyond that . . . well, each of us knows that point beyond which we stand alone. Elsie Bengough sometimes said that had she had one-tenth part of Oleron's genius there were few things she could not have done—thus making that genius a quantitatively divisible thing, a sort of ingredient, to be added to or to be subtracted from in the admixture of his work. That it was a qualitative thing, essential, indivisible, informing, passed her comprehension. Their spirits parted company at that point. Oleron knew it. She did not appear to know it.

''Yes, yes, yes,'' he said a little wearily, by-and-by, ''practically you're quite right, entirely right, and I haven't a word to say. If I could only turn *Romilly* over to you you'd make an enormous success of her. But that can't be, and I, for my part, am seriously doubting whether she's worth my while. You know what that means.''

''What does it mean?'' she demanded bluntly.

''Well,'' he said, smiling wanly, ''what *does* it mean when you're convinced a thing isn't worth doing? You simply don't do it.''

Miss Bengough's eyes swept the ceiling for assistance against this impossible man.

''What utter rubbish!'' she broke out at last. ''Why, when I saw you last you were simply oozing *Romilly*; you were turning her off at the rate of four chapters a week; if you hadn't moved you'd have had her three parts done by now. What on earth possessed you to move right in the middle of your most important work?''

Oleron tried to put her off with a recital of inconveniences, but she wouldn't have it. Perhaps in her heart she partly suspected the reason. He was simply mortally weary of the narrow circumstances of his life. He had had twenty years of it—twenty years of garrets and roof-chambers and dingy flats and shabby lodgings, and he was tired of dinginess and shabbiness. The reward was as far off as ever—or if it was not, he no longer cared as once he would have cared to put out his hand and take it. It is all very well to tell a man who is at the point of exhaustion that only another effort is required of him; if he cannot make it he is as far off as ever. . . .

''Anyway,'' Oleron summed up, ''I'm happier here than I've been for a long time. That's some sort of a justification.''

''And doing no work,'' said Miss Bengough pointedly.

At that a trifling petulance that had been gathering in Oleron came to a head.

''And why should I do nothing but work?'' he demanded. ''How much happier am I for it? I don't say I don't love my work—when it's done; but I hate doing it. Sometimes it's an intolerable burden that I simply long to be rid of. Once in many weeks it has a moment, one moment, of glow and thrill for me; I remember the days when it was all glow and thrill; and now I'm forty-four, and it's becoming drudgery. Nobody wants it; I'm ceasing to want it myself; and if any ordinary sensible man were to ask me whether I didn't think I was a fool to go on, I think I should agree that I was.''

Miss Bengough's comely pink face was serious.

''But you knew all that, many, many years ago, Paul—and still you chose it,'' she said in a low voice.

''Well, and how should I have known?'' he demanded. ''I didn't know. I was told so. My heart, if you like, told me so, and I thought I knew. Youth always thinks it knows; then one day it discovers that it is nearly fifty————''

''Forty-four, Paul————''

''—forty-four, then—and it finds that the glamour isn't in front, but behind. Yes, I knew and chose, if *that's* knowing and choosing . . . but it's a costly choice we're called on to make when we're young!''

Miss Bengough's eyes were on the floor. Without moving them she said: "You're not regretting it, Paul?"

"Am I not?" he took her up. "Upon my word, I've lately thought I am! What *do* I get in return for it all?"

"You know what you get," she replied.

He might have known from her tone what else he could have had for the holding up of a finger—herself. She knew, but could not tell him, that he could have done no better thing for himself. Had he, any time these ten years, asked her to marry him, she would have replied quietly, "Very well; when?" He had never thought of it. . . .

"Yours is the real work," she continued quietly. "Without you we jackals couldn't exist. You and a few like you hold everything upon your shoulders."

For a minute there was a silence. Then it occurred to Oleron that this was common vulgar grumbling. It was not his habit. Suddenly he rose and began to stack cups and plates on the tray.

"Sorry you catch me like this, Elsie," he said, with a little laugh. . . . "No, I'll take them out; then we'll go for a walk, if you like. . . ."

He carried out the tray, and then began to show Miss Bengough round his flat. She made few comments. In the kitchen she asked what an old faded square of reddish frieze was, that Mrs. Barrett used as a cushion for her wooden chair.

"That? I should be glad if you could tell *me* what it is," Oleron replied as he unfolded the bag and related the story of its finding in the window-seat.

"I think I know what it is," said Miss Bengough. "It's been used to wrap up a harp before putting it into its case."

"By Jove, that's probably just what it was," said Oleron. "I could make neither head nor tail of it. . . ."

They finished the tour of the flat, and returned to the sitting-room.

"And who lives in the rest of the house?" Miss Bengough asked.

"I dare say a tramp sleeps in the cellar occasionally. No-body else."

"Hm! . . . Well, I'll tell you what I think about it, if you like."

"I should like."

"You'll never work here."

"Oh?" said Oleron quickly. "Why not?"

"You'll never finish *Romilly* here. Why, I don't know, but you won't. I know it. You'll have to leave before you get on with that book."

He mused for a moment, and then said:

"Isn't that a little—prejudiced, Elsie?"

"Perfectly ridiculous. As an argument it hasn't a leg to stand on. But there it is," she replied, her mouth once more full of the large-headed hat pins.

Oleron was reaching down his hat and coat. He laughed.

"I can only hope you're entirely wrong," he said, "for I shall be in a serious mess if *Romilly* isn't out in the autumn."

4

As Oleron sat by his fire that evening, pondering Miss Bengough's prognostication that difficulties awaited him in his work, he came to the conclusion that it would have been far better had she kept her beliefs to herself. No man does a thing better for having his confidence damped at the outset, and to speak of difficulties is in a sense to make them. Speech itself becomes a deterrent act, to which other discouragements accrete until the very event of which warning is given is as likely as not to come to pass. He heartily confounded her. An influence hostile to the completion of *Romilly* had been born.

And in some illogical, dogmatic way women seem to have, she had attached this antagonistic influence to his new abode. Was ever anything so absurd! "You'll never finish *Romilly* here." . . . Why not? Was this her idea of the luxury that saps the spring of action and brings a man down to indolence and dropping out of the race? The place was well enough—

it was entirely charming, for that matter—but it was not so demoralizing as all that! No; Elsie had missed the mark that time. . . .

He moved his chair to look round the room that smiled, positively smiled, in the firelight. He too smiled, as if pity was to be entertained for a maligned apartment. Even that slight lack of robust color he had remarked was not noticeable in the soft glow. The drawn chintz curtains—they had a flowered and trellised pattern, with baskets and oaten pipes—fell in long quiet folds to the window-seats; the rows of bindings in old bookcases took the light richly; the last trace of sallowness had gone with the daylight; and, if the truth must be told, it had been Elsie herself who had seemed a little out of the picture.

That reflection struck him a little, and presently he returned to it. Yes, the room had, quite accidentally, done Miss Bengough a disservice that afternoon. It had, in some subtle but unmistakable way, placed her, marked a contrast of qualities. Assuming for the sake of argument the slightly ridiculous proposition that the room in which Oleron sat *was* characterized by a certain sparsity and lack of vigor; so much the worse for Miss Bengough; she certainly erred on the side of redundancy and general muchness. And if one must contrast abstract qualities, Oleron inclined to the austere in taste. . . .

Yes, here Oleron had made a distinct discovery; he wondered he had not made it before. He pictured Miss Bengough again as she had appeared that afternoon—large, showy, moistly pink, with that quality of the prize bloom exuding, as it were, from her; and instantly she suffered in his thought. He even recognized now that he had noticed something odd at the time, and that unconsciously his attitude, even while she had been there, had been one of criticism. The mechanism of her was a little obvious; her melting humidity was the result of analyzable processes; and behind her there had seemed to lurk some dim shape emblematic of mortality. He had never, during the ten years of their intimacy, dreamed for a moment of asking her to marry him; nonetheless, he now felt for the first time a thankfulness that he had not done so. . . .

Then, suddenly and swiftly, his face flamed that he should be thinking thus of his friend. What! Elsie Bengough, with whom he had spent weeks and weeks of afternoons—she, the good chum, on whose help he would have counted had all the rest of the world failed him—she, whose loyalty to him would not, he knew, swerve as long as there was breath in her—Elsie to be even in thought dissected thus! He was an ingrate and a cad. . . .

Had she been there in that moment he would have abased himself before her.

For ten minutes and more he sat, still gazing into the fire, with that humiliating red fading slowly from his cheeks. All was still within and without, save for a tiny musical tinkling that came from his kitchen—the dripping of water from an imperfectly turned-off tap into the vessel beneath it. Mechanically he began to beat with his fingers to the faintly heard falling of the drops; the tiny regular movement seemed to hasten that shameful withdrawal from his face. He grew cool once more; and when he resumed his meditation he was all unconscious that he took it up again at the same point. . . .

It was not only her florid superfluity of build that he had approached in the attitude of criticism; he was conscious also of the wide differences between her mind and his own. He felt no thankfulness that up to a certain point their natures had ever run companionably side by side; he was now full of questions beyond that point. Their intellects diverged; there was no denying it; and, looking back, he was inclined to doubt whether there had been any real coincidence. True, he had read his writings to her and she had appeared to speak comprehendingly and to the point; but what can a man do who, having assumed that another sees as he does, is suddenly brought up sharp by something that falsifies and discredits all that has gone before? He doubted all now. . . . It did for a moment occur to him that the man who demands of a friend more than can be given to him is in danger of losing that friend, but he put the thought aside.

Again he ceased to think, and again moved his finger to the distant dripping of the tap. . . .

And now (he resumed by-and-by), if these things were true of Elsie Bengough, they were also true of the creation of which she was the prototype—Romilly Bishop. And since he could say of Romilly what for very shame he could not say of Elsie, he gave his thoughts rein. He did so in that smiling, fire-lighted room, to the accompaniment of the faintly heard tap.

There was no longer any doubt about it; he hated the central character of his novel. Even as he had described her physically she overpowered the senses; she was coarse-fibered, overcolored, rank. It became true the moment he formulated his thought; Gulliver had described the Brobdingnagian maids-of-honor thus: and mentally and spiritually she corresponded—was unsensitive, limited, common. The model (he closed his eyes for a moment)—the model stuck out through fifteen vulgar and blatant chapters to such a pitch that, without seeing the reason, he had been unable to begin the sixteenth. He marveled that it had only just dawned upon him.

And *this* was to have been his Beatrice, his vision! As Elsie she was to have gone into the furnace of his art, and she was to have come out the Woman all men desire! Her thoughts were to have been culled from his own finest, her form from his dearest dreams, and her setting wherever he could find one fit for her worth. He had brooded long before making the attempt; then one day he had felt her stir within him as a mother feels a quickening, and he had begun to write; and so he had added chapter to chapter. . . .

And those fifteen sodden chapters were what he had produced!

Again he sat softly moving his finger. . . .

Then he bestirred himself.

She must go, all fifteen chapters of her. That was settled. For what was to take her place his mind was a blank; but one thing at a time; a man is not excused from taking the wrong course because the right one is not immediately revealed to him. Better would come if it was to come; in the meantime—

He rose, fetched the fifteen chapters, and read them over before he should drop them into the fire.

But instead of putting them into the fire he let them fall from his hand. He became conscious of the dripping of the tap again. It had a tinkling gamut of four or five notes, on which it rang irregular changes, and it was foolishly sweet and dulcimer-like. In his mind Oleron could see the gathering of each drop, its little tremble on the lip of the tap, and the tiny percussion of its fall "Plink—plunk," minimized almost to inaudibility. Following the lowest note there seemed to be a brief phrase, irregularly repeated; and presently Oleron found himself waiting for the recurrence of this phrase. It was quite pretty. . . .

But it did not conduce to wakefulness, and Oleron dozed over his fire.

When he awoke again the fire had burned low and the flames of the candles were licking the rims of the Sheffield sticks. Sluggishly he rose, yawned, went his nightly round of door-locks, and window-fastenings, and passed into his bedroom. Soon, he slept soundly.

But a curious little sequel followed on the morrow. Mrs. Barrett usually tapped, not at his door, but at the wooden wall beyond which lay Oleron's bed; and then Oleron rose, put on his dressing-gown, and admitted her. He was not conscious that as he did so that morning he hummed an air; but Mrs. Barrett lingered with her hand on the doorknob and her face a little averted and smiling.

"De-ar me!" her soft falsetto rose. "But that will be a very o-ald tune, Mr. Oleron. I will not have heard it this forty years!"

"What tune?" Oleron asked.

"The tune, indeed, that you was humming, sir."

Oleron had his thumb in the flap of a letter. It remained there.

"*I* was humming? . . . Sing it, Mrs. Barrett."

Mrs. Barrett prut-prutted.

"I have no voice for singing, Mr. Oleron; it was Ann Pugh was the singer of our family; but the tune will be very o-ald, and it is called 'The Beckoning Fair One.' "

"Try to sing it," said Oleron, his thumb still in the envelope; and Mrs. Barrett, with much dimpling and confusion, hummed the air.

"They do say it was sung to a harp, Mr. Oleron, and it will be very o-ald," she concluded.

"And *I* was singing that?"

"Indeed you was. I would not be likely to tell you lies."

With a "Very well—let me have breakfast," Oleron opened his letter; but the trifling circumstance struck him as more odd than he would have admitted to himself. The phrase he had hummed had been that which he had associated with the falling from the tap on the evening before.

5

Even more curious than that the commonplace dripping of an ordinary water-tap should have tallied so closely with an actually existing air was another result it had, namely, that it awakened, or seemed to awaken, in Oleron an abnormal sensitiveness to other noises of the old house. It has been remarked that silence obtains its fullest and most impressive quality when it is broken by some minute sound; and, truth to tell, the place was never still. Perhaps the mildness of the spring air operated on its torpid old timbers; perhaps Oleron's fires caused it to stretch its old anatomy; and certainly a whole world of insect life bored and burrowed in its baulks and joists. At any rate Oleron had only to sit quietly in his chair and to wait for a minute or two in order to become aware of such a change in the auditory scale as comes upon a man who, conceiving the midsummer woods to be motionless and still, all at once finds his ear sharpened to the crepitation of a myriad insects.

And he smiled to think of man's arbitrary distinction between that which has life and that which has not. Here, quite apart from such recognizable sounds as the scampering of mice, the falling of plaster behind his paneling, and the popping of purses or coffins from his fire, was a whole house talking to him had he but known its language. Beams settled with a tired sigh into their old mortises; creatures ticked in the walls; joists cracked, boards complained; with no palpable stirring of the air window-sashes changed their positions with a soft knock in their frames. And whether the place had life in this sense or not, it had at all events a winsome personality. It needed but an hour of musing for Oleron to conceive the idea that, as his own body stood in friendly relation to his soul, so, by an extension and an attenuation, his habitation might fantastically be supposed to stand in some relation to himself. He even amused himself with the farfetched fancy that he might so identify himself with the place that some future tenant, taking possession, might regard it as in a sense haunted. It would be rather a joke if he, a perfectly harmless author, with nothing on his mind worse than a novel he had discovered he must begin again, should turn out to be laying the foundation of a future ghost! . . .

In proportion, however, as he felt this growing attachment to the fabric of his abode, Elsie Bengough, from being merely unattracted, began to show a dislike of the place that was more and more marked. And she did not scruple to speak of her aversion.

"It doesn't belong to today at all, for you especially it's bad," she said with decision. "You're only too ready to let go your hold on actual things and to slip into apathy; *you* ought to be in a place with concrete floors and a patent gasmeter and a tradesman's lift. And it would do you all the good in the world if you had a job that made you scramble and rub elbows with your fellow-men. Now, if I could get you a job, for, say, two or three days a week, one that would allow you heaps of time for your proper work—would you take it?"

Somehow, Oleron resented a little being diagnosed like this. He thanked Miss Bengough, but without a smile.

"Thank you, but I don't think so. After all each of us has his own life to live," he could not refrain from adding.

"His own life to live! . . . How long is it since you were out, Paul?"

"About two hours."

"I don't mean to buy stamps or to post a letter. How long is it since you had anything like a stretch?"

"Oh, some little time perhaps. I don't know."

"Since I was here last?"

"I haven't been out much."

"And has *Romilly* progressed much better for your being cooped up?"

"I think she has. I'm laying the foundations of her. I shall begin the actual writing presently."

It seemed as if Miss Bengough had forgotten their tussle about the first *Romilly*. She frowned, turned half away, and then quickly turned again.

"Ah! . . . So you've still got that ridiculous idea in your head?"

"If you mean," said Oleron slowly, "that I've discarded the old *Romilly*, and am at work on a new one, you're right. I have still got that idea in my head."

Something uncordial in his tone struck her; but she was a fighter. His own absurd sensitiveness hardened her. She gave a "Pshaw!" of impatience.

"Where is the old one?" she demanded abruptly.

"Why?" asked Oleron.

"I want to see it. I want to show some of it to you. I want, if you're not wool-gathering entirely, to bring you back to your senses."

This time it was he who turned his back. But when he turned round again he spoke more gently.

"It's no good, Elsie. I'm responsible for the way I go, and you must allow me to go it—even if it should seem wrong to you. Believe me, I am giving thought to it. . . . The manuscript? I was on the point of burning it, but I didn't. It's in that window-seat, if you must see it."

Miss Bengough crossed quickly to the window-seat, and lifted the lid. Suddenly she gave a little exclamation, and put the back of her hand to her mouth. She spoke over her shoulder:

"You ought to knock those nails in, Paul," she said.

He strode to her side.

"What? What is it? What's the matter?" he asked. "I did knock them in—or, rather, pulled them out."

"You left enough to scratch with," she replied, showing her hand. From the upper wrist to the knuckle of the little finger a welling red wound showed.

"Good—Gracious!" Oleron ejaculated. . . . "Here, come to the bathroom and bathe it quickly—"

He hurried her to the bathroom, turned on warm water, and bathed and cleansed the bad gash. Then, still holding the hand, he turned cold water on it, uttering broken phrases of astonishment and concern.

"Good Lord, how did that happen! As far as I knew I'd . . . is this water too cold? Does that hurt? I can't imagine how on earth . . . there; that'll do—"

"No—one moment longer—I can bear it," she murmured, her eyes closed. . . .

Presently he led her back to the sitting-room and bound the hand in one of his handkerchiefs; but his face did not lose its expression of perplexity. He had spent half a day in opening and making serviceable the three windowboxes, and he could not conceive how he had come to leave an inch and a half of rusty nail standing in the wood. He himself had opened the lids of each of them a dozen times and had not noticed any nail; but there it was. . . .

"It shall come out now, at all events," he muttered, as he went for a pair of pincers. And he made no mistake about it that time.

Elsie Bengough had sunk into a chair, and her face was rather white; but in her hand was the manuscript of *Romilly*. She had not finished with *Romilly* yet. Presently she returned to the charge.

"Oh, Paul, it will be the greatest mistake you ever, *ever* made if you do not publish this!" she said.

He hung his head, genuinely distressed. He couldn't get that incident of the nail out of his head, and *Romilly* occupied a second place in his thoughts for the moment. But still she insisted: and when presently he spoke it was almost as if he asked her pardon for something.

"What can I say, Elsie? I can only hope that when you see

the new version, you'll see how right I am. And if in spite of all you *don't* like her, well . . .'' he made a hopeless gesture. "Don't you see that I *must* be guided by my own lights?''

She was silent.

"Come, Elsie," he said gently. "We've got along well so far; don't let us split on this."

The last words had hardly passed his lips before he regretted them. She had been nursing her injured hand, with her eyes once more closed; but her lips and lids quivered simultaneously. Her voice shook as she spoke.

"I can't help saying it, Paul, but you are so greatly changed."

"Hush, Elsie," he murmured soothingly; "you've had a shock; rest for a while. How could I change?''

"I don't know, but you are. You've not been yourself ever since you came here. I wish you'd never seen the place. It's stopped your work, it's making you into a person I hardly know, and it's made me horribly anxious about you. . . . Oh, how my hand is beginning to throb!''

"Poor child!" he murmured. "Will you let me take you to a doctor and have it properly dressed?''

"No—I shall be all right presently—I'll keep it raised—''

She put her elbow on the back of her chair, and the bandaged hand rested lightly on his shoulder.

At that touch an entirely new anxiety stirred suddenly within him. Hundreds of times previously, on their jaunts and excursions, she had slipped her hand within his arm as she might have slipped it into the arm of a brother, and he had accepted the little affectionate gesture as a brother might have accepted it. But now, for the first time, there rushed into his mind a hundred startling questions. Her eyes were still closed, and her head had fallen pathetically back; and there was a lost and ineffable smile on her parted lips. The truth broke in upon him. Good God! . . . And he had never divined it!

And stranger than all was that, now that he did see that she was lost in love of him, there came to him, not sorrow and humility and abasement, but something else that he struggled in vain against—something entirely strange and new, that, had he analyzed it, he would have found to be petulance and irritation and resentment and ungentleness. The sudden selfish prompting mastered him before he was aware. He all but gave it words. What was she doing there at all? Why was she not getting on with her own work? Why was she here interfering with his? Who had given her this guardianship over him that lately she had put forward so assertively?—"Changed?" It was she, not himself, who had changed. . . .

But by the time she had opened her eyes again he had overcome his resentment sufficiently to speak gently, albeit with reserve.

"I wish you would let me take you to a doctor."

She rose.

"No, thank you, Paul," she said. "I'll go now. If I need a dressing I'll get one; take the other hand, please. Goodby—"

He did not attempt to detain her. He walked with her to the foot of the stairs. Halfway along the narrow alley she turned.

"It would be a long way to come if you happened not to be in," she said: "I'll send you a postcard the next time."

At the gate she turned again.

"Leave here, Paul," she said, with a mournful look. "Everything's wrong with this house."

Then she was gone.

Oleron returned to his room. He crossed straight to the windowbox. He opened the lid and stood long looking at it. Then he closed it again and turned away.

"That's rather frightening," he muttered. "It's simply not possible that I should not have removed that nail. . . ."

6

Oleron knew very well what Elsie had meant when she had said that her next visit would be preceded by a postcard. She, too, had realized that at last, at last he knew—knew, and didn't want her. It gave him a miserable, pitiful pang, therefore, when she came again within a week, knocking at the door unannounced. She spoke from the landing; she did not intend to stay, she said; and he had to press her before she would so much as enter.

Her excuse for calling was that she had heard of an inquiry for short stories that he might be wise to follow up. He thanked her. Then, her business over, she seemed anxious to get away again. Oleron did not seek to detain her; even he saw through the pretext of the stories; and he accompanied her down the stairs.

But Elsie Bengough had no luck whatever in that house. A second accident befell her. Halfway down the staircase there was the sharp sound of splintering wood, and she checked a loud cry. Oleron knew the woodwork to be old, but he himself had ascended and descended frequently enough without mishap. . . .

Elsie had put her foot through one of the stairs.

He sprang to her side in alarm.

"Oh, I say! My poor girl!"

She laughed hysterically.

"It's my weight—I know I'm getting fat—"

"Keep still—let me clear these splinters away," he muttered between his teeth.

She continued to laugh and sob that it was her weight—she was getting fat—

He thrust downward at the broken boards. The extrication was no easy matter, and her torn boot showed him how badly the foot and ankle within it must be abraded.

"Good God—good God!" he muttered over and over again.

"I shall be too heavy for anything soon," she sobbed and laughed.

But she refused to reascend and to examine her hurt.

"No, let me go quickly—let me go quickly," she repeated.

"But it's a frightful gash!"

"No—not so bad—let me get away quickly—I'm—I'm not wanted."

At her words, that she was not wanted, his head dropped as if she had given him a buffet.

"Elsie!" he choked, brokenly and shocked.

But she too made a quick gesture, as if she put something violently aside.

"Oh, Paul, not *that*—not *you*—of course I do mean that too in a sense—oh, you know what I mean! . . . But if the other can't be, spare me this now! I—I wouldn't have come, but—but oh, I did, I *did* try to keep away!"

It was intolerable, heartbreaking; but what could he do—what could he say? He did not love her. . . .

"Let me go—I'm not wanted—let me take away what's left of me—"

"Dear Elsie—you are very dear to me—"

But again she made the gesture, as of putting something violently aside.

"No, not that—not anything less—don't offer me anything less—leave me a little pride—"

"Let me get my hat and coat—let me take you to a doctor," he muttered.

But she refused. She refused even the support of his arm. She gave another unsteady laugh.

"I'm sorry I broke your stairs, Paul. . . . You will go and see about the short stories, won't you?"

He groaned.

"Then if you won't see a doctor, will you go across the square and let Mrs. Barrett look at you? Look, there's Barrett passing now—"

The long-nosed Barrett was looking curiously down the alley, but as Oleron was about to call him he made off without a word. Elsie seemed anxious for nothing so much as to be clear of the place, and finally promised to go straight to a doctor, but insisted on going alone.

"Good-by," she said.

And Oleron watched her until she was past the hatchet-like "To Let" boards, as if he feared that even they might fall upon her and maim her.

That night Oleron did not dine. He had far too much on his mind. He walked from room to room of his flat, as if he could have walked away from Elsie Bengough's haunting cry that still rang in his ears. "I'm not wanted—don't offer me anything less—let me take away what's left of me—"

Oh, if he could only have persuaded himself that he loved her!

He walked until twilight fell, then, without lighting candles, he stirred up the fire, and flung himself into a chair.

Poor, poor Elsie! . . .

But even while his heart ached for her, it was out of the question. If only he had known! If only he had used common observation! But those walks, those sisterly takings of the arm—what a fool he had been! . . . Well, it was too late now. It was she, not he, who must now act—act by keeping away. He would help her all he could. He himself would not sit in her presence. If she came, he would hurry her out again as fast as he could. . . . Poor, poor Elsie!

His room grew dark; the fire burned dead; and he continued to sit, wincing from time to time as a fresh tortured phrase rang again in his ears.

Then suddenly, he knew not why, he found himself anxious for her in a new sense—uneasy about her personal safety. A horrible fancy that even then she might be looking over an embankment down into dark water, that she might even now be glancing up at the hook on the door, took him. Women had been known to do those things. . . . Then there would be an inquest, and he himself would be called upon to identify her, and would be asked how she had come by an ill-healed wound on the hand and a bad abrasion of the ankle. Barret would say that he had seen her leaving his house. . . .

Then he recognized that his thoughts were morbid. By an effort of will he put them aside, and sat for a while listening to the faint creakings and tickings and rappings within his paneling. . . .

If only he could have married her! . . . But he couldn't. Her face had risen before him again as he had seen it on the stairs, drawn with pain and ugly and swollen with tears. Ugly—yes, positively blubbered; if tears were women's weapons, as they were said to be, such tears were weapons turning against themselves . . . suicide again. . . .

Then all at once he found himself attentively considering her two accidents.

Extraordinary they had been, both of them. He *could not* have left that old nail standing in the wood; why, he had fetched tools specially from the kitchen; and he was convinced that that step that had broken beneath her weight had been as sound as the others. It was inexplicable. If these things could happen, anything could happen. There was not a beam nor a jamb in the place that might not fall without warning, not a plank that might not crash inward, not a nail that might not become a dagger. The whole place was full of life even now; as he sat there in the dark he heard its crowds of noises as if the house had been one great microphone. . . .

Only half conscious that he did so, he had been sitting for some time identifying these noises, attributing to each crack or creak or knock its material cause; but there was one noise which, again not fully conscious of the omission, he had not sought to account for. It had last come some minutes ago; it came again now—a sort of soft sweeping rustle that seemed to hold an almost inaudible minute crackling. For half a minute or so it had Oleron's attention; then his heavy thoughts were of Elsie Bengough again.

He was nearer to loving her in that moment than he had ever been. He thought how to some men their loved ones were but the dearer for those poor mortal blemishes that tell us we are but sojourners on earth, with a common fate not far distant that makes it hardly worth while to do anything but love for the time remaining. Strangling sobs, blearing tears, bodies buffeted by sickness, hearts and minds callous and hard with the rubs of the world—how little love there would be were these things a barrier to love! In that sense he did love Elsie Bengough. What her happiness had never moved in him her sorrow almost woke. . . .

Suddenly his meditation went. His ear had once more become conscious of that soft and repeated noise—the long sweep with the almost inaudible crackle in it. Again and again it came, with a curious insistence, and urgency. It quickened a little as he became increasingly attentive . . . it seemed to Oleron that it grew louder. . . .

All at once he started bolt upright in his chair, tense and listening. The silky rustle came again; he was trying to attach it to something. . . .

The next moment he had leapt to his feet, unnerved and terrified. His chair hung poised for a moment, and then went over, setting the fire-irons clattering as it fell. There was only one noise in the world like that which had caused him to spring thus to his feet. . . .

The next time it came Oleron felt behind him at the empty air with his hand, and backed slowly until he found himself against the wall.

"God in Heaven!" The ejaculation broke from Oleron's lips. The sound had ceased.

The next moment he had given a high cry.

"What is it? What's there? *Who's* there?"

A sound of scuttling caused his knees to bend under him for a moment; but that, he knew, was a mouse. That was not something that his stomach turned sick and his mind reeled to entertain. That other sound, the like of which was not in the world, had now entirely ceased; and again he called. . . .

He called and continued to call; and then another terror, a terror of the sound of his own voice, seized him. He did not dare to call again. His shaking hand went to his pocket for a match, but found none. He thought there might be matches on the mantelpiece—

He worked his way to the mantelpiece round a little recess, without for a moment leaving the wall. Then his hand encountered the mantelpiece, and groped along it. A box of matches fell to the hearth. He could just see them in the firelight, but his hand could not pick them up until he had cornered them inside the fender.

Then he rose and struck a light.

The room was as usual. He struck a second match. A candle stood on the table. He lighted it, and the flame sank for a moment and then burned up clear. Again he looked round.

There was nothing.

There was nothing; but there had been something, and might still be something. Formerly, Oleron had smiled at the fantastic thought that, by a merging and interplay of identities between himself and his beautiful room, he might be preparing a ghost for the future; it had not occurred to him *that there might have been a similar merging and coalescence in the past*. Yet with this staggering impossibility he was now face to face. Something did persist in the house; it had a tenant other than himself; and that tenant, whatsoever or whosoever, had appalled Oleron's soul by producing the sound of a woman brushing her hair.

7

Without quite knowing how he came to be there Oleron found himself striding over the loose board he had temporarily placed on the step broken by Miss Bengough. He was hatless and descending the stairs. Not until later did there return to him a hazy memory that he had left the candle burning on the table, had opened the door no wider than was necessary to allow the passage of his body, and had sidled out, closing the door softly behind him. At the foot of the stairs another shock awaited him. Something dashed with a flurry up from the disused cellars and disappeared out of the door. It was only a cat, but Oleron gave a childish sob.

He passed out of the gate, and stood for a moment under the "To Let" boards, plucking foolishly at his lip and looking up at the glimmer of light behind one of his red blinds. Then, still looking over his shoulder, he moved stumblingly up the square. There was a small public-house round the corner; Oleron had never entered it; but he entered it now, and put down a shilling that missed the counter by inches.

"B—b—bran—brandy," he said, and then stooped to look for the shilling.

He had the little sawdusted bar to himself; what company there was—carters and laborers and the small tradesmen of the neighborhood—was gathered in the farther compartment, beyond the space where the white-haired landlady moved among her taps and bottles. Oleron sat down on a hardwood settee with a perforated seat, drank half his brandy, and then, thinking he might as well drink it as spill it, finished it.

Then he fell to wondering which of the men whose voices he heard across the public-house would undertake the removal of his effects on the morrow.

In the meantime he ordered more brandy.

For he did not intend to go back to that room where he had left the candle burning. Oh no! He couldn't have faced even the entry and the staircase with the broken step—certainly not that pith-white, fascinating room. He would go back for the present to his old arrangement, of workroom and separate sleeping-quarters; he would go to his old landlady at once—presently—when he had finished his brandy—and see if she could put him up for the night. His glass was empty now. . . .

He rose, had it refilled, and sat down again.

And if anybody asked his reason for removing again? Oh, he had reason enough—reason enough! Nails that put themselves back into wood again and gashed people's hands, steps that broke when you trod on them, and women who came into a man's place and brushed their hair in the dark, were reasons enough! He was querulous and injured about it all. He had taken the place for himself, not for invisible women to brush their hair in; that lawyer fellow in Lincoln's Inn should be told so, too, before many hours were out; it was outrageous, letting people in for agreements like that!

A cut-glass partition divided the compartment where Oleron sat from the space where the white-haired landlady moved; but it stopped seven or eight inches above the level of the counter. There was no partition at the further bar. Presently Oleron, raising his eyes, saw that faces were watching him through the aperture. The faces disappeared when he looked at them.

He moved to a corner where he could not be seen from the other bar; but this brought him into line with the white-haired landlady.

She knew him by sight—had doubtless seen him passing and repassing; and presently she made a remark on the weather. Oleron did not know what he replied, but it sufficed to call forth the further remark that the winter had been a bad one for influenza, but that the spring weather seemed to be coming at last. . . . Even this slight contact with the commonplace steadied Oleron a little; an idle, nascent wonder whether the landlady brushed her hair every night, and, if so, whether it gave out those little electric cracklings, was shut down with a snap; and Oleron was better. . . .

With his next glass of brandy he was all for going back to his flat. Not go back? Indeed, he would go back! They should very soon see whether he was going to be turned out of his place like that! He began to wonder why he was doing the rather unusual thing he was doing at that moment, unusual for him—sitting hatless, drinking brandy, in a public-house. Suppose he were to tell the white-haired landlady all about it—to tell her that a caller had scratched her hand on a nail, had later had the back luck to put her foot through a rotten stair, and that he himself, in an old house full of squeaks and creaks and whispers, had heard a minute noise and had bolted from it in fright—what would she think of him? That he was mad, of course. . . . Pshaw! The real truth of the matter was that he hadn't been doing enough work to occupy him. He had been dreaming his days away, filling his head with a lot of moonshine about a new *Romilly* (as if the old one was not good enough), and now he was surprised that the devil should enter an empty head!

Yes, he would go back. He would take a walk in the air first—he hadn't walked enough lately—and then he would take himself in hand, settle the hash of that sixteenth chapter of *Romilly* (fancy, he had actually been fool enough to think of destroying fifteen chapters!) and thenceforward he would remember that he had obligations to his fellow men and work to do in the world. There was the matter in a nutshell.

He finished his brandy and went out.

He had walked for some time before any other bearing of the matter than that on himself occurred to him. At first, the fresh air had increased the heady effect of the brandy he had drunk; but afterwards his mind grew clearer than it had been since morning. And the clearer it grew, the less final did his boastful self-assurances become, and the firmer his conviction that, when all explanations had been made, there remained something that could not be explained. His hysteria of an hour before had passed; he grew steadily calmer; but the disquieting conviction remained. A deep fear took possession of him. It was a fear for Elsie.

For something in his place was inimical to her safety. Of themselves, her two accidents might not have persuaded him of this; but she herself had said it. *"I'm not wanted here. . . ."* And she had declared that there was something wrong with the place. She had seen it before he had. Well and good. One thing stood out clearly: namely, that if this was so, she must be kept away for quite another reason than that which had so confounded and humiliated Oleron. Luckily she had expressed her intention of staying away; she must be held to that intention. He must see to it.

And he must see to it all the more that he now saw his first example, never to set foot in the place again, was absurd. People did not do that kind of thing. With Elsie made secure, he could not with any respect to himself suffer himself to be turned out by a shadow, nor even by a danger merely because it was a danger. He had to live somewhere, and he would live there. He must return.

He mastered the faint chill of fear that came with the decision, and turned in his walk abruptly. Should fear grow on him again he would, perhaps, take one more glass of brandy. . . .

But by the time he reached the short street that led to the square he was too late for more brandy. The little public-house was still lighted, but closed, and one or two men were standing talking on the curb. Oleron noticed that a sudden silence fell on them as he passed, and he noticed further that the long-nosed Barrett, whom he passed a little lower down, did not return his good-night. He turned in at the broken gate, hesitated merely an instant in the alley, and then mounted his stairs again.

Only an inch of candle remained in the Sheffield stick, and Oleron did not light another one. Deliberately he forced himself to take it up and to make the tour of his five rooms before retiring. It was as he returned from the kitchen across his little hall that he noticed that a letter lay on the floor. He carried it into his sitting-room, and glanced at the envelope before opening it.

It was unstamped, and had been put into the door by hand. Its handwriting was clumsy, and it ran from beginning to end without comma or period. Oleron read the first line, turned to the signature, and then finished the letter.

It was from the man Barrett, and it informed Oleron that he, Barrett, would be obliged if Mr. Oleron would make other arrangements for the preparing of his breakfasts and the cleaning-out of his place. The sting lay in the tail, that is to say, the postscript. This consisted of a text of Scripture. It embodied an allusion that could only be to Elsie Bengough. . . .

A seldom-seen frown had cut deeply into Oleron's brow. So! That was it! Very well; they would see about that on the morrow. . . . For the rest, this seemed merely another reason why Elsie should keep away. . . .

Then his suppressed rage broke out. . . .

The foul-minded lot! The devil himself could not have given a leer at anything that had ever passed between Paul Oleron and Elsie Bengough, yet this nosing rascal must be prying and talking! . . .

Oleron crumpled the paper up, held it in the candle flame, and then ground the ashes under his heel.

One useful purpose, however, the letter had served: it had created in Oleron a wrathful blaze that effectually banished pale shadows. Nevertheless, one other puzzling circumstance was to close the day. As he undressed, he chanced to glance at his bed. The coverlets bore an impress as if somebody had lain on them. Oleron could not remember that he himself had lain down during the day—offhanded, he would have said that certainly he had not; but after all, he could not be positive. His indignation for Elsie, acting possibly with the residue of the brandy in him, excluded all other considerations; and he put out his candle, lay down, and passed immediately into a deep and dreamless sleep, which, in the absence of Mrs. Barrett's morning call, lasted almost once round the clock.

8

To the man who pays heed to that voice within him which warns him that twilight and danger are settling over his soul, terror is apt to appear an absolute thing, against which his heart must be safeguarded in a twink unless there is to take place an alteration in the whole range and scale of his nature. Mercifully, he has never far to look for safeguards. Of the immediate and small and common and momentary things of life, of usages and observances and modes and conventions, he builds up fortifications against the powers of darkness. He is even content that, not terror only, but joy also, should for working purposes be placed in the category of the absolute things; and the last treason he will commit will be that breaking down of terms and limits that strikes, not at one man, but at the welfare of the souls of all.

In his own person, Oleron began to commit this treason. He began to commit it by admitting the inexplicable and horrible to an increasing familiarity. He did it insensibly, unconsciously, by a neglect of the things that he now regarded it as an impertinence in Elsie Bengough to have prescribed. Two months before, the words "a haunted house," applied to his lovely bemusing dwelling, would have chilled his marrow; now his scale of sensation becoming depressed, he could ask "Haunted by what?" and remain unconscious that horror, when it can be proved to be relative, by so much loses its proper quality. He was setting aside the landmarks. Mists and confusion had begun to enwrap him.

And he was conscious of nothing so much as of a voracious inquisitiveness. He wanted *to know*. He was resolved to know. Nothing but the knowlege would satisfy him; and craftily he cast about for means whereby he might attain it.

He might have spared his craft. The matter was the easiest imaginable. As in time past he had known, in his writing, moments when his thoughts had seemed to rise of themselves and to embody themselves in words not to be altered afterwards, so now the questions he put himself seemed to be answered even in the moment of their asking. There was exhilaration in the swift, easy processes. He had known no such joy in his own power since the days when his writing had been a daily freshness and a delight to him. It was almost as if the course he must pursue was being dictated to him.

And the first thing he must do, of course, was to define the problem. He defined it in terms of mathematics. Granted that he had not the place to himself; granted that the old house had inexpressibly caught and engaged his spirit; granted that, by virtue of the common denominator of the place, this unknown co-tenant stood in some relation to himself: what next? Clearly, the nature of the other numerator must be ascertained.

And how? Ordinarily this would not have seemed simple, but to Oleron it was now pellucidly clear. The key, *of course*, lay in his half-written novel—or rather, in both *Romillys*, the old and the proposed new one.

A little while before, Oleron would have thought himself mad to have embraced such an opinion; now he accepted the dizzying hypothesis without a quiver.

He began to examine the first and second *Romillys*.

From the moment of his doing so the thing advanced by leaps and bounds. Swiftly he reviewed the history of the *Romilly* of the fifteen chapters. He remembered clearly now that he had found her insufficient on the very first morning on which he had sat down to work in his new place. Other instances of his aversion leaped up to confirm his obscure investigation. There had come the night when he had hardly forborne to throw the whole thing into the fire; and the next morning he had begun the planning of the new *Romilly*. It had been on that morning that Mrs. Barrett, overhearing him humming a brief phrase that the dripping of a tap the night before had suggested, had informed him that he was singing some air he had never in his life heard before, called "The Beckoning Fair One." . . .

The Beckoning Fair One! . . .

With scarcely a pause in thought he continued:

The first *Romilly* having been definitely thrown over, the second had instantly fastened herself upon him, clamoring for birth in his brain. He even fancied now, looking back, that there had been something like passion, hate almost, in the supplanting, and that more than once a stray thought given to his discarded creation had—(it was astonishing how credible Oleron found the almost unthinkable idea)—had offended the supplanter.

Yet that a malignancy almost homicidal should be extended to his fiction's poor mortal prototype. . . .

In spite of his inuring to a scale in which the horrible was now a thing to be fingered and turned this way and that, a "Good God!" broke from Oleron.

This intrusion of the first *Romilly*'s prototype into his thought again was a factor that for the moment brought his inquiry into the nature of his problem to a termination; the mere thought of Elsie was fatal to anything abstract. For another thing, he could not yet think of that letter of Barrett's, nor of a little scene that had followed it, without a mounting of color and a quick contraction of the brow. For wisely or not, he had had that argument out at once. Striding across the square on the following morning, he had bearded Barrett on his own doorstep. Coming back again a few minutes later, he had been strongly of opinion that he had only made matters worse. The man had been vagueness itself. He had not been able to be either challenged or brow-beaten into anything more definite than a muttered farrago in which the words "Certain things . . . Mrs. Barrett . . . respectable house . . . if the cap fits . . . proceedings that shall be nameless," had been constantly repeated.

"Not that I make any charge—" he had concluded.

"Charge!" Oleron had cried.

"I 'ave my idears of things, as I don't doubt you 'ave yours—"

"Ideas—mine!" Oleron had cried wrathfully, immediately dropping his voice as heads had appeared at windows of the square. "Look you here, my man; you've an unwholesome mind, which probably you can't help, but a tongue which you can help, and shall! If there is a breath of this repeated . . ."

"I'll not be talked to on my own doorstep like this by anybody . . ." Barrett had blustered. . . .

"You shall, and I'm doing it . . ."

"Don't you forget there's a Gawd above all, Who 'as said . . ."

"You're a low scandalmonger! . . ."

And so forth, continuing badly what was already badly begun. Oleron had returned wrathfully to his own house and thenceforward, looking out of his windows, had seen Barrett's face at odd times, lifting blinds or peering round curtains, as if he sought to put himself in possession of Heaven knew what evidence, in case it should be required of him.

The unfortunate occurrence made certain minor differences in Oleron's domestic arrangements. Barrett's tongue, he gathered, had already been busy; he was looked at askance by the dwellers of the square; and he judged it better, until he should be able to obtain other help, to make his purchases of provisions a little farther afield rather than at the small shops of the immediate neighborhood. For the rest, housekeeping was no new thing to him, and he would resume his old bachelor habits. . . .

Besides, he was deep in certain rather abstruse investigations, in which it was better that he should not be disturbed. He was looking out of his window one midday rather tired, not very well, and glad that it was not very likely he would have to stir out of doors, when he saw Elsie Bengough crossing the square towards his house. The weather had broken; it was a raw and gusty day; and she had to force her way against the wind that set her ample skirts bellying about her opulent figure and her veil spinning and streaming behind her.

Oleron acted swiftly and instinctively. Seizing his hat, he sprang to the door and descended the stairs at a run. A sort of panic had seized him. She must be prevented from setting foot in the place. As he ran along the alley he was conscious that his eyes went up to the eaves as if something drew them. He did not know that a slate might not accidentally fall. . . .

He met her at the gate, and spoke with curious volubleness.

"This is really too bad, Elsie! Just as I'm urgently called away! I'm afraid it can't be helped though, and that you'll have to think me an inhospitable beast." He poured it out just as it came into his head.

She asked if he was going to town.

"Yes, yes—to town," he replied. "I've got to call on—on Chambers. You know Chambers, don't you? No, I remember you don't; a big man you once saw me with. . . . I ought to have gone yesterday, and—" this he felt to be a brilliant effort—"and he's going out of town this afternoon. To Brighton. I had a letter from him this morning."

He took her arm and led her up the square. She had to remind him that his way to town lay in the other direction.

"Of course—how stupid of me!" he said, with a little loud laugh. "I'm so used to going the other way with you— of course; it's the other way to the bus. Will you come along with me? I am so awfully sorry it's happened like this. . . ."

They took the street to the bus terminus.

This time Elsie bore no signs of having gone through interior struggles. If she detected anything unusual in his manner she made no comment, and he, seeing her calm, began to talk less recklessly through silences. By the time they reached the bus terminus, nobody, seeing the pallid-faced man without an overcoat and the large ample-skirted girl at his side, would have supposed that one of them was ready to sink on his knees for thankfulness that he had, as he believed, saved the other from a wildly unthinkable danger.

They mounted to the top of the bus, Oleron protesting that he should not miss his overcoat, and that he found the day, if anything, rather oppressively hot. They sat down on a front seat.

Now that this meeting was forced upon him, he had something else to say that would make demands upon his tact. It had been on his mind for some time, and was, indeed, peculiarly difficult to put. He revolved it for some minutes, and then, remembering the success of his story of a sudden call to town, cut the knot of his difficulty with another lie.

"I'm thinking of going away for a little while, Elsie," he said.

She merely said: "Oh?"

"Somewhere for a change. I need a change. I think I shall go tomorrow, or the day after. Yes, tomorrow, I think."

"Yes," she replied.

"I don't quite know how long I shall be," he continued. "I shall have to let you know when I am back."

"Yes, let me know," she replied in an even tone.

The tone was, for her, suspiciously even. He was a little uneasy.

"You don't ask me where I'm going," he said, with a little cumbrous effort to rally her.

She was looking straight before her, past the bus-driver.

"I know," she said.

He was startled. "How, you know?"

"You're not going anywhere," she replied.

He found not a word to say. It was a minute or so before she continued, in the same controlled voice she had employed from the start.

"You're not going anywhere. You weren't going out this morning. You only came out because I appeared; don't behave as if we were strangers, Paul."

A flush of pink had mounted to his cheeks. He noticed that the wind had given her the pink of early rhubarb. Still he found nothing to say.

"Of course, you ought to go away," she continued. "I don't know whether you look at yourself often in the glass, but you're rather noticeable. Several people have turned to look at you this morning. So, of course, you ought to go away. But you won't, and I know why."

He shivered, coughed a little, and then broke silence.

"Then if you know, there's no use in continuing this discussion," he said curtly.

"Not for me, perhaps, but there is for you," she replied. "Shall I tell you what I know?"

"No," he said in a voice slightly raised.

"No?" she asked, her round eyes earnestly on him.

"No."

Again he was getting out of patience with her; again he was conscious of the strain. Her devotion and fidelity and love plagued him; she was only humiliating both herself and him.

It would have been bad enough had he ever, by word or deed, given her cause for thus fastening herself on him . . . but there; that was the worst of that kind of life for a woman. Women such as she, business women, in and out of offices all the time, always, whether they realized it or not, made comradeship a cover for something else. They accepted the unconventional status, came and went freely, as men did, were honestly taken by men at their own valuation—and then it turned out to be the other thing after all, and they went and fell in love. No wonder there was gossip in shops and squares and public houses! In a sense the gossipers were in the right of it. Independent, yet not efficient; with some of womanhood's graces forgone, and yet with all the woman's hunger and need; half sophisticated yet not wise; Oleron was tired of it all. . . .

And it was time he told her so.

"I suppose," he said trembling, looking down between his knees, "I suppose the real trouble is in the life women who earn their own living are obliged to lead."

He could not tell in what sense she took the lame generality; she merely replied: "I suppose so."

"It can't be helped," he continued, "but you do sacrifice a good deal."

She agreed: a good deal; and then she added after a moment: "What, for instance?"

"You may or may not be gradually attaining a new status, but you're in a false position today."

It was very likely, she said; she hadn't thought of it much in that light—

"And," he continued desperately, "you're bound to suffer. Your most innocent acts are misunderstood; motives you never dreamed of are attributed to you; and in the end it comes to"—he hesitated a moment and then took the plunge—"to the sidelong look and the leer."

She took his meaning with perfect ease. She merely shivered a little as she pronounced the name.

"Barrett?"

His silence told her the rest.

Anything further that was to be said must come from her.

It came as the bus stopped at a stage and fresh passengers mounted the stairs.

"You'd better get down here and go back, Paul," she said. "I understand perfectly—perfectly. It isn't Barrett. You'd be able to deal with Barrett. It's merely convenient for you to say it's Barrett. I know what it is . . . but you said I wasn't to tell you that. Very well. But before you go let me tell you why I came up this morning."

In a dull tone he asked her why. Again she looked straight before as she replied:

"I came to force your hand. Things couldn't go on as they have been going, you know; and now that's all over."

"All over," he repeated stupidly.

"All over. I want you now to consider yourself, as far as I'm concerned, perfectly free. I make only one reservation."

He hardly had the spirit to ask her what that was.

"If *I* merely need *you*," she said, "please don't give that a thought; that's nothing; I shan't come near for that. But," she dropped her voice, "if *you're* in need of *me*, Paul—I shall know if you are, *and you will be*—then I shall come at no matter what cost. You understand that?"

He could only groan.

"So that's understood," she concluded. "And I think that's all. Now go back. I should advise you to walk back, for you're shivering—good-by—"

She gave him a cold hand, and he descended. He turned on the edge of the curb as the bus started again. For the first time in all the years he had known her, she parted from him with no smile and no wave of her long arm.

9

He stood on the curb plunged in misery, looking after her as long as she remained in sight; but almost instantly with her disappearance he felt the heaviness lift a little from his spirit. She had given him his liberty; true, there was a sense in which he had never parted with it, but now was no time for splitting hairs; he was free to act, and all was clear ahead.

Swiftly the sense of lightness grew on him: it became a positive rejoicing in his liberty; and before he was halfway home he had decided what must be done next.

The vicar of the parish in which his dwelling was situated lived within ten minutes of the square. To his house Oleron turned his steps. It was necessary that he should have all the information he could get about this old house with the insurance marks and the sloping "To Let" boards, and the vicar was the person most likely to be able to furnish it. This last preliminary out of the way, and—aha! Oleron chuckled—things might be expected to happen!

But he gained less information than he had hoped for. The house, the vicar said, was old—but there needed no vicar to tell Oleron that; it was reputed (Oleron pricked up his ears) to be haunted—but there were few old houses about which some such rumor did not circulate among the ignorant; and the deplorable lack of Faith of the modern world, the vicar thought, did not tend to dissipate these superstitions. For the rest, his manner was the soothing manner of one who prefers not to make statements without knowing how they will be taken by his hearer. Oleron smiled as he perceived this.

"You may leave my nerves out of the question," he said. "How long has the place been empty?"

"A dozen years, I should say," the vicar replied.

"And the last tenant—did you know him—or her?" Oleron was conscious of a tingling of his nerves as he offered the vicar the alternative of sex.

"Him," said the vicar. "A man. If I remember rightly, his name was Madley; an artist. He was a great recluse; seldom went out of the place, and"—the vicar hesitated and then broke into a little gush of candor—"and since you appear to have come for this information, and since it is better that the truth should be told than that garbled versions should get about, I don't mind saying that this man Madley died there, under somewhat unusual circumstances. It was ascertained at the post-mortem that there was not a particle of food in his stomach, although he was found to be not without money. And his frame was simply worn out. Suicide was spoken of, but you'll agree with me that deliberate starvation is, to say the least, an uncommon form of suicide. An open verdict was returned.''

''Ah!'' said Oleron. . . . ''Does there happen to be any comprehensive history of this parish?''

''No; partial ones only. I myself am not guiltless of having made a number of notes on its purely ecclesiastical history, its registers and so forth, which I shall be happy to show you if you would care to see them; but it is a large parish, I have only one curate, and my leisure, as you will readily understand . . .''

The extent of the parish and the scantiness of the vicar's leisure occupied the remainder of the interview, and Oleron thanked the vicar, took his leave, and walked slowly home.

He walked slowly for a reason, twice turning away from the house within a stone's-throw of the gate and taking another turn of twenty minutes or so. He had a very ticklish piece of work now before him; it required the greatest mental concentration; it was nothing less than to bring his mind, if he might, into such a state of unpreoccupation and receptivity that he should see the place as he had seen it on that morning when, his removal accomplished, he had sat down to begin the sixteenth chapter of the first *Romilly*.

For, could he recapture that first impression, he now hoped for far more from it. Formerly, he had carried no end of mental lumber. Before the influence of the place had been able to find him out at all, it had had the inertia of those dreary chapters to overcome. No results had shown. The process had been one of slow saturation, charging, filling up to a brim. But now he was light, unburdened, rid at last both of that *Romilly* and of her prototype. Now for the new unknown, coy, jealous, bewitching Beckoning Fair! . . .

At half-past two of the afternoon he put his key into the Yale lock, entered, and closed the door behind him. . . .

His fantastic attempt was instantly and astonishingly successful. He could have shouted with triumph as he entered the room; it was as if he had *escaped* into it. Once more, as in the days when his writing had had a daily freshness and wonder and promise for him, he was conscious of that new ease and mastery and exhilaration and release. The air of the place seemed to hold more oxygen; as if his own specific gravity had changed, his very tread seemed less ponderable. The flowers in the bowls, the fair proportions of the meadowsweet-colored panels and moldings, the polished floor, and the lofty and faintly starred ceiling, fairly laughed their welcome. Oleron actually laughed back, and spoke aloud.

"Oh, you're pretty, pretty!" he flattered it.

Then he lay down on his couch.

He spent that afternoon as a convalescent who expected a dear visitor might have spent it—in a delicious vacancy, smiling now and then as if in his sleep, and ever lifting drowsy and contented eyes to his alluring surroundings. He lay thus until darkness came, and, with darkness, the nocturnal noises of the old house. . . .

But if he waited for any specific happening, he waited in vain.

He waited similarly in vain on the morrow, maintaining, though with less ease, that sensitized late-like condition of his mind. Nothing occurred to give it an impression. Whatever it was which he so patiently wooed, it seemed to be both shy and exciting.

Then on the third day he thought he understood. A look of gentle drollery and cunning came into his eyes, and he chuckled.

"Oho, oho! . . . Well, if the wind sits in *that* quarter we must see what else there is to be done. What is there, now? . . . No, I won't send for Elsie; we don't need a wheel to break the butterfly on; we won't go to those lengths, my butterfly. . . ."

He was standing musing, thumbing his lean jaw, looking aslant; suddenly he crossed to his hall, took down his hat, and went out.

"My lady is coquettish, is she? Well, we'll see what a little neglect will do," he chuckled as he went down the stairs.

He sought a railway station, got into a train, and spent the rest of the day in the country. Oh, yes: Oleron thought *he* was the man to deal with Fair Ones who beckoned, and invited, and then took refuge in shyness and hanging back!

He did not return until after eleven that night.

"*Now*, my Fair Beckoner!" he murmured as he walked along the alley and felt in his pocket for his keys. . . .

Inside his flat, he was perfectly composed, perfectly deliberate, exceedingly careful not to give himself away. As if to intimate that he intended to retire immediately, he lighted only a single candle; and as he set out with it on his nightly round he affected to yawn. He went first into his kitchen. There was a full moon, and a lozenge of moonlight, almost peacock-blue by contrast with his candle-flame, lay on the floor. The window was uncurtained, and he could see the reflection of the candle, and, faintly, that of his own face, as he moved about. The door of the powder-closet stood a little ajar, and he closed it before sitting down to remove his boots on the chair with the cushion made of the folded harp-bag. From the kitchen he passed to the bathroom. There, another slant of blue moonlight cut the window-sill and lay across the pipes on the wall. He visited his seldom-used study, and stood for a moment gazing at the silvered roofs across the square. Then, walking straight through his sitting-room, his stockinged feet making no noise, he entered his bedroom and put the candle on the chest of drawers. His face all this time wore no expression save that of tiredness. He had never been wilier nor more alert.

His small bedroom fireplace was opposite the chest of drawers on which the mirror stood, and his bed and the window occupied the remaining sides of the room. Oleron drew down his blind, took off his coat, and then stooped to get his slippers from under the bed.

He could have given no reason for the conviction, but that the manifestation that for two days had been withheld was close at hand he never for an instant doubted. Nor, though he could not form the faintest guess of the shape it might take, did he experience fear. Startling or surprising it might be; he was prepared for that; but that was all; his scale of sensation had become depressed. His hand moved this way and that under the bed in search of his slippers. . . .

But for all this caution and method and preparedness, his heart all at once gave a leap and a pause that was almost horrid. His hand had found the slippers, but he was still on his knees; save for the circumstance he would have fallen. The bed was a low one; the groping for the slippers accounted for the turn of his head to one side; and he was careful to keep the attitude until he had partly recovered his self-possession. When presently he rose there was a drop of blood on his lower lip where he had caught at it with his teeth, and his watch had jerked out of the pocket of his waistcoat and was dangling at the end of its short leather guard. . . .

Then, before the watch had ceased its little oscillation, he was himself again.

In the middle of his mantelpiece there stood a picture, a portrait of his grandmother; he placed himself before this picture, so that he could see in the glass of it the steady flame of the candle that burned behind him on the chest of drawers. He could see also in the picture-glass the little glancings of light from the bevels and facets of the objects about the mirror and candle. But he could see more. These twinklings and reflections and re-reflections did not change their position; but there was one gleam that had motion. It was fainter than the rest, and it moved up and down through the air. It was the reflection of the candle on Oleron's black vulcanite comb, and each of its downward movements was accompanied by a silky and crackling rustle.

Oleron, watching what went on in the glass of his grandmother's portrait, continued to play his part. He felt for his dangling watch and began slowly to wind it up. Then, for a moment ceasing to watch, he began to empty his trousers pockets and to place methodically in a little row on the mantelpiece the pennies and half-pennies he took from them. The sweeping, minutely electric noise filled the whole bedroom, and had Oleron altered his point of observation, he could have brought the dim gleam of the moving comb so into position that it would almost have outlined his grandmother's head.

Any other head of which it might have been following the outline was invisible.

Oleron finished the emptying of his pockets; then, under

cover of another simulated yawn, not so much summoning his resolution as overmastered by an exorbitant curiosity, he swung suddenly round. That which was being combed was still not to be seen, but the comb did not stop. It had altered its angle a little, and had moved a little to the left. It was passing, in fairly regular sweeps, from a point rather more than five feet from the ground, in a direction roughly vertical, to another point a few inches below the level of the chest of drawers.

Oleron continued to act to admiration. He walked to his little washstand in the corner, poured out water, and began to wash his hands. He removed his waistcoat, and continued his preparations for bed. The combing did not cease, and he stood for a moment in thought. Again his eyes twinkled. The next was very cunning—

"Hm! . . . *I think I'll read for a quarter of an hour*," he said aloud. . . .

He passed out of the room.

He was away a couple of minutes; when he returned again the room was suddenly silent. He glanced at the chest of drawers; the comb lay still, between the collar he had removed and a pair of gloves. Without hesitation Oleron put out his hand and picked it up. It was an ordinary eighteen-penny comb, taken from a card in a chemist's shop, of a substance of a definite specific gravity, and no more capable of rebellion against the Laws by which it existed than are the worlds that keep their orbits through the void. Oleron put it down again; then he glanced at the bundle of papers he held in his hand. What he had gone to fetch had been the fifteen chapters of the original *Romilly*.

"Hm!" he muttered as he threw the manuscript into a chair. . . . "As I thought. . . . She's just blindly, ragingly, murderously jealous."

On the night after that, and on the following night, and for many nights and days, so many that he began to be uncertain about the count of them, Oleron, courting, cajoling, neglecting, threatening, beseeching, eaten out with unappeased curiosity and regardless that his life was becoming one consuming passion and desire, continued his search for the unknown co-numerator of his abode.

10

As time went on, it came to pass that few except the postman mounted Oleron's stairs; and since men who do not write letters receive few, even the postman's tread became so infrequent that it was not heard more than once or twice a week. There came a letter from Oleron's publishers, asking when they might expect to receive the manuscript of his new book; he delayed for some days to answer it, and finally forgot it. A second letter came, which also he failed to answer. He received no third.

The weather grew bright and warm. The privet bushes among the chopper-like notice-boards flowered, and in the streets where Oleron did his shopping the baskets of flower-women lined the curbs. Oleron purchased flowers daily; his room clamored for flowers, fresh and continually renewed; and Oleron did not stint its demands. Nevertheless, the necessity for going out to buy them began to irk him more and more, and it was with a greater and ever greater sense of relief that he returned home again. He began to be conscious that again his scale of sensation had suffered a subtle change—a change that was not restoration to its former capacity, but an extension and enlarging that once more included terror. It admitted it in an entirely new form. *Lux orco, tenebroe Jovi.* The name of this terror was agoraphobia. Oleron had begun to dread air and space and the horror that might pounce upon the unguarded back.

Presently he so contrived it that his food and flowers were delivered daily at his door. He rubbed his hands when he had hit upon this expedient. That was better! Now he could please himself whether he went out or not. . . .

Quickly he was confirmed in his choice. It became his pleasure to remain immured.

But he was not happy—or, if he was, his happiness took an extraordinary turn. He fretted discontentedly, could sometimes have wept for mere weakness and misery; and yet he was dimly conscious that he would not have exchanged his sadness for all the noisy mirth of the world outside. And speaking of noise: noise, much noise, now caused him the acutest discomfort. It was hardly more to be endured than that new-born fear that kept him, on the increasingly rare occasions when he did go out, sidling close to walls and feeling friendly railings with his hand. He moved from room to room softly and in slippers, and sometimes stood for many seconds closing a door so gently that not a sound broke the stillness that was in itself a delight. Sunday now became an intolerable day to him, for, since the coming of the fine weather, there had begun to assemble in the square under his windows each Sunday morning certain members of the sect to which the long-nosed Barrett adhered. These came with a great drum and large brass-bellied instruments; men and women uplifted anguished voices, struggling with their God; and Barrett himself, with upraised face and closed eyes and working brows, prayed that the sound of his voice might penetrate the ears of all unbelievers—as it certainly did Oleron's. One day, in the middle of one of these rhapsodies, Oleron sprang to his blind and pulled it down, and heard, as he did so, his own name made the object of a fresh torrent of outpouring.

And sometimes, but not as expecting a reply, Oleron stood still and called softly. Once or twice he called "Romilly!" and then waited; but more often his whispering did not take the shape of a name.

There was one spot in particular of his abode that he began to haunt with increasing persistency. This was just within the opening of his bedroom door. He had discovered one day that by opening every door in his place (always excepting the outer one, which he only opened unwillingly) and by placing himself on this particular spot, he could actually see to a greater or less extent into each of his five rooms without changing his position. He could see the whole of his sitting-room, all of his bedroom except the part hidden by the open door, and glimpses of his kitchen, bathroom, and of his rarely used study. He was often in this place, breathless and with his finger on his lip. One day, as he stood there, he suddenly found himself wondering whether this Madley, of whom the vicar had spoken, had ever discovered the strategic importance of the bedroom entry.

Light, moreover, now caused him greater disquietude than did darkness. Direct sunlight, of which as the sun passed daily round the house, each of his rooms had now its share, was like a flame in his brain; and even diffused light was a dull and numbing ache. He began, at successive hours of the day, one after another, to lower his crimson blinds. He made short and daring excursions in order to do this; but he was ever careful to leave his retreat open, in case he should have sudden need of it. Presently this lowering of the blinds had become a daily methodical exercise, and his rooms, when he had been his round, had the blood-red half-light of a photographer's darkroom.

One day, as he drew down the blind of his little study and backed in good order out of the room again, he broke into a soft laugh.

"*That* bilks Mr. Barret!" he said; and the baffling of Barrett continued to afford him mirth for an hour.

But on another day, soon after, he had a fright that left him trembling also for an hour. He had seized the cord to darken the window over the seat in which he had found the harp-bag, and was standing with his back well protected in the embrasure, when he thought he saw the tail of a black-and-white check skirt disappear round the corner of the house. He could not be sure—had he run to the window of the other wall, which was blinded, the skirt must have been already past—but he was *almost* sure that it was Elsie. He listened in an agony of suspense for her tread on the stairs.

But no tread came, and after three or four minutes he drew a long breath of relief.

"By Jove, but that would have compromised me horribly!" he muttered. . . .

And he continued to mutter from time to time: "Horribly compromising . . . *no* woman would stand that . . . not *any* kind of woman . . . oh, compromising in the extreme!"

Yet he was not happy. He could not have assigned the

cause of the fits of quiet weeping which took him sometimes; they came and went, like the fitful illumination of the clouds that travelled over the square; and perhaps, after all, if he was not happy, he was not unhappy. Before he could be unhappy something must have been withdrawn, and nothing had been granted. He was waiting for that granting, in that flower-laden, frightfully enticing apartment of his, with the pith-white walls tinged and subdued by the crimson blinds to a blood-like gloom.

He paid no heed to it that his stock of money was running perilously low, nor that he had ceased to work. Ceased to work? He had not ceased to work. They knew very little about it who supposed that Oleron had ceased to work! He was in truth only now beginning to work. He was preparing such a work . . . such a work . . . such a Mistress was a-making in the gestation of his Art. . . . Let him but get this period of probation and poignant waiting over and men should see. . . . How *should* men know her, this Fair One of Oleron's, until Oleron himself knew her? Lovely radiant creations are not thrown off like How-d'ye-do's. The men to whom it is committed to father them must weep wretched tears, as Oleron did, must swell with vain presumptuous hopes, as Oleron did, must pursue, as Oleron pursued, the capricious, fair, mocking, slippery, eager Spirit that, ever eluding, ever sees to it that the chase does not slacken. Let Oleron but hunt this Huntress a little longer . . . he would have her sparkling and panting in his arms yet. . . . Oh, no: they were very far from the truth who supposed that Oleron had ceased to work!

And if all else was falling away from Oleron, gladly he was letting it go. So do we all when our Fair Ones beckon. Quite at the beginning we wink, and promise ourselves that we will put Her Ladyship through her paces, neglect her for a day, turn her own jealous wiles against her, flout and ignore her when she comes wheedling; perhaps there lurks within us all the time a heartless sprite who is never fooled; but in the end all falls away. She beckons, beckons, and all goes. . . .

And so Oleron kept his strategic post within the frame of

his bedroom door, and watched, and waited, and smiled, with his finger on his lips. . . . It was his duteous service, his worship, his troth-plighting, all that he had ever known of Love. And when he found himself, as he now and then did, hating the dead man Madley, and wishing that he had never lived, he felt that that, too, was an acceptable service. . . .

But, as he thus prepared himself, as it were, for a Marriage, and moped and chafed more and more that the Bride made no sign, he made a discovery that he ought to have made weeks before.

It was through a thought of the dead Madley that he made it. Since that night when he had thought in his greenness that a little studied neglect would bring the lovely Beckoner to her knees, and had made use of her own jealousy to banish her, he had not set eyes on those fifteen discarded chapters of *Romilly*. He had thrown them back into the window seat, forgotten their very existence. But his own jealousy of Madley put him in mind of hers, of her jilted rival of flesh and blood, and he remembered them. . . . Fool that he had been! Had he, then, expected his Desire to manifest herself while there still existed the evidence of his divided allegiance? What, and she with a passion so fierce and centered that it had not hesitated at the destruction, twice attempted, of her rival? Fool that he had been! . . .

But if *that* was all the pledge and sacrifice she required she should have it—ah, yes, and quickly!

He took the manuscript from the window seat, and brought it to the fire.

He kept his fire always burning now; the warmth brought out the last vestige of odor of the flowers with which his room was banked. He did not know what time it was; long since he had allowed his clock to run down—it had seemed a foolish measurer of time in regard to the stupendous things that were happening to Oleron; but he knew it was late. He took the *Romilly* manuscript and knelt before the fire.

But he had not finished removing the fastening that held the sheets together before he suddenly gave a start, turned his head over his shoulder, and listened intently. The sound he had heard had not been loud—it had been, indeed, no more than a tap, twice or thrice repeated—but it had filled Oleron with alarm. His face grew dark as it came again.

He heard a voice outside on his landing.

"Paul! . . . Paul! . . ."

It was Elsie's voice.

"Paul! . . . I know you're in . . . I want to see you. . . ."

He cursed her under his breath, but kept perfectly still. He did not intend to admit her.

"Paul! . . . You're in trouble . . . I believe you're in danger . . . at least come to the door! . . ."

Oleron smothered a low laugh. It somehow amused him that she, in such danger herself, should talk to him of *his* danger! . . . Well, if she was, serve her right; she knew, or said she knew, all about it. . . .

"Paul! . . . Paul! . . ."

"*Paul! . . . Paul! . . .*" He mimicked her under his breath.

"Oh, Paul, it's *horrible*! . . ."

Horrible was it? thought Oleron. Then let her get away. . . .

"I only want to help you, Paul. . . . I didn't promise not to come if you needed me. . . ."

He was impervious to the pitiful sob that interrupted the low cry. The devil take the woman! Should he shout to her to go away and not come back? No: let her call and knock and sob. She had a gift for sobbing; she mustn't think her sobs would move him. They irritated him, so that he set his teeth and shook his fist at her, but that was all. Let her sob.

"*Paul! . . . Paul! . . .*"

With his teeth hard set, he dropped his first page of *Romilly* into the fire. Then he began to drop the rest in, sheet by sheet.

For many minutes the calling behind his door continued; then suddenly it ceased. He heard the sound of feet slowly descending the stairs. He listened for the noise of a fall or a cry or the crash of a piece of the handrail of the upper landing; but none of these things came. She was spared. Apparently her rival suffered her to crawl abject and beaten away. Oleron heard the passing of her steps under the window; then she was gone.

He dropped the last page into the fire, and then, with a low laugh, rose. He looked fondly round his room.

"Lucky to get away like that," he remarked. "She wouldn't have got away if I'd given her as much as a word or a look! What devils these women are! . . . But no; I oughtn't to say that; one of 'em showed forbearance. . . ."

Who showed forbearance? And what was forborne? Ah, Oleron knew! . . . Contempt, no doubt, had been at the bottom of it, but that didn't matter: the pestering creature had been allowed to go unharmed. Yes, she was lucky; Oleron hoped she knew it. . . .

And now, now, now for his reward!

Oleron crossed the room. All his doors were open; his eyes shone as he placed himself within that of his bedroom.

Fool that he had been, not to think of destroying the manuscript sooner! . . .

How, in a houseful of shadows, should he know his own Shadow? How, in a houseful of noises, distinguish the summons he felt to be at hand? Ah, trust him! He would know! The place was full of a jugglery of dim lights. The blind at his elbow that allowed the light of a street lamp to struggle vaguely through—the glimpse of greeny blue moonlight seen through the distant kitchen door—the sulky glow of the fire under the black ashes of the burnt manuscript—the glimmering of the tulips and the moon-daisies and narcissi in the bowls and jugs and jars—these did not so trick and bewilder his eyes that he would not know his Own! It was he, not she, who had been delaying the shadowy Bridal; he hung his head for a moment in mute acknowledgment; then he bent his eyes on the deceiving, puzzling gloom again. He would have called her name had he known it—but now he would not ask her to share even a name with the other. . . .

His own face, within the frame of the door, glimmered white as the narcissi in the darkness. . . .

A shadow, light as fleece, seemed to take shape in the kitchen (the time had been when Oleron would have said that

a cloud had passed over the unseen moon). The low illumination on the blind at his elbow grew dimmer (the time had
been when Oleron would have concluded that the lamplighter
going his round had turned low the flame of the lamp). The
fire settled, letting down the black and charred papers; a
flower fell from a bowl, and lay indistinct upon the floor; all
was still; and then a stray draught moved through the old
house, passing before Oleron's face. . . .

Suddenly, inclining his head, he withdrew a little from the
doorjamb. The wandering draught caused the door to move
a little on its hinges. Oleron trembled violently, stood for a
moment longer, and then, putting his hand out to the knob,
softly drew the door to, sat on the nearest chair, and waited,
as a man might await the calling of his name that should
summon him to some weighty, high and privy Audience. . . .

11

One knows not whether there can be human compassion
for anemia of the soul. When the pitch of Life is dropped,
and the spirit is so put over and reversed that that only is
horrible which before was sweet and worldly and of the day,
the human relation disappears. The sane soul turns appalled
away, lest not merely itself, but sanity should suffer. We are
not gods. We cannot drive our devils. We must see selfishly
to it that devils do not enter into ourselves.

And this we must do even though Love so transfuse us that
we may well deem our nature to be half divine. We shall but
speak of honor and duty in vain. The letter dropped within
the dark door will lie unregarded, or, if regarded for a brief
instant between two unspeakable lapses, left and forgotten
again. The telegram will be undelivered, nor will the whistling messenger (wiselier guided than he knows to whistle)
be conscious as he walks away of the drawn blind that is
pushed aside an inch by a finger and then fearfully replaced
again. No: let the miserable wrestle with his own shadows;
let him, if indeed he be so mad, clip and strain and enfold
and crouch the succubus; but let him do so in a house into

which not an air of Heaven penetrates, nor a bright finger of the sun pierces the filthy twilight. The lost must remain lost. Humanity has other business to attend to.

For the handwriting of the two letters that Oleron, stealing noiselessly one June day into his kitchen to rid his sitting-room of an armful of fetid and decaying flowers, had seen on the floor within his door, had had no more meaning for him than if it had belonged to some dim and far-away dream. And at the beating of the telegraph-boy upon the door, within a few feet of the bed where he lay, he had gnashed his teeth and stopped his ears. He had pictured the lad standing there, just beyond his partition, among packets of provisions and bundles of dead and dying flowers. For his outer landing was littered with these. Oleron had feared to open his door to take them in. After a week, the errand lads had reported that there must be some mistake about the order, and had left no more. Inside, in the red twilight, the old flowers turned brown and fell and decayed where they lay.

Gradually his power was draining away. The Abomination fastened on Oleron's power. The steady sapping sometimes left him for many hours of prostration gazing vacantly up at his red-tinged ceiling; idly suffering such fancies as came of themselves to have their way with him. Even the strongest of his memories had no more than a precarious hold upon his attention. Sometimes a flitting half-memory, of a novel to be written, a novel it was important that he should write, tantalized him for a space before vanishing again; and sometimes whole novels, perfect, splendid, established to endure, rose magically before him. And sometimes the memories were absurdly remote and trivial, of garrets he had inhabited and lodgings that had sheltered him, and so forth. Oleron had known a good deal about such things in his time, but all that was now past. He had at last found a place which he did not intend to leave until they fetched him out—a place that some might have thought a little on the green-sick side, that others might have considered to be a little too redolent of long-dead and morbid things for a living man to be mewed up in, but ah, so irresistible, with such an authority of its own, with such an associate of its own, and a place of such delights when once a man had ceased to struggle against its inexorable will! A novel? Somebody ought to write a novel about a place like that! There must be lots to write about in a place like that if one could but get to the bottom of it! It had probably already been painted, by a man called Madley who had lived there . . . but Oleron had not known this Madley—had a strong feeling that he wouldn't have liked him— would rather he had lived somewhere else—really couldn't stand the fellow—hated him, Madley, in fact. (Aha! That was a joke!) He seriously doubted whether the man had led the life he ought; Oleron was in two minds sometimes whether he wouldn't tell that long-nosed guardian of the public morals across the way about him; but probably he knew, and had made his praying hullabaloos for him also. That was his line. Why, Oleron himself had had a dust-up with him about something or other . . . some girl or other . . . Elsie Bengough her name was, he remembered. . . .

Oleron had moments of deep uneasiness about this Elsie Bengough. Or rather, he was not so much uneasy about her as restless about the things she did. Chief of these was the way in which she persisted in thrusting herself into his thoughts; and, whenever he was quick enough, he sent her packing the moment she made her appearance there. The truth was that she was not merely a bore; she had always been that; it had now come to the pitch where her very presence in his fancy was inimical to the full enjoyment of certain experiences. . . . She had no tact; really ought to have known that people are not at home to the thoughts of everybody all the time; ought in mere politeness to have allowed him certain seasons quite to himself; and was monstrously ignorant of things if she did not know, as she appeared not to know, that there were certain special hours when a man's veins ran with fire and daring and power, in which . . . well, in which he had a reasonable right to treat folk as he had treated that prying Barrett—to shut them out completely. . . . But no, up she popped: the thought of her, and ruined all. Bright towering fabrics, by the side of which even those perfect, magical novels of which he dreamed were dun and gray, vanished utterly at her intrusion. It was as if a fog should suddenly quench some fair-beaming star, as if at the threshold of some golden portal prepared for Oleron a pit should suddenly gape, as if a bat-like shadow should turn the growning dawn to murk and darkness again. . . . Therefore, Oleron strove to stifle even the nascent thought of her.

Nevertheless, there came an occasion on which this woman Bengough absolutely refused to be suppressed. Oleron could not have told exactly when this happened; he only knew by the glimmer of the street lamp on his blind that it was some time during the night, and that for some time she had not presented herself.

He had no warning, none, of her coming; she just came—was there. Strive as he would, he could not shake off the thought of her nor the image of her face. She haunted him.

But for her to come at *that* moment of all moments! . . . Really, it was past belief! How *she* could endure it, Oleron could not conceive! Actually, to look on, as it were, at the triumph of a Rival. . . . Good God! It was monstrous! tact—reticence—he had never credited her with an overwhelming amount of either: but he had never attributed mere—oh, there was no word for it! Monstrous—monstrous! Did she intend thenceforward. . . . Good God! To look on! . . .

Oleron felt the blood rush up to the roots of his hair with anger against her.

"Damnation take her!" he choked. . . .

But the next moment his heat and resentment had changed to a cold sweat of cowering fear. Panic-stricken, he strove to comprehend what he had done. For though he knew not what, he knew he had done something, something fatal, irreparable, blasting. Anger he had felt, but not *this* blaze of ire that suddenly flooded the twilight of his consciousness with a white infernal light. *That* appalling flash was not his—not his *that* open rift of bright and searing Hell—not his, not his! His had been the hand of a child, preparing a puny blow; but what was *this other* horrific hand that was drawn back to strike in the same place? Had *he* set that in motion? Had *he* provided the spark that had touched off the whole accumulated power of that formidable and relentless place? He did not know. He only knew that that poor igniting particle in himself was blown out, that—Oh, impossible!—a clinging kiss (how else to express it?) had changed on his very lips to a gnashing and a removal, and that for very pity of the awful odds he must cry out to her against whom he had lately raged to guard herself. . . . guard herself. . . .

"Look out!" he shrieked aloud. . . .

The revulsion was instant. As if a cold slow billow had broken over him, he came to find that he was lying in his bed, that the mist and horror that had for so long enwrapped him had departed, that he was Paul Oleron, and that he was sick, naked, helpless, and unutterably abandoned and alone. His faculties, though weak, answered at last to his calls upon them; and he knew that it must have been a hideous nightmare that had left him sweating and shaking thus.

Yes, he was himself, Paul Oleron, a tired novelist, already past the summit of his best work, and slipping downhill again empty-handed from it all. He had struck short in his life's aim. He had tried too much, had overestimated his strength, and was a failure, a failure. . . .

It all came to him in the single word, enwrapped and complete; it needed no sequential thought; he was a failure. He had missed. . . .

And he had missed not one happiness, but two. He had missed the ease of this world, which men love, and he had missed also that other shining prize for which men forgo ease, the snatching and holding and triumphant bearing up aloft of which is the only justification of the mad adventurer who hazards the enterprise. And there was no second attempt. Fate has no morrow. Oleron's morrow must be to sit down to profitless, ill-done, unrequired work again, and so on the morrow after that, the morrow after that, and as many morrows as there might be. . . .

He lay there, weakly yet sanely considering it. . . .

And since the whole attempt had failed, it was hardly worth while to consider whether a little might not be saved from the general wreck. No good would ever come out of that half-finished novel. He had intended that it should appear in the autumn; was under contract that it should appear; no matter;

it was better to pay forfeit to his publishers than to waste what days were left. He was spent; age was not far off; and paths of wisdom and sadness were the properest for the remainder of the journey. . . .

If only he had chosen the wife, the child, the faithful friend at the fireside, and let them follow an *ignis fatuus* that list! . . .

In the meantime it began to puzzle him exceedingly why he should be so weak, that his room should smell so overpoweringly of decaying vegetable matter, and that his hand, chancing to stray to his face in the darkness, should encounter a beard.

"Most extraordinary!" he began to mutter to himself. "Have I been ill? Am I ill now? And if so, why have they left me alone? . . . Extraordinary! . . ."

He thought he heard a sound from the kitchen or bathroom. He rose a little on his pillow, and listened. . . . Ah! He was not alone, then! It certainly would have been extraordinary if they had left him ill and alone——Alone? Oh, no. He would be looked after. He wouldn't be left, ill, to shift for himself. If everybody else had forsaken him, he could trust Elsie Bengough, the dearest chum he had, for that . . . bless her faithful heart!

But suddenly a short, stifled, spluttering cry rang sharply out:

"Paul!"

It came from the kitchen.

And in the same moment it flashed upon Oleron, he knew not how, that two, three, five, he knew not how many minutes before, another sound, unmarked at the time, but suddenly transfixing his attention now, had striven to reach his intelligence. This sound had been the slight touch of metal on metal—just such a sound as Oleron made when he put his key into the lock.

"Hallo! . . . Who's that?" he called sharply from his bed.

He had no answer.

He called again. "Hallo! . . . Who's there? . . . Who is it?"

This time he was sure he heard noises, soft and heavy, in the kitchen.

"This is a queer thing altogether," he muttered. "By Jove, I'm as weak as a kitten, too. . . . Hallo, there! Somebody called, didn't they? . . . Elsie! Is that you? . . ."

Then he began to knock with his hand on the wall at the side of his bed.

"Elsie! . . . Elsie! . . . You called, didn't you? . . . Please come here, whoever it is! . . ."

There was a sound as of a closing door, and then silence. Oleron began to get rather alarmed.

"It may be a nurse," he muttered: "Elsie'd have to get me a nurse, of course. She'd sit with me as long as she could spare the time, brave lass, and she'd get a nurse for the rest. . . . But it was awfully like her voice. . . . Elsie, or whoever it is! . . . I can't make this out at all. I must go and see what's the matter. . . ."

He put one leg out of bed. Feeling its feebleness, he reached with his hand for the additional support of the wall. . . .

But before putting out the other leg he stopped and considered, picking at his new-found beard. He was suddenly wondering whether he *dared* go into the kitchen. It was such a frightfully long way; no man knew what horror might not leap and huddle on his shoulders if he went so far; when a man has an overmastering impulse to get back into bed he ought to take heed of the warning and obey it. Besides, why should he go? What was there to go for? If it was that Bengough creature again, let her look after herself; Oleron was not going to have things cramp themselves on his defenseless back for the sake of such a spoil-sport as *she*! . . . If she was in, let her let herself out again, and the sooner the better for her! Oleron simply couldn't be bothered. He had his work to do. On the morrow, he must set about the writing of a novel with a heroine so winsome, capricious, adorable, jealous, wicked, beautiful, inflaming, and altogether evil, that men should stand amazed. She was coming over him now; he knew by the alteration of the very air of the room when she was near him; and that soft thrill of bliss that had begun to stir in him never came unless she was beckoning, beckoning. . . .

He let go of the wall and fell back into bed again as—oh, unthinkable!—the other half of that kiss that a gnash had interrupted was placed (how else convey it?) on his lips, robbing him of very breath. . . .

12

In the bright June sunlight a crowd filled the square, and looked up at the windows of the old house with the antique insurance marks on its walls of red brick and the agents' notice-boards hanging like wooden choppers over the paling. Two constables stood at the broken gate of the narrow entrance alley, keeping folk back. The women kept to the outskirts of the throng, moving now and then as if to see the drawn red blinds of the old house from a new angle, and talking in whispers. The children were in the houses, behind closed doors.

A long-nosed man had a little group about him, and he was telling some story over and over again; and another man, little and fat and wide-eyed, sought to capture the long-nosed man's audience with some relation in which a key figured.

". . . and it was revealed to me that there'd been something that very afternoon," the long-nosed man was saying. "I was standing there, where Constable Saunders is—or rather, I was passing about my business, when they came out. There was no deceiving me, oh, no deceiving *me*! I saw her face. . . ."

"What was it like, Mr. Barrett?" a man asked.

"It was like hers whom our Lord said to, 'Woman, doth any man accuse thee?'—white as paper, and no mistake! Don't tell *me*! . . . And so I walks straight across to Mrs. Barrett, and 'Jane,' I says, 'this must stop, and stop at once; we are commanded to avoid evil,' I says, 'and it must come to an end now; let him get help elsewhere.' And she says to me, 'John,' she says, 'it's four-and-sixpence a week'—them was her words. 'Jane,' I says, 'if it was forty-six thousand pounds it should stop' . . . and from that day to this she hasn't set foot inside that gate.''

There was a short silence: then,

"Did Mrs. Barrett ever . . . *see* anything, like?'' somebody vaguely inquired.

Barrett turned austerely on the speaker.

"What Mrs. Barrett saw and Mrs. Barrett didn't see shall not pass these lips; even as it is written, keep thy tongue from speaking evil," he said.

Another man spoke.

"He was pretty near canned up in the *Wagon and Horses* that night, weren't he, Jim?''

"Yes, 'e 'adn't 'alf copped it. . . .''

"Not standing treat much, neither; he was in the bar, all on his own. . . .''

"So 'e was; we talked about it. . . .''

The fat, scared-eyed man made another attempt.

"She got the key off of me—she 'ad the number of it—she came into my shop of a Tuesday evening. . . .''

Nobody heeded him.

"Shut your heads,'' a heavy laborer commented gruffly, "she hasn't been found yet. 'Ere's the inspectors; we shall know more in a bit.''

Two inspectors had come up and were talking to the constables who guarded the gate. The little fat man ran eagerly forward, saying that she had bought the key of him. "I remember the number, because of its being three ones and three threes—111333!'' he exclaimed excitedly.

An inspector put him aside.

"Nobody's been in?'' he asked of one of the constables.

"No, sir.''

"Then you, Brackley, come with us; you, Smith, keep the gate. There's a squad on its way.''

The two inspectors and the constable passed down the alley and entered the house. They mounted the wide carved staircase.

"This don't look as if he'd been out much lately,'' one of the inspectors muttered as he kicked aside a litter of dead leaves and paper that lay outside Oleron's door. "I don't think we need knock—break a pane, Brackley."

The door had two glazed panels; there was a sound of shattered glass; and Brackley put his hand through the hole his elbow had made and drew back the latch.

"Faugh!" . . . choked one of the inspectors as they entered. "Let some light and air in, quick. It stinks like a hearse——"

The assembly out in the square saw the red blinds go up and the windows of the old house flung open.

"That's better," said one of the inspectors, putting his head out of a window and drawing a deep breath. . . . "That seems to be the bedroom in there; will you go in, Simms, while I go over the rest? . . ."

They had drawn up the bedroom blind also, and the waxy-white, emaciated man on the bed had made a blinker of his hand against the torturing flood of brightness. Nor could he believe that his hearing was not playing tricks with him, for there were two policemen in his room, bending over him and asking where "she" was. He shook his head.

"This woman Bengough . . . goes by the name of Miss Elsie Bengough . . . d'ye hear? Where is she? . . . No good, Brackley; get him up; be careful with him; I'll just shove *my* head out of the window, I think. . . ."

The other inspector had been through Oleron's study and had found nothing, and was now in the kitchen, kicking aside an ankle-deep mass of vegetable refuse that cumbered the floor. The kitchen window had no blind, and was overshadowed by the blank end of the house across the alley. The kitchen appeared to be empty.

But the inspector, kicking aside the dead flowers, noticed that a shuffling track that was not of his making had been swept to a cupboard in the corner. In the upper part of the door of the cupboard was a square panel that looked as if it slid on runners. The door itself was closed.

The inspector advanced, put out his hand to the little knob, and slid the hatch along its groove.

Then he took an involuntary step back again.

Framed in the aperture, and falling forward a little before

it jammed again in its frame, was something that resembled a large lumpy pudding, done up in a pudding-bag of faded browny red frieze.

"Ah!" said the inspector.

To close the hatch again he would have had to thrust that pudding back with his hand; and somehow he did not quite like the idea of touching it. Instead, he turned the handle of the cupboard itself. There was weight behind it, so much weight that, after opening the door three or four inches and peering inside, he had to put his shoulder to it in order to close it again. In closing it he left sticking out, a few inches from the floor, a triangle of black and white check skirt.

He went into the small hall.

"All right!" he called.

They had got Oleron into his clothes. He still used his hands as blinkers, and his brain was very confused. A number of things were happening that he couldn't understand. He couldn't understand the extraordinary mess of dead flowers there seemed to be everywhere; he couldn't understand why there should be police officers in his room; he couldn't understand why one of these should be sent for a four-wheeler and a stretcher; and he couldn't understand what heavy article they seemed to be moving about in the kitchen—his kitchen . . .

"What's the matter?" he muttered sleepily. . . .

Then he heard a murmur in the square, and the stopping of a four-wheeler outside. A police officer was at his elbow again, and Oleron wondered why, when he whispered something to him, he should run off a string of words—something about "used in evidence against you." They had lifted him to his feet, and were assisting him towards the door. . . .

No, Oleron couldn't understand it at all.

They got him down the stairs and along the alley. Oleron was aware of confused angry shoutings; he gathered that a number of people wanted to lynch somebody or other. Then his attention became fixed on a little fat frightened-eyed man who appeared to be making a statement that an officer was taking down in a notebook.

"I'd seen her with him . . . they was often together . . .

she came into my shop and said it was for him . . . I thought it was all right . . . 111333 the number was,'' the man was saying.

The people seemed to be very angry; many police were keeping them back; but one of the inspectors had a voice that Oleron thought quite kind and friendly. He was telling somebody to get somebody else into the dab before something or other was brought out; and Oleron noticed that a four-wheeler was drawn up at the gate. It appeared that it was himself who was to be put into it; and as they lifted him up he saw that the inspector tried to stand between him and something that stood behind the cab, but was not quick enough to prevent Oleron seeing that this something was a hooded stretcher. The angry voices sounded like a sea, something hard, like a stone, hit the back of the cab; and the inspector followed Oleron in and stood with his back to the window nearer the side where the people were. The door they had put Oleron in at remained open, apparently till the other inspector should come; and through the opening Oleron had a glimpse of the hatchet-like "To Let" boards among the privet-trees. One of them said that the key was at Number Six. . . .

Suddenly the raging of voices was hushed. Along the entrance-alley shuffling steps were heard, and the other inspector appeared at the cab door.

"Right away," he said to the driver.

He entered, fastened the door after him, and blocked up the second window with his back. Between the two inspectors Oleron slept peacefully. The cab moved down the square, the other vehicle went up the hill. The mortuary lay that way.

Fitz-James O'Brien

WHAT WAS IT?

Fitz-James O'Brien was regarded as the heir apparent to Poe in America before his early death in the Civil War. He left behind only the excellent stories collected in his single, posthumous compilation *(The Life, Poems and Stories of . . .)*. Three of his nine stories are significant contributions to the evolution of science fiction ("The Diamond Lens," "The Wondersmith," and "What Was It?"), but "What Was It?" is indeed a horror story of the physical sciences, and moreover a tale that catalogs other writers of the fantastic, from the Shakespeare of "The Tempest," and E.T.A. Hoffmann, to Mrs. Crowe, Charles Brockden Brown and Bulwer-Lytton. O'Brien manages to tame his invisible horror through science, rejecting the supernatural, which makes the story in a way an antihorror piece, but the juxtaposition of science and horror persists, from Poe through Lovecraft and beyond. "What Was It?" is a story substantially ahead of its time, with much of the feel of the 1890s fiction to come.

I t is, I confess, with considerable difference that I approach the strange narrative which I am about to relate. The events which I purpose detailing are of so extraordinary a character that I am quite prepared to meet with an unusual amount of incredulity and scorn. I accept all such beforehand. I have, I trust, the literary courage to face unbelief. I have, after mature consideration, resolved to narrate, in as simple and straightforward a manner as I can compass, some facts that passed under my observation, in the month of July last, and which, in the annals of the mysteries of physical science, are wholly unparalleled.

I live at No.—Twenty-sixth Street, in New York. The house is in some respects a curious one. It has enjoyed for the last two years the reputation of being haunted. It is a large and stately residence, surrounded by what was once a garden, but which is now only a green enclosure used for bleaching clothes. The dry basin of what has been a fountain, and a few fruit-trees ragged and unpruned, indicate that this spot in past days was a pleasant, shady retreat, filled with fruits and flowers and the sweet murmur of waters.

The house is very spacious. A hall of noble size leads to a large spiral staircase winding through its centre, while the various apartments are of imposing dimensions. It was built some fifteen or twenty years since by Mr. A——, the well-known New York merchant, who five years ago threw the commercial world into convulsions by a stupendous bank fraud. Mr. A——, as every one knows, escaped to Europe, and died not long after, of a broken heart. Almost immediately after the news of his decease reached this country and was verified, the report spread in Twenty-sixth Street that No.—was haunted. Legal measures had dispossessed the widow of its former owner, and it was inhabited merely by a care-taker and his wife, placed there by the house-agent in whose hands it had passed for purposes of renting or sale. These people declared that they were troubled with unnatural noises. Doors were opened without any visible agency. The remnants of furniture scattered through the various rooms were, during the night, piled one upon the other by unknown hands. Invisible feet passed up and down the stairs in broad daylight, accompanied by the rustle of unseen silk dresses, and the gliding of viewless hands along the massive balusters. The care-taker and his wife declared they would live there no longer. The house-agent laughed, dismissed them, and put others in their place. The noises and supernatural manifestations continued. The neighborhood caught up the story, and the house remained untenanted for three years. Several per-

sons negotiated for it; but, somehow, always before the bargain was closed they heard the unpleasant rumors and declined to treat any further.

It was in this state of things that my landlady, who at that
time kept a boarding-house in Bleecker Street, and who
wished to move father up town, conceived the bold idea of
renting No.—Twenty-sixth Street. Happening to have in her
house rather a plucky and philosophical set of boarders, she
laid her scheme before us, stating candidly everything she
had heard respecting the ghostly qualities of the establishment to which she wished to remove us. With the exception
of two timid persons,—a sea-captain and a returned Califor-
nian, who immediately gave notice that they would leave,—all
of Mrs. Moffat's guests declared that they would accompany
her in her chivalric incursion into the abode of spirits.

Our removal was effected in the month of May, and we
were charmed with our new residence. The portion of
Twenty-sixth Street where our house is situated, between
Seventh and Eighth Avenues, is one of the pleasantest local-
ities in New York. The gardens back of the house, running
down nearly to the Hudson, form, in the summer time, a
perfect avenue of verdure. The air is pure and invigorating,
sweeping, as it does, straight across the river from the Wee-
hawken heights, and even the ragged garden which surrounded the house, although displaying on washing days
rather too much clothes-line, still gave us apiece of green-
sward to look at, and a cool retreat in the summer evenings,
where we smoked our cigars in the dusk, and watched the
fireflies flashing their dark-lanterns in the long grass.

Of course we had no sooner established ourselves at No.—
then we began to expect the ghosts. We absolutely awaited
their advent with eagerness. Our dinner conversation was supernatural. One of the boarders, who had purchased Mrs.
Crowe's "Night Side of Nature" for his own private delec-
tation, was regarded as a public enemy by the entire household for not having bought twenty copies. The man led a life
of supreme wretchedness while he was reading this volume.
A system of espionage was established, of which he was the
victim. If he incautiously laid the book down for an instant

and left the room, it was immediately seized and read aloud in secret places to a select few. I found myself a person of immense importance, it having leaked out that I was tolerably well versed in the history of supernaturalism, and had once written a story the foundation of which was a ghost. If a table or a wainscot panel happened to warp when we were assembled in the large drawing-room, there was an instant silence, and every one was prepared for an immediate clanking of chains and a spectral form.

After a month of psychological excitement, it was with the utmost dissatisfaction that we were forced to acknowledge that nothing in the remotest degree approaching the supernatural had manifested itself. Once the black butler asseverated that his candle had been blown out by some invisible agency while he was undressing himself for the night; but as I had more than once discovered this colored gentleman in a condition when one candle must have appeared to him like two, I thought it possible that, by going a step further in his potations, he might have reversed this phenomenon, and seen no candle at all where he ought to have beheld one.

Things were in this state when an incident took place so awful and inexplicable in its character that my reason fairly reels at the bare memory of the occurrence. It was the tenth of July. After dinner was over I repaired, with my friend Dr. Hammond, to the garden to smoke my evening pipe. Independent of certain mental sympathies which existed between the Doctor and myself, we were linked together by a vice. We both smoked opium. We knew each other's secret, and respected it. We enjoyed together that wonderful expansion of thought, that marvellous intensifying of the perceptive faculties, that boundless feeling of existence when we seem to have points of contact with the whole universe,—in short, that unimaginable spiritual bliss, which I would not surrender for a throne, and which I hope you, reader, will never—never taste.

Those hours of opium happiness which the Doctor and I spent together in secret were regulated with a scientific accuracy. We did not blindly smoke the drug of paradise, and leave our dreams to chance. While smoking, we carefully steered our conversation through the brightest and calmest channels of thought. We talked of the East, and endeavored to recall the magical panorama of its glowing scenery. We criticised the most sensuous poets,—those who painted life ruddy with health, brimming with passion, happy in the possession of youth and strength. If we talked of Shakespeare's "Tempest," we lingered over Ariel, and avoided Caliban. Like the Guebers, we turned our faces to the east, and saw only the sunny side of the world.

This skilful coloring of our train of thought produced in our subsequent visions a corresponding tone. The splendor of Arabian fairy-land dyed our dreams. We paced that narrow strip of grass with the tread and port of kings. The song of the *rana arborea*, while he clung to the bark of the ragged plum-tree, sounded like the strains of divine musicians. Houses, walls, and streets melted like rain-clouds, and vistas of unimaginable glory stretched away before us. It was a rapturous companionship. We enjoyed the vast delight more perfectly because, even in our most ecstatic moments, we were conscious of each other's presence. Our pleasures, while individual, were still twin, vibrating and moving in musical accord.

On the evening in question, the tenth of July, the Doctor and myself drifted into an unusually meta-physical mood. We lit our large meer-schaums, filled with fine Turkish tobacco, in the core of which burned a little black nut of opium, that, like the nut in the fairy tale, held within its narrow limits wonders beyond the reach of kings; we paced to and fro, conversing. A strange perversity dominated the currents of our thought. They would *not* flow through the sun-lit channels into which we strove to divert them. For some unaccountable reason, they constantly diverged into dark and lonesome beds, where a continual gloom brooded. It was in vain that, after our old fashion, we flung ourselves on the shores of the East, and talked of its gay bazaars, of the splendors of the time of Haroun, of harems and golden palaces. Black afreets continually arose from the depths of our talk, and expanded, like the one the fisherman released from the copper vessel, until they blotted everything bright from our vision. Insensibly, we yielded to the occult force that swayed us, and indulged in gloomy speculation. We had talked some time upon the proneness of the human mind to mysticism, and the almost universal love of the terrible, when Hammond suddenly said to me, "What do you consider to be the greatest element of terror?"

The question puzzled me. That many things were terrible, I knew. Stumbling over a corpse in the dark; beholding, as I once did, a woman floating down a deep and rapid river, with wildly lifted arms, and awful, upturned face, uttering, as she drifted, shrieks that rent one's heart, while we, the spectators, stood frozen at a window which overhung the river at a height of sixty feet, unable to make the slightest effort to save her, but dumbly watching her last supreme agony and her disappearance. A shattered wreck, with no life visible, encountered floating listlessly on the ocean, is a terrible object, for it suggests a huge terror, the proportions of which are veiled. But now struck me, for the first time, that there must be one great and ruling embodiment of fear,—a King of Terrors, to which all others must succumb. What might it be? To what train of circumstances would it owe its existence?

"I confess, Hammond," I replied to my friend, "I never considered the subject before. That there must be one Something more terrible than any other thing, I feel. I cannot attempt, however, even the most vague definition."

"I am somewhat like you, Harry," he answered. "I feel my capacity to experience a terror greater than anything yet conceived by the human mind;—something combining in fearful and unnatural amalgamation hitherto supposed incompatible elements. The calling of the voices in Brockden Brown's novel of 'Wieland' is awful; so is the picture of the Dweller of the Threshold, in Bulwer's 'Zanoni'; but," he added, shaking his head gloomily, "there is something more terrible still than these."

"Look here, Hammond," I rejoined, "let us drop this kind of talk, for heaven's sake! We shall suffer for it, depend on it."

"I don't know what's the matter with me tonight," he replied, "but my brain is running upon all sorts of weird and awful thoughts. I feel as if I could write a story like Hoffman, to-night, if I were only master of a literary style.''

"Well, if we are going to be Hoffmanesque in our talk, I'm off to bed. Opium and nightmares should never be brought together. How sultry it is! Good-night, Hammond.''

"Good-night, Harry. Pleasant dreams to you.''

"To you, gloomy wretch, afreets, ghouls, and enchanters.''

We parted, and each sought his respective chamber. I undressed quickly and got into bed, taking with me, according to my usual custom, a book, over which I generally read myself to sleep. I opened the volume as soon as I had laid my head upon the pillow, and instantly flung it to the other side of the room. It was Goudon's "History of Monsters,''— a curious French work, which I had lately imported from Paris, but which, in the state of mind I had then reached, was anything but an agreeable companion. I resolved to go to sleep at once; so, turning down my gas until nothing but a little blue point of light glimmered on the top of the tube, I composed myself to rest.

The room was in total darkness. The atom of gas that still remained alight did not illuminate a distance of three inches round the burner. I desperately drew my arms across my eyes, as if to shut out the darkness, and tried to think of nothing. It was in vain. The confounded themes touched on by Hammond in the garden kept obtruding themselves on my brain. I battled against them. I erected ramparts of would-be blankness of intellect to keep them out. They still crowded upon me. While I was lying still as a corpse, hoping that by a perfect physical inaction I should hasten mental repose, an awful incident occurred. A Something dropped, as it seemed, from the ceiling, plum upon my chest, and the next instant I felt two bony hands encircling my throat, endeavoring to choke me.

I am no coward, and am possessed of considerable physical strength. The suddenness of the attack, instead of stunning me, strung every nerve to its highest tension. My body acted from instinct, before my brain had time to realize the terrors of my position. In an instant I wound two muscular arms around the creature, and squeezed it, with all the strength of despair, against my chest. In a few seconds the bony hands that had fastened on my throat loosened their hold, and I was free to breathe once more. Then commenced a struggle of awful intensity. Immersed in the most profound darkness, totally ignorant of the nature of the Thing by which I was so suddenly attacked, finding my grasp slipping every moment, by reason, it seemed to me, of the entire nakedness of my assailant, bitten with sharp teeth in the shoulder, neck, and chest, having every moment to protect my throat against a pair of sinewy, agile hands, which my utmost efforts could not confine,—these were a combination of circumstances to combat which required all the strength, skill and courage that I possessed.

At last, after a silent, deadly, exhausting struggle, I got my assailant under by a series of incredible efforts of strength. Once pinned, with my knee on what I made out to be its chest, I knew that I was victor. I rested for a moment to breathe. I heard the creature beneath me panting in the darkness, and felt the violent throbbing of a heart. It was apparently as exhausted as I was; that was one comfort. At this moment I remembered that I usually placed under my pillow, before going to bed, a large yellow silk pocket-handkerchief. I felt for it instantly; it was there. In a few seconds more I had, after a fashion, pinioned the creature's arms.

I now felt tolerably secure. There was nothing more to be done but to turn on the gas, and, having first seen what my midnight assailant was like, arouse the household. I will confess to being actuated by a certain pride in not giving the alarm before; I wished to make the capture alone and unaided.

Never losing my hold for an instant, I slipped from the bed to the floor, dragging my captive with me. I had but a few steps to make to reach the gas-burner; these I made with the greatest caution, holding the creature in a grip like vise. At last I got within arms'-length of the tiny speck of blue light which told me where the gas-burner lay. Quick as lightning I released my grasp with one hand and let on the full flood of light. Then I turned to look at my captive.

I cannot even attempt to give any definition of my sensations the instant after I turned on the gas. I suppose I must have shrieked with terror, for in less than a minute afterward my room was crowded with the inmates of the house. I shudder now as I think of that awful moment. *I saw nothing!* Yes; I had one arm firmly clasped round a breathing, panting, corporeal shape, my other hand gripped with all its strength a throat as warm, and apparently fleshy, as my own; and yet, with this living substance in my grasp, with its body pressed against my own, and all in the bright glare of a large jet of gas, I absolutely beheld nothing! Not even an outline,—a vapor!

I do not, even at this hour, realize the situation in which I found myself. Imagination in vain tries to compass the awful paradox.

It breathed. I felt its warm breath upon my cheek. It struggled fiercely. It had hands. They clutched me. Its skin was smooth, like my own. There it lay, pressed close up against me, solid as stone,—and yet utterly invisible!

I wonder that I did not faint or go mad on the instant. Some wonderful instinct must have sustained me; for, absolutely, in place of loosening my hold on the terrible Enigma, I seemed to gain an additional strength in my moment of horror, and tightened my grasp with such wonderful force that I felt the creature shivering with agony.

Just then Hammond entered the room at the head of the household. As soon as he beheld my face—which, I suppose, must have been an awful sight to look at—he hastened forward, crying, "Great heaven, Harry! what has happened?"

"Hammond! Hammond!" I cried, "come here. O, this is awful! I have been attacked in bed by something or other, which I have hold of; but I can't see it,—I can't see it!"

Hammond, doubtless struck by the unfeigned horror expressed in my countenance, made one or two steps forward with an anxious yet puzzled expression. A very audible titter burst from the remainder of my visitors. This suppressed laughter made me furious. To laugh at a human being in my position! It was the worst species of cruelty. *Now*, I can understand why the appearance of a man struggling violently, as it would seem, with an airy nothing, and calling for assistance against a vision, should have appeared ludicrous. *Then*, so great was my rage against the mocking crowd that had I the power, I would have stricken them dead where they stood.

"Hammond! Hammond!" I cried again, despairingly, "for God's sake come to me. I can hold the—the thing but a short while longer. It is over-powering me. Help me! Help me!"

"Harry," whispered Hammond, approaching me, "you have been smoking too much opium."

"I swear to you, Hammond, that this is no vision," I answered, in the same low tone. "Don't you see how it shakes my whole frame with its struggles? If you don't believe me, convince yourself. Feel it,—touch it."

Hammond advanced and laid his hand in the spot I indicated. A Wild cry of horror burst from him. He had felt it!

In a moment he had discovered somewhere in my room a long piece of cord, and was the next instant winding it and knotting it about the body of the unseen being that I clasped in my arms.

"Harry," he said, in a hoarse, agitated voice, for, though he preserved his presence of mind, he was deeply moved, "Harry, it's all safe now. You may let go, old fellow, if you're tired. The Thing can't move."

I was utterly exhausted, and I gladly loosed my hold.

Hammond stood holding the ends of the cord that bound the Invisible, twisted round his hand, while before him, self-supporting as it were, he beheld a rope laced and interlaced, and stretching tightly around a vacant space. I never saw a man look so thoroughly stricken with awe. Nevertheless his face expressed all the courage and determination which I knew him to possess. His lips, although white, were set firmly, and one could perceive at a glance that, although stricken with fear, he was not daunted.

The confusion that ensued among the guests of the house who were witnesses of this extraordinary scene between Hammond and myself,—who beheld the pantomime of binding this struggling Something,—who beheld me almost sinking from physical exhaustion when my task of jailer was over,—the confusion and terror that took possession of the bystanders, when they saw all this, was beyond description. The weaker ones fled from the apartment. The few who remained clustered near the door and could not be induced to approach Hammond and his Charge. Still, incredulity broke out through their terror. They had not the courage to satisfy themselves, and yet they doubted. It was in vain that I begged of some of the men to come near and convince themselves by touch of the existence in that room of a living being which was invisible. They were incredulous, but did not dare to undeceive themselves. How could a solid, living, breathing body be invisible, they ask. My reply was this. I gave a sign to Hammond, and both of us—conquering our fearful repugnance to touch the invisible creature—lifted it from the ground, manacled as it was, and took it to my bed. Its weight was about that of a boy of fourteen.

"Now, my friends," I said, as Hammond and myself held the creature suspended over the bed, "I can give you self-evident proof that here is a solid, ponderable body, which, nevertheless, you cannot see. Be good enough to watch the surface of the bed attentively."

I was astonished at my own courage in treating this strange event so calmly; but I had recovered from my first terror, and felt a sort of scientific pride in the affair, which dominated every other feeling.

The eyes of the bystanders were immediately fixed on my bed. At a given signal Hammond and I let the creature fall. There was the dull sound of a heavy body alighting on a soft mass. The timbers of the bed creaked. A deep impression marked itself distinctly on the pillow, and on the bed itself. The crowd who witnessed this gave a low cry, and rushed from the room. Hammond and I were left alone with our Mystery.

We remained silent for some time, listening to the low, irregular breathing of the creature on the bed, and watching the rustle of the bed-clothes as it impotently struggled to free itself from confinement. Then Hammond spoke.

"Harry, this is awful."

"Ay, awful."

"But not unaccountable."

"Not unaccountable! What do you mean? Such a thing has never occurred since the birth of the world. I know not what to think, Hammond. God grant that I am not mad, and that this is not an insane fantasy!"

"Let us reason a little, Harry. Here is a solid body which we touch, but which we cannot see. The fact is so unusual that it strikes us with terror. Is there no parallel, though, for such a phenomenon? Take a piece of pure glass. It is tangible and transparent. A certain chemical coarseness is all that prevents its being so entirely transparent as to be totally invisible. It is not *theoretically impossible*, mind you, to make a glass which shall not reflect a single ray of light,—a glass so pure and homogeneous in its atoms that the rays from the sun will pass through it as they do through the air, refracted but not reflected. We do not see the air, and yet we feel it."

"That's all very well, Hammond, but these are inanimate substances. Glass does not breathe, air does not breathe. This *thing* has a heart that palpitates,—a will that moves it,—lungs that play, and inspire and respire."

"You forget the phenomena of which we have so often heard of late," answered the Doctor, gravely. "At the meetings called 'spirit circles,' invisible hands have been thrust into the hands of those persons round the table,—warm, fleshy hands that seemed to pulsate with mortal life."

"What? Do you think, then, that this thing is—"

"I don't know what it is," was the solemn reply; "but please the gods I will, with your assistance, thoroughly investigate it."

We watched together, smoking many pipes, all night long, by the bedside of the unearthly being that tossed and panted until it was apparently wearied out. Then we learned by the low, regular breathing that it slept.

The next morning the house was all astir. The boarders congregated on the landing outside my room, and Hammond and myself were lions. We had to answer a thousand questions as to the state of our extraordinary prisoner, for as yet not one person in the house except ourselves could be induced to set foot in the apartment.

The creature was awake. This was evidenced by the convulsive manner in which the bed-clothes were moved in its efforts to escape. There was something truly terrible in beholding, as it were, those second-hand indications of the terrible writhings and agonized struggles for liberty which themselves were invisible.

Hammond and myself had racked our brains during the long night to discover some means by which we might realize the shape and general appearance of the Enigma. As well as we could make out by passing our hands over the creature's form, its outlines and lineaments were human. There was a mouth; a round, smooth head without hair; a nose, which, however, was little elevated above the cheeks; and its hands and feet felt like those of a boy. At first we thought of placing the being on a smooth surface and tracing its outline with chalk, as shoemakers trace the outline of the foot. This plan was given up as being of no value. Such an outline would give not the slightest idea of its conformation.

A happy thought struck me. We could take a cast of it in plaster of Paris. This would give us the solid figure, and satisfy all our wishes. But how to do it? The movements of the creature would disturb the setting of the plastic covering, and distort the mould. Another thought. Why not give it chloroform? It had respiratory organs,—that was evident by its breathing. Once reduced to a state of insensibility, we could do with it what we would. Doctor X——was sent for; and after the worthy physician had recovered from the first shock of amazement, he proceeded to administer the chloroform. In three minutes afterward we were enabled to remove the fetters from the creature's body, and a modeller was busily engaged in covering the invisible form with the moist clay. In five minutes more we had a mould, and before evening a rough facsimile of the Mystery. It was shaped like a man,— distorted, uncouth, and horrible, but still a man. It was small, not over four feet and some inches in height, and its limbs revealed a muscular development that was unparalleled. Its face surpassed in hideousness anything I had ever seen. Gustave Doré, or Callot, or Tony Johannot, never conceived anything so horrible. There is a face in one of the latter's illustrations to *Un Voyage où il vous plaira* which somewhat approaches the countenance of this creature, but does not equal it. It was the physiognomy of what I should fancy a ghoul might be. It looked as if it was capable of feeding on human flesh.

Having satisfied our curiosity, and bound every one in the house to secrecy, it became a question what was to be done with our Enigma? It was impossible that we should keep such a horror in our house; it was equally impossible that such an awful being should be let loose upon the world. I confess that I would have gladly voted for the creature's destruction. But who would shoulder the responsibility? Who would undertake the execution of this horrible semblance of a human being? Day after day this question was deliberated gravely. The boarders all left the house. Mrs. Moffat was in despair, and threatened Hammond and myself with all sorts of legal penalties if we did not remove the Horror. Our answer was, "We will go if you like, but we decline taking this creature with us. Remove it yourself if you please. It appeared in your house. On you the responsibility rests." To this there was, of course, no answer. Mrs. Moffat could not obtain for love or money a person who would even approach the Mystery.

The most singular part of the affair was that we were entirely ignorant of what the creature habitually fed on. Everything in the way of nutriment that we could think of was placed before it, but was never touched. It was awful to stand by, day after day, and see the clothes toss, and hear the hard breathing, and know that it was starving.

Ten, twelve days, a fortnight passed, and it still lived. The pulsations of the heart, however, were daily growing fainter, and had now nearly ceased. It was evident that the creature was dying for want of sustenance. While this terrible life-struggle was going on, I felt miserable. I could not sleep. Horrible as the creature was, it was pitiful to think of the pangs it was suffering.

At last it died. Hammond and I found it cold and stiff one morning in the bed. The heart had ceased to beat, the lungs to inspire. We hastened to bury it in the garden. It was a strange funeral, the dropping of that viewless corpse into the damp hole. The cast of its form I gave to Doctor X——, who keeps it in his museum in Tenth Street.

As I am on the eve of a long journey from which I may not return, I have drawn up this narrative of an event the most singular that has ever come to my knowledge.

Shirley Jackson

THE BEAUTIFUL STRANGER

Shirley Jackson's "The Beautiful Stranger" is an enigmatic, fantastic tale, a middle-class paranoid fantasy of utopia denied, perhaps a parody of the women's gothic romance, a tale of dread and doubt. Stephen King, in *Danse Macabre*, credits Jackson with influencing the invention of "the new American gothic," which is characterized as "a symbolic mirror," and summarizes a perceptive article by the scholar, John G. Park, about the growing obsession with the self-evident in the new gothic form, especially in Jackson's work. For our purposes in this anthology, though, it is Jackson's balancing of the psychological versus the supernatural in horror that is most salient. It is the tension created by the mysterious atmosphere, by the doubt as to the accuracy of the character's perception that leaves the reader in anxiety and wonder in *The Haunting of Hill House* and "The Beautiful Stranger," that is at the heart of the horroripilation. Jackson's best work is as complex and many-leveled as "The Turn of the Screw."

What might be called the first intimation of strangeness occurred at the railroad station. She had come with her children, Smalljohn and her baby girl, to meet her husband when he returned from a business trip to Boston. Because she had been oddly afraid of being late, and perhaps even seeming uneager to encounter her husband after a week's separation, she dressed the children and put them into the car at

home a long half hour before the train was due. As a result,
of course, they had to wait interminably at the station, and
what was to have been a charmingly staged reunion, family
embracing husband and father, became at last an ill-timed
and awkward performance. Smalljohn's hair was mussed, and
he was sticky. The baby was cross, pulling at her pink bonnet
and her dainty lace-edged dress, whining. The final arrival
of the train caught them in mid-movements, as it were; Margaret was tying the ribbons on the baby's bonnet, Smalljohn
was half over the back of the car seat. They scrambled out
of the car, cringing from the sound of the train, hopelessly
out of sorts.

John Senior waved from the high steps of the train. Unlike
his wife and children, he looked utterly prepared for his return, as though he had taken some pains to secure a meeting
at least painless, and had, in fact, stood just so, waving cordially from the steps of the train, for perhaps as long as half
an hour, ensuring that he should not be caught half-ready,
his hand not lifted so far as to over-emphasize the extent of
his delight in seeing them again.

His wife had an odd sense of lost time. Standing now on
the platform with the baby in her arms and Smalljohn beside
her, she could not for a minute remember clearly whether he
was coming home, or whether they were yet standing here to
say good-bye to him. They had been quarreling when he left,
and she had spent the week of his absence determining to
forget that in his presence she had been frightened and hurt.
This will be a good time to get things straight, she had been
telling herself; while John is gone I can try to get hold of
myself again. Now, unsure at last whether this was an arrival
or a departure, she felt afraid again, straining to meet an
unendurable tension. This will not do, she thought, believing
that she was being honest with herself, and as he came down
the train steps and walked toward them she smiled, holding
the baby tightly against her so that the touch of its small
warmth might bring some genuine tenderness into her smile.

This will not do, she thought, and smiled more cordially
and told him ''hello'' as he came to her. Wondering, she
kissed him and then when he held his arm around her and

the baby for a minute the baby pulled back and struggled, screaming. Everyone moved in anger, and the baby kicked and screamed, "No, no, no."

"What a way to say hello to Daddy," Margaret said, and she shook the baby, half-amused, and yet grateful for the baby's sympathetic support. John turned to Smalljohn and lifted him, Smalljohn kicking and laughing helplessly. "Daddy, Daddy," Smalljohn shouted, and the baby screamed, "No, no."

Helplessly, because no one could talk with the baby screaming so, they turned and went to the car. When the baby was back in her pink basket in the car, and Smalljohn was settled with another lollipop beside her, there was an appalling quiet which would have to be filled as quickly as possible with meaningful words. John had taken the driver's seat in the car while Margaret was quieting the baby, and when Margaret got in beside him she felt a little chill of animosity at the sight of his hands on the wheel; I can't bear to relinquish even this much, she thought; for a week no one has driven the car except me. Because she could see so clearly that this was unreasonable—John owned half the car, after all—she said to him with bright interest, "And how was your trip? The weather?"

"Wonderful," he said, and again she was angered at the warmth in his tone; if she was unreasonable about the car, he was surely unreasonable to have enjoyed himself quite so much. "Everything went very well. I'm pretty sure I got the contract, everyone was very pleasant about it, and I go back in two weeks to settle everything."

The stinger is in the tail, she thought. He wouldn't tell it all so hastily if he didn't want me to miss half of it; I am supposed to be pleased that he got the contract and that everyone was so pleasant, and the part about going back is supposed to slip past me painlessly.

"Maybe I can go with you, then," she said. "Your mother will take the children."

"Fine," he said, but it was much too late; he hesitated noticeably before he spoke.

"I want to go too," said Smalljohn. "Can I go with Daddy?"

They came into their house, Margaret carrying the baby, and John carrying his suitcase and arguing delightedly with Smalljohn over which of them was carrying the heavier weight of it. The house was ready for them; Margaret had made sure that it was cleaned and emptied of the qualities which attached so surely to her position of wife alone with small children; the toys which Smalljohn had thrown around with unusual freedom were picked up, the baby's clothes (no one, after all, came to call when John was gone) were taken from the kitchen radiator where they had been drying. Aside from the fact that the house gave no impression of waiting for any particular people, but only for anyone well-bred and clean enough to fit within its small trim walls, it could have passed for a home, Margaret thought, even for a home where a happy family lived in domestic peace. She set the baby down in the playpen and turned with the baby's bonnet and jacket in her hand and saw her husband, head bent gravely as he listened to Smalljohn. Who? she wondered suddenly; is he taller? That is not my husband.

She laughed, and they turned to her, Smalljohn curious, and her husband with a quick bright recognition; she thought, why, it is *not* my husband, and he knows that I have seen it. There was no astonishment in her; she would have thought perhaps thirty seconds before that such a thing was impossible, but since it was now clearly possible, surprise would have been meaningless. Some other emotion was necessary, but she found at first only peripheral manifestations of one. Her heart was beating violently, her hands were shaking, and her fingers were cold. Her legs felt weak and she took hold of the back of a chair to steady herself. She found that she was still laughing, and then her emotion caught up with her and she knew what it was: it was relief.

"I'm glad you came," she said. She went over and put her head against his shoulder. "It was hard to say hello in the station," she said.

Smalljohn looked on for a minute and then wandered off to his toybox. Margaret was thinking, this is not the man who enjoyed seeing me cry; I need not be afraid. She caught her breath and was quiet; there was nothing that needed saying.

For the rest of the day she was happy. There was a constant delight in the relief from her weight of fear and unhappiness, it was pure joy to know that there was no longer any residue of suspicion and hatred; when she called him "John" she did so demurely, knowing that he participated in her secret amusement; when he answered her civilly there was, she thought, an edge of laughter behind his words. They seemed to have agreed soberly that mention of the subject would be in bad taste, might even, in fact, endanger their pleasure.

They were hilarious at dinner. John would not have made her a cocktail, but when she came downstairs from putting the children to bed the stranger met her at the foot of the stairs, smiling up at her, and took her arm to lead her into the living room where the cocktail shaker and glasses stood on the low table before the fire.

"How nice," she said, happy that she had taken a moment to brush her hair and put on fresh lipstick, happy that the coffee table which she had chosen with John and the fireplace which had seen many fires built by John and the low sofa where John had slept sometimes, had all seen fit to welcome the stranger with grace. She sat on the sofa and smiled at him when he handed her a glass; there was an odd illicit excitement in all of it; she was "entertaining" a man. The scene was a little marred by the fact that he had given her a martini with neither olive nor onion; it was the way she preferred her martini, and yet he should not have, strictly, known this, but she reassured herself with the thought that naturally he would have taken some pains to inform himself before coming.

He lifted his glass to her with a smile; he is here only because I am here, she thought.

"It's nice to be here," he said. He had, then, made one attempt to sound like John, in the car coming home. After he knew that she had recognized him for a stranger, he had never made any attempt to say words like "coming home" or "getting back," and of course she could not, not without pointing her lie. She put her hand in his and lay back against the sofa, looking into the fire.

"Being lonely is worse than anything in the world," she said.

"You're not lonely now?"

"Are you going away?"

"Not unless you come too." They laughed at his parody of John.

They sat next to each other at dinner; she and John had always sat at formal opposite ends of the table, asking one another politely to pass the salt and the butter.

"I'm going to put in a little set of shelves over there," he said, nodding toward the corner of the dining room. "It looks empty here, and it needs things. Symbols."

"Like?" She liked to look at him; his hair, she thought, was a little darker than John's, and his hands were stronger; this man would build whatever he decided he wanted built.

"We need things together. Things we like, both of us. Small delicate pretty things. Ivory."

With John she would have felt it necessary to remark at once that they could not afford such delicate pretty things, and put a cold finish to the idea, but with the stranger she said, "We'd have to look for them; not everything would be right."

"I saw a little creature once," he said. "Like a tiny little man, only colored all purple and blue and gold."

She remembered this conversation; it contained the truth like a jewel set in the evening. Much later, she was to tell herself that it was true; John could not have said these things.

She was happy, she was radiant, she had no conscience. He went obediently to his office the next morning, saying good-bye at the door with a rueful smile that seemed to mock the present necessity for doing the things that John always did, and as she watched him go down the walk she reflected that this was surely not going to be permanent; she could not endure having him gone for so long every day, although she had felt little about parting from John; moreover, if he kept doing John's things he might grow imperceptibly more like John. We will simply have to go away, she thought. She was pleased, seeing him get into the car; she would gladly share with him—indeed, give him outright—all that had been John's, so long as he stayed her stranger.

She laughed while she did her housework and dressed the baby. She took satisfaction in unpacking his suitcase, which he had abandoned and forgotten in a corner of the bedroom, as though prepared to take it up and leave again if she had not been as he thought her, had not wanted him to stay. She put away his clothes, so disarmingly like John's, and wondered for a minute at the closet; would there be a kind of delicacy in him about John's things? Then she told herself no, not so long as he began with John's wife, and laughed again.

The baby was cross all day, but when Smalljohn came home from nursery school his first question was—looking up eagerly—"Where is Daddy?"

"Daddy has gone to the office," and again she laughed, at the moment's quick sly picture of the insult to John.

Half a dozen times during the day she went upstairs, to look at his suitcase and touch the leather softly. She glanced constantly as she passed through the dining room into the corner where the small shelves would be someday, and told herself that they would find a tiny little man, all purple and blue and gold, to stand on the shelves and guard them from intrusion.

When the children awakened from their naps she took them for a walk and then, away from the house and returned violently to her former lonely pattern (walk with the children, talk meaninglessly of Daddy, long for someone to talk to in the evening ahead, restrain herself from hurrying home: he might have telephoned), she began to feel frightened again; suppose she had been wrong? It could not be possible that she was mistaken; it would be unutterably cruel for John to come tonight.

Then, she heard the car stop and when she opened the door and looked up she thought, no, it is not my husband, with a return of gladness. She was aware from his smile that he had perceived her doubts, and yet he was so clearly a stranger that, seeing him, she had no need of speaking.

She asked him, instead, almost meaningless questions during that evening, and his answers were important only because she was storing them away to reassure herself while he was away. She asked him what was the name of their Shakespeare professor in college, and who was that girl he liked so before he met Margaret. When he smiled and said that he had no idea, that he would not recognize the name if she told him, she was in delight. He had not bothered to master all of the past, then; he had learned enough (the names of the children, the location of the house, how she liked her cocktails) to get to her, and after that, it was not important, because either she would want him to stay, or she would, calling upon John, send him away again.

"What is your favorite food?" she asked him. "Are you fond of fishing? Did you ever have a dog?"

"Someone told me today," he said once, "that he had heard I was back from Boston, and I distinctly thought he said that he heard I was dead in Boston."

He was lonely, too, she thought with sadness, and that is why he came, bringing a destiny with him: now I will see him come every evening through the door and think, this is not my husband, and wait for him, remembering that I am waiting for a stranger.

"At any rate," she said, "*you* were not dead in Boston, and nothing else matters."

She saw him leave in the morning with a warm pride, and she did her housework and dressed the baby; when Smalljohn came home from nursery school he did not ask, but looked with quick searching eyes and then sighed. While the children were taking their naps she thought that she might take them to the park this afternoon, and then the thought of another such afternoon, another long afternoon with no one but the children, another afternoon of widowhood, was more than she could submit to; I have done this too much, she thought, I must see something today beyond the faces of my children. No one should be so much alone.

Moving quickly, she dressed and set the house to rights. She called a high-school girl and asked if she would take the children to the park; without guilt, she neglected the thousand small orders regarding the proper jacket for the baby, whether Smalljohn might have popcorn, when to bring them home. She fled, thinking, I must be with people.

She took a taxi into town, because it seemed to her the only possible thing to do was to seek out a gift for him, her first gift to him, and she thought she would find him, perhaps, a little creature all blue and purple and gold.

She wandered through the strange shops in the town, choosing small lovely things to stand on the new shelves, looking long and critically at ivories, at small statues, at brightly colored meaningless expensive toys, suitable for giving to a stranger.

It was almost dark when she started home, carrying her packages. She looked from the window of the taxi into the dark streets, and thought with pleasure that the stranger would be home before her, and look from the window to see her hurrying to him; he would think, this is a stranger, I am waiting for a stranger, as he saw her coming. "Here," she said, tapping on the glass, "right here, driver." She got out of the taxi and paid the driver, and smiled as he drove away. I must look well, she thought, the driver smiled back at me.

She turned and started for the house, and then hesitated; surely she had come too far? This is not possible, she thought, this cannot be; surely our house was white?

The evening was very dark, and she could see only the houses going in rows, with more rows beyond them and more rows beyond that, and somewhere a house which was hers, with the beautiful stranger inside, and she lost out here.

Ambrose Bierce

THE DAMNED THING

Ambrose Bierce is, after Poe, the greatest American horror writer of the nineteenth century. He is one of the conduits through which Poe influenced Robert W. Chambers. He is relatively underrated nevertheless, since a large portion of his horror fiction is not supernatural at all but psychological fiction and is of a brutally and grotesquely ironic cast, darkly humorous stories of the absurd and surreal. "The Damned Thing" is one of his most impressive works, another in the hybrid line of O'Brien and Chambers that leads all the way to A. E. Van Vogt's "Black Destroyer" and John W. Campbell's "Who Goes There" and defines the sub-genre of "invisible, nonsupernatural horrific menace," one of the primary forms of the monster story that is also, characteristically, concerned with reality and perception. As the ghost and, indeed, the supernatural entirely have become less central to horror fiction, their place is in part taken by the newly imagined realities of SF (the first single author collection in the SF genre in the 1930s was *The Horror on the Asteroid* by Edmund Hamilton). Lovecraft's "At the Mountains of Madness," a sequel to Poe's "Narrative of Arthur Gordon Pym," was published in *Astounding*, an SF magazine in the 1930s, and Hugo Gernsback, the man who invented the idea of SF as a genre, mentioned H. G. Wells, Jules Verne and Edgar Allan Poe as the models for writers to follow, in the April 1926 editorial of his first issue of *Amazing Stories*. But it was O'Brien and Bierce (and, indeed, Wells) who are the virtual models, who took the seed from Poe and grew the first fertile forms. The evolution sketched in here spreads into substantial branches of horror fiction in the latter half of the twentieth century, an underemphasized but significant part of the SF genre worth a book in itself.

I: One Does Not Always Eat What is on the Table

By the light of a tallow candle which had been placed on one end of a rough table a man was reading something written in a book. It was an old account book, greatly worn; and the writing was not, apparently, very legible, for the man sometimes held the page close to the flame of the candle to get a stronger light on it. The shadow of the book would then throw into obscurity a half of the room, darkening a number of faces and figures; for besides the reader, eight other men were present. Seven of them sat against the rough log walls, silent, motionless, and the room being small, not very far from the table. By extending an arm anyone of them could have touched the eighth man, who lay on the table, face upward, partly covered by a sheet, his arms at his sides. He was dead.

The man with the book was not reading aloud, and no one spoke; all seemed to be waiting for something to occur; the dead man only was without expectation. From the blank darkness outside came in, through the aperture that served for a window, all the ever unfamiliar noises of night in the wilderness—the long nameless note of a distant coyote; the stilly pulsing trill of tireless insects in trees; strange cries of night birds, so different from those of the birds of day; the drone of great blundering beetles, and all that mysterious chorus of small sounds that seem always to have been but half heard when they have suddenly ceased, as if conscious of an indiscretion. But nothing of all this was noted in that company; its members were not overmuch addicted to idle interest in matters of no practical importance; that was obvious in every line of their rugged faces—obvious even in the dim light of the single candle. They were evidently men of the vicinity—farmers and woodsmen.

The person reading was a trifle different; one would have said of him that he was of the world, worldly, albeit there was that in his attire which attested a certain fellowship with the organisms of his environment. His coat would hardly have passed muster in San Francisco; his foot-gear was not of urban origin, and the hat that lay by him on the floor (he was the only one uncovered) was such that if one had considered it as an article of mere personal adornment he would have missed its meaning. In countenance the man was rather prepossessing, with just a hint of sternness; though that he may have assumed or cultivated, as appropriate to one in authority. For he was a coroner. It was by virtue of his office that he had possession of the book in which he was reading; it had been found among the dead man's effects—in his cabin, where the inquest was now taking place.

When the coroner had finished reading he put the book into his breast pocket. At that moment the door was pushed open and a young man entered. He, clearly, was not of mountain birth and breeding: he was clad as those who dwell in cities. His clothing was dusty, however, as from travel. He had, in fact, been riding hard to attend the inquest.

The coroner nodded; no one else greeted him.

"We have waited for you," said the coroner. "It is necessary to have done with this business to-night."

The young man smiled. "I am sorry to have kept you," he said. "I went away, not to evade your summons, but to post to my newspaper an account of what I suppose I am called back to relate."

The coroner smiled.

"The account that you posted to your newspaper," he said, "differs, probably, from that which you will give here under oath."

"That," replied the other, rather hotly and with a visible flush, "is as you please. I used manifold paper and have a copy of what I sent. It was not written as news, for it is incredible, but as fiction. It may go as a part of my testimony under oath.''

''But you say it is incredible.''

''That is nothing to you, sir, if I also swear that it is true.''

The coroner was silent for a time, his eyes upon the floor. The men about the sides of the cabin talked in whispers, but seldom withdrew their gaze from the face of the corpse. Presently the coroner lifted his eyes and said: ''We will resume the inquest.''

The men removed their hats. The witness was sworn.

''What is your name?'' the coroner asked.

''William Harker.''

''Age?''

''Twenty-seven.''

''You knew the deceased, Hugh Morgan?''

''Yes.''

''You were with him when he died?''

''Near him.''

''How did that happen—your presence, I mean?''

''I was visiting him at this place to shoot and fish. A part of my purpose, however, was to study him and his odd, solitary way of life. He seemed a good model for a character in fiction. I sometimes write stories.''

''I sometimes read them.''

''Thank you.''

''Stories in general—not yours.''

Some of the jurors laughed. Against a sombre background humour shows high lights. Soldiers in intervals of battle laugh easily, and a jest in the death chamber conquers by surprise.

''Relate the circumstances of this man's death,'' said the coroner. ''You may use any notes or memoranda that you please.''

The witness understood. Pulling a manuscript from his breast pocket he held it near the candle and turning the leaves until he found the passage that he wanted to read.

2: What May Happen in a Field of Wild Oats

" . . . The sun had hardly risen when we left the house. We were looking for quail, each with a shotgun, but we had only one dog. Morgan said that our best ground was beyond a certain ridge that he pointed out, and we crossed it by a trail through the *chaparral*. On the other side was comparatively level ground, thickly covered with wild oats. As we emerged from the *chaparral* Morgan was but a few yards in advance. Suddenly we heard, at a little distance to our right and partly in front, a noise as of some animal thrashing about in the bushes, which we could see were violently agitated.

" 'We've started a deer,' I said. 'I wish we had brought a rifle.'

"Morgan, who had stopped and was intently watching the agitated *chaparral*, said nothing, but had cocked both barrels of his gun and was holding it in readiness to aim. I thought him a trifle excited, which surprised me, for he had a reputation for exceptional coolness, even in moments of sudden and imminent peril.

" 'Oh, come,' I said. 'You are not going to fill up a deer with quail-shot, are you?'

"Still he did not reply; but catching a sight of his face as he turned it slightly toward me, I was struck by the intensity of his look. Then I understood that we had serious business in hand, and my first conjecture was that we had 'jumped' a grizzly. I advanced to Morgan's side, cocking my piece as I moved.

"The bushes were now quiet and the sounds had ceased, but Morgan was as attentive to the place as before.

" 'What is it? What the devil is it?' I asked.

" 'That Damned Thing!' he replied, without turning his head. His voice was husky and unnatural. He trembled visibly.

"I was about to speak further, when I observed the wild oats near the place of the disturbance moving in the most inexplicable way. I can hardly describe it. It seemed as if stirred by a streak of wind, which not only bent it, but pressed it down—crushed it so that it did not rise; and this movement was slowly prolonging itself directly toward us.

"Nothing that I had ever seen had affected me so strangely as this unfamiliar and unaccountable phenomenon, yet I am unable to recall any sense of fear. I remember—and tell it here because, singularly enough, I recollected it then—that once in looking carelessly out of an open window I momentarily mistook a small tree close at hand for one of a group of larger trees at a little distance away. It looked the same size as the others, but being more distinctly and sharply defined in mass and detail seemed out of harmony with them. It was a mere falsification of the law of aerial perspective, but it startled, almost terrified me. We so rely upon the orderly operation of familiar natural laws that any seeming suspension of them is noted as a menace to our safety, a warning of unthinkable calamity. So now the apparently causeless movement of the herbage and the slow, undeviating approach of the line of disturbance were distinctly disquieting. My companion appeared actually frightened, and I could hardly credit my senses when I saw him suddenly throw his gun to his shoulder and fire both barrels at the agitated grain! Before the smoke of the discharge had cleared away I heard a loud savage cry—a scream like that of a wild animal—and flinging his gun upon the ground, Morgan sprang away and ran swiftly from the spot. At the same instant I was thrown violently to the ground by the impact of something unseen in the smoke— some soft, heavy substance that seemed thrown against me with great force.

"Before I could get upon my feet and recover my gun, which seemed to have been struck from my hands, I heard Morgan crying out as if in mortal agony, and mingling with his cries were such hoarse, savage sounds as one hears from fighting dogs. Inexpressibly terrified, I struggled to my feet and looked in the direction of Morgan's retreat; and may Heaven in mercy spare me from another sight like that! At a distance of less than thirty yards was my friend, down upon one knee, his head thrown back at a frightful angle, hatless, his long hair in disorder and his whole body in violent move-

ment from side to side, backward and forward. His right arm
was lifted and seemed to lack the hand—at least, I could see
none. The other arm was invisible. At times, as my memory
now reports this extraordinary scene, I could discern but a
part of his body; it was as if he had been partly blotted out—
I cannot otherwise express it—then a shifting of his position
would bring it all into view again.

"All this must have occurred within a few seconds, yet in
that time Morgan assumed all the postures of a determined
wrestler vanquished by superior weight and strength. I saw
nothing but him, and him not always distinctly. During the
entire incident his shouts and curses were heard, as if through
an enveloping uproar of such sounds of rage and fury as I
had never heard from the throat of man or brute!

"For a moment only I stood irresolute, then throwing down
my gun, I ran forward to my friend's assistance. I had a vague
belief that he was suffering from a fit, or some form of convulsion. Before I could reach his side he was down and quiet.
All sounds had ceased, but with a feeling of such terror as
even these awful events had not inspired I now saw again the
mysterious movement of the wild oats, prolonging itself from
the trampled area about the prostrate man toward the edge of
a wood. It was only when it had reached the wood that I was
able to withdraw my eyes and look at my companion. He was
dead."

3: A Man Though Naked May Be in Rags

The coroner rose from his seat and stood beside the dead
man. Lifting an edge of the sheet, he pulled it away, exposing
the entire body, altogether naked and showing in the candlelight a clay-like yellow. It had, however, broad maculations
of bluish black, obviously caused by extravasated blood from
contusions. The chest and sides looked as if they had been
beaten with a bludgeon. There were dreadful lacerations; the
skin was torn in strips and shreds.

The coroner moved round to the end of the table and undid
a silk handkerchief which had been passed under the chin

and knotted on the top of the head. When the handkerchief was drawn away it exposed what had been the throat. Some of the jurors who had risen to get a better view repented their curiosity and turned away their faces. Witness Harker went to the open window and leaned out across the sill, faint and sick. Dropping the handkerchief upon the dead man's neck, the coroner stepped to an angle of the room and from a pile of clothing produced one garment after another, each of which he held up a moment for inspection. All were torn, and stiff with blood. The jurors did not make a closer inspection. They seemed rather uninterested. They had, in truth, seen all this before; the only thing that was new to them being Harker's testimony.

"Gentlemen," the coroner said, "we have no more evidence, I think. Your duty has been already explained to you; if there is nothing you wish to ask you may go outside and consider your verdict."

The foreman rose—a tall, bearded man of sixty, coarsely clad.

"I should like to ask one question, Mr. Coroner," he said. "What asylum did this yer last witness escape from?"

"Mr. Harker," said the coroner gravely and tranquilly, "from what asylum did you last escape?"

Harker flushed crimson again, but said nothing, and the seven jurors rose and solemnly filed out of the cabin.

"If you have done insulting me, sir," said Harker, as soon as he and the officer were left alone with the dead man, "I suppose I am at liberty to go?"

"Yes."

Harker started to leave, but paused, with his hand on the door latch. The habit of his profession was strong in him—stronger than his sense of personal dignity. He turned about and said:

"The book that you have there—I recognize it as Morgan's diary. You seemed greatly interested in it; you read in it while I was testifying. May I see it? The public would like—"

"The book will cut no figure in this matter," replied the official, slipping it into his coat pocket; "all the entries in it were made before the writer's death."

As Harker passed out of the house the jury reentered and stood about the table, on which the now covered corpse showed under the sheet with sharp definition. The foreman seated himself near the candle, produced from his breast pocket a pencil and scrap of paper and wrote rather laboriously the following verdict, which with various degrees of effort all signed:

"We, the jury, do find that the remains come to their death at the hands of a mountain lion, but some of us thinks, all the same, they had fits."

4:   An Explanation from the Tomb

In the diary of the late Hugh Morgan are certain interesting entries having, possibly, a scientific value as suggestions. At the inquest upon his body the book was not put in evidence; possibly the coroner thought it not worth while to confuse the jury. The date of the first of the entries mentioned cannot be ascertained; the upper part of the leaf is torn away; the part of the entry remaining follows:

". . . would run in a half-circle, keeping his head turned always toward the centre, and again he would stand still, barking furiously. At last he ran away into the brush as fast as he could go. I thought at first that he had gone mad, but on returning to the house found no other alteration in his manner than what was obviously due to fear of punishment.

"Can a dog see with his nose? Do odours impress some cerebral centre with images of the thing that emitted them? . . .

"*Sept. 2.*—Looking at the stars last night as they rose above the crest of the ridge east of the house, I observed them successively disappear—from left to right. Each was eclipsed but an instant, and only a few at the same time, but along the entire length of the ridge all that were within a degree or two of the crest were blotted out. It was as if something had passed along between me and them; but I could not see it, and the stars were not thick enough to define its outline. Ugh! don't like this." . . .

Several weeks' entries are missing, three leaves being torn from the book.

"*Sept. 27.*—It has been about here again—I find evidences of its presence every day. I watched again all last night in the same cover, gun in hand, double-charged with buckshot. In the morning the fresh footprints were there, as before. Yet I would have sworn that I did not sleep—indeed, I hardly sleep at all. It is terrible, insupportable! If these amazing experiences are real I shall go mad; if they are fanciful I am mad already.

"*Oct. 3.*—I shall not go—it shall not drive me away. No, this is *my* house, *my* land. God hates a coward. . . .

"*Oct. 5.*—I can stand it no longer; I have invited Harker to pass a few weeks with me—he has a level head. I can judge from his manner if he thinks me mad.

"*Oct. 7.*—I have the solution of the mystery; it came to me last night—suddenly, as by revelation. How simple—how terribly simple!

"There are sounds that we cannot hear. At either end of the scale are notes that stir no chord of that imperfect instrument, the human ear. They are too high or too grave. I have observed a flock of blackbirds occupying an entire tree-top—the tops of several trees—and all in full song. Suddenly—in a moment—at absolutely the same instant—all spring into the air and fly away. How? They could not all see one another—whole tree-tops intervened. At no point could a leader have been visible to all. There must have been a signal of warning or command, high and shrill above the din, but by me unheard. I have observed, too, the same simultaneous flight when all were silent, among not only blackbirds, but other birds—quail, for example, widely separated by bushes—even on opposite sides of a hill.

"It is known to seamen that a school of whales basking or sporting on the surface of the ocean, miles apart, with the convexity of the earth between, will sometimes dive at the same instant—all gone out of sight in a moment. The signal has been sounded—too grave for the ear of the sailor at the masthead and his comrades on the deck—who nevertheless feel its vibrations in the ship as the stones of a cathedral are stirred by the bass of the organ.

"As with sounds, so with colours. At each end of the solar spectrum the chemist can detect the presence of what are known as 'actinic' rays. They represent colours—integral colours in the composition of light—which we are unable to discern. The human eye is an imperfect instrument; its range is but a few octaves of the real 'chromatic scale.' I am not mad; there are colours that we cannot see.

"And, God help me! the Damned Thing is of such a colour!"

Edith Wharton

AFTERWARD

Edith Wharton, one of the great American writers in the tradition of realism, a close friend of Henry James, is also one of the finest of all American writers of supernatural fiction. James and Walter de la Mare are her models. Had John W. Campbell chosen, he could have used her as one of the models for the kind of tales he wanted to find for *Unknown*, ghost stories with a finely depicted everyday contemporary setting, except that her stories are basically for and of the upper and upper middle classes and Campbell produced for the "pulp" audience. Her influence on succeeding writers is difficult to trace, but her stories (collected in *Ghosts*) are masterful and endure. "Afterward" is indeed in the manner of de la Mare. Wharton gives us a character portrayal of meticulous clarity and substantial psychological depth, but the events are unsettling and ambiguous enough to impel the story over the border into our third category. It is essentially a story about perception and the nature of reality.

I

"Oh, there *is* one, of course, but you'll never know it."
   The assertion, laughingly flung out six months earlier in a bright June garden, came back to Mary Boyne with a new perception of its significance as she stood, in the De-

cember dusk, waiting for the lamps to be brought into the library.

The words had been spoken by their friend Alida Stair, as they sat at tea on her lawn at Pangbourne, in reference to the very house of which the library in question was the central, the pivotal, "feature." Mary Boyne and her husband, in quest of a country place in one of the southern or southwestern counties, had, on their arrival in England, carried their problem straight to Alida Stair, who had successfully solved it in her own case; but it was not until they had rejected, almost capriciously, several practical and judicious suggestions that she threw out: "Well, there's Lyng, in Dorsetshire. It belongs to Hugo's cousins, and you can get it for a song."

The reason she gave for its being obtainable on these terms—its remoteness from a station, its lack of electric light, hot-water pipes, and other vulgar necessities—were exactly those pleading in its favour with two romantic Americans perversely in search of the economic drawbacks which were associated, in their tradition, with unusual architectural felicities.

"I should never believe I was living in an old house unless I was thoroughly uncomfortable," Ned Boyne, the more extravagant of the two, had jocosely insisted; "the least hint of 'convenience' would make me think it had been bought out of an exhibition, with the pieces numbered, and set up again." And they had proceeded to enumerate, with humorous precision, their various doubts and demands, refusing to believe that the house their cousin recommended was *really* Tudor till they learned it had no heating system, or that the village church was literally in the grounds till she assured them of the deplorable uncertainty of the water-supply.

"It's too uncomfortable to be true!" Edward Boyne had continued to exult as the avowal of each disadvantage was successively wrung from her; but he had cut short his rhapsody to ask, with a relapse to distrust: "And the ghost? You've been concealing from us the fact that there is no ghost!"

Mary, at the moment, had laughed with him, yet almost with her laugh, being possessed of several sets of independent perceptions, had been struck by a note of flatness in Alida's answering hilarity.

"Oh, Dorsetshire's full of ghosts, you know."

"Yes, yes; but that won't do. I don't want to have to drive ten miles to see somebody else's ghost. I want one of my own on the premises. *Is* there a ghost at Lyng?"

His rejoinder had made Alida laugh again, and it was then that she had flung back tantalizingly: "Oh, there *is* one, of course, but you'll never know it."

"Never know it?" Boyne pulled her up. "But what in the world constitutes a ghost except the fact of its being known for one?"

"I can't say. But that's the story."

"That there's a ghost, but that nobody knows it's a ghost?"

"Well—not till afterward, at any rate."

"Till afterward?"

"Not till long, long afterward."

"But if it's once been identified as an unearthly visitant, why hasn't its *signalement* been handed down in the family? How has it managed to preserve its incognito?"

Alida could only shake her head. "Don't ask me. But it has."

"And then suddenly—" Mary spoke up as if from cavernous depths of divination—"suddenly, long afterward, one says to one's self: *'That was it?'*"

She was startled at the sepulchral sound with which her question fell on the banter of the other two, and she saw the shadow of the same surprise flit across Alida's pupils. "I suppose so. One just has to wait."

"Oh, hang waiting!" Ned broke in. "Life's too short for a ghost who can only be enjoyed in retrospect. Can't we do better than that, Mary?"

But it turned out that in the event they were not destined to, for within three months of their conversation with Mrs. Stair they were settled at Lyng, and the life they had yearned for, to the point of planning it in advance in all its daily details, had actually begun for them.

It was to sit, in the thick December dusk, by just such a wide-hooded fireplace, under just such black oak rafters, with the sense that beyond the mullioned panes the downs were darkened to a deeper solitude: it was for the ultimate indulgence of such sensations that Mary Boyne, abruptly exiled from New York by her husband's business, had endured for nearly fourteen years the soul-deadening ugliness of a Middle Western town, and that Boyne had ground on doggedly at his engineering till, with a suddenness that still made her blink, the prodigious windfall of the Blue Star Mine had put them at a stroke in possession of life and the leisure to taste it. They had never for a moment meant their new state to be one of idleness; but they meant to give themselves only to harmonious activities. She had her vision of painting and gardening (against a background of gray walls), he dreamed of the production of his long-planned book on the "Economic Basis of Culture"; and with such absorbing work ahead no existence could be too sequestered: they could not get far enough from the world, or plunge deep enough into the past.

Dorsetshire had attracted them from the first by an air of remoteness out of all proportion to its geographical position. But to the Boynes it was one of the ever-recurring wonders of the whole incredibly compressed island—a nest of counties, as they put it—that for the production of its effect so little of a given quality went so far: that so few miles made a distance, and so short a distance a difference.

"It's that," Ned had once enthusiastically explained, "that gives such depth to their effects, such relief to their contrasts. They've been able to lay the butter so thick on every delicious mouthful."

The butter had certainly been laid on thick at Lyng: the old house hidden under a shoulder of the downs had almost all the finer marks of commerce with a protracted past. The mere fact that it was neither large nor exceptional made it, to the Boynes, abound the more completely in its special charm—the charm of having been for centuries a deep dim reservoir of life. The life had probably not been of the most vivid order: for long periods, no doubt, it had fallen as noiselessly into the past as the quiet drizzle of autumn fell, hour after hour, into the fish-pond between the yews; but these back-waters of existence sometimes breed, in their sluggish depths, strange acuities of emotion, and Mary Boyne had felt from the first the mysterious stir of intenser memories.

The feeling had never been stronger than on this particular afternoon when, waiting in the library for the lamps to come, she rose from her seat and stood among the shadows of the hearth. Her husband had gone off, after luncheon, for one of his long tramps on the downs. She had noticed of late that he preferred to go alone; and, in the tried security of their personal relations, had been driven to conclude that his book was bothering him, and that he needed the afternoons to turn over in solitude the problems left from the morning's work. Certainly the book was not going as smoothly as she had thought it would, and there were lines of perplexity between his eyes such as had never been there in his engineering days. He had often, then, looked fagged to the verge of illness, but the native demon of "worry" had never branded his brow. Yet the few pages he had so far read to her—the introduction, and a summary of the opening chapter—showed a firm hold on this subject, and an increasing confidence in his powers.

The fact threw her into deeper perplexity, since, now that he had done with "business" and its disturbing contingencies, the one other possible source of anxiety was eliminated. Unless it were his health, then? But physically he had gained since they had come to Dorsetshire, grown robuster, ruddier and fresher-eyed. It was only within the last week that she had felt in him the undefinable change which made her restless in his absence, and as tongue-tied in his presence as though it were *she* who had a secret to keep from him!

The thought that there *was* a secret somewhere between them struck her with a sudden rap of wonder, and she looked about her down the long room.

"Can it be the house?" she mused.

The room itself might have been full of secrets. They seemed to be piling themselves up, as evening fell, like the layers and layers of velvet shadow dropping from the low ceiling, the rows of books, the smoke-blurred sculpture of the hearth.

"Why, of course—the house is haunted!" she reflected.

The ghost—Alida's imperceptible ghost—after figuring

largely in the banter of their first month or two at Lyng, had been gradually left aside as too ineffectual for imaginative use. Mary had, indeed, as became the tenant of a haunted house, made the customary inquiries among her rural neighbours, but, beyond a vague "They dü say so, ma'am," the villagers had nothing to impart. The elusive spectre had apparently never had sufficient identity for a legend to crystallize about it, and after a time the Boynes had set the matter down to their profit-and-loss account, agreeing that Lyng was one of the few houses good enough in itself to dispense with supernatural enhancements.

"And I suppose, poor ineffectual demon, that's why it beats its beautiful wings in vain in the void," Mary had laughingly concluded.

"Or, rather," Ned answered in the same strain, "why, amid so much that's ghostly, it can never affirm its separate existence as *the* ghost." And thereupon their invisible housemate had finally dropped out of their references, which were numerous enough to make them soon unaware of the loss.

Now, as she stood on the hearth, the subject of their earlier curiosity revived in her with a new sense of its meaning—a sense gradually acquired through daily contact with the scene of the lurking mystery. It was the house itself, of course, that possessed the ghost-seeing faculty, that communed visually but secretly with its own past; if one could only get into close enough communion with the house, one might surprise its secret, and acquire the ghost-sight on one's own account. Perhaps, in his long hours in this very room, where she never trespassed till the afternoon, her husband *had* acquired it already, and was silently carrying about the weight of whatever it had revealed to him. Mary was too well versed in the code of the spectral world not to know that one could not talk about the ghosts one saw: to do so was almost as great a breach of taste as to name a lady in a club. But this explanation did not really satisfy her. "What, after all, except for the fun of the shudder," she reflected, "would he really care for any of their old ghosts?" And thence she was thrown back once more on the fundamental dilemma: the fact that one's greater or less susceptibility to spectral influences had no particular bearing on the case, since, when one *did* see a ghost at Lyng, one did not know it.

"Not till long afterward," Alida Stair had said. Well, supposing Ned *had* seen one when they first came, and had known only within the last week what had happened to him? More and more under the spell of the hour, she threw back her thoughts to the early days of their tenancy, but at first only to recall a lively confusion of unpacking, settling, arranging of books, and calling to each other from remote corners of the house as, treasure after treasure, it revealed itself to them. It was in this particular connection that she presently recalled a certain soft afternoon of the previous October, when, passing from the first rapturous flurry of exploration to a detailed inspection of the old house, she had pressed (like a novel heroine) a panel that opened on a flight of corkscrew stairs leading to a flat ledge of the roof—the roof which, from below, seemed to slope away on all sides too abruptly for any but practised feet to scale.

The view from this hidden coign was enchanting, and she had flown down to snatch Ned from his papers and give him the freedom of her discovery. She remembered still how, standing at her side, he had passed his arm about her while their gaze flew to the long tossed horizon-line of the downs, and then dropped contentedly back to trace the arabesque of yew hedges about the fish-pond, and the shadow of the cedar on the lawn.

"And now the other way," he had said, turning her about within his arm; and closely pressed to him, she had absorbed, like some long satisfying draught, the picture of the gray-walled court, the squat lions on the gates, and the lime-avenue reaching up to the highroad under the downs.

It was just then, while they gazed and held each other, that she had felt his arm relax, and heard a sharp "Hullo!" that made her turn to glance at him.

Distinctly, yes, she now recalled that she had seen, as she glanced, a shadow of anxiety, of perplexity, rather, fall across his face; and, following his eyes, had beheld the figure of a man—a man in loose grayish clothes, as it appeared to her—who was sauntering down the lime-avenue to the court with the doubtful gait of a stranger who seeks his way. Her short-sighted eyes had given her but a blurred impression of slightness and grayishness, with something foreign, or at least unlocal, in the cut of the figure or its dress; but her husband had apparently seen more—seen enough to make him push past her with a hasty "Wait!" and dash down the stairs without pausing to give her a hand.

A slight tendency to dizziness obliged her, after a provisional clutch at the chimney against which they had been leaning, to follow him first more cautiously; and when she had reached the landing she paused again, for a less definite reason, leaning over the banister to strain her eyes through the silence of the brown sun-flecked depths. She lingered there till, somewhere in those depths, she heard the closing of a door; then, mechanically impelled, she went down the shallow flights of steps till she reached the lower hall.

The front door stood open on the sunlight of the court, and hall and court were empty. The library door was open, too, and after listening in vain for any sound of voices within, she crossed the threshold, and found her husband alone, vaguely fingering the papers on his desk.

He looked up, as if surprised at her entrance, but the shadow of anxiety had passed from his face, leaving it even, as she fancied, a little brighter and clearer than usual.

"What was it? Who was it?" she asked.

"Who?" he repeated, with the surprise still all on his side.

"The man we saw coming toward the house."

He seemed to reflect. "The man? Why, I thought I saw Peters; I dashed after him to say a word about the stable drains, but he had disappeared before I could get down."

"Disappeared? But he seemed to be walking so slowly when we saw him."

Boyne shrugged his shoulders. "So I thought; but he must have got up steam in the interval. What do you say to our trying a scramble up Meldon Steep before sunset?"

That was all. At the time the occurrence had been less than nothing, had, indeed, been immediately obliterated by the magic of their first vision from Meldon Steep, a height which they had dreamed of climbing ever since they had first seen its bare spine rising above the roof of Lyng. Doubtless it was the mere fact of the other incident's having occurred on the very day of their ascent to Meldon that had kept it stored away in the fold of memory from which it now emerged; for in itself it had no mark of the portentous. At the moment there could have been nothing more natural than that Ned should dash himself from the roof in the pursuit of dilatory tradesmen. It was the period when they were always on the watch for one or the other of the specialists employed about the place; always lying in wait for them, and rushing out at them with questions, reproaches or reminders. And certainly in the distance the gray figure had looked like Peters.

Yet now, as she reviewed the scene, she felt her husband's explanation of it to have been invalidated by the look of anxiety on his face. Why had the familiar appearance of Peters made him anxious? Why, above all, if it was of such prime necessity to confer with him on the subject of the stable drains, had the failure to find him produced such a look of relief? Mary could not say that any one of these questions had occurred to her at the time, yet from the promptness with which they now marshalled themselves at her summons, she had a sense that they must all along have been there, waiting their hour.

II

Weary with her thoughts, she moved to the window. The library was now quite dark, and she was surprised to see how much faint light the outer world still held.

As she peered out into it across the court, a figure shaped itself far down the perspective of bare limes: it looked a mere blot of deeper gray in the grayness, and for an instant, as it moved toward her, her heart thumped to the thought, "It's the ghost!"

She had time, in that long instant, to feel suddenly that the man of whom, two months earlier, she had had a distant vision from the roof, was now, at his predestined hour, about to reveal himself as *not* having been Peters; and her spirit sank under the impending fear of the disclosure. But almost with the next tick of the clock the figure, gaining substance and character, showed itself even to her weak sight as her husband's; and she turned to meet him, as he entered, with the confession of her folly.

"It's really too absurd," she laughed out, "but I never *can* remember!"

"Remember what?" Boyne questioned as they drew together.

"That when one sees the Lyng ghost one never knows it."

Her hand was on his sleeve, and he kept it there, but with no response in his gesture or in the lines of his preoccupied face.

"Did you think you'd seen it?" he asked, after an appreciable interval.

"Why, I actually took *you* for it, my dear, in my mad determination to spot it!"

"Me—just now?" His arm dropped away, and he turned from her with a faint echo of her laugh. "Really, dearest, you'd better give it up, if that's the best you can do."

"Oh, yes, I give it up. Have *you*?" she asked, turning round on him abruptly.

The parlour-maid had entered with letters and a lamp, and the light struck up into Boyne's face as he bent above the tray she presented.

"Have *you*?" Mary perversely insisted, when the servant had disappeared on her errand of illumination.

"Have I what?" he rejoined absently, the light bringing out the sharp stamp of worry between his brows as he turned over the letters.

"Given up trying to see the ghost." Her heart beat a little at the experiment she was making.

Her husband, laying his letters aside, moved away into the shadow of the hearth.

"I never tried," he said, tearing open the wrapper of a newspaper.

"Well, of course," Mary persisted, "the exasperating thing is that there's no use trying, since one can't be sure till so long afterward."

He was unfolding the paper as if he had hardly heard her; but after a pause, during which the sheets rustled spasmodically between his hands, he looked up to ask, "Have you any idea *how long*?"

Mary had sunk into a low chair beside the fireplace. From her seat she glanced over, startled, at her husband's profile, which was projected against the circle of lamplight.

"No; none. Have *you*?" she retorted, repeating her former phrase with an added stress of intention.

Boyne crumpled the paper into a bunch, and then, inconsequently, turned back with it toward the lamp.

"Lord, no! I only meant," he explained, with a faint tinge of impatience, "is there any legend, any tradition, as to that?"

"Not that I know of," she answered; but the impulse to add "What makes you ask?" was checked by the reappearance of the parlour-maid, with tea and a second lamp.

With the dispersal of shadows, and the repetition of the daily domestic office, Mary Boyne felt herself less oppressed by that sense of something mutely imminent which had darkened her afternoon. For a few moments she gave herself to the details of her task, and when she looked up from it she was struck to the point of bewilderment by the change in her husband's face. He had seated himself near the farther lamp, and was absorbed in the perusal of his letters; but was it something he had found in them, or merely the shifting of her own point of view, that had restored his features to their normal aspect? The longer she looked the more definitely the change affirmed itself. The lines of tension had vanished, and such traces of fatigue as lingered were of the kind easily attributable to steady mental effort. He glanced up, as if drawn by her gaze, and met her eyes with a smile.

"I'm dying for my tea, you know; and here's a letter for you," he said.

She took the letter he held out in exchange for the cup she proffered him, and, returning to her seat, broke the seal with the languid gesture of the reader whose interests are all enclosed in the circle of one cherished presence.

Her next conscious motion was that of starting to her feet,

the letter falling to them as she rose, while she held out to her husband a newspaper clipping.

"Ned! What's this? What does it mean?"

He had risen at the same instant, almost as if hearing her cry before she uttered it; and for a perceptible space of time he and she studied each other, like adversaries watching for an advantage, across the space between her chair and his desk.

"What's what? You fairly made me jump!" Boyne said at length, moving toward her with a sudden half-exasperated laugh. The shadow of apprehension was on his face again, not now a look of fixed foreboding, but a shifting vigilance of lips and eyes that gave her the sense of his feeling himself invisibly surrounded.

Her hand shook so that she could hardly give him the clipping.

"This article—from the *Waukesha Sentinel*—that a man named Elwell has brought suit against you—that there was something wrong about the Blue Star Mine. I can't understand more than half."

They continued to face each other as she spoke, and to her astonishment she saw that her words had the almost immediate effect of dissipating the strained watchfulness of his look.

"Oh, *that*!" He glanced down the printed slip, and then folded it with the gesture of one who handles something harmless and familiar. "What's the matter with you this afternoon, Mary? I thought you'd got bad news."

She stood before him with her undefinable terror subsiding slowly under the reassurance of his tone.

"You knew about this, then—it's all right?"

"Certainly I knew about it; and it's all right."

"But what *is* it? I don't understand. What does this man accuse you of?"

"Pretty nearly every crime in the calendar." Boyne had tossed the clipping down, and thrown himself into an arm-chair near the fire. "Do you want to hear the story? It's not particularly interesting—just a squabble over interests in the Blue Star."

"But who is this Elwell? I don't know the name."

"Oh, he's a fellow I put into it—gave him a hand up. I told you all about him at the time."

"I daresay. I must have forgotten." Vainly she strained back among her memories. "But if you helped him, why does he make this return?"

"Probably some shyster lawyer got hold of him and talked him over. It's all rather technical and complicated. I thought that kind of thing bored you."

His wife felt a sting of compunction. Theoretically, she deprecated the American wife's detachment from her husband's professional interests, but in practice she had always found it difficult to fix her attention on Boyne's report of the transactions in which his varied interests involved him. Besides, she had felt during their years of exile, that, in a community where the amenities of living could be obtained only at the cost of efforts as arduous as her husband's professional labours, such brief leisure as he and she could command should be used as an escape from immediate preoccupations, a flight to the life they always dreamed of living. Once or twice, now that this new life had actually drawn its magic circle about them, she had asked herself if she had done right; but hitherto such conjectures had been no more than the retrospective excursions of an active fancy. Now, for the first time, it startled her a little to find how little she knew of the material foundation on which her happiness was built.

She glanced at her husband, and was again reassured by the composure of his face; yet she felt the need of more definite grounds for her reassurance.

"But doesn't this suit worry you? Why have you never spoken to me about it?"

He answered both questions at once. "I didn't speak of it at first because it *did* worry me—annoyed me, rather. But it's all ancient history now. Your correspondent must have got hold of a back number of the *Sentinel*."

She felt a quick thrill of relief. "You mean it's over? He's lost his case?"

"There was just a perceptible delay in Boyne's reply. "The suit's been withdrawn—that's all."

But she persisted, as if to exonerate herself from the inward charge of being too easily put off. "Withdrawn it because he saw he had no chance?"

"Oh, he had no chance," Boyne answered.

She was still struggling with a dimly felt perplexity at the back of her thoughts.

"How long ago was it withdrawn?"

He paused, as if with a slight return of his former uncertainty. "I've just had the news now; but I've been expecting it."

"Just now—in one of your letters?"

"Yes; in one of my letters."

She made no answer, and was aware only, after a short interval of waiting, that he had risen, and, strolling across the room, had placed himself on the sofa at her side. She felt him, as he did so, pass an arm about her, she felt his hand seek hers and clasp it, and turning slowly, drawn by the warmth of his cheek, she met his smiling eyes.

"It's all right—it's all right?" she questioned, through the flood of her dissolving doubts; and "I give you my word it was never righter!" he laughed back at her, holding her close.

III

One of the strangest things she was afterward to recall out of all the next day's strangeness was the sudden and complete recovery of her sense of security.

It was in the air when she woke in her low-ceiled, dusky room; it went with her downstairs to the breakfast-table, flashed out at her from the fire, and reduplicated itself from the flanks of the urn and the sturdy flutings of the Georgian teapot. It was as if, in some roundabout way, all her diffused fears of the previous day, with their moment of sharp concentration about the newspaper article—as if this dim questioning of the future, and startled return upon the past, had between them liquidated the arrears of some haunting moral obligation. If she had indeed been careless of her husband's affairs, it was, her new state seemed to prove, because her faith in him instinctively justified such carelessness; and his right to her faith had now affirmed itself in the very face of menace and suspicion. She had never seen him more untroubled, more naturally and unconsciously himself, than after the cross-examination to which she had subjected him: it was almost as if he had been aware of her doubts and had wanted the air cleared as much as she did.

It was as clear, thank Heaven! as the bright outer light that surprised her almost with a touch of summer when she issued from the house for her daily round of the gardens. She had left Boyne at his desk, indulging herself, as she passed the library door, by a last peep at his quiet face, where he bent, pipe in mouth, above his papers; and now she had her own morning's task to perform. The task involved, on such charmed winter days, almost as much happy loitering about the different quarters of her demesne as if spring were already at work there. There were such endless possibilities still before her, such opportunities to bring out the latent graces of the old place, without a single irreverent touch of alteration, that the winter was all too short to plan what spring and autumn executed. And her recovered sense of safety gave, on this particular morning, a peculiar zest to her progress through the sweet still place. She went first to the kitchen-garden, where the espaliered pear trees drew complicated patterns on the walls, and pigeons were fluttering and preening about the silvery-slated roof of their cot. There was something wrong about the piping of the hot-house, and she was expecting an authority from Dorchester, who was to drive out between trains and make a diagnosis of the boiler. But when she dipped into the damp heat of the greenhouses, among the spiced scents and waxy pinks and reds of old-fashioned exotics—even the flora of Lyng was in the note!—she learned that the great man had not arrived, and, the day being too rare to waste in an artificial atmosphere, she came out again and paced along the springy turf of the bowling-green to the gardens behind the house. At their farther end rose a grass terrace, looking across the fish-pond and yew hedges to the long house-front with its twisted chimney-stacks and blue roof angles all drenched in the pale gold moisture of the air.

Seen thus, across the level tracery of the gardens, it sent her, from open windows and hospitably smoking chimneys, the look of some warm human presence, of a mind slowly ripened on a sunny wall of experience. She had never before had such a sense of her intimacy with it, such a conviction that its secrets were all beneficent, kept, as they said to children, "for one's good," such a trust in its power to gather up her life and Ned's into the harmonious pattern of the long long story it sat there weaving in the sun.

She heard steps behind her, and turned, expecting to see the gardener accompanied by the engineer from Dorchester. But only one figure was in sight, that of a youngish slightly built man, who, for reasons she could not on the spot have given, did not remotely resemble her notion of an authority on hot-house boilers. The new-comer, on seeing her, lifted his hat, and paused with the air of a gentleman—perhaps a traveller—who wishes to make it known that his intrusion is involuntary. Lyng occasionally attracted the more cultivated traveller, and Mary half expected to see the stranger dissemble a camera, or justify his presence by producing it. But he made no gesture of any sort, and after a moment she asked, in a tone responding to the courteous hesitation of his attitude: "Is there any one you wish to see?"

"I came to see Mr. Boyne," he answered. His intonation, rather than his accent, was faintly American, and Mary, at the note, looked at him more closely. The brim of his soft felt hat cast a shade on his face, which, thus obscured, wore to her short-sighted gaze a look of seriousness, as of a person arriving "on business," and civilly but firmly aware of his rights.

Past experience had made her equally sensible to such claims; but she was jealous of her husband's morning hours, and doubtful of his having given any one the right to intrude on them.

"Have you an appointment with my husband?" she asked.

The visitor hesitated, as if unprepared for the question.

"I think he expects me," he replied.

It was Mary's turn to hesitate. "You see, this is his time for work: he never sees any one in the morning."

He looked at her a moment without answering; then, as if accepting her decision, he began to move away. As he turned, Mary saw him pause and glance up at the peaceful house-front. Something in his air suggested weariness and disappointment, the dejection of the traveller who has come from far off and whose hours are limited by the time-table. It occurred to her that if this were the case her refusal might have made his errand vain, and a sense of compunction caused her to hasten after him.

"May I ask if you have come a long way?"

He gave her the same grave look. "Yes—I have come a long way."

"Then, if you'll go to the house, no doubt my husband will see you now. You'll find him in the library."

She did not know why she had added the last phrase, except from a vague impulse to atone for her previous inhospitality. The visitor seemed about to express his thanks, but her attention was distracted by the approach of the gardener with a companion who bore all the marks of being the expert from Dorchester.

"This way," she said, waving the stranger to the house; and an instant later she had forgotten him in the absorption of her meeting with the boiler-maker.

The encounter led to such far-reaching results that the engineer ended by finding it expedient to ignore his train, and Mary was beguiled into spending the remainder of the morning in absorbed confabulation among the flower-pots. When the colloquy ended, she was surprised to find that it was nearly luncheon time, and she half expected, as she hurried back to the house, to see her husband coming out to meet her. But she found no one in the court but an under-gardener raking the gravel, and the hall, when she entered it, was so silent that she guessed Boyne to be still at work.

Not wishing to disturb him, she turned into the drawing-room, and there, at her writing table, lost herself in renewed calculations of the outlay to which the morning's conference had pledged her. The fact that she could permit herself such follies had not yet lost its novelty; and somehow, in contrast to the vague fears of the previous days, it now seemed an element of her recovered security, of the sense that, as Ned had said, things in general had never been "righter."

She was still luxuriating in a lavish play of figures when the parlour-maid, from the threshold, roused her with an enquiry as to the expediency of serving luncheon. It was one of their jokes that Trimmle announced luncheon as if she were divulging a state secret, and Mary, intent upon her papers, merely murmured an absent-minded assent.

She felt Trimmle wavering doubtfully on the threshold, as if in rebuke of such unconsidered assent; then her retreating steps sounded down the passage, and Mary, pushing away her papers, crossed the hall and went to the library door. It was still closed, and she wavered in her turn, disliking to disturb her husband, yet anxious that he should not exceed his usual measure of work. As she stood there, balancing her impulses, Trimmle returned with the announcement of luncheon, and Mary, thus impelled, opened the library door.

Boyne was not at his desk, and she peered about her, expecting to discover him before the book-shelves, somewhere down the length of the room; but her call brought no response, and gradually it became clear to her that he was not there.

She turned back to the parlour-maid.

"Mr. Boyne must be upstairs. Please tell him that luncheon is ready."

Trimmle appeared to hesitate between the obvious duty of obedience and an equally obvious conviction of the foolishness of injunction laid on her. The struggle resulted in her saying: "If you please, madam, Mr. Boyne's not upstairs."

"Not in his room? Are you sure?"

"I'm sure, madam."

Mary consulted the clock. "Where is he, then?"

"He's gone out," Trimmle announced, with the superior air of one who has respectfully waited for the question that a well-ordered mind would have put first.

Mary's conjecture had been right, then. Boyne must have gone to the gardens to meet her, and since she had missed him, it was clear that he had taken the shorter way by the south door, instead of going round to the court. She crossed the hall to the French window opening directly on the yew garden, but the parlourmaid, after another moment of inner conflict, decided to bring out: "Please, madam, Mr. Boyne didn't go that way."

Mary turned back. "Where *did* he go? And when?"

"He went out of the front door, up the drive, madam." It was a matter of principle with Trimmle never to answer more than one question at a time.

"Up the drive? At this hour?" Mary went to the door herself, and glanced across the court through the tunnel of bare limes. But its perspective was as empty as when she had scanned it on entering.

"Did Mr. Boyne leave no message?"

Trimmle seemed to surrender herself to a last struggle with the forces of chaos.

"No, madam. He just went out with the gentleman."

"The gentleman? What gentleman?" Mary wheeled about, as if to front this new factor.

"The gentleman who called, madam," said Trimmle resignedly.

"When did a gentleman call? Do explain yourself, Trimmle!"

Only the fact that Mary was very hungry, and that she wanted to consult her husband about the greenhouses, would have caused her to lay so unusual an injunction on her attendant; and even now she was detached enough to note in Trimmle's eye the dawning defiance of the respectful subordinate who has been pressed too hard.

"I couldn't exactly say the hour, madam, because I didn't let the gentleman in," she replied, with an air of discreetly ignoring the irregularity of her mistress's course.

"You didn't let him in?"

"No, madam. When the bell rang I was dressing, and Agnes—"

"Go and ask Agnes, then," said Mary.

Trimmle still wore her look of patient magnanimity. "Agnes would not know, madam, for she had unfortunately burnt her hand in trimming the wick of the new lamp from town"—Trimmle, as Mary was aware, had always been opposed to the new lamp—"and so Mrs. Dockett sent the kitchen-maid instead."

Mary looked again at the clock. "It's after two! Go and ask the kitchen-maid if Mr. Boyne left any word."

She went in to luncheon without waiting, and Trimmle presently brought her there the kitchenmaid's statement that the gentleman had called about eleven o'clock, and that Mr. Boyne had gone out with him without leaving any message. The kitchen-maid did not even know the caller's name, for he had written it on a slip of paper, which he had folded and handed to her, with the injunction to deliver it at once to Mr. Boyne.

Mary finished her luncheon, still wondering, and when it was over, and Trimmle had brought the coffee to the drawing-room, her wonder had deepened to a first faint tinge of disquietude. It was unlike Boyne to absent himself without explanation at so unwonted an hour, and the difficulty of identifying the visitor whose summons he had apparently obeyed made his disappearance the more unaccountable. Mary Boyne's experience as the wife of a busy engineer, subject to sudden calls and compelled to keep irregular hours, had trained her to the philosophic acceptance of surprises; but since Boyne's withdrawal from business he had adopted a Benedictine regularity of life. As if to make up for the dispersed and agitated years, with their "stand-up" lunches, and dinners rattled down to the joltings of the dining-cars, he cultivated the last refinements of punctuality and monotony, discouraging his wife's fancy for the unexpected, and declaring that to a delicate taste there were infinite gradations of pleasure in the recurrences of habit.

Still, since no life can completely defend itself from the unforeseen, it was evident that all Boyne's precautions would sooner or later prove unavailable, and Mary concluded that he had cut short a tiresome visit by walking with his caller to the station, or at least accompanying him for part of the way.

This conclusion relieved her from further preoccupation, and she went out herself to take up her conference with the gardener. Thence she walked to the village post office, a mile or so away; and when she turned toward home the early twilight was setting in.

She had taken a foot-path across the downs, and as Boyne, meanwhile, had probably returned from the station by the highroad, there was little likelihood of their meeting. She felt sure, however, of his having reached the house before her; so sure that, when she entered it herself, without even pausing to enquire of Trimmle, she made directly for the library. But the library was still empty, and with an unwonted exactness of visual memory she observed that the papers on her husband's desk lay precisely as they had lain when she had gone in to call him to luncheon.

Then of a sudden she was seized by a vague dread of the unknown. She had closed the door behind her on entering, and as she stood alone in the long silent room, her dread seemed to take shape and sound, to be there breathing and lurking among the shadows. Her short-sighted eyes strained through them, half-discerning an actual presence, something aloof, that watched and knew; and in the recoil from that intangible presence she threw herself on the bell-rope and gave it a sharp pull.

The sharp summons brought Trimmle in precipitately with a lamp, and Mary breathed again at this sobering reappearance of the usual.

"You may bring tea if Mr. Boyne is in," she said, to justify her ring.

"Very well, madam. But Mr. Boyne is not in," said Trimmle, putting down the lamp.

"Not in? You mean he's come back and gone out again?"

"No, madam. He's never been back."

The dread stirred again, and Mary knew that now it had her fast.

"Not since he went out with—the gentleman?"

"Not since he went out with the gentleman."

"But who *was* the gentleman?" Mary insisted, with the shrill note of some one trying to be heard through a confusion of noises.

"That I couldn't say, madam." Trimmle, standing there by the lamp, seemed suddenly to grow less round and rosy, as though eclipsed by the same creeping shade of apprehension.

"But the kitchen-maid knows—wasn't it the kitchen-maid who let him in?"

"She doesn't know either, madam, for he wrote his name on a folded paper."

Mary, through her agitation, was aware that they were both designating the unknown visitor by a vague pronoun, instead of the conventional formula which, till then, had kept their allusions within the bounds of conformity. And at the same moment her mind caught at the suggestion of the folded paper.

"But he must have a name! Where's the paper?"

She moved to the desk, and began to turn over the documents that littered it. The first that caught her eye was an unfinished letter in her husband's hand, with his pen lying across it, as though dropped there at a sudden summons.

"My dear Parvis"—who was Parvis?—"I have just received your letter announcing Elwell's death, and while I suppose there is now no further risk of trouble, it might be safer—"

She tossed the sheet aside, and continued her search; but no folded paper was discoverable among the letters and pages of manuscript which had been swept together in a heap, as if by a hurried or a startled gesture.

"But the kitchen-maid *saw* him. Send her here," she commanded, wondering at her dullness in not thinking sooner of so simple a solution.

Trimmle vanished in a flash, as if thankful to be out of the room, and when she reappeared, conducting the agitated underling, Mary had regained her self-possession, and had her questions ready.

The gentleman was a stranger, yes—that she understood. But what had he said? And, above all, what had he looked like? The first question was easily enough answered, for the disconcerting reason that he had said so little—had merely asked for Mr. Boyne, and, scribbling something on a bit of paper, had requested that it should at once be carried in to him.

"Then you don't know what he wrote? You're not sure it *was* his name?"

The kitchen-maid was not sure, but supposed it was, since he had written it in answer to her enquiry as to whom she should announce.

"And when you carried the paper in to Mr. Boyne, what did he say?"

The kitchen-maid did not think that Mr. Boyne had said anything, but she could not be sure, for just as she had handed him the paper and he was opening it, she had become aware that the visitor had followed her into the library, and she had slipped out, leaving the two gentlemen together.

"But then, if you left them in the library, how do you know that they went out of the house?"

This question plunged the witness into a momentary inarticulateness, from which she was rescued by Trimmle, who, by means of ingenious circumlocutions, elicited the statement that before she could cross the hall to the back passage she had heard the two gentlemen behind her, and had seen them go out of the front door together.

"Then, if you saw the strange gentleman twice, you must be able to tell me what he looked like."

But with this final challenge to her powers of expression it became clear that the limit of the kitchen-maid's endurance had been reached. The obligation of going to the front door to "show in" a visitor was in itself so subversive of the fundamental order of things that it had thrown her faculties into hopeless disarray, and she could only stammer out, after various panting efforts: "His hat, mum, was different-like, as you might say—"

"Different? How different?" Mary flashed out, her own mind, in the same instant, leaping back to an image left on it that morning, and then lost under layers of subsequent impressions.

"His hat had a wide brim, you mean? and his face was pale—a youngish face?" Mary pressed her, with a white-lipped intensity of interrogation. But if the kitchen-maid found any adequate answer to this challenge, it was swept away for her listener down the rushing current of her own convictions. The stranger—the stranger in the garden! Why had Mary not thought of him before? She needed no one now to tell her that it was he who had called for her husband and gone away with him. But who was he, and why had Boyne obeyed him?

IV

It leaped out at her suddenly, like a grin out of the dark, that they had often called England so little—"such a confoundedly hard place to get lost in."

A confoundedly hard place to get lost in! That had been her husband's phrase. And now, with the whole machinery of official investigation sweeping its flashlights from shore to shore, and across the dividing straits; now, with Boyne's name blazing from the walls of every town and village, his portrait (how that wrung her!) hawked up and down the country like the image of a hunted criminal; now the little compact populous island, so policed, surveyed and administered, revealed itself as a Sphinx-like guardian of abysmal mysteries, staring back into his wife's anguished eyes as if with the wicked joy of knowing something they would never know!

In the fortnight since Boyne's disappearance there had been no word of him, no trace of his movements. Even the usual misleading reports that raise expectancy in tortured bosoms had been few and fleeting. No one but the kitchen-maid had seen Boyne leave the house, and no one else had seen "the gentleman" who accompanied him. All enquiries in the neighbourhood failed to elicit the memory of a stranger's presence that day in the neighbourhood of Lyng. And no one had met Edward Boyne, either alone or in company, in any of the neighbouring villages, or on the road across the downs, or at either of the local railway-stations. The sunny English noon had swallowed him as completely as if he had gone out into Cimmerian night.

Mary, while every official means of investigation was working at its highest pressure, had ransacked her husband's papers for any trace of antecedent complications, of entanglements or obligations unknown to her, that might throw a ray into the darkness. But if any such had existed in the background of Boyne's life, they had vanished like the slip of paper on which the visitor had written his name. There remained no possible thread of guidance except—if it were indeed an exception—the letter which Boyne had apparently been in the act of writing when he received his mysterious summons. That letter, read and reread by his wife, and submitted by her to the police, yielded little enough to feed conjecture.

"I have just heard of Elwell's death, and while I suppose there is now no further risk of trouble, it might be safer—" That was all. The "risk of trouble" was easily explained by the newspaper clipping which had apprised Mary of the suit brought against her husband by one of his associates in the Blue Star enterprise. The only new information conveyed by the letter was the fact of its showing Boyne, when he wrote it, to be still apprehensive of the results of the suit, though he had told his wife that it had been withdrawn, and though the letter itself proved that the plaintiff was dead. It took several days of cabling to fix the identity of the "Parvis" to whom the fragment was addressed, but even after these enquiries had shown him to be a Waukesha lawyer, no new facts concerning the Elwell suit were elicited. He appeared to have had no direct concern in it, but to have been conversant with the facts merely as an acquaintance, and possible intermediary; and he declared himself unable to guess with what object Boyne intended to seek his assistance.

This negative information, sole fruit of the first fortnight's search, was not increased by a jot during the slow weeks that followed. Mary knew that the investigations were still being carried on, but she had a vague sense of their gradually slackening, as the actual march of time seemed to slacken. It was as though the days, flying horror-struck from the shrouded image of the one inscrutable day, gained assurance as the distance lengthened, till at last they fell back into their normal gait. And so with the human imaginations at work on the dark event. No doubt it occupied them still, but week by week and hour by hour it grew less absorbing, took up less space, was slowly but inevitably crowded out of the foreground of consciousness by the new problems perpetually bubbling up from the cloudy cauldron of human experience.

Even Mary Boyne's consciousness gradually felt the same lowering of velocity. It still swayed with the incessant oscillations of conjecture; but they were slower, more rhythmical in their beat. There were even moments of weariness when, like the victim of some poison which leaves the brain clear, but holds the body motionless, she saw herself domesticated with the Horror, accepting its perpetual presence as one of the fixed conditions of life.

These moments lengthened into hours and days, till she passed into a phase of stolid acquiescence. She watched the routine of daily life with the incurious eye of a savage on whom the meaningless processes of civilization make but the faintest impression. She had come to regard herself as part of the routine, a spoke of the wheel, revolving with its motion; she felt almost like the furniture of the room in which she sat, an insensate object to be dusted and pushed about with the chairs and tables. And this deepening apathy held her fast at Lyng, in spite of the entreaties of friends and the usual medical recommendation of "change." Her friends supposed that her refusal to move was inspired by the belief that her husband would one day return to the spot from which he had vanished, and a beautiful legend grew up about this imaginary state of waiting. But in reality she had no such belief: the depths of anguish enclosing her were no longer lighted by flashes of hope. She was sure that Boyne would never come back, that he had gone out of her sight as completely as if Death itself had waited that day on the threshold. She had even renounced, one by one, the various theories as to his disappearance which had been advanced by the press, the police, and her own agonised imagination. In sheer lassitude her mind turned from these alternatives of horror, and sank back into the blank fact that he was gone.

No, she would never know what had become of him—no one would ever know. But the house *knew*; the library in which she spent her long lonely evenings knew. For it was here that the last scene had been enacted, here that the stranger had come, and spoken the word which had caused Boyne to rise and follow him. The floor she trod had felt his tread; the books on the shelves had seen his face; and there were moments when the intense consciousness of the old dusky walls seemed about to break out into some audible revelation of their secret. But the revelation never came, and she knew it would never come. Lyng was not one of the garrulous old houses that betray the secrets entrusted to them. Its very legend proved that it had always been the mute accomplice, the incorruptible custodian, of the mysteries it had surprised. And Mary Boyne, sitting face to face with its silence, felt the futility of seeking to break it by any human means.

V

"I don't say it *wasn't* straight, and yet I don't say it *was* straight. It was business."

Mary, at the words, lifted her head with a start, and looked intently at the speaker.

When, half an hour before, a card with "Mr. Parvis" on it had been brought up to her, she had been immediately aware that the name had been a part of her consciousness ever since she had read it at the head of Boyne's unfinished letter. In the library she had found awaiting her a small sallow man with a bald head and gold eyeglasses, and it sent a tremor through her to know that this was the person to whom her husband's last known thought had been directed.

Parvis, civilly, but without vain preamble—in the manner of a man who has his watch in his hand—had set forth the object of his visit. He had "run over" to England on business, and finding himself in the neighbourhood of Dorchester, had not wished to leave it without paying his respects to Mrs. Boyne; and without asking her, if the occasion offered, what she meant to do about Bob Elwell's family.

The words touched the spring of some obscure dread in Mary's bosom. Did her visitor, after all, know what Boyne had meant by his unfinished phrase? She asked for an elucidation of his question, and noticed at once that he seemed surprised at her continued ignorance of the subject. Was it possible that she really knew as little as she said?

"I know nothing—you must tell me," she faltered out; and her visitor thereupon proceeded to unfold his story. It threw, even to her confused perceptions, and imperfectly initiated vision, a lurid glare on the whole hazy episode of the Blue Star Mine. Her husband had made his money in that brilliant speculation at the cost of "getting ahead" of someone less alert to seize the chance; and the victim of his ingenuity was young Robert Elwell, who had "put him on" to the Blue Star scheme.

Parvis, at Mary's first cry, had thrown her a sobering glance through his impartial glasses.

"Bob Elwell wasn't smart enough, that's all; if he had been, he might have turned round and served Boyne the same way. It's the kind of thing that happens every day in business. I guess it's what the scientists call the survival of the fittest—see?" said Mr. Parvis, evidently pleased with the aptness of his analogy.

Mary felt a physical shrinking from the next question she tried to frame: it was as though the words on her lips had a taste that nauseated her.

"But then—you accuse my husband of doing something dishonourable?"

Mr. Parvis surveyed the question dispassionately. "Oh, no, I don't. I don't even say it wasn't straight." He glanced up and down the long lines of books, as if one of them might have supplied him with the definition he sought. "I don't say it *wasn't* straight, and yet I don't say it *was* straight. It was business." After all, no definition in his category could be more comprehensive than that.

Mary sat staring at him with a look of terror. He seemed to her like the indifferent emissary of some evil power.

"But Mr. Elwell's lawyers apparently did not take your view, since I suppose the suit was withdrawn by their advice."

"Oh, yes; they knew he hadn't a leg to stand on, technically. It was when they advised him to withdraw the suit that he got desperate. You see, he'd borrowed most of the money he lost in the Blue Star, and he was up a tree. That's why he shot himself when they told him he had no show.''

The horror was sweeping over Mary in great deafening waves.

"He shot himself? He killed himself because of *that*?"

"Well, he didn't kill himself, exactly. He dragged on two months before he died." Parvis emitted the statement as unemotionally as a gramophone grinding out its "record."

"You mean that he tried to kill himself, and failed? And tried again?"

"Oh, he didn't have to *try* again," said Parvis grimly.

They sat opposite each other in silence, he swinging his eyeglasses thoughtfully about his finger, she, motionless, her arms stretched along her knees in an attitude of rigid tension.

"But if you knew all this," she began at length, hardly able to force her voice above a whisper, "how is it that when I wrote you at the time of my husband's disappearance you said you didn't understand this letter?"

Parvis received this without perceptible embarrassment: "Why, I didn't understand it—strictly speaking. And it wasn't the time to talk about it, if I had. The Elwell business was settled when the suit was withdrawn. Nothing I could have told you would have helped you to find your husband."

Mary continued to scrutinize him. "Then why are you telling me now?"

Still Parvis did not hesitate. "Well, to begin with, I supposed you knew more than you appear to—I mean about the circumstances of Elwell's death. And then people are talking of it now; the whole matter's been raked up again. And I thought if you didn't know you ought to."

She remained silent, and he continued: "You see, it's only come out lately what a bad state Elwell's affairs were in. His wife's a proud woman, and she fought on as long as she could, going out to work, and taking sewing at home when she got too sick—something with the heart, I believe. But she had his mother to look after, and the children, and she broke down under it, and finally had to ask for help. That called attention to the case, and the papers took it up, and a subscription was started. Everybody out there liked Bob Elwell, and most of the prominent names in the place are down on the list, and people began to wonder why—''

Parvis broke off to fumble in an inner pocket. "Here," he continued, "here's an account of the whole thing from the *Sentinel*—a little sensational, of course. But I guess you'd better took it over.''

He held out a newspaper to Mary, who unfolded it slowly, remembering, as she did so, the evening when, in that same room, the perusal of a clipping from the *Sentinel* had first shaken the depths of her security.

As she opened the paper, her eyes, shrinking from the glaring head-lines, "Widow of Boyne's Victim Forced to Appeal for Aid,'' ran down the column of text to two portraits inserted in it. The first was her husband's, taken from a photograph made the year they had come to England. It was the picture of him that she liked best, the one that stood on the writing table upstairs in her bedroom. As the eyes in the photograph met hers, she felt it would be impossible to read what was said of him, and closed her lids with the sharpness of the pain.

"I thought if you felt disposed to put your name down—'' she heard Parvis continue.

She opened her eyes with an effort, and they fell on the other portrait. It was that of a youngish man, slightly built, with features somewhat blurred by the shadow of a projecting hat-brim. Where had she seen that outline before? She stared at it confusedly, her heart hammering in her ears. Then she gave a cry.

"This is the man—the man who came for my husband!''

She heard Parvis start to his feet, and was dimly aware that she had slipped backward into the corner of the sofa, and that he was bending above her in alarm. She straightened herself, and reached out for the paper which she had dropped.

"It's the man! I should know him anywhere!'' she persisted in a voice that sounded to her own ears like a scream.

Parvis's answer seemed to come to her from far off, down endless fog-muffled windings.

"Mrs. Boyne, you're not very well. Shall I call somebody? Shall I get a glass of water?"

"No, no, no!" She threw herself toward him, her hand frantically clutching the newspaper. "I tell you, it's the man! I *know* him! He spoke to me in the garden!"

Parvis took the journal from her, directing his glasses to the portrait. "It can't be, Mrs. Boyne. It's Robert Elwell."

"Robert Elwell?" Her white stare seemed to travel into space. "Then it was Robert Elwell who came for him."

"Came for Boyne? The day he went away from here?" Parvis's voice dropped as hers rose. He bent over, laying a fraternal hand on her, as if to coax her gently back into her seat. "Why, Elwell was dead! Don't you remember?"

Mary sat with her eyes fixed on the picture, unconscious of what he was saying.

"Don't you remember Boyne's unfinished letter to me—the one you found on his desk that day? It was written just after he'd heard of Elwell's death." She noticed an odd shake in Parvis's unemotional voice. "Surely you remember!" he urged her.

Yes, she remembered: that was the profoundest horror of it. Elwell had died the day before her husband's disappearance; and this was Elwell's portrait; and it was the portrait of the man who had spoken to her in the garden. She lifted her head and looked slowly about the library. The library could have borne witness that it was also the portrait of the man who had come in that day to call Boyne from his unfinished letter. Through the misty surgings of her brain she heard the faint boom of half-forgotten words—words spoken by Alida Stair on the lawn at Pangbourne before Boyne and his wife had ever seen the house at Lyng, or had imagined that they might one day live there.

"This was the man who spoke to me," she repeated.

She looked again at Parvis. He was trying to conceal his disturbance under what he probably imagined to be an expression of indulgent commiseration; but the edges of his lips were blue. "He thinks me mad; but I'm not mad," she reflected; and suddenly there flashed upon her a way of justifying her strange affirmation.

She sat quiet, controlling the quiver of her lips, and waiting till she could trust her voice; then she said, looking straight at Parvis: "Will you answer me one question, please? When was it that Robert Elwell tried to kill himself?"

"When—when?" Parvis stammered.

"Yes; the date. Please try to remember."

She saw that he was growing still more afraid of her. "I have a reason," she insisted.

"Yes, yes. Only I can't remember. About two months before, I should say."

"I want the date," she repeated.

Parvis picked up the newspaper. "We might see here," he said, still humouring her. He ran his eyes down the page. "Here it is. Last October—the—"

She caught the words from him. "The 20th, wasn't it?" With a sharp look at her, he verified. "Yes, the 20th. Then you *did* know?"

"I know now." Her gaze continued to travel past him. "Sunday, the 20th—that was the day he came first."

Parvis's voice was almost inaudible. "Came *here* first?"

"Yes."

"You saw him twice, then?"

"Yes, twice." She just breathed it at him. "He came first on the 20th of October. I remember the date because it was the day we went up Meldon Steep for the first time." She felt a faint gasp of inward laughter at the thought that but for that she might have forgotten.

Parvis continued to scrutinize her, as if trying to intercept her gaze.

"We saw him from the roof," she went on. "He came down the lime-avenue toward the house. He was dressed just as he is in that picture. My husband saw him first. He was frightened, and ran down ahead of me; but there was no one there. He had vanished."

"Elwell had vanished?" Parvis faltered.

"Yes." Their two whispers seemed to grope for each other. "I couldn't think what had happened. I see now. He *tried* to come then; but he wasn't dead enough—he couldn't reach us.

He had to wait for two months to die; and then he came back again—and Ned went with him.''

She nodded at Parvis with the look of triumph of a child who has worked out a difficult puzzle. But suddenly she lifted her hands with a desperate gesture, pressing them to her temples.

"Oh, my God! I sent him to Ned—I told him where to go! I sent him to this room!'' she screamed.

She felt the walls of books rush toward her, like inward falling ruins; and she heard Parvis, a long way off, through the ruins, crying to her, and struggling to get at her. But she was numb to his touch, she did not know what he was saying. Through the tumult she heard but one clear note, the voice of Alida Stair, speaking on the lawn at Pangbourne.

"You won't know till afterward,'' it said. "You won't know till long, long afterward.''

Algernon Blackwood

THE WILLOWS

Algernon Blackwood was one of the most prolific writers in all horror literature, and has been considered by some enthusiasts and experts as the greatest. H. P. Lovecraft (who did not impress Blackwood) called him "the one absolute and unquestioned master of weird atmosphere." His contributions to horror are many, but principally that he wrote many of his best works set outdoors, while horror had before him usually been set indoors. His nature or outdoor horror atmosphere is nowhere stronger than in "The Willows," which has been called the finest supernatural horror story in English. It stands in the center of the nature-of-reality stream in horror, midway between Bierce's "The Damned Thing" and Stephen King's "The Mist," closer to science fiction than the classic ghost story. In it, Blackwood captures part of the absolute essence of all horror literature: "And altogether the fear that hovered about me was such an unknown and immense kind of fear, so unlike anything I had ever felt before, that it woke a sense of awe and wonder in me that did much to counteract its worst effects." Horror, at its best, moves beyond fear to awe and wonder.

I

After leaving Vienna, an long before you come to Buda-Pesth, the Danube enters a region of singular loneliness and desolation, where its waters spread away on all sides regardless of a main channel, and the country becomes a swamp for miles upon miles, covered by a vast sea of low willow-bushes. On the big maps this deserted area is painted in a fluffy blue, growing fainter in color as it leaves the banks, and across it may be seen in large straggling letters the word *Sümpfe*, meaning marshes.

In high flood this great acreage of sand, shingle-beds, and willow-grown islands is almost topped by the water, but in normal seasons the bushes bend and rustle in the free winds, showing their silver leaves to the sunshine in an ever-moving plain of bewildering beauty. These willows never attain to the dignity of trees; they have no rigid trunks; they remain humble bushes, with rounded tops and soft outline, swaying on slender stems that answer to the least pressure of the wind; supple as grasses, and so continually shifting that they somehow give the impression that the entire plain is moving and *alive*. For the wind sends waves rising and falling over the whole surface, waves of leaves instead of waves of water, green swells like the sea, too, until the branches turn and lift, and then silvery white as their under-side turns to the sun.

Happy to slip beyond the control of stern banks, the Danube here wanders about at will among the intricate network of channels intersecting the islands everywhere with broad avenues down which the waters pour with a shouting sound; making whirlpools, eddies, and foaming rapids; tearing at the sandy banks; carrying away masses of shore and willow-clumps; and forming new islands innumerable which shift daily in size and shape and possess at best an impermanent life, since the flood-time obliterates their very existence.

Properly speaking, this fascinating part of the river's life begins soon after leaving Pressburg, and we, in our Canadian canoe, with gipsy tent and frying-pan on board, reached it on the crest of a rising flood about mid-July. That very same morning, when the sky was reddening before sunrise, we had slipped swiftly through still-sleeping Vienna, leaving it a couple of hours later a mere patch of smoke against the blue hills of the Wienerwald on the horizon; we had breakfasted below Fischeramend under a grove of birch trees roaring in the wind; and had then swept on the tearing current past Orth, Hainburg, Petronell (the old Roman Carnuntum of Marcus Aurelius), and so under the frowning heights of Theben on a spur of the Carpathians, where the March steals in quietly from the left and the frontier is crossed between Austria and Hungary.

Racing along at twelve kilometers an hour soon took us well into Hungary, and the muddy waters—sure sign of flood—sent us aground on many a shingle-bed, and twisted us like a cork in many a sudden belching whirlpool before the towers of Pressburg (Hungarian, Poszony) showed against the sky; and then the canoe, leaping like a spirited horse, flew at top speed under the gray walls, negotiated safely the sunken chain of the Fliegende Brücke ferry, turned the corner sharply to the left, and plunged on yellow foam into the wilderness of islands, sand-banks, and swamp-land beyond—the land of the willows.

The change came suddenly, as when a series of bioscope pictures snaps down on the streets of a town and shifts without warning into the scenery of lake and forest. We entered the land of desolation on wings, and in less than half an hour there was neither boat nor fishing-hut nor red roof, nor any single sign of human habitation and civilization within sight. The sense of remoteness from the world of human kind, the utter isolation, the fascination of this singular world of willows, winds, and waters, instantly laid its spell upon us both, so that we allowed laughingly to one another that we ought by rights to have held some special kind of passport to admit us, and that we had, somewhat audaciously, come without asking leave into a separate little kingdom of wonder and magic—a kingdom that was reserved for the use of others who had a right to it, with everywhere unwritten warnings to trespassers for those who had the imagination to discover them.

Though still early in the afternoon, the ceaseless buffetings of a most tempestuous wind made us feel weary, and we at once began casting about for a suitable camping-ground for the night. But the bewildering character of the islands made landing difficult; the swirling flood carried us in-shore and then swept us out again; the willow branches tore our hands as we seized them to stop the canoe, and we pulled many a yard of sandy bank into the water before at length we shot with a great sideways blow from the wind into a backwater and managed to beach the bows in a cloud of spray. Then we lay panting and laughing after our exertions on hot yellow sand, sheltered from the wind, and in the full blaze of a scorching sun, a cloudless blue sky above, and an immense army of dancing, shouting willow bushes, closing in from all sides, shining with spray and clapping their thousand little hands as though to applaud the success of our efforts.

"What a river!" I said to my companion, thinking of all the way we had traveled from the source in the Black Forest, and how we had often been obliged to wade and push in the upper shallows at the beginning of June.

"Won't stand much nonsense now, will it?" he said, pulling the canoe a little farther into safety up the sand, and then composing himself for a nap.

I lay by his side, happy and peaceful in the bath of the elements—water, wind, sand, and the great fire of the sun— thinking of the long journey that lay behind us, and of the great stretch before us to the Black Sea, and how lucky I was to have such a delightful and charming traveling companion as my friend, the Swede.

We had made many similar journeys together, but the Danube, more than any other river I knew, impressed us from the very beginning with its *aliveness*. From its tiny bubbling entry into the world among the pinewood gardens of Donaueschingen, until this moment when it began to play the great river-game of losing itself among the deserted swamps, unobserved, unrestrained, it had seemed to us like following the growth of some living creature. Sleepy at first, but later developing violent desires as it became conscious of its deep soul, it rolled, like some huge fluid being, through all the countries we had passed, holding our little craft on its mighty shoulders, playing roughly with us sometimes, yet always friendly and well-meaning, till at length we had come inevitably to regard it as a Great Personage.

How, indeed, could it be otherwise, since it told us so

much of its secret life? At night we heard it singing to the moon as we lay in our tent, uttering that odd sibilant note peculiar to itself and said to be caused by the rapid tearing of the pebbles along its bed, so great is its hurrying speed. We knew, too, the voice of its gurgling whirlpools, suddenly bubbling up on a surface previously quite calm; the roar of its shallows and swift rapids; its constant steady thundering below all mere surface sounds; and that ceaseless tearing of its icy waters at the banks. How it stood up and shouted when the rains fell flat upon its face! And how its laughter roared out when the wind blew upstream and tried to stop its growing speed! We knew all its sounds and voices, its tumblings and foamings, its unnecessary splashing against the bridges; that self-conscious chatter when there were hills to look on; the affected dignity of its speech when it passed through the little towns, far too important to laugh; and all these faint, sweet whisperings when the sun caught it fairly in some slow curve and poured down upon it till the steam rose.

It was full of tricks, too, in its early life before the great world knew it. There were places in the upper reaches among the Swabian forests, when yet the first whispers of its destiny had not reached it, where it elected to disappear through holes in the ground, to appear again on the other side of the porous limestone hills and start a new river with another name; leaving, too, so little water in its own bed that we had to climb out and wade and push the canoe through miles of shallows!

And a chief pleasure, in those early days of its irresponsible youth, was to lie low, like Brer Fox, just before the little turbulent tributaries came to join it from the Alps, and to refuse to acknowledge them when in, but to run for miles side by side, the dividing line well marked, the very levels different, the Danube utterly declining to recognize the newcomer. Below Passau, however, it gave up this particular trick, for there the Inn comes in with a thundering power impossible to ignore, and so pushes and incommodes the parent river that there is hardly room for them in the long twisting gorge that follows, and the Danube is shoved this way and that against the cliffs, and forced to hurry itself with great waves and much dashing to and fro in order to get through in time. And during the fight our canoe slipped down from its shoulder to its breast, and had the time of its life among the struggling waves. But the Inn taught the old river a lesson, and after Passau it no longer pretended to ignore new arrivals.

This was many days back, of course, and since then we had come to know other aspects of the great creature, and across the Bavarian wheat plain of Straubing she wandered so slowly under the blazing June sun that we could well imagine only the surface inches were water, while below there moved, concealed as by a silken mantle, a whole army of Undines, passing silently and unseen down to the sea, and very leisurely too, lest they be discovered.

Much, too, we forgave her because of her friendliness to the birds and animals that haunted the shores. Cormorants lined the banks in lonely places in rows like short black palings; gray crows crowded the shingle-beds; storks stood fishing in the vistas of shallower water that opened up between the islands, and hawks, swans, and marsh birds of all sorts filled the air with glinting wings and singing, petulant cries. It was impossible to feel annoyed with the river's vagaries after seeing a deep leap with a splash into the water at sunrise and swim past the bows of the canoe; and often we saw fawns peering at us from the underbrush, or looked straight into the brown eyes of a stag as we charged full tilt round a corner and entered another reach of the river. Foxes, too, everywhere haunted the banks, tripping daintily among the driftwood and disappearing so suddenly that it was impossible to see how they managed it.

But now, after leaving Pressburg, everything changed a little, and the Danube became more serious. It ceased trifling. It was halfway to the Black Sea, within scenting distance almost of other, stranger countries where no tricks would be permitted or understood. It became suddenly grown-up, and claimed our respect and even our awe. It broke out into three arms, for one thing, that only met again a hundred kilometers farther down, and for a canoe there were no indications which one was intended to be followed.

"If you take a side channel," said the Hungarian officer

we met in the Pressburg shop while buying provisions, "you may find yourselves, when the flood subsides, forty miles from anywhere, high and dry, and you may easily starve. There are no people, no farms, no fishermen. I warn you not to continue. The river, too, is still rising, and this wind will increase."

The rising river did not alarm us in the least, but the matter of being left high and dry by a sudden subsidence of the waters might be serious, and we had consequently laid in an extra stock of provisions. For the rest, the officer's prophecy held true, and the wind, blowing down a perfectly clear sky, increased steadily till it reached the dignity of a westerly gale.

It was earlier than usual when we camped, for the sun was a good hour or two from the horizon, and leaving my friend still asleep on the hot sand, I wandered about in desultory examination of our hotel. The island, I found, was less than an acre in extent, a mere sandy bank standing some two or three feet above the level of the river. The far end, pointing into the sunset, was covered with flying spray which the tremendous wind drove off the crests of the broken waves. It was triangular in shape, with the apex upstream.

I stood there for several minutes, watching the impetuous crimson flood bearing down with a shouting roar, dashing in waves against the bank as though to sweep it bodily away, and then swirling by in two foaming streams on either side. The ground seemed to shake with the shock and rush, while the furious movement of the willow bushes as the wind poured over them increased the curious illusion that the island itself actually moved. Above, for a mile or two, I could see the great river descending upon me; it was like looking up the slope of a sliding hill, white with foam, and leaping up everywhere to show itself to the sun.

The rest of the island was too thickly grown with willows to make walking pleasant, but I made the tour, nevertheless. From the lower end the light, of course, changed, and the river looked dark and angry. Only the backs of the flying waves were visible, streaked with foam, and pushed forcibly by the great puffs of wind that fell upon them from behind.

For a short mile it was visible, pouring in and out among the islands, and then disappearing with a huge sweep into the willows, which closed about it like a herd of monstrous antediluvian creatures crowding down to drink. They made me think of gigantic sponge-like growths that sucked the river up into themselves. They caused it to vanish from sight. They herded there together in such overpowering numbers.

Altogether it was an impressive scene, with its utter loneliness, its bizarre suggestion; and as I gazed, long and curiously, a singular emotion began to stir somewhere in the depths of me. Midway in my delight of the wild beauty, there crept, unbidden and unexplained, a curious feeling of disquietude, almost of alarm.

A rising river, perhaps, always suggests something of the ominous: many of the little islands I saw before me would probably have been swept away by the morning; this resistless, thundering flood of water touched the sense of awe. Yet I was aware that my uneasiness lay deeper far than the emotions of awe and wonder. It was not that I felt. Nor had it directly to do with the power of the driving wind—this shouting hurricane that might almost carry up a few acres of willows into the air and scatter them like so much chaff over the landscape. The wind was simply enjoying itself, for nothing rose out of the flat landscape to stop it, and I was conscious of sharing its great game with a kind of pleasurable excitement. Yet this novel emotion had nothing to do with the wind. Indeed, so vague was the sense of distress I experienced, that it was impossible to trace it to its source and deal with it accordingly, though I was aware somehow that it had to do with my realization of our utter insignificance before this unrestrained power of the elements about me. The huge-grown river had something to do with it too—a vague, unpleasant idea that we had somehow trifled with these great elemental forces in whose power we lay helpless every hour of the day and night. For here, indeed, they were gigantically at play together, and the sight appealed to the imagination.

But my emotion, so far as I could understand it, seemed to attach itself more particularly to the willow bushes, to these acres and acres of willows, crowding, so thickly growing there, swarming everywhere the eye could reach, pressing upon the river as though to suffocate it, standing in dense array mile after mile beneath the sky, watching, waiting, listening. And, apart quite from the elements, the willows connected themselves subtly with my malaise, attacking the mind insidiously somehow by reason of their vast numbers, and contriving in some way or other to represent to the imagination a new and mighty power, a power, moreover, not altogether friendly to us.

Great revelations of nature, of course, never fail to impress in one way or another, and I was no stranger to moods of the kind. Mountains overawe and oceans terrify, while the mystery of great forests exercises a spell peculiarly its own. But all these, at one point or another, somewhere link on intimately with human life and human experience. They stir comprehensible, even if alarming, emotions. They tend on the whole to exalt.

With this multitude of willows, however, it was something far different, I felt. Some essence emanated from them that besieged the heart. A sense of awe awakened, true, but of awe touched somewhere by a vague terror. Their serried ranks growing everywhere darker about me as the shadows deepened, moving furiously yet softly in the wind, woke in me the curious and unwelcome suggestion that we had trespassed here upon the borders of an alien world, a world where we were intruders, a world where we were not wanted or invited to remain—where we ran grave risks perhaps!

The feeling, however, though it refused to yield its meaning entirely to analysis, did not at the time trouble me by passing into menace. Yet it never left me quite, even during the very practical business of putting up the tent in a hurricane of wind and building a fire for the stew-pot. It remained, just enough to bother and perplex, and to rob a most delightful camping-ground of a good portion of its charm. To my companion, however, I said nothing, for he was a man I considered devoid of imagination. In the first place, I could never have explained to him what I meant, and in the second, he would have laughed stupidly at me if I had.

There was a slight depression in the center of the island,

and here we pitched the tent. The surrounding willows broke the wind a bit.

"A poor camp," observed the imperturbable Swede when at last the tent stood upright; "no stones and precious little firewood. I'm for moving on early to-morrow—eh? This sand won't hold anything."

But the experience of a collapsing tent at midnight had taught us many devices, and we made the cosy gipsy house as safe as possible, and then set about collecting a store of wood to last till bedtime. Willow bushes drop no branches, and driftwood was our only source of supply. We hunted the shores pretty thoroughly. Everywhere the banks were crumbling as the rising flood tore at them and carried away great portions with a splash and a gurgle.

"The island's much smaller than when we landed," said the accurate Swede. "It won't last long at this rate. We'd better drag the canoe close to the tent, and be ready to start at a moment's notice. *I* shall sleep in my clothes."

He was a little distance off, climbing along the bank, and I heard this rather jolly laugh as he spoke.

"By Jove!" I heard him call, a moment later, and turned to see what had caused his exclamation; but for the moment he was hidden by the willows, and I could not find him.

"What in the world's this?" I heard him cry again, and this time his voice had become serious.

I ran up quickly and joined him on the bank. He was looking over the river, pointing at something in the water.

"Good Heavens, it's a man's body!" he cried excitedly. "Look!"

A black thing, turning over and over in the foaming waves, swept rapidly past. It kept disappearing and coming up to the surface again. It was about twenty feet from the shore, and just as it was opposite to where we stood it lurched round and looked straight at us. We saw its eyes reflecting the sunset, and gleaming an odd yellow as the body turned over. Then it gave a swift, gulping plunge, and dived out of sight in a flash.

"An otter, by gad!" we exclaimed in the same breath, laughing.

It *was* an otter, alive, and out on the hunt; yet it had looked exactly like the body of a drowned man turning helplessly in the current. Far below, it came to the surface once again, and we saw its black skin, wet and shining in the sunlight.

Then, too, just as we turned back, our arms full of drift-wood, another thing happened to recall us to the river bank. This time it really was a man, and what was more, a man in a boat. Now a small boat on the Danube was an unusual sight at any time, but here in this deserted region, and at flood time, it was so unexpected as to constitute a real event. We stood and stared.

Whether it was due to the slanting sunlight, or the refraction from the wonderfully illumined water, I cannot say, but, whatever the cause, I found it difficult to focus my sight properly upon the flying apparition. It seemed, however, to be a man standing upright in a sort of flat-bottomed boat, steering with a long oar, and being carried down the opposite shore at a tremendous pace. He apparently was looking across in our direction, but the distance was too great and the light too uncertain for us to make our very plainly what he was about. It seemed to me that he was gesticulating and making signs at us. His voice came across the water to us shouting something furiously but the wind drowned it so that no single word was audible. There was something curious about the whole appearance—man, boat, signs, voice—that made an impression on me out of all proportion to its cause.

"He's crossing himself!" I cried. "Look, he's making the sign of the cross!"

"I believe you're right," the Swede said, shading his eyes with his hand and watching the man out of sight. He seemed to be gone in a moment, melting away down there into the sea of willows where the sun caught them in the bend of the river and turned them into a great crimson wall of beauty. Mist, too, had begun to rise, so that the air was hazy.

"But what in the world is he doing at nightfall on this flooded river?" I said, half to myself. "Where is he going at such a time, and what did he mean by his signs and shouting? D'you think he wished to warn us about something?"

"He saw our smoke, and thought we were spirits probably," laughed my companion. "These Hungarians believe in all sorts of rubbish: you remember the shopwoman at Pressburg warning us that no one ever landed here because it belonged to some sort of beings outside man's world! I suppose they believe in fairies and elementals, possibly demons too. That peasant in the boat saw people on the islands for the first time in his life," he added, after a slight pause, "and it scared him, that's all." The Swede's tone of voice was not convincing, and his manner lacked something that was usually there. I noted the change instantly while he talked, though without being able to label it precisely.

"If they had enough imagination," I laughed loudly—I remember trying to make as much *noise* as I could—"they might well people a place like this with the gods of antiquity. The Romans must have haunted all this region more or less with their shrines and sacred groves and elemental deities."

The subject dropped and we returned to our stew-pot, for my friend was not given to imaginative conversation as a rule. Moreover, just then I remember feeling distinctly glad that he was not imaginative; his stolid, practical nature suddenly seemed to me welcome and comforting. It was an admirable temperament, I felt: he could steer down rapids like a red Indian, shoot dangerous bridges and whirlpools better than any white man I ever saw in a canoe. He was a grand fellow for an adventurous trip, a tower of strength when untoward things happened. I looked at his strong face and light curly hair as he staggered along under his pile of driftwood (twice the size of mine!), and I experienced a feeling of relief. Yes, I was distinctly glad just then that the Swede was—what he was, and that he never made remarks that suggested more than they said.

"The river's still rising, though," he added, as if following out some thoughts of his own, and dropping his load with a gasp. "This island will be under water in two days if it goes on."

"I wish the *wind* would go down," I said. "I don't care a fig for the river."

The flood, indeed, had no terrors for us; we could get off at ten minutes' notice, and the more water the better we liked it. It meant an increasing current and the obliteration of the treacherous shingle-beds that so often threatened to tear the bottom out of our canoe.

Contrary to our expectations, the wind did not go down with the sun. It seemed to increase with the darkness, howling overhead and shaking the willows round us like straws. Curious sounds accompanied it sometimes, like the explosion of heavy guns, and it fell upon the water and the island in great flat blows of immense power. It made me think of the sounds a planet must make, could we only hear it, driving along through space.

But the sky kept wholly clear of clouds, and soon after supper the full moon rose up in the east and covered the river and the plain of shouting willows with a light like the day.

We lay on the sandy patch beside the fire, smoking, listening to the noises of the night round us, and talking happily of the journey we had already made, and of our plans ahead. The map lay spread in the door of the tent, but the high wind made it hard to study, and presently we lowered the curtain and extinguished the lantern. The firelight was enough to smoke and see each other's face by, and the sparks flew about overhead like fireworks. A few yards beyond, the river gurgled and hissed, and from time to time a heavy splash announced the falling away of further portions of the bank.

Our talk, I noticed, had to do with the far-away scenes and incidents of our first camps in the Black Forest, or of other subjects altogether remote from the present setting, for neither of us spoke of the actual moment more than was necessary—almost as though we had agreed tacitly to avoid discussion of the camp and its incidents. Neither the otter nor the boatman, for instance, received the honor of a single mention, though ordinarily these would have furnished discussion for the greater part of the evening. They were, of course, distinct events in such a place.

The scarcity of wood made it a business to keep the fire going, for the wind, that drove the smoke in our faces wherever we sat, helped at the same time to make a forced draught. We took it in turn to make foraging expeditions into the darkness, and the quantity the Swede brought back always made me feel that he took an absurdly long time finding it; for the fact was I did not care much about being left alone, and yet it always seemed to be my turn to grub about among the bushes or scramble along the slippery banks in the moonlight. The long day's battle with wind and water—such wind and such water!—had tired us both, and an early bed was the obvious program. Yet neither of us made the move for the tent. We lay there, tending the fire, talking in desultory fashion, peering about us into the dense willow bushes, and listening to the thunder of wind and river. The loneliness of the place had entered our very bones, and silence seemed natural, for after a bit the sound of our voices became a trifle unreal and forced; whispering would have been the fitting mode of communication, I felt, and the human voice, always rather absurd amid the roar of the elements, now carried with it something almost illegitimate. It was like talking out loud in church, or in some place where it was not lawful, perhaps not quite *safe*, to be overheard.

The eeriness of this lonely island, set among a million willows, swept by a hurricane, and surrounded by hurrying deep waters, touched us both, I fancy. Untrodden by man, almost unknown to man, it lay there beneath the moon, remote from human influence, on the frontier of another world, an alien world, a world tenanted by willows only and the souls of willows. And we, in our rashness, had dared to invade it, even to make use of it! Something more than the power of its mystery stirred in me as I lay on the sand, feet to fire, and peered up through the leaves at the stars. For the last time I rose to get firewood.

"When this has burnt up," I said firmly, "I shall turn in," and my companion watched me lazily as I moved off into the surrounding shadows.

For an unimaginative man I thought he seemed unusually receptive that night, unusually open to suggestion of things other than sensory. He too was touched by the beauty and loneliness of the place. I was not altogether pleased, I remember, to recognize this slight change in him, and instead of immediately collecting sticks, I made my way to the far point of the island where the moonlight on plain and river could be seen to better advantage. The desire to be alone had come suddenly upon me; my former dread returned in force; there was a vague feeling in me I wished to face and probe to the bottom.

When I reached the point of sand jutting out among the waves, the spell of the place descended upon me with a positive shock. No mere "scenery" could have produced such an effect. There was something more here, something to alarm.

I gazed across the waste of wild waters; I watched the whispering willows; I heard the ceaseless beating of the tireless wind; and, one and all, each in its own way, stirred in me this sensation of a strange distress. But the *willows* especially: for ever they went on chattering and talking among themselves, laughing a little, shrilly crying out, sometimes sighing—but what it was they made so much to-do about belonged to the secret life of the great plain they inhabited. And it was utterly alien to the world I knew, or to that of the wild yet kindly elements. They made me think of a host of beings from another plane of life, another evolution altogether, perhaps, all discussing a mystery known only to themselves. I watched them moving busily together, oddly shaking their big bushy heads, twirling their myriad leaves even when there was no wind. They moved of their own will as though alive, and they touched, by some incalculable method, my own keen sense of the *horrible*.

There they stood in the moonlight, like a vast army surrounding our camp, shaking their innumerable silver spears defiantly, formed all ready for an attack.

The psychology of places, for some imaginations at least, is very vivid; for the wanderer, especially, camps have their "note" either of welcome or rejection. At first it may not always be apparent, because the busy preparations of tent and cooking prevent, but with the first pause—after supper usually—it comes and announces itself. And the note of this willow-camp now became unmistakably plain to me: we were interlopers, trespassers; we were not welcomed. The sense of unfamiliarity grew upon me as I stood there watching. We touched the frontier of a region where our presence was resented. For a night's lodging we might perhaps be tolerated; but for a prolonged and inquisitive stay—No! by all the gods of the trees and the wilderness, no! We were the first human influences upon this island, and we were not wanted. *The willows were against us.*

Strange thoughts like these, bizarre fancies, borne I know not whence, found lodgment in my mind as I stood listening. What, I thought, if, after all, these crouching willows proved to be alive; if suddenly they should rise up, like a swarm of living creatures, marshaled by the gods whose territory we had invaded, sweep towards us off the vast swamps, booming overhead in the night—and then *settle down*! As I looked it was so easy to imagine they actually moved, crept nearer, retreated a little, huddled together in masses, hostile, waiting for the great wind that should finally start them a-running. I could have sworn their aspect changed a little, and their ranks deepened and pressed more closely together.

The melancholy shrill cry of a night bird sounded overhead, and suddenly I nearly lost my balance as the piece of bank I stood upon fell with a great splash into the river, undermined by the flood. I stepped back just in time, and went on hunting for firewood again, half laughing at the odd fancies that crowded so thickly into the mind and cast their spell upon me. I recalled the Swede's remark about moving on next day, and I was just thinking that I fully agreed with him, when I turned with a start and saw the subject of my thoughts standing immediately in front of me. He was quite close. The roar of the elements had covered his approach.

"You've been gone so long," he shouted above the wind, "I thought something must have happened to you."

But there was that in his tone, and a certain look in his face as well, that conveyed to me more than his actual words, and in a flash I understood the real reason for his coming. It was because the spell of the place had entered his soul too, and he did not like being alone.

"River still rising," he cried, pointing to the flood in the moonlight, "and the wind's simply awful."

He always said the same things, but it was the cry for companionship that gave the real importance to his words.

"Lucky," I cried back, "our tent's in the hollow. I think it'll hold all right." I added something about the difficulty of finding wood, in order to explain my absence, but the wind caught my words and flung them across the river, so that he did not hear, but just looked at me through the branches, nodding his head.

"Lucky if we get away without disaster!" he shouted, or words to that effect; and I remember feeling half angry with him for putting the thought into words, for it was exactly what I felt myself. There was disaster impending somewhere, and the sense of presentiment lay unpleasantly upon me.

We went back to the fire and made a final blaze, poking it up with our feet. We took a last look round. But for the wind the heat would have been unpleasant. I put this thought into words, and I remember my friend's reply struck me oddly: that he would rather have the heat, the ordinary July weather, than this "diabolical wind."

Everything was snug for the night; the canoe lying turned over beside the tent, with both yellow paddles beneath her; the provision sack hanging from a willow stem, and the washed-up dishes moved to a safe distance from the fire, all ready for the morning meal.

We smothered the embers of the fire with sand, and then turned in. The flap of the tent door was up, and I saw the branches and the stars and the white moonlight. The shaking willows and the heavy buffetings of the wind against our taut little house were the last things I remembered as sleep came down and covered all with its soft and delicious forgetfulness.

II

Suddenly I found myself lying awake, peering from my sandy mattress through the door of the tent. I looked at my watch pinned against the canvas, and saw by the bright moonlight that it was past twelve o'clock—the threshold of a new day—and I had therefore slept a couple of hours. The Swede was asleep still beside me; the wind howled as before; something plucked at my heart and made me feel afraid.

There was a sense of disturbance in my immediate neighborhood.

I sat up quickly and looked out. The trees were swaying violently to and fro as the gusts smote them, but our little bit of green canvas lay snugly safe in the hollow, for the wind passed over it without meeting enough resistance to make it vicious. The feeling of disquietude did not pass, however, and I crawled quietly out of the tent to see if our belongings were safe. I moved carefully so as not to waken my companion. A curious excitement was on me.

I was halfway out, kneeling on all fours, when my eye first took in that the tops of the bushes opposite, with their moving tracery of leaves, made shapes against the sky. I sat back on my haunches and stared. It was incredible, surely, but there, opposite and slightly above me, were shapes of some indeterminate sort among the willows, and as the branches swayed in the wind they seemed to group themselves about these shapes, forming a series of monstrous outlines that shifted rapidly beneath the moon. Close, about fifty feet in front of me, I saw these things.

My first instinct was to waken my companion, that he too might see them, but something made me hesitate—the sudden realization, probably, that I should not welcome corroboration; and meanwhile I crouched there staring in amazement with smarting eyes. I was wide awake. I remember saying to myself that I was *not* dreaming.

They first became properly visible, these huge figures, just within the tops of the bushes—immense, bronze-colored, moving, and wholly independent of the swaying of the branches. I saw them plainly and noted, now I came to examine them more calmly, that they were very much larger than human, and indeed that something in their appearance proclaimed them to be *not human* at all. Certainly they were not merely the moving tracery of the branches against the moonlight. They shifted independently. They rose upwards in a continuous stream from earth to sky, vanishing utterly as soon as they reached the dark of the sky. They were interlaced one with another, making a great column, and I saw their limbs and huge bodies melting in and out of each other, forming this serpentine line that bent and swayed and twisted spirally with the contortions of the wind-tossed trees. They were nude, fluid shapes, passing up the bushes, *within* the leaves almost—rising up in a living column into the heavens. Their faces I never could see. Unceasingly they poured upwards, swaying in great bending curves, with a hue of dull bronze upon their skins.

I stared, trying to force every atom of vision from my eyes. For a long time I thought they *must* every moment disappear and resolve themselves into the movements of the branches and prove to be an optical illusion. I searched everywhere for a proof of reality, when all the while I understood quite well that the standard of reality had changed. For the longer I looked the more certain I became that these figures were real and living, though perhaps not according to the standards that the camera and the biologist would insist upon.

Far from feeling fear, I was possessed with a sense of awe and wonder such as I have never known. I seemed to be gazing at the personified elemental forces of this haunted and primeval region. Our intrusion had stirred the powers of the place into activity. It was we who were the cause of the disturbance, and my brain filled to bursting with stories and legends of the spirits and deities of places that have been acknowledged and worshiped by men in all ages of the world's history. But, before I could arrive at any possible explanation, something impelled me to go farther out, and I crept forward on to the sand and stood upright. I felt the ground still warm under my bare feet; the wind tore at my hair and face; and the sound of the rive burst upon my ears with a sudden roar. These things, I knew, were real, and proved that my senses were acting normally. Yet the figures still rose from the earth to heaven, silent, majestically, in a great spiral of grace and strength that overwhelmed me at length with a genuine deep emotion of worship. I felt that I must fall down and worship—absolutely worship.

Perhaps in another minute I might have done so, when a gust of wind swept against me with such force that it blew me sideways, and I nearly stumbled and fell. It seemed to shake the dream violently out of me. At least it gave me another point of view somehow. The figures still remained, still ascended into heaven from the heat of the night, but my reason at last began to assert itself. It must be a subjective experience, I argued—none the less real for that, but still subjective. The moonlight and the branches combined to work out these pictures upon the mirror of my imagination, and for some reason I projected them outwards and made them appear objective. I knew this must be the case, of course. I was the subject of a vivid and interesting hallucination. I took courage, and began to move forward across the open patches of sand. By Jove, though, was it all hallucination? Was it merely subjective? Did not my reason argue in the old futile way from the little standard of the known?

I only know that great column of figures ascended darkly into the sky for what seemed a very long period of time, and with a very complete measure of reality as most men are accustomed to gauge reality. Then suddenly they were gone!

And, once they were gone and the immediate wonder of their great presence had passed, fear came down upon me with a cold rush. The esoteric meaning of this lonely and haunted region suddenly flamed up within me and I began to tremble dreadfully. I took a quick look round—a look of horror that came near to panic—calculating vainly ways of escape; and then, realizing how helpless I was to achieve anything really effective, I crept back silently into the tent and lay down again upon my sandy mattress, first lowering the door-curtain to shut out the sight of the willows in the moonlight, and then burying my head as deeply as possible beneath the blankets to deaden the sound of the terrifying wind.

III

As though further to convince me that I had not been dreaming, I remember that it was a long time before I fell again into a troubled and restless sleep; and even then only the upper crust of me slept, and underneath there was something that never quite lost consciousness, but lay alert and on the watch.

But this second time I jumped up with a genuine start of terror. It was neither the wind nor the river that woke me, but the slow approach of something that caused the sleeping portion of me to grow smaller and smaller till at last it vanished altogether, and I found myself sitting bolt upright—listening.

Outside there was a sound of multitudinous little patterings. They had been coming, I was aware, for a long time, and in my sleep they had first become audible. I sat there nervously wide awake as though I had not slept at all. It seemed to me that my breathing came with difficulty, and that there was a great weight upon the surface of my body. In spite of the hot night, I felt clammy with cold and shivered. Something surely was pressing steadily against the sides of the tent and weighing down upon it from above. Was it the body of the wind? Was this the pattering rain, the dripping of the leaves? The spray blown from the river by the wind and gathering in big drops? I thought quickly of a dozen things.

Then suddenly the explanation leaped into my mind: a bough from the poplar, the only large tree on the island, had fallen with the wind. Still half caught by the other branches, it would fall with the next gust and crush us, and meanwhile its leaves brushed and tapped upon the tight canvas surface of the tent. I raised the loose flap and rushed out, calling to the Swede to follow.

But when I got out and stood upright I saw that the tent was free. There was no hanging bough; there was no rain or spray; nothing approached.

A cold, gray light filtered down through the bushes and lay on the faintly gleaming sand. Stars still crowded the sky directly overhead, and the wind howled magnificently, but the fire no longer gave out any glow, and I saw the east reddening in streaks through the trees. Several hours must have passed since I stood there before, watching the ascending figures, and the memory of it now came back to me horribly, like an evil dream. Oh, how tired it made me feel, that ceaseless raging wind! Yet, though the deep lassitude of a sleepless night was on me, my nerves were tingling with the activity of an equally tireless apprehension, and all idea of repose was out of the question. The river, I saw, had risen further. Its thunder filled the air, and a fine spray made itself felt through my thin sleeping shirt.

Yet nowhere did I discover the slightest evidences of anything to cause alarm. This deep, prolonged disturbance in my heart remained wholly unaccounted for.

My companion had not stirred when I called him, and there was no need to waken him now. I looked about me carefully, noting everything: the turned-over canoe; the yellow paddles—two of them, I'm certain; the provision sack and the extra lantern hanging together from the tree; and, crowding everywhere about me, enveloping all, the willows, those endless, shaking willows. A bird uttered its morning cry, and a string of ducks passed with whirring flight overhead in the twilight. The sand whirled, dry and stinging, about my bare feet in the wind.

I walked round the tent and then went out a little way into the bush, so that I could see across the river to the farther landscape, and the same profound yet indefinable emotion of distress seized upon me again as I saw the interminable sea of bushes stretching to the horizon, looking ghostly and unreal in the wan light of dawn. I walked softly here and there, still puzzling over that odd sound of infinite pattering, and of that pressure upon the tent that had wakened me. It *must* have been the wind, I reflected—the wind beating upon the loose, hot sand, driving the dry particles smartly against the taut canvas—the wind dropping heavily upon our fragile roof.

Yet all the time my nervousness and malaise increased appreciably.

I crossed over to the farther shore and noted how the coast line had altered in the night, and what masses of sand the river had torn away. I dipped my hands and feet into the cool current, and bathed my forehead. Already there was a glow of sunrise in the sky and the exquisite freshness of coming day. On my way back I passed purposely beneath the very bushes where I had seen the column of figures rising into the air, and midway among the clumps I suddenly found myself overtaken by a sense of vast terror. From the shadows a large figure went swiftly by. Some one passed me, as sure as ever man did. . . .

It was a great staggering blow from the wind that helped me forward again, and once out in the more open space, the sense of terror diminished strangely. The winds were about and walking, I remember saying to myself; for the winds often move like great presences under the trees. And altogether the fear that hovered about me was such an unknown and immense kind of fear, so unlike anything I had ever felt before, that it woke a sense of awe and wonder in me that did much to counteract its worst effects; and when I reached a high point in the middle of the island from which I could see the wide stretch of river, crimson in the sunrise, the whole magical beauty of it all was so overpowering that a sort of wild yearning woke in me and almost brought a cry up into the throat.

But this cry found no expression, for as my eyes wandered from the plain beyond to the island round me and noted our little tent half hidden among the willows, a dreadful discovery leaped out at me, compared to which my terror of the walking winds seemed as nothing at all.

For a change, I thought, had somehow come about in the arrangement of the landscape. It was not that my point of vantage gave me a different view, but that an alteration had apparently been effected in the relation of the tent to the willows, and of the willows to the tent. Surely the bushes now crowded much closer—unnecessarily, unpleasantly close. *They had moved nearer.*

Creeping with silent feet over the shifting sands, drawing imperceptibly nearer by soft, unhurried movements, the willows had come closer during the night. But had the wind moved them, or had they moved of themselves? I recalled the sound of infinite small patterings and the pressure upon the tent and upon my own heart that caused me to wake in terror. I swayed for a moment in the wind like a tree, finding it hard to keep my upright position on the sandy hillock. There was a suggestion here of personal agency, of deliberate intention, f aggressive hostility, and it terrified me into a sort of rigidity.

Then the reaction followed quickly. The idea was so bizarre, so absurd, that I felt inclined to laugh. But the laughter came no more readily than the cry, for the knowledge that my mind was so receptive to such dangerous imaginings brought the additional terror that it was through our minds and not through our physical bodies that the attack would come, and was coming.

The wind buffeted me about, and, very quickly it seemed, the sun came up over the horizon, for it was after four o'clock, and I must have stood on that little pinnacle of sand longer than I knew, afraid to come down at close quarters with the willows. I returned quietly, creepily, to the tent, first taking another exhaustive look round and—yes, I confess it—making a few measurements. I paced out on the warm sand the distances between the willows and the tent, making a note of the shortest distance particularly.

I crawled stealthily into my blankets. My companion, to all appearances, still slept soundly, and I was glad that this was so. Provided my experiences were not corroborated, I could find strength somehow to deny them, perhaps. With the daylight I could persuade myself that it was all a subjective hallucination, a fantasy of the night, a projection of the excited imagination.

Nothing further came to disturb me, and I fell asleep almost at once, utterly exhausted, yet still in dread of hearing again that weird sound of multitudinous pattering, or of feeling the pressure upon my heart that had made it difficult to breathe.

IV

The sun was high in the heavens when my companion woke me from a heavy sleep and announced that the porridge was cooked and there was just time to bathe. The grateful smell of frizzling bacon entered the tent door.

"River still rising," he said, "and several islands out in

midstream have disappeared altogether. Our own island" much smaller."

"Any wood left?" I asked sleepily.

"The wood and the island will finish to-morrow in a dead heat," he laughed, "but there's enough to last us till then."

I plunged in the river from the point of the island, which had indeed altered a lot in size and shape during the night and was swept down in a moment to the landing place opposite the tent. The water was icy, and the banks flew by like the country from an express train. Bathing under such conditions was an exhilarating operation, and the terror of the night seemed cleansed out of me by a process of evaporation in the brain. The sun was blazing hot; not a cloud showed itself anywhere; the wind, however, had not abated one little jot.

Quite suddenly then the implied meaning of the Swede's words flashed across me, showing that he no longer wished to leave post-haste, and had changed his mind. "Enough to last till to-morrow"—he assumed we should stay on the island another night. It struck me as odd. The night before he was so positive the other way. How had the change come about?

Great crumblings of the banks occurred at breakfast, with heavy splashings and clouds of spray which the wind brought into our frying-pan, and my fellow-traveler talked incessantly about the difficulty the Vienna-Pesth steamers must have to find the channel in flood. But the state of his mind interested and impressed me far more than the state of the river or the difficulties of the steamers. He had changed somehow since the evening before. His manner was different—a trifle excited, a trifle shy, with a sort of suspicion about his voice and gestures. I hardly know how to describe it now in cold blood, but at the time I remember being quite certain of one thing, viz., that he had become frightened!

He ate very little breakfast, and for once omitted to smoke his pipe. He had the map spread open beside him, and kept studying its markings.

"We'd better get off sharp in an hour," I said presently, feeling for an opening that must bring him indirectly to a partial confession at any rate. And his answer puzzled me uncomfortably: "Rather! If they'll let us."

"Who'll let us? The elements?" I asked quickly, with affected indifference.

"The powers of this awful place, whoever they are," he replied, keeping his eyes on the map. "The gods are here, if they are anywhere at all in the world."

"The elements are always the true immortals," I replied, laughing as naturally as I could manage, yet knowing quite well that my face reflected my true feelings when he looked up gravely at me and spoke across the smoke:

"We shall be fortunate if we get away without further disaster."

This was exactly what I had dreaded, and I screwed myself up to the point of the direct question. It was like agreeing to allow the dentist to extract the tooth; it *had* to come anyhow in the long run, and the rest was all pretense.

"Further disaster! Why, what's happened?"

"For one thing—the steering paddle's gone," he said quietly.

"The steering paddle gone!" I repeated, greatly excited, for this was our rudder, and the Danube in flood without a rudder was suicide. "But what——"

"And there's a tear in the bottom of the canoe," he added, with a genuine little tremor in his voice.

I continued staring at him, able only to repeat the words in his face somewhat foolishly. There, in the heat of the sun, and on this burning sand, I was aware of a freezing atmosphere descending round us. I got up to follow him, for he merely nodded his head gravely and led the way towards the tent a few yards on the other side of the fireplace. The canoe still lay there as I had last seen her in the night, ribs uppermost, the paddles, or rather, *the* paddle, on the sand beside her.

"There's only one," he said, stooping to pick it up. "And here's the rent in the base-board."

It was on the tip of my tongue to tell him that I had clearly noticed *two* paddles a few hours before, but a second impulse made me think better of it, and I said nothing. I approached to see.

There was a long, finely made tear in the bottom of the canoe where a little slither of wood had been neatly taken clean out; it looked as if the tooth of a sharp rock or snag had eaten down her length, and investigation showed that the hole went through. Had we launched out in her without observing it we must inevitably have foundered. At first the water would have made the wood swell so as to close the hole, but once out in midstream the water must have poured in, and the canoe, never more than two inches above the surface, would have filled and sunk very rapidly.

"There, you see, an attempt to prepare a victim for the sacrifice," I heard him saying, more to himself than to me, "two victims rather," he added as he bent over and ran his fingers along the slit.

I began to whistle—a thing I always do unconsciously when utterly nonplussed—and purposely paid no attention to his words. I was determined to consider them foolish.

"It wasn't there last night," he said presently, straightening up from his examination and looking anywhere but at me.

"We must have scratched her in landing, of course," I stopped whistling to say, "The stones are very sharp——"

I stopped abruptly, for at that moment he turned round and met my eye squarely. I knew just as well as he did how impossible my explanation was. There were no stones, to begin with.

"And then there's this to explain too," he added quietly, handing me the paddle and pointing to the blade.

A new and curious emotion spread freezingly over me as I took and examined it. The blade was scraped down all over, beautifully scraped, as though someone had sand-papered it with care, making it so thin that the first vigorous stroke must have snapped it off at the elbow.

"One of us walked in his sleep and did this thing," I said feebly, "or—or it has been filed by the constant stream of sand particles blown against it by the wind, perhaps."

"Ah," said the Swede, turning away, laughing a little, "you can explain everything!"

"The same wind that caught the steering paddle and flung it so near the bank that it fell in with the next lump that crumbled," I called out after him, absolutely determined to find an explanation for everything he showed me.

"I see," he shouted back, turning his head to look at me before disappearing among the willow bushes.

Once alone with these perplexing evidences of personal agency, I think my first thought took the form of "One of us must have done this thing, and it certainly was not I." But my second thought decided how impossible it was to suppose, under all the circumstances, that either of us had done it. That my companion, the trusted friend of a dozen similar expeditions, could have knowingly had a hand in it, was a suggestion not to be entertained for a moment. Equally absurd seemed the explanation that this imperturbable and densely practical nature had suddenly become insane and was busied with insane purposes.

Yet the fact remained that what disturbed me most, and kept my fear actively alive even in this blaze of sunshine and wild beauty, was the clear certainty that some curious alteration had come about in his *mind*—that he was nervous, timid, suspicious, aware of goings on he did not speak about, watching a series of secret and hitherto unmentionable events—waiting, in a word, for a climax that he expected, and, I thought, expected very soon. This grew up in my mind intuitively—I hardly knew how.

I made a hurried examination of the tent and its surroundings, but the measurements of the night remained the same. There were deep hollows formed in the sand, I now noticed for the first time, basin-shaped and of various depths and sizes, varying from that of a teacup to a large bowl. The wind, no doubt, was responsible for these miniature craters, just as it was for lifting the paddle and tossing it towards the water. The rent in the canoe was the only thing that seemed quite inexplicable; and, after all, it *was* conceivable that a sharp point had caught it when we landed. The examination I made of the shore did not assist this theory, but all the same

I clung to it with that diminishing portion of my intelligence which I called "my reason." An explanation of some kind was an absolute necessity, just as some working explanation of the universe is necessary—however absurd—to the happiness of every individual who seeks to do his duty in the world and face the problems of life. The simile seemed to me at the time an exact parallel.

I at once set the pitch melting, and presently the Swede joined me at the work, though under the best conditions in the world the canoe could not be safe for traveling till the following day. I drew his attention casually to the hollows in the sand.

"Yes," he said, "I know. They're all over the island. But *you* can explain them, no doubt!"

"Wind, of course," I answered without hesitation. "Have you never watched those little whirlwinds in the street that twist and twirl everything into a circle? This sand's loose enough to yield, that's all."

He made no reply, and we worked on in silence for a bit. I watched him surreptitiously all the time, and I had an idea he was watching me. He seemed, too, to be always listening attentively to something I could not hear, or perhaps for something that he expected to hear, for he kept turning about and staring into the bushes, and up into the sky, and out across the water where it was visible through the openings among the willows. Sometimes he even put his hand to his ear and held it there for several minutes. He said nothing to me, however, about it, and I asked no questions. And meanwhile, as he mended that torn canoe with the skill and address of a red Indian, I was glad to notice his absorption in the work, for there was a vague dread in my heart that he would speak of the changed aspect of the willows. And, if he had noticed *that*, my imagination could no longer be held a sufficient explanation of it.

At length, after a long pause, he began to talk.

"Queer thing," he added in a hurried sort of voice, as though he wanted to say something and get it over. "Queer thing, I mean, about that otter last night."

I had expected something so totally different that he caught me with surprise, and I looked up sharply.

"Shows how lonely this place is. Otters are awfully shy things—"

"I don't mean that, of course," he interrupted. "I mean—do you think—did you think it really *was* an otter?"

"What else, in the name of heaven, what else?"

"You know, I saw it before you did, and at first it seemed—so *much* bigger than an otter."

"The sunset as you looked upstream magnified it, or something," I replied.

He looked at me absently a moment, as though his mind were busy with other thoughts.

"It had such extraordinary yellow eyes," he went on half to himself.

"That was the sun too," I laughed, a trifle boisterously. "I suppose you'll wonder next if that fellow in the boat——"

I suddenly decided not to finish the sentence. He was in the act again of listening, turning his head to the wind, and something in the expression of his face made me halt. The subject dropped, and we went on with our caulking. Apparently he had not noticed my unfinished sentence. Five minutes later, however, he looked at me across the canoe, the smoking pitch in his hand, his face exceedingly grave.

"I *did* rather wonder, if you want to know," he said slowly, "what that thing in the boat was. I remember thinking at the time it was not a man. The whole business seemed to rise quite suddenly out of the water."

I laughed again boisterously in his face, but this time there was impatience, and a strain of anger too, in my feeling.

"Look here now," I cried, "this place is quite queer enough without going out of our way to imagine things! That boat was an ordinary boat, and the man in it was an ordinary man, and they were both going downstream as fast as they could lick. And that otter *was* an otter, so don't let's play the fool about it!"

He looked steadily at me with the same grave expression.

He was not in the least annoyed. I took courage from his silence.

"And for heaven's sake," I went on, "don't keep pretending you hear things, because it only gives me the jumps, and there's nothing to hear but the river and this cursed old thundering wind."

"You *fool*!" he answered in a low, shocked voice, "you utter fool. That's just the way all victims talk. As if you didn't understand just as well as I do!" he sneered with scorn in his voice, and a sort of resignation. "The best thing you can do is to keep quiet and try to hold your mind as firm as possible. This feeble attempt at self-deception only makes the truth harder when you're forced to meet it."

My little effort was over, and I found nothing more to say, for I knew quite well his words were true, and that *I* was the fool, not *he*. Up to a certain stage in the adventure he kept ahead of me easily, and I think I felt annoyed to be out of it, to be thus proved less psychic, less sensitive than himself to these extraordinary happenings, and half ignorant all the time of what was going on under my very nose. *He knew* from the very beginning, apparently. But at the moment I wholly missed the point of his words about the necessity of there being a victim, and that we ourselves were destined to satisfy the want. I dropped all pretense thenceforward, but thenceforward likewise my fear increased steadily to the climax.

"But you're quite right about one thing," he added, before the subject passed, "and that is that we're wiser not to talk about it, or even to think about it, because what one *thinks* finds expression in words, and what one *says*, happens."

That afternoon, while the canoe dried and hardened, we spent trying to fish, testing the leak, collecting wood, and watching the enormous flood of rising water. Masses of driftwood swept near our shores sometimes, and we fished for them with long willow branches. The island grew perceptibly smaller as the banks were torn away with great gulps and splashes. The weather kept brilliantly fine till about four o'clock, and then for the first time for three days the wind showed signs of abating. Clouds began to gather in the southwest, spreading thence slowly over the sky.

This lessening of the wind came as a great relief, for the incessant roaring, banging, and thundering had irritated our nerves. Yet the silence that came about five o'clock with its sudden cessation was in a manner quite as oppressive. The booming of the river had everything its own way then: it filled the air with deep murmurs, more musical than the wind noises, but infinitely more monotonous. The wind held many notes, rising, falling, always beating out some sort of great elemental tune; whereas the river's song lay between three notes at most—dull pedal notes, that held a lugubrious quality foreign to the wind, and somehow seemed to me, in my then nervous state, to sound wonderfully well the music of doom.

It was extraordinary, too, how the withdrawal suddenly of bright sunlight took everything out of the landscape that made for cheerfulness; and since this particular landscape had already managed to convey the suggestion of something sinister, the change of course was all the more unwelcome and noticeable. For me, I know, the darkening outlook became distinctly more alarming, and I found myself more than once calculating how soon after sunset the full moon would get up in the east, and whether the gathering clouds would greatly interfere with her lighting of the little island.

With this general hush of the wind—though it still indulged in occasional brief gusts—the river seemed to me to grow blacker, the willows to stand more densely together. The latter, too, kept up a sort of independent movement of their own, rustling among themselves when no wind stirred, and shaking oddly from the roots upwards. When common objects in this way become charged with the suggestion of horror, they stimulate the imagination far more than things of unusual appearance; and these bushes, crowding huddled about us, assumed for me in the darkness a bizarre *grotesquerie* of appearance that lent to them somehow the aspect of purposeful and living creatures. Their very ordinariness, I felt, masked what was malignant and hostile to us. The forces of the region drew nearer with the coming of night. They were focusing upon our island, and more particularly upon ourselves. For thus, somehow, in the terms of the imagination, did my really indescribable sensations in this extraordinary place present themselves.

I had slept a good deal in the early afternoon, and had thus recovered somewhat from the exhaustion of a disturbed night, but this only served apparently to render me more susceptible than before to the obsessing spell of the haunting. I fought against it, laughing at my feelings as absurd and childish, with very obvious physiological explanations, yet, in spite of every effort, they gained in strength upon me so that I dreaded the night as a child lost in a forest must dread the approach of darkness.

The canoe we had carefully covered with a waterproof sheet during the day, and the one remaining paddle had been securely tied by the Swede to the base of a tree, lest the wind should rob us of that too. From five o'clock onwards I busied myself with the stew-pot and preparations for dinner, it being my turn to cook that night. We had potatoes, onions, bits of bacon fat to add flavour, and a general thick residue from former stews at the bottom of the pot; with black bread broken up into it, the result was most excellent, and it was followed by a stew of plums with sugar and a brew of strong tea with dried milk. A good pile of wood lay close at hand, and the absence of wind made my duties easy. My companion sat lazily watching me, dividing his attentions between cleaning his pipe and giving useless advice—an admitted privilege of the off-duty man. He had been very quiet all the afternoon, engaged in re-caulking the canoe, strengthening the tent ropes, and fishing for driftwood while I slept. No more talk about undesirable things had passed between us, and I think his only remarks had to do with the gradual destruction of the island, which he declared was now fully a third smaller than when we first landed.

The pot had just began to bubble when I heard his voice calling to me from the bank, where he had wandered away without my noticing. I ran up.

"Come and listen," he said, "and see what you make of it." He held his hand cupwise to his ear, as so often before.

"*Now* do you hear anything?" he asked, watching me curiously.

We stood there, listening attentively together. At first I heard only the deep note of the water and the hissings rising from its turbulent surface. The willows, for once, were motionless and silent. Then a sound began to reach my ears faintly, a peculiar sound—something like the humming of a distant gong. It seemed to come across to us in the darkness from the waste of swamps and willows opposite. It was repeated at regular intervals, but it was certainly neither the sound nor the hooting of a distant steamer. I can liken it to nothing so much as to the sound of an immense gong, suspended far up in the sky, repeating incessantly its muffled metallic note, soft and musical, as it was repeatedly struck. My heart quickened as I listened.

"I've heard it all day," said my companion. "While you slept this afternoon it came all round the island. I hunted it down, but could never get near enough to see—to localize it correctly. Sometimes it was overhead, and sometimes it seemed under the water. Once or twice, too, I could have sworn it was not outside at all, but *within myself*—you know—the way a sound in the fourth dimension is supposed to come."

I was too much puzzled to pay much attention to his words. I listened carefully, striving to associate it with any known familiar sound I could think of, but without success. It changed in direction, too, coming nearer, and then sinking utterly away into remote distance. I cannot say that it was ominous in quality, because to me it seemed distinctly musical, yet I must admit it set going a distressing feeling that made me wish I had never heard it.

"The wind blowing in those sand-funnels," I said, determined to find an explanation, "or the bushes rubbing together after the storm perhaps."

"It comes off the whole swamp," my friend answered. "It comes from everywhere at once." He ignored my explanations. "It comes from the willow bushes somehow——"

"But now the wind has dropped," I objected. "The willows can hardly make a noise by themselves, can they?"

His answer frightened me, first because I had dreaded it, and secondly, because I knew intuitively it was true.

"It is *because* the wind has dropped we now hear it. It was drowned before. It is the cry, I believe of the——"

I dashed back to my fire, warned by a sound of bubbling that the stew was in danger, but determined at the same time to escape from further conversation. I was resolute, if possible, to avoid the exchanging of views. I dreaded, too, that he would begin again about the gods, or the elemental forces, or something else disquieting, and I wanted to keep myself well in hand for what might happen later. There was another night to be faced before we escaped from this distressing place, and there was no knowing yet what it might bring forth.

"Come and cut up bread for the pot," I called to him, vigorously stirring the appetizing mixture. That stew-pot held sanity for us both, and the thought made me laugh.

He came over slowly and took the provision sack from the tree, fumbling in its mysterious depths, and then emptying the entire contents upon the ground-sheet at his feet.

"Hurry up!" I cried; "it's boiling."

The Swede burst out into a roar of laughter that startled me. It was forced laughter, not artificial exactly, but mirthless.

"There's nothing here!" he shouted, holding his sides.

"Bread, I mean."

"It's gone. There is no bread. They've taken it!"

I dropped the long spoon and ran up. Everything the sack contained lay upon the ground-sheet, but there was no loaf.

The whole dead weight of my growing fear fell upon me and shook me. Then I burst out laughing too. It was the only thing to do: and the sound of my own laughter also made me understand his. The strain of physical pressure caused it—this explosion of unnatural laughter in both of us; it was an effort of repressed forces to seek relief; it was a temporary safety valve. And with both of us it ceased quite suddenly.

"How criminally stupid of me!" I cried, still determined to be consistent and find an explanation. "I clean forgot to buy a loaf at Pressburg. That chattering woman put everything out of my head, and I must have left it lying on the counter or——"

"The oatmeal, too, is much less than it was this morning," the Swede interrupted.

Why in the world need he draw attention to it? I thought angrily.

"There's enough for to-morrow," I said, stirring vigorously, "and we can get lots more at Komorn or Gran. In twenty-four hours we shall be miles from here."

"I hope so—to God," he muttered, putting the things back into the sack, "unless we're claimed first as victims for the sacrifice," he added with a foolish laugh. He dragged the sack into the tent, for safety's sake, I suppose, and I heard him mumbling on to himself, but so indistinctly that it seemed quite natural for me to ignore his words.

Our meal was beyond question a gloomy one, and we ate it almost in silence, avoiding one another's eyes, and keeping the fire bright. Then we washed up and prepared for the night, and, once smoking, our minds unoccupied with any definite duties, the apprehension I had felt all day long became more and more acute. It was not then active fear, I think, but the very vagueness of its origin distressed me far more than if I had been able to ticket and face it squarely. The curious sound I have likened to the note of a gong became now almost incessant, and filled the stillness of the night with a faint, continuous ringing rather than a series of distinct notes. At one time it was behind and at another time in front of us. Sometimes I fancied it came from the bushes on our left, and then again from the clumps on our right. More often it hovered directly overhead like the whirring of wings. It was really everywhere at once, behind, in front, at our sides and over our heads, completely surrounding us. The sound really defies description. But nothing within my knowledge is like that ceaseless muffled humming rising off the deserted world of swamps and willows.

We sat smoking in comparative silence, the strain growing every minute greater. The worst feature of the situation seemed to me that we did not know what to expect, and could therefore make no sort of preparation by way of defense. We could anticipate nothing. My explanations made in the sunshine, moreover, now came to haunt me with their foolish and wholly unsatisfactory nature, and it was more and more clear to me that some kind of plain talk with my companion was inevitable, whether I liked it or not. After all, we had to spend the night together, and to sleep in the same tent side by side. I saw that I could not get along much longer without the support of his mind, and for that, of course, plain talk was imperative. As long as possible, however, I postponed this little climax, and tried to ignore or laugh at the occasional sentences he flung into the emptiness.

Some of these sentences, moreover, were confoundedly disquieting to me, coming as they did to corroborate much that I felt myself: corroboration, too—which made it so much more convincing—from a totally different point of view. He composed such curious sentences, and hurled them at me in such an inconsequential sort of way, as though his main line of thought was secret to himself, and these fragments were the bits he found it impossible to digest. He got rid of them by uttering them. Speech relieved him. It was like being sick.

"There are things about us, I'm sure, that make for disorder, disintegration, destruction, *our* destruction," he said once, while the fire blazed between us. "We've strayed out of a safe line somewhere."

And another time, when the gong sounds had come nearer, ringing much louder than before, and directly over our heads, he said, as though talking to himself:

"I don't think a phonograph would show any record of that. The sound doesn't come to me by the ears at all. The vibrations reach me in another manner altogether, and seem to be within me, which is precisely how a fourth dimension sound might be supposed to make itself heard."

I purposely made no reply to this, but I sat up a little closer to the fire and peered about me into the darkness. The clouds were massed all over the sky and no trace of moonlight came through. Very still, too, everything was, so that the river and the frogs had things all their own way.

"It has that about it," he went on, "which is utterly out of common experience. It is *unknown*. Only one thing describes it really: it is a non-human sound; I mean a sound outside humanity."

Having rid himself of this indigestible morsel, he lay quiet for a time; but he had so admirably expressed my own feeling that it was a relief to have the thought out, and to have confined it by the limitation of words from dangerous wandering to and fro in the mind.

The solitude of that Danube camping-place, can I ever forget it? The feeling of being utterly alone on an empty planet! My thoughts ran incessantly upon cities and the haunts of men. I would have given my soul, as the saying is, for the "feel" of those Bavarian villages we had passed through by the score; for the normal, human commonplaces: peasants drinking beer, tables beneath the trees, hot sunshine, and a ruined castle on the rocks behind the red-roofed church. Even the tourists would have been welcome.

Yet what I felt of dread was no ordinary ghostly fear. It was infinitely greater, stranger, and seemed to arise from some dim ancestral sense of terror more profoundly disturbing than anything I had known or dreamed of. We had "strayed," as the Swede put it, into some region or some set of conditions where the risks were great, yet unintelligible to us; where the frontiers of some unknown world lay close about us. It was a spot held by the dwellers in some outer space, a sort of peephole whence they could spy upon the earth, themselves unseen, a point where the veil between had torn a little thin. As the final result of too long a sojourn here, we should be carried over the border and deprived of what we called "our lives," yet by mental, not physical, processes. In that sense, as he said, we should be the victims of our adventure—a sacrifice.

It took us in different fashion, each according to the measure of his sensitiveness and powers of resistance. I translated it vaguely into a personification of the mightily disturbed elements, investing them with the horror of a deliberate and malefic purpose, resentful of our audacious intrusion into their breeding-place; whereas my friend threw it into the unoriginal form at first of a trespass on some ancient shrine, some place where the old gods still held sway, where the emotional forces of former worshipers still clung, and the ancestral portion of him yielded to the old pagan spell.

At any rate, here was a place unpolluted by men, kept clean by the winds from coarsening human influences, a place where spiritual agencies were within reach and aggressive. Never, before or since, have I been so attacked by indescribable suggestions of a "beyond region," of another scheme of life, another evolution not parallel to the human. And in the end our minds would succumb under the weight of the awful spell, and we should be drawn across the frontier into *their* world.

Small things testified to this amazing influence of the place, and now in the silence round the fire they allowed themselves to be noted by the mind. The very atmosphere had proved itself a magnifying medium to distort every indication: the otter rolling in the current, the hurrying boatman making signs, the shifting willows, one and all had been robbed of its natural character, and revealed in something of its other aspect—as it existed across the border in that other region. And this changed aspect I felt was new not merely to me, but to the race. The whole experience whose verge we touched was unknown to humanity at all. It was a new order of experience, and in the true sense of the word *unearthly*.

"It's the deliberate, calculating purpose that reduces one's courage to zero," the Swede said suddenly, as if he had been actually following my thoughts. "Otherwise imagination might count for much. But the paddle, the canoe, the lessening food——"

"Haven't I explained all that once?" I interrupted viciously.

"You have," he answered dryly; "you have indeed."

He made other remarks too, as usual, about what he called the "plain determination to provide a victim"; but, having now arranged my thoughts better, I recognized that his was simply the cry of his frightened soul against the knowledge that he was being attacked in a vital part, and that he would be somehow taken or destroyed. The situation called for a courage and calmness of reasoning that neither of us could compass, and I have never before been so clearly conscious of two persons in me—the one that explained everything, and the other that laughed at such foolish explanations, yet was horribly afraid.

Meanwhile, in the pitchy night the fire died down and the woodpile grew small. Neither of us moved to replenish the stock, and the darkness consequently came up very close to our faces. A few feet beyond the circle of firelight it was inky black. Occasionally a stray puff of wind set the willows shivering about us, but apart from this not very welcome sound a deep and depressing silence reigned, broken only by the gurgling of the river and the humming in the air overhead.

We both missed, I think, the shouting company of the winds.

At length, at a moment when a stray puff prolonged itself as though the wind were about to rise again, I reached the point for me of saturation, the point where it was absolutely necessary to find relief in plain speech, or else to betray myself by some hysterical extravagance that must have been far worse in its effect upon both of us. I kicked the fire into a blaze, and turned to my companion abruptly. He looked up with a start.

"I can't disguise it any longer," I said; "I don't like this place, and the darkness, and the noises, and the awful feeling I get. There's something here that beats me utterly. I'm in a blue funk, and that's the plain truth. If the other shore was—different, I swear I'd be inclined to swim for it!"

The Swede's face turned very white beneath the deep tan of sun and wind. He stared straight at me and answered quietly, but his voice betrayed his huge excitement by its unnatural calmness. For the moment, at any rate, he was the strong man of the two. He was more phlegmatic, for one thing.

"It's not a physical condition we can escape from by running away," he replied, in the tone of a doctor diagnosing some grave disease; "we must sit tight and wait. There are forces close here that could kill a herd of elephants in a second as easily as you or I could squash a fly. Our only chance is to keep perfectly still. Our insignificance perhaps may save us."

I put a dozen questions into my expression of face, but

found no words. It was precisely like listening to an accurate description of a disease whose symptoms had puzzled me.

"I mean that so far, although aware of our disturbing presence, they have not *found* us—not 'located' us, as the Americans say," he went on. "They're blundering about like men hunting for a leak of gas. The paddle and canoe and provisions prove that. I think they *feel* us, but cannot actually see us. We must keep our minds quiet—it's our minds they feel. We must control our thoughts, or it's all up with us."

"Death you mean?" I stammered, icy with the horror of his suggestion.

"Worse—by far," he said. "Death, according to one's belief, means either annihilation or release from the limitations of the senses, but it involves no change of character. *You* don't suddenly alter just because the body's gone. But this means a radical alteration, a complete change, a horrible loss of oneself by substitution—far worse than death, and not even annihilation. We happen to have camped in a spot where their region touches ours, where the veil between has worn thin"— horrors! he was using my very own phrase, my actual words— "so that they are aware of our being in their neighborhood."

"But *who* are aware?" I asked.

I forgot the shaking of the willows in the windless calm, the humming overhead, everything except that I was waiting for an answer that I dreaded more than I can possibly explain.

He lowered his voice at once to reply, leaning forward a little over the fire, an indefinable change in his face that made me avoid his eyes and look down upon the ground.

"All my life," he said, "I have been strangely, vividly, conscious of another region—not far removed from our own world in one sense, yet wholly different in kind—where great things go on unceasingly, where immense and terrible personalities hurry by, intent on vast purposes compared to which earthly affairs, the rise and fall of nations, the destinies of empires, the fate of armies and continents, are all as dust in the balance; vast purposes, I mean, that deal directly with the soul, and not indirectly with mere expressions of the soul——"

"I suggest just now—" I began, seeking to stop him, feeling as though I was face to face with a madman. But he instantly overbore me with his torrent that *had* to come.

"You think," he said, "it is the spirits of the elements, and I thought perhaps it was the old gods. But I tell you now it is—*neither*. These would be comprehensible entities, for they have relations with men, depending upon them for worship or sacrifice, whereas these beings who are now about us have absolutely nothing to do with mankind, and it is mere chance that their space happens just at this spot to touch our own."

The mere conception, which his words somehow made so convincing, as I listened to them there in the dark stillness of that lonely island, set me shaking a little all over. I found it impossible to control my movements.

"And what do you propose?" I began again.

"A sacrifice, a victim, might save us by distracting them until we could get away," he went on, "just as the wolves stop to devour the dogs and give the sleigh another start. But—I see no chance of any other victim now."

I stared blankly at him. The gleam in his eyes was dreadful. Presently he continued.

"It's the willows, of course. The willows *mask* the others, but the others are feeling about for us. If we let our minds betray out fear, we're lost, lost utterly." He looked at me with an expression so calm, so determined, so sincere, that I no longer had any doubts as to his sanity. He was as sane as any man ever was. "If we can hold out through the night," he added, "we may get off in the daylight unnoticed, or rather, *undiscovered*."

"But you really think a sacrifice would——"

That gong-like humming came down very close over our heads as I spoke, but it was my friend's scared face that really stopped my mouth.

"Hush!" he whispered, holding up his hand. "Do not mention them more than you can help. Do not refer to them *by name*. To name is to reveal: it is the inevitable clue, and our only hope lies in ignoring them, in order that they may ignore us."

"Even in thought?" He was extraordinarily agitated.

"Especially in thought. Our thoughts make spirals in their world. We must keep them *out of our minds* at all costs if possible."

I raked the fire together to prevent the darkness having everything its own way. I never longed for the sun as I longed for it then in the awful blackness of that summer night.

"Were you awake all last night?" he went on suddenly.

"I slept badly a little after dawn," I replied evasively, trying to follow his instructions, which I knew instinctively were true, "but the wind, of course——"

"I know. But the wind won't account for all the noises."

"Then you heard it too?"

"The multiplying countless little footsteps I heard," he said, adding, after a moment's hesitation, "and that other sound——"

"You mean above the tent, and the pressing down upon us of something tremendous, gigantic?"

He nodded significantly.

"It was like the beginning of a sort of inner suffocation?" I said.

"Partly, yes. It seemed to me that the weight of the atmosphere had been altered—had increased enormously, so that we should be crushed."

"And *that*," I went on, determined to have it all out, pointing upwards where the gong-like note hummed ceaselessly, rising and falling like wind. "What do you make of that?"

"It's *their* sound," he whispered gravely. "It's the sound of their world, the humming in their region. The division here is so thin that it leaks through somehow. But, if you listen carefully, you'll find it's not above so much as around us. It's in the willows. It's the willows themselves humming, because here the willows have been made symbols of the forces that are against us."

I could not follow exactly what he meant by this, yet the thought and idea in my mind were beyond question the thought and idea in his. I realized what he realized, only with less power of analysis than his. It was on the tip of my tongue to tell him at last about my hallucination of the ascending figures and the moving bushes, when he suddenly thrust his face again close into mine across the firelight and began to speak in a very earnest whisper. He amazed me by his calmness and pluck, his apparent control of the situation. This man I had for years deemed unimaginative, stolid!

"Now listen," he said. "The only thing for us to do is to go on as though nothing had happened, follow our usual habits, go to bed, and so forth; pretend we feel nothing and notice nothing. It is a question wholly of the mind, and the less we think about them the better our chance of escape. Above all, don't *think*, for what you think happens!"

"All right," I managed to reply, simply breathless with his words and the strangeness of it all; "all right, I'll try, but tell me one thing more first. Tell me what you make of those hollows in the ground all about us, those sand-funnels?"

"No!" he cried, forgetting to whisper in his excitement. "I dare not, simply dare not, put the thought into words. If you have not guessed, I am glad. Don't try to. *They* have put it into my mind; try your hardest to prevent their putting it into yours."

He sank his voice again to a whisper before he finished, and I did not press him to explain. There was already just about as much horror in me as I could hold. The conversation came to an end, and we smoked our pipes busily in silence.

Then something happened, something unimportant apparently, as the way it is when the nerves are in a very great state of tension, and this small thing for a brief space gave me an entirely different point of view. I chanced to look down at my sand-shoe—the sort we used for the canoe—and something to do with the hole at the toe suddenly recalled to me the London shop where I had bought them, the difficulty the man had in fitting me, and other details of the uninteresting but practical operation. At once, in its train, followed a wholesome view of the modern skeptical world I was accustomed to move in at home. I thought of roast beef and ale, motor-cars, policemen, brass bands, and a dozen other things that proclaimed the soul of ordinariness or utility. The effect was immediate and astonishing even to myself. Psychologically, I suppose, it was simply a sudden and violent reaction after the strain of living in an atmosphere of things that to the normal consciousness must seem impossible and incredible. But, whatever the cause, it momentarily lifted the spell from my heart, and left me for the short space of a minute feeling free and utterly unafraid. I looked up at my friend opposite.

"You damned old pagan!" I cried, laughing aloud in his face. "You imaginative idiot! You superstitious idolator! You——"

I stopped in the middle, seized anew by the old horror. I tried to smother the sound of my voice as something sacrilegious. The Swede, of course, heard it too—that strange cry overhead in the darkness—and that sudden drop in the air as though something had come nearer.

He had turned ashen white under the tan. He stood bolt upright in front of the fire, stiff as a rod, staring at me.

"After that," he said in a sort of helpless, frantic way, "we must go! We can't stay now; we must strike camp this very instant and go on—down the river."

He was talking, I saw, quite wildly, his words dictated by abject terror—the terror he had resisted so long, but which had caught him at last.

"In the dark?" I exclaimed, shaking with fear after my hysterical outburst, but still realizing our position better than he did. "Sheer madness. The river's in flood, and we've only got a single paddle. Besides, we only go deeper into their country! There's nothing ahead for fifty miles but willows, willows, willows!"

He sat down again in a state of semi-collapse. The positions, by one of those kaleidoscopic changes nature loves, were suddenly reversed, and the control of our forces passed over into my hands. His mind at last had reached the point where it was beginning to weaken.

"What on earth possessed you to do such a thing?" he whispered, with awe of genuine terror in his voice and face.

I crossed round to his side of the fire. I took both his hands in mine, kneeling down beside him and looking straight into his frightened eyes.

"We'll make one more blaze," I said firmly, "and then turn in for the night. At sunrise we'll be off full speed for Komorn. Now, pull yourself together a bit, and remember your own advice about *not thinking fear*!"

He said no more, and I saw that he would agree and obey. In some measure, too, it was a sort of relief to get up and make an excursion into the darkness for more wood. We kept close together, almost touching, groping among the bushes and along the bank. The humming overhead never ceased, but seemed to me to grow louder as we increased our distance from the fire. It was shivery work!

We were grubbing away in the middle of a thickish clump of willows where some driftwood from a former flood had caught high among the branches, when my body was seized in a grip that made me half drop upon the sand. It was the Swede. He had fallen against me, and was clutching me for support. I heard his breath coming and going in short gasps.

"Look! By my soul!" he whispered, and for the first time in my experience I knew what it was to hear tears of terror in a human voice. He was pointing to the fire, some fifty feet away. I followed the direction of his finger, and I swear my heart missed a beat.

There, in front of the dim glow, *something was moving*.

I saw it through a veil that hung before my eyes like the gauze drop-curtain used at the back of a theater—hazily a little. It was neither a human figure nor an animal. To me it gave the strange impression of being as large as several animals grouped together, like horses, two or three, moving slowly. The Swede, too, got a similar result, though expressing it differently, for he thought it was shaped and sized like a clump of willow bushes, rounded at the top, and moving all over upon its surface—"coiling upon itself like smoke," he said afterwards.

"I watched it settle downwards through the bushes," he sobbed at me. "Look, by God! It's coming this way! Oh, oh!"—he gave a kind of whistling cry. *"They've found us."*

I gave one terrified glance, which just enabled me to see that the shadowy form was swinging towards us through the bushes, and then I collapsed backwards with a crash into the branches. These failed, of course, to support my weight, so that with the Swede on the top of me we fell in a struggling heap upon the sand. I really hardly knew what was happening. I was conscious only of a sort of enveloping sensation of icy fear that plucked the nerves out of their fleshy covering, twisted them this way and that, and replaced them quivering. My eyes were tightly shut; something in my throat choked me; a feeling that my consciousness was expanding, extending out into space, swiftly gave way to another feeling that I was losing it altogether, and about to die.

An acute spasm of pain passed through me, and I was aware that the Swede had hold of me in such a way that he hurt me abominably. It was the way he caught at me in falling.

But it was this pain, he declared afterwards, that saved me: it caused me to *forget them* and think of something else at the very instant when they were about to find me. It concealed my mind from them at the moment of discovery, yet just in time to evade their terrible seizing of me. He himself, he says, actually swooned at the same moment, and that was what saved him.

I only know that at a later time, how long or short is impossible to say, I found myself scrambling up out of the slippery network of willow branches, and saw my companion standing in front of me holding out a hand to assist me. I stared at him in a dazed way, rubbing the arm he had twisted for me. Nothing came to me to say, somehow.

"I lost consciousness for a moment or two," I heard him say. "That's what saved me. It made me stop thinking about them."

"You nearly broke my arm in two," I said, uttering my only connected thought at the moment. A numbness came over me.

"That's what saved *you*!" he replied. "Between us, we've managed to set them off on a false tack somewhere. The humming has ceased. It's gone—for the moment at any rate!"

A wave of hysterical laughter seized me again, and this time spread to my friend too—great healing gusts of shaking laughter that brought a tremendous sense of relief in their train. We made our way back to the fire and put the wood on so that it blazed at once. Then we saw that the tent had fallen over and lay in a tangled heap upon the ground.

We picked it up, and during the process tripped more than once and caught our feet in sand.

"It's those sand-funnels," exclaimed the Swede, when the tent was up again and the firelight lit up the ground for several yards about us. "And look at the size of them!"

All round the tent and about the fireplace where we had seen the moving shadows there were deep funnel-shaped hollows in the sand, exactly similar to the ones we had already found over the island, only far bigger and deeper, beautifully formed, and wide enough in some instances to admit the whole of my foot and leg.

Neither of us said a word. We both knew that sleep was the safest thing we could do, and to bed we went accordingly without further delay, having first thrown sand on the fire and taken the provision sack and the paddle inside the tent with us. The canoe, too, we propped in such a way at the end of the tent that our feet touched it, and the least motion would disturb and wake us.

In case of emergency, too, we again went to bed in our clothes, ready for a sudden start.

V

It was my firm intention to lie awake all night and watch, but the exhaustion of nerves and body decreed otherwise, and sleep after a while came over me with a welcome blanket of oblivion. The fact that my companion also slept quickened its approach. At first he fidgeted and constantly sat up, asking me if I "heard this" or "heard that." He tossed about his cork mattress, and said the tent was moving and the river had risen over the point of the island; but each time I went out to look I returned with the report that all was well, and finally he grew calmer and lay still. Then at length his breathing became regular and I heard unmistakable sounds of snoring—

the first and only time in my life when snoring has been a welcome and calming influence.

This, I remember, was the last thought in my mind before dozing off.

A difficulty in breathing woke me, and I found the blanket over my face. But something else besides the blanket was pressing upon me, and my first thought was that my companion had rolled off his mattress on to my own in his sleep. I called to him and sat up, and at the same moment it came to me that the tent was *surrounded*. That sound of multitudinous soft pattering was again audible outside, filling the night with horror.

I called again to him, louder than before. He did not answer, but I missed the sound of his snoring, and also noticed that the flap of the tent door was down. This was the unpardonable sin. I crawled out in the darkness to hook it back securely, and it was then for the first time I realized positively that the Swede was not there. He had gone.

I dashed out in a mad run, seized by a dreadful agitation, and the moment I was out I plunged into a sort of torrent of humming that surrounded me completely and came out of every quarter of the heavens at once. It was that same familiar humming—gone mad! A swarm of great invisible bees might have been about me in the air. The sound seemed to thicken the very atmosphere, and I felt that my lungs worked with difficulty.

But my friend was in danger, and I could not hesitate.

The dawn was just about to break, and a faint whitish light spread upwards over the clouds from a thin strip of clear horizon. No wind stirred. I could just make out the bushes and river beyond, and the pale sandy patches. In my excitement I ran frantically to and fro about the island, calling him by name, shouting at the top of my voice the first words that came into my head. But the willows smothered my voice, and the humming muffled it, so that the sound only traveled a few feet round me. I plunged among the bushes, tripping headlong, tumbling over roots, and scraping my face as I tore this way and that among the preventing branches.

Then, quite unexpectedly, I came out upon the island's

point and saw a dark figure outlined between the water and the sky. It was the Swede. And already he had one foot in the river! A moment more and he would have taken the plunge.

I threw myself upon him, flinging my arms about his waist and dragging him shorewards with all my strength. Of course he struggled furiously, making a noise all the time just like that cursed humming, and using the most outlandish phrases in his anger about "going *inside* to Them," and "taking the way of the water and the wind," and God only knows what more besides, that I tried in vain to recall afterwards, but which turned me sick with horror and amazement as I listened. But in the end I managed to get him into the comparative safety of the tent, and flung him breathless and cursing upon the mattress, where I held him until the fit had passed.

I think the suddenness with which it all went and he grew calm, coinciding as it did with the equally abrupt cessation of the humming and pattering outside—I think this was almost the strangest part of the whole business perhaps. For he just opened his eyes and turned his tired face up to me so that the dawn threw a pale light upon it through the doorway, and said, for all the world just like a frightened child:

"My life, old man—it's my life I owe you. But it's all over now anyhow. They've found a victim in our place!"

Then he dropped back upon his blankets and went to sleep literally under my eyes. He simply collapsed, and began to snore again as healthily as though nothing had happened and he had never tried to offer his own life as a sacrifice by drowning. And when the sunlight woke him three hours later—hours of ceaseless vigil for me—it became so clear to me that he remembered absolutely nothing of what he had attempted to do that I deemed it wise to hold my peace and ask no dangerous questions.

He woke naturally and easily, as I have said, when the sun was already high in a windless hot sky, and he at once got up and set about the preparation of the fire for breakfast. I followed him anxiously at bathing, but he did not attempt to plunge in, merely dipping his head and making some remark about the extra coldness of the water.

"River's falling at last," he said, "and I'm glad of it."

"The humming has stopped too," I said.

He looked up at me quietly with his normal expression. Evidently he remembered everything except his own attempt at suicide.

"Everything has stopped," he said, "because——"

He hesitated. But I knew some reference to that remark he had made just before he fainted was in his mind, and I was determined to know it.

"Because 'They've found another victim'?" I said, forcing a little laugh.

"Exactly," he answered, "exactly! I feel as positive of it as though—as though—I feel quite safe again, I mean," he finished.

He began to look curiously about him. The sunlight lay in hot patches on the sand. There was no wind. The willows were motionless. He slowly rose to his feet.

"Come," he said; "I think if we look, we shall find it."

He started off on a run, and I followed him. He kept to the banks, poking with a stick among the sandy bays and caves and little back-waters, myself always close on his heels.

"Ah!" he exclaimed presently, "ah!"

The tone of his voice somehow brought back to me a vivid sense of the horror of the last twenty-four hours, and I hurried up to join him. He was pointing with his stick at a large black object that lay half in the water and half on the sand. It appeared to be caught by some twisted willow roots so that the river could not sweep it away. A few hours before the spot must have been under water.

"See," he said quietly, "the victim that made our escape possible!"

And when I peered across his shoulder I saw that his stick rested on the body of a man. He turned it over. It was the corpse of a peasant, and the face was hidden in the sand. Clearly the man had been drowned but a few hours before, and his body must have been swept down upon our island somewhere about the hour of the dawn—*at the very time the fit had passed.*

"We must give it a decent burial, you know."

"I suppose so," I replied. I shuddered a little in spite of myself, for there was something about the appearance of that poor drowned man that turned me cold.

The Swede glanced up sharply at me, and began clambering down the bank. I followed him more leisurely. The current, I noticed, had torn away much of the clothing from the body, so that the neck and part of the chest lay bare.

Halfway down the bank my companion suddenly stopped and held up his hand in warning; but either my foot slipped, or I had gained too much momentum to bring myself quickly to a halt, for I bumped into him and sent him forward with a sort of leap to save himself. We tumbled together on to the hard sand so that our feet splashed into the water. And, before anything could be done, we had collided a little heavily against the corpse.

The Swede uttered a sharp cry. And I sprang back as if I had been shot.

At the moment we touched the body there arose from its surface the loud sound of humming—the sound of several hummings—which passed with a vast commotion as of winged things in the air about us and disappeared upwards into the sky, growing fainter and fainter till they finally ceased in the distance. It was exactly as though we had disturbed some living yet invisible creatures at work.

My companion clutched me, and I think I clutched him, but before either of us had time properly to recover from the unexpected shock, we saw that a movement of the current was turning the corpse round so that it became released from the grip of the willow roots. A moment later it had turned completely over, the dead face uppermost, staring at the sky. It lay on the edge of the main stream. In another moment it would be swept away.

The Swede started to save it, shouting again something I did not catch about a "proper burial" and then abruptly dropped upon his knees on the sand and covered his eyes with his hands. I was beside him in an instant.

I saw what he had seen.

For just as the body swung round to the current the face and the exposed chest turned full towards us, and showed plainly how the skin and flesh were indented with small hollows, beautifully formed, and exactly similar in shape and kind to the sand-funnels that we had found all over the island.

"Their mark!" I heard my companion mutter under his breath. "Their awful mark!"

And when I turned my eyes again from his ghastly face to the river, the current had done its work, and the body had been swept away into midstream and was already beyond our reach and almost out of sight, turning over and over on the waves like an otter.

Thomas M. Disch

THE ASIAN SHORE

Thomas M. Disch's "The Asian Shore" is an extraordinary work of contemporary fiction about the nature of reality, about a singular transformation that is unsettling, disturbing, perhaps horrifying. It goes one step beyond Henry James' "The Jolly Corner," portraying a unique doppelganger situation that is altogether beyond conventional psychological investigation of character. It is not a "category" story, neither supernatural nor science fiction, though it emerged originally out of SF, where it was first published. It is printed here comfortably among its kin in our third stream of horror, where it represents the ambiguous boundary of horror with existential dread. Disch is not often mentioned as a horror writer, but he has in fact a significant body of fiction in such collections as *Fun With Your New Head* (1971), *Getting Into Death* (1976), *102 H-Bombs* (1966), and the novel, *The Businessman* (1984), a body of work that seems of growing importance to the contemporary horror field.

1

There were voices on the cobbled street, and the sounds of motors. Footsteps, slamming doors, whistles, footsteps. He lived on the ground floor, so there was no way to avoid these evidences of the city's too abundant life. They accumulated in the room like so much dust, like the heaps of unanswered correspondence on the mottled tablecloth.

Every night he would drag a chair into the unfurnished back room—the guest room, as he liked to think of it—and look out over the tiled roofs and across the black waters of the Bosphorus at the lights of Üsküdar. But the sounds penetrated this room too. He would sit there, in the darkness, drinking wine, waiting for her knock on the back door.

Or he might try to read: histories, books of travel, the long dull biography of Atatürk. A kind of sedation. Sometimes he would even begin a letter to his wife:

> Dear Janice,
>   No doubt you've been wondering what's become of me these last few months. . . .

But the trouble was that once that part had been written, the frail courtesies, the perfunctory reportage, he could not bring himself to say what *had* become of him.

Voices. . . .

It was just as well that he couldn't speak the language. For a while he had studied it, taxiing three times a week to Robert College in Bebek, but the grammar, based on assumptions wholly alien to any other language he knew, with its wavering boundaries between verbs and nouns, nouns and adjectives, withstood every assault of his incorrigibly Aristotelian mind. He sat at the back of the classroom, behind the rows of American teen-agers, as sullen as convicts, as comically out of context as the machineries melting in a Dali landscape—sat there and parroted innocuous dialogues after the teacher, taking both roles in turn, first the trustful, inquisitive John, forever wandering alone and lost in the streets of Istanbul and Ankara, then the helpful, knowing Ahmet Bay. Neither of these interlocutors would admit what had become increasingly evident with each faltering word that John spoke—that he would wander these same streets for years, inarticulate, cheated, and despised.

But these lessons, while they lasted, had one great advantage. They provided an illusion of activity, an obelisk upon which the eye might focus amid the desert of each new day, something to move toward and then something to leave behind.

After the first month it had rained a great deal, and this provided him with a good excuse for staying in. He had mopped up the major attractions of the city in one week, and he persisted at sightseeing long afterward, even in doubtful weather, until at last he had checked off every mosque and ruin, every museum and cistern cited in boldface in the pages of his Hachette. He visited the cemetery of Eyüp, and he devoted an entire Sunday to the land walls, carefully searching for, though he could not read Greek, the inscriptions of the various Byzantine emperors. But more and more often on these excursions he would see the woman or the child or the woman and the child together, until he came almost to dread the sight of any woman or any child in the city. It was not an unreasonable dread.

And always, at nine o'clock, or ten at the very latest, she would come knocking at the door of the apartment. Or, if the outer door of the building had not been left ajar by the people upstairs, at the window of the front room. She knocked patiently, in little clusters of three or four raps spaced several seconds apart, never very loud. Sometimes, but only if she were in the hall, she would accompany her knocking with a few words in Turkish, usually *Yavuz! Yavuz!* He had asked the clerk at the mail desk of the consulate what this meant, for he couldn't find it in his dictionary. It was a common Turkish name, a man's name.

His name was John. John Benedict Harris. He was an American.

She seldom stayed out there for more than half an hour any one night, knocking and calling to him, or to this imaginary Yavuz, and he would remain all that while in the chair in the unfurnished room, drinking Kavak and watching the ferries move back and forth on the dark water between Kabatas and Usküdar, the European and the Asian shore.

He had seen her first outside the fortress of Rumeli Hisar. It was the day, shortly after he'd arrived in the city, that he had come out to register at Robert College. After paying his fees and inspecting the library, he had come down the hill by the wrong path, and there it had stood, mammoth and majestically improbable, a gift. He did not know its name, and his Hachette was at the hotel. There was just the raw fact of the fortress, a mass of gray stone, its towers and crenelations, the gray Bosphorus below. He angled for a photograph, but even that far away it was too big—one could not frame the whole of it in a single shot.

He left the road, taking a path through dry brush that promised to circle the fortress. As he approached, the walls reared higher and higher. Before such walls there could be no question of an assault.

He saw her when she was about fifty feet away. She came toward him on the footpath, carrying a large bundle wrapped in newspaper and bound with twine. Her clothes were the usual motley of washed-out cotton prints that all the poorer women of the city went about in, but she did not, like most other women of her kind, attempt to pull her shawl across her face when she noticed him.

But perhaps it was only that her bundle would have made this conventional gesture of modesty awkward, for after that first glance she did at least lower her eyes to the path. No, it was hard to discover any clear portent in this first encounter.

As they passed each other he stepped off the path, and she did mumble some word in Turkish. Thank you, he supposed. He watched her until she reached the road, wondering whether she would look back, and she didn't.

He followed the walls of the fortress down the steep crumbling hillside to the shore road without finding an entrance. It amused him to think that there might not be one. Between the water and the barbicans there was only a narrow strip of highway.

An absolute daunting structure.

The entrance, which did exist, was just to the side of the central tower. He paid five lire admission and another two and a half lire to bring in his camera.

Of the three principal towers, visitors were allowed to climb only the one at the center of the eastern wall that ran along the Bosphorus. He was out of condition and mounted the enclosed spiral staircase slowly. The stone steps had evidently been pirated from other buildings. Every so often he recognized a fragment of a classic entablature of a wholly inappropriate intaglio design—a Greek cross or some crude Byzantine eagle. Each footfall became a symbolic conquest: one could not ascend these stairs without becoming implicated in the fall of Constantinople.

The staircase opened out into a kind of wooden catwalk clinging to the inner wall of the tower at a height of about sixty feet. The silolike space was resonant with the coo and flutter of invisible pigeons, and somewhere the wind was playing with a metal door, creaking it open, banging it shut. Here, if he so wished, he might discover portents.

He crept along the wooden platform, both hands grasping the iron rail stapled to the stone wall, feeling just an agreeable amount of terror, sweating nicely. It occurred to him how much this would have pleased Janice, whose enthusiasm for heights had equaled his. He wondered when, if ever, he would see her again, and what she would be like. By now undoubtedly she had begun divorce proceedings. Perhaps she was already no longer his wife.

The platform led to another stone staircase, shorter than the first, which ascended to the creaking metal door. He pushed it open and stepped out amid a flurry of pigeons into the full dazzle of the noon, the wide splendor of the elevation, sunlight above and the bright bow of water beneath—and, beyond the water, the surreal green of the Asian hills, hundred-breasted Cybele. It seemed, all of this, to demand some kind of affirmation, a yell. But he didn't feel up to yelling, or large gestures. He could only admire, at this distance, the illusion of tactility, hills as flesh, an illusion that could be heightened if he laid his hands, still sweaty from his passage along the catwalk, on the rough warm stone of the balustrade.

Looking down the side of the tower at the empty road he saw her again, standing at the very edge of the water. She was looking up at him. When he noticed her she lifted both hands above her head, as though signaling, and shouted something that, even if he could have heard it properly, he would surely not have understood. He supposed that she was asking to have her picture taken, so he turned the setting ring to the fastest speed to compensate for the glare from the water. She stood directly below the tower, and there seemed no way to frame an interesting composition. He released the shutter. Woman, water, asphalt road: it would be a snapshot, not a photograph, and he didn't believe in taking snapshots.

The woman continued to call up to him, arms raised in that same hieratic gesture. It made no sense. He waved to her and smiled uncertainly. It was something of a nuisance, really. He would have preferred to have this scene to himself. One climbed towers, after all, in order to be alone.

Altin, the man who had found his apartment for him, worked as a commission agent for carpet and jewelry shops in the Grand Bazaar. He would strike up conversations with English and American tourists and advise them what to buy, and where, and how much to pay. They spent one day looking and settled on an apartment building near Taksim, the commemorative traffic circle that served the European quarter of the city as a kind of Broadway. The several banks of Istanbul demonstrated their modern character here with neon signs, and in the center of the traffic circle, life-size, Atatürk led a small but representative group of his countrymen toward their bright, Western destiny.

The apartment was thought (by Altin) to partake of this same advanced spirit: it had central heating, a sit-down toilet, a bathtub, and a defunct but prestigious refrigerator. The rent was six hundred lire a month, which came to sixty-six dollars at the official rate but only fifty dollars at the rate Altin gave. He was anxious to move out of the hotel, so he agreed to a six-month lease.

He hated it from the day he moved in. Except for the shreds of a lousy sofa in the guest room, which he obliged the landlord to remove, he left everything as he found it. Even the blurry pinups from a Turkish girlie magazine remained where they were to cover the cracks in the new plaster. He was determined to make no accommodations: he might have to live in this city; it was not required that he *enjoy* it.

Every day he picked up his mail at the consulate. He sampled a variety of restaurants. He saw the sights and made notes for his book.

On Thursdays he visited a *hamam* to sweat out the accumulated poisons of the week and to be kneaded and stomped by a masseur.

He supervised the growth of his young mustache.

He rotted, like a jar of preserves left open and forgotten on the top shelf of a cupboard.

He learned that there was a special Turkish word for the rolls of dirt that are scraped off the skin after a steambath, and another that imitated the sound of boiling water: *fuker, fuker, fuker*. Boiling water signified, to the Turkish mind, the first stages of sexual arousal. It was roughly equivalent to the stateside notion of "electricity."

Occasionally, as he began to construct his own internal map of the unpromising alleyways and ruinous staircase streets of his neighborhood, he fancied that he saw her, that same woman. It was hard to be certain. She would always be some distance away, or he might catch just a glimpse out of the corner of his eye. If it were the same woman, nothing at this stage suggested that she was pursuing him. It was, at most, a coincidence.

In any case, he could not be certain. Her face had not been unusual, and he did not have the photograph to consult, for he had spoiled the entire roll of film removing it from the camera.

Sometimes after one of these failed encounters he would feel a slight uneasiness. It amounted to no more than that.

He met the boy in Usküdar. It was during the first severe cold spell, in mid-November. His first trip across the Bosphorus, and when he stepped off the ferry onto the very soil (or, anyhow, the very asphalt) of this new continent, the largest of all, he could feel the great mass of it beckoning him toward its vast eastward vortex, tugging at him, sucking at his soul.

It had been his first intention, back in New York, to stop two months at most in Istanbul, learn the language; then into

Asia. How often he had mesmerized himself with the litany of its marvels: the grand mosques of Kayseri and Sivas, of Beysehir and Afyon Karahisar; the isolate grandeur of Ararat and then, still moving east, the shores of the Caspian; Meshed, Kabul, the Himalayas. It was all these that reached out to him now, singing, stretching forth their siren arms, inviting him to their whirlpool.

And he? He refused. Though he could feel the charm of the invitation, he refused. Though he might have wished very much to unite with them, he still refused. For he had tied himself to the mast, where he was proof against their call. He had his apartment in that city which stood just outside their reach, and he would stay there until it was time to return. In the spring he was going back to the States.

But he did allow the sirens this much—that he would abandon the rational mosque-to-mosque itinerary laid down by his Hachette and entrust the rest of the day to serendipity. While the sun still shone that afternoon they might lead him where they would.

Asphalt gave way to cobbles, and cobbles to packed dirt. The squalor here was on a much less majestic scale than in Stambul, where even the most decrepit hovels had been squeezed by the pressure of population to heights of three and four stories. In Usküdar the same wretched buildings sprawled across the hills like beggars whose crutches had been kicked out from under them, supine; through their rags of unpainted wood one could see the scabbed flesh of mud-and-wattle. As he threaded his way from one dirt street to the next and found each of them sustaining this one unvarying tone, without color, without counterpoint, he began to conceive a new Asia, not of mountains and vast plains, but this same slum rolling on perpetually across grassless hills, a continuum of drabness, of sheer dumb extent.

Because he was short and because he would not dress the part of an American, he could go through these streets without calling attention to himself. The mustache too, probably, helped. Only his conscious, observing eyes (the camera had spoiled a second roll of film and was being repaired) would have betrayed him as a tourist today. Indeed, Altin had assured him (intending, no doubt, a compliment) that as soon as he learned to speak the language he would pass for a Turk.

It grew steadily colder throughout the afternoon. The wind moved a thick veil of mist over the sun and left it there. As the mists thinned and thickened, as the flat disk of sun, sinking westward, would fade and brighten, the vagaries of light whispered conflicting rumors about these houses and their dwellers. But he did not wish to stop and listen. He already knew more concerning these things than he wanted to. He set off at a quicker pace in the supposed direction of the landing stage.

The boy stood crying beside a public fountain, a water faucet projecting from a crude block of concrete, at the intersection of two narrow streets. Five years old, perhaps six. He was carrying a large plastic bucket of water in each hand, one bright red, the other turquoise. The water had splashed over his thin trousers and bare feet.

At first he supposed the boy cried only because of the cold. The damp ground must be near to freezing. To walk on it in bare wet feet. . . .

Then he saw the slippers. They were what he would have called shower slippers, small die-stamped ovals of blue plastic with single thongs that had to be grasped between the first and second toes.

The boy would stoop over and force the thongs between his stiff, cold-reddened toes, but after only a step or two the slippers would again fall off his numb feet. With each frustrated progress more water would slop over the sides of the buckets. He could not keep the slippers on his feet, and he would not walk off without them.

With this understanding came a kind of horror, a horror of his own helplessness. He could not go up to the boy and ask him where he lived, lift him and carry him—he was so small—to his home. Nor could he scold the child's parents for having sent him out on this errand without proper shoes or winter clothes. He could not even take up the buckets and have the child lead him to his home. For each of these possibilities demanded that he be able to *speak* to the boy, and this he could not do.

What *could* he do? Offer money? As well offer him, at such a moment, a pamphlet from the U.S. Information Agency!

There was, in fact, nothing, *nothing* he could do.

The boy had become aware of him. Now that he had a sympathetic audience he let himself cry in earnest. Lowering the two buckets to the ground and pointing at these and at the slippers, he spoke pleadingly to this grown-up stranger, to this rescuer, words in Turkish.

He took a step backward, a second step, and the boy shouted at him, what message of pain or uncomprehending indignation he would never know. He turned away and ran back along the street that had brought him to this crossway. It was another hour before he found the landing stage. It had begun to snow.

As he took his seat inside the ferry he found himself glancing at the other passengers, as though expecting to find her there among them.

The next day he came down with a cold. The fever rose through the night. He woke several times, and it was always their two faces that he carried with him from the dreams, like souvenirs whose origin and purpose have been forgotten; the woman at Rumeli Hisar, the child in Usküdar: some part of his mind had already begun to draw the equation between them.

2

It was the thesis of his first book that the quiddity of architecture, its chief claim to an esthetic interest, was its arbitrariness. Once the lintels were lying on the posts, once some kind of roof had been spread across the hollow space, then anything else that might be done was gratuitous. Even the lintel and the post, the roof, the space below, these were gratuitous as well. Stated thus it was a mild enough notion; the difficulty was in training the eye to see the whole world of usual forms—patterns of brick, painted plaster, carved and carpentered wood—not as ''buildings'' and ''streets'' but as an infinite series of free and arbitrary choices. There was no place in such a scheme for orders, styles, sophistication, taste. Every artifact of the city was anomalous, unique, but living there in the midst of it all you could not allow yourself too fine a sense of this fact. If you did . . .

It had been his task, these last three or four years, to re-educate his eye and mind to just this condition, of innocence. His was the very reverse of the Romantics' aims, for he did not expect to find himself, when this ideal state of "raw" perception was reached (it never would be, of course, for innocence, like justice, is an absolute; it may be approached but never attained), any closer to nature. Nature, as such, did not concern him. What he sought, on the contrary, was a sense of the great artifice of things, of structures, of the immense interminable wall that has been built just to exclude nature.

The attention that his first book had received showed that he had been at least partially successful, but he knew (and who better?) how far short his aim had fallen, how many clauses of the perceptual social contract he had never even thought to question.

So, since it was now a matter of ridding himself of the sense of the familiar, he had had to find some better laboratory for this purpose than New York, somewhere that he could be, more naturally, an alien. This much seemed obvious to him.

It had not seemed so obvious to his wife.

He did not insist. He was willing to be reasonable. He would talk about it. He talked about it whenever they were together—at dinner, at her friends' parties (his friends didn't seem to give parties), in bed—and it came down to this, that Janice objected not so much to the projected trip as to his entire program, the thesis itself.

No doubt her reasons were sound. The sense of the arbitrary did not stop at architecture; it embraced—or it would, if he let it—all phenomena. If there were no fixed laws that governed the furbelows and arabesques out of which a city is composed, there were equally no laws (or only arbitrary laws, which is the same as none at all) to define the relationships woven into the lattice of that city, relationships between man and man, man and woman, John and Janice.

And indeed this had already occurred to him, though he had not spoken of it to her before. He had often had to stop, in the midst of some quotidian ritual like dining out, and take his bearings. As the thesis developed, as he continued to sift away layer after layer of preconception, he found himself more and more astonished at the size of the demesne that recognized the sovereignty of convention. At times he even thought he could trace in his wife's slightest gesture or in her aptest phrase or in a kiss some hint of the Palladian rule book from which it had been derived. Perhaps with practice one would be able to document the entire history of her styles— here an echo of the Gothic Revival, there an imitation of Mies.

When his application for a Guggenheim was rejected, he decided he would make the trip by himself, using the bit of money that was still left from the book. Though he saw no necessity for it, he had agreed to Janice's request for a divorce. They parted on the best of terms. She had even seen him to the boat.

The wet snow would fall for a day, two days, forming knee-deep drifts in the open spaces of the city, in paved courtyards, on vacant lots. Cold winds polished the slush of streets and sidewalks to dull-gleaming lumpy ice. The steeper hills became impassable. The snow and the ice would linger a few days and then a sudden thaw would send it all pouring down the cobbled hillside in a single afternoon, brief alpine cataracts of refuse and brown water. A patch of tolerable weather might follow this flood, and then another blizzard. Altin assured him that this was an unusually fierce winter, unprecedented.

A spiral diminishing.

A tightness.

And each day the light fell more obliquely across the white hills and was more quickly spent.

One night, returning from a movie, he slipped on the iced cobbles just outside the door of his building, tearing both knees of his trousers beyond any possibility of repair. It was the only winter suit he had brought. Altin gave him the name of a tailor who could make another suit quickly and for less money than he would have to pay for a readymade. Altin did all the bargaining with the tailor and even selected the fabric, a heavy wool-rayon blend of a sickly and slightly iridescent blue, the muted, imprecise color of the more unhappy breeds of pigeons. He understood nothing of the fine points of tailoring, and so he could not decide what it was about this suit—whether the shape of the lapels, the length of the back vent, the width of the pantlegs—that made it seem so different from other suits he had worn, so much . . . smaller. And yet it fitted his figure with the exactness one expects of a tailored suit. If he looked smaller now, and thicker, perhaps that was how he *ought* to look and his previous suits had been telling lies about him all these years. The color too performed some nuance of metamorphosis: his skin, balanced against his blue-gray sheen, seemed less "tan" than sallow. When he wore it he became, to all appearances, a Turk.

Not that he wanted to look like a Turk. Turks were, by and large, a homely lot. He only wished to avoid the other Americans who abounded here even at this nadir of the off-season. As their numbers decreased, their gregariousness grew more implacable. The smallest sign—a copy of *Newsweek* or the *Herald-Tribune*, a word of English, an airmail letter with its telltale canceled stamp—could bring them down at once in the full fury of their good-fellowship. It was convenient to have some kind of camouflage, just as it was necessary to learn their haunts in order to avoid them: Divan Yolu and Cumhuriyet Cadessi, the American Library and the consulate, as well as some eight or ten of the principal well-touristed restaurants.

Once the winter had firmly established itself he also put a stop to his sightseeing. Two months of Ottoman mosques and Byzantine rubble had brought his sense of the arbitrary to so fine a pitch that he no longer required the stimulus of the monumental. His own rooms—a rickety table, the flowered drapes, the blurry lurid pinups, the intersecting planes of walls and ceilings—could present as great a plenitude of "problems" as the grand mosques of Suleiman or Sultan Ahmet with all their mihrabs and minbers, their stalactite niches and faienced walls.

Too great a plenitude, actually. Day and night the rooms nagged at him. They diverted his attention from anything else he might try to do. He knew them with the enforced intimacy with which a prisoner knows his cell—every defect of construction, every failed grace, the precise incidence of the light at each hour of the day. Had he taken the trouble to rearrange the furniture, to put up his own prints and maps, to clean the windows and scrub the floors, to fashion some kind of bookcase (all his books remained in their two shipping cases), he might have been able to blot out these alien presences by the sheer strength of self-assertion, as one can mask bad odors with incense or the smell of flowers. But this would have been admitting defeat. It would have shown how unequal he was to his own thesis.

As a compromise he began to spend his afternoons in a café a short distance down the street on which he lived. There he would sit, at the table nearest the front window, contemplating the spirals of steam that rose from the small corolla of his tea glass. At the back of the long room, beneath the tarnished brass tea urn, there were always two old men playing backgammon. The other patrons sat by themselves and gave no indication that their thoughts were in any way different from his. Even when no one was smoking, the air was pungent with the charcoal fires of nargilehs. Conversation of any kind was rare. The nargilehs bubbled, tiny dice rattled in a leather cup, a newspaper rustled, a glass chinked against its saucer.

His red notebook always lay ready at hand on the table, and on the notebook his ballpoint pen. Once he had placed them there, he never touched them again till it was time to leave.

Though less and less in the habit of analyzing sensation and motive, he was aware that the special virtue of this café was as a bastion, the securest he possessed, against the new omnipresent influence of the arbitrary. If he sat here peacefully, observing the requirements of the ritual, a decorum as simple as the rules of backgammon, gradually the elements in the space about him would cohere. Things settled, unproblematically, into their own contours. Taking the flower-shaped glass as its center, this glass that was now only and exactly a glass of tea, his perceptions slowly spread out through the room, like the concentric ripples passing across the surface of an ornamental pond, embracing all its objects at last in a firm, noumenal grasp. Just so. The room was just what a room should be. It contained him.

He did not take notice of the first rapping on the café window, though he was aware, by some small cold contraction of his thoughts, of an infringement of the rules. The second time he looked up.

They were together. The woman and the child.

He had seen them each on several occasions since his trip to Üsküdar three weeks before. The boy once on the torn-up sidewalk outside the consulate, and another time sitting on the railing of the Karaköy bridge. Once, riding in a *dolmus* to Taksim, he had passed within a scant few feet of the woman and they had exchanged a glance of unambiguous recognition. But he had never seen them together before.

But could he be certain, now, that it *was* those two? He saw a woman and a child, and the woman was rapping with one bony knuckle on the window for someone's attention. For his? If he could have seen her face. . . .

He looked at the other occupants of the café. The backgammon players. A fat, unshaven man reading a newspaper. A dark-skinned man with spectacles and a flaring mustache. The two old men, on opposite sides of the room, puffing on nargilehs. None of them paid any attention to the woman's rapping.

He stared resolutely at his glass of tea, no longer a paradigm of its own necessity. It had become a foreign object, an artifact picked up out of the rubble of a buried city, a shard.

The woman outside continued to rap at the window. At last the owner of the café went outside and spoke a few sharp words to her. She left without making a reply.

He sat with his cold tea another fifteen minutes. Then he went out into the street. There was no sign of them. He returned the hundred yards to his apartment as calmly as he could. Once inside he fastened the chain lock. He never went back to the café.

When the woman came that night, knocking at his door, it was not a surprise.

And every night, at nine or, at the very latest, ten o'clock. *Yavuz! Yavuz!* Calling to him.

He stared at the black water, the lights of the other shore. He wondered, often, when he would give in, when he would open the door.

But it was surely a mistake. Some accidental *resemblance*. He was not Yavuz.

John Benedict Harris. An American.

If there had ever been one, if there had ever been a Yavuz.

The man who had tacked the pinups on the walls?

Two women, they might have been twins, in heavy eye make-up, garter belts, mounted on the same white horse. Lewdly smiling.

A bouffant hairdo, puffy lips. Drooping breasts with large brown nipples. A couch.

A beachball. Her skin dark. Bikini. Laughing. Sand. The water unnaturally blue.

Snapshots.

Had these ever been *his* fantasies? If not, why could he not bring himself to take them off the walls? He had prints by Piranesi. A blowup of Sagrada Familia in Barcelona. The Tchernikov sketch. He could have covered the walls.

He found himself trying to imagine this Yavuz . . . what he must be like.

3

Three days after Christmas he received a card from his wife, postmarked Nevada. Janice, he knew, did not believe in Christmas cards. It showed an immense stretch of white desert—a salt-flat, he supposed—with purple mountains in the distance, and above the purple mountains, a heavily retouched sunset. Pink. There were no figures in this landscape, or any sign of vegetation. Inside she had written:

"Merry Christmas! Janice."

The same day he received a manila envelope with a copy of *Art News*. A noncommittal note from his friend Raymond was paperclipped to the cover: "Thought you might like to see this. R."

In the back pages of the magazine there was a long and unsympathetic review of his book by F.R. Robertson. Robertson was known as an authority on Hegel's esthetics. He maintained that *Homo Arbitrans* was nothing but a conpendium of truisms and—without seeming to recognize any contradiction in this—a hopelessly muddled reworking of Hegel.

Years ago he had dropped out of a course taught by Robertson after attending the first two lectures. He wondered if Robertson could have remembered this.

The review contained several errors of fact, one misquotation, and failed to mention his central argument, which was not, admittedly, dialectical. He decided he should write a reply and laid the magazine beside his typewriter to remind himself. The same evening he spilled the better part of a bottle of wine on it, so he tore out the review and threw the magazine into the garbage with his wife's card.

The necessity for a movie had compelled him into the streets and kept him in the streets, wandering from marquee to marquee, long after the drizzle of the afternoon had thickened to rain. In New York when this mood came over him he would take in a double bill of science-fiction films or Westerns on 42nd Street, but here, though cinemas abounded in the absence of television, only the glossiest Hollywood kitsch was presented with the original soundtrack. B-movies were invariably dubbed in Turkish.

So obsessive was this need that he almost passed the man in the skeleton suit without noticing him. He trudged back and forth on the sidewalk, a sodden refugee from Halloween, followed by a small Hamelin of excited children. The rain had curled the corners of his poster (it served him now as an umbrella) and caused the inks to run. He could make out:

KIL G

STA   LDA

After Atatürk, the skeleton-suited Kiling was the principal figure of the new Turkish folklore. Every newsstand was heaped with magazines and comics celebrating his adventures, and here he was himself, or his avatar at least, advertising his latest movie. Yes, and there, down the side street, was the theater where it was playing: *Kiling Istanbulda*. Or: *Kiling in Istanbul*. Beneath the colossal letters a skull-masked Kiling threatened to kiss a lovely and obviously reluctant blonde, while on the larger poster across the street he gunned down two well-dressed men. One could not decide, on the evidence of such tableaux as these, whether Kiling was fundamentally good, like Batman, or bad, like Fantomas. So. . . .

He bought a ticket. He would find out. It was the name that intrigued him. It was, distinctly, an English name.

He took a seat four rows from the font just as the feature began, immersing himself gratefully into the familiar urban imagery. Reduced to black and white and framed by darkness, the customary vistas of Istanbul possessed a heightened reality. New American cars drove through the narrow streets at perilous speeds. An old doctor was strangled by an unseen assailant. Then for a long while nothing of interest happened. A tepid romance developed between the blond singer and the young architect, while a number of gangsters, or diplomats, tried to obtain possession of the doctor's black valise. After a confusing sequence in which four of these men were killed in an explosion, the valise fell into the hands of Kiling. But it proved to be empty.

The police chased Kiling over tiled rooftops. But this was a proof only of his agility, not of his guilt: the police can often make mistakes in these matters. Kiling entered, through a window, the bedroom of the blond singer, waking her.

Contrary to the advertising posters outside, he made no attempt to kiss her. He addressed her in a hollow bass voice. The editing seemed to suggest that Kiling was actually the young architect whom the singer loved, but as his mask was never removed, this too remained in doubt.

He felt a hand on his shoulder.

He was certain it was she and he would not turn around. Had she followed him to the theater? If he rose to leave, would she make a scene? He tried to ignore the pressure of the hand, staring at the screen where the young architect had just received a mysterious telegram. His hands gripped tightly into his thighs. His hands: the hands of John Benedict Harris.

"Mr. Harris, hello!"

A man's voice. He turned around. It was Altin.

"Altin."

Altin smiled. His face flickered. "Yes. Do you think it is anyone?"

"Anyone else?"

"Yes."

"No."

"You are seeing this movie?"

"Yes."

"It is not in English. It is in Turkish."

"I know."

Several people in nearby rows were hissing for them to be quiet. The blond singer had gone down into one of the city's large cisterns. Binbirdirek. He himself had been there. The editing created an illusion that it was larger than it actually was.

"We will come up there," Altin whispered.

He nodded.

Altin sat on his right, and Altin's friend took the seat remaining empty on his left. Altin introduced his friend in a whisper. His name was Yavuz. He did not speak English.

Reluctantly he shook hands with Yavuz.

It was difficult, thereafter, to give his full attention to the film. He kept glancing sideways at Yavuz. He was about his own height and age, but then this seemed to be true of half the men in Istanbul. An unexceptional face, eyes that glistened moistly in the half-light reflected from the screen.

Kiling was climbing up the girders of the building being constructed on a high hillside. In the distance the Bosphorous snaked past misted hills.

There was something so unappealing in almost every Turkish face. He had never been able to pin it down: some weaknesses of bone structure, the narrow cheekbones; the strong vertical lines that ran down from the hollows of the eyes to the corner of the mouth; the mouth itself, narrow, flat, inflexible. Or some subtler disharmony among all these elements.

Yavuz. A common name, the mail clerk had said.

In the last minutes of the movie there was a fight between two figures dressed in skeleton suits, a true and a false Kiling. One of them was thrown to his death from the steel beams of the unfinished building. The villain, surely—but had it been the true or the false Kiling who died? And come to think of it, which of them had frightened the singer in her bedroom, strangled the old doctor, stolen the valise?

"Did you like it?" Altin asked as they crowded toward the exit.

"Yes, I did."

"And did you understand what the people said?"

"Some of it. Enough."

Altin spoke for a while to Yavuz, who then turned to address his new friend from America in rapid Turkish.

He shook his head apologetically. Altin and Yavuz laughed.

"He says to you that you have the same suit."

"Yes, I noticed that as soon as the light came on."

"Where do you go now, Mr. Harris?"

"What time is it?"

They were outside the theater. The rain had moderated to a drizzle. Altin looked at his watch. "Seven o'clock. And a half."

"I must go home now."

"We will come with you and buy a bottle of wine. Yes?"

He looked uncertainly at Yavuz. Yavuz smiled.

And when she came tonight, knocking at his door and calling for Yavuz?

"Not tonight, Altin."

"No?"

"I am a little sick."

"Yes?"

"Sick. I have a fever. My head aches." He put his hand, mimetically, to his forehead, and as he did he *could* feel both the fever and the headache. "Some other time perhaps. I'm sorry."

Altin shrugged skeptically.

He shook hands with Altin and then with Yavuz. Clearly, they both felt they had been snubbed.

Returning to his apartment, he took an indirect route that avoided the dark side streets. The tone of the movie lingered, like the taste of a liqueur, to enliven the rhythm of cars and crowds, deepen the chiaroscuro of headlights and shop windows. Once, leaving the Eighth Street Cinema after *Jules et Jim*, he had discovered all the street signs of the Village translated into French; now the same law of magic allowed him to think that he could understand the fragmented conversation of passers-by. The meaning of an isolated phrase registered with the self-evident uninterpreted immediacy of "fact," the nature of the words mingling with the nature of things. Just so. Each knot in the net of language slipped, without any need of explication, into place. Every nuance of glance and inflection fitted, like a tailored suit, the contours of that moment, this street, the light, his conscious mind.

Inebriated by this fictive empathy, he turned into his own darker street at last and almost walked past the woman—who fitted, like every other element of the scene, so well the corner where she'd taken up her watch—without noticing her.

"You!" he said and stopped.

They stood four feet apart, regarding each other carefully. Perhaps she had been as little prepared for this confrontation as he.

Her thick hair was combed back in stiff waves from a low forehead, falling in massive parentheses to either side of her thin face. Pitted skin, flesh wrinkled in concentration around small pale lips. And tears—yes, tears—just forming in the corners of her staring eyes. With one hand she held a small parcel wrapped in newspaper and string, with the other she clutched the bulky confusion of her skirts. She wore several layers of clothing, rather than a coat, against the cold.

A slight erection stirred and tangled in the flap of his cotton underpants. He blushed. Once, reading a paperback edition of Krafft-Ebing, the same embarrassing thing had happened. That time it had been a description of necrophilia.

God, he thought, *if she notices!*

She whispered to him, lowering her gaze. To him, to Yavuz.

To come home with her . . . Why did he? . . . Yavuz, Yavuz, Yavuz . . . she needed . . . and his son. . . .

"I don't *understand* you," he insisted. "Your words make no sense to me. I am an American. My name is John Benedict Harris, not Yavuz. You're making a mistake—can't you see that?"

She nodded her head. "Yavuz."

"Not Yavuz! *Yok! Yok, yok!"*

And a word that meant "love" but not exactly that. Her hand tightened in the folds of her several skirts, raising them to show the thin, black-stockinged ankles.

"No!"

She moaned.

. . . wife . . . his home . . . Yalova . . . his life.

"Damn you, go away!"

Her hand let go her skirts and darted quickly to his shoulder, digging into the cheap cloth. Her other hand shoved the wrapped parcel at him. He pushed her back but she clung fiercely, shrieking his name: *Yavuz!* He struck her face.

She fell on the wet cobbles. He backed away. The greasy parcel was in his left hand. She pushed herself up to her feet. Tears flowed along the vertical channels from eyes to mouth. A Turkish face. Blood dripped slowly out of one nostril. She began to walk away in the direction of Taksim.

"And don't return, do you understand? Stay away from me!" His voice cracked.

When she was out of sight he looked at the parcel in his hands. He knew he ought not to open it, that the wisest course was to throw it into the nearest garbage can. But even as he warned himself, his fingers had snapped the string.

A large lukewarm doughy mass of *borek*. And an orange. The saliva sprouted in his mouth at the acrid smell of the cheese.

No!

He had not had dinner that night. He was hungry. He ate it. Even the orange.

During the month of January he made only two entries in his notebook. The first, undated, was a long extract copied from A. H. Lybyer's book on the Janissaries, the great slave-corps of the sultans, *The Government of the Ottoman Empire in the Time of Suleiman the Magnificent*. The passage read:

Perhaps no more daring experiment has been tried on a large scale upon the face of the earth than that embodied in the Ottoman Ruling Institution. Its nearest ideal analogue is found in the Republic of Plato, its nearest actual parallel in the Mamluk system of Egypt; but it was not restrained within the aristocratic Hellenic limitations of the first, and it subdued and outlived the second. In the United States of America men have risen from the rude work of the backwoods to the presidential chair, but they have done so by their own effort and not through the gradations of a system carefully organized to push them forward. The Roman Catholic Church can still train a peasant to become a pope, but it has never begun by choosing its candidates almost exclusively from families which profess a hostile religion. The Ottoman system deliberately took slaves and made them ministers of state. It took boys from the sheep-run and the plough-tail and made them courtiers and the husbands of princesses; it took young men whose ancestors had borne the Christian name for centuries and made them rulers in the greatest of Muhammadan states, and soldiers and generals in invincible armies whose chief joy it was to beat down the Cross and elevate the Crescent. It never asked its novices "Who was your father?" or "What do you know?" or even "Can you speak our tongue?" but it studied their faces and their frames and said: "You shall be a soldier and, if you show yourself worthy, a general," or "You shall be a scholar and a gentleman and, if the ability lies in you, a governor and a prime minister." Gradually disregarding the fabric of fundamental customs which is called "human nature," and those religious and social prejudices which are thought to be almost as deep as life itself, the Ottoman system took children forever from parents, discouraged family cares among its members through their most active years, allowed them no certain hold on property, gave them no definite promise that their sons and daughters would profit by their success and sacrifice, raised and lowered them with no regard for ancestry or previous distinction, taught them a strange law, ethics, and religion, and ever kept them conscious of a sword raised above their heads which might put an end at any moment to a brilliant career along a matchless path of human glory.

The second and briefer entry was dated the twenty-third of January and read as follows:

Heavy rains yesterday. I stayed in drinking. She came around at her usual hour. This morning when I put on my brown shoes to go out shopping they were wet through. Two hours to dry them out over the heater. Yesterday I wore only my sheepskin slippers—I did not leave the building once.

4

A human face is a construction, an artifact. The mouth is a little door, and the eyes are windows that look at the street, and all the rest of it, the flesh, the bone beneath, is a wall to which any manner of ornament may be affixed, gewgaws of whatever style or period one takes a fancy to—swags hung below the cheeks and chin, lines chiseled or smoothed away, a recession emphasized, a bit of vegetation here and there. Each addition or subtraction, however minor in itself, will affect the entire composition. Thus, the hair that he had trimmed a bit closer to the temples restores hegemony to the vertical elements of a face that is now noticeably *narrower*. Or is this exclusively a matter of proportion and emphasis? For he has lost weight too (one cannot stop eating regularly without some shrinkage), and the loss has been appreciable. A new darkness has given definition to the always incipient pouches below his eyes, a darkness echoed by the new hollowness of his cheeks.

But the chief agent of metamorphosis is the mustache, which has grown full enough now to obscure the modeling of his upper lip. The ends, which had first shown a tendency to droop, have developed, by his nervous habit of twisting them about his fingers, the flaring upward curve of a scimitar (or *pala*, after which in Turkey this style of mustache is named: *pala biyik*). It is this, the baroque mustache, not a face, that he sees when he looks in a mirror.

Then there is the whole question of "expression," its quickness, constancy, the play of intelligence, the characteristic "tone" and the hundreds upon hundreds of possible gradations within the range of that tone, the eyes' habits of irony and candor, the betraying tension or slackness of a lip. Yet it is scarcely necessary to go into this at all, for his face, when he sees it, or when anyone sees it, could not be said to *have* an expression. What was there, after all, for him to express?

The blurring of edges, whole days lost, long hours awake in bed, books scattered about the room like little animal corpses to be nibbled at when he grew hungry, the endless cups of tea, the tasteless cigarettes. Wine, at least, did what it was supposed to do—it took away the sting. Not that he felt the sting these days with any poignance. But perhaps without the wine he would have.

He piled the nonreturnable bottles in the bathtub, exercising in this act (if in no other) the old discrimination, the "compulsive tact" he had made so much of in his book.

The drapes were always drawn. The lights were left burning at all hours, even when he slept, even when he was out, three sixty-watt bulbs in a metal chandelier hanging just out of plumb.

Voices from the street impinged. Vendors in the morning, and the metallic screak of children. At night the radio in the apartment below, drunken arguments. Scatterings of words, like illuminated signs glimpsed driving on a thruway, at high speeds, at night.

Two bottles of wine were not enough if he started early in the afternoon, but three could make him sick.

And though the hours crawled, like wounded insects, so slowly across the floor, the days rushed by in a torrent. The sunlight slipped across the Bosphorus so quickly that there was scarcely time to rise and see it.

One morning when he woke there was a balloon on a stick propped in the dusty flower vase atop his dresser. A crude Mickey Mouse was stenciled on the bright red rubber. He left it there, bobbing in the vase, and watched it shrivel day by day, the face turning small and black and wrinkled.

The next time it was ticket stubs, two of them, from the Kabatas-Usküdar ferry.

Till that moment he had told himself it was a matter only of holding out until the spring. He had prepared himself for a siege, believing that an assault was not possible. Now he realized that he would actually have to go out there and fight.

Though it was mid-February, the weather accommodated his belated resolution with a series of bright blue days, a wholly unseasonable warmth that even tricked early blossoms from a few unsuspecting trees. He went through Topkapi once again, giving a respectful, indiscriminate and puzzled attention to the celadon ware, to golden snuffboxes, to pearly-embroidered pillows, to the portrait miniatures of the sultans, to the fossil footprint of the Prophet, to Iznik tiles, to the lot. There it was, all spread out before him, heaps and masses of it: beauty. Like a salesclerk tying price tags to items of merchandise, he would attach this favorite word of his, provisionally, to these sundry bibelots, then step back a pace or two to see how well or poorly it "matched." Was *this* beautiful? Was *that*?

Amazingly, none of it was beautiful. The priceless baubles all just sat there on their shelves, behind the thick glass, as unrespondent as the drab furniture back in his own room.

He tried the mosques: Sultan Ahmet, Beyazit, Sehazade, Yeni Camii, Laleli Camii. The old magic, the Vitruvian trinity of "commodity, firmness, and delight," had never failed him so enormously before. Even the shock of scale, the gapemouthed peasant reverence before thick pillars and high domes, even this deserted him. Go where he would through the city, he could not get out of his room.

Then the land walls, where months before he had felt himself rubbing up against the very garment of the past. He stood at the same spot where he had stood then, at the point where Mehmet the Conqueror had breached the walls. Quincunxes of granite cannonballs decorated the grass; they reminded him of the red balloon.

As a last resort he returned to Eyüp. The false spring had reached a tenuous apogee, and the February light flared with deceiving brilliance from the thousand facets of white stone blanketing the steep hillside. Small flocks of three or four sheep browsed between the graves. The turbaned shafts of marble jutted in every direction but the vertical (which it was given to the cypresses to define) or lay, higgledy-piggledy, one atop another. No walls, no ceilings, scarcely a path through the litter: this was an architecture supremely abstract. It seemed to him to have been piled up here, over the centuries, just to vindicate the thesis of his book.

And it worked. It worked splendidly. His mind and his eye came alive. Ideas and images coalesced. The sharp slanting light of the late afternoon caressed the jumbled marble with a cold careful hand, like a beautician adding the last touches to an elaborate coiffure. Beauty? Here it was. Here it was abundantly!

He returned the next day with his camera, redeemed from

the repair shop where it had languished for two months. To be on the safe side he had asked the repairman to load it for him. He composed each picture with mathematical punctilio, fussing over the depth of field, crouching or climbing atop sepulchers for a better angle, checking each shot against the reading on the light meter, deliberately avoiding picturesque solutions and easy effects. Even taking these pains he found that he'd gone through the twenty exposures in under two hours.

He went up to the small café on the top of the hill. Here, his Hachette had noted respectfully, the great Pierre Loti had been wont to come of a summer evening, to drink a glass of tea and took down the sculptured hills and through the pillars of cypress at the Fresh Waters of Europe and the Golden Horn. The café perpetuated the memory of this vanished glory with pictures and mementos. Loti, in a red fez and savage mustachios, glowered at the contemporary patrons from every wall. During the First World War, Loti had remained in Istanbul, taking the part of his friend, the Turkish sultan, against his native France.

He ordered a glass of tea from a waitress who had been got up as a harem girl. Apart from the waitress he had the café to himself. He sat on Pierre Loti's favorite stool. It was delicious. He felt right at home.

He opened his notebook and began to write.

Like an invalid taking his first walk out of doors after a long convalescence, his renascent energies caused him not only the predictable and welcome euphoria of resurrection but also a pronounced intellectual giddiness, as though by the simple act of rising to his feet he had thrust himself up to some really dangerous height. This dizziness became most acute when, in trying to draft a reply to Robertson's review, he was obliged to return to passages in his own book. Often as not what he found there struck him as incomprehensible. There were entire chapters that might as well have been written in ideograms or futhorc, for all the sense they made to him now. But occasionally, cued by some remark so irrelevant to any issue at hand as to be squeezed into an embarrassed parenthesis, he would spring off toward the most unforeseen—and undesirable—conclusions. Or rather, each of these tangents led, asymptotically, to a single conclusion: to wit, that his book, or any book he might conceive, was worthless, and worthless not because his thesis was wrong but precisely because it might be right.

There was a realm of judgment and a realm of fact. His book, if only because it was a book, existed within the bounds of the first. There was the trivial fact of its corporeality, but, in this case as in most others, he discounted that. It was a work of criticism, a systematization of judgment, and to the extent that his system was complete, its critical apparatus must be able to measure its own scales of mensuration and judge the justice of its own decree. But could it? Was not his "system" as arbitrary a construction as any silly pyramid? What was it, after all? A string of words, of more or less agreeable noises, politely assumed to correspond to certain objects and classes of objects, actions and groups of actions, in the realm of fact. And by what subtle magic was this correspondence to be verified? Why, by just the assertion that it was so!

This, admittedly, lacked clarity. It had come to him thick and fast, and it was colored not a little by cheap red wine. To fix its outlines a bit more firmly in his own mind he tried to "get it down" in his letter to *Art News*:

Sirs:

I write to you concerning F.R. Robertson's review of my book, though the few words I have to say bear but slightly upon Mr. Robertson's oracles, as slightly perhaps as these bore upon *Homo Arbitrans*.

Only this—that, as Gódel has demonstrated in mathematics, Wittgenstein in philosophy, and Duchamp, Cage, and Ashbery in their respective fields, the final statement of any system is a self-denunciation, a demonstration of how its particular little tricks are done— not by magic (as magicians have always known) but by the readiness of the magician's audience to be deceived, which readiness is the very glue of the social contract.

Every system, including my own and Mr. Robertson's, is a system of more or less interesting lies, and if one begins to call these lies into question, then one ought really to begin with the first. That is to say, with the very questionable proposition on the title page: *Homo Arbitrans* by John Benedict Harris.

Now I ask you, Mr. Robertson, what could be more improbable than that? More tentative? More arbitrary?

He sent the letter off, unsigned.

5

He had been promised his photos by Monday, so Monday morning, before the frost had thawed on the plate-glass window, he was at the shop. The same immodest anxious interest to see his pictures of Eyüp possessed him as once he had felt to see an essay or a review in print. It was as though these items, the pictures, the printed words, had the power to rescind, for a little while, his banishment to the realm of judgment, as though they said to him: "Yes, look, here we are, right in your hand. We're real, and so you must be too."

The old man behind the counter, a German, looked up mournfully to gargle a mournful *ach*. "Ach, Mr. Harris! Your pictures are not ready yet. Come back soon at twelve o'clock."

He walked through the melting streets that were, this side of the Golden Horn, jokebooks of eclecticism. No mail at the consulate, which was only to be expected. Half-past ten.

A pudding at a pudding shop. Two lire. A cigarette. A few more jokes: a bedraggled caryatid, an Egyptian tomb, a Greek temple that had been changed by some Circean wand into a butcher shop. Eleven.

He looked, in the bookshop, at the same shopworn selection of books that he had looked at so often before. Eleven-thirty. Surely, they would be ready by now.

"You are here, Mr. Harris. Very good."

Smiling in anticipation, he opened the envelope, removed the slim, warped stack of prints.

No.

"I'm afraid these aren't mine." He handed them back. He didn't want to feel them in his hand.

"What?"

"Those are the wrong pictures. You've made a mistake."

The old man put on a pair of dirty spectacles and shuffled through the prints. He squinted at the name on the envelope. "You are Mr. Harris."

"Yes, that is the name on the envelope. The envelope's all right, the pictures aren't."

"It is not a mistake."

"These are *somebody else's* snapshots. Some family picnic. You can see that."

"I myself took out the roll of film from your camera. Do you remember, Mr. Harris?"

He laughed uneasily. He hated scenes. He considered just walking out of the shop, forgetting all about the pictures. "Yes, I do remember. But I'm afraid you must have gotten that roll of film confused with another. I *didn't* take these pictures. I took pictures at the cemetery in Eyüp. Does that ring a bell?"

Perhaps, he thought, "ring a bell" was not an expression a German would understand.

As a waiter whose honesty has been called into question will go over the bill again with exaggerated attention, the old man frowned and examined each of the pictures in turn. With a triumphant clearing of his throat he laid one of the snapshots face up on the counter. "Who is that, Mr. Harris?"

It was the boy.

"Who! I . . . I don't know his name."

The old German laughed theatrically, lifting his eyes to a witnessing heaven. "It is you, Mr. Harris! It is you!"

He bent over the counter. His fingers still refused to touch the print. The boy was held up in the arms of a man whose head was bent forward as though he were examining the close-cropped scalp for lice. Details were fuzzy, the lens having been mistakenly set at infinity.

Was it his face? The mustache resembled his mustache, the crescents under his eyes, the hair falling forward. . . .

But the angle of the head, the lack of focus—there was room for doubt.

"Twenty-four lire please, Mr. Harris."

"Yes. Of course." He took a fifty-lire note from his billfold. The old man dug into a lady's plastic coin purse for change.

"Thank you, Mr. Harris."

"Yes. I'm . . . sorry."

The old man replaced the prints in the envelope, handed them across the counter.

He put the envelope in the pocket of his suit. "It was my mistake."

"Good-bye."

"Yes, good-bye."

He stood on the street, in the sunlight, exposed. Any moment either of them might come up to him, lay a hand on his shoulder, tug at his pantleg. He could not examine the prints here. He returned to the sweetshop and spread them out in four rows on a marble-topped table.

Twenty photographs. A day's outing, as commonplace as it had been impossible.

Of these twenty, three were so overexposed as to be meaningless, and should not have been printed at all. Three others showed what appeared to be islands or different sections of a very irregular coastline. They were unimaginatively composed, with great expanses of bleached-out sky and glaring water. Squeezed between these, the land registered merely as long dark blotches flecked with tiny gray rectangles of buildings. There was also a view up a steep street of wooden houses and naked wintry gardens.

The remaining thirteen pictures showed various people, and groups of people, looking at the camera. A heavyset woman in black, with black teeth, squinting into the sun—standing next to a pine tree in one picture, sitting uncomfortably on a natural stone formation in the second. An old man, dark-skinned, bald, with a flaring mustache and several days' stubble of beard. Then these two together—a very blurred print. Three little girls standing in front of a middle-aged woman, who regarded them with a pleased, proprietorial air. The same three girls grouped around the old man, who seemed to take no notice of them whatever. And a group of five men: the spread-legged shadow of the man taking this picture was roughly stenciled across the pebbled foreground.

And the woman. Alone. The wrinkled sallow flesh abraded to a smooth white mask by the harsh midday light.

Then the boy snuggling beside her on a blanket. Nearby small waves lapped at a narrow shingle.

Then these two still together with the old woman and the three little girls. The contiguity of the two women's faces suggested a family resemblance.

The figure that could be identified as himself appeared in only three of the pictures: once holding the boy in his arms; once with his arm around the woman's shoulders, while the boy stood before them scowling; once in a group of thirteen people, all of whom had appeared in one or another of the previous shots. Only the last of these three were in focus. He was one of the least noticeable figures in this group, but the mustached face smiling so rigidly into the camera was undeniably his own.

He had never seen these people, except, of course, for the woman and the boy. Though he had, hundreds of times, seen people just like them in the streets of Istanbul. Nor did he recognize the plots of grass, the stands of pine, the boulders, the shingle beach, though once again they were of such a generic type that he might well have passed such places a dozen times without taking any notice of them. Was the world of fact really as characterless as *this*? That it *was* the world of fact he never for a moment doubted.

And what had *he* to place in the balance against these evidences? A name? A face?

He scanned the walls of the sweetshop for a mirror. There was none. He lifted the spoon, dripping, from his glass of tea to regard the reflection of his face, blurred and inverted, in the concave surface. As he brought the spoon closer, the image grew less distinct, then rotated through one hundred eighty degrees to present, upright, the mirror image of his staring, dilated eyes.

He stood on the open upper deck as the ferry churned, hooting, from the deck. Like a man stepping out of doors on a blustery day, the ferry rounded the peninsular tip of the old city, leaving the quiet of the Horn for the rough wind-whitened waters of the Sea of Marmara. A cold south wind stiffened the scarlet star and crescent on the stern mast.

From this vantage the city showed its noblest silhouette: first the great gray horizontal mass of the Topkapi walls, then the delicate swell of the dome of St. Irena, which had been built (like a friend carefully chosen to demonstrate, by contrast, one's own virtues) just to point up the swaggering impossibility of the neighboring Holy Wisdom, that graceless and abstract issue of the union commemorated on every capital within by the twined monograms of the demon-emperor Justinian and his whore and consort Theodora; then, bringing both the topographic and historic sequence to an end, the proud finality of the Blue Mosque.

The ferry began to roll in the rougher water of the open sea. Clouds moved across the sun at quicker intervals to mass in the north above the dwindling city. It was four-thirty. By five o'clock he would reach Heybeli, the island identified by both Atlin and the mail clerk at the consulate as the setting of the photographs.

The airline ticket to New York was in his pocket. His bags, all but the one he would take on the plane, had been packed and shipped off in a single afternoon and morning of head-long drunken fear. Now he was safe. The certain knowledge that tomorrow he would be thousands of miles away had shored up the crumbling walls of confidence like the promise of a prophet who cannot err, Tiresias in balmy weather. Admittedly this was the shameful safety of a rout so complete that the enemy had almost captured his baggage train—but it was safety for all that, as definite as tomorrow. Indeed, this "tomorrow" was more definite, more present to his mind and senses, than the actual limbo of its preparation, just as, when a boy, he had endured the dreadful tedium of Christmas

Eve by projecting himself into the morning that would have to follow and which, when it did finally arrive, was never so real, by half, as his anticipations.

Because he was this safe, he dared today confront the enemy (if the enemy would confront *him*) head on. It risked nothing, and there was no telling what it might yield. Though if it were the *frisson* that he was after, then he should have stayed and seen the thing through to its end. No, this last excursion was more a gesture than an act, bravado rather than bravery. The very self-consciousness with which he had set out seemed to ensure that nothing really disastrous could happen. Had it not always been their strategy before to catch him unaware?

Finally, of course, he could not explain to himself why he had gone to the ferry, bought his ticket, embarked, except that each successive act seemed to heighten the delectable sense of his own inexorable advance, a sensation at once of almost insupportable tension and of dreamlike lassitude. He could no more have turned back along this path, once he had entered on it, than at the coda of a symphony he could have refused to listen. Beauty? Oh yes, intolerably! He had *never* known anything so beautiful as this.

The ferry pulled into the quay of Kinali Ada, the first of the islands. People got on and off. Now the ferry turned directly into the wind, toward Burgaz. Behind them the European coast vanished into the haze.

The ferry had left the Burgaz dock and was rounding the tiny islet of Kasik. He watched with fascination as the dark hills of Kasik, Burgaz, and Kinali slipped slowly into perfect alignment with their positions in the photograph. He could almost hear the click of the shutter.

And the other relationships between these simple sliding planes of sea and land—was there not something nearly as *familiar* in each infinitesimal shift of perspective? When he looked at these islands with his eyes half-closed, attention unfocused, he could almost . . .

But whenever he tried to take this up, however gently, between the needle-tipped compasses of analysis, it crumbled into dust.

It began to snow just as the ferry approached Heybeli. He stood at the end of the pier. The ferry was moving eastward, into the white air, toward Büyük Ada.

He looked up a steep street of wooden houses and naked wintry gardens. Clusters of snowflakes fell on the wet cobbles and melted. At irregular intervals street lamps glowed yellow in the dusk, but the houses remained dark. Heybeli was a summer resort. Few people lived here in the winter months. He walked halfway up the hill, then turned to the right. Certain details of woodwork, the proportion of a window, a sagging roof caught his attention momentarily, like the flicker of wings in the foliage of a tree twenty, fifty, a hundred yards ahead.

The houses were fewer, spaced farther apart. In the gardens snow covered the leaves of cabbages. The road wound up the hill toward a stone building. It was just possible to make out the flag waving against the gray sky. He turned onto a footpath that skirted the base of the hill. It led into the pines. The thick carpet of fallen needles was more slippery than ice. He rested his cheek against the bark of a tree and heard, again, the camera's click, systole and diastole of his heart.

He heard the water, before he saw it, lapping on the beach. He stopped. He focused. He recognized the rock. He walked toward it. So encompassing was his sense of this scene, so inclusive, that he could feel the footsteps he left behind in the snow, feel the snow slowly covering them again. He stopped.

It was here he had stood with the boy in his arms. The woman had held the camera to her eye with reverent awkwardness. He had bent his head forward to avoid looking directly into the glare of the setting sun. The boy's scalp was covered with the scabs of insect bites.

He was ready to admit that all this had happened, the whole impossible event. He did admit it. He lifted his head proudly and smiled, as though to say: *All right—and then? No matter what you do, I'm safe! Because, really, I'm not here at all. I'm already in New York.*

He laid his hands in a gesture of defiance on the outcropping of rock before him. His fingers brushed the resilient thong of the slipper. Covered with snow, the small oval of blue plastic had completely escaped his attention.

He spun around to face the forest, then round again to stare at the slipper lying there. He reached for it, thinking to throw it into the water, then drew his hand back.

He turned back to the forest. A man was standing just outside the line of the trees, on the path. It was too dark to discern any more of his features than that he had a mustache.

On his left the snowy beach ended in a wall of sandstone. To his right the path swung back into the forest, and behind him the sea dragged the shingle back and forth.

"Yes?"

The man bent his head attentively, but said nothing.

"Well, yes? Say it."

The man walked back into the forest.

The ferry was just pulling in as he stumbled up to the quay. He ran onto it without stopping at the booth to buy a ticket. Inside under the electric light he could see the tear in his trousers and a cut on the palm of his right hand. He had fallen many times, on the pine needles, over rocks in furrowed fields, on cobbles.

He took a seat by the coal stove. When his breath returned to him, he found that he was shivering violently. A boy came round with a tray of tea. He bought a glass for one lire. He asked the boy, in Turkish, what time it was. It was ten o'clock.

The ferry pulled up to the dock. The sign over the ticket book said BÜYÜK ADA. The ferry pulled away from the dock.

The ticket taker came for his ticket. He held out a ten-lire note and said, "Istanbul."

The ticket taker nodded his head, which meant no.

"*Yok.*"

"No? How much then? *Kac para?*"

"Yok. Istanbul—Yalova." He took the money offered him and gave him back in exchange eight lire and a ticket to Yalova on the Asian coast.

He had got onto a ferry going in the wrong direction. He was not returning to Istanbul, but to Yalova.

He explained, first in slow precise English, then in a desperate fragmentary Turkish, that he could not go to Yalova, that it was impossible. He produced his airline ticket, pointed at the eight o'clock departure time, but he could not remember the Turkish word for "tomorrow." Even in his desperation he could see the futility of all this: between BÜYÜK ADA and Yalova there were no more stops, and there would be no ferries returning to Istanbul that night. When he got to Yalova he would have to get off the boat.

A woman and a boy stood at the end of the wooden dock, at the base of a cone of snowy light. The lights were turned off on the middle deck of the ferry. The man who had been standing so long at the railing stepped, stiffly, down to the dock. He walked directly toward the woman and the boy. Scraps of paper eddied about his feet then, caught up in a strong gust, sailed out at a great height over the dark water.

The man nodded sullenly at the woman, who mumbled a few rapid words of Turkish. Then they set off, as they had so many times before, toward their home, the man leading the way, his wife and son following a few paces behind, taking the road along the shore.

Robert Aickman

THE HOSPICE

Robert Aickman's stories always maintain a certain level of doubt as to the nature of what is literally going on. He builds an atmosphere of growing dread and fear out of this doubt and never for a moment reveals whatever firm grounding might explain the events rationally. Horrifying things are glimpsed out of the corner of the eye but when the head turns to look at them, they are gone. This is a story of a man who has lost his way and wandered over the border into the absurd and the surreal. Both the reader and the viewpoint-character experience simultaneous disorientation and in the end more questions are raised than answered. "The Hospice" is classic Aickman, a paradigm of our third variety of horror, wherein the moral structures are deconstructed (as in Jackson's "The Summer People") and the psychological conceits unreliable—all details and every effect contribute to profound and unsettling instability suggestive of undefinable horror, which is most certainly there.

It was somewhere at the back of beyond. Maybury would have found it difficult to be more precise.

He was one who, when motoring outside his own territory, preferred to follow a route "given" by one of the automobile organizations, and, on this very occasion, as on other previous ones, he had found reasons to deplore all deviation. This time it had been the works manager's fault. The man had not only poured ridicule on the official route, but had stood at the yard gate in order to make quite certain that Maybury set off by the short cut which, according to him, all the fellows in the firm used, and which departed in the exactly opposite direction.

The most that could be said was that Maybury was presumably at the outer edge of the immense West Midlands conurbation. The outer edge it by now surely must be, as he seemed to have been driving for hours since he left the works, going round and round in large or small circles, asking the way and being unable to understand the answers (when answers were vouchsafed), all the time seemingly more off-course than ever.

Maybury looked at his watch. He *had* been driving for hours. By rights he should have been more than halfway home—considerably more. Even the dashboard light seemed feebler than usual; but by it Maybury saw that soon he would be out of petrol. His mind had not been on that particular matter of petrol.

Dark though it was, Maybury was aware of many trees, mountainous and opaque. It was not, however, that there were no houses. Houses there must be, because on both sides of the road, there were gates; broad single gates, commonly painted white: and, even where there were no gates, there were dim entrances. Presumably it was a costly nineteenth-century housing estate. Almost indentical roads seemed to curve away in all directions. The straightforward had been genteelly avoided. As often in such places, the racer-through, the taker of a short cut, was quite systematically penalized. Probably this attitude accounted also for the failure to bring the street lighting fully up-to-date.

Maybury came to a specific bifurcation. It was impossible to make any reasoned choice, and he doubted whether it mattered much in any case.

Maybury stopped the car by the side of the road, then stopped the engine in order to save the waning petrol while he thought. In the end, he opened the door and stepped out into the road. He looked upwards. The moon and stars were almost hidden by the thick trees. It was quiet. The houses were set too far back from the road for the noise of the television sets to be heard, or the blue glare thereof seen. Pedestrians are nowadays rare in such a district at any hour, but now there was no traffic either, nor sound of traffic more remote. Maybury was disturbed by the silence.

He advanced a short distance on foot, as one does at such times. In any case, he had no map, but only a route, from which he had departed quite hopelessly. None the less, even that second and locally preferred route, the one used by all the fellows, had seemed perfectly clear at the time, and as the manager had described it. He supposed that otherwise he might not have been persuaded to embark upon it; not even overpersuaded. As things were, his wonted expedient of merely driving straight ahead until one found some definite sign or other indication would be dubious, because the petrol might run out first.

Parallel with each side of each road was a narrow made-up footway, with a central gravelly strip. Beyond the strip to Maybury's left was a wilderness of vegetation, traversed by a ditch, beyond which was the hedge-line of the different properties. By the light of the occasional street-lamp, Maybury could see that sometimes there was an owner who had his hedge trimmed, and sometimes an owner who did not. It would be futile to walk any further along the road, though the air was pleasantly warm and aromatic. There were Angela and their son, Tony, awaiting him; and he must resume the fight to rejoin them.

Something shot out at him from the boskage on his left.

He had disturbed a cat, returned to its feral habitude. The first he knew of it was its claws, or conceivably its teeth, sunk into his left leg. There had been no question of ingratiation or cuddling up. Maybury kicked out furiously. The strange sequel was total silence. He must have kicked the cat a long way, because on the instant there was no hint of it. Nor had he seen the color of the cat, though there was a pool of light at that point on the footway. He fancied he had seen two flaming eyes, but he was not sure even of that. There had been no mew, no scream.

Maybury faltered. His leg really hurt. It hurt so much that

he could not bring himself to touch the limb, even to look at it in the lamplight.

He faltered back to the car, and, though his leg made difficulties even in starting it, set off indecisively down the road along which he had just walked. It might well have become a case of its being wise for him to seek a hospital. The deep scratch or bite of a cat might well hold venom, and it was not pleasant to think where the particular cat had been treading, or what it might have been devouring. Maybury again looked at his watch. It was fourteen minutes past eight. Only nine minutes had passed since he had looked at it last.

The road was beginning to straighten out, and the number of entrances to diminish, though the trees remained dense. Possibly, as so often happens, the money had run out before the full development had reached this region of the property. There were still occasional houses, with entries at long and irregular intervals. Lamp posts were becoming fewer also, but Maybury saw that one of them bore a hanging sign of some kind. It was most unlikely to indicate a destination, let alone a destination of use to Maybury, but he eased and stopped none the less, so urgently did he need a clue of some kind. The sign was shaped like a club in a pack of cards, and read:

THE HOSPICE

$$S_{O_{M_E}} \quad \text{GOOD FARE} \quad {}_{I}{}^{N}_{O}$$

ACCOMMODA^T

The modest words relating to accommodation were curved round the downward pointing extremity of the club.

Maybury decided almost instantly. He was hungry. He was injured. He was lost. He was almost without petrol.

He would enquire for dinner and, if he could telephone home, might even stay the night, though he had neither pyjamas nor electric razor. The gate, made of iron, and more suited, Maybury would have thought, to a farmyard bullpen, was, none the less, wide open. Maybury drove through.

The drive had likewise been surfaced with rather unattractive concrete, and it appeared to have been done some time ago, since there were now many potholes, as if heavy vehicles passed frequently. Maybury's headlights bounced and lurched disconcertingly as he proceeded, but suddenly the drive, which had run quite straight, again as on a modern farm, swerved, and there, on Maybury's left, was The Hospice. He realized that the drive he had come down, if indeed it had been a drive, was not the original main entrance. There was an older, more traditional drive, winding away between rhododendron bushes. All this was visible in bright light from a fixture high above the cornice of the building: almost a floodlight, Maybury thought. He supposed that a new entry had been made for the vehicles of the various suppliers when the place had become—whatever exactly it had become, a private hotel? a guest house? a club? No doubt the management aspired to cater for the occupants of the big houses, now that there were no longer servants in the world.

Maybury locked the car and pushed at the door of the house. It was a solid Victorian door, and it did not respond to Maybury's pressure. Maybury was discouraged by the need to ring, but he rang. He noticed that there was a second bell, lower down, marked NIGHT. Surely it could not yet be Night? The great thing was to get in, to feed (the works had offered only packeted sandwiches and flavourless coffee by way of luncheon), to ingratiate himself: before raising questions of petrol, whereabouts, possible accommodation for the night, a telephone call to Angela, disinfectant for his leg. He did not much care for standing alone in a strange place under the bright floodlight, uncertain what was going to happen.

But quite soon the door was opened by a lad with curly fair hair and an untroubled face. He looked like a young athlete, as Maybury at once thought. He was wearing a white jacket and smiling helpfully.

"Dinner? Yes, certainly, sir. I fear we've just started, but I'm sure we can fit you in."

To Maybury, the words brought back the seaside boarding houses where he had been taken for holidays when a boy.

Punctuality in those days had been almost as important as sobriety.

"If you can give me just a couple of minutes to wash . . ."

"Certainly, sir. This way, please."

Inside, it was not at all like those boarding houses of Maybury's youth. Maybury happened to know exactly what it *was* like. The effect was that produced by the efforts of an expensive and, therefore, rather old-fashioned furniture emporium if one placed one's whole abode and most of one's chequebook in its hands. There were hangings on all the walls, and every chair and sofa was upholstered. Colours and fabrics were harmonious but rich. The several standard lamps had immense shades. The polished tables derived from Italian originals. One could perhaps feel that a few upholstered occupants should have been designed and purveyed to harmonize also. As it was, the room was empty, except for the two of them.

The lad held open the door marked "Gentlemen" in script, but then followed Maybury in, which Maybury had not particularly expected. But the lad did not proceed to fuss tiresomely, with soap and towel, as happens sometimes in very expensive hotels, and happened formerly in clubs. All he did was stand about. Maybury reflected that doubtless he was concerned to prevent all possible delay, dinner having started.

The dining-room struck Maybury, immediately he entered, as rather too hot. The central heating must be working with full efficiency. The room was lined with hangings similar to those Maybury had seen in the hall, but apparently even heavier. Possibly noise reduction was among the objects. The ceiling of the room had been brought down in the modern manner, as if to serve the stunted; and any window or windows had disappeared behind swathes.

It is true that knives and forks make a clatter, but there appeared to be no other immediate necessity for costly noise abatement, as the diners were all extremely quiet; which at first seemed the more unexpected in that most of them were seated, fairly closely packed, at a single long table running down the central axis of the room. Maybury soon reflected, however, that if he had been wedged together with a party of otal strangers, he might have found little to say to them either.

This was not put to the test. On each side of the room were four smaller tables, set endways against the walls, every table set for a single person, even though big enough to accommodate four, two on either side; and at one of these, Maybury was settled by the handsome lad in the white jacket.

Immediately, soup arrived.

The instantaneity of the service (apart from the fact that Maybury was late) could be accounted for by the large number of the staff. There were quite certainly four men, all, like the lad, in white jackets; and two women, both in dark blue dresses. The six of them were noticeably deft and well set-up, though all were past their first youth. Maybury could not see more because he had been placed with his back to the end wall which contained the service door (as well as, on the other side, the door by which the guests entered from the lounge). At every table, the single place had been positioned in that way, so that the occupant saw neither the service door opening and shutting, nor, in front of him, the face of another diner.

As a matter of fact, Maybury was the only single diner on that side of the room (he had been given the second table down, but did not think that anyone had entered to sit behind him at the first table); and, on the other side of the room, there was only a single diner also, he thought, a lady, seated at the second table likewise, and thus precisely parallel with him.

There was an enormous quantity of soup, in what Maybury realized was an unusually deep and wide plate. The amplitude of the plate had at first been masked by the circumstance that round much of its wide rim was inscribed, in large black letters, THE HOSPICE; rather in the style of a baby's plate, Maybury thought, if both lettering and plate had not been so immense. The soup itself was unusually weighty too: it undoubtedly contained eggs as well as pulses, and steps had been taken to add "thickening" also.

Maybury was hungry, as has been said, but he was faintly disconcerted to realize that one of the middle-aged women was standing quietly behind him as he consumed the not inconsiderable number of final spoonfuls. The spoons seemed very large also, at least for modern usages. The woman removed the empty plate with a reassuring smile.

The second course was there. As she set it before him, the woman spoke confidentially in his ear of the third course: "It's turkey tonight." Her tone was exactly that in which promise is conveyed to a little boy of his favourite dish. It was as if she were Maybury's nanny; even though Maybury had never had a nanny, not exactly. Meanwhile, the second course was a proliferating elaboration of pasta; plainly homemade pasta, probably fabricated that morning. Cheese, in fairly large granules, was strewn across the heap from a large porcelain bowl without Maybury being noticeably consulted.

"Can I have something to drink? A lager will do."

"We have nothing like that, sir." It was as if Maybury knew this perfectly well, but she was prepared to play with him. There might, he thought, have been some warning that the place was unlicensed.

"A pity," said Maybury.

The woman's inflections were beginning to bore him; and he was wondering how much the rich food, all palpably fresh, and home-grown, and of almost unattainable quality, was about to cost him. He doubted very much whether it would be sensible to think of staying the night at The Hospice.

"When you have finished your second course, you may have the opportunity of a word with Mr. Falkner." Maybury recollected that, after all, he had started behind all the others. He must doubtless expect to be a little hustled while he caught up with them. In any case, he was not sure whether or not the implication was that Mr. Falkner might, under certain circumstances, unlock a private liquor store.

Obviously it would help the catching-up process if Maybury ate no more than two-thirds of the pasta fantasy. But the woman in the dark blue dress did not seem to see it like that.

"Can't you eat any more?" she enquired baldly, and no longer addressing Maybury as sir.

"Not if I'm to attempt another course," replied Maybury, quite equably.

"It's turkey tonight," said the woman. "You know how turkey just slips down you?" She still had not removed his plate.

"It's very good," said Maybury firmly. "But I've had enough."

It was as if the woman were not used to such conduct, but, as this was no longer a nursery, she took the plate away.

There was even a slight pause, during which Maybury tried to look round the room without giving an appearance of doing so. The main point seemed to be that everyone was dressed rather formally: all the men in "dark suits," all the women in "long dresses." There was a wide variety of age, but, curiously again, there were more men than women. Conversation still seemed far from general. Maybury could not help wondering whether the solidity of the diet did not contribute here. Then it occurred to him that it was as if most of these people had been with one another for a long time, during which things to talk about might have run out, and possibly with little opportunity for renewal through fresh experience. He had met that in hotels. Naturally, Maybury could not, without seeming rude, examine the one-third of the assembly which was seated behind him.

His slab of turkey appeared. He had caught up, even though by cheating. It was an enormous pile, steaming slightly, and also seeping slightly with a colourless, oily fluid. With it appeared five separate varieties of vegetable in separate dishes, brought on a tray; and a sauceboat, apparently for him alone, of specially compounded fluid, dark red and turgid. A sizeable mound of stuffing completed the repast. The middle-aged woman set it all before him swiftly but, this time, silently, with unmistakable reserve.

The truth was that Maybury had little appetite left. He gazed around, less furtively, to see how the rest were managing. He had to admit that, as far as he could see, they were one and all eating as if their lives depended on it: old as well as young, female as well as male; it was as if all had spent a long, unfed day in the hunting field. "Eating as if their lives depended on it," he said again to himself; then, struck by the absurdity of the phrase when applied to eating, he picked up his knife and fork with resolution.

"Is everything to your liking, Mr. Maybury?"

Again he had been gently taken by surprise. Mr. Falkner was at his shoulder: a sleek man in the most beautiful dinner jacket, an instantly ameliorative maître d'hôtel.

"Perfect, thank you," said Maybury. "But how did you know my name?"

"We like to remember the names of all our guests," said Falkner, smiling.

"Yes, but how did you find out *my* name in the first place?"

"We like to think we are proficient at that too, Mr. Maybury."

"I am much impressed," said Maybury. Really he felt irritated (irritated, at least), but his firm had trained him never to display irritation outside the family circle.

"Not at all," said Falkner genially. "Whatever our vocation in life, we may as well do what we can to excel." He settled the matter by dropping the subject. "Is there anything I can get for you? Anything you would like?"

"No, thank you very much. I have plenty."

"Thank *you*, Mr. Maybury. If you wish to speak to me at any time, I am normally available in my office. Now I will leave you to the enjoyment of your meal. I may tell you, in confidence, that there is steamed fruit pudding to follow."

He went quietly forward on his round of the room, speaking to perhaps one person in three at the long, central table; mainly, it seemed, to the older people, as was no doubt to be expected. Falkner wore very elegant black suède shoes, which reminded Maybury of the injury to his own leg, about which he had done nothing, though it might well be septic, even endangering the limb itself, perhaps the whole system.

He was considerably enraged by Falkner's performance about his name, especially as he could find no answer to the puzzle. He felt that he had been placed, almost deliberately, at an undignified disadvantage. Falkner's patronizing conduct in this trifling matter was of a piece with the nannying attitude of the waitress. Moreover, was the unexplained discovery of his name such a trifle, after all? Maybury felt that it had made him vulnerable in other matters also, however undefined. It was the last straw in the matter of his eating any more turkey. He no longer had any appetite whatever.

He began to pass everything systematically through his mind, as he had been trained to do; and almost immediately surmised the answer. In his car was a blue-bound file which on its front bore his name: "Mr. Lucas Maybury"; and this file he supposed that he must have left, name-upwards, on the driving seat, as he commonly did. All the same, the name was merely typed on a sticky label, and would not have been easy to make out through the car window. But he then remembered the floodlight. Even so, quite an effort had been necessary on someone's part, and he wondered who had made that effort. Again he guessed the answer: it was Falkner himself who had been snooping. What would Falkner have done if Maybury had parked the car outside the floodlighted area, as would have been perfectly possible? Used a torch? Perhaps even skeleton keys?

That was absurd.

And how much did the whole thing matter? People in business often had these little vanities, and often had he encountered them. People would do almost anything to feed them. Probably he had one or two himself. The great thing when meeting any situation was to extract the essentials and to concentrate upon them.

To some of the people Falkner was speaking for quite a period of time, while, as Maybury noticed, those seated next to them, previously saying little in most cases, now said nothing at all, but confined themselves entirely to eating. Some of the people at the long table were not merely elderly, he had observed, but positively senile: drooling, watery-eyed, and almost hairless; but even they seemed to be eating away with the best. Maybury had the horrid idea about them that eating was all they did do. "They lived for eating": another nursery expression, Maybury reflected; and at last he had come upon those of whom it might be true. Some of these people might well relate to rich foods as alcoholics relate to excisable spirits. He found it more nauseating than any sottishness; of which he had seen a certain amount.

Falkner was proceeding so slowly, showing so much professional consideration, that he had not yet reached the lady who sat by herself parallel with Maybury, on the other side of the room. At her Maybury now stared more frankly. Black hair reached her shoulders, and she wore what appeared to be a silk evening dress, a real "model," Maybury thought (though he did not really know), in many colours; but her expression was of such sadness, suffering, and exhaustion that Maybury was sincerely shocked, especially as once she must, he was sure, have been beautiful, indeed, in a way, still was. Surely so unhappy, even tragic, a figure as that could not be ploughing through a big slab of turkey with five vegetables? Without caution or courtesy, Maybury half rose to his feet in order to look.

"Eat up, sir. Why you've hardly started!" His tormentor had quietly returned to him. What was more, the tragic lady *did* appear to be eating.

"I've had enough. I'm sorry, it's very good, but I've had enough."

"You said that before, sir, and, look, here you are, still eating away." He knew that he had, indeed, used those exact words. Crises are met by clichés.

"I've eaten quite enough."

"That's not necessarily for each of us to say, is it?"

"I want no more to eat of any kind. Please take all this away and just bring me a black coffee. When the time comes, if you like. I don't mind waiting." Though Maybury did mind waiting, it was necessary to remain in control.

The woman did the last thing Maybury could have expected her to do. She picked up his laden plate (he had at least helped himself to everything) and, with force, dashed it on the floor. Even then the plate itself did not break, but gravy and five vegetables and rich stuffing spread across the thick, patterned, wall-to-wall carpet. Complete, in place of comparative, silence followed in the whole room; though there was still, as Maybury even then observed, the muted clashing of cutlery. Indeed, his own knife and fork were still in his hands.

Falkner returned round the bottom end of the long table.

"Mulligan," he asked, "how many more times?" His tone was as quiet as ever. Maybury had not realized that the alarming woman was Irish.

"Mr. Maybury," Falkner continued. "I entirely understand your difficulty. There is naturally no obligation to partake of anything you do not wish. I am only sorry for what has happened. It must seem very poor service on our part. Perhaps you would prefer to go into our lounge? Would you care simply for some coffee?"

"Yes," said Maybury, concentrating upon the essential. "I should, please. Indeed, I had already ordered a black coffee. Could I possibly have a pot of it?"

He had to step with care over the mess on the floor, looking downwards. As he did so, he saw something most curious. A central rail ran the length of the long table a few inches above the floor. To this rail, one of the male guests was attached by a fetter round his left ankle.

Maybury, now considerably shaken, had rather expected to be alone in the lounge until the coffee arrived. But he had no sooner dropped down upon one of the massive sofas (it could easily have seated five in a row, at least two of them stout) than the handsome boy appeared from somewhere and proceeded merely to stand about, as at an earlier phase of the evening. There were no illustrated papers to be seen, nor even brochures about Beautiful Britain, and Maybury found the lad's presence irksome. All the same, he did not quite dare to say, "There's nothing I want." He could think of nothing to say or to do; nor did the boy speak, or seem to have anything particular to do either. It was obvious that his presence could hardly be required there when everyone was in the dining room. Presumably they would soon be passing on to fruit pudding. Maybury was aware that he had yet to pay his bill. There was a baffled but considerable pause.

Much to his surprise, it was Mulligan who in the end brought him the coffee. It was a single cup, not a pot; and even the cup was of such a size that Maybury, for once that evening, could have done with bigger. At once he divined that coffee was outside the régime of the place, and that he was being specially compensated, though he might well have to pay extra for it. He had vaguely supposed that Mulligan would have been helping to mop up in the dining-room. Mulligan, in fact, seemed quite undisturbed.

"Sugar, sir?" she said.

"One lump, please," said Maybury, eyeing the size of the cup.

He did not fail to notice that, before going, she exchanged a glance with the handsome lad. He was young enough to be her son, and the glance might mean anything or nothing.

While Maybury was trying to make the most of his meagre coffee and to ignore the presence of the lad, who must surely be bored, the door from the dining-room opened, and the tragic lady from the other side of the room appeared.

"Close the door, will you?" she said to the boy. The boy closed the door, and then stood about again, watching them.

"Do you mind if I join you?" the lady asked Maybury.

"I should be delighted."

She was really rather lovely in her melancholy way, her dress was as splendid as Maybury had supposed, and there was in her demeanour an element that could only be called stately. Maybury was unaccustomed to that.

She sat, not at the other end of the sofa, but at the centre of it. It struck Maybury that the rich way she was dressed might almost have been devised to harmonize with the rich way the room was decorated. She wore complicated, oriental-looking earrings, with pink translucent stones, like rosé diamonds (perhaps they *were* diamonds); and silver shoes. Her perfume was heavy and distinctive.

"My name is Cécile Céliména," she said. "How do you do? I am supposed to be related to the composer, Chaminade."

"How do you do?" said Maybury. "My name is Lucas Maybury, and my only important relation is Solway Short. In fact, he's my cousin."

They shook hands. Her hand was very soft and white, and she wore a number of rings, which Maybury thought looked real and valuable (though he could not really tell). In order to shake hands with him, she turned the whole upper part of her body towards him.

"Who is that gentleman you mention?" she asked.

"Solway Short? The racing motorist. You must have seen him on the television."

"I do not watch the television."

"Quite right. It's almost entirely a waste of time."

"If you do not wish to waste time, why are you at The Hospice?"

The lad, still observing them, shifted, noticeably, from one leg to the other.

"I am here for dinner. I am just passing through."

"Oh! You are going then?"

Maybury hesitated. She was attractive and, for the moment, he did not wish to go. "I suppose so. When I've paid my bill and found out where I can get some petrol. My tank's almost empty. As a matter of fact, I'm lost. I've lost my way."

"Most of us here are lost."

"Why here? What makes you come here?"

"We come for the food and the peace and the warmth and the rest."

"A tremendous *amount* of food, I thought."

"That's necessary. It's the restorative, you might say."

"I'm not sure that I quite fit in," said Maybury. And then he added: "I shouldn't have thought that you did either."

"Oh, but I do! Whatever makes you think not?" She seemed quite anxious about it, so that Maybury supposed he had taken the wrong line.

He made the best of it. "It's just that you seem a little different from what I have seen of the others."

"In what way, different?" she asked, really anxious, and looking at him with concentration.

"To start with, more beautiful. You are very beautiful," he said, even though the lad was there, certainly taking in every word.

"That is kind of you to say." Unexpectedly she stretched across the short distance between them and took his hand. "What did you say your name was?"

"Lucas Maybury."

"Do people call you Luke?"

"No, I dislike it. I'm not a Luke sort of person."

"But your wife can't call you Lucas?"

"I'm afraid she does." It was a fishing question he could have done without.

"Lucas? Oh no, it's such a cold name." She was still holding his hand.

"I'm very sorry about it. Would you like me to order you some coffee?"

"No, no. Coffee is not right; it is stimulating, wakeful, overexciting, unquiet." She was gazing at him again with sad eyes.

"This is a curious place," said Maybury, giving her hand a squeeze. It was surely becoming remarkable that none of the other guests had yet appeared.

"I could not live without The Hospice," she replied.

"Do you come here often?" It was a ludicrously conventional form of words.

"Of course. Life would be impossible otherwise. All those people in the world without enough food, living without love, without even proper clothes to keep the cold out."

During dinner it had become as hot in the lounge, Maybury thought, as it had been in the dining-room.

Her tragic face sought his understanding. None the less, the line she had taken up was not a favourite of his. He preferred problems to which solutions were at least possible. He had been warned against the other kind.

"Yes," he said. "I know what you mean, of course."

"There are millions and millions of people all over the world with no clothes at all," she cried, withdrawing her hand.

"Not quite," Maybury said, smiling. "Not quite that. Or not yet."

He knew the risks perfectly well, and thought as little about them as possible. One had to survive, and also to look after one's dependents.

"In any case," he continued, trying to lighten the tone, "that hardly applies to you. I have seldom seen a more gorgeous dress."

"Yes," she replied with simple gravity. "It comes from Rome. Would you like to touch it?"

Naturally, Maybury would have liked, but, equally naturally, was held back by the presence of the watchful lad.

"Touch it," she commanded in a low voice. "God, what are you waiting for? Touch it." She seized his left hand again and forced it against her warm, silky breast. The lad seemed to take no more and no less notice than of anything else.

"Forget. Let go. What is life for, for God's sake?" There was a passionate earnestness about her which might rob any such man as Maybury of all assessment, but he was still essentially outside the situation. As a matter of fact, he had never in his life lost *all* control, and he was pretty sure by now that, for better or for worse, he was incapable of it.

She twisted round until her legs were extended the length of the sofa, and her head was on his lap, or more precisely on his thighs. She had moved so deftly as not even to have disordered her skirt. Her perfume wafted upwards.

"Stop glancing at Vincent," she gurgled up at him. "I'll tell you something about Vincent. Though you may think he looks like a Greek God, the simple fact is that he hasn't got what it takes, he's impotent."

Maybury was embarrassed, of course. All the same, what he reflected was that often there were horses for courses, and often no more to be said about a certain kind of situation than that one thing.

It did not matter much what he reflected, because when she had spoken, Vincent had brusquely left the room through what Maybury supposed to be the service door.

"Thank the Lord," he could not help remarking naïvely.

"He's gone for reinforcements," she said. "We'll soon see."

Where were the other guests? Where, by now, could they be? All the same, Maybury's spirits were authentically rising, and he began caressing her more intimately.

Then, suddenly, it seemed that everyone was in the room at once, and this time all talking and fussing.

She sat herself up, none to precipitately, and with her lips close to his ear, said, "Come to me later. Number 23."

It was quite impossible for Maybury to point out that he was not staying the night in The Hospice.

Falkner had appeared.

"To bed, all," he cried genially, subduing the crepitation on the instant.

Maybury, unentangled once more, looked at his watch. It seemed to be precisely ten o'clock. That, no doubt, was the point. Still, it seemed very close upon a heavy meal.

No one moved much, but no one spoke either.

"To bed, all of you," said Falkner again, this time in a tone which might almost be described as roguish. Maybury's lady rose to her feet.

All of them filtered away, Maybury's lady among them. She had spoken no further word, made no further gesture.

Maybury was alone with Falkner.

"Let me remove your cup," said Falkner courteously.

"Before I ask for my bill," said Maybury, "I wonder if you could tell me where I might possibly find some petrol at this hour?"

"Are you out of petrol?" enquired Falkner.

"Almost."

"There's nothing open at night within twenty miles. Not nowadays. Something to do with our new friends, the Arabs, I believe. All I can suggest is that I syphon some petrol from the tank of our own vehicle. It is a quite large vehicle and it has a large tank."

"I couldn't possibly put you to that trouble." In any case, he, Maybury, did not know exactly how to do it. He had heard of it, but it had never arisen before in his own life.

The lad, Vincent, reappeared, still looking pink, Maybury thought, though it was difficult to be sure with such a glowing skin. Vincent began to lock up; a quite serious process, it seemed, rather as in great-grandparental days, when prowling desperadoes were to be feared.

"No trouble at all, Mr. Maybury," said Falkner. "Vincent here can do it easily, or another member of my staff."

"Well," said Maybury, "if it would be all right . . ."

"Vincent," directed Falkner, "don't bolt and padlock the front door yet. Mr. Maybury intends to leave us."

"Very good," said Vincent, gruffly.

"Now if we could go to your car, Mr. Maybury, you could then drive it round to the back. I will show you the way. I must apologise for putting you to this extra trouble, but the other vehicle takes some time to start, especially at night."

Vincent had opened the front door for them.

"After you, Mr. Maybury," said Falkner.

Where it had been excessively hot within, it duly proved to be excessively cold without. The floodlight had been turned off. The moon had "gone in," as Maybury believed the saying was; and all the stars had apparently gone in with it.

Still, the distance to the car was not great. Maybury soon found it in the thick darkness, with Falkner coming quietly step by step behind him.

"Perhaps I had better go back and get a torch?" remarked Falkner.

So there duly was a torch. It brought to Maybury's mind the matter of the office file with his name on it, and, as he unlocked the car door, there the file was, exactly as he had supposed, and, assuredly, name uppermost. Maybury threw it across to the back seat.

Falkner's electric torch was a heavy service object which drenched a wide area in cold, white light.

"May I sit beside you, Mr. Maybury?" He closed the offside door behind him.

Maybury had already turned on the headlights, torch or no torch, and was pushing at the starter, which seemed obdurate.

It was not, he thought, that there was anything wrong with it, but rather that there was something wrong with him. The sensation was exactly like a nightmare. He had of course done it hundreds of times, probably thousands of times; but now, when after all it really mattered, he simply could not manage it, had, quite incredibly, somehow lost the simple knack of it. He often endured bad dreams of just this kind. He found time with part of his mind to wonder whether this was not a bad dream. But it was to be presumed not, since now he did not wake, as we soon do when once we realize that we are dreaming.

"I wish I could be of some help," remarked Falkner, who had shut off his torch, "but I am not accustomed to the make of car. I might easily do more harm than good." He spoke with his usual bland geniality.

Maybury was irritated again. The make of car was one of the commonest there is: trust the firm for that. All the same, he knew it was entirely his own fault that he could not make the car start, and not in the least Falkner's. He felt as if he were going mad. "I don't quite know what to suggest," he said; and added: "If, as you say, there's no garage."

"Perhaps Cromie could be of assistance," said Falkner. "Cromie has been with us quite a long time and is a wizard with any mechanical problem."

No one could say that Falkner was pressing Maybury to stay the night, or even hinting towards it, as one might expect. Maybury wondered whether the funny place was not, in fact, full up. It seemed the most likely answer. Not that Maybury wished to stay the night: far from it.

"I'm not sure," he said, "that I have the right to disturb anyone else."

"Cromie is on night duty," replied Falkner. "He is always on night duty. That is what we employ him for. I will fetch him."

He turned on the torch once more, stepped out of the car, and disappeared into the house, shutting the front door behind him, lest the cold air enter.

In the end, the front door reopened, and Falkner re-emerged. He still wore no coat over his dinner suit, and seemed to ignore the cold. Falkner was followed by a burly but shapeless and shambling figure, whom Maybury first saw indistinctly standing behind Falkner in the light from inside the house.

"Cromie will soon put things to rights," said Falkner, opening the door of the car. "Won't you, Cromie?" It was much as one speaks to a friendly retriever.

But there was little, Maybury felt, that was friendly about Cromie. Maybury had to admit to himself that on the instant he found Cromie alarming, even though, what with one thing and another, there was little to be seen of him.

"Now what exactly seems wrong, Mr. Maybury?" asked Falkner. "Just tell Cromie what it is."

Falkner himself had not attempted to re-enter the car, but Cromie forced himself in and was sprawling in the front seat, next to Maybury, where Angela normally sat. He really did seem a very big, bulging person, but Maybury decisively preferred not to look at him, though the glow cast backwards from the headlights provided a certain illumination.

Maybury could not acknowledge that for some degrading reason he was unable to operate the starter, and so had to claim there was something wrong with it. He was unable not to see Cromie's huge, badly misshapen, yellow hands, both of them, as he tugged with both of them at the knob, forcing it in and out with such violence that Maybury cried out: "Less force. You'll wreck it."

"Careful, Cromie," said Falkner from outside the car. "Most of Cromie's work is on a big scale," he explained to Maybury.

But violence proved effective, as so often. Within seconds, the car engine was humming away.

"Thank you very much," said Maybury.

Cromie made no detectable response, nor did he move.

"Come on out, Cromie," said Falkner. "Come on out of it."

Cromie duly extricated himself and shambled off into the darkness.

"Now," said Maybury, brisking up as the engine purred. "Where do we go for the petrol?"

There was the slightest of pauses. Then Falkner spoke from the dimness outside. "Mr. Maybury, I have remembered something. It is not petrol that we have in our tank. It is, of course, diesel oil. I must apologise for such a stupid mistake."

Maybury was not merely irritated, not merely scared: he was infuriated. With rage and confusion he found it impossible to speak at all. No one in the modern world could confuse diesel oil and petrol in that way. But what could he possibly do?

Falkner, standing outside the open door of the car, spoke

again. "I am extremely sorry, Mr. Maybury. Would you permit me to make some amends by inviting you to spend the night with us free of charge, except perhaps for the dinner?"

Within the last few minutes Maybury had suspected that this moment was bound to come in one form or another.

"Thank you," he said less than graciously. "I suppose I had better accept."

"We shall try to make you comfortable," said Falkner.

Maybury turned off the headlights, climbed out of the car once more, shut and, for what it was worth, locked the door, and followed Falkner back into the house. This time Falkner completed the locking and bolting of the front door that he had instructed Vincent to omit.

"I have no luggage of any kind," remarked Maybury, still very much on the defensive.

"That may solve itself," said Falkner, straightening up from the bottom bolt and smoothing his dinner jacket. "There's something I ought to explain. But will you first excuse me a moment?" He went out through the door at the back of the lounge.

Hotels really have become far too hot, thought Maybury. It positively addled the brain.

Falkner returned. "There is something I ought to explain," he said again. "We have no single rooms, partly because many of our visitors prefer not to be alone at night. The best we can do for you in your emergency, Mr. Maybury, is to offer you the share of a room with another guest. It is a large room and there are two beds. It is a sheer stroke of good luck that at present there is only one guest in the room, Mr. Bannard. Mr. Bannard will be glad of your company, I am certain, and you will be quite safe with him. He is a very pleasant person, I can assure you. I have just sent a message up asking him if he can possibly come down, so that I can introduce you. He is always very helpful, and I think he will be here in a moment. Mr. Bannard has been with us for some time, so that I am sure he will be able to fit you up with pyjamas and so forth."

It was just about the last thing that Maybury wanted from any point of view, but he had learned that it was of a kind

hat is peculiarly difficult to protest against, without somehow
utting oneself in the wrong with other people. Besides, he
upposed that he was now committed to a night in the place,
and therefore to all the implications, whatever they might be,
or very nearly so.

"I should like to telephone my wife, if I may," Maybury
said. Angela had been steadily on his mind for some time.

"I fear that's impossible, Mr. Maybury," replied Falkner.
"I'm so sorry."

"How can it be impossible?"

"In order to reduce tension and sustain the atmosphere that
our guests prefer, we have no external telephone. Only an
internal link between my quarters and the proprietors."

"But how can you run a hotel in the modern world without
a telephone?"

"Most of our guests are regulars. Many of them come
again and again, and the last thing they come for is to hear
a telephone ringing the whole time with all the strain it involves."

"They must be half round the bend," snapped Maybury,
before he could stop himself.

"Mr. Maybury," replied Falkner, "I have to remind you
of two things. The first is that I have invited you to be our
guest in the fuller sense of the word. The second is that,
although you attach so much importance to efficiency, you
none the less appear to have set out on a long journey at night
with very little petrol in your tank. Possibly you should think
yourself fortunate that you are not spending the night stranded
on some motorway."

"I'm sorry," said Maybury, "but I simply must telephone
my wife. Soon she'll be out of her mind with worry."

"I shouldn't think so, Mr. Maybury," said Falkner smiling. "Concerned, we must hope; but not quite out of her
mind."

Maybury could have hit him, but at that moment a stranger
entered.

"Ah, Mr. Bannard," said Falkner, and introduced them.
They actually shook hands. "You won't mind, Mr. Bannard,
if Mr. Maybury shares your room?"

Bannard was a slender, bony little man, of about Maybury's age. He was bald, with a rim of curly red hair. He had slightly glaucous grey-green eyes of the kind that often go with red hair. In the present environment, he was quite perky, but Maybury wondered how he would make out in the world beyond. Perhaps, however, this was because Bannard was too shrimp-like to look his best in pyjamas.

"I should be delighted to share my room with anyone," replied Bannard. "I'm lonely by myself."

"Splendid," said Falkner coolly. "Perhaps you'd lead Mr. Maybury upstairs and lend him some pyjamas? You must remember that he is a stranger to us and doesn't yet know all our ways."

"Delighted, delighted," exclaimed Bannard.

"Well, then," said Falkner. "Is there anything you would like, Mr. Maybury, before you go upstairs?"

"Only a telephone," rejoined Maybury, still recalcitrant. He simply did not believe Falkner. No one in the modern world could live without a telephone, let alone run a business without one. He had begun uneasily to wonder if Falkner had spoken the whole truth about the petrol and the diesel fuel either.

"Anything you would like that we are in a position to provide, Mr. Maybury?" persisted Falkner, with offensive specificity.

"There's no telephone *here*," put in Bannard, whose voice was noticeably high, even squeaky.

"In that case, nothing," said Maybury. "But I don't know what my wife will do with herself."

"None of us knows that," said Bannard superfluously, and cackled for a second.

"Good-night, Mr. Maybury. Thank you, Mr. Bannard."

Maybury was almost surprised to discover, as he followed Bannard upstairs, that it seemed a perfectly normal hotel, though overheated and decorated over-heavily. On the first landing was a full-size reproduction of a chieftain in scarlet tartan by Raeburn. Maybury knew the picture, because it had been chosen for the firm's calendar one year, though ever since they had used girls. Bannard lived on the second floor, where the picture on the landing was smaller, and depicted ladies and gentlemen in riding dress taking refreshments together.

"Not too much noise," said Bannard. "We have some very light sleepers amongst us."

The corridors were down to half-illumination for the night watches, and distinctly sinister. Maybury crept foolishly along and almost stole into Bannard's room.

"No," said Bannard in a giggling whisper. "Not Number 13, not yet. Number 12 A."

As a matter of fact Maybury had not noticed the number on the door that Bannard was now cautiously closing, and he did not feel called upon to rejoin.

"Do be quiet taking your things off, old man," said Bannard softly. "When once you've woken people who've been properly asleep, you can never quite tell. It's a bad thing to do."

It was a large square room, and the two beds were in exactly opposite corners, somewhat to Maybury's relief. The light had been on when they entered. Maybury surmised that even the unnecessary clicking of switches was to be eschewed.

"That's your bed," whispered Bannard, pointing jocularly.

So far Maybury had removed only his shoes. He could have done without Bannard staring at him and without Bannard's affable grin.

"Or perhaps you'd rather we did something before settling down?" whispered Bannard.

"No, thank you," replied Maybury. "It's been a long day." He was trying to keep his voice reasonably low, but he absolutely refused to whisper.

"To be sure it has," said Bannard, rising to much the volume that Maybury had employed. "Night-night then. The best thing is to get to sleep quickly." His tone was similar to that which seemed habitual with Falkner.

Bannard climbed agilely into his own bed, and lay on his back peering at Maybury over the sheets.

"Hang your suit in the cupboard," said Bannard, who had already done likewise. "There's room."

"Thank you," said Maybury. "Where do I find the pyjamas?"

"Top drawer," said Bannard. "Help yourself. They're all alike."

And, indeed, the drawer proved to be virtually filled with apparently identical suits of pyjamas.

"It's between seasons," said Bannard. "Neither proper summer, nor proper winter."

"Many thanks for the loan," said Maybury, though the pyjamas were considerably too small for him.

"The bathroom's in there," said Bannard.

When Maybury returned, he opened the door of the cupboard. It was a big cupboard and it was almost filled by a long line of (presumably) Bannard's suits.

"There's room," said Bannard once more. "Find yourself an empty hanger. Make yourself at home."

While balancing his trousers on the hanger and suspending it from the rail, Maybury again became aware of the injury to his leg. He had hustled so rapidly into Bannard's pyjamas that, for better or for worse, he had not even looked at the scar.

"What's the matter?" asked Bannard on the instant. "Hurt yourself, have you?"

"It was a damned cat scratched me," replied Maybury, without thinking very much.

But this time he decided to look. With some difficulty and some pain, he rolled up the tight pyjama leg. It was a quite nasty gash and there was much dried blood. He realized that he had not even thought about washing the wound. In so far as he had been worrying about anything habitual, he had been worrying about Angela.

"Don't show it to me," squeaked out Bannard, forgetting not to make a noise. All the same, he was sitting up in bed and staring as if his eyes would pop. "It's bad for me to see things like that. I'm upset by them."

"Don't worry," said Maybury. "I'm sure it's not as serious as it looks." In fact, he was far from sure; and he was aware also that it had not been quite what Bannard was concerned about.

"I don't want to know anything about it," said Bannard.

Maybury made no reply but simply rolled down the pyjama leg. About his injury too there was plainly nothing to be done. Even a request for Vaseline might lead to hysterics. Maybury tried to concentrate upon the reflection that if nothing worse had followed from the gash by now, then nothing worse might ever follow.

Bannard, however, was still sitting up in bed. He was looking pale. "I come here to forget things like that," he said. "We all do." His voice was shaking.

"Shall I turn the light out?" enquired Maybury. "As I'm the one who's still up?"

"I don't usually do that," said Bannard, reclining once more, none the less. "It can make things unnecessarily difficult. But there's you to be considered too."

"It's your room," said Maybury, hesitating.

"All right," said Bannard. "If you wish. Turn it out. Tonight anyway." Maybury did his injured leg no good when stumbling back to his bed. All the same, he managed to arrive there.

"I'm only here for one night," he said more to the darkness than to Bannard. "You'll be on your own again tomorrow."

Bannard made no reply, and, indeed, it seemed to Maybury as if he were no longer there, that Bannard was not an organism that could function in the dark. Maybury refrained from raising any question of drawing back a curtain (the curtains were as long and heavy as elsewhere), or of letting in a little night air. Things, he felt, were better left more or less as they were.

It was completely dark. It was completely silent. It was far too hot.

Maybury wondered what the time was. He had lost all touch. Unfortunately, his watch lacked a luminous dial.

He doubted whether he would ever sleep, but the night had to be endured somehow. For Angela it must be even harder—far harder. At the best, he had never seen himself as a first-class husband, able to provide a superfluity, eager to be protective. Things would become quite impossible, if he were to lose a leg. But, with modern medicine, that might be avoidable, even at the worst: he should be able to continue struggling on for some time yet.

As stealthily as possible he insinuated himself from between the burning blankets and sheets on to the surface of the bed. He lay there like a dying fish, trying not to make another movement of any kind.

He became almost cataleptic with inner exertion. It was not a promising recipe for slumber. In the end, he thought he could detect Bannard's breathing, far, far away. So Bannard was still there. Fantasy and reality are different things. No one could tell whether Bannard slept or waked, but it had in any case become a quite important aim not to resume general conversation with Bannard. Half a lifetime passed.

There could be no doubt, now, that Bannard was both still in the room and also awake. Perceptibly, he was on the move. Maybury's body contracted with speculation as to whether Bannard in the total blackness was making towards his corner. Maybury felt that he was only half his normal size.

Bannard edged and groped interminably. Of course Maybury had been unfair to him in extinguishing the light, and the present anxiety was doubtless no more than the price to be paid.

Bannard himself seemed certainly to be entering into the spirit of the situation: possibly he had not turned the light on because he could not reach the switch; but there seemed more to it than that. Bannard could be thought of as committed to a positive effort in the direction of silence, in order that Maybury, the guest for a night, should not be disturbed. Maybury could hardly hear him moving at all, though perhaps it was a gamble whether this was consideration or menace. Maybury would hardly have been surprised if the next event had been hands on his throat.

But, in fact, the next event was Bannard reaching the door and opening it, with vast delicacy and slowness. It was a considerable anticlimax, and not palpably outside the order of nature, but Maybury did not feel fully reassured as he rigidly watched the column of dim light from the passage slowly widen and then slowly narrow until it vanished with the faint click of the handle. Plainly there was little to worry about, after all, but Maybury had probably reached that level of anxiety where almost any new event merely causes new stress. Soon, moreover, there would be the stress of Bannard's return. Maybury half realized that he was in a grotesque condition to be so upset, when Bannard was, in fact, showing him all possible consideration. Once more he reflected that poor Angela's plight was far worse.

Thinking about Angela's plight, and how sweet, at the bottom of everything, she really was, Maybury felt more wakeful than ever, as he awaited Bannard's return, surely imminent, surely. Sleep was impossible until Bannard had returned.

But still Bannard did not return. Maybury began to wonder whether something had gone wrong with his own time faculty, such as it was; something, that is, of medical significance. That whole evening and night, from soon after his commitment to the recommended route, he had been in doubt about his place in the universe, about what people called the state of his nerves. Here was evidence that he had good reason for anxiety.

Then, from somewhere within the house, came a shattering, earpiercing scream, and then another, and another. It was impossible to tell whether the din came from near or far; still less whether it was female or male. Maybury had not known that the human organism could make so loud a noise, even in the bitterest distress. It was shattering to listen to; especially in the enclosed, hot, total darkness. And this was nothing momentary: the screaming went on and on, a paroxysm, until Maybury had to clutch at himself not to scream in response.

He fell off the bed and floundered about for the heavy curtains. Some light on the scene there must be; if possible, some new air in the room. He found the curtains within a moment, and dragged back first one, and then the other.

There was no more light than before.

Shutters, perhaps? Maybury's arm stretched out gingerly. He could feel neither wood nor metal.

The light switch. It must be found.

While Maybury fell about in the darkness, the screaming stopped on a ghoulish gurgle: perhaps as if the sufferer had vomited immensely and then passed out; or perhaps as if the sufferer had in mercy passed away altogether. Maybury continued to search.

It was harder than ever to say how long it took, but in the end he found the switch, and the immediate mystery was explained. Behind the drawn-back curtains was, as the children say, just wall. The room apparently had no window. The curtains were mere decoration.

All was silent once more: once more extremely silent. Bannard's bed was turned back as neatly as if in the full light of day.

Maybury cast off Bannard's pyjamas and, as quickly as his state permitted, resumed his own clothes. Not that he had any very definite course of action. Simply it seemed better to be fully dressed. He looked vaguely inside his pocket-book to confirm that his money was still there.

He went to the door and made cautiously to open it and seek some hint into the best thing for him to do, the best way to make off.

The door was unopenable. There was no movement in it at all. It had been locked at the least; perhaps more. If Bannard had done it, he had been astonishingly quiet about it: conceivably experienced.

Maybury tried to apply himself to thinking calmly.

The upshot was that once more, and even more hurriedly, he removed his clothes, disposed of them suitably, and resumed Bannard's pyjamas.

It would be sensible once more to turn out the light; to withdraw to bed, between the sheets, if possible; to stand by, as before. But Maybury found that turning out the light, the resultant total blackness, were more than he could face, however expedient.

Ineptly, he sat on the side of his bed, still trying to think things out, to plan sensibly. Would Bannard, after all this time, ever, in fact, return? At least during the course of that night?

He became aware that the electric light bulb had begun to crackle and fizzle. Then, with no further sound, it simply failed. It was not, Maybury thought, some final authoritative lights-out all over the house. It was merely that the single bulb had given out, however unfortunately from his own point of view: an isolated industrial accident.

He lay there, half in and half out, for a long time. He concentrated on the thought that nothing had actually happened that was dangerous. Ever since his schooldays (and, indeed, during them) he had become increasingly aware that there were many things strange to him, most of which had proved in the end to be apparently quite harmless.

Then Bannard was creeping back into the dark room. Maybury's ears had picked up no faint sound of a step in the passage, and, more remarkable, there had been no noise, either, of a turned key, let alone, perhaps, of a drawn bolt. Maybury's view of the bulb failure was confirmed by a repetition of the widening and narrowing column of light, dim, but probably no dimmer than before. Up to a point, lights were still on elsewhere. Bannard, considerate as before, did not try to turn on the light in the room. He shut the door with extraordinary skill, and Maybury could just, though only just, hear him slithering into his bed.

Still, there was one unmistakable development: at Bannard's return, the dark room had filled with perfume; the perfume favoured, long ago, as it seemed, by the lady who had been so charming to Maybury in the lounge. Smell is, in any case, notoriously the most recollective of the senses.

Almost at once, this time, Bannard not merely fell obtrusively asleep, but was soon snoring quite loudly.

Maybury had every reason to be at least irritated by everything that was happening, but instead he soon fell asleep himself. So long as Bannard was asleep, he was at least in abeyance as an active factor in the situation; and many perfumes have their own drowsiness, as Iago remarked. Angela passed temporarily from the forefront of Maybury's mind.

Then he was awake again. The light was on once more,

and Maybury supposed that he had been awakened deliberately, because Bannard was standing there by his bed. Where
and how had he found a new light bulb? Perhaps he kept a
supply in a drawer. This seemed so likely that Maybury
thought no more of the matter.

It was very odd, however, in another way also.

When Maybury had been at school, he had sometimes
found difficulty in distinguishing certain boys from certain
other boys. It had been a very large school, and boys do often
look alike. None the less, it was a situation that Maybury
thought best to keep to himself, at the time and since. He
had occasionally made responses or approaches based upon
misidentifications: but had been fortunate in never being made
to suffer for it bodily, even though he had suffered much in
his self-regard.

And now it was the same. Was the man standing there
really Bannard? One obvious thing was that Bannard had an
aureole or fringe of red hair, whereas this man's fringe was
quite grey. There was also a different expression and general
look, but Maybury was more likely to have been mistaken
about that. The pyjamas seemed to be the same, but that
meant little.

"I was just wondering if you'd care to talk for a bit," said
Bannard. One had to assume that Bannard it was; at least to
start off with. "I didn't mean to wake you up. I was just
making sure."

"That's all right, I suppose," said Maybury.

"I'm over my first beauty sleep," said Bannard. "It can
be lonely during the night." Under all the circumstances it
was a distinctly absurd remark, but undoubtedly it was in
Bannard's idiom.

"What was all that screaming?" enquired Maybury.

"I didn't hear anything," said Bannard. "I suppose I slept
through it. But I can imagine. We soon learn to take no notice. There are sleepwalkers for that matter, from time to
time."

"I suppose that's why the bedroom doors are so hard to
open?"

"Not a bit," said Bannard, but he then added, "Well,

partly, perhaps. Yes, partly. I think so. But it's just a knack really. We're not actually locked in, you know.'' He giggled. ''But what makes you ask? You don't need to leave the room in order to go to the loo. I showed you, old man.''

So it really must be Bannard, even though his eyes seemed to be a different shape, and even a different colour, as the hard light caught them when he laughed.

''I expect I was sleepwalking myself,'' said Maybury warily.

''There's no need to get the wind up,'' said Bannard, ''like a kid at a new school. All that goes on here is based on the simplest of natural principles: eating good food regularly, sleeping long hours, not taxing the overworked brain. The food is particularly important. You just wait for breakfast, old man, and see what you get. The most tremendous spread, I promise you.''

''How do you manage to eat it all?'' asked Maybury. ''Dinner alone was too much for me.''

''We simply let Nature have its way. Or rather, perhaps, *her* way. We give Nature her head.''

''But it's not *natural* to eat so much.''

''That's all you know,'' said Bannard. ''What you are, old man, is effete.'' He giggled as Bannard had giggled, but he looked somehow unlike Maybury's recollection of Bannard. Maybury was almost certain there was some decisive difference.

The room still smelt of the woman's perfume; or perhaps it was largely Bannard who smelt of it, Bannard who now stood so close to Maybury. It was embarrassing that Bannard, if he really had to rise from his bed and wake Maybury up, did not sit down; though preferably not on Maybury's blanket.

''I'm not saying there's no suffering here,'' continued Bannard. ''But where in the world are you exempt from suffering? At least no one rots away in some attic—or wretched bed-sitter, more likely. Here there are no single rooms. We all help one another. What can you and I do for one another, old man?''

He took a step nearer and bent slightly over Maybury's face. His pyjamas really reeked of perfume.

It was essential to be rid of him; but essential to do it uncontentiously. The prospect should accept the representative's point of view as far as possible unawares.

"Perhaps we could talk for just five or ten minutes more," said Maybury, "and then I should like to go to sleep again, if you will excuse me. I ought to explain that I slept very little last night owing to my wife's illness."

"Is your wife pretty?" asked Bannard. "Really pretty? With this and that?" He made a couple of gestures, quite conventional though not aforetime seen in drawing rooms.

"Of course she is," said Maybury. "What do you think?"

"Does she really turn you on? Make you lose control of yourself?"

"Naturally," said Maybury. He tried to smile, to show he had a sense of humour which could help him to cope with tasteless questions.

Bannard now not merely sat on Maybury's bed, but pushed his frame against Maybury's legs, which there was not much room to withdraw, owing to the tightness of the blanket, as Bannard sat on it.

"Tell us about it," said Bannard. "Tell us exactly what it's like to be a married man. Has it changed your whole life? Transformed everything?"

"Not exactly. In any case, I married years ago."

"So now there is someone else. *I* understand."

"No, actually there is not."

"Love's old sweet song still sings to you?"

"If you like to put it like that, yes. I love my wife. Besides, she's ill. And we have a son. There's him to consider too."

"How old is your son?"

"Nearly sixteen."

"What colour are his hair and eyes?"

"Really, I'm not sure. No particular colour. He's not a baby, you know."

"Are his hands still soft?"

"I shouldn't think so."

"Do you love your son, then?"

"In his own way, yes, of course."

"I should love him were he mine, and my wife too." It seemed to Maybury that Bannard said it with real sentiment. What was more, he looked at least twice as sad as when Maybury had first seen him: twice as old, and twice as sad. It was all ludicrous, and Maybury at last felt really tired, despite the lump of Bannard looming over him, and looking different.

"Time's up for me," said Maybury. "I'm sorry. Do you mind if we go to sleep again?"

Bannard rose at once to his feet, turned his back on Maybury's corner, and went to his bed without a word, thus causing further embarrassment.

It was again left to Maybury to turn out the light, and to shove his way back to bed through the blackness.

Bannard had left more than a waft of the perfume behind him; which perhaps helped Maybury to sleep once more almost immediately, despite all things.

Could the absurd conversation with Bannard have been a dream? Certainly what happened next was a dream: for there was Angela in her nightdress with her hands on her poor head, crying out "Wake up! Wake up! Wake up!" Maybury could not but comply, and in Angela's place, there was the boy, Vincent, with early morning tea for him. Perforce the light was on once more: but that was not a matter to be gone into.

"Good morning, Mr. Maybury."

"Good morning, Vincent."

Bannard already had his tea.

Each of them had a pot, a cup, jugs of milk and hot water, and a plate of bread and butter, all set on a tray. There were eight large triangular slices each.

"No sugar," cried out Bannard genially. "Sugar kills appetite."

Perfect rubbish, Maybury reflected; and squinted across at Bannard, recollecting his last rubbishy conversation. By the

light of morning, even if it were but the same electric light,
Bannard looked much more himself, fluffy red aureole and
all. He looked quite rested. He munched away at his bread
and butter. Maybury thought it best to go through the mo-
tions of following suit. From over there Bannard could hardly
see the details.

"Race you to the bathroom, old man," Bannard cried out.

"Please go first," responded Maybury soberly. As he had
no means of conveying the bread and butter off the premises,
he hoped, with the aid of the towel, to conceal it in his skimpy
pyjamas jacket, and push it down the water closet. Even Bannard would probably not attempt to throw his arms round
him and so uncover the offence.

Down in the lounge, there they all were, with Falkner pre-
siding indefinably but genially. Wan though authentic sunlight trickled in from the outer world, but Maybury observed
that the front door was still bolted and chained. It was the
first thing he looked for. Universal expectation was detectable: of breakfast, Maybury assumed. Bannard, at all times
shrimpish, was simply lost in the throng. Cécile he could not
see, but he made a point of not looking very hard. In any
case, several of the people looked new, or at least different.
Possibly it was a further example of the phenomenon Maybury had encountered with Bannard.

Falkner crossed to him at once: the recalcitrant but still
privileged outsider. "I can promise you a good breakfast,
Mr. Maybury," he said confidentially. "Lentils. Fresh fish.
Rump steak. Apple pie made by ourselves, with lots and lots
of cream."

"I mustn't stay for it," said Maybury. "I simply mustn't.
I have my living to earn. I must go at once."

He was quite prepared to walk a couple of miles; indeed,
all set for it. The automobile organisation, which had given
him the route from which he should never have diverged,
could recover his car. They had done it for him before, several times.

A faint shadow passed over Falkner's face, but he merely
said in a low voice, "If you really insist, Mr. Maybury—"

"I'm afraid I have to," said Maybury.

"Then I'll have a word with you in a moment."

None of the others seemed to concern themselves. Soon they all filed off, talking quietly among themselves, or, in many cases, saying nothing.

"Mr. Maybury," said Falkner, "you can respect a confidence?"

"Yes," said Maybury steadily.

"There was an incident here last night. A death. We do not talk about such things. Our guests do not expect it."

"I am sorry," said Maybury.

"Such things still upset me," said Falkner. "None the less I must not think about that. My immediate task is to dispose of the body. While the guests are preoccupied. To spare them all knowledge, all pain."

"How is that to be done?" enquired Maybury.

"In the usual manner, Mr. Maybury. The hearse is drawing up outside the door even as we speak. Where you are concerned, the point is this. If you wish for what in other circumstances I could call a lift, I could arrange for you to join the vehicle. It is travelling quite a distance. We find that best." Falkner was progressively unfastening the front door. "It seems the best solution, don't you think, Mr. Maybury? At least it is the best I can offer. Though you will not be able to thank Mr. Bannard, of course."

A coffin was already coming down the stairs, borne on the shoulders of four men in black, with Vincent, in his white jacket, coming first, in order to leave no doubt of the way and to prevent any loss of time.

"I agree," said Maybury. "I accept. Perhaps you would let me know my bill for dinner?"

"I shall waive that too, Mr. Maybury," replied Falkner, "in the present circumstances. We have a duty to hasten. We have others to think of. I shall simply say how glad we have all been to have you with us." He held out his hand. "Goodbye, Mr. Maybury."

Maybury was compelled to travel with the coffin itself, because there simply was not room for him on the front seat, where a director of the firm, a corpulent man, had to be accommodated with the driver. The nearness of death compelled a respectful silence among the company in the rear compartment, especially when a living stranger was in the midst; and Maybury alighted unobtrusively when a bus stop was reached. One of the undertaker's men said that he should not have to wait long.

Philip K. Dick

A LITTLE SOMETHING FOR US TEMPUNAUTS

Philip K. Dick was often regarded as the greatest science fiction writer in English during the 1960s and 1970s. Many of his most famous novels and stories are in the horror mode—yet he is rarely discussed as a horror writer of great powers and achievement—worthy of a place beside Robert Aickman and at the same time a legitimate heir of Robert W. Chambers and Ambrose Bierce. Science fiction has a long tradition of stories that question the nature of reality but none is more disturbing than "A Little Something for Us Tempunauts," written at the height of Dick's career. Bodies of work from such writers as Dick and Wolfe and Disch in the SF field in recent decades demand the broadening of the older definitions of horror literature, and require discarding criteria based on content in favor of the effect itself.

Wearily, Addison Doug plodded up the long path of synthetic redwood rounds, step by step, his head down a little, moving as if he were in actual physical pain. The girl watched him, wanting to help him, hurt within her to see how worn and unhappy he was, but at the same time she rejoiced that he was there at all. On and on, toward her, without glancing up, going by feel . . . like he's done this many times, she thought suddenly. Knows the way too well. Why?

"Addi," she called, and ran toward him. "They said on the TV you were dead. All of you were killed!"

He paused, wiping back his dark hair which was no longer long; just before launch they had cropped it. But he had evidently forgotten. "You believe everything you see on TV?" he said, and came on again, haltingly, but smiling now. And reaching up for her.

God, it felt good to hold him, and to have him clutch at her again, with more strength than she had expected. "I was going to find somebody else," she gasped. "To replace you."

"I'll knock your head off if you do," he said. "Anyhow, that isn't possible; nobody could replace me."

"But what about the implosion?" she said. "On re-entry, they said—"

"I forget," Addison said, in the tone he used when he meant, I'm not going to discuss it. The tone had always angered her before, but not now. This time she sensed how awful the memory was. "I'm going to stay at your place a couple days," he said, as together they moved up the path toward the open front door of the tilted A-frame house. "If that's okay. And Benz and Crayne will be joining me, later on; maybe even as soon as tonight. We've got a lot to talk over and figure out."

"Then all three of you survived." She gazed up into his careworn face. "Everything they said on TV . . ." She understood, then. Or believed she did. "It was a cover story. For—political purposes, to fool the Russians. Right? I mean, the Soviet Union'll think the launch was a failure because on re-entry—"

"No," he said. "A chrononaut will be joining us, most likely. To help figure out what happened. General Toad said one of them is already on his way here; they got clearance already. Because of the gravity of the situation."

"Jesus," the girl said, stricken. "Then who's the cover story for?"

"Let's have something to drink," Addison said. "And then I'll outline it all for you."

"Only thing I've got at the moment is California brandy."

Addison Doug said, "I'd drink anything right now, the way I feel." He dropped to the couch, leaned back, and sighed a ragged, distressed sigh, as the girl hurriedly began fixing both of them a drink.

The FM-radio in the car yammered, ". . . grieves at the stricken turn of events precipitating out of an unheralded . . ."

"Official nonsense babble," Crayne said, shutting off the radio. He and Benz were having trouble finding the house, having only been there once before. It struck Crayne that this was a somewhat informal way of convening a conference of this importance, meeting at Addison's chick's pad out here in the boondocks of Ojai. On the other hand, they wouldn't be pestered by the curious. And they probably didn't have much time. But that was hard to say; about that no one knew for sure.

The hills on both sides of the road had once been forests, Crayne observed. Now housing tracts and their melted, irregular, plastic roads marred every rise in sight. "I'll bet this was nice once," he said to Benz, who was driving.

"The Los Padres National Forest is near here," Benz said. "I got lost in there when I was eight. For hours I was sure a rattler would get me. Every stick was a snake."

"The rattler's got you now," Crayne said.

"All of us," Benz said.

"You know," Crayne said, "it's a hell of an experience to be dead."

"Speak for yourself."

"But technically—"

"If you listen to the radio and TV." Benz turned toward him, his big gnome face bleak with admonishing sternness. "We're no more dead than anyone else on the planet. The difference for us is that our death date is in the past, whereas everyone else's is set somewhere at an uncertain time in the future. Actually, some people have it pretty damn well set, like people in cancer wards; they're as certain as we are. More so. For example, how long can we stay here before we go back? We have a margin, a latitude that a terminal cancer victim doesn't have."

Crayne said caustically, "The next thing you'll be telling us to cheer us up is that we're in no pain."

"Addi is. I watched him lurch off earlier today. He's got it psychosomatically—made it into a physical complaint. Like God's kneeling on his neck; you know, carrying a much-too-great burden that's unfair, only he won't complain out loud . . . just points now and then at the nail hole in his hand." He grinned.

"Addi has got more to live for than we do."

"Every man has more to live for than any other man. I don't have a cute chick to sleep with, but I'd like to see the semi's rolling along the Riverside Freeway at sunset a few more times. It's not what you have to live for; it's that you want to live to see it, to be there—that's what is so damn sad."

They rode on in silence.

In the quiet living room of the girl's house the three tempunauts sat around smoking, taking it easy; Addison Doug thought to himself that the girl looked unusually foxy and desirable in her stretched-tight white sweater and micro-skirt and he wished, wistfully, that she looked a little less interesting. He could not really afford to get embroiled in such stuff at this point. He was too tired.

"Does she know," Benz said, indicating the girl, "what this is all about? I mean, can we talk openly? It won't wipe her out?"

"I haven't explained it to her yet," Addison said.

"You goddam well better," Crayne said.

"What is it?" the girl said, stricken, sitting upright with one hand directly between her breasts. As if clutching at a religious artifact that isn't there, Addison thought.

"We got snuffed on re-entry," Benz said. He was, really, the cruelest of the three. Or at least the most blunt. "You see, Miss . . ."

"Hawkins," the girl whispered.

"Glad to meet you, Miss Hawkins." Benz surveyed her in his cold, lazy fashion. "You have a first name?"

"Merry Lou."

"Okay, Merry Lou," Benz said. To the other two men he observed, "Sounds like the name a waitress has stitched on her blouse. Merry Lou's my name and I'll be serving you dinner and breakfast and lunch and dinner and breakfast for the next few days or however long it is before you all give up and go back to your own time; that'll be fifty-three dollars and eight cents, please, not including tip. And I hope y'all never come back, y'hear?" His voice had begun to shake; his cigarette, too. "Sorry, Miss Hawkins," he said then. "We're all screwed up by the implosion at re-entry time. As soon as we got here in ETA we learned about it. We've known longer than anyone else; we knew as soon as we hit Emergence Time."

"But there's nothing we could do," Crayne said.

"There's nothing anyone can do," Addison said to her, and put his arm around her. It felt like a déjà vu thing but then it hit him. *We're in a closed time loop,* he thought, *we keep going through this again and again, trying to solve the re-entry problem, each time imagining it's the first time, the only time . . . and never succeeding. Which attempt is this? Maybe the millionth; we have sat here a million times, raking the same facts over and over again and getting nowhere.* He felt bony-weary, thinking that. *And he felt a sort of vast philosophical hate toward all other men, who did not have this enigma to deal with. We all go to one place,* he thought, *as the Bible says. But . . . for the three of us, we have been there already. Are lying there now. So it's wrong to ask us to stand around on the surface of Earth afterward and argue and worry about it and try to figure out what malfunctioned. That should be, rightly, for our heirs to do. We've had enough already.*

He did not say this aloud, though—for their sake.

"Maybe you bumped into something," the girl said.

Glancing at the others, Benz said sardonically, "Maybe we 'bumped into something.' "

"The TV commentators keep saying that," Merry Lou said, "about the hazard in re-entry of being out of phase spatially and colliding right down to the molecular level with tangent objects, any one of which—" She gestured. "You know. 'No two objects can occupy the same space at the same time.' So everything blew up, for that reason.'' She glanced around questioningly.

"That is the major risk factor," Crayne acknowledged. "At least theoretically, as Doctor Fein at Planning calculated when they got into the hazard question. But we had a variety of safety locking devices provided that functioned automatically. Re-entry couldn't occur unless these assists had stabilized us spatially so we would not overlap. Of course, all those devices, in sequence, might have failed. One after the other. I was watching my feedback 'metric scopes on launch, and they agreed, every one of them, that we were phased properly at that time. And I heard no warning tones. Saw none, neither." He grimaced. "At least it didn't happen then."

Suddenly Benz said, "Do you realize that our next-of-kin are now rich? All our Federal and commercial life insurance payoff. Our 'next of kin'—God forbid, that's us, I guess. We can apply for tens of thousands of dollars, cash on the line. Walk into our brokers' offices and say, 'I'm dead; lay the heavy bread on me.' ''

Addison Doug was thinking, the public memorial services. That they have planned, after the autopsies. That long line of black-draped Cads going down Pennsylvania Avenue, with all the government dignitaries and double-domed scientist types—*and we'll be there*. Not once but twice. Once in the oak hand-rubbed brass-fitted flag-draped caskets, but also . . . maybe riding in open limos, waving at the crowds of mourners.

"The ceremonies," he said aloud.

The others stared at him, angrily, not comprehending. And then, one by one, they understood; he saw it on their faces.

"No," Benz grated. "That's—impossible."

Crayne shook his head emphatically. "They'll order us to be there, and we will be. Obeying orders."

"Will we have to *smile*?" Addison said. "To fucking *smile*?"

"No," General Toad said slowly, his great wattled head shivering about on his broomstick neck, the color of his skin dirty and mottled, as if the mass of decorations on his stiff-board collar had started part of him decaying away. "You are not to smile, but on the contrary are to adopt a properly grief-stricken manner. In keeping with the national mood of sorrow at this time."

"That'll be hard to do," Crayne said.

The Russian chrononaut showed no response; his thin beaked face, narrow within his translating earphones, remained strained with concern.

"The nation," General Toad said, "will become aware of your presence among us once more for this brief interval; cameras of all major TV networks will pan up on you without warning, and at the same time, the various commentators have been instructed to tell their audiences something like the following." He got out a piece of typed material, put on his glasses, cleared his throat and said, " 'We seem to be focusing on three figures riding together. Can't quite make them out. Can you?' " General Toad lowered the paper. "At this point they'll interrogate their colleagues extempore. Finally they'll exclaim, 'Why Roger,' or Walter or Ned, as the case may be, according to the individual network—"

"Or Bill," Crayne said. "In case it's the Bufonidae network, down there in the swamp."

General Toad ignored him. "They will severally exclaim, "Why Roger, I believe we're seeing the three tempunauts themselves! Does this indeed mean that somehow the difficulty—?" And then the colleague commentator says in his somewhat more somber voice, 'What we're seeing at this time I think, David,' or Henry or Pete or Ralph, whichever it is, 'consists of mankind's first verified glimpse of what the technical people refer to as Emergence Time Activity or ETA. Contrary to what might seem to be the case at first sight, these are *not*—repeat not—our three valiant tempunauts as such, as we would ordinarily experience them, but more likely picked up by our cameras as the three of them are temporarily suspended in their voyage to the future, which we initially had reason to hope would take place in a time continuum roughly a hundred years from now . . . but it would seem that they somehow undershot and are here now, at this moment, which of course is, as we know, our present.' "

Addison Doug closed his eyes and thought, Crayne will ask him if he can be panned up on by the TV cameras holding a balloon and eating cotton candy. I think we're all going nuts from this, all of us. And then he wondered, How many times have we gone through this idiotic exchange?

I can't prove it, he thought wearily. But I know it's true. We've sat here, done this miniscule scrabbling, listened to and said all this crap, many times. He shuddered. Each rinky dink word . . .

"What's the matter?" Benz said acutely.

The Soviet chrononaut spoke up for the first time. "What is the maximum interval of ETA possible to your three-man team? And how large a percent has been exhausted by now?"

After a pause Crayne said, "They briefed us on that before we came in here today. We've consumed approximately one-half of our maximum total ETA interval."

"However," General Toad rumbled, "we have scheduled the Day of National Mourning to fall within the expected period remaining to them of ETA time. This required us to speed up the autopsy and other forensic findings, but in view of public sentiment, it was felt . . ."

The autopsy, Addison Doug thought, and again he shuddered; this time he could not keep his thoughts within himself and he said, "Why don't we adjourn this nonsense meeting and drop down to Pathology and view a few tissue sections enlarged and in color, and maybe we'll brainstorm a couple of vital concepts that'll aid medical science in its quest for explanations? Explanations—that's what we need. Explanations for problems that don't exist yet; we can develop the problems later." He paused. "Who agrees?"

"I'm not looking at my spleen up there on the screen," Benz said. "I'll ride in the parade but I won't participate in my own autopsy."

"You could distribute microscopic purple-stained slices of your own gut to the mourners along the way," Crayne said. "They could provide each of us with a doggy bag; right,

General? We can strew tissue sections like confetti. I still think we should smile.''

"I have researched all the memoranda about smiling," General Toad said, riffling the pages stacked before him, "and the consensus at policy is that smiling is not in accord with national sentiment. So that issue must be ruled closed. As far as your participating in the autopsical procedures which are now in progress—"

"We're missing out as we sit here," Crayne said to Addison Doug. "I always miss out."

Ignoring him, Addison addressed the Soviet chrononaut. "Officer N. Gauki," he said in his microphone, dangling on his chest, "what in your mind is the greatest terror facing a time traveler? That there will be an implosion due to coincidence on re-entry, such as has occurred in our launch? Or did other traumatic obsessions bother you and your comrade during your own brief but highly successful time flight?"

N. Gauki after a pause answered, "R. Plenya and I exchanged views at several informal times. I believe I can speak for us both when I respond to your question by emphasizing our perpetual fear that we had inadvertently entered a closed time loop and would never break out."

"You'd repeat it forever?" Addison Doug asked.

"Yes, Mr. A. Doug," the chrononaut said, nodding somberly.

A fear that he had never experienced before overcame Addison Doug. He turned helplessly to Benz and muttered, "Shit." They gazed at each other.

"I really don't believe this is what happened," Benz said to him in a low voice, putting his hand on Doug's shoulder; he gripped hard, the grip of friendship. "We just imploded on re-entry, that's all. Take it easy."

"Could we adjourn soon?" Addison Doug said in a hoarse, strangling voice, half-rising from his chair. He felt the room and the people in it rushing in at him, suffocating him. Claustrophobia, he realized. Like when I was in grade school, when they flashed a surprise test on our teaching machines, and I saw I couldn't pass it. "Please," he said simply, standing. They were all looking at him, with different expressions.

The Russian's face was especially sympathetic, and deeply lined with care. Addison wished—"I want to go home," he said to them all, and felt stupid.

He was drunk. It was late at night, at a bar on Hollywood Boulevard; fortunately Merry Lou was with him, and he was having a good time. Everyone was telling him so, anyhow. He clung to Merry Lou and said, "The great unity in life, the supreme unity and meaning, is man and woman. Their absolute unity; right?"

"I know," Merry Lou said. "We studied that in class." Tonight, at his request, Merry Lou was a small blonde girl, wearing purple bellbottoms and high heels and an open midriff blouse. Earlier she had had a lapis lazuli in her navel, but during dinner at Ting Ho's it had popped out and been lost. The owner of the restaurant had promised to keep on searching for it, but Merry Lou had been gloomy ever since. It was, she said, symbolic. But of what she did not say. Or anyhow he could not remember; maybe that was it. She had told him what it meant, and he had forgotten.

An elegant young black at a nearby table, with an Afro and striped vest and overstuffed red tie, had been staring at Addison for some time. He obviously wanted to come over to their table but was afraid to; meanwhile, he kept on staring.

"Did you ever get the sensation," Addison said to Merry Lou, "that you knew exactly what was about to happen? What someone was going to say? Word for word? Down to the slightest detail? As if you had already lived through it once before?"

"Everybody gets into that space," Merry Lou said. She sipped a Bloody Mary.

The black rose and walked toward them. He stood by Addison. "I'm sorry to bother you, sir."

Addison said to Merry Lou, "He's going to say, 'Don't I know you from somewhere? Didn't I see you on TV?'"

"That was precisely what I intended to say," the black said.

Addison said, "You undoubtedly saw my picture on page

forty-six of the current issue of *Time*, the section on new medical discoveries. I'm the G.P. from a small town in Iowa catapulted to fame by my invention of a widespread, easily available cure for eternal life. Several of the big pharmaceutical houses are already bidding on my vaccine.''

"That might have been where I saw your picture," the black said, but he did not appear convinced. Nor did he appear drunk; he eyed Addison Doug intensely. "May I seat myself with you and the lady?"

"Sure," Addison Doug said. He now saw, in the man's hand, the ID of the U.S. security agency that had ridden herd on the project from the start.

"Mr. Doug," the security agent said as he seated himself beside Addison, "you really shouldn't be here shooting off your mouth like this. If I recognized you, some other dude might and freak out. It's all classified until the Day of Mourning. Technically, you're in violation of a Federal Statute by being here; did you realize that? I should haul you in. But this is a difficult situation; we don't want to do something uncool and make a scene. Where are your two colleagues?"

"At my place," Merry Lou said. She had obviously not seen the ID. "Listen," she said sharply to the agent, "why don't you get lost? My husband here has been through a grueling ordeal, and this is his only chance to unwind."

Addison looked at the man. "I knew what you were going to say before you came over here." Word for word, he thought. I am right, and Benz is wrong and this will keep happening, this replay.

"Maybe," the security agent said, "I can induce you to go back to Miss Hawkins' place voluntarily. Some info arrived—" he tapped the tiny earphone in his right ear—"just a few minutes ago, to all of us, to deliver to you, marked urgent, if we located you. At the launch site ruins . . . they've been combing through the rubble, you know?"

"I know," Addison said.

"They think they have their first clue. Something was brought back by one of you. From ETA, over and above what you took, in violation of all your pre-launch training."

"Let me ask you this," Addison Doug said. "Suppose

somebody does see me? Suppose somebody does recognize me? So what?''

"The public believes that even though re-entry failed, the flight into time, the first American time-travel launch, was successful. Three U.S. tempunauts were thrust a hundred years into the future—roughly twice as far as the Soviet launch of last year. That you only went a *week* will be less of a shock if it's believed that you three chose deliberately to re-manifest at this continuum because you wished to attend, in fact felt compelled to attend—''

"We wanted to be in the parade," Addison interrupted. "Twice."

"You were drawn to the dramatic and somber spectacle of your own funeral procession, and will be glimpsed there by the alert camera crews of all major networks. Mr. Doug, really, an awful lot of high-level planning and expense have gone into this to help correct a dreadful situation; trust us, believe me. It'll be easier on the public, and that's vital, if there's ever to be another U.S. time shot. And that is, after all, what we all want.''

Addison Doug stared at him. "We want what?"

Uneasily, the security agent said, "To take further trips into time. As you have done. Unfortunately, you yourself cannot ever do so again, because of the tragic implosion and death of the three of you. But other tempunauts—''

"We want what? Is that what we want?" Addison's voice rose; people at nearby tables were watching now. Nervously.

"Certainly," the agent said. "And keep your voice down."

"I don't want that," Addison said. "I want to stop. To stop forever. To just lie in the ground, in the dust, with everyone else. To see no more summers—the *same* summer.''

"Seen one, you've seen them all," Merry Lou said hysterically. "I think he's right, Addi; we should get out of here. You've had too many drinks, and it's late, and this news about the—''

Addison broke in, "What was brought back? How much extra mass?"

The security agency said, "Preliminary analysis shows that machinery weighing about one hundred pounds was lugged back into the time-field of the module and picked up along with you. This much mass—'' The agent gestured. ''That blew up the pad right on the spot. It couldn't begin to compensate for that much more than had occupied its open area at launch time.''

''Wow!'' Merry Lou said, eyes wide. ''Maybe somebody sold one of you a quadraphonic phono for a dollar ninety-eight including fifteen-inch air-suspension speakers and a lifetime supply of Neil Diamond records.'' She tried to laugh, but failed; her eyes dimmed over. ''Addi,'' she whispered, ''I'm sorry. But it's sort of—weird. I mean, it's absurd; you all were briefed, weren't you, about your return weight? You weren't even to add so much as a piece of paper to what you took. I even saw Doctor Fein demonstrating the reasons on TV. And one of you hoisted a hundred pounds of machinery into the field? You must have been trying to self-destruct, to do that!'' Tears slid from her eyes; one tear rolled out onto her nose and hung there. He reached reflexively to wipe it away, as if helping a little girl rather than a grown one.

''I'll fly you to the analysis site,'' the security agent said, standing up. He and Addison helped Merry Lou to her feet; she trembled as she stood a moment, finishing her Bloody Mary. Addison felt acute sorrow for her, but then, almost at once, it passed. He wondered why. One can weary even of that, he conjectured. Of caring for someone. If it goes on too long—on and on. Forever. And, at last, even after that, into something no one before, not God Himself, maybe, had ever had to suffer and in the end, for all His great heart, succumb to.

As they walked through the crowded bar toward the street, Addison Doug said to the security agent, ''Which one of us—''

''They know which one,'' the agent said as he held the door to the street open for Merry Lou. The agent stood, now, behind Addison, signaling for a gray Federal car to land at the red parking area. Two other security agents, in uniform, hurried toward them.

''Was it me?'' Addison Doug asked.

''You better believe it,'' the security agent said.

* * *

The funeral procession moved with aching solemnity down Pennsylvania Avenue, three flag-draped caskets and dozens of black limousines passing between rows of heavily coated, shivering mourners. A low haze hung over the day, gray outlines of buildings faded into the rain-drenched murk of the Washington March day.

Scrutinizing the lead Cadillac through prismatic binoculars, TV's top news and public events commentator Henry Cassidy droned on at his vast unseen audience. ". . . sad recollections of that earlier train among the wheatfields carrying the coffin of Abraham Lincoln back to burial and the nation's capital. And what a sad day this is, and what appropriate weather, with its dour overcast and sprinkles!" In his monitor he saw the zoomar lens pan up on the fourth Cadillac, as it followed those with the caskets of the dead tempunauts.

His engineer tapped him on the arm.

"We appear to be focusing on three unfamiliar figures so far not identified, riding together," Henry Cassidy said into his neck mike, nodding agreement. "So far I'm unable to quite make them out. Are your location and vision any better from where you're placed, Everett?" he inquired of his colleague and pressed the button that notified Everett Branton to replace him on the air.

"Why, Henry," Branton said in a voice of growing excitement, "I believe we're actually eyewitness to the three American tempunauts as they remanifest themselves on their historic journey into the future!"

"Does this signify," Cassidy said, "that somehow they have managed to solve and overcome the—"

"Afraid not, Henry," Branton said in his slow, regretful voice. "What we're eyewitnessing to our complete surprise consists of the Western world's first verified glimpse of what the technical people refer to as Emergence Time Activity."

"Ah yes, ETA," Cassidy said brightly, reading it off the official script the Federal authorities had handed him before air time.

"Right, Henry. Contrary to what *might* seem to be the case

at first sight, these are not—repeat *not*—our three brave tempunauts as such, as we would ordinarily experience them—"

"I grasp it now, Everett," Cassidy broke in excitedly, since his authorized script read CASS BREAKS IN EXCITEDLY. "Our three tempunauts have momentarily suspended in their historic voyage to the future, which we believe will span across to a time-continuum roughly a century from now. . . . It would seem that the overwhelming grief and drama of this unanticipated day of mourning has caused them to . . ."

"Sorry to interrupt, Henry," Everett Branton said, "but I think, since the procession has momentarily halted on its slow march forward, that we might be able to . . ."

"No!" Cassidy said, as a note was handed him in a swift scribble, reading: *Do not interview 'nauts. Urgent. Dis. previous inst.* "I don't think we're going to be able to . . ." he continued, ". . . to speak briefly with tempunauts Benz, Crayne, and Doug, as you had hoped, Everett. As we had all briefly hoped to." He wildly waved the boom-mike back; it had already begun to swing out expectantly toward the stopped Cadillac. Cassidy shook his head violently at the mike technician and his engineer.

Perceiving the boom-mike swinging at them, Addison Doug stood up in the back of the open Cadillac. Cassidy groaned. He wants to speak, he realized. Didn't they reinstruct *him*? Why am I the only one they get across to? Other boom-mikes representing other networks plus radio station interviewers on foot now were rushing out to thrust up their microphones into the faces of the three tempunauts, especially Addison Doug's. Doug was already beginning to speak, in response to a question shouted up to him by a reporter. With his boom-mike off, Cassidy couldn't hear the question, nor Doug's answer. With reluctance, he signaled for his own boom-mike to trigger on.

". . . before," Doug was saying loudly.

"In what manner, 'All this has happened before'?" the radio reporter, standing close to the car, was saying.

"I mean," U.S. tempunaut Addison Doug declared, his face red and strained, "that I have stood here in this spot and said again and again, and all of you have viewed this parade and our deaths at re-entry endless times, a closed cycle of trapped time which must be broken."

"Are you seeking," another reporter jabbered up at Addison Doug, "for a solution to the re-entry implosion disaster which can be applied in retrospect so that when you do return to the past you will be able to correct the malfunction and avoid the tragedy which cost—or for you three, will cost—your lives?"

Tempunaut Benz said, "We are doing that, yes."

"Trying to ascertain the cause of the violent implosion and eliminate the cause before we return," tempunaut Crayne added, nodding. "We have learned already that for reasons unknown, a mass of nearly one hundred pounds of miscellaneous Volkswagen motor parts, including cylinders, the head . . ."

This is awful, Cassidy thought. "This is amazing!" he said aloud, into his neck mike. "The already tragically deceased U.S. tempunauts, with a determination that could emerge only from the rigorous training and discipline to which they were subjected—and we wondered why at the time but can clearly see why now—have already analyzed the mechanical slipup responsible, evidently, for their own deaths, and have begun the laborious process of sifting through and eliminating causes of that slipup so that they can return to their original launch site and re-enter without mishap."

"One wonders," Branton mumbled onto the air and into his feedback earphone, "what the consequences of this alteration of the near past will be. If in re-entry they do *not* implode and are *not* killed, then they will not—well, it's too complex for me, Henry, these time paradoxes that Doctor Fein at the Time Extrusion Labs in Pasadena has so frequently and eloquently brought to our attention."

Into all the microphones available, of all sorts, tempunaut Addison Doug was saying, more quietly now, "We must now eliminate the cause of re-entry implosion. The only way out of this trap is for us to die. Death is the only solution for this. For the three of us." He was interrupted as the procession of Cadillacs began to move forward.

Shutting off his mike momentarily, Henry Cassidy said to his engineer, "Is he nuts?"

"Only time will tell," his engineer said in a hard-to-hear voice.

"An extraordinary moment in the history of the Unites States' involvement in time travel," Cassidy said then, into his now live mike. "Only time will tell—if you will pardon the inadvertent pun—whether tempunaut Doug's cryptic remarks, uttered impromptu at this moment of supreme suffering for him, as in a sense to a lesser degree it is for all of us, are the words of a man deranged by grief or an accurate insight into the macabre dilemma that in theoretical terms we knew all along might eventually confront—confront and strike down with its lethal blow—a time-travel launch, either ours or the Russians'."

He segued then, to a commercial.

"You know," Branton's voice muttered in his ear, not on the air but just to the control room and to him, "if he's right they ought to let the poor bastards die."

"They ought to release them," Cassidy agreed. "My God, the way Doug looked and talked, you'd imagine he'd gone through this for a thousand years and then some! I wouldn't be in his shoes for anything."

"I'll bet you fifty bucks," Branton said, "they have gone through this before. Many times."

"Then we have, too," Cassidy said.

Rain fell now, making all the lined-up mourners shiny. Their faces, their eyes, even their clothes—everything glistened in wet reflections of broken, fractured light, bent and sparkling, as, from gathering gray formless layers above them, the day darkened.

"Are we on the air?" Branton asked.

Who knows? Cassidy thought. He wished the day would end.

The Soviet chrononaut N. Gauki lifted both hands impassionedly and spoke to the Americans across the table from him in a voice of extreme urgency. "It is the opinion of myself and my colleague R. Plenya, who for his pioneering achievements in time travel has been certified a Hero of the Soviet People, and rightly so, that based on our own experience and on theoretical material developed both in your own academic circles and in the Soviet Academy of Sciences of the USSR, we believe that tempunaut A. Doug's fears may be justified. And his deliberate destruction of himself and his team mates at re-entry, by hauling a huge mass of auto back with him from ETA, in violation of his orders, should be regarded as the act of a desperate man with no other means of escape. Of course, the decision is up to you. We have only advisory position in this matter.''

Addison Doug played with his cigarette lighter on the table and did not look up. His ears hummed, and he wondered what that meant. It had an electronic quality. Maybe we're within the module again, he thought. But he did not perceive it; he felt the reality of the people around him, the table, the blue plastic lighter between his fingers. No smoking in the module during re-entry, he thought. He put the light carefully away in his pocket.

''We've developed no concrete evidence whatsoever,'' General Toad said, ''that a closed-time loop has been set up. There's only the subjective feelings of fatigue on the part of Mr. Doug. Just his belief that he's done all this repeatedly. As he says, it is very probably psychological in nature.'' He rooted pig-like among the papers before him. ''I have a report, not disclosed to the media, from four psychiatrists at Yale on his psychological makeup. Although unusually stable, there is a tendency toward cyclothymia on his part, culminating in acute depression. This naturally was taken into account long before the launch, but it was calculated that the joyful qualities of the two others in the team would offset this functionally. Anyhow, that depressive tendency in him is exceptionally high, now.'' He held the paper out, but no one at the table accepted it. ''Isn't it true, Doctor Fein,'' he said, ''that an acutely depressed person experiences time in a peculiar way, that is, circular time, time repeating itself, getting nowhere, around and around? The person gets so psychotic that he refuses to let go of the past. Re-runs it in his head constantly.''

"But you see," Dr. Fein said, "this subjective sensation of being trapped is perhaps all we would have." This was the research physicist whose basic work had laid the theoretical foundation for the project. "If a closed loop did unfortunately lock into being."

"The general," Addison Doug said, "is using words he doesn't understand."

"I researched the ones I was unfamiliar with," General Toad said. "The technical psychiatric terms . . . I know what they mean."

To Addison Doug, Benz said, "Where'd you get all those VW parts, Addi?"

"I don't have them yet," Addison Doug said.

"Probably picked up the first junk he could lay his hands on," Crayne said. "Whatever was available, just before we started back."

"Will start back," Addison Doug corrected.

"Here are my instructions to the three of you," General Toad said. "You are not in any way to attempt to cause damage or implosion or malfunction during re-entry, either by lugging back extra mass or by any other method that enters your mind. You are to return as scheduled and in replica of the prior simulations. This especially applies to you, Mr. Doug." The phone by his right arm buzzed. He frowned, picked up the receiver. An interval passed, and then he scowled deeply and set the receiver back down, loudly.

"You've been overruled," Dr. Fein said.

"Yes, I have," General Toad said. "And I must say at this time that I am personally glad because my decision was an unpleasant one."

"Then we can arrange for implosion at re-entry," Benz said after a pause.

"The three of you are to make the decision," General Toad said. "Since it involves your lives. It's been entirely left up to you. Whichever way you want it. If you're convinced you're in a closed time loop, and you believe a massive implosion at re-entry will abolish it—" He ceased talking, as tempunaut Doug rose to his feet. "Are you going to make another speech, Doug?" he said.

"I just want to thank everyone involved," Addison Doug said. "For letting us decide." He gazed haggard-faced and wearily around at all the individuals seated at the table. "I really appreciate it."

"You know," Benz said slowly, "blowing us up at re-entry could add nothing to the chances of abolishing a closed loop. In fact that could do it, Doug."

"Not if it kills us all," Crayne said.

"You agree with Addi?" Benz said.

"Dead is dead," Crayne said. "I've been pondering it. What other way is more likely to get us out of this? Than if we're dead? What possible other way?"

"You may be in no loop," Dr. Fein pointed out.

"But we may be," Crayne said.

Doug, still on his feet, said to Crayne and Benz, "Could we include Merry Lou in our decision-making?"

"Why?" Benz said.

"I can't think too clearly any more," Doug said. "Merry Lou can help me; I depend on her."

"Sure," Crayne said. Benz, too, nodded.

General Toad examined his wristwatch stoically and said, "Gentlemen, this concludes our discussion."

Soviet chrononaut Gauki removed his headphones and neck mike and hurried toward the three U.S. tempunauts, his hand extended; he was apparently saying something in Russian, but none of them could understand it. They moved away somberly, clustering close.

"In my opinion you're nuts, Addi," Benz said. "But it would appear that I'm the minority now."

"If he *is* right," Crayne said, "if—one chance in a billion—if we are going back again and again forever, that would justify it."

"Could we go see Merry Lou?" Addison Doug said. "Drive over to her place now?"

"She's waiting outside," Crayne said.

Striding up to stand beside the three tempunauts, General Toad said, "You know, what made the determination go the way it did was the public reaction to how you, Doug, looked and behaved during the funeral procession. The NSC advisors came to the conclusion that the public would, like you, rather be certain it's over for all of you. That it's more of a relief to them to know you're free of your mission than to save the project and obtain a perfect re-entry. I guess you really made a lasting impression on them, Doug. That whining you did.'' He walked away then, leaving the three of them standing there alone.

''Forget him,'' Crayne said to Addison Doug. ''Forget everyone like him. We've got to do what we have to.''

''Merry Lou will explain it to me,'' Doug said. She would know what to do, what would be right.

''I'll go get her,'' Crayne said, ''and after that the four of us can drive somewhere, maybe to her place, and decide what to do. Okay?''

''Thank you,'' Addison Doug said, nodding; he glanced around for her hopefully, wondering where she was. In the next room, perhaps, somewhere close. ''I appreciate that,'' he said.

Benz and Crayne eyed each other. He saw that, but did not know what it meant. He knew only that he needed someone. Merry Lou most of all, to help him understand what the situation was. And what to finalize on to get them out of it.

Merry Lou drove them north from Los Angeles in the superfast lane of the freeway toward Ventura, and after that inland to Ojai. The four of them said very little. Merry Lou drove well, as always; leaning against her, Addison Doug felt himself relax into a temporary sort of peace.

''There's nothing like having a chick drive you,'' Crayne said, after many miles had passed in silence.

''It's an aristocratic sensation,'' Benz murmured. ''To have a woman do the driving. Like you're nobility being chauffeured.''

Merry Lou said, ''Until she runs into something. Some big slow object.''

Addison Doug said, ''When you saw me trudging up to your place . . . up the redwood round path the other day. What did you think? Tell me honestly.''

''You looked,'' the girl said, ''as if you'd done it many times. You looked worn and tired and—ready to die. At the end." She hesitated. "I'm sorry, but that's how you looked, Addi. I thought to myself, he knows the way too well."

"Like I'd done it too many times."

"Yes," she said.

"Then you vote for implosion," Addison Doug said.

"Well—"

"Be honest with me," he said.

Merry Lou said, "Look in the back seat. The box on the floor."

With a flashlight from the glove compartment the three men examined the box. Addison Doug, with fear, saw its contents. VW motor parts, rusty and worn. Still oily.

"I got them from behind a foreign car garage near my place," Merry Lou said. "On the way to Pasadena. The first junk I saw that seemed as if it'd be heavy enough. I had heard them say on TV at launch time that anything over fifty pounds up to—"

"It'll do it," Addison Doug said. "It did do it."

"So there's no point in going to your place," Crayne said. "It's decided. We might as well head south toward the module. And initiate the procedure for getting out of ETA. And back to re-entry." His voice was heavy but evenly pitched. "Thanks for your vote, Miss Hawkins."

She said, "You are all so tired."

"I'm not," Benz said. "I'm mad. Mad as hell."

"At me?" Addison Doug said.

"I don't know," Benz said. "It just—Hell." He lapsed into brooding silence then. Hunched over, baffled and inert. Withdrawn as far as possible from the others in the car.

At the next freeway junction she turned the car south. A sense of freedom seemed now to fill her, and Addison Doug felt some of the weight, the fatigue, ebbing already.

On the wrist of each of the three men the emergency alert receiver buzzed its warning tone; they all started.

"What's that mean?" Merry Lou said, slowing the car.

"We're to contact General Toad by phone as soon as possible," Crayne said. He pointed. "There's a Standard Station over there; take the next exit, Miss Hawkins. We can phone in from there."

A few minutes later Merry Lou brought her car to a halt beside the outdoor phone booth. "I hope it's not bad news," she said.

"I'll talk first," Doug said, getting out. Bad news, he thought with labored amusement. Like what? He crunched stiffly across to the phone booth, entered, shut the door behind him, dropped in a dime and dialed the toll-free number.

"Well, do I have news!" General Toad said when the operator had put him on the line. "It's a good thing we got hold of you. Just a minute—I'm going to let Doctor Fein tell you this himself. You're more apt to believe him than me." Several clicks, and then Doctor Fein's reedy, precise, scholarly voice, but intensified by urgency.

"What's the bad news?" Addison Doug said.

"Not bad, necessarily," Dr. Fein said. "I've had computations run since our discussion, and it would appear—by that I mean it is statistically probable but still unverified for a certainty—that you are right, Addison. You are in a closed time loop."

Addison Doug exhaled raggedly. You nowhere autocratic mother, he thought. You probably knew all along.

"However," Dr. Fein said excitedly, stammering a little, "I also calculate—we jointly do, largely through Cal Tech—that the greatest likelihood of maintaining the loop is to implode on re-entry. Do you understand, Addison? If you lug all those rusty VW parts back and implode, then your statistical chances of closing the loop forever is greater than if you simply re-enter and all goes well."

Addison Doug said nothing.

"In fact, Addi—and this is the severe part that I have to stress—implosion at re-entry, especially a massive, calculated one of the sort we seem to see shaping up—do you grasp all this, Addi? Am I getting through to you? For Chrissake, Addi? Virtually *guarantees* the locking in of an absolutely unyielding loop such as you've got in mind. Such as we've all been worried about from the start." A pause. "Addi? Are you there?"

Addison Doug said, "I want to die."

"That's your exhaustion from the loop. God knows how

many repetitions there've been already of the three of you—"

"No," he said and started to hang up.

"Let me speak with Benz and Crayne," Dr. Fein said rapidly. "Please, before you go ahead with re-entry. Especially Benz; I'd like to speak with him in particular. Please, Addison. For their sake; your almost total exhaustion has—"

He hung up. Left the phone booth, step by step.

As he climbed back into the car, he heard their two alert receivers still buzzing. "General Toad said the automatic call for us would keep your two receivers doing that for a while," he said. And shut the car door after him. "Let's take off."

"Doesn't he want to talk to us?" Benz said.

Addison Doug said, "General Toad wanted to inform us that they have a little something for us. We've been voted a special Congressional Citation for valor or some damn thing like that. A special medal they never voted anyone before. To be awarded posthumously."

"Well, hell—that's about the only way it can be awarded," Crayne said.

Merry Lou, as she started up the engine, began to cry.

"It'll be a relief," Crayne said presently, as they returned bumpily to the freeway, "when it's over."

It won't be long now, Addison Doug's mind declared.

On their wrists the emergency alert receivers continued to put out their combined buzzing.

"They will nibble you to death," Addison Doug said. "The endless wearing down by various bureaucratic voices."

The others in the car turned to gaze at him inquiringly, with uneasiness mixed with perplexity.

"Yeah," Crayne said. "These automatic alerts are really a nuisance." He sounded tired. As tired as I am, Addison Doug thought. And, realizing this, he felt better. It showed how right he was.

Great drops of water struck the windshield; it had now begun to rain. That pleased him too. It reminded him of that most exalted of all experiences with the shortness of his life: the funeral procession moving slowly down Pennsylvania Avenue, the flag-draped caskets. Closing his eyes, he leaned back and felt good at last. And heard, all around him once again, the sorrow-bent people. And, in his head, dreamed of the special Congressional Medal. For weariness, he thought. A medal for being tired.

He saw, in his head, himself in other parades too, and in the deaths of many. But really it was one death and one parade. Slow cars moving along the street in Dallas, and with Dr. King as well. . . . He saw himself return again and again, in his closed cycle of life, to the national mourning that he could not and they could not forget. He would be there; they would always be there; it would always be, and every one of them would return together again and again forever. To the place, the moment, they wanted to be. The event which meant the most to all of them.

This was his gift to them, the people, his country. He had bestowed upon the world a wonderful burden. The dreadful and weary miracle of eternal life.

Contents of *THE COLOR OF EVIL*
Volume 1 of THE DARK DESCENT
edited by David G. Hartwell

Now available from Tor Books

Contents of *THE MEDUSA IN THE SHIELD*
Volume 2 of THE DARK DESCENT
edited by David G. Hartwell

Now available from Tor Books

SPINE-TINGLING HORROR
FROM TOR

GENE WOLFE

☐ ☐	50625-1	CASTLEVIEW	$4.95 Canada $5.95
☐ ☐	50718-5	ENDANGERED SPECIES	$4.95 Canada $5.95
☐ ☐	55813-8	FREE LIVE FREE	$3.95 Canada $4.95
☐ ☐	51155-7	SOLDIER OF ARETE	$4.95 Canada $5.95
☐ ☐	55815-4	SOLDIER OF THE MIST	$3.95 Canada $4.95
☐ ☐	50301-5	THERE ARE DOORS	$4.95 Canada $5.95
☐ ☐	55817-0	THE URTH OF THE NEW SUN	$3.95 Canada $4.95

HORROR FROM RAMSEY CAMPBELL

☐ ☐	50263-9	ANCIENT IMAGES	$4.95 Canada $5.95
☐ ☐	51652-4	DARK COMPANIONS	$3.50 Canada $3.95
☐ ☐	51670-2	FINE FRIGHTS	$3.95 Canada $4.95
☐ ☐	51662-1	THE HUNGRY MOON	$4.50 Canada $5.95
☐ ☐	51650-8	INCARNATE	$3.95 Canada $4.50
☐ ☐	51638-9	INFLUENCE	$4.50 Canada $5.50
☐ ☐	51664-8	THE NAMELESS	$3.95 Canada $4.95
☐ ☐	51656-7	OBSESSION	$3.95 Canada $4.95
☐ ☐	51668-0	THE PARASITE	$4.95 Canada $5.95

Buy them at your local bookstore or use this handy coupon:
Clip and mail this page with your order.

Publishers Book and Audio Mailing Service
P.O. Box 120159, Staten Island, NY 10312-0004

Please send me the book(s) I have checked above. I am enclosing $ _____
(please add $1.25 for the first book, and $.25 for each additional book to cover postage and handling.
Send check or money order only—no CODs).

Name _____
Address _____
City _____ State/Zip _____
Please allow six weeks for delivery. Prices subject to change without notice.

T.M. WRIGHT

☐ ☐	50992-7	BOUNDARIES	$4.95 Canada $5.95
☐ ☐	52765-8	THE ISLAND	$3.95 Canada $4.95
☐ ☐	52750-X	MANHATTAN GHOST STORY	$3.95 Canada $4.95
☐ ☐	52768-2	THE PEOPLE OF THE DARK	$3.95 Canada $4.95
☐ ☐	50294-9	THE PLACE	$4.95 Canada $5.95
☐ ☐	52748-8	THE PLAYGROUND	$3.95 Canada $4.95
☐ ☐	52762-3	STRANGE SEED	$3.95 Canada $4.95
☐ ☐	52744-5	THE WOMAN NEXT DOOR	$3.95 Canada $4.95

Buy them at your local bookstore or use this handy coupon:
Clip and mail this page with your order.

Publishers Book and Audio Mailing Service
P.O. Box 120159, Staten Island, NY 10312-0004

Please send me the book(s) I have checked above. I am enclosing $ _____
(please add $1.25 for the first book, and $.25 for each additional book to cover postage and handling.
Send check or money order only—no CODs).

Name _____
Address _____
City _____ State/Zip _____
Please allow six weeks for delivery. Prices subject to change without notice.